BOOK TWO

LIGHTFALL

SHADOW OF THE BIRD

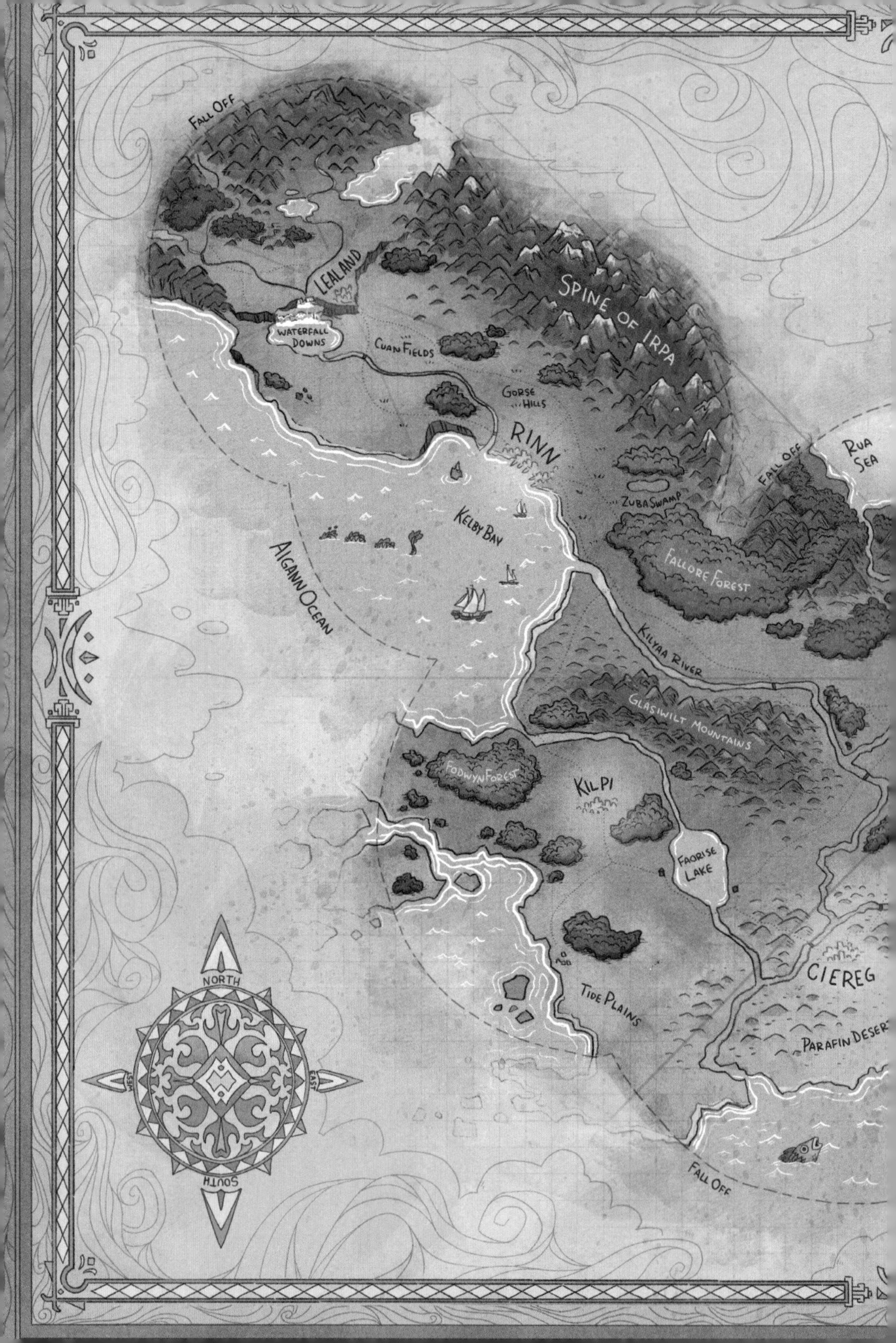

Fall Off
Lealand
Waterfall Downs
Cuan Fields
Spine of Irpa
Gorse Hills
Rinn
Rua Sea
Fall Off
Zuba Swamp
Kelby Bay
Fallore Forest
Aigann Ocean
Kilyaa River
Glasiwilt Mountains
Fodwyn Forest
Kilpi
Faorise Lake
Ciereg
Tide Plains
Parafin Desert
North
West
East
South
Fall Off

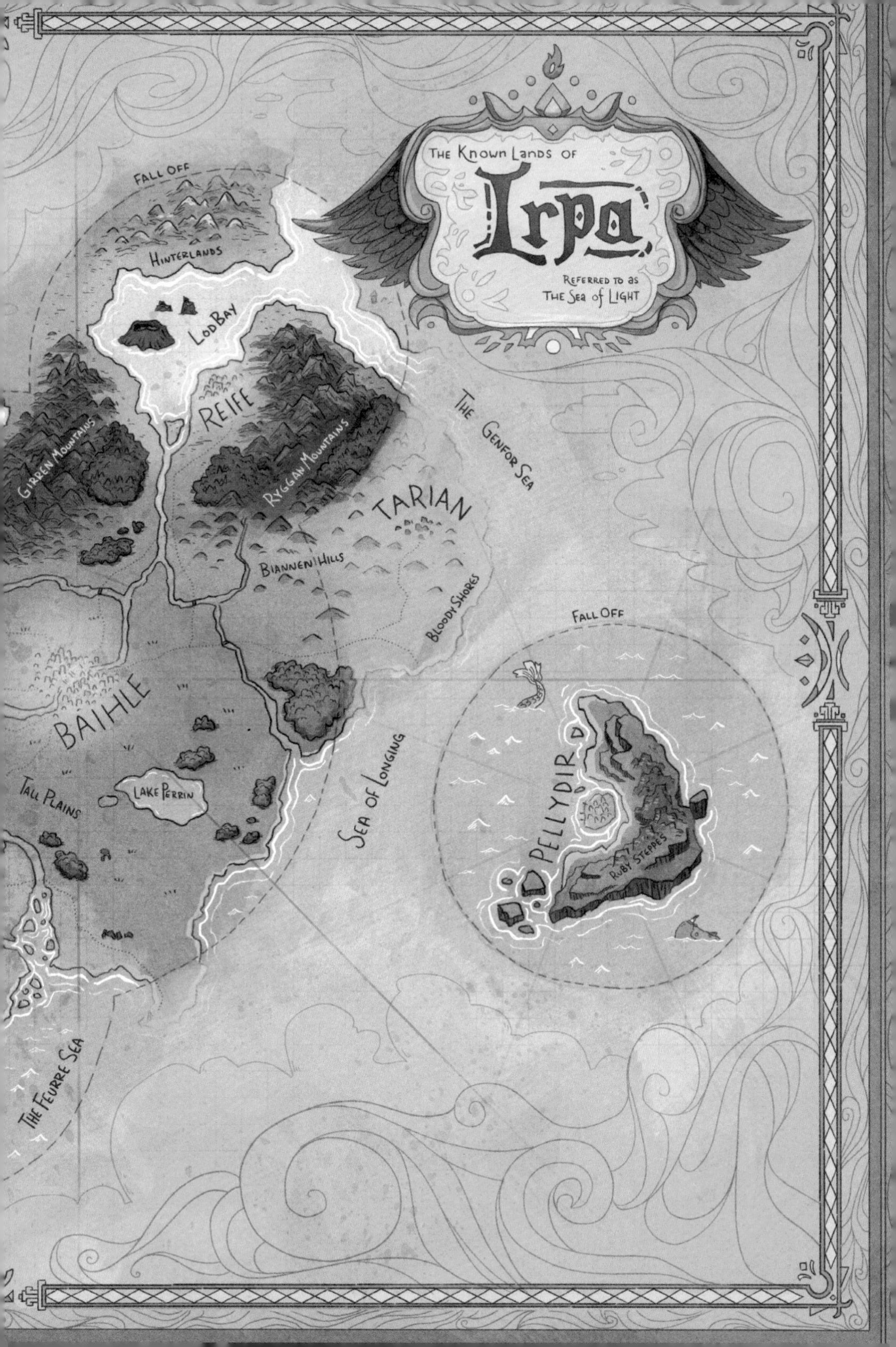

The Known Lands of
Irpa
Referred to as
The Sea of Light
Fall Off
Hinterlands
Lod Bay
Reife
Girren Mountains
Ryggan Mountains
The Genfor Sea
Tarian
Biannen Hills
Bloody Shores
Fall Off
Baihle
Sea of Longing
Tall Plains
Lake Perrin
Pellydir
Ruby Steppes
The Feurre Sea

You know, Hobbes, some days even my
lucky rocketship underpants don't help.

—Bill Watterson

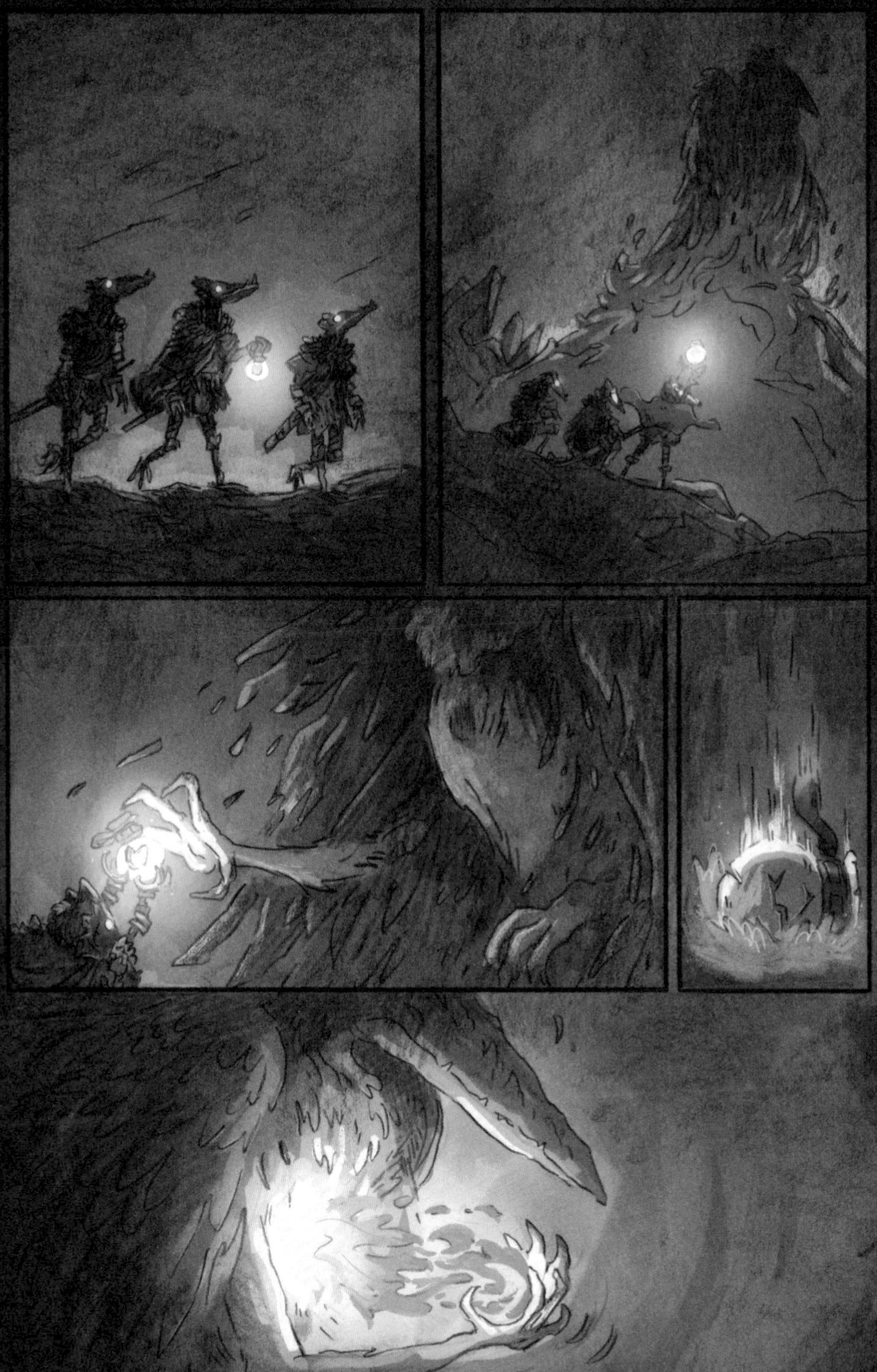

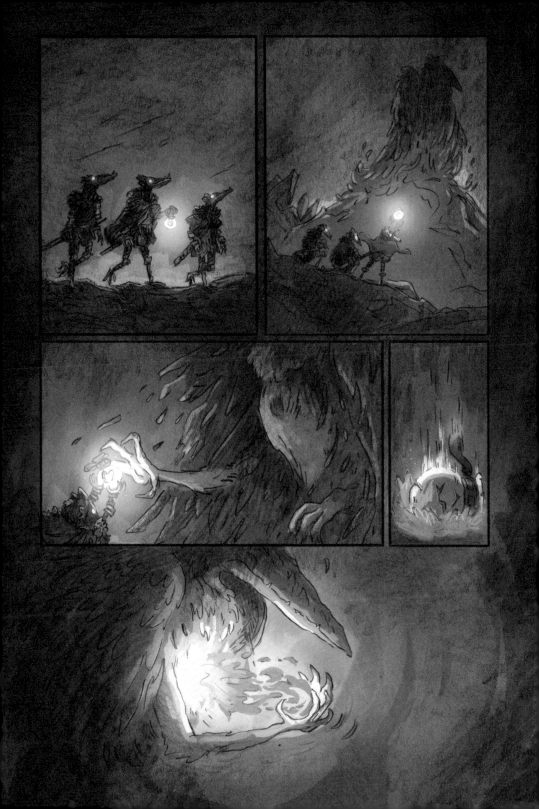

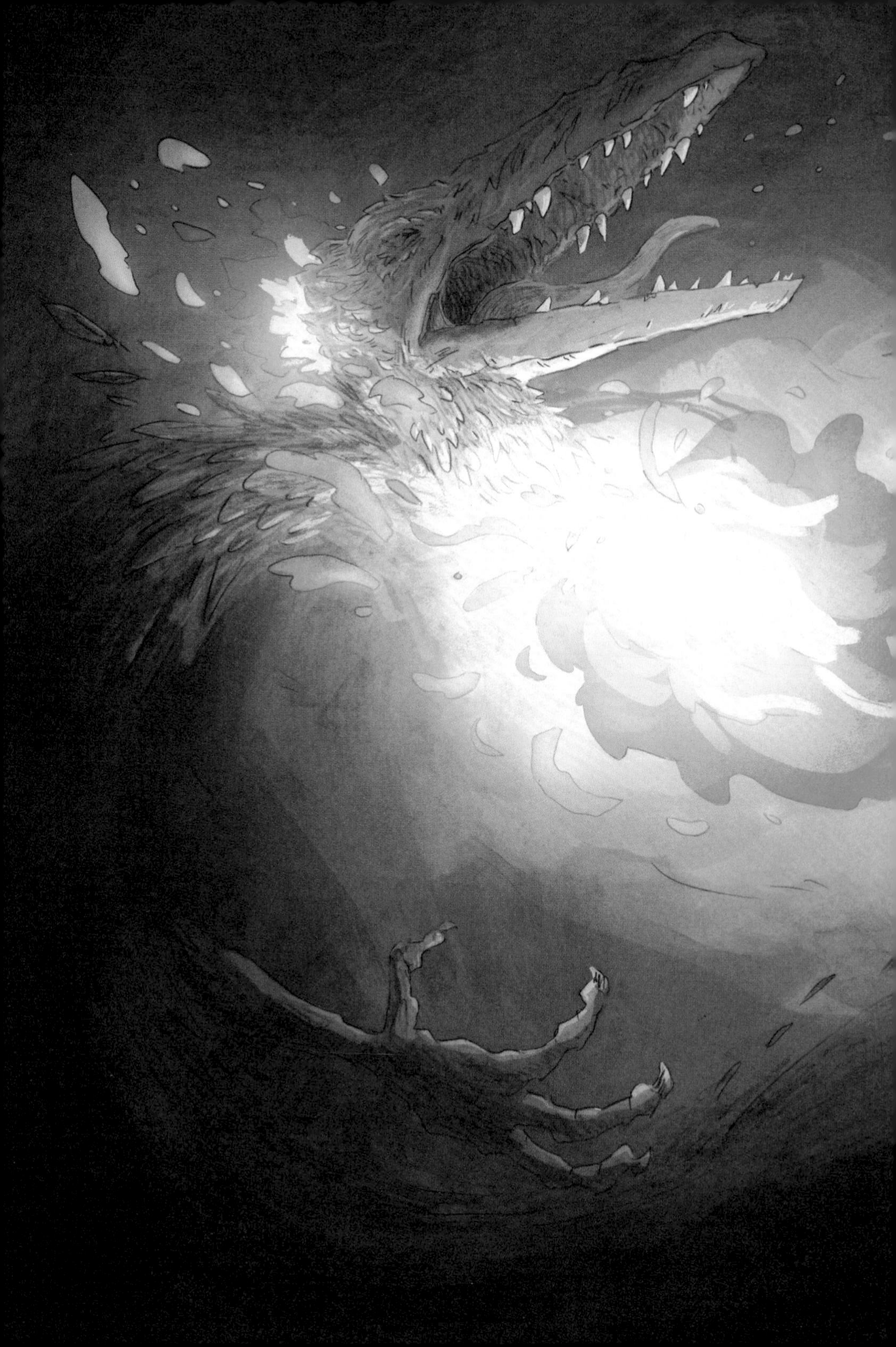

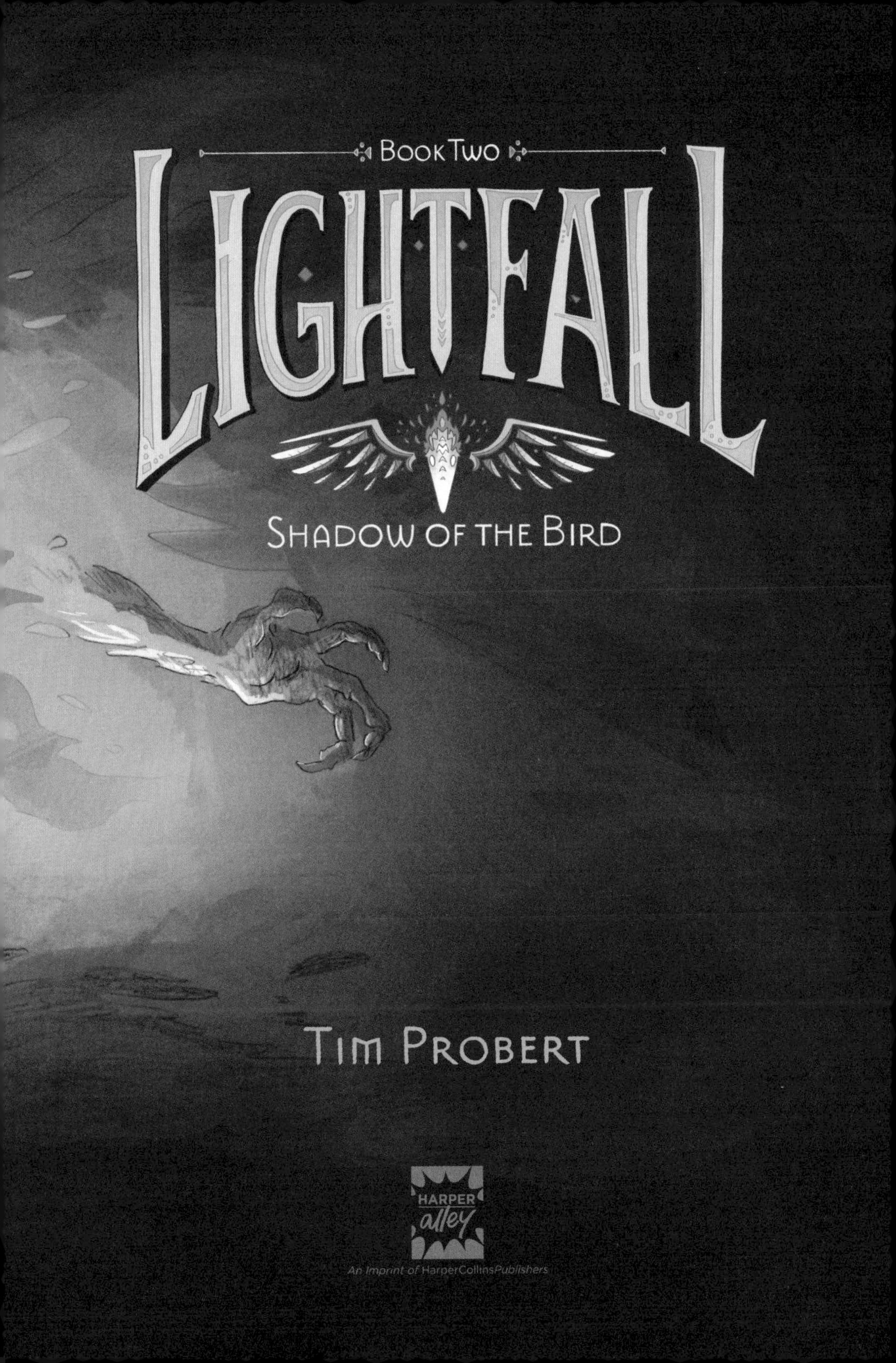

Book Two

Lightfall

Shadow of the Bird

Tim Probert

Harper Alley
An Imprint of HarperCollinsPublishers

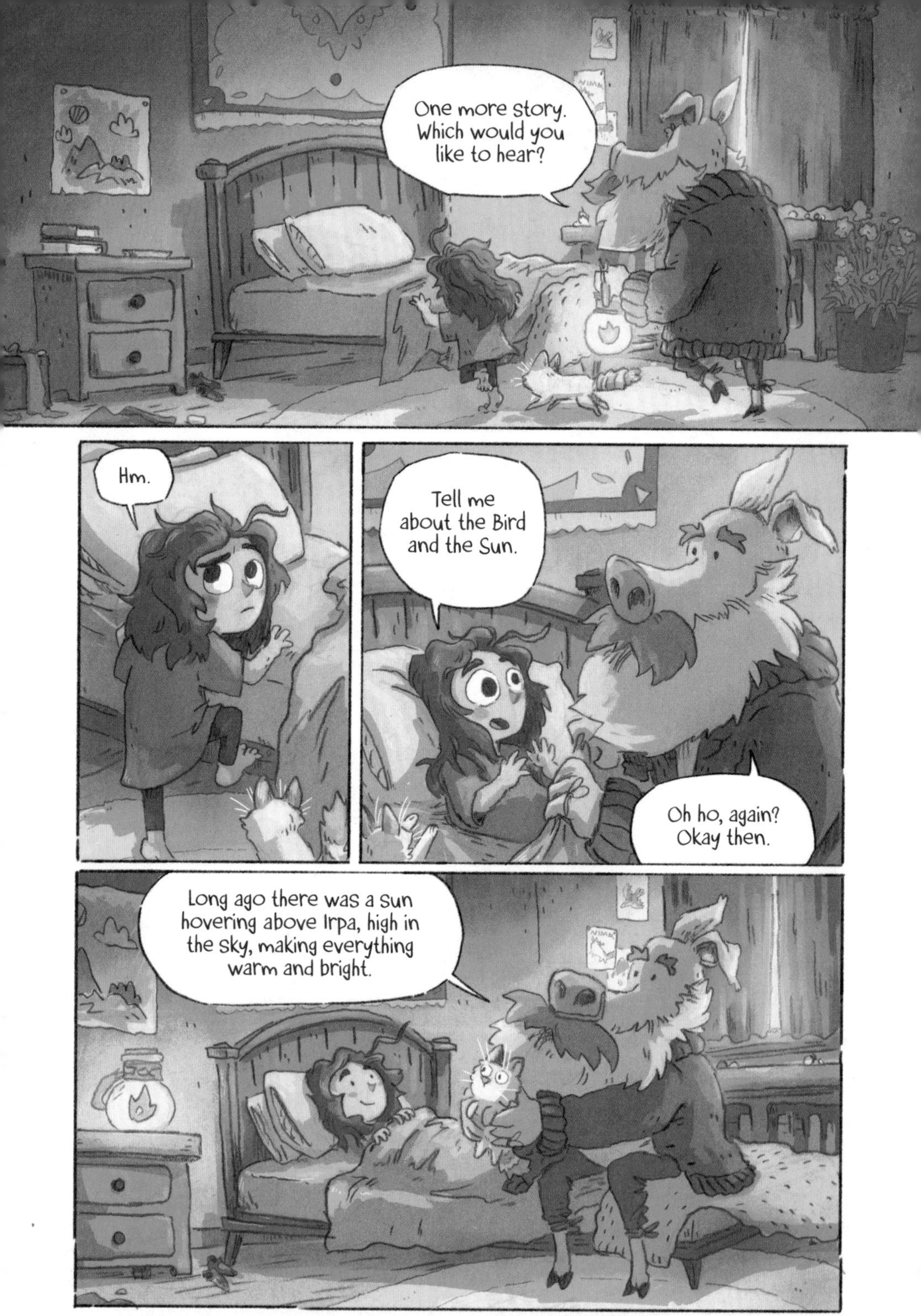
One more story. Which would you like to hear?
Hm.
Tell me about the Bird and the Sun.
Oh ho, again? Okay then.
Long ago there was a sun hovering above Irpa, high in the sky, making everything warm and bright.

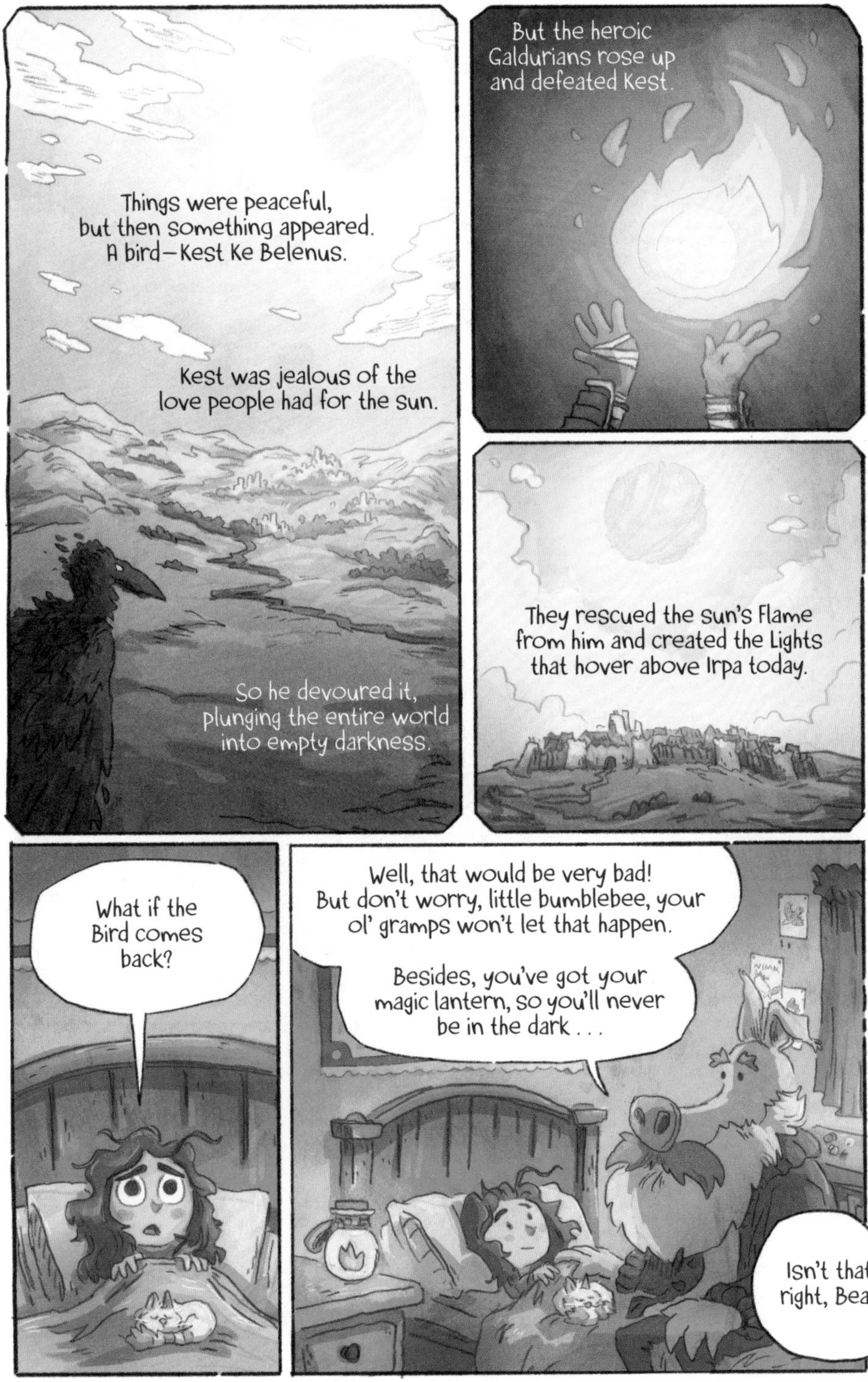
Things were peaceful, but then something appeared. A bird—Kest Ke Belenus.
Kest was jealous of the love people had for the sun.
So he devoured it, plunging the entire world into empty darkness.
But the heroic Galdurians rose up and defeated Kest.
They rescued the sun's Flame from him and created the Lights that hover above Irpa today.
What if the Bird comes back?
Well, that would be very bad! But don't worry, little bumblebee, your ol' gramps won't let that happen.
Besides, you've got your magic lantern, so you'll never be in the dark . . .
Isn't that right, Bea?

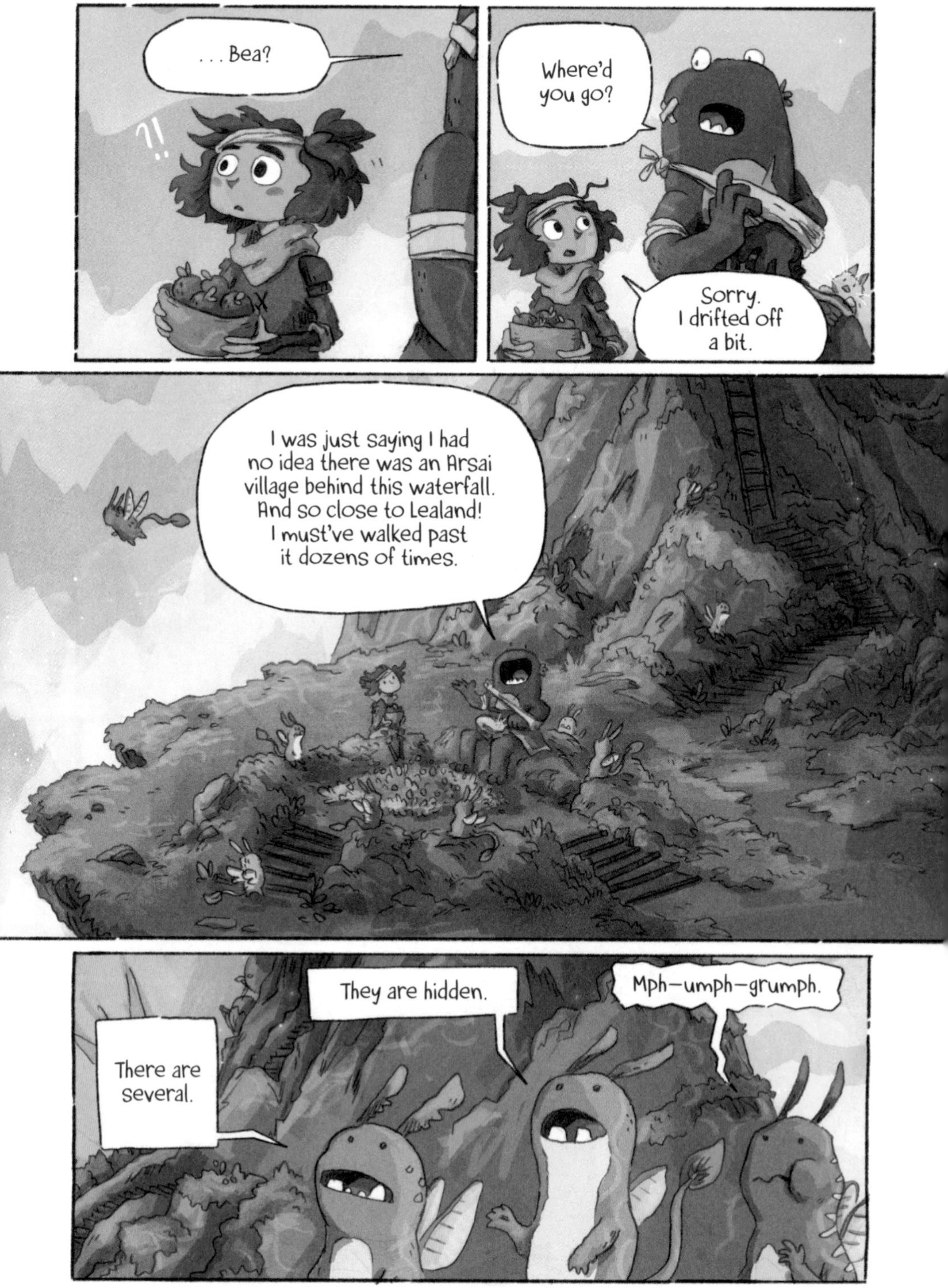
. . . Bea?
?!
Where'd you go?
Sorry. I drifted off a bit.
I was just saying I had no idea there was an Arsai village behind this waterfall. And so close to Lealand! I must've walked past it dozens of times.
There are several.
They are hidden.
Mph—umph—grumph.

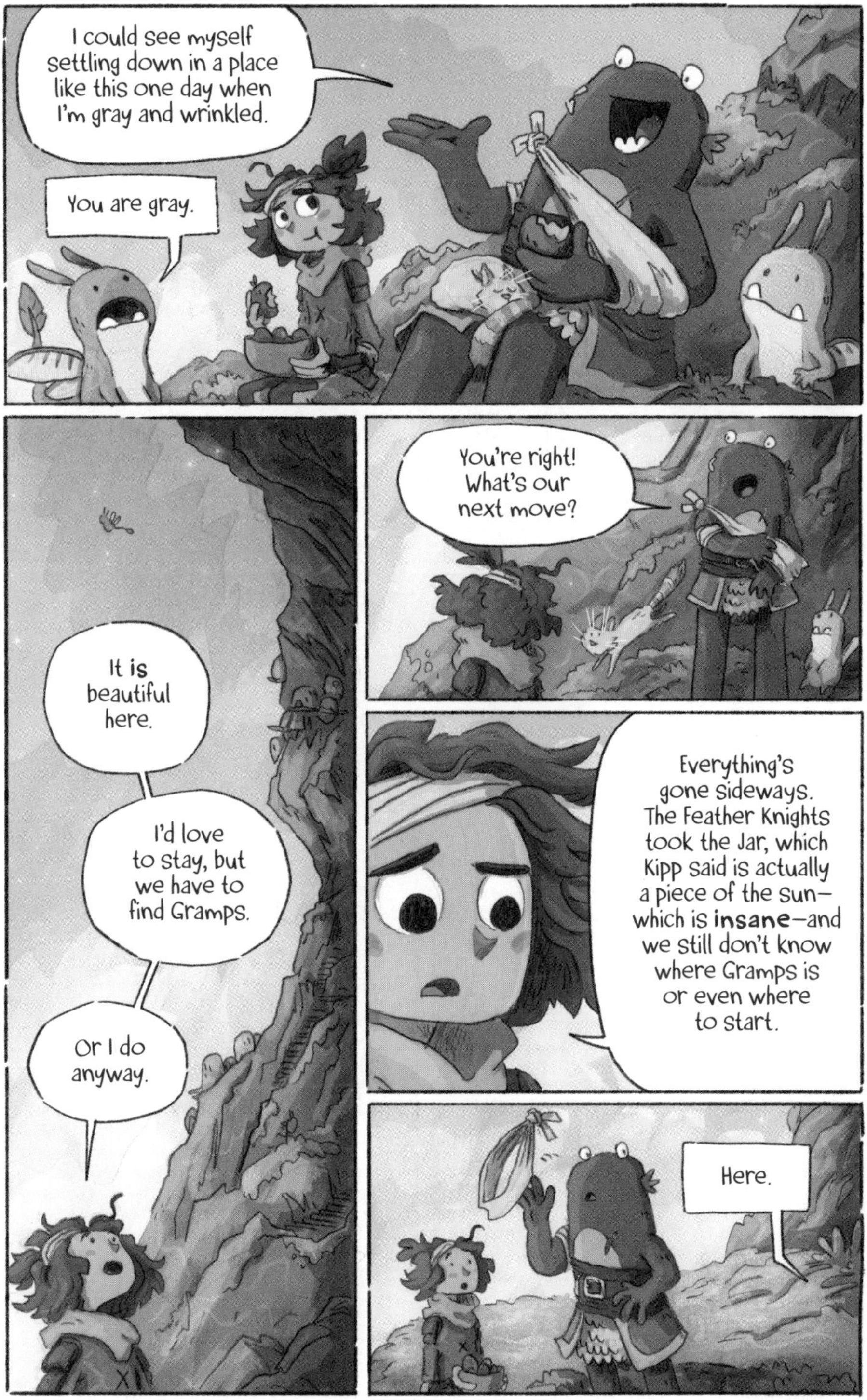
I could see myself settling down in a place like this one day when I'm gray and wrinkled.
You are gray.
It **is** beautiful here.
I'd love to stay, but we have to find Gramps.
Or I do anyway.
You're right! What's our next move?
Everything's gone sideways. The Feather Knights took the Jar, which Kipp said is actually a piece of the sun—which is **insane**—and we still don't know where Gramps is or even where to start.
Here.

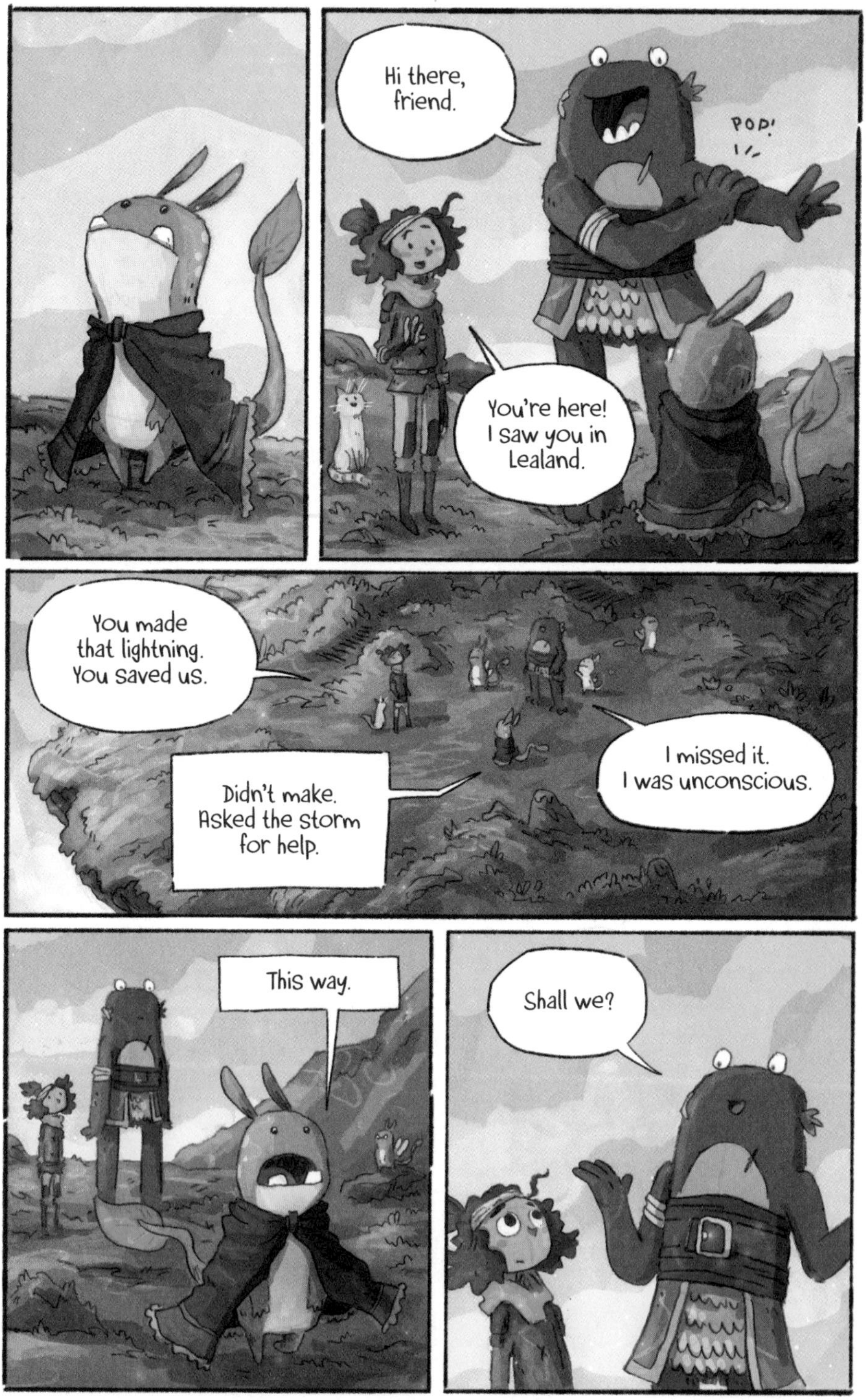
Hi there, friend.
POP!
You're here! I saw you in Lealand.
You made that lightning. You saved us.
I missed it. I was unconscious.
Didn't make. Asked the storm for help.
This way.
Shall we?

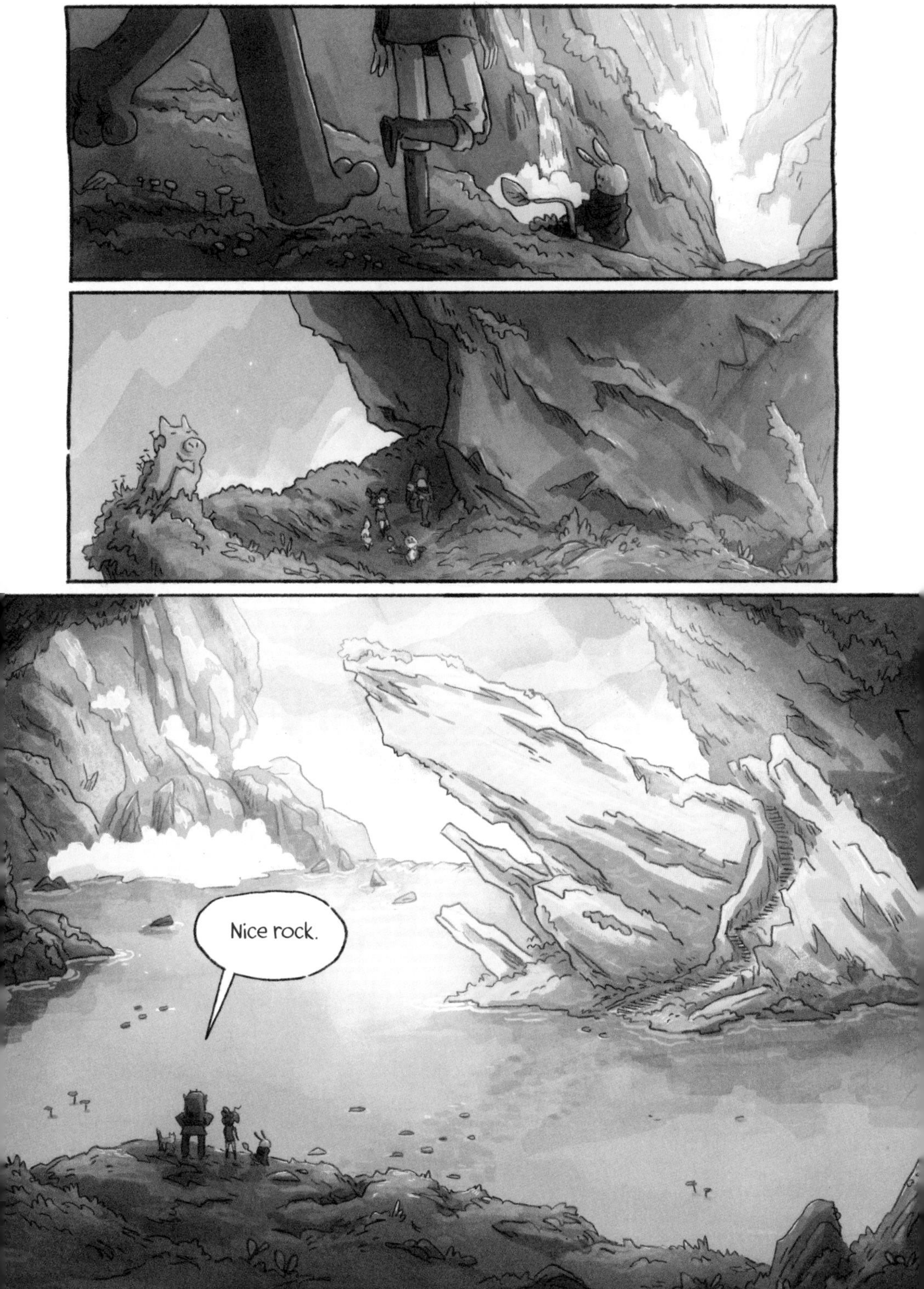
Nice rock.

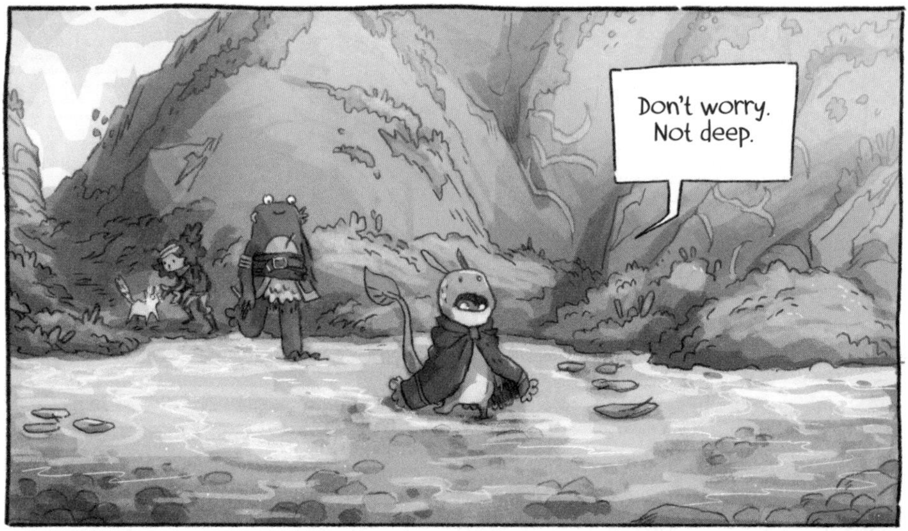
Don't worry.
Not deep.

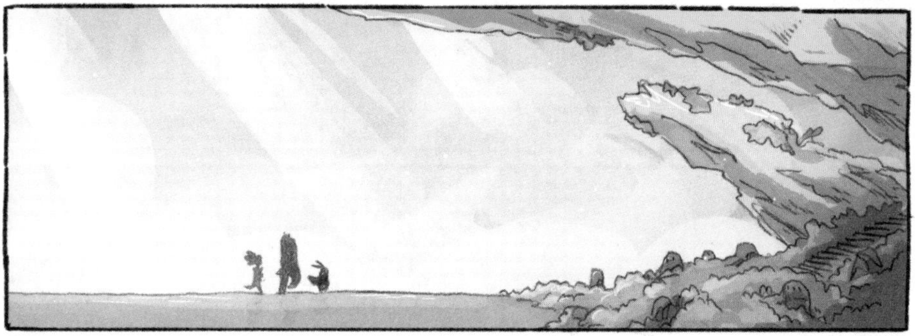

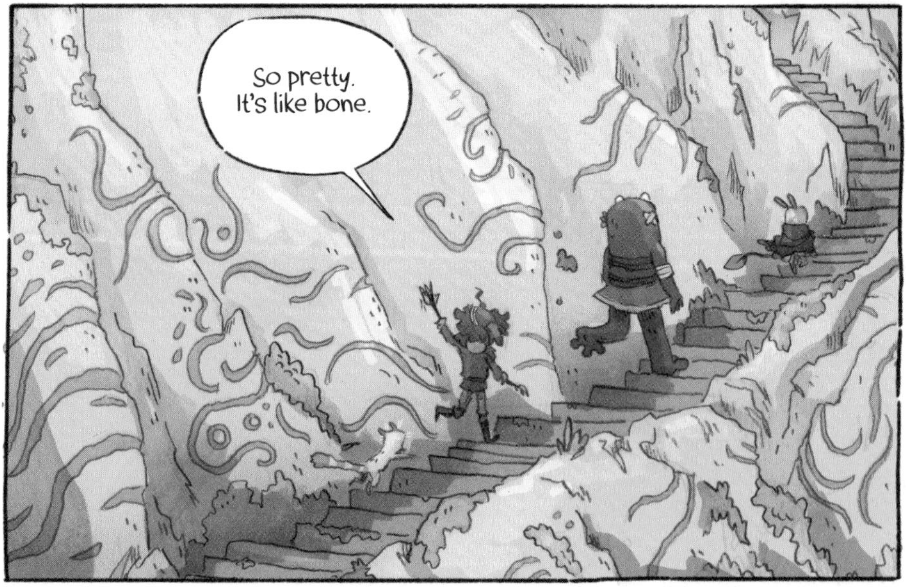
So pretty.
It's like bone.

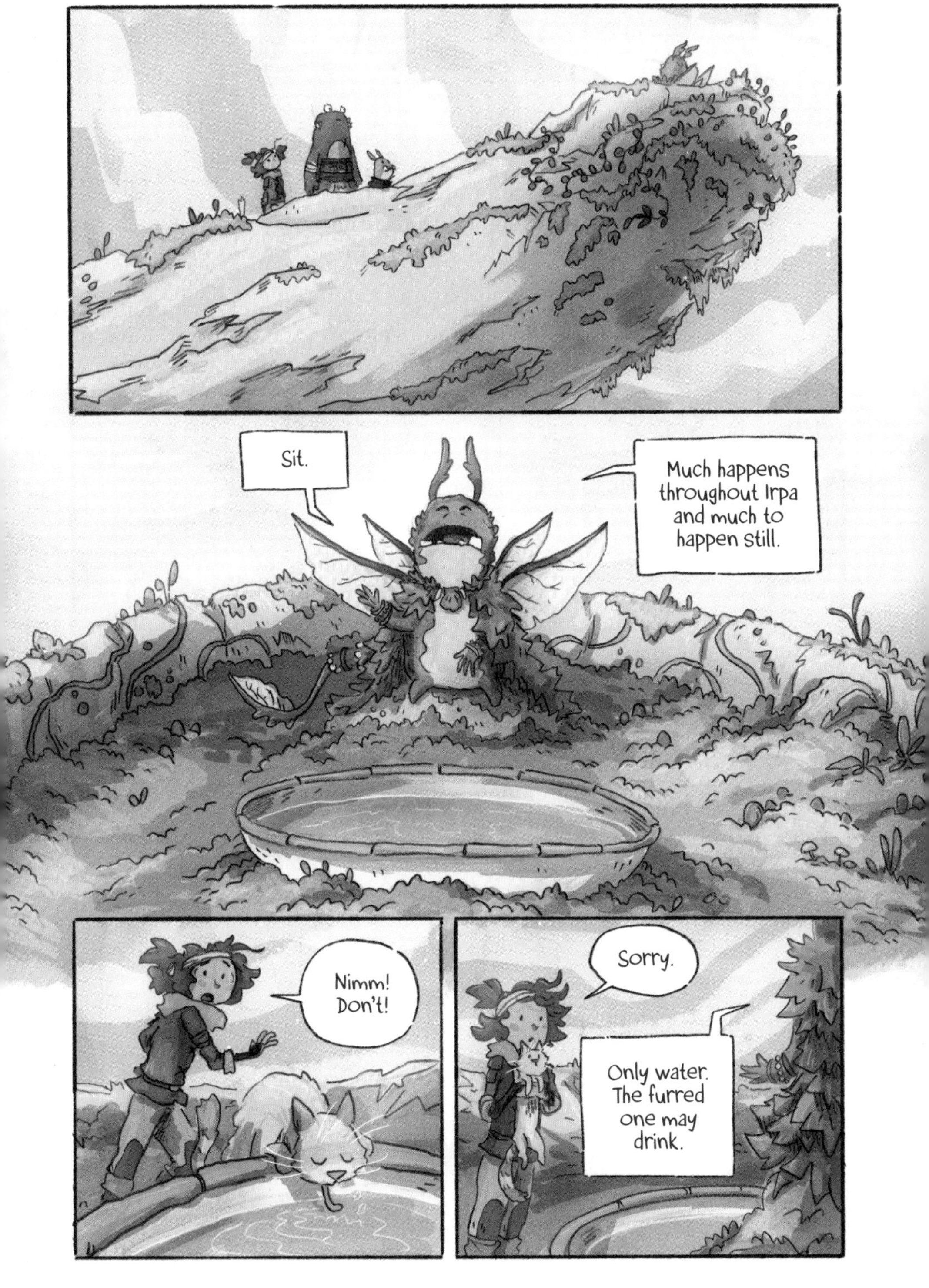
Sit.
Much happens throughout Irpa and much to happen still.
Nimm! Don't!
Sorry.
Only water. The furred one may drink.

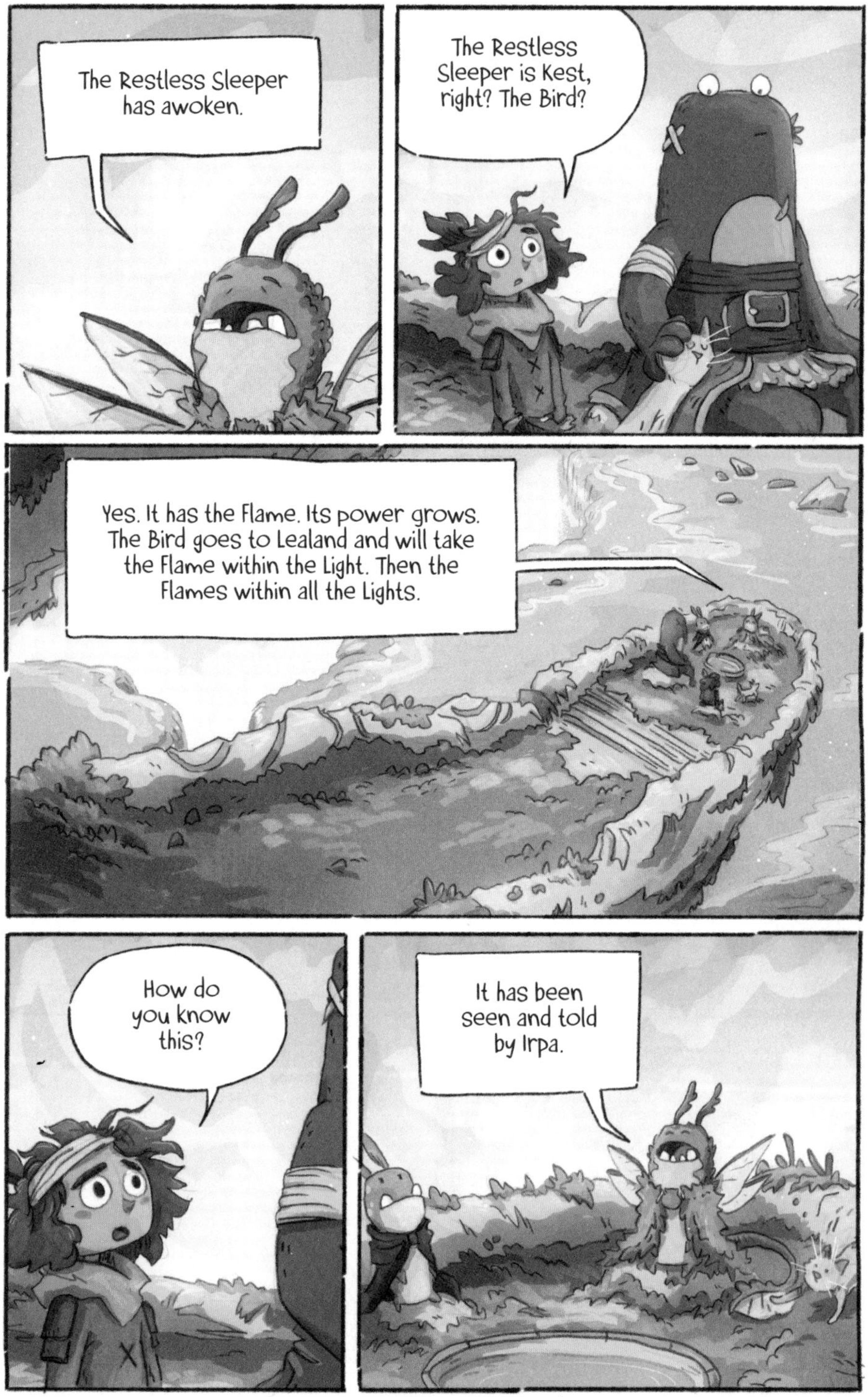
The Restless Sleeper has awoken.
The Restless Sleeper is Kest, right? The Bird?
Yes. It has the Flame. Its power grows. The Bird goes to Lealand and will take the Flame within the Light. Then the Flames within all the Lights.
How do you know this?
It has been seen and told by Irpa.

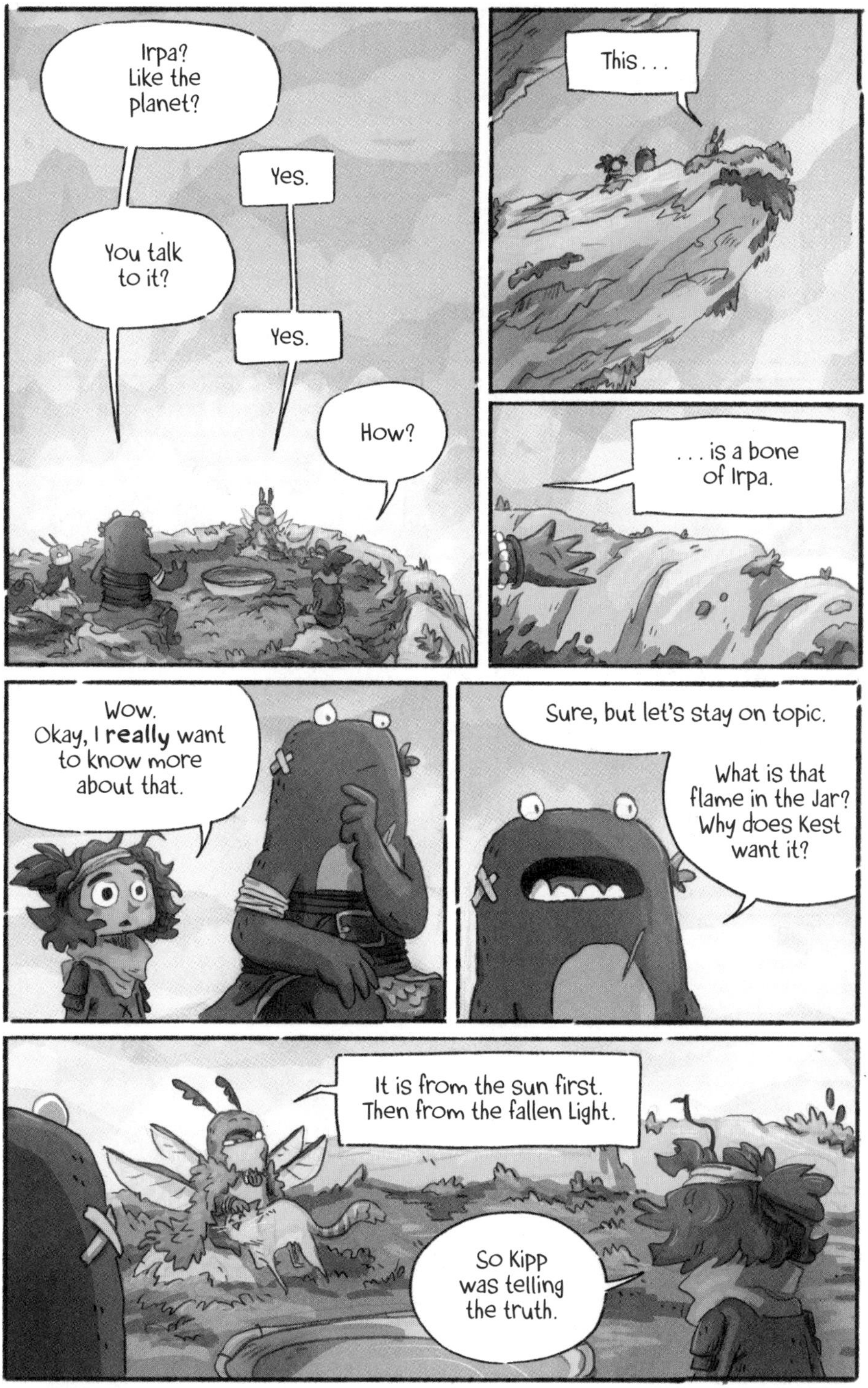

Irpa? Like the planet?
Yes.
You talk to it?
Yes.
How?
This...
...is a bone of Irpa.
Wow. Okay, I **really** want to know more about that.
Sure, but let's stay on topic.
What is that flame in the Jar? Why does Kest want it?
It is from the sun first. Then from the fallen Light.
So Kipp was telling the truth.

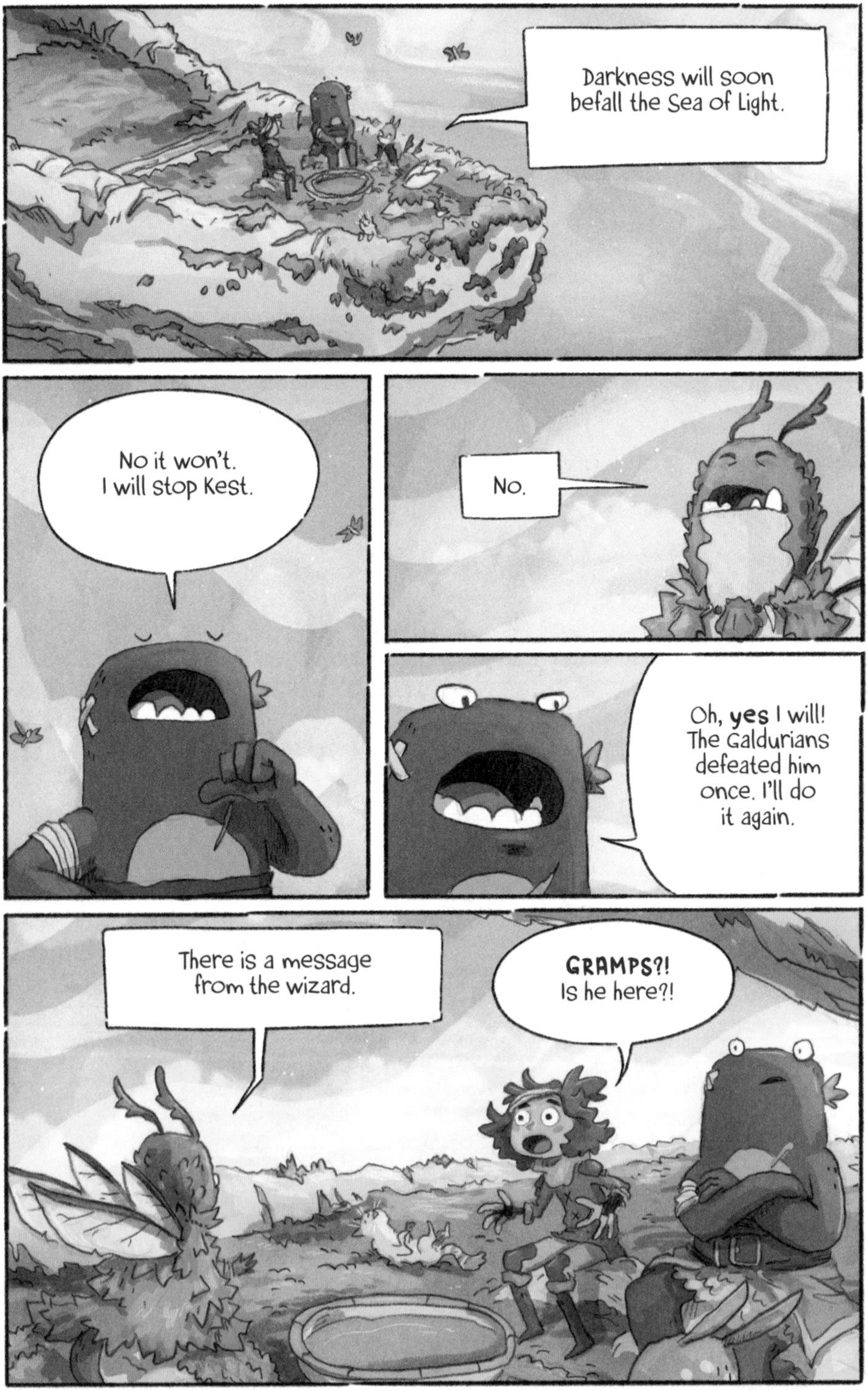
Darkness will soon befall the Sea of Light.
No it won't. I will stop Kest.
No.
Oh, **yes** I will! The Galdurians defeated him once. I'll do it again.
There is a message from the wizard.
GRAMPS?! Is he here?!

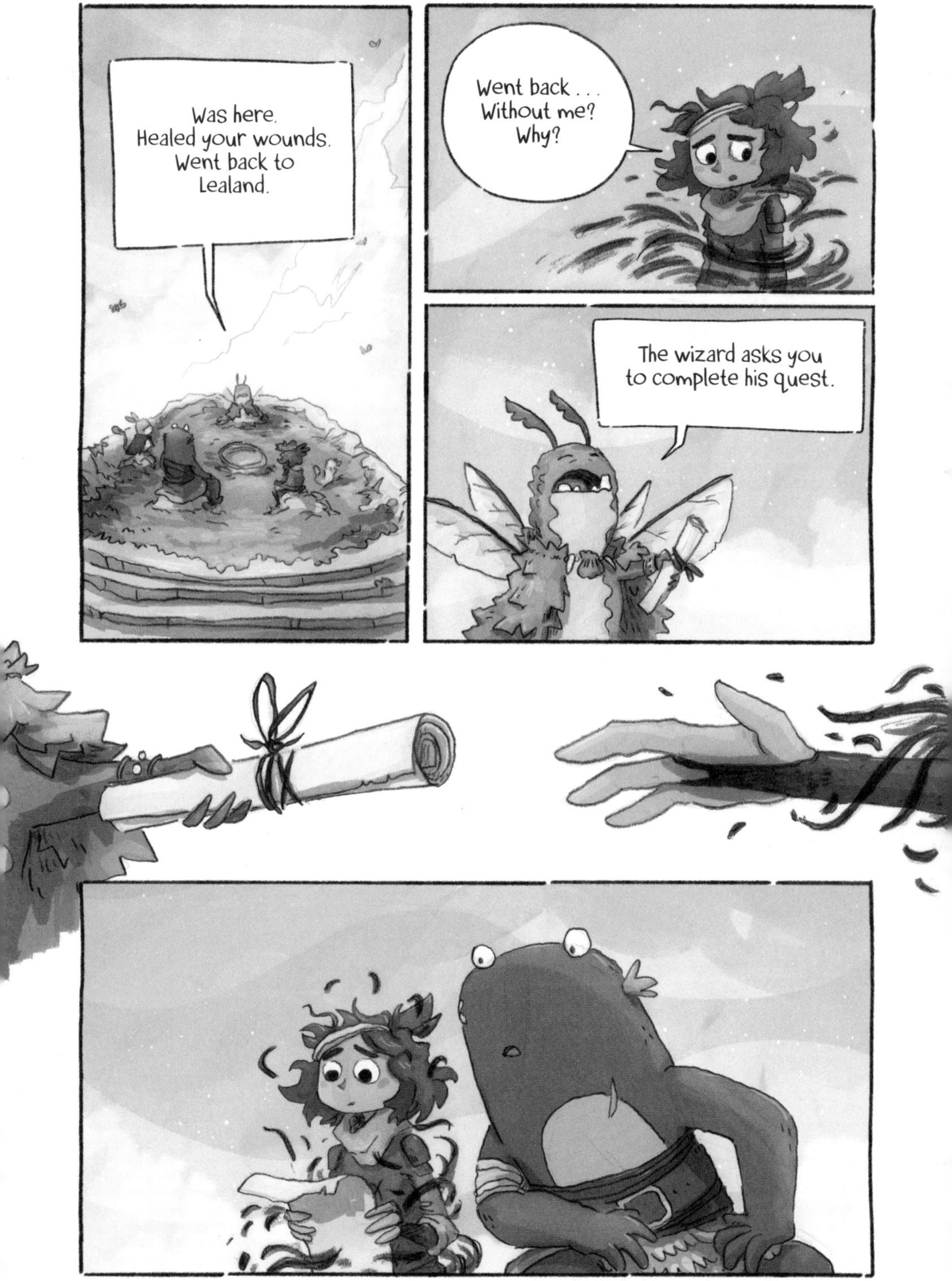
Was here.
Healed your wounds.
Went back to
Lealand.
Went back . . .
Without me?
Why?
The wizard asks you
to complete his quest.

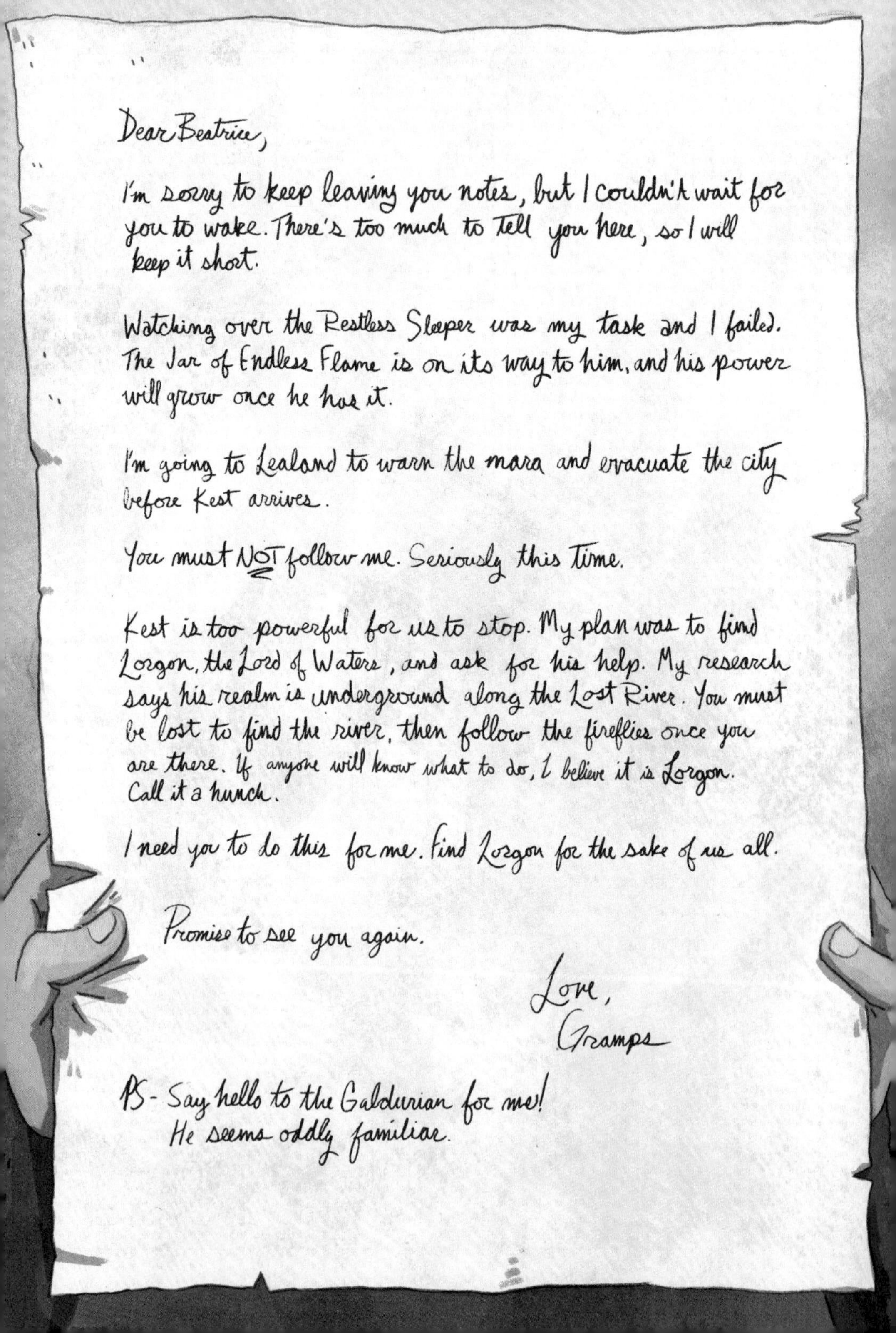

Dear Beatrice,

I'm sorry to keep leaving you notes, but I couldn't wait for you to wake. There's too much to tell you here, so I will keep it short.

Watching over the Restless Sleeper was my task and I failed. The Jar of Endless Flame is on its way to him, and his power will grow once he has it.

I'm going to Lealand to warn the mara and evacuate the city before Kest arrives.

You must NOT follow me. Seriously this time.

Kest is too powerful for us to stop. My plan was to find Lorgon, the Lord of Waters, and ask for his help. My research says his realm is underground along the Lost River. You must be lost to find the river, then follow the fireflies once you are there. If anyone will know what to do, I believe it is Lorgon. Call it a hunch.

I need you to do this for me. Find Lorgon for the sake of us all.

Promise to see you again.

Love,
Gramps

PS- Say hello to the Galdurian for me!
He seems oddly familiar.

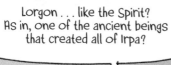

Lorgon . . . like the Spirit?
As in, one of the ancient beings
that created all of Irpa?

Yes.

How?!
Nobody's ever seen
a Spirit. And we're supposed
to find one and ask it for help?!
They might not be around
anymore. Or they might
not even be real!

They said the same thing about
Galdurians, to be fair. But even still,
I don't think searching for Lorgon
is the answer.

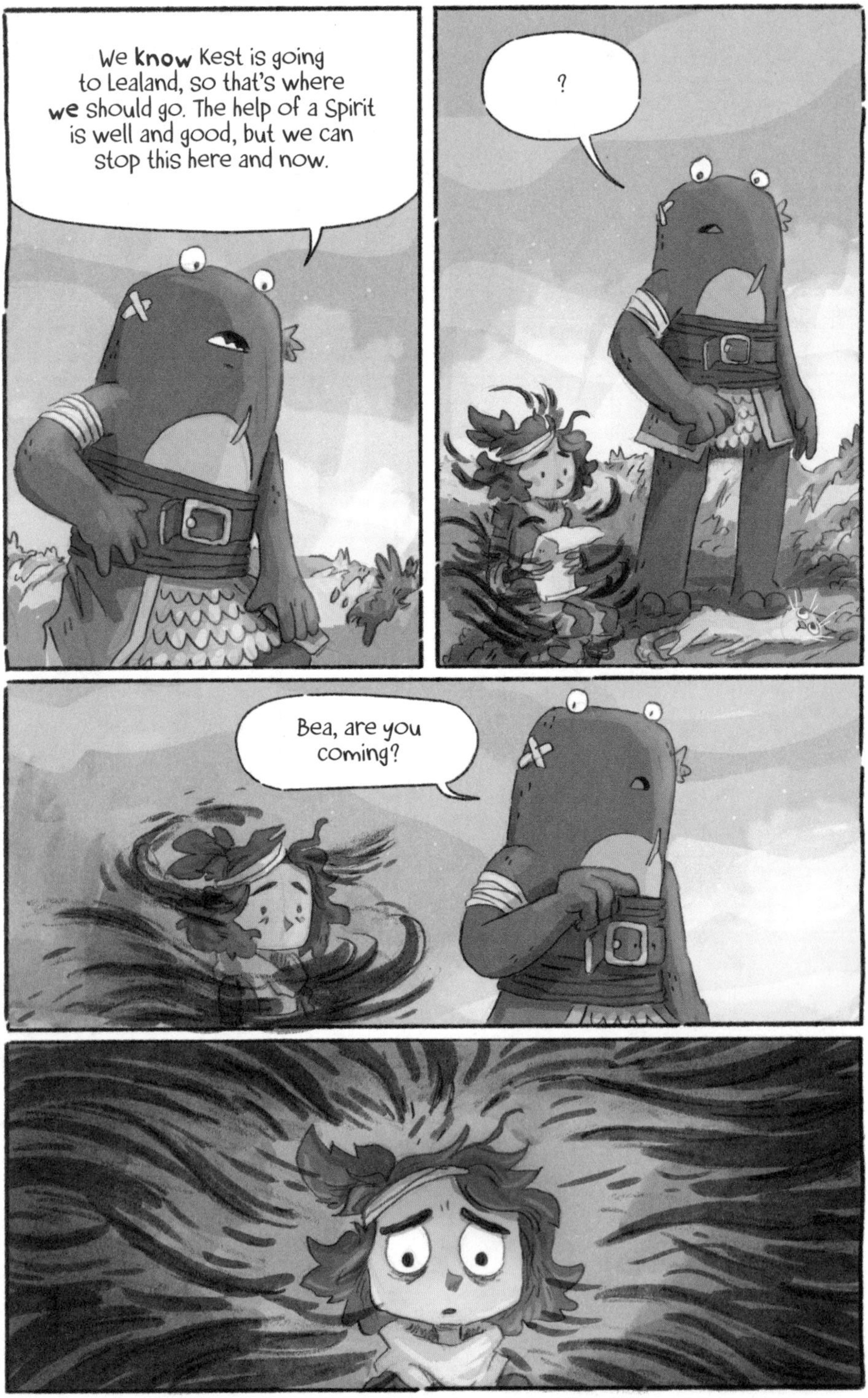
We **know** Kest is going to Lealand, so that's where **we** should go. The help of a Spirit is well and good, but we can stop this here and now.
?
Bea, are you coming?

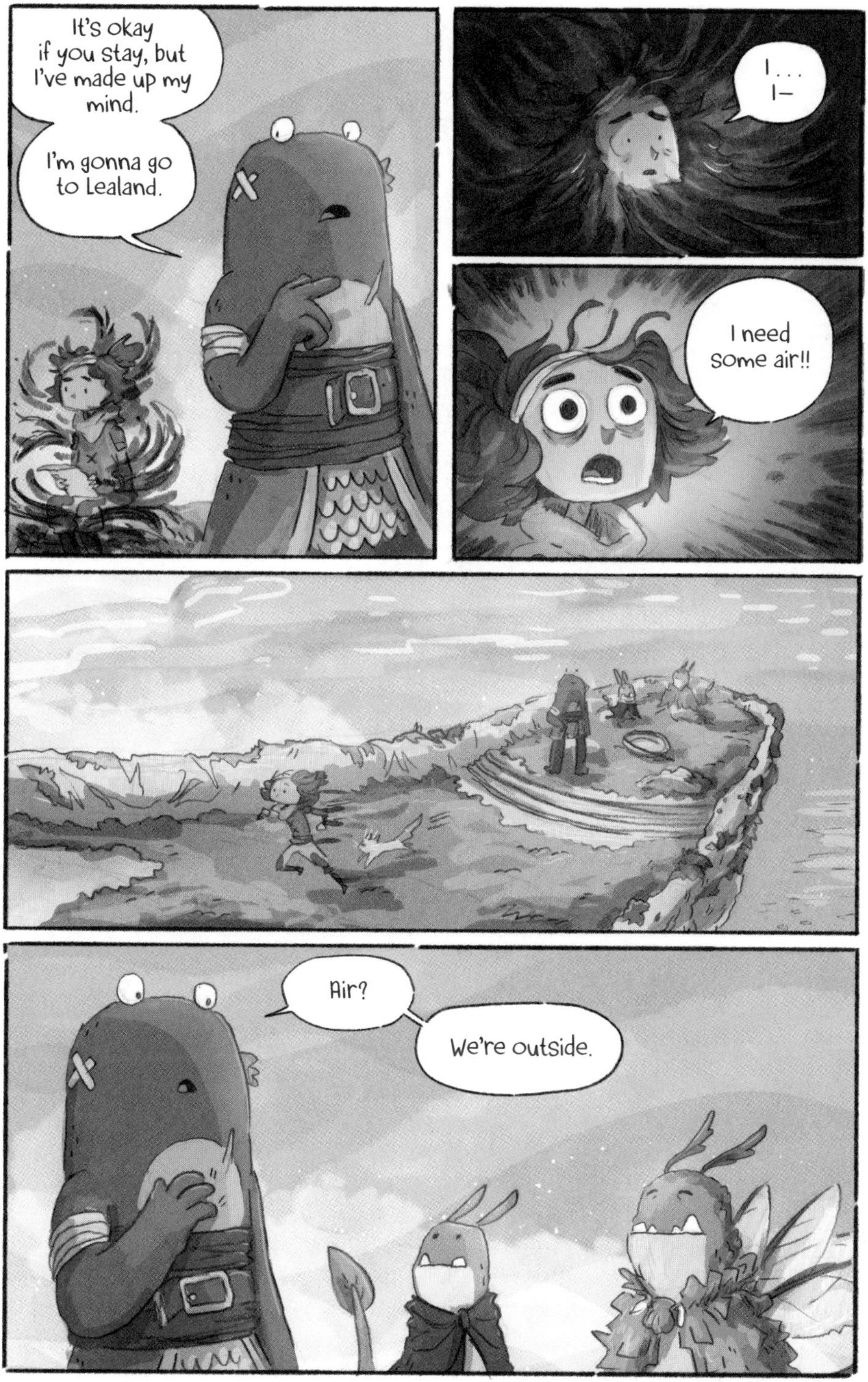
It's okay if you stay, but I've made up my mind.
I'm gonna go to Lealand.
I . . .
I—
I need some air!!
Air?
We're outside.

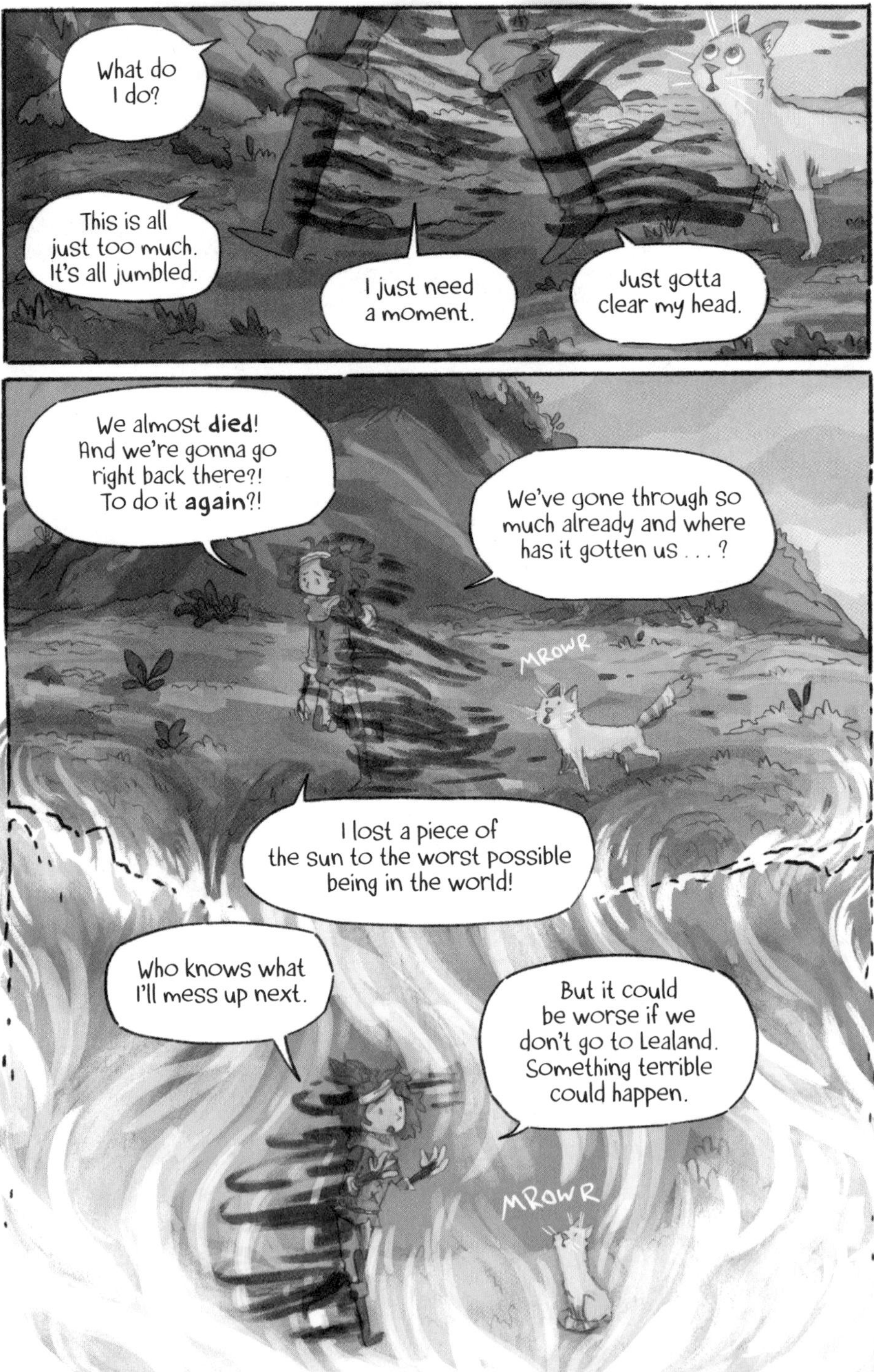
What do I do?
This is all just too much. It's all jumbled.
I just need a moment.
Just gotta clear my head.
We almost **died**! And we're gonna go right back there?! To do it **again**?!
We've gone through so much already and where has it gotten us . . . ?
MROWR
I lost a piece of the sun to the worst possible being in the world!
Who knows what I'll mess up next.
But it could be worse if we don't go to Lealand. Something terrible could happen.
MROWR

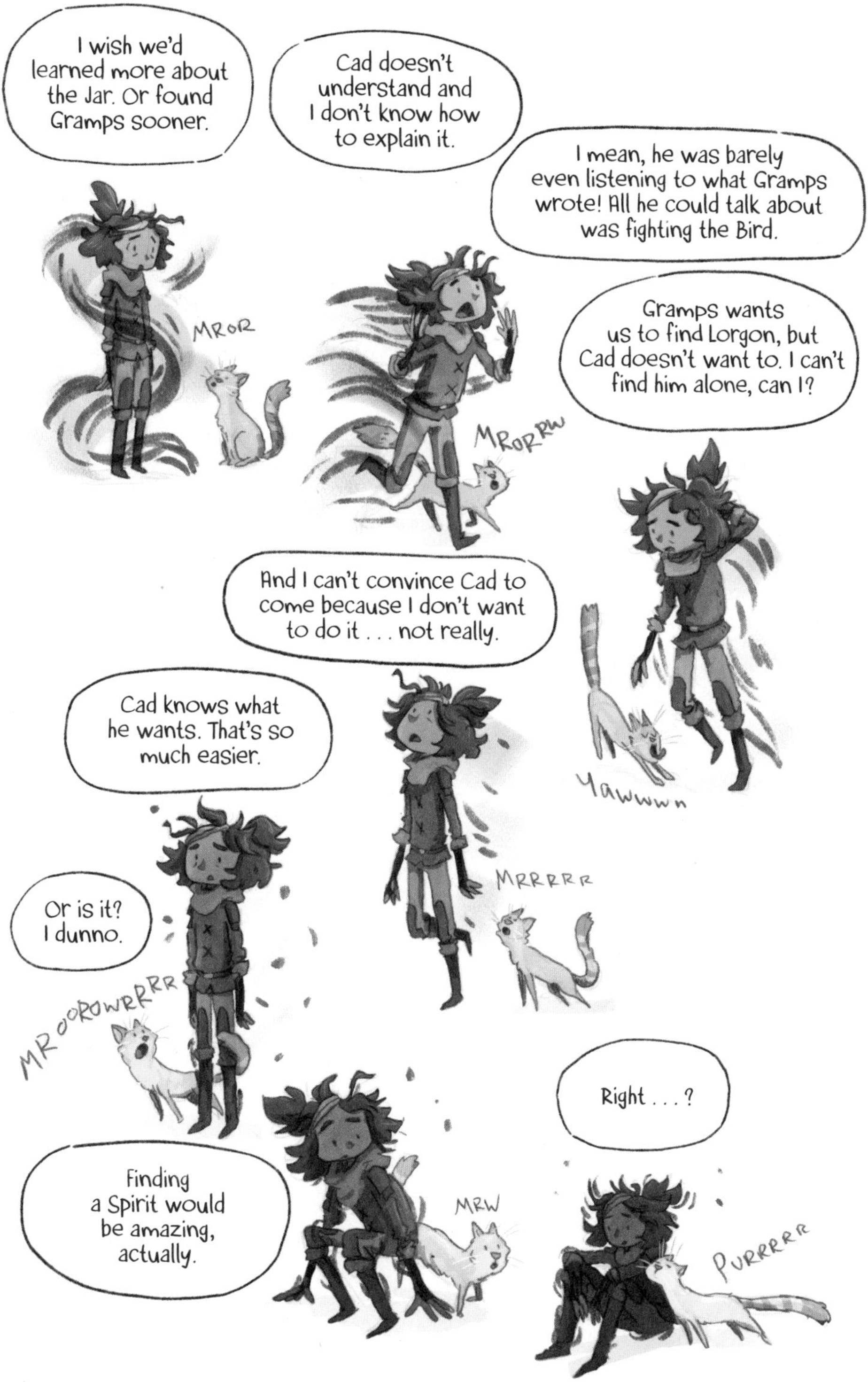
I wish we'd learned more about the Jar. Or found Gramps sooner.
Cad doesn't understand and I don't know how to explain it.
I mean, he was barely even listening to what Gramps wrote! All he could talk about was fighting the Bird.
MROR
MRORRW
Gramps wants us to find Lorgon, but Cad doesn't want to. I can't find him alone, can I?
And I can't convince Cad to come because I don't want to do it . . . not really.
Yawwwn
Cad knows what he wants. That's so much easier.
MRRRRR
Or is it? I dunno.
MROOROWRRRR
Right . . . ?
Finding a Spirit would be amazing, actually.
MRW
PURRRRR

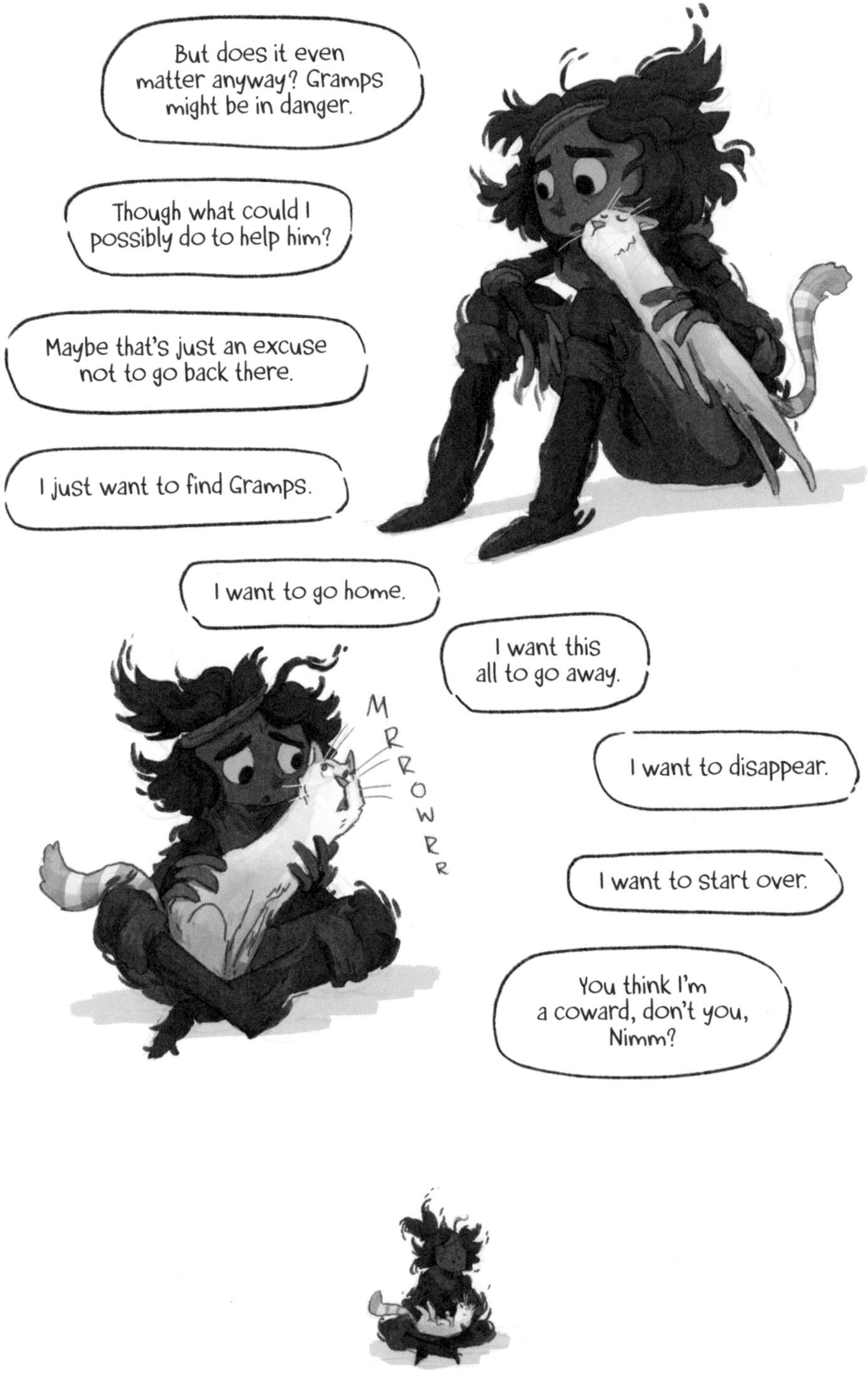
But does it even matter anyway? Gramps might be in danger.
Though what could I possibly do to help him?
Maybe that's just an excuse not to go back there.
I just want to find Gramps.
I want to go home.
I want this all to go away.
MRROWRR
I want to disappear.
I want to start over.
You think I'm a coward, don't you, Nimm?

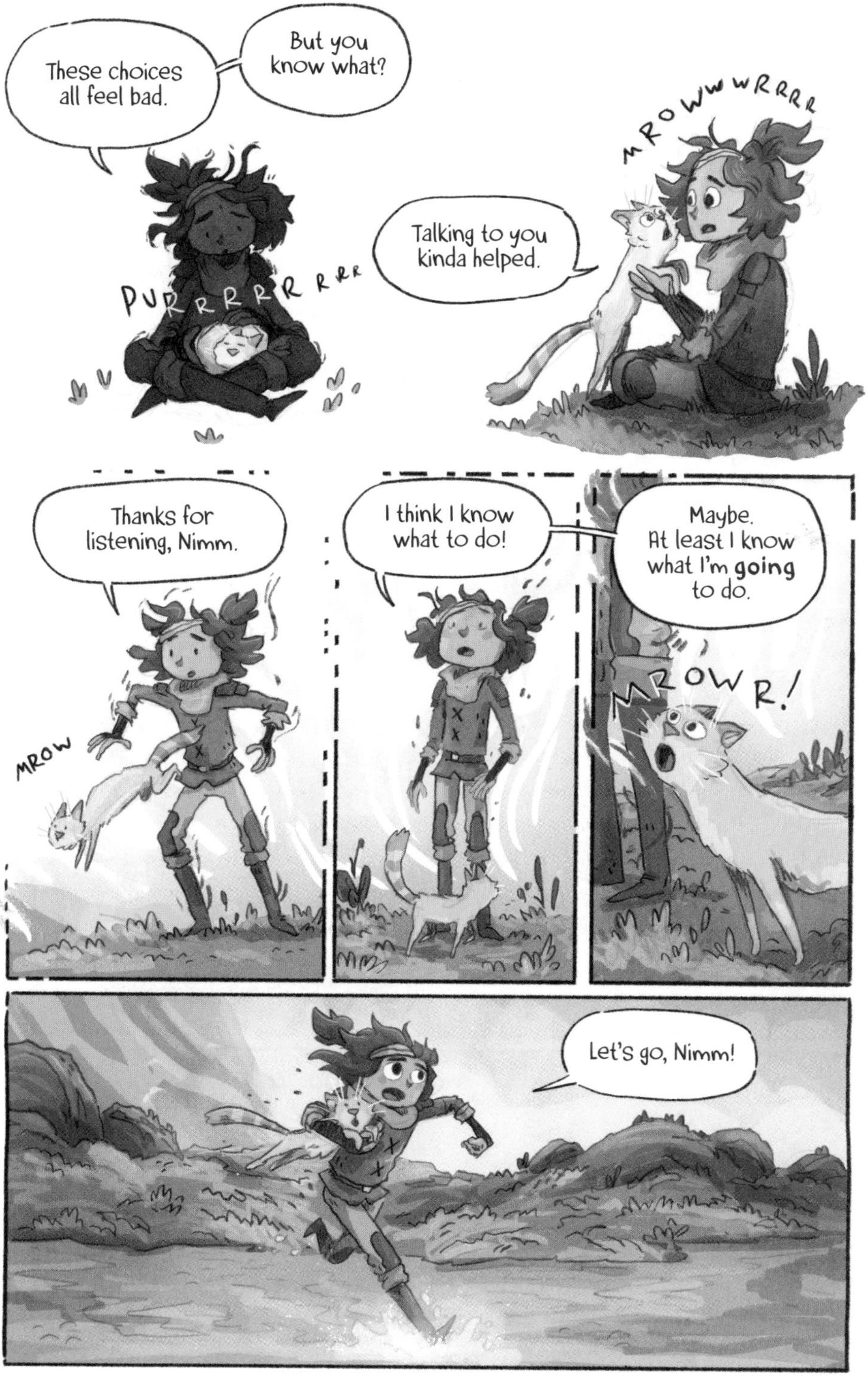
These choices all feel bad.
But you know what?
PURRRRRRRR
Talking to you kinda helped.
MROWWWWRRRRR
Thanks for listening, Nimm.
MROW
I think I know what to do!
Maybe. At least I know what I'm **going** to do.
MROWR!
Let's go, Nimm!

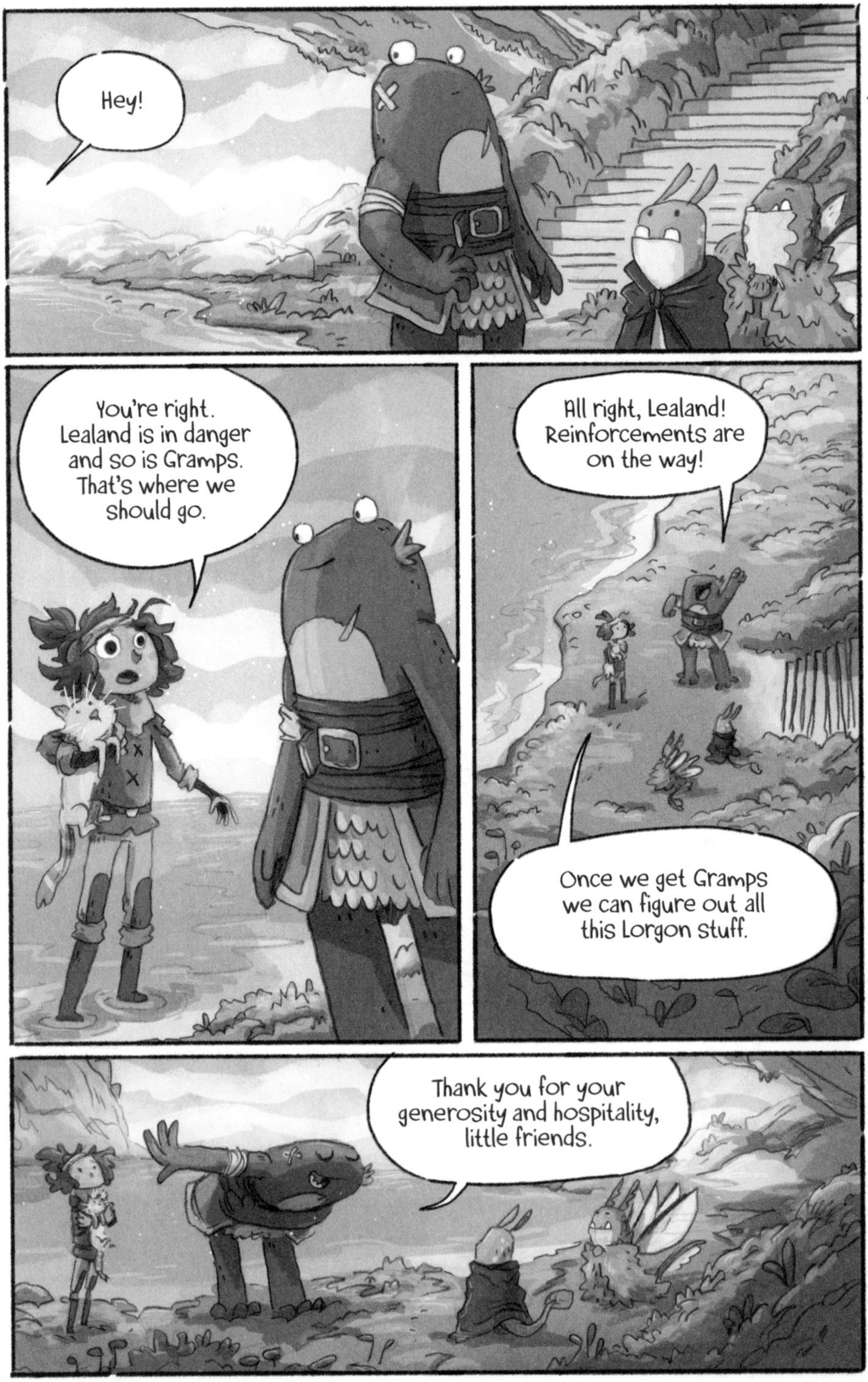
Hey!
You're right. Lealand is in danger and so is Gramps. That's where we should go.
All right, Lealand! Reinforcements are on the way!
Once we get Gramps we can figure out all this Lorgon stuff.
Thank you for your generosity and hospitality, little friends.

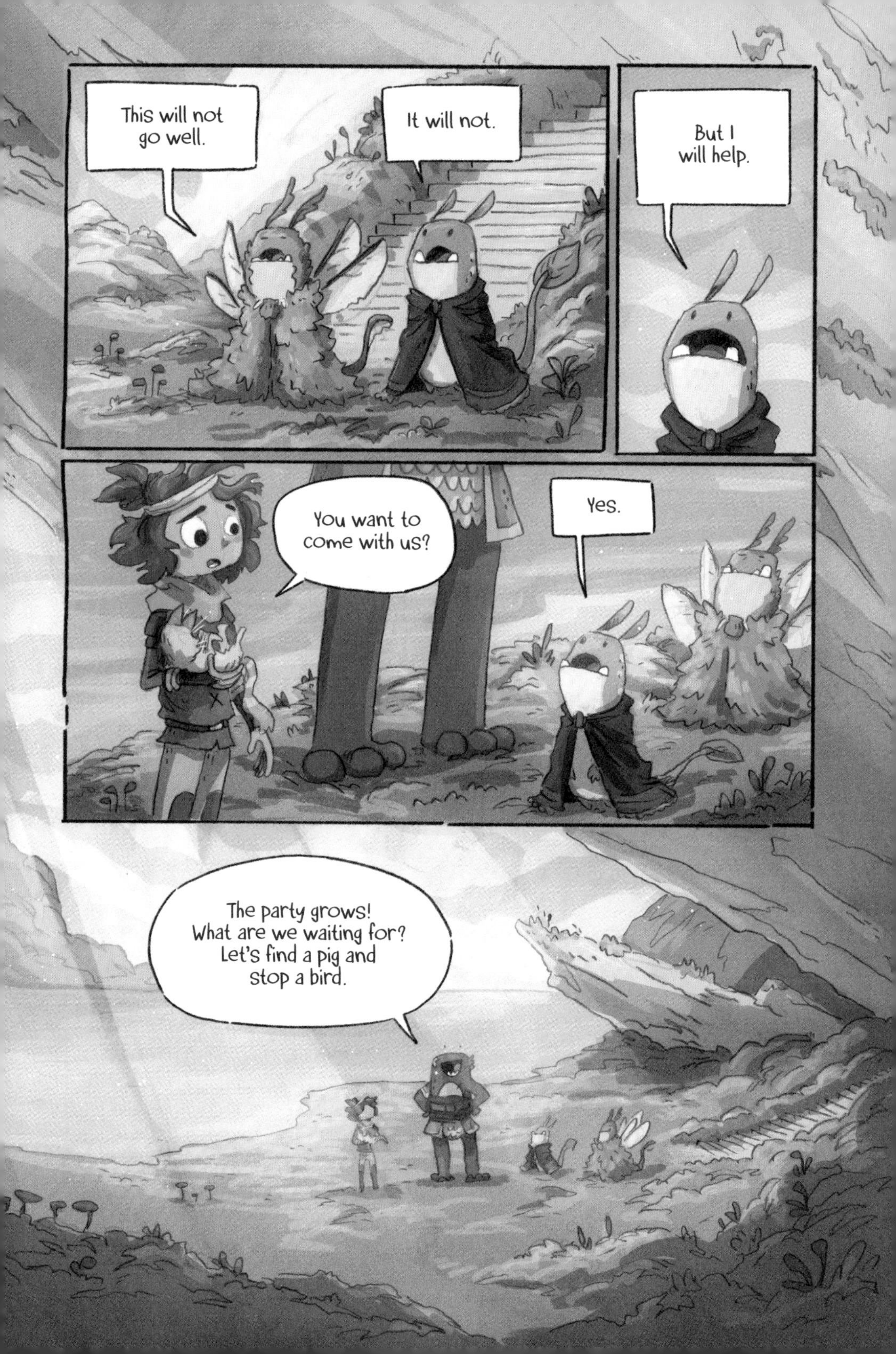
This will not go well.
It will not.
But I will help.
You want to come with us?
Yes.
The party grows! What are we waiting for? Let's find a pig and stop a bird.

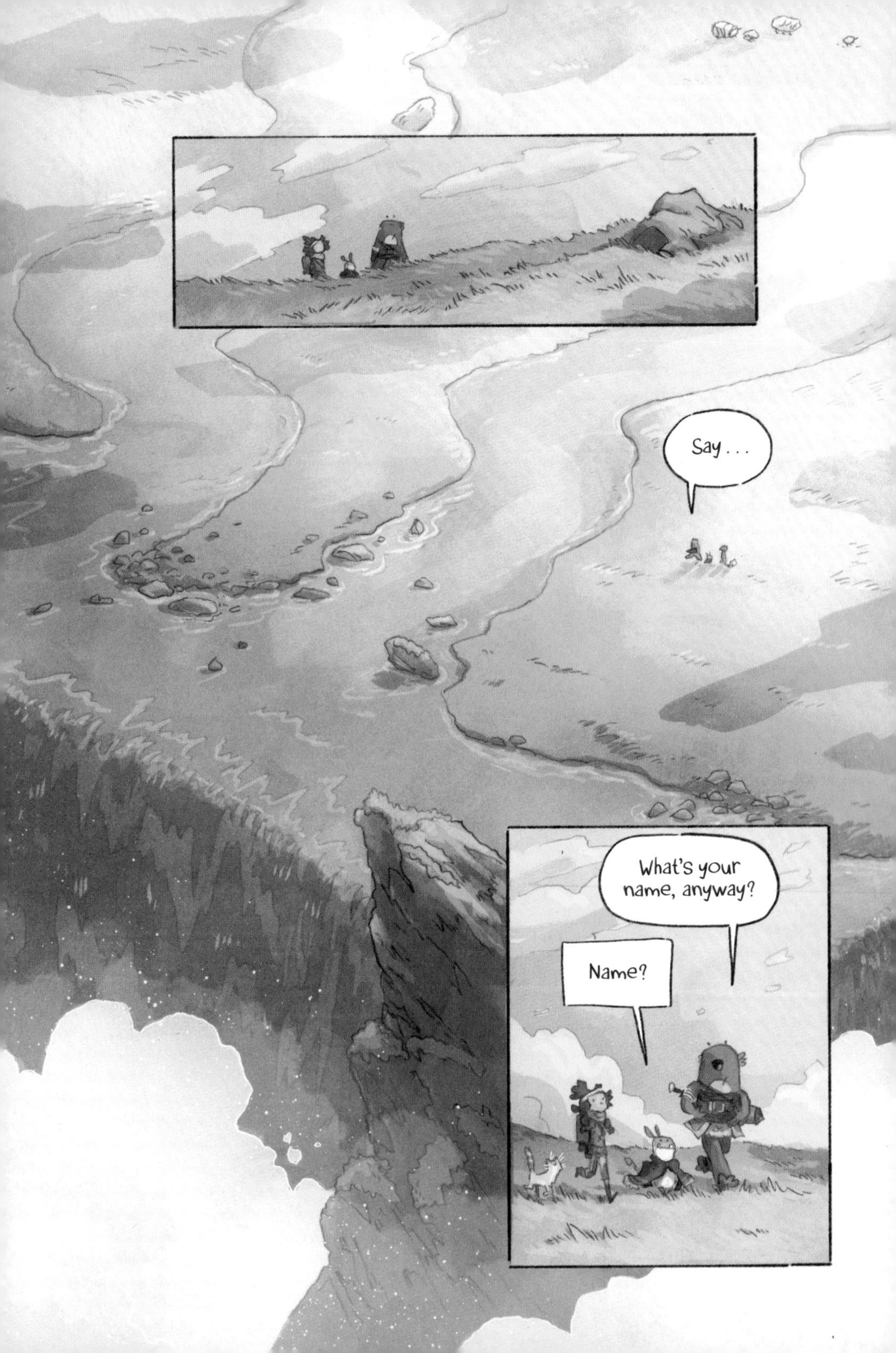
Say . . .
What's your name, anyway?
Name?

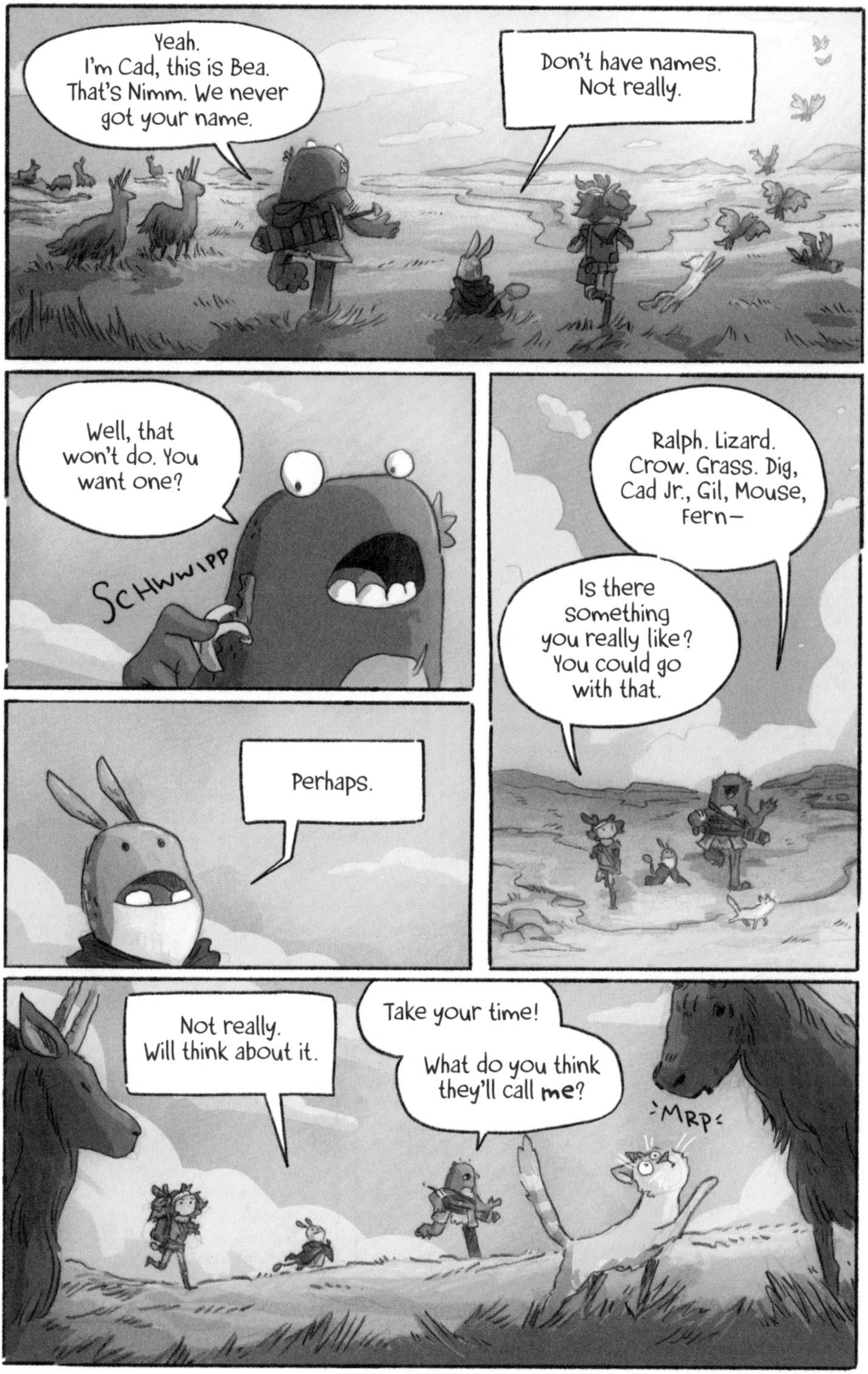
Yeah.
I'm Cad, this is Bea.
That's Nimm. We never
got your name.
Don't have names.
Not really.
Well, that
won't do. You
want one?
SCHWWIPP
Ralph. Lizard.
Crow. Grass. Dig,
Cad Jr., Gil, Mouse,
Fern—
Is there
something
you really like?
You could go
with that.
Perhaps.
Not really.
Will think about it.
Take your time!
What do you think
they'll call **me**?
MRP

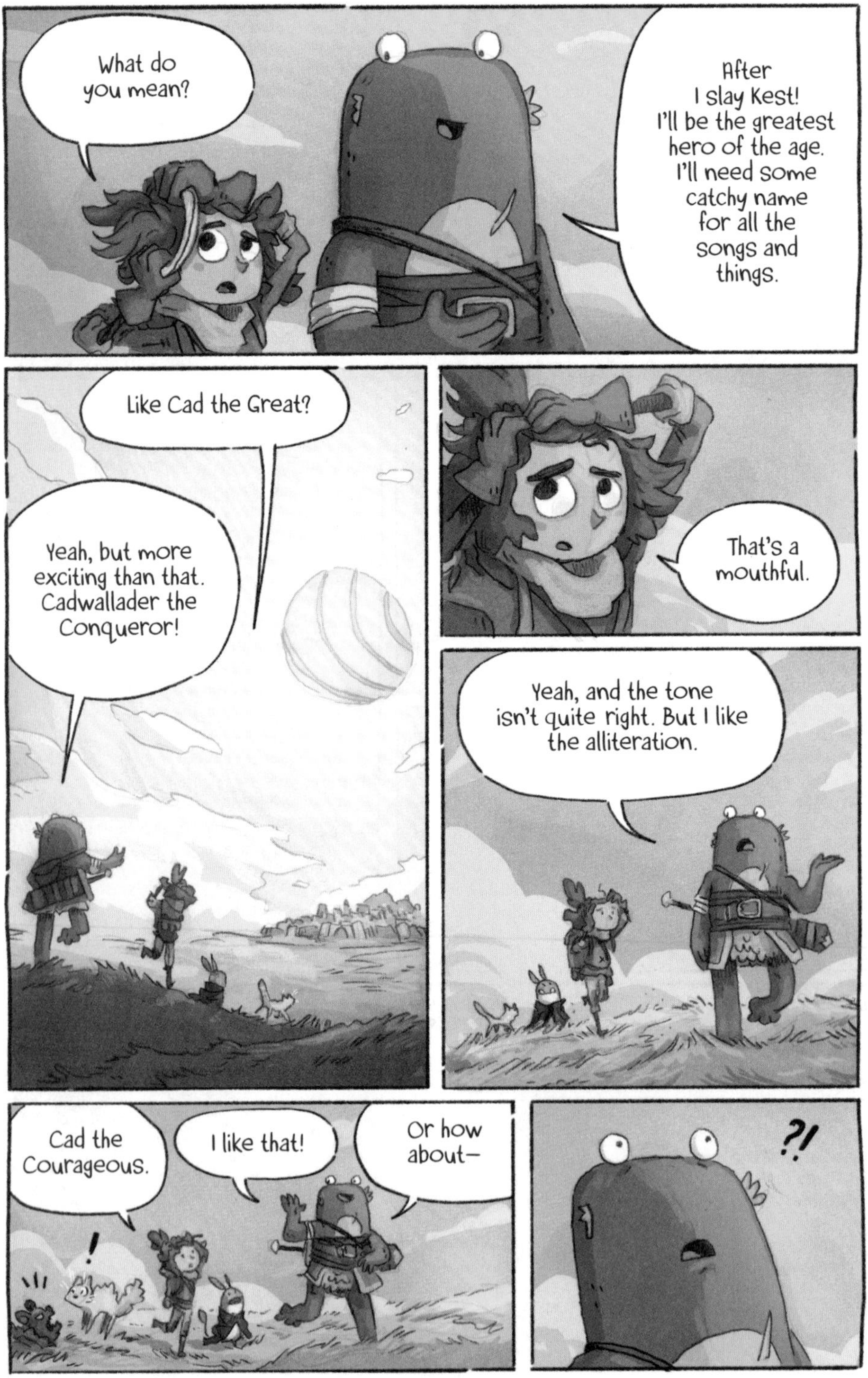
What do you mean?
After I slay Kest! I'll be the greatest hero of the age. I'll need some catchy name for all the songs and things.
Like Cad the Great?
Yeah, but more exciting than that. Cadwallader the Conqueror!
That's a mouthful.
Yeah, and the tone isn't quite right. But I like the alliteration.
Cad the Courageous.
I like that!
Or how about—
!
?!

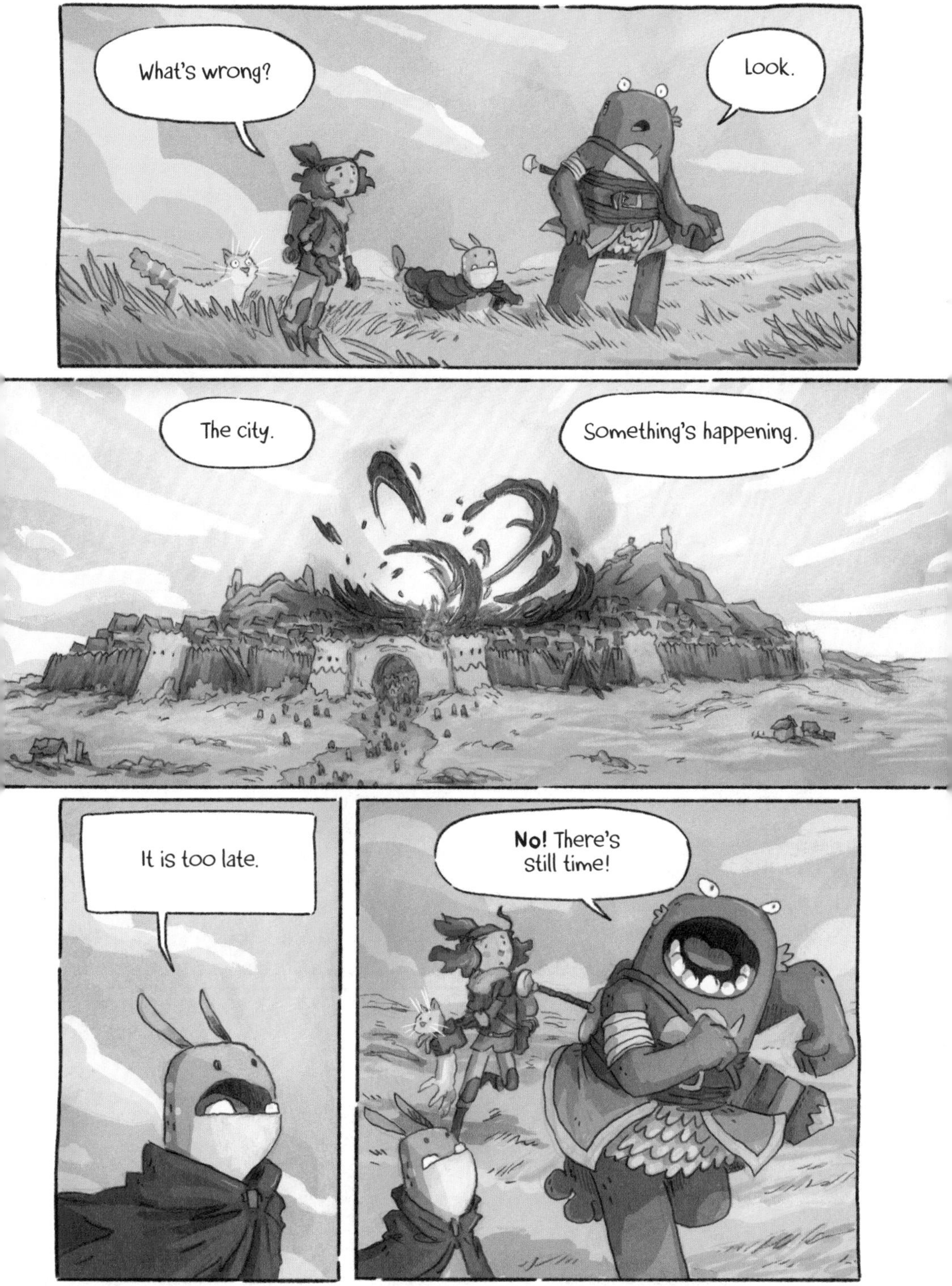
What's wrong?
Look.
The city.
Something's happening.
It is too late.
No! There's still time!

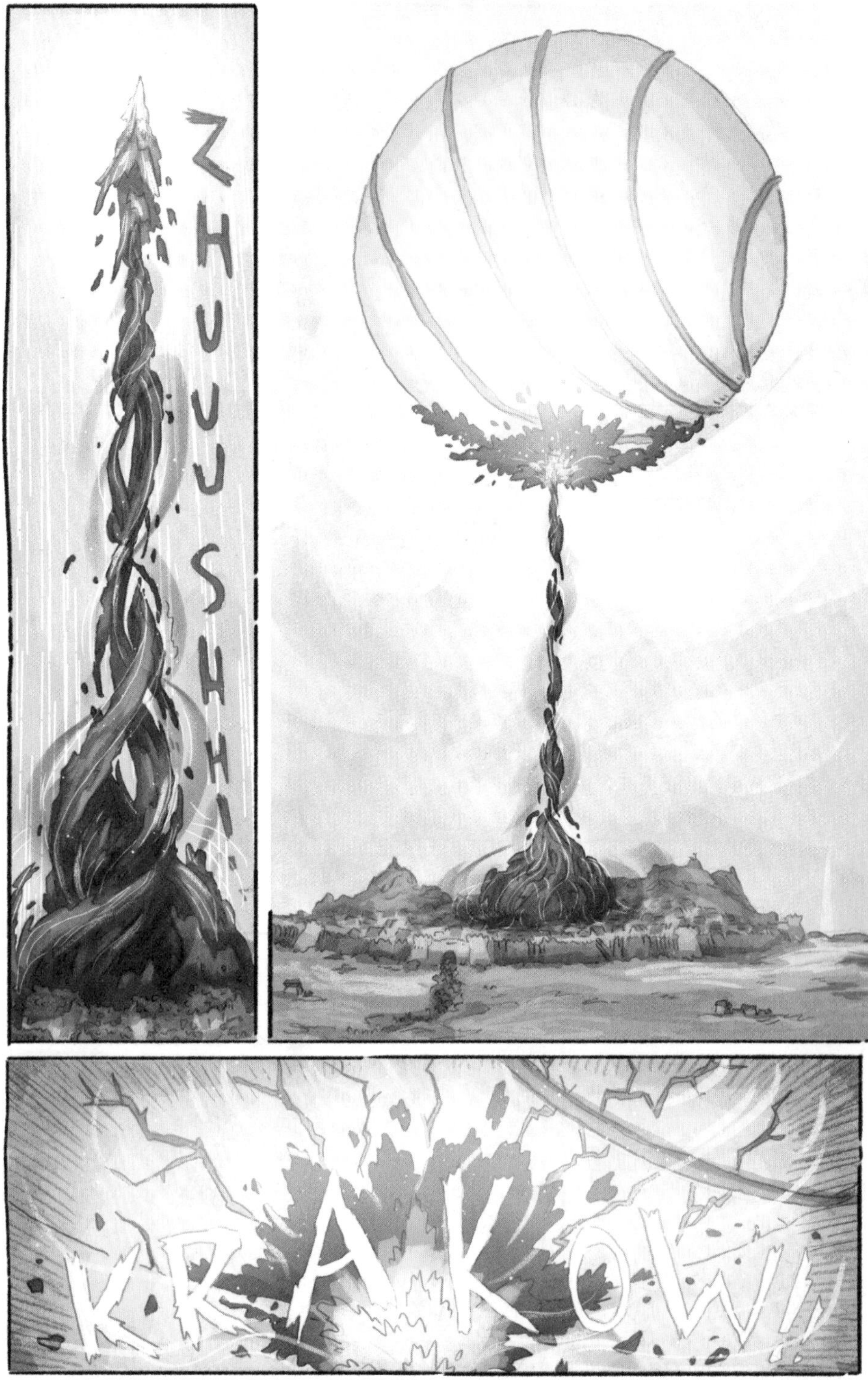
ZHUUUSHHH!
KRAKOW!

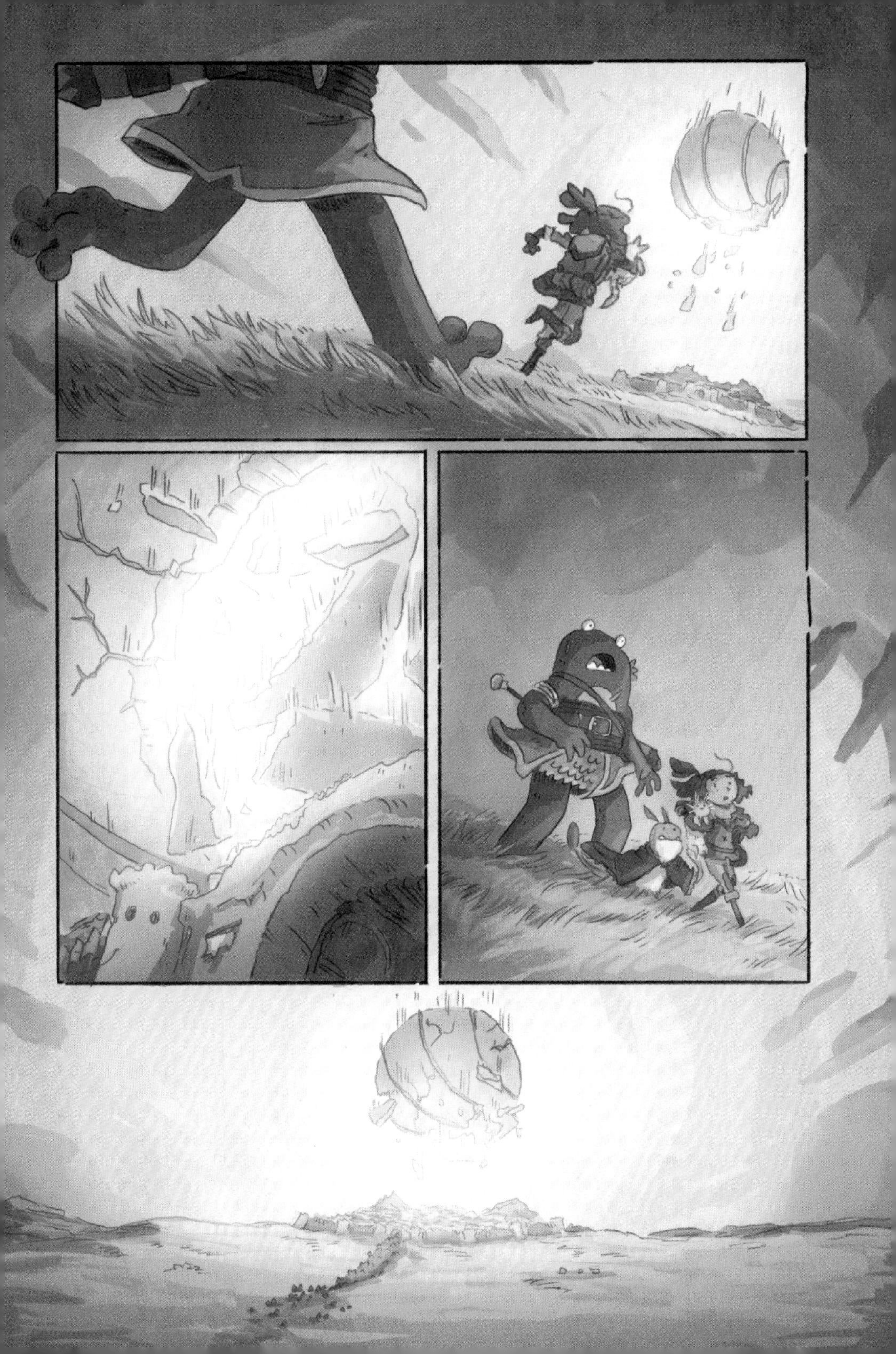

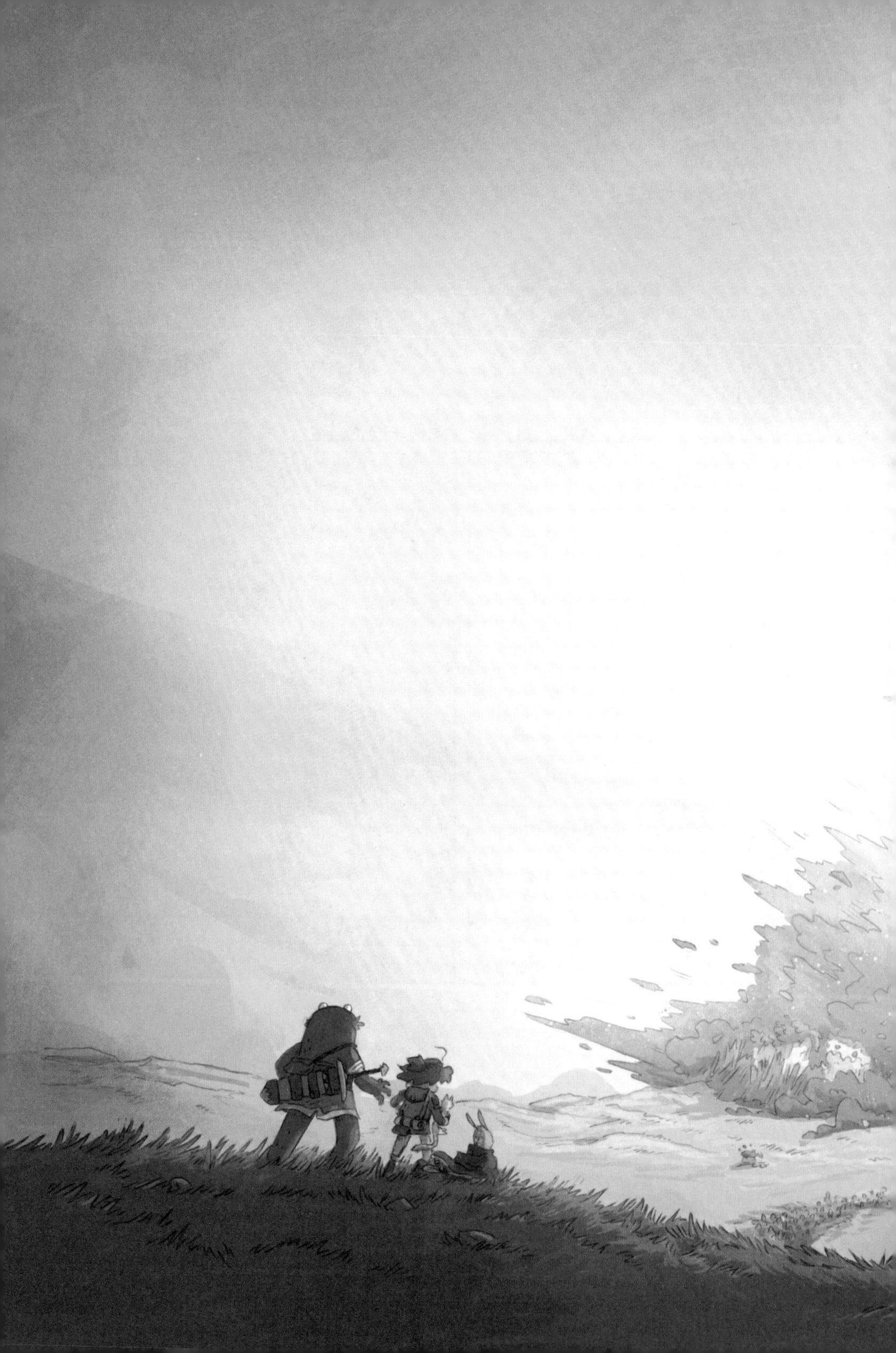

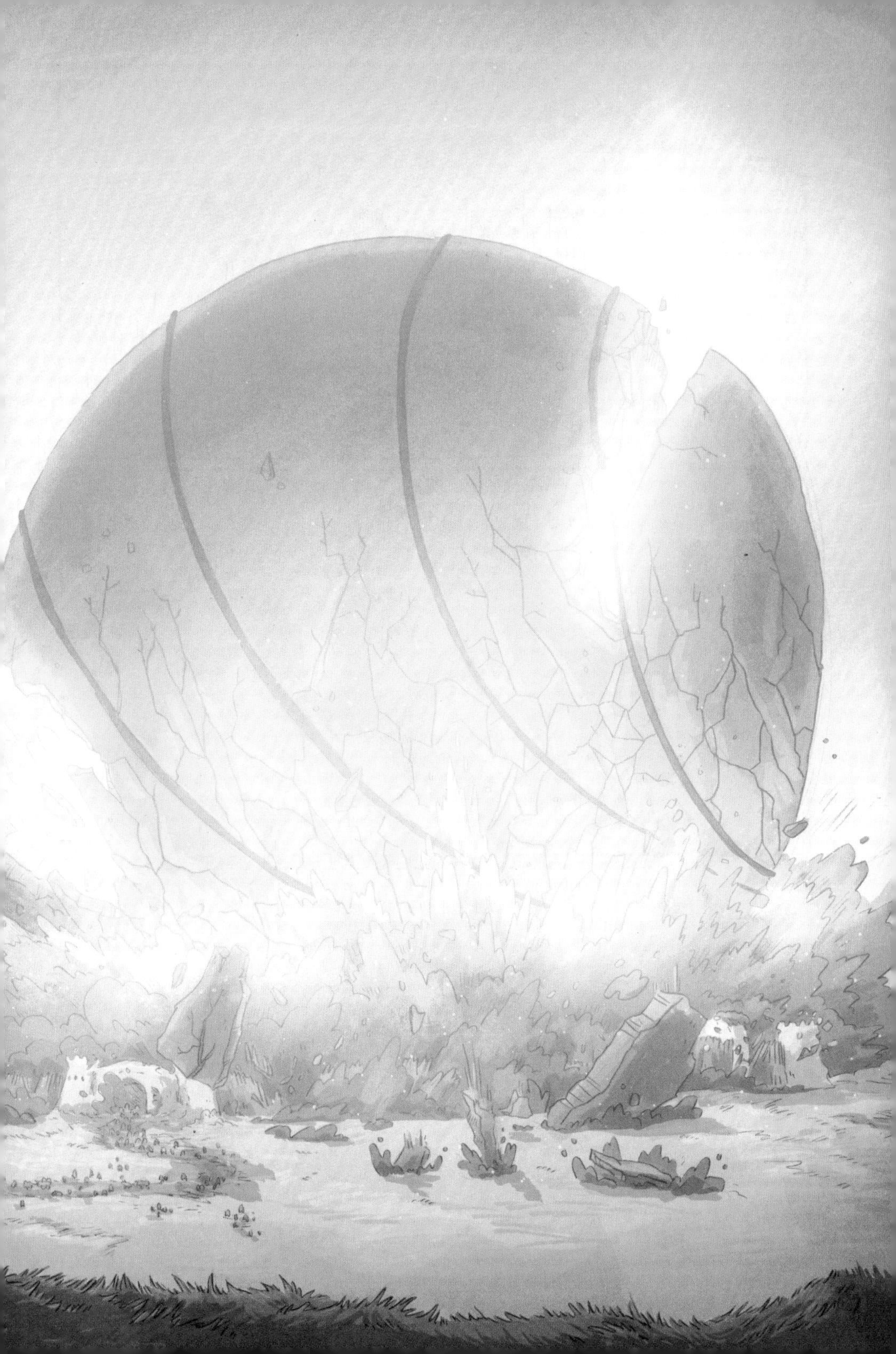

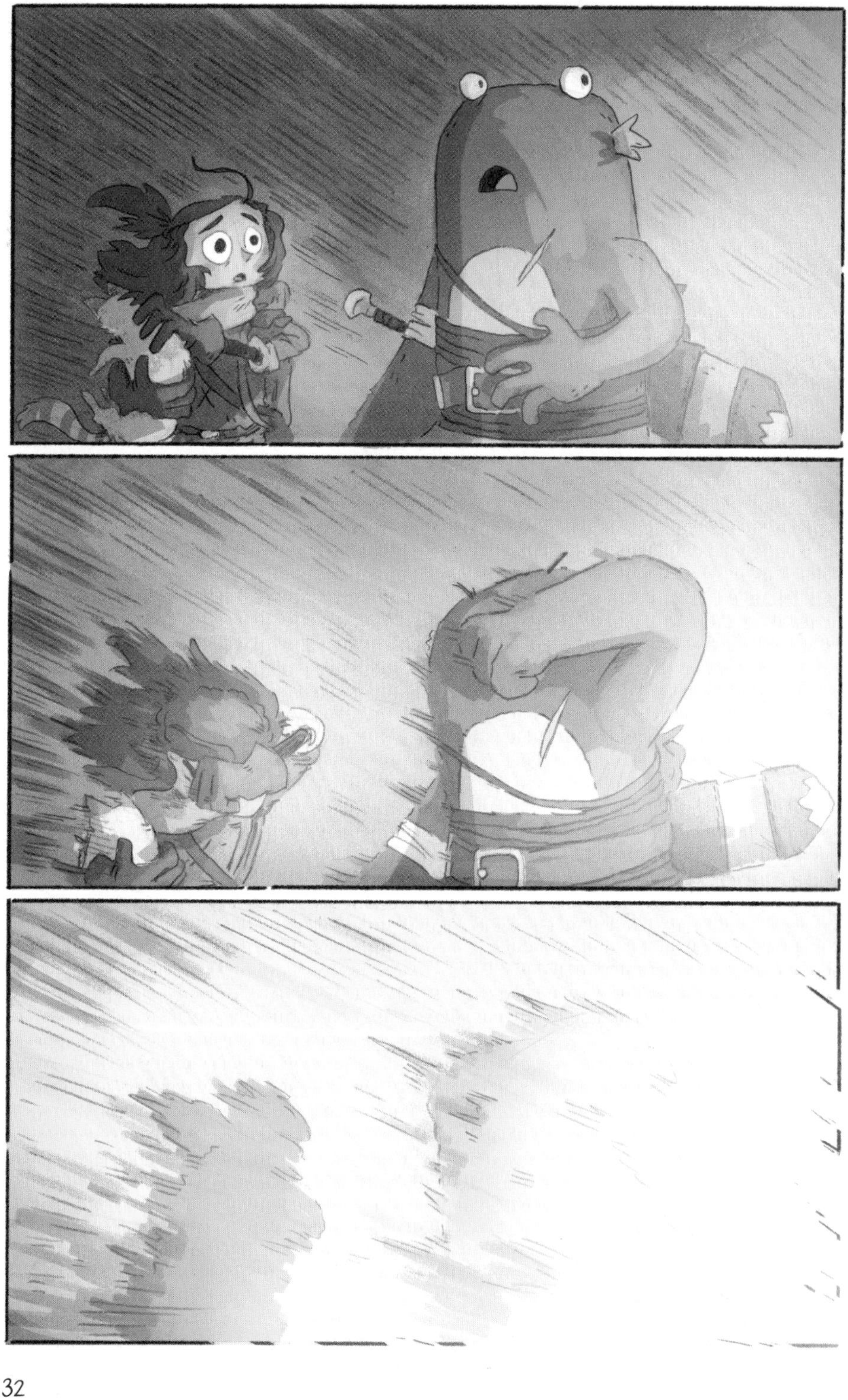

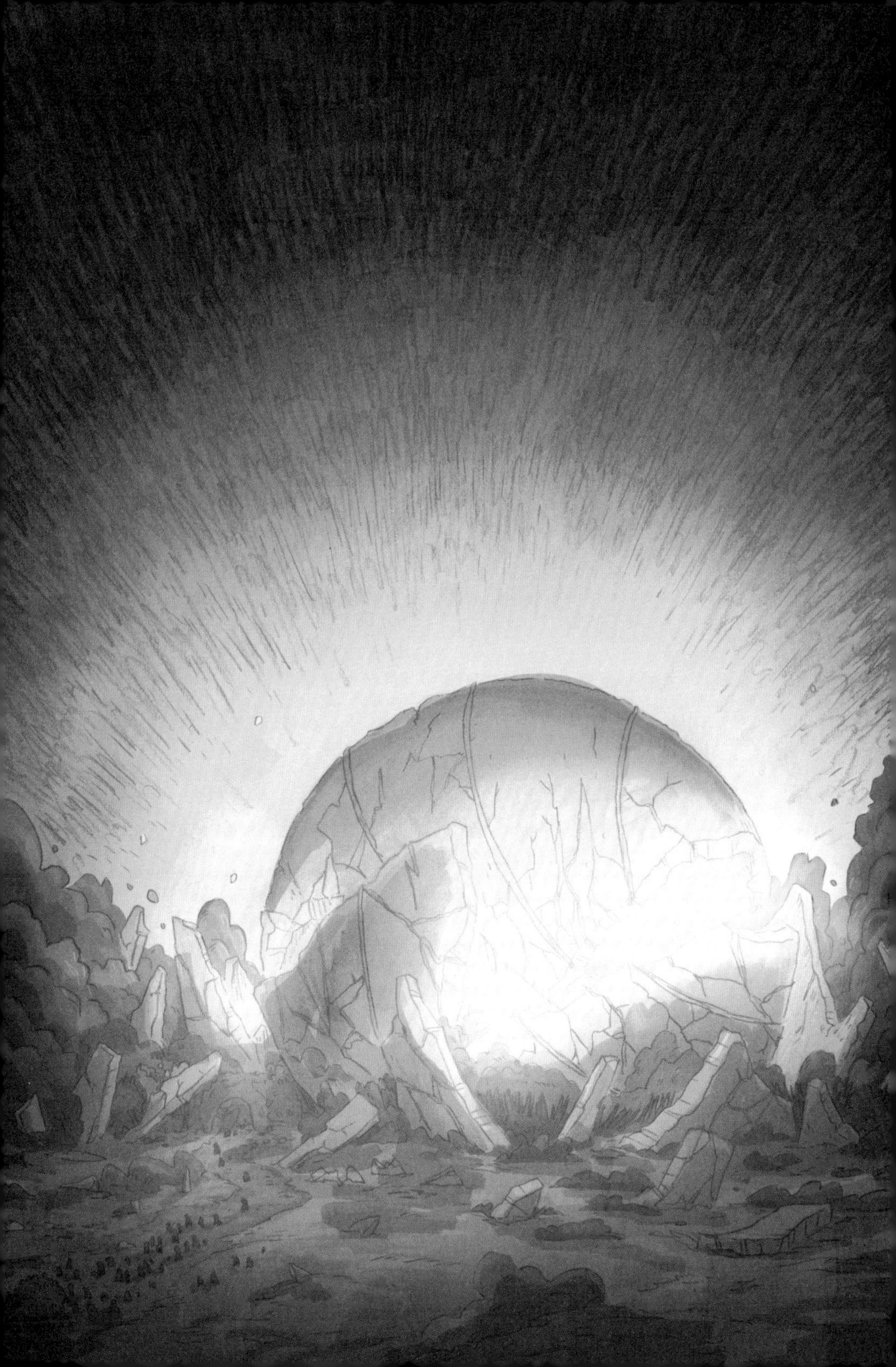

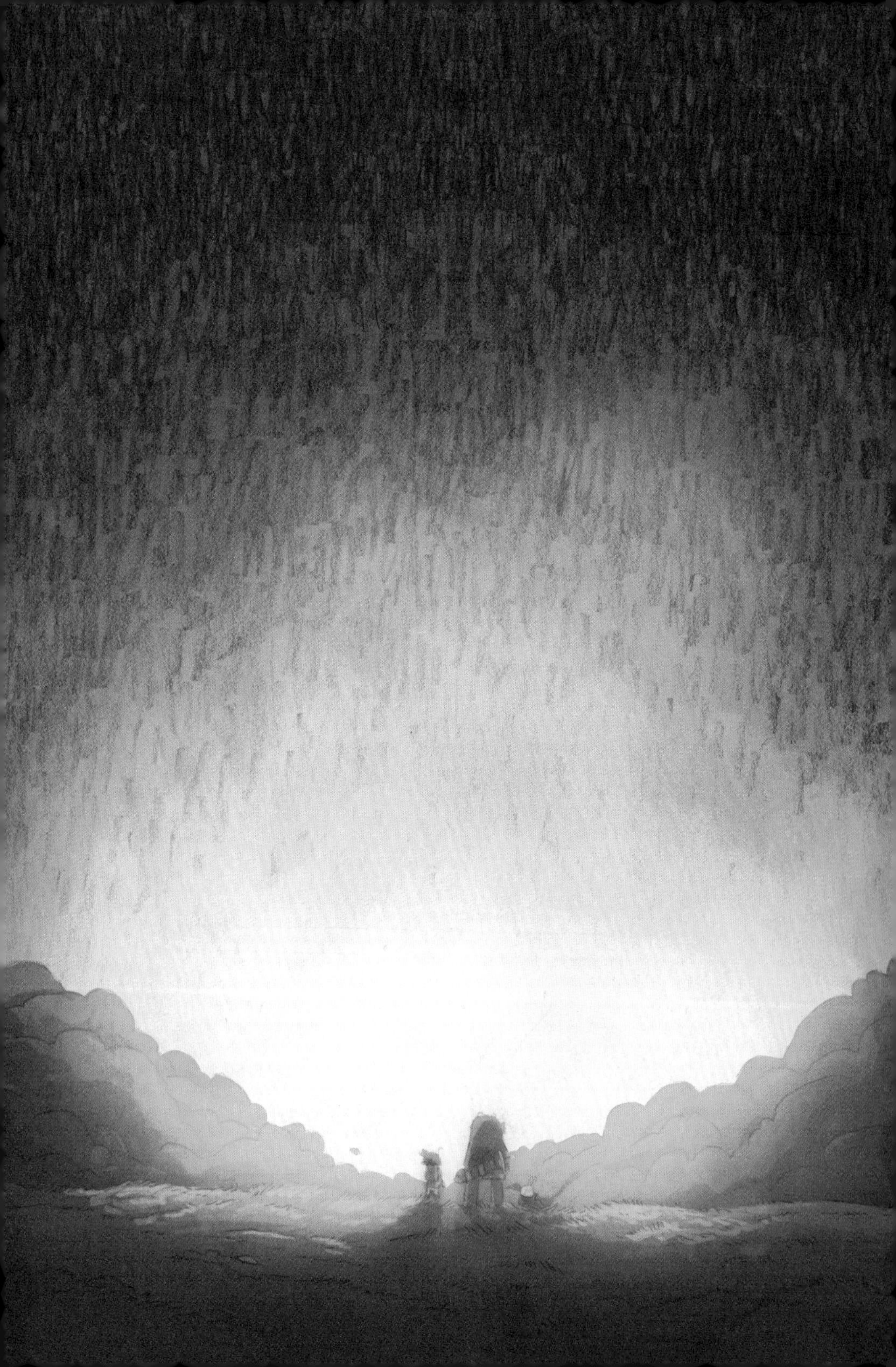

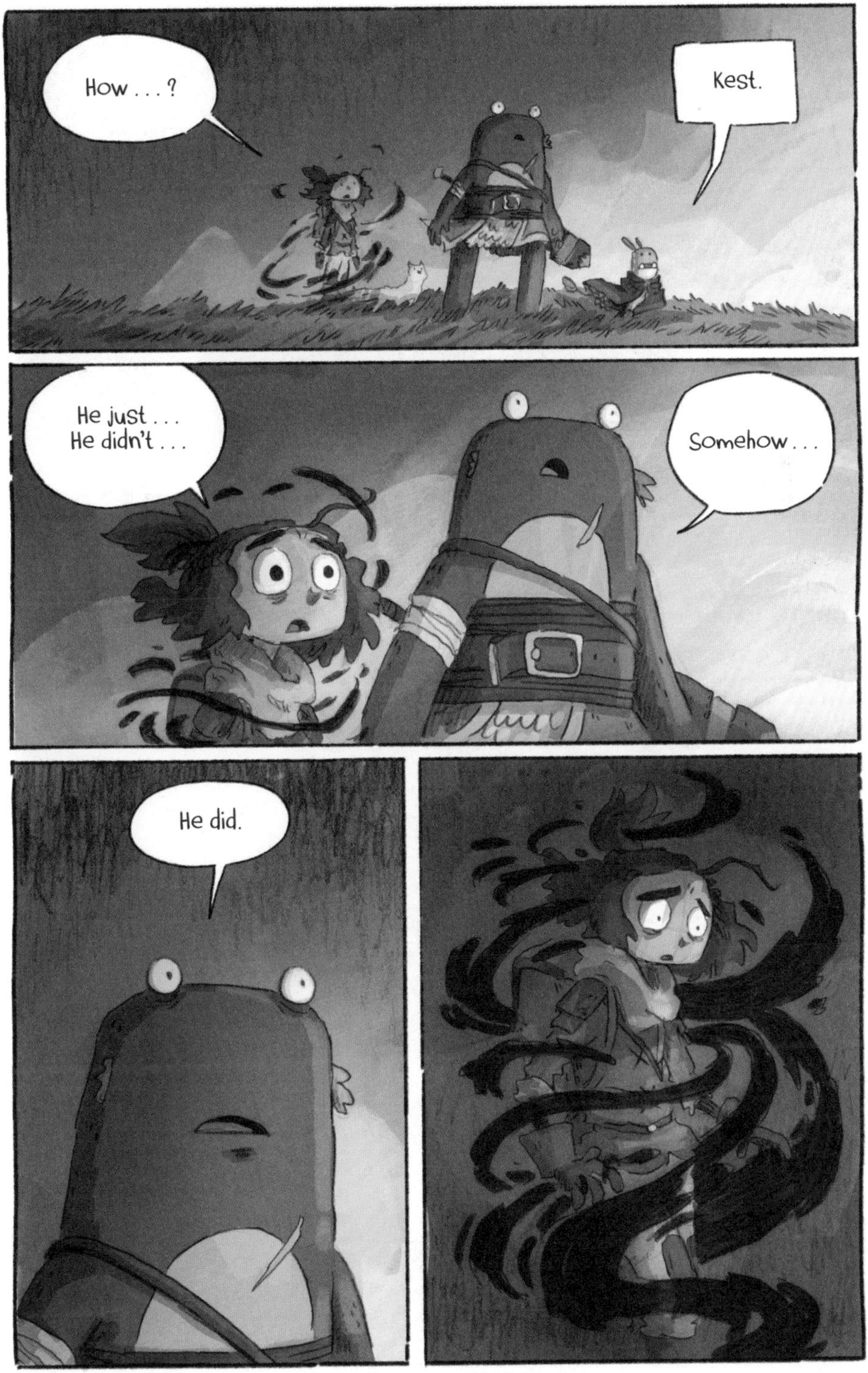
How . . . ?
Kest.
He just . . .
He didn't . . .
Somehow . . .
He did.

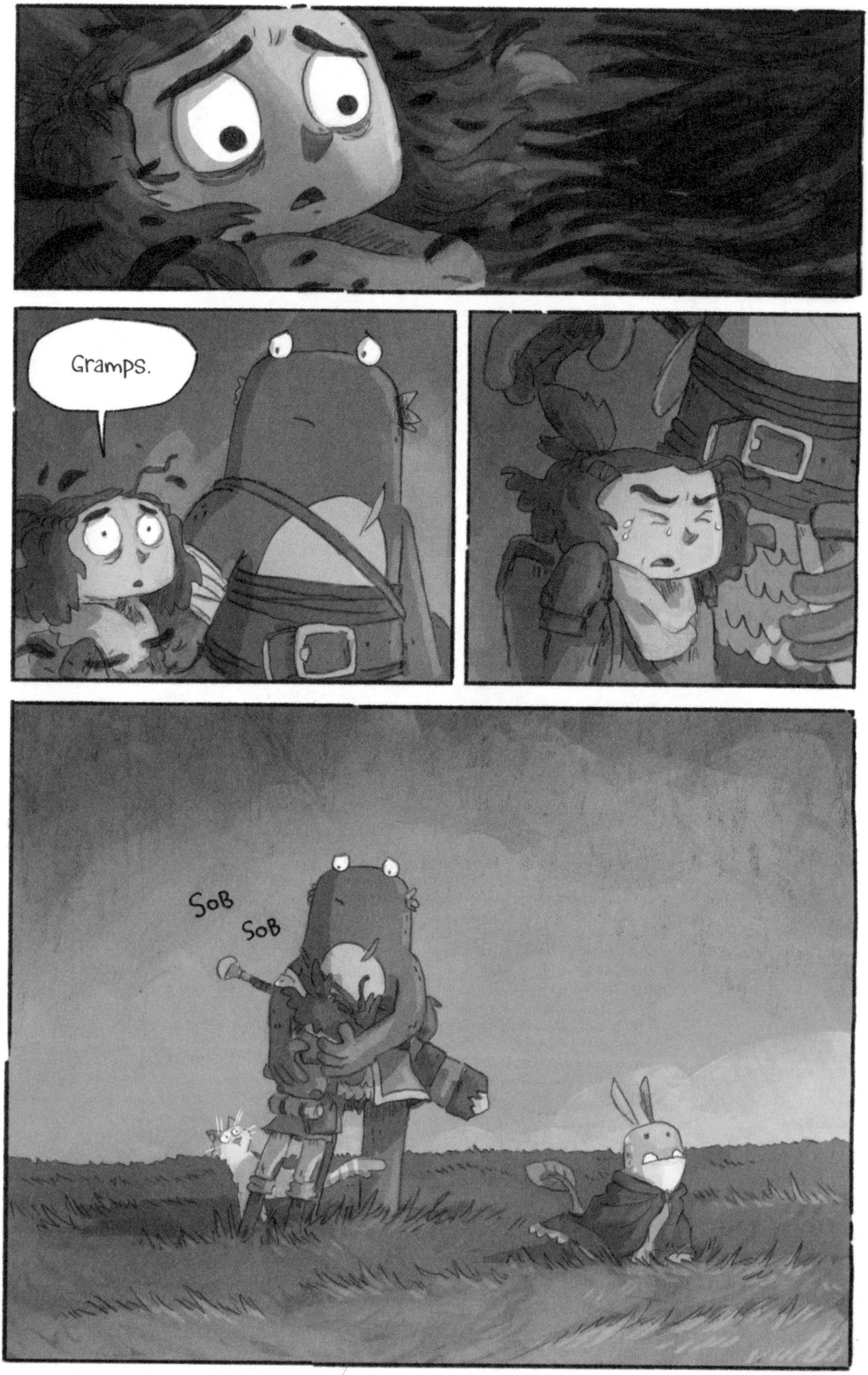
Gramps.
SOB
SOB

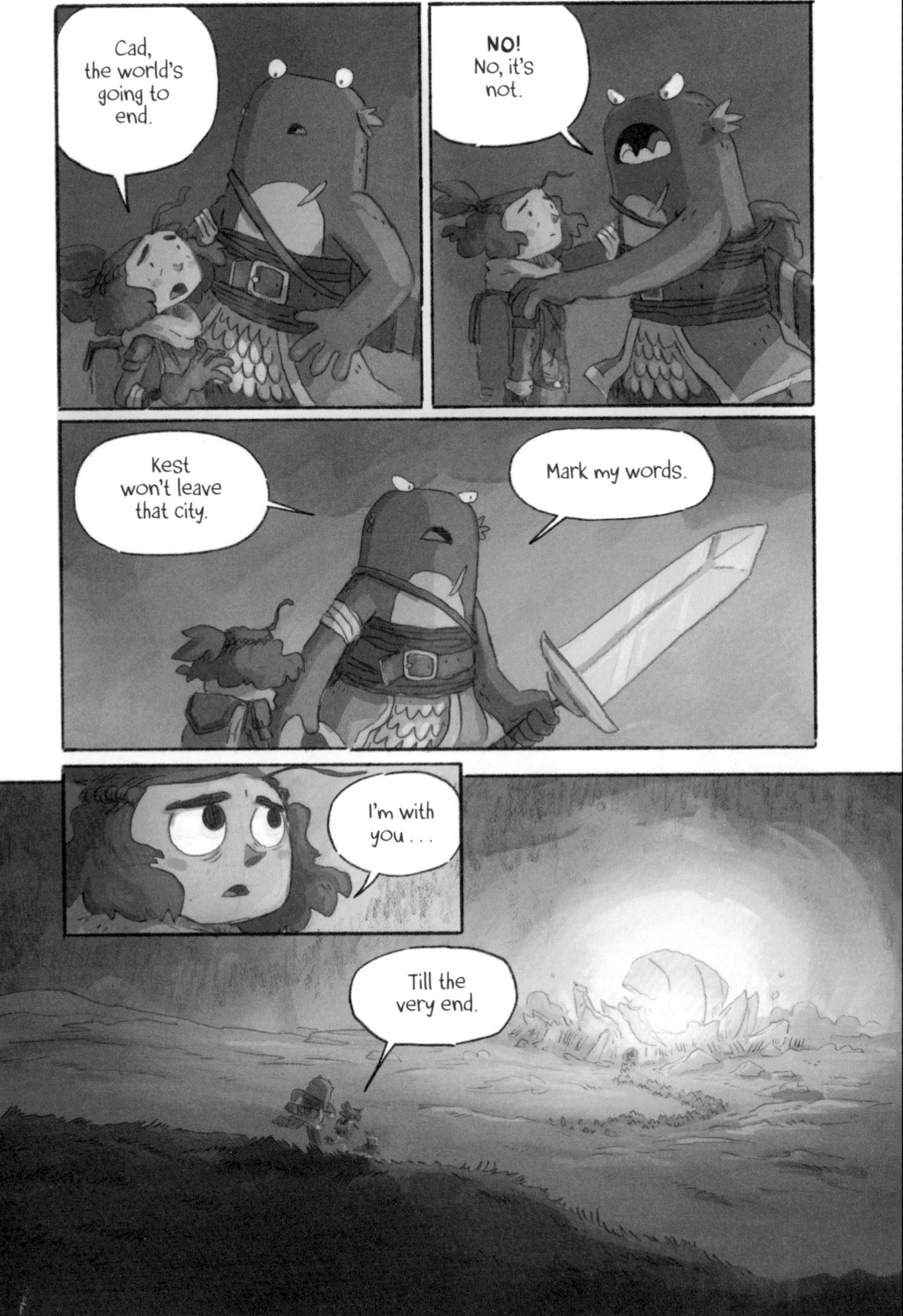
Cad, the world's going to end.
NO! No, it's not.
Kest won't leave that city.
Mark my words.
I'm with you . . .
Till the very end.

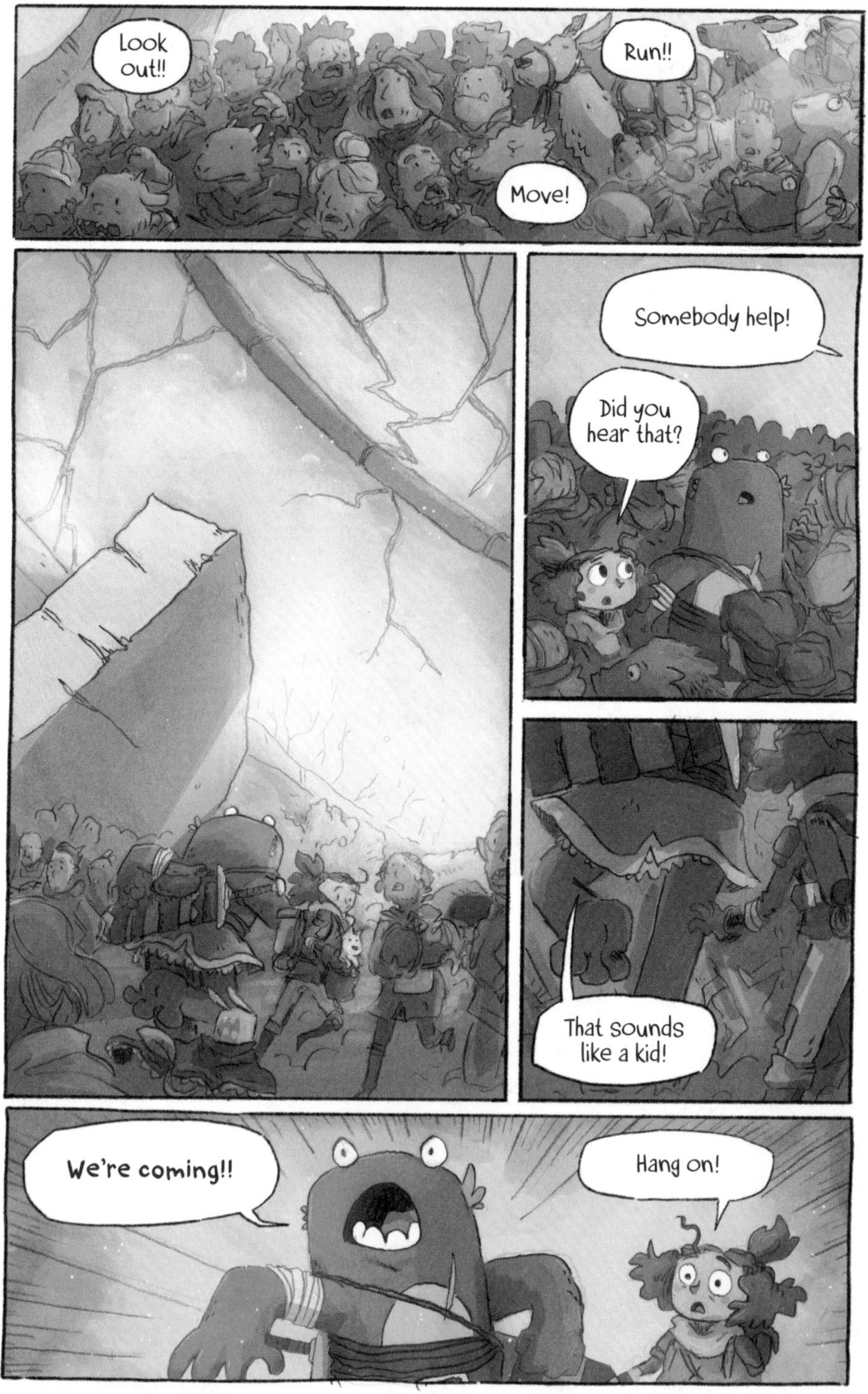
Look out!!
Run!!
Move!
Somebody help!
Did you hear that?
That sounds like a kid!
We're coming!!
Hang on!

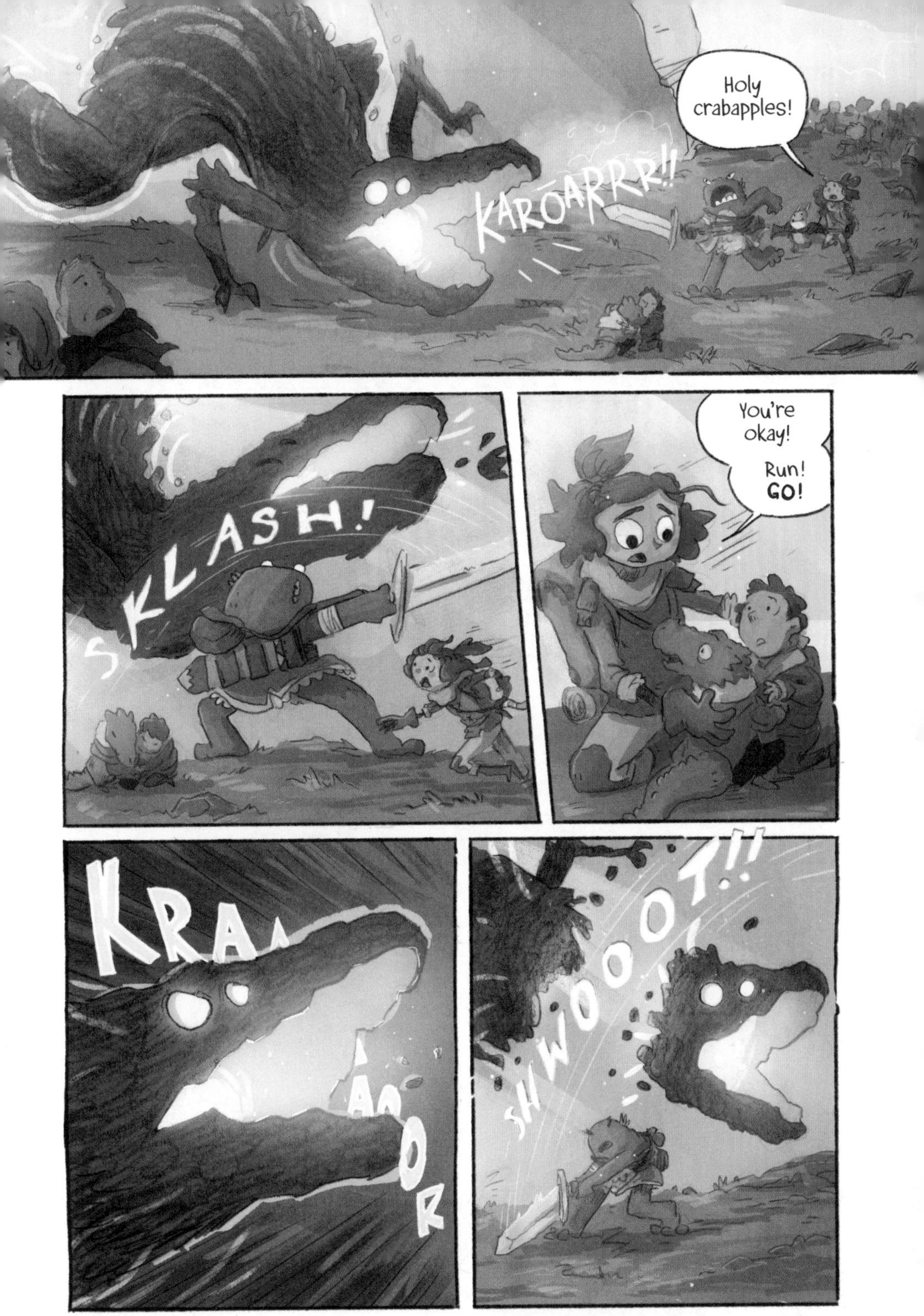

Holy crabapples!
KAROARRR!!
SKLASH!
You're okay!
Run! GO!
KRA
OR
SHWOOOT!!

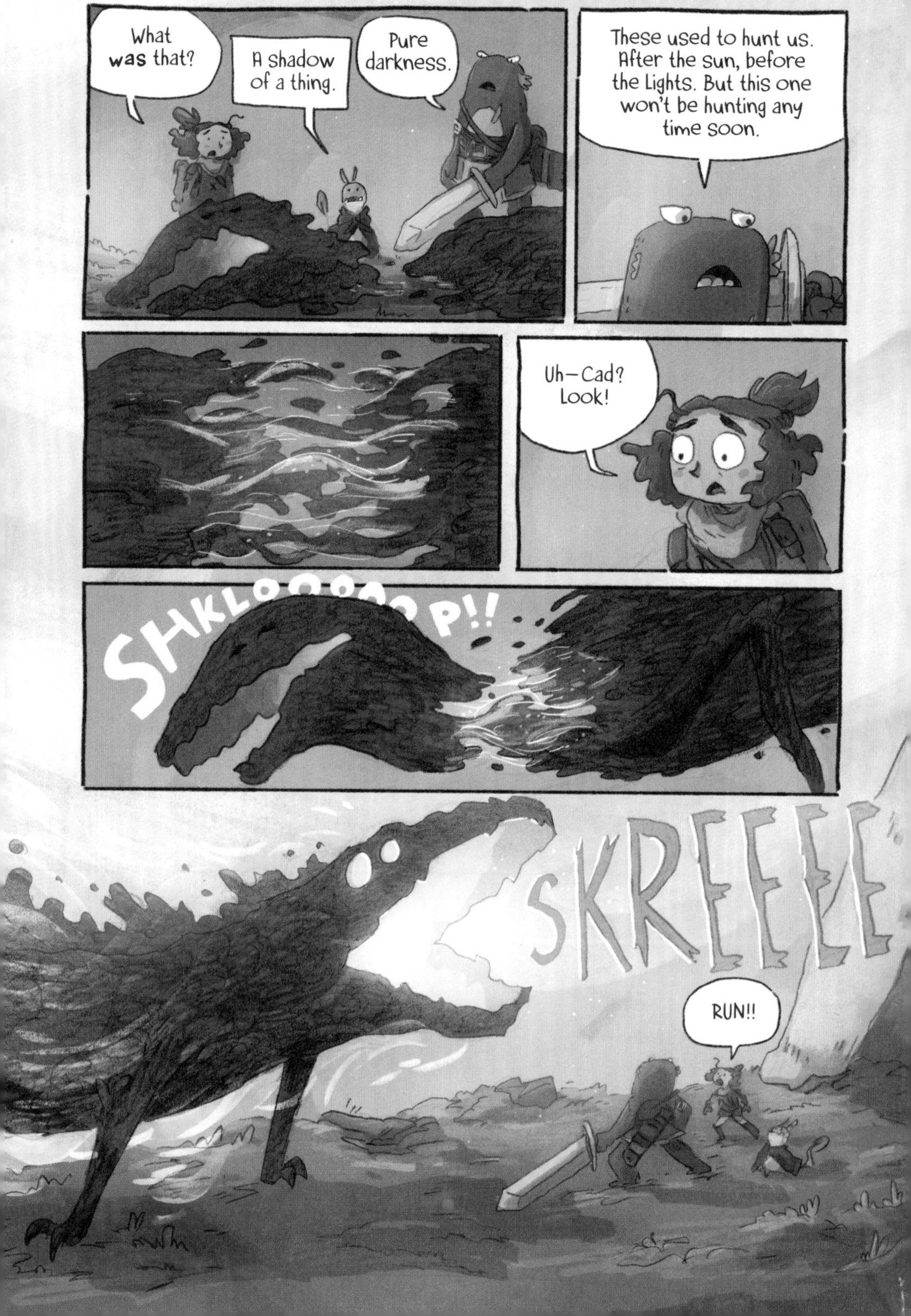
What was that?
A shadow of a thing.
Pure darkness.
These used to hunt us. After the sun, before the Lights. But this one won't be hunting any time soon.
Uh—Cad? Look!
SHKLOOOOOOP!!
SKREEEE
RUN!!

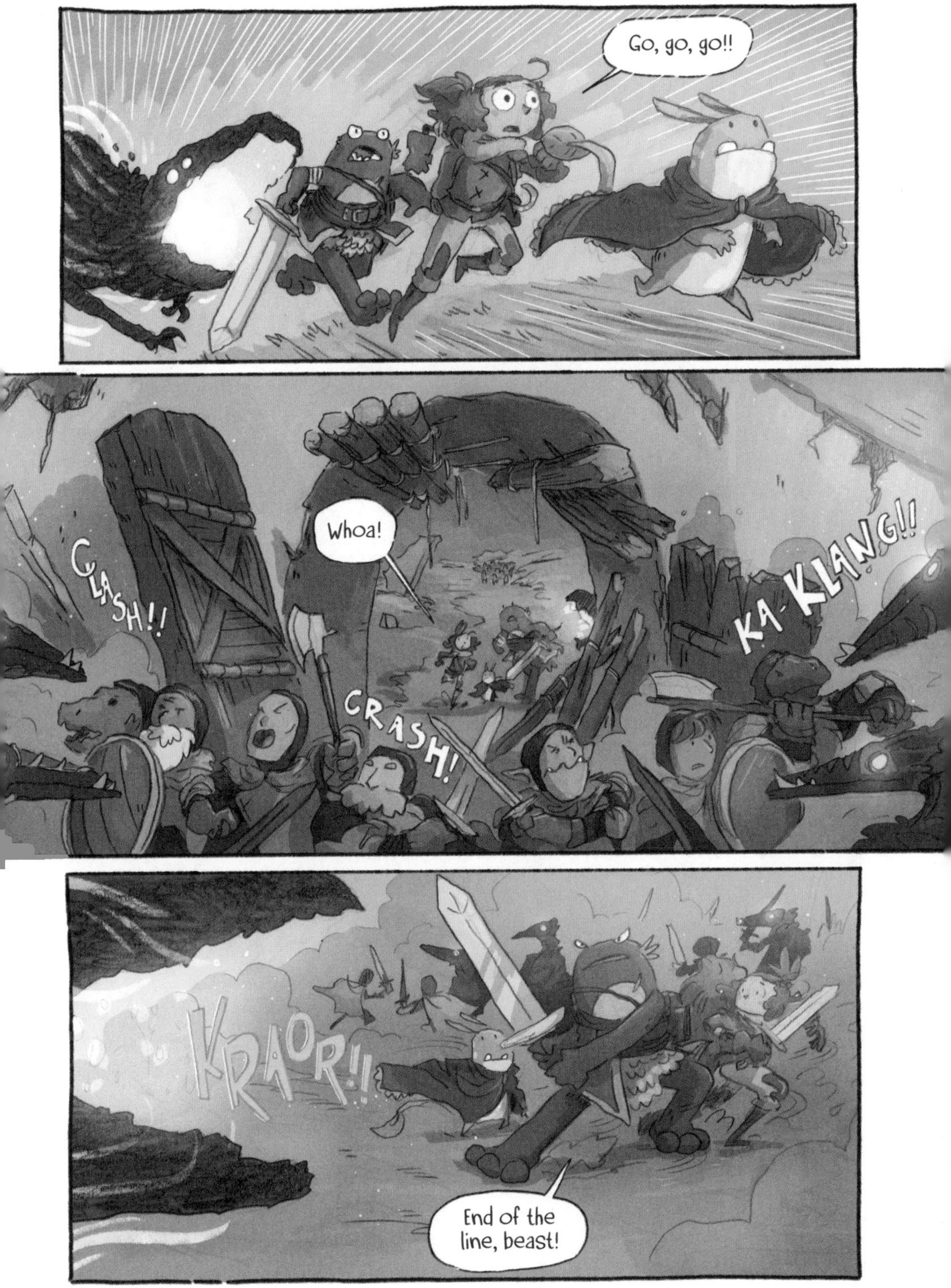
Go, go, go!!
Whoa!
CLASH!!
CRASH!
KA-KLANG!!
KRAOR!!
End of the line, beast!

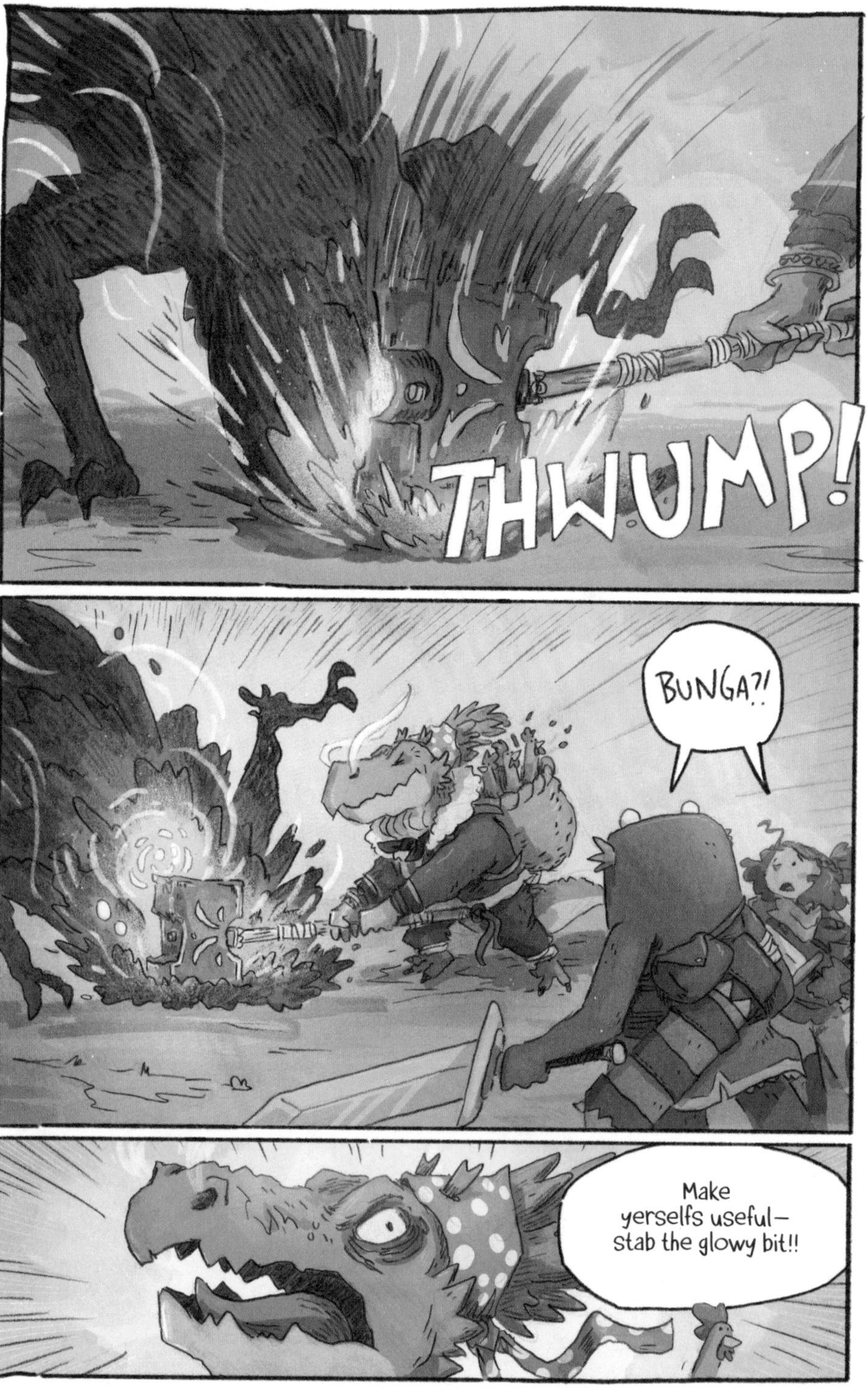
THWUMP!
BUNGA?!
Make yerselfs useful— stab the glowy bit!!

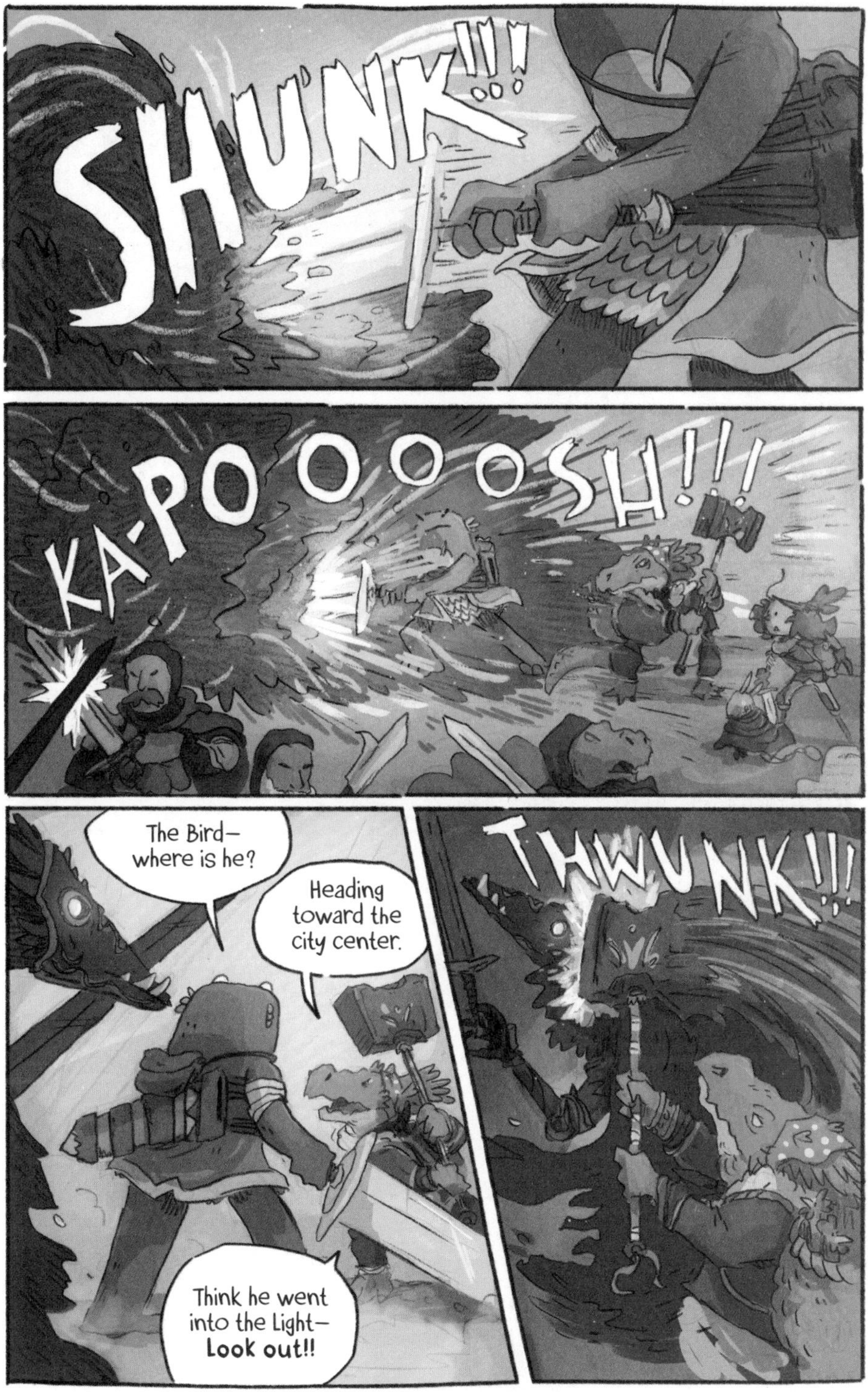
SHUNK!!!
KA-POOOOOSH!!!
The Bird—
where is he?
Heading
toward the
city center.
Think he went
into the Light—
Look out!!
THWUNK!!!

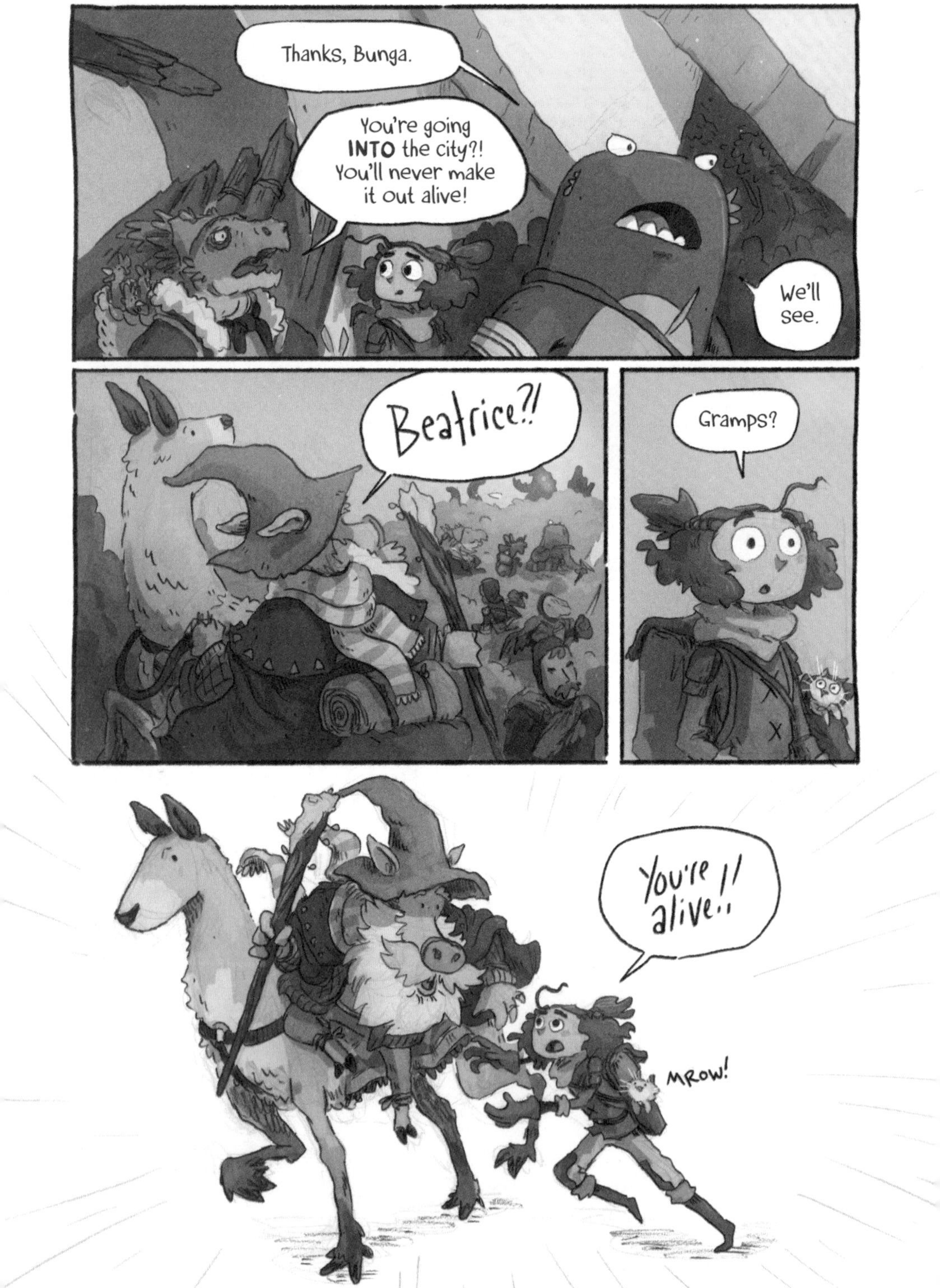
Thanks, Bunga.
You're going INTO the city?! You'll never make it out alive!
We'll see.
Beatrice?!
Gramps?
You're alive!!
MROW!

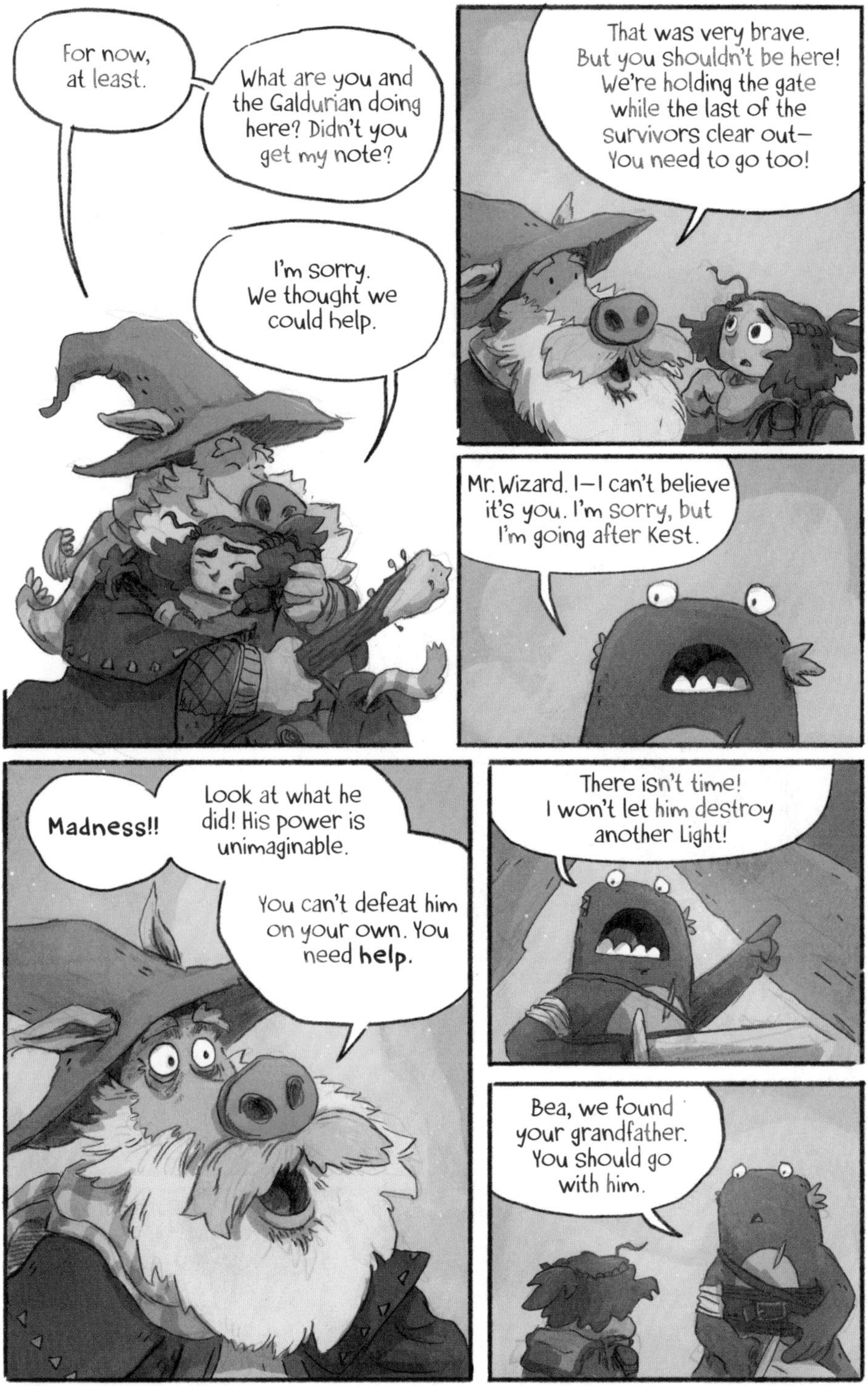
For now, at least.
What are you and the Galdurian doing here? Didn't you get my note?
I'm sorry. We thought we could help.
That was very brave. But you shouldn't be here! We're holding the gate while the last of the survivors clear out— You need to go too!
Mr. Wizard. I—I can't believe it's you. I'm sorry, but I'm going after Kest.
Madness!!
Look at what he did! His power is unimaginable.
You can't defeat him on your own. You need **help.**
There isn't time! I won't let him destroy another Light!
Bea, we found your grandfather. You should go with him.

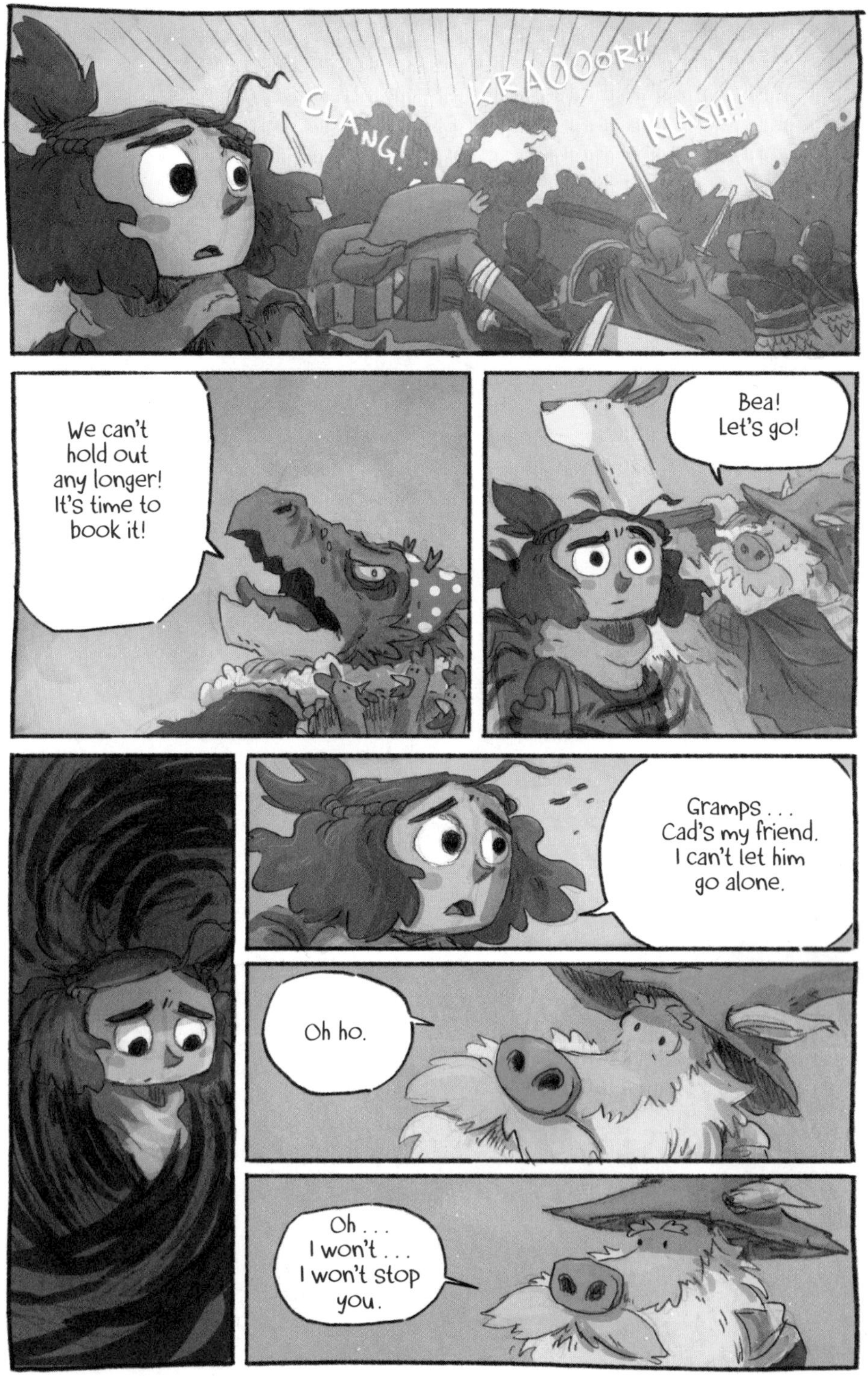
CLANG!
KRAOOOR!!
KLASH!!
We can't hold out any longer! It's time to book it!
Bea! Let's go!
Gramps . . . Cad's my friend. I can't let him go alone.
Oh ho.
Oh . . . I won't . . . I won't stop you.

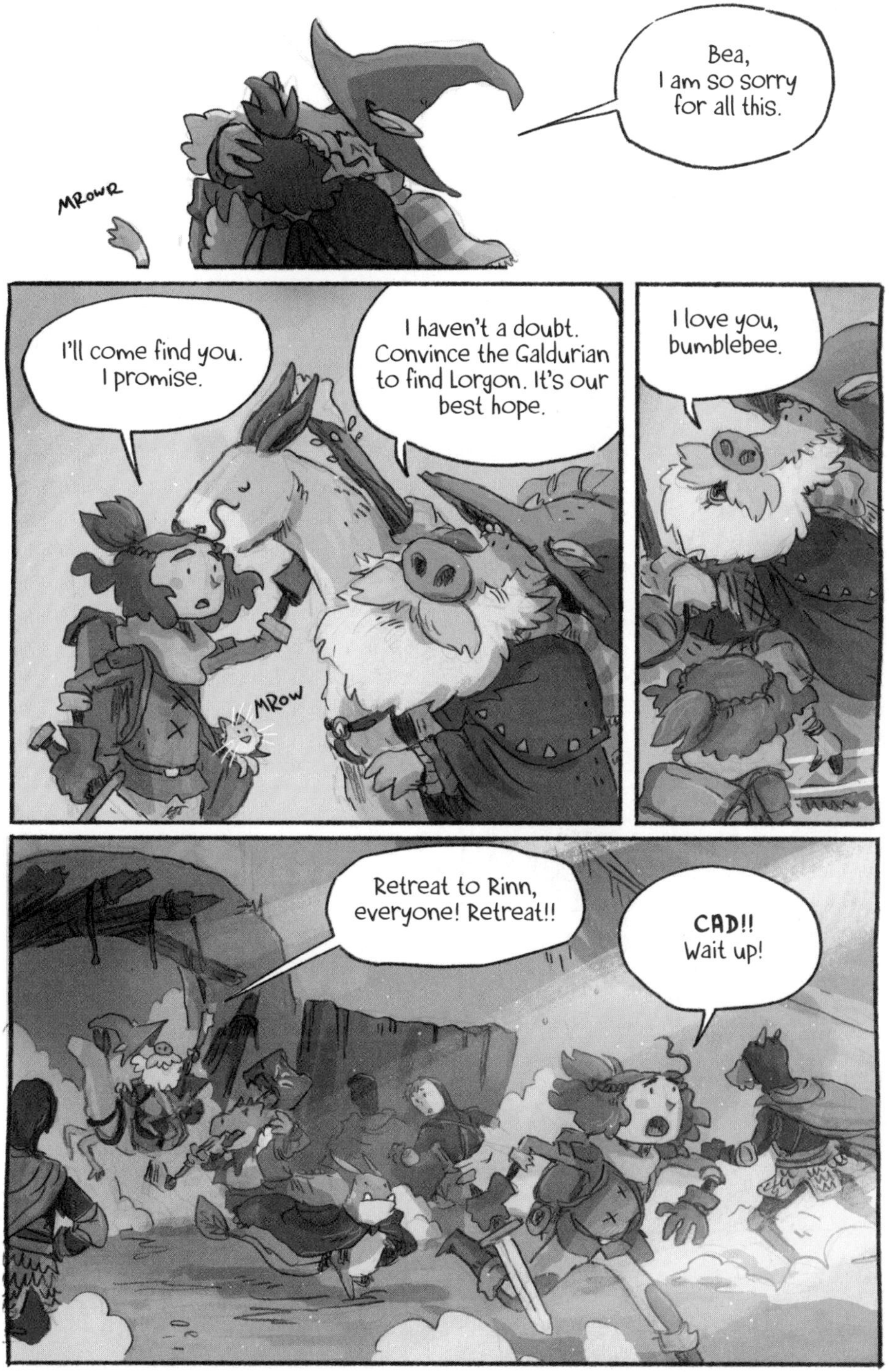
Bea,
I am so sorry for all this.
MROWR
I'll come find you. I promise.
I haven't a doubt. Convince the Galdurian to find Lorgon. It's our best hope.
MROW
I love you, bumblebee.
Retreat to Rinn, everyone! Retreat!!
CAD!!
Wait up!

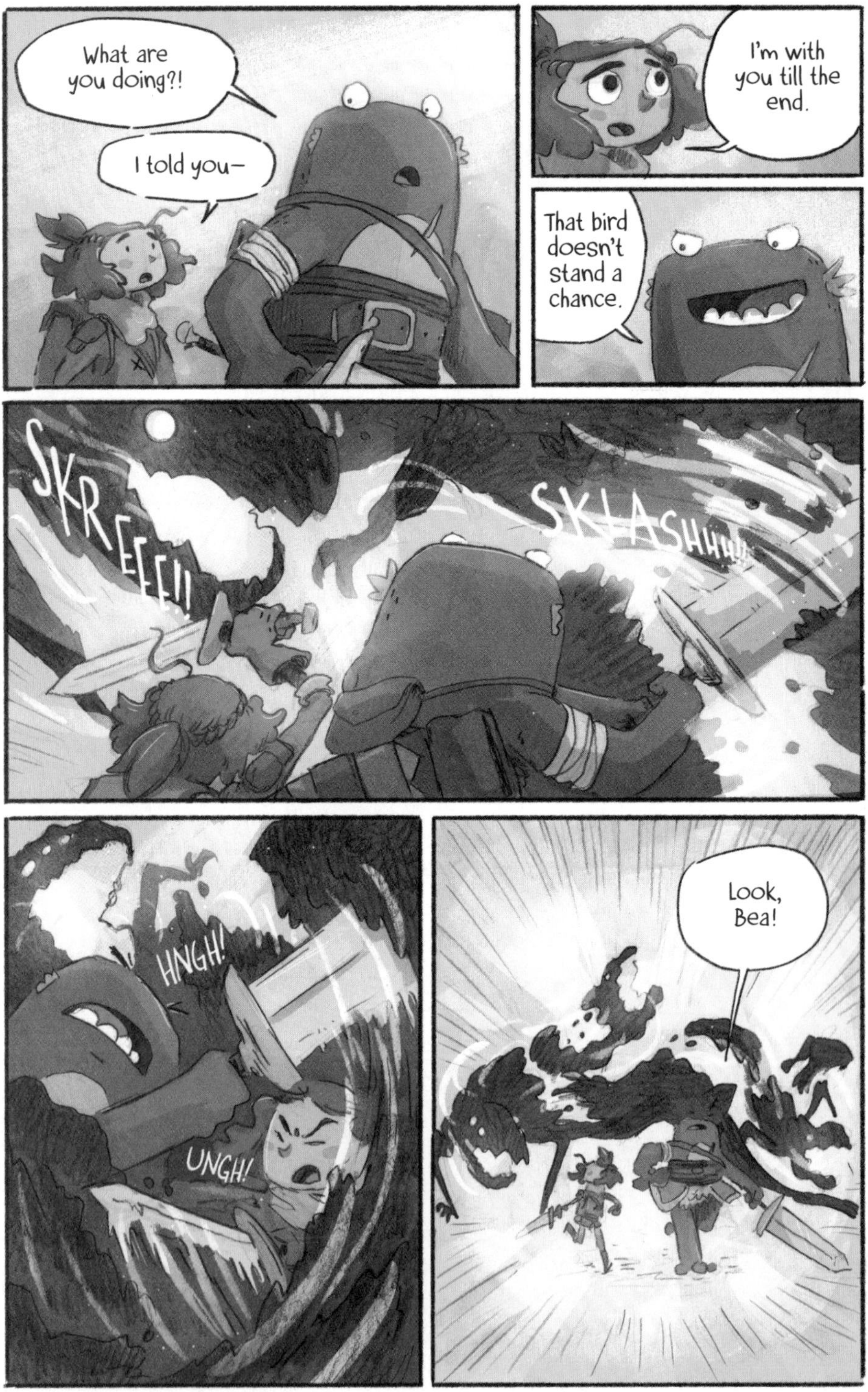
What are you doing?!
I told you–
I'm with you till the end.
That bird doesn't stand a chance.
SKREEEE!!
SKLASHHH!!
HNGH!
UNGH!
Look, Bea!

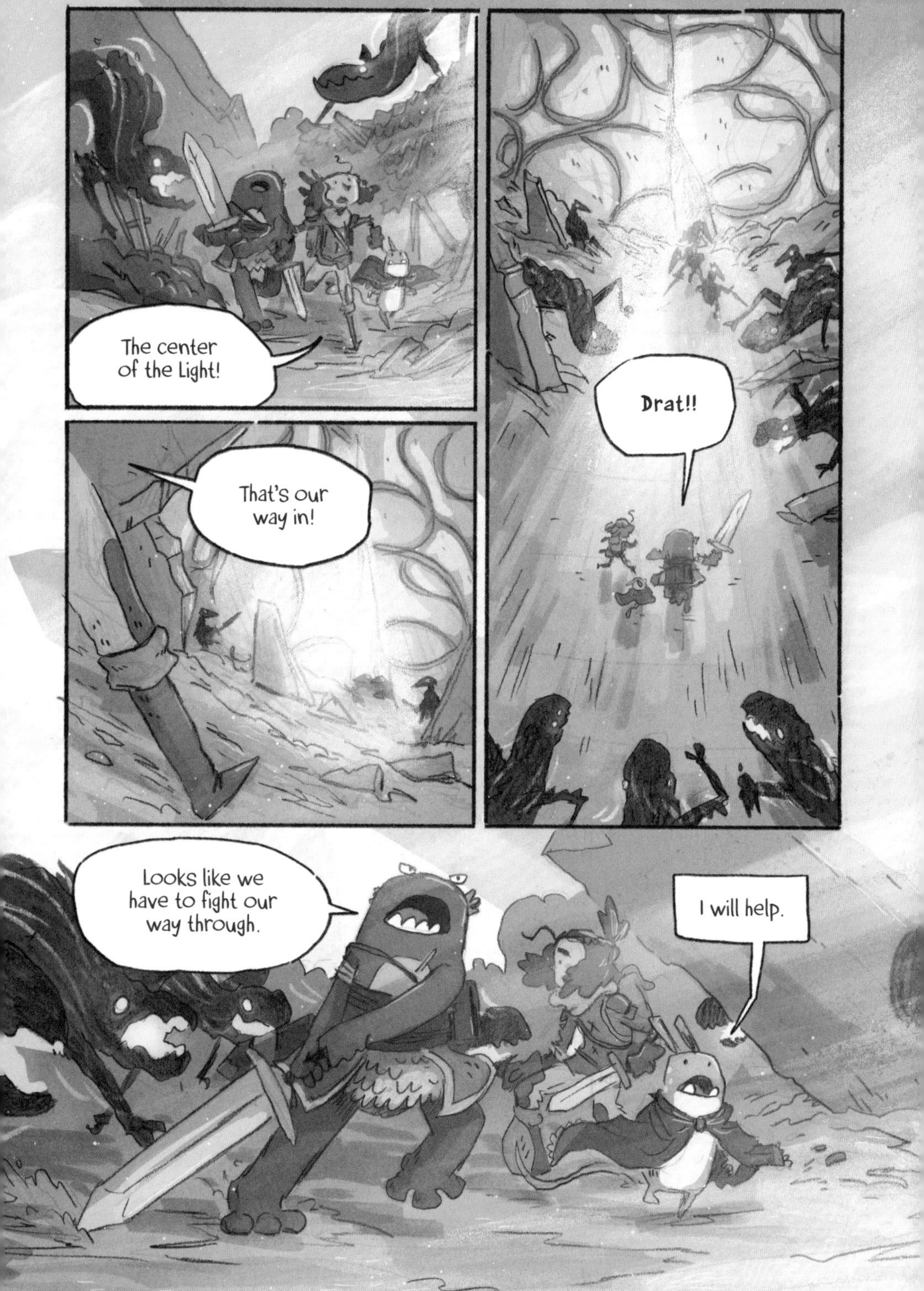
The center of the Light!
That's our way in!
Drat!!
Looks like we have to fight our way through.
I will help.

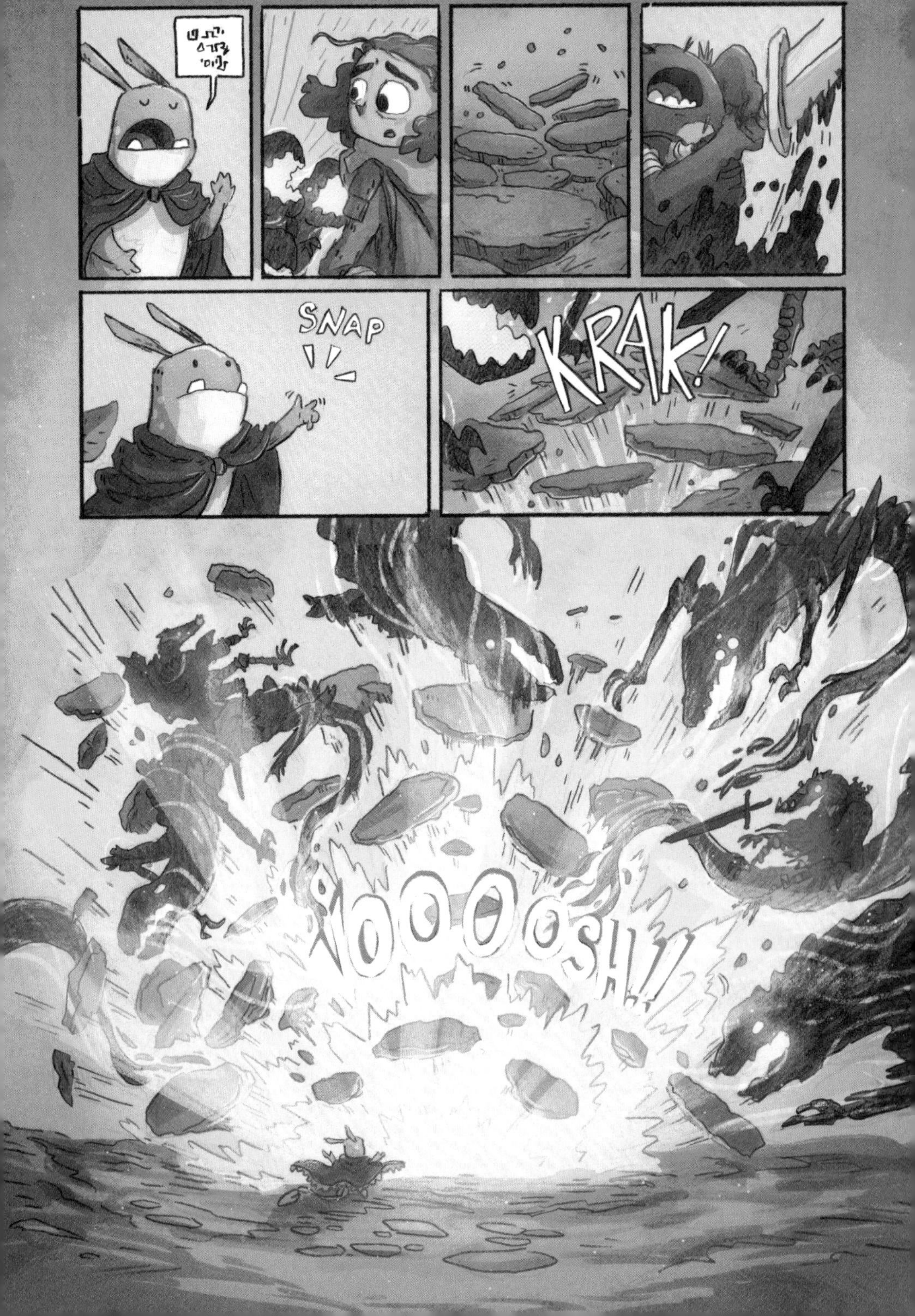
SNAP
KRAK!
WOOOOSH!!

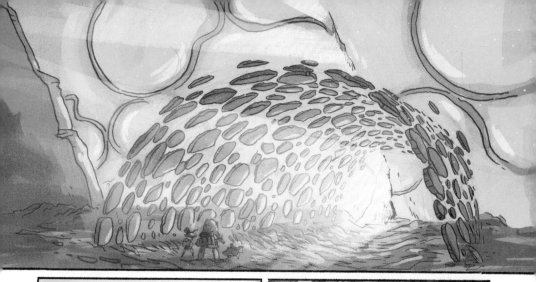

GO.

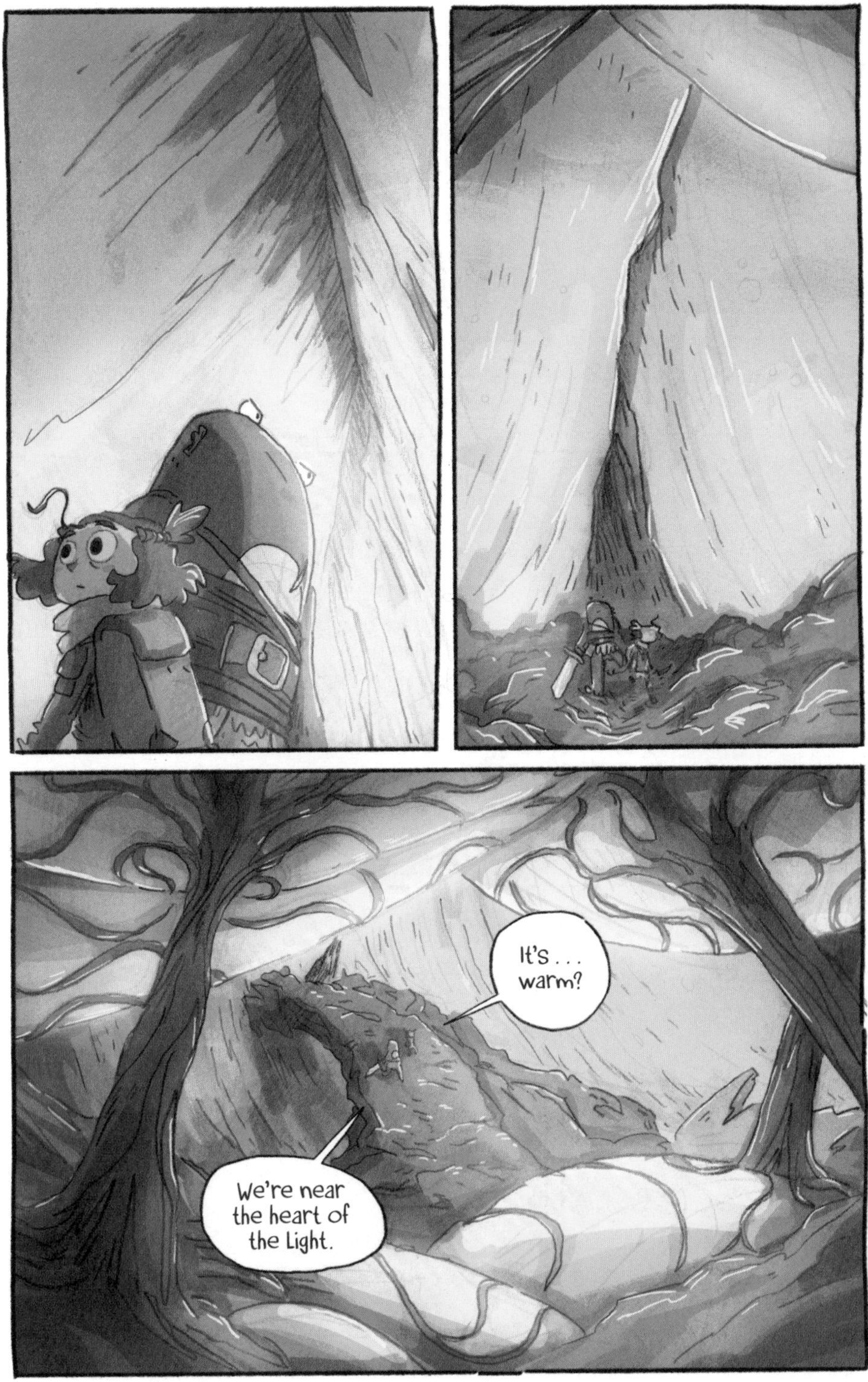
It's . . . warm?
We're near the heart of the Light.

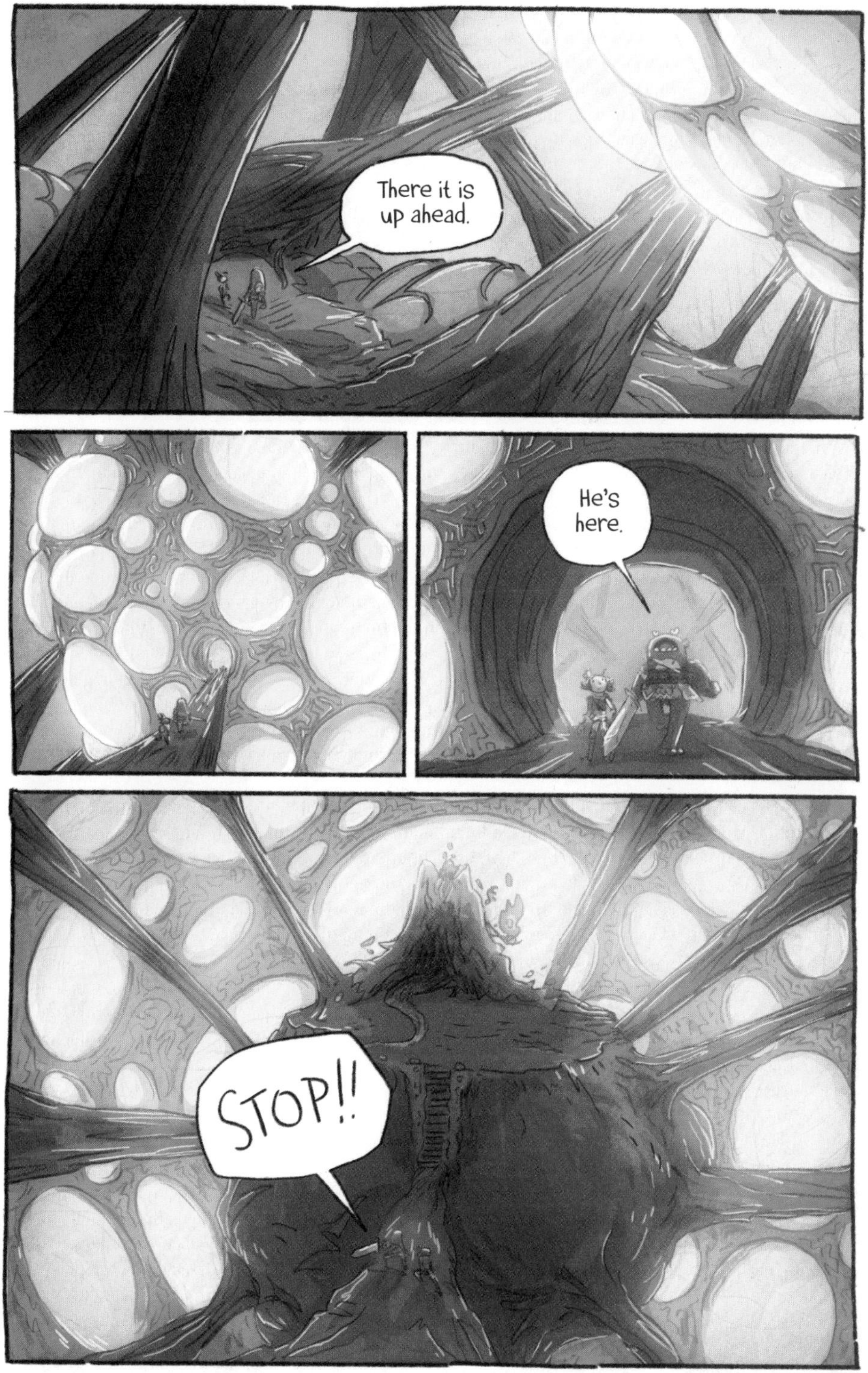
There it is up ahead.
He's here.
STOP!!

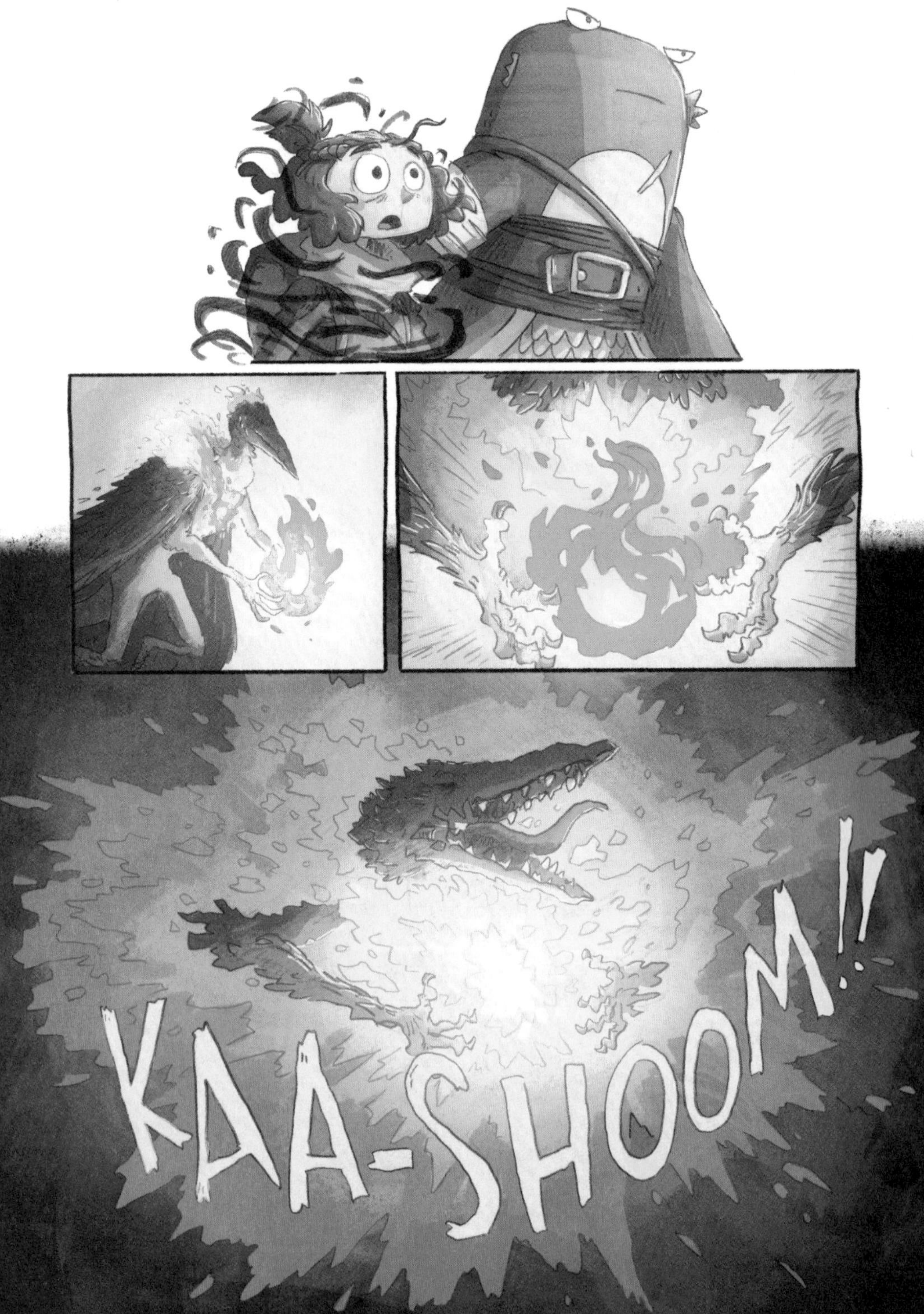
KAA-SHOOM!!

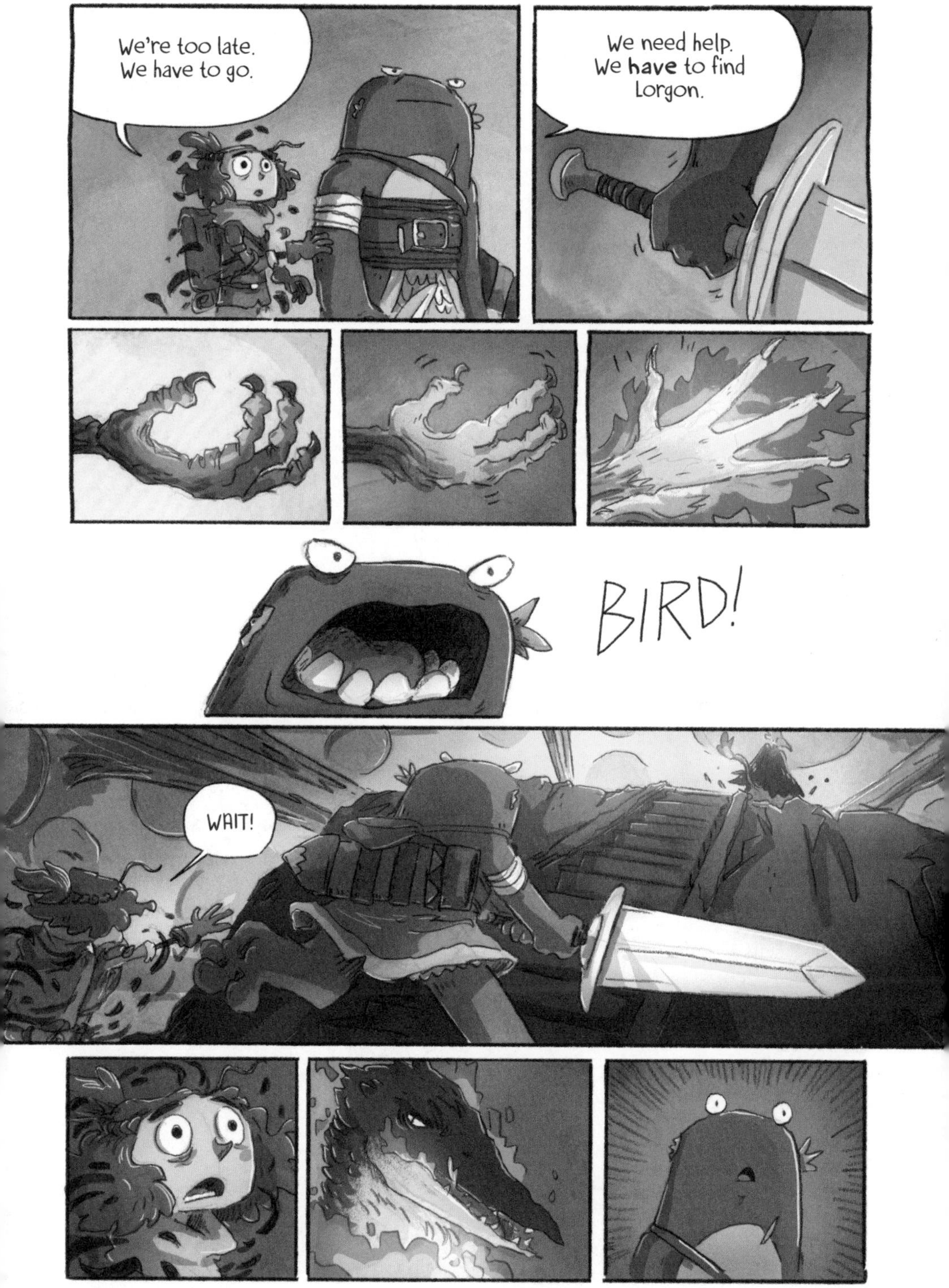
We're too late.
We have to go.
We need help.
We **have** to find Lorgon.
BIRD!
WAIT!

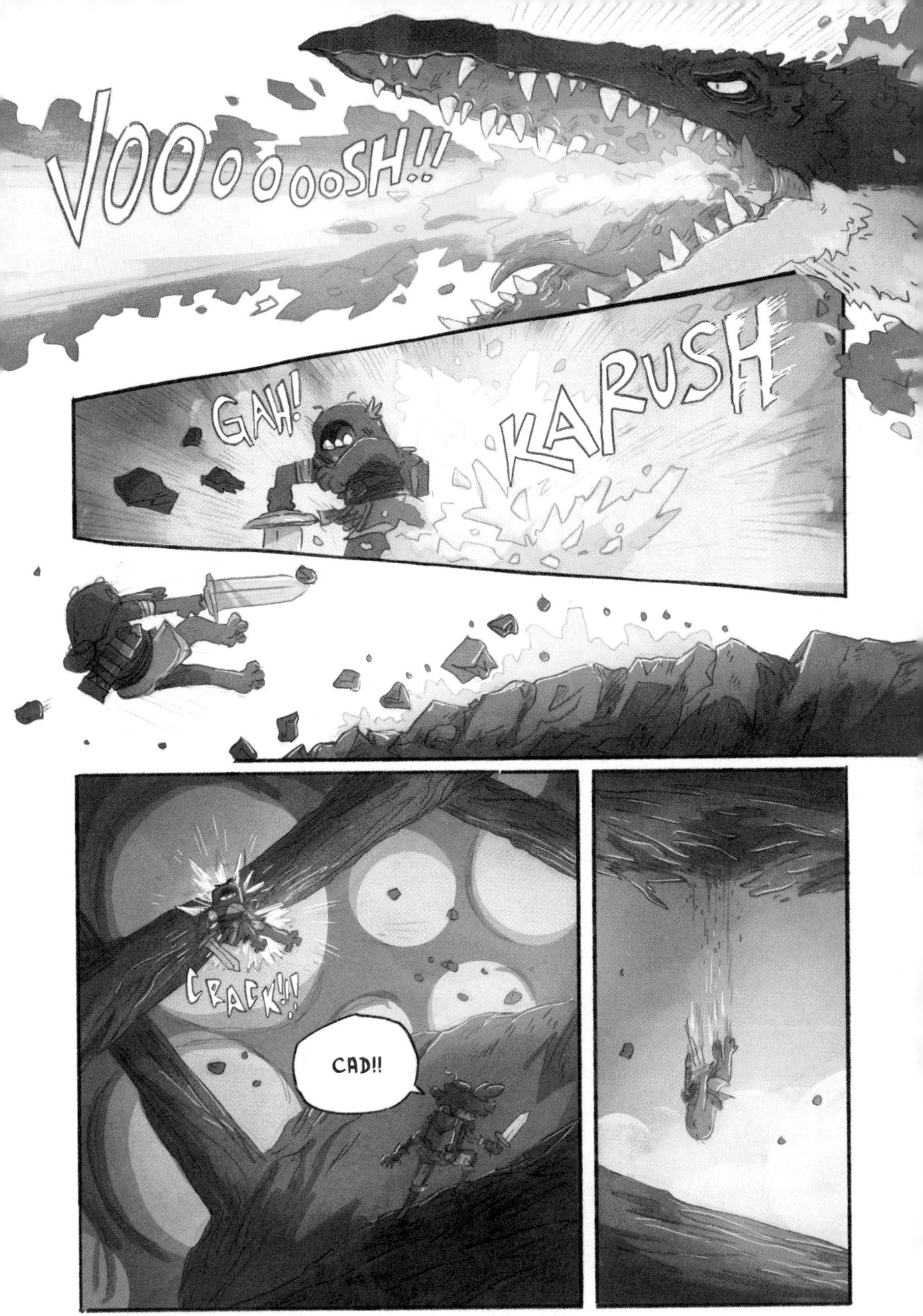
VOOOOOOOSH!!
GAH!
KARUSH
CRACK!!!
CAD!!

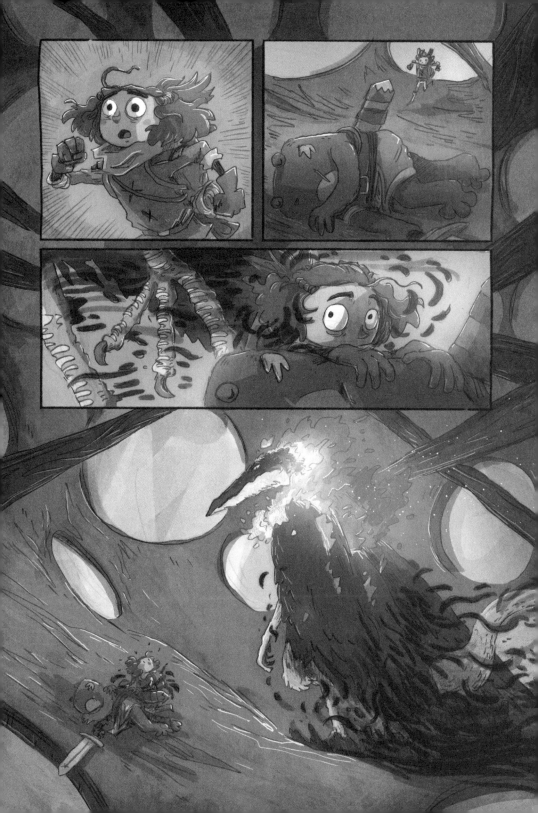

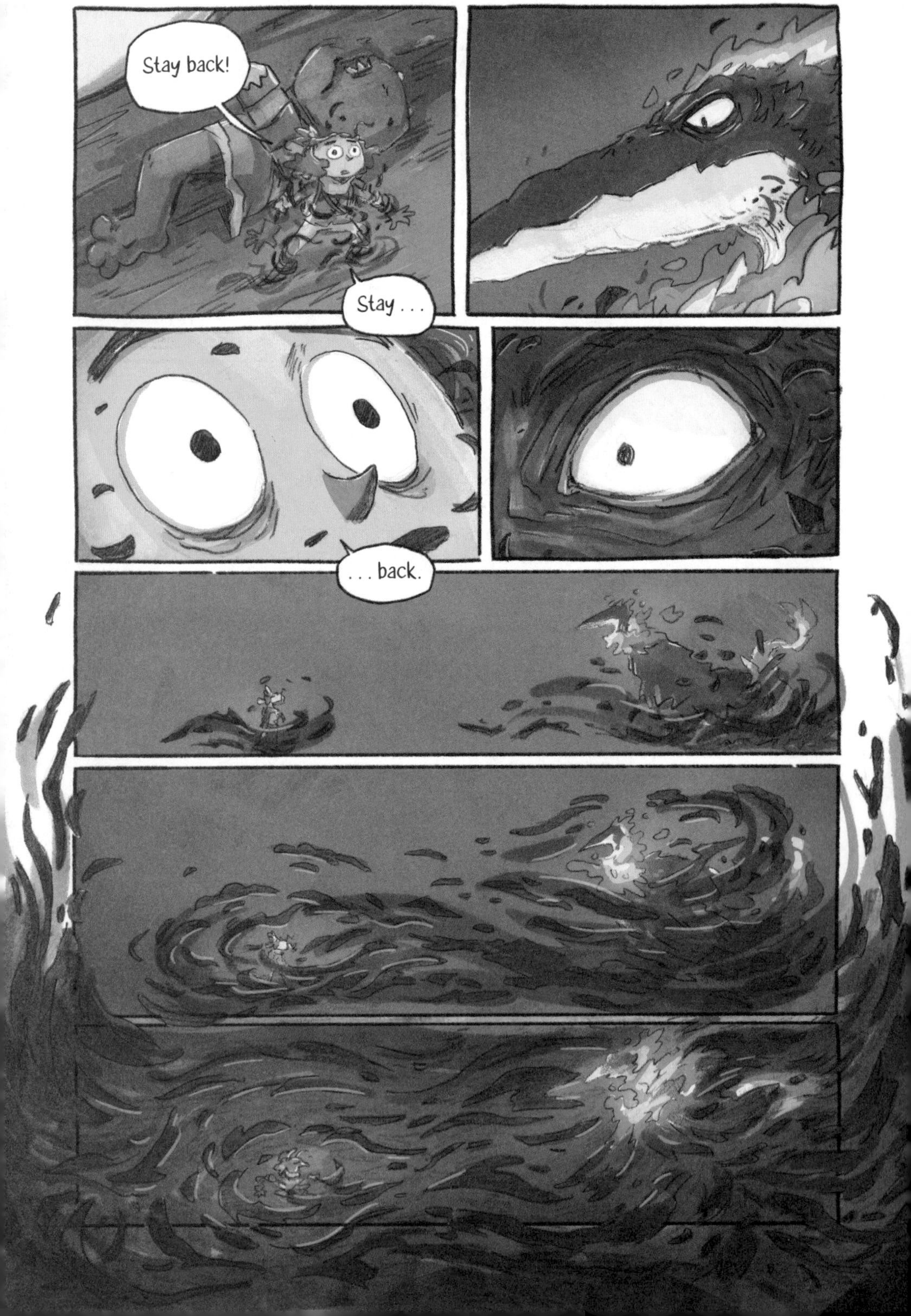
Stay back!
Stay . . .
. . . back.

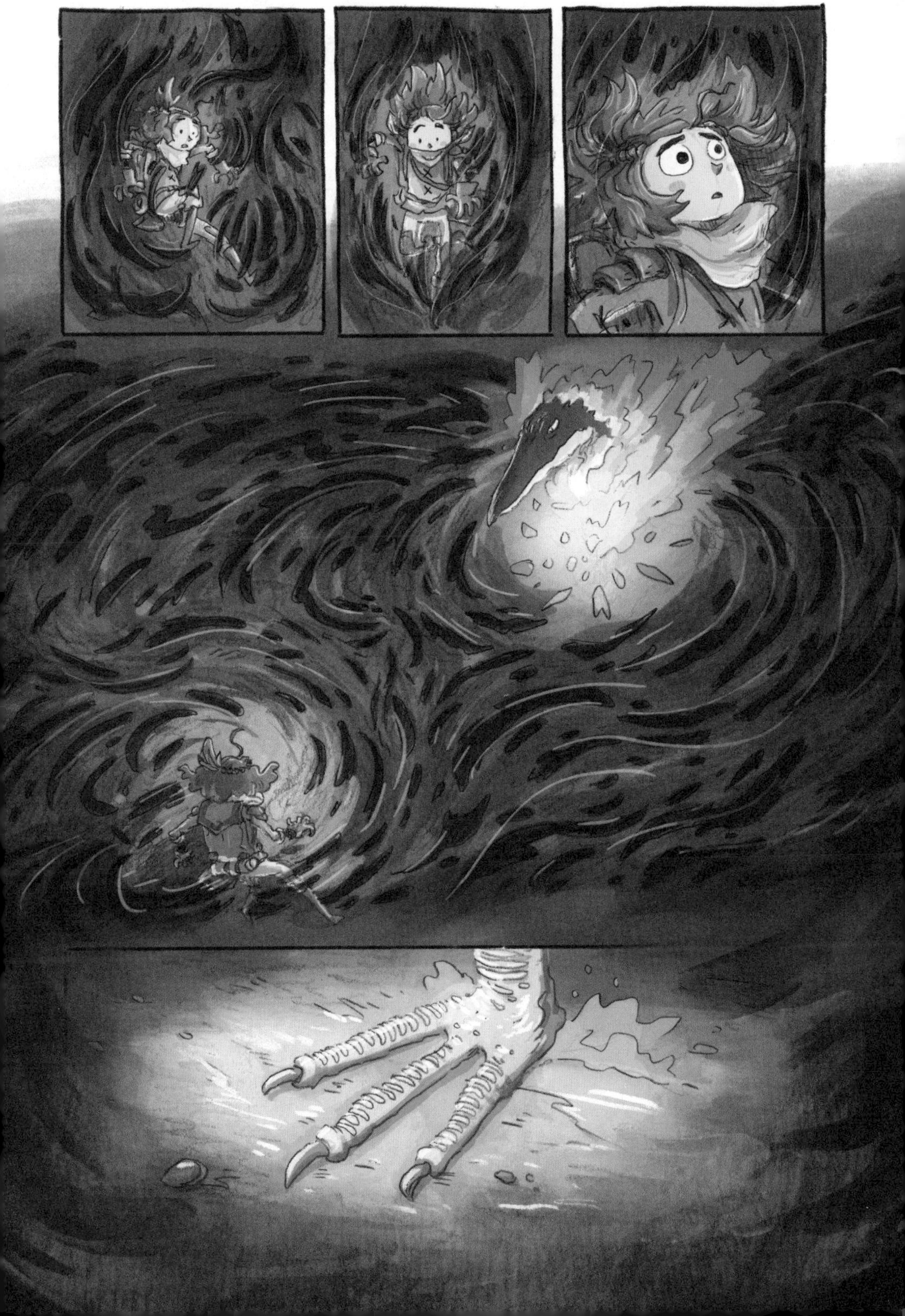

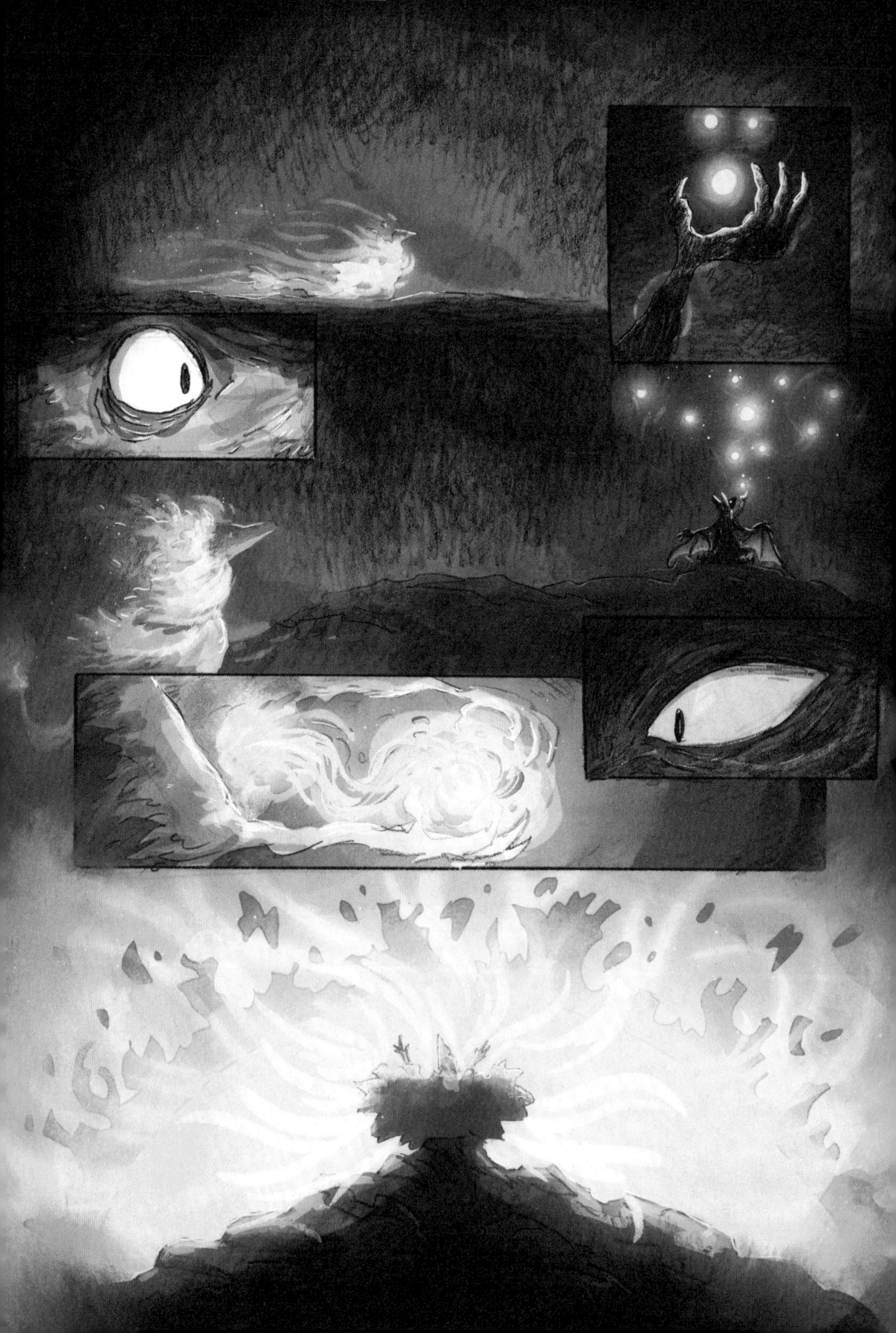

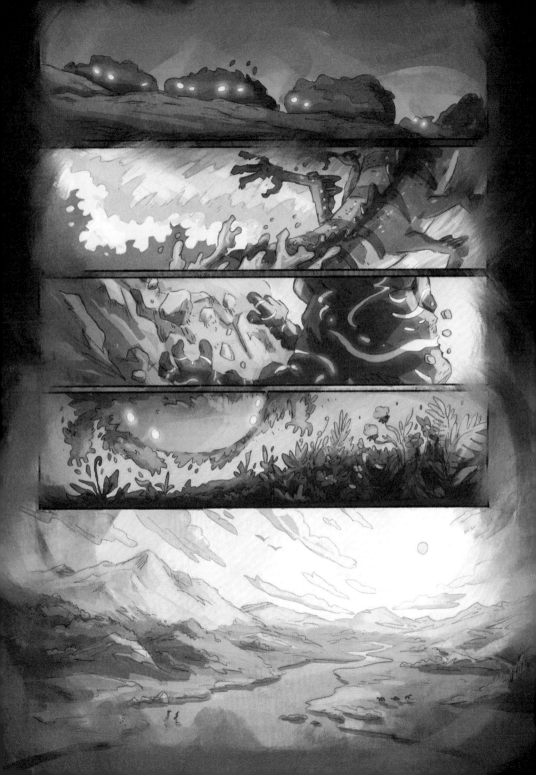

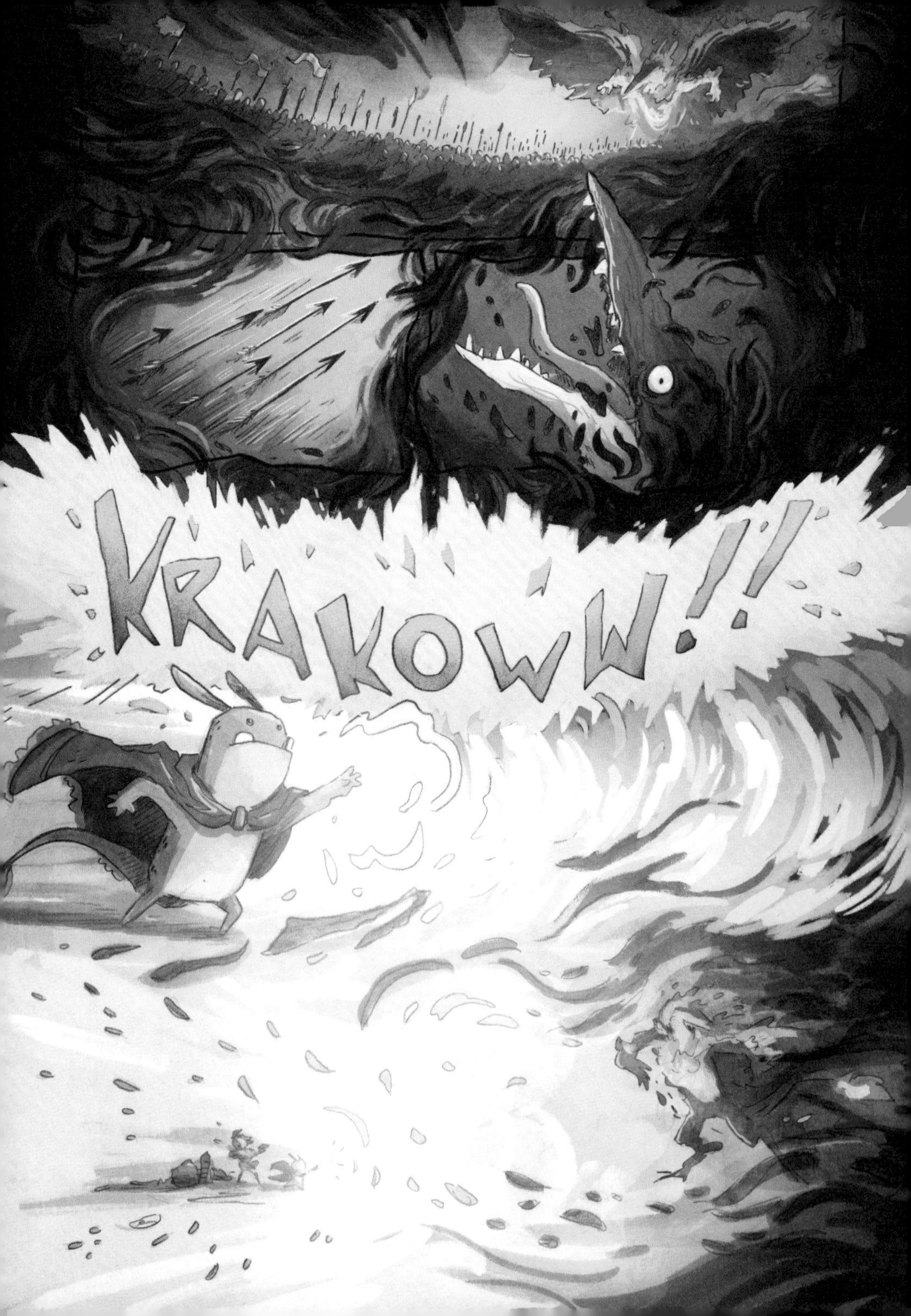
KRAKOWW!!

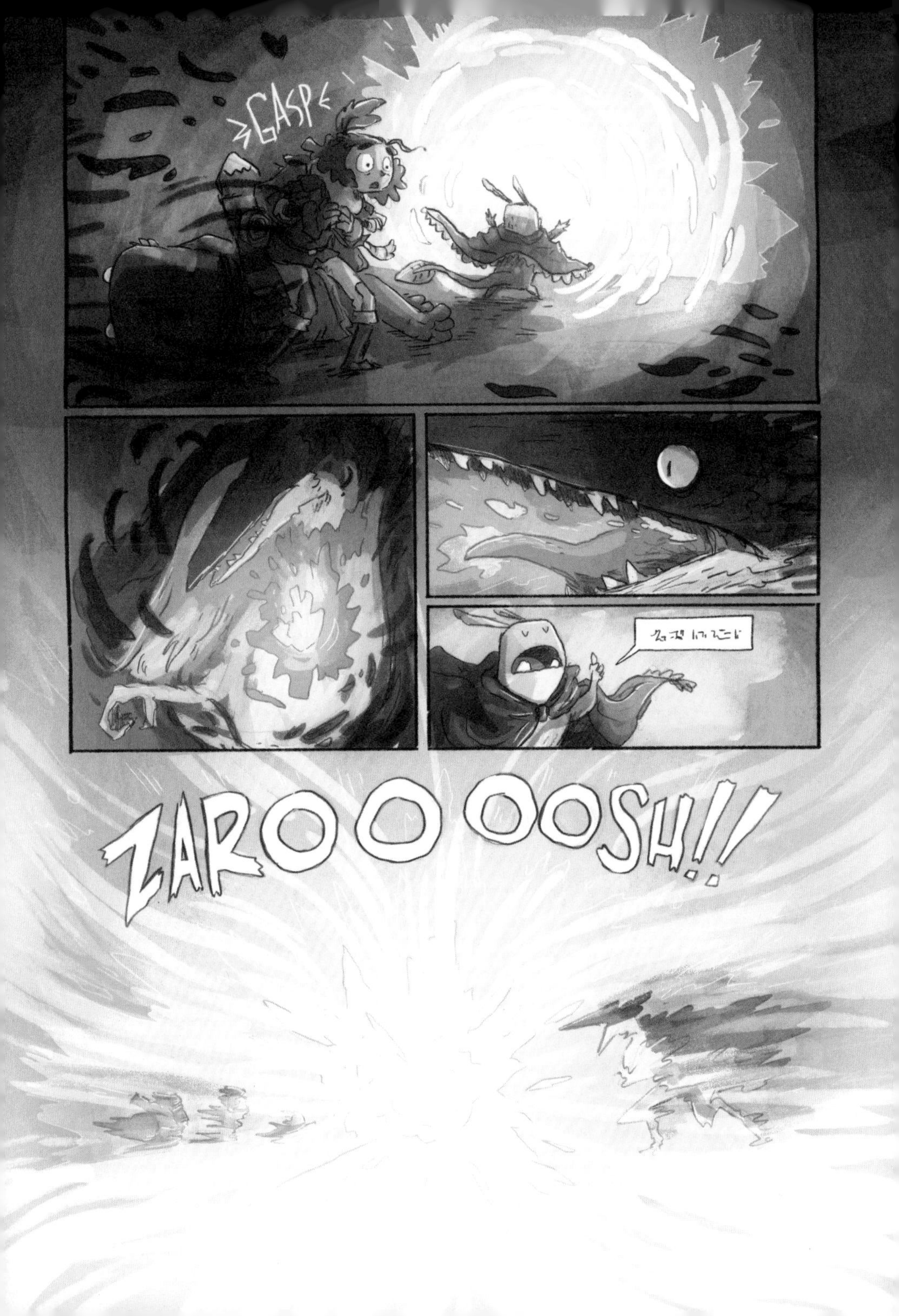
GASP
ZAROOOOOSH!!

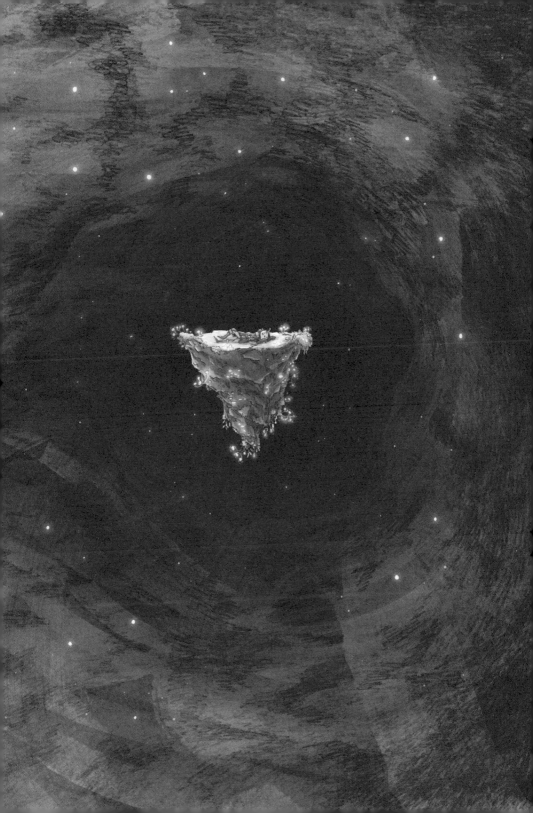

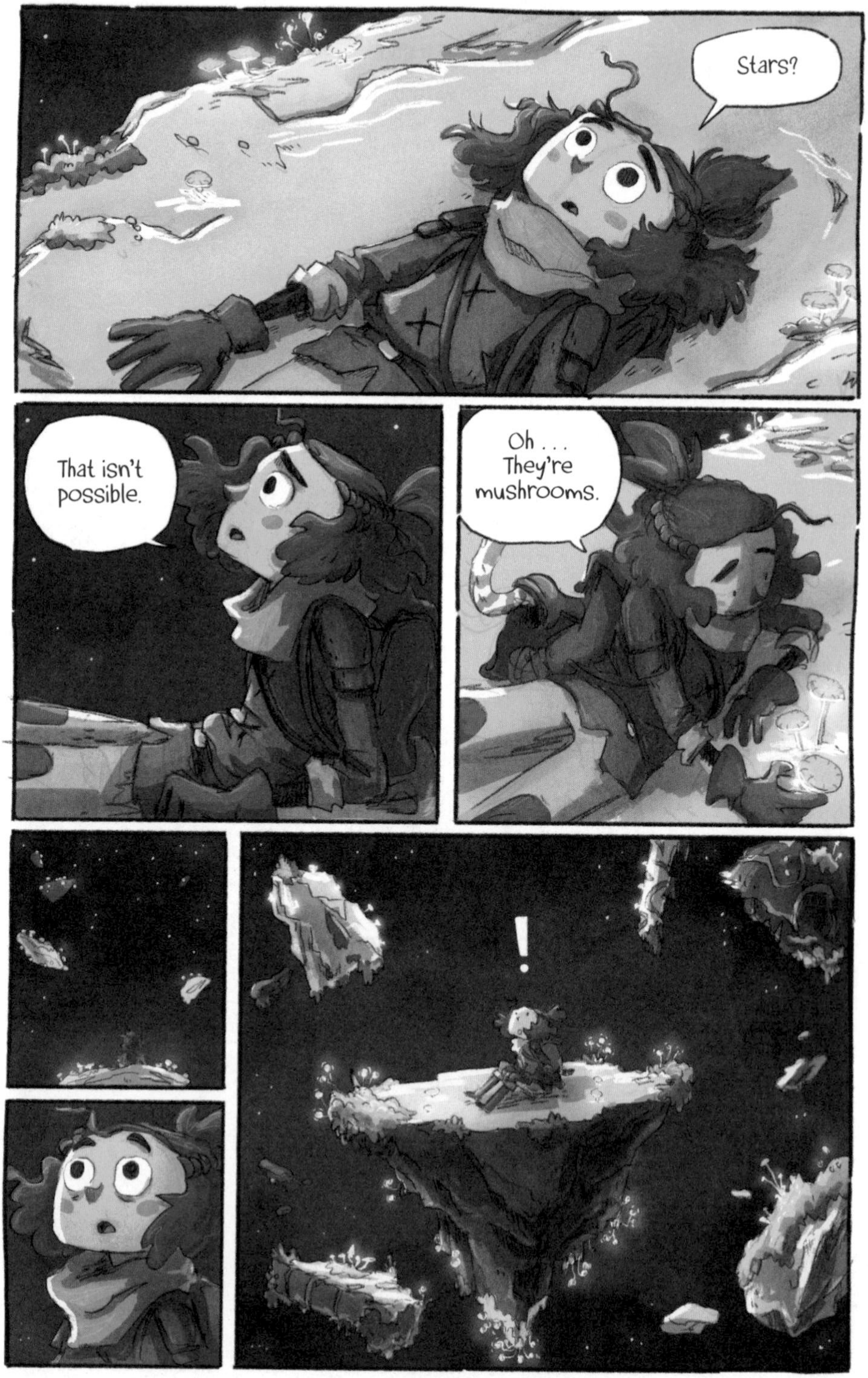
Stars?
That isn't possible.
Oh . . . They're mushrooms.
!

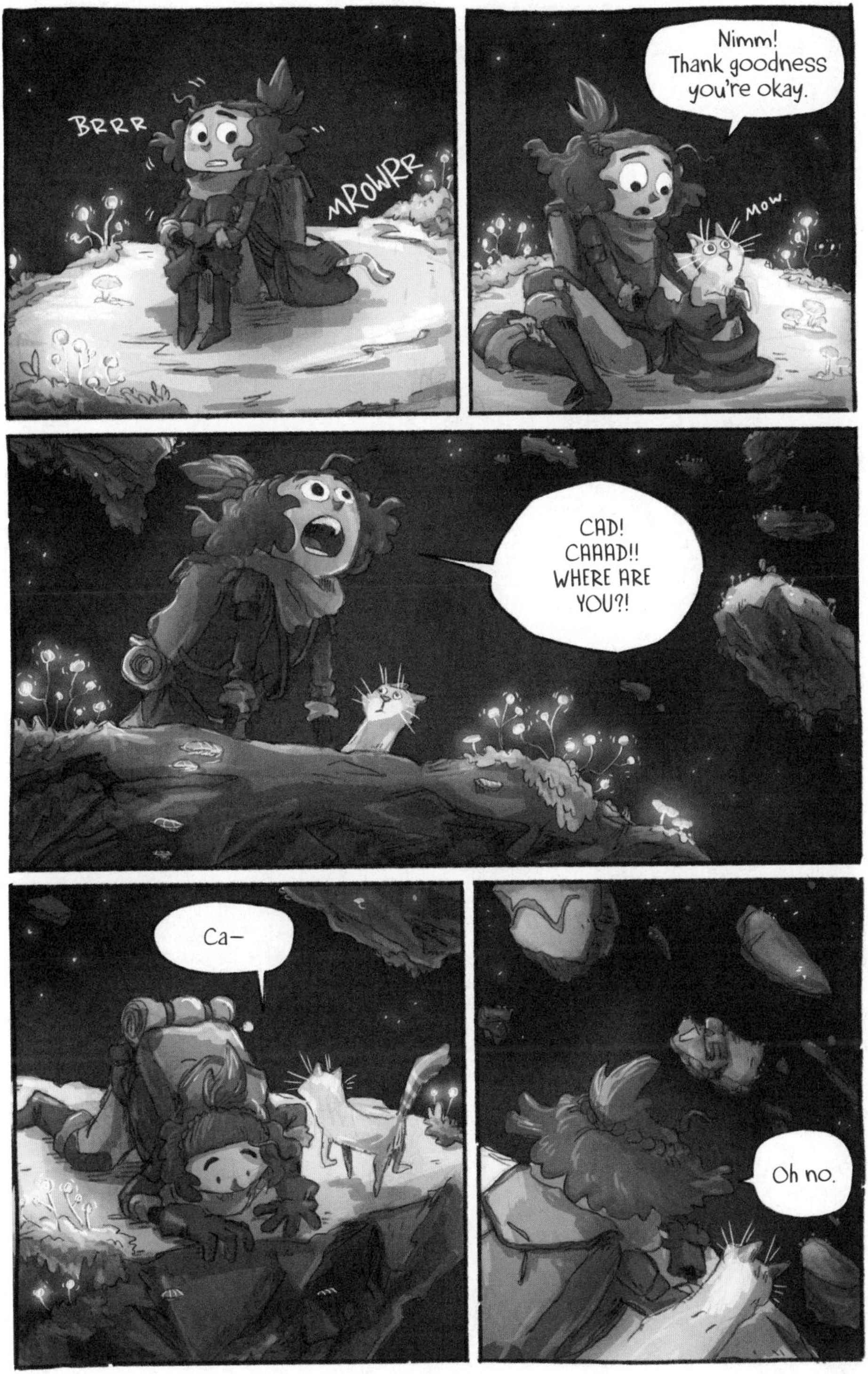
BRRR
MROWRR
Nimm! Thank goodness you're okay.
MOW.
CAD! CAAAD!! WHERE ARE YOU?!
Ca—
Oh no.

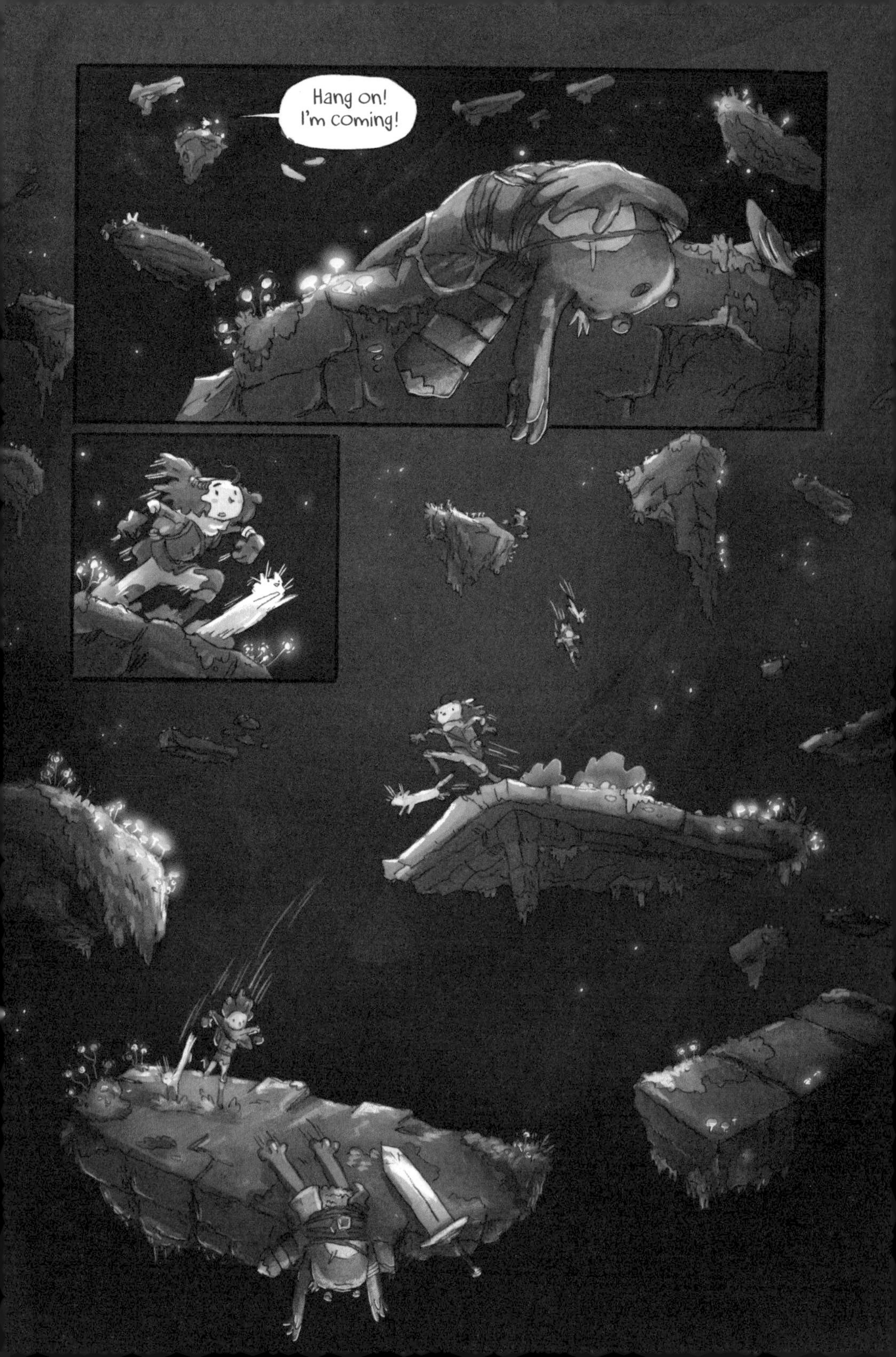
Hang on!
I'm coming!

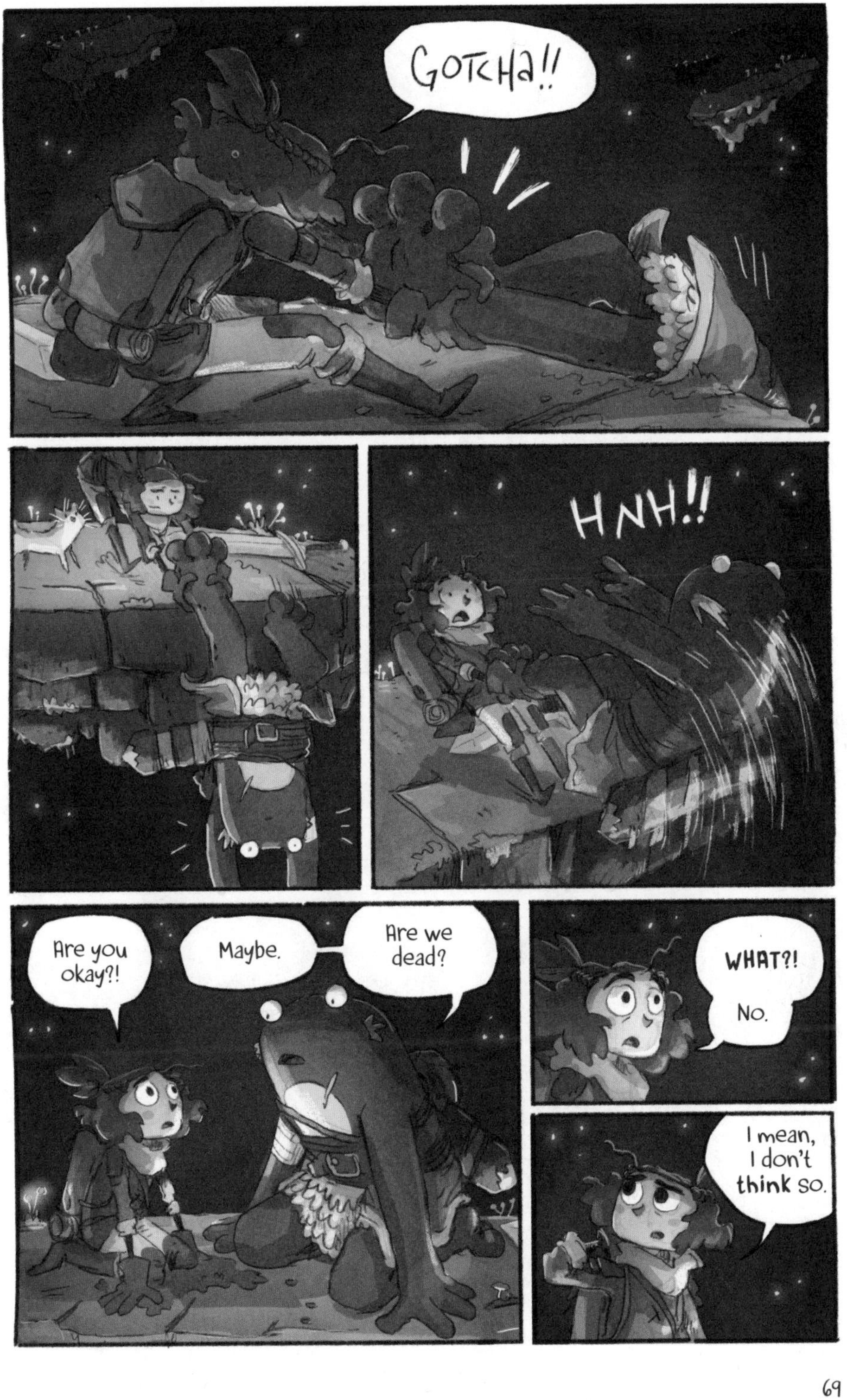
GOTCHA!!
HNH!!
Are you okay?!
Maybe.
Are we dead?
WHAT?!
No.
I mean, I don't think so.

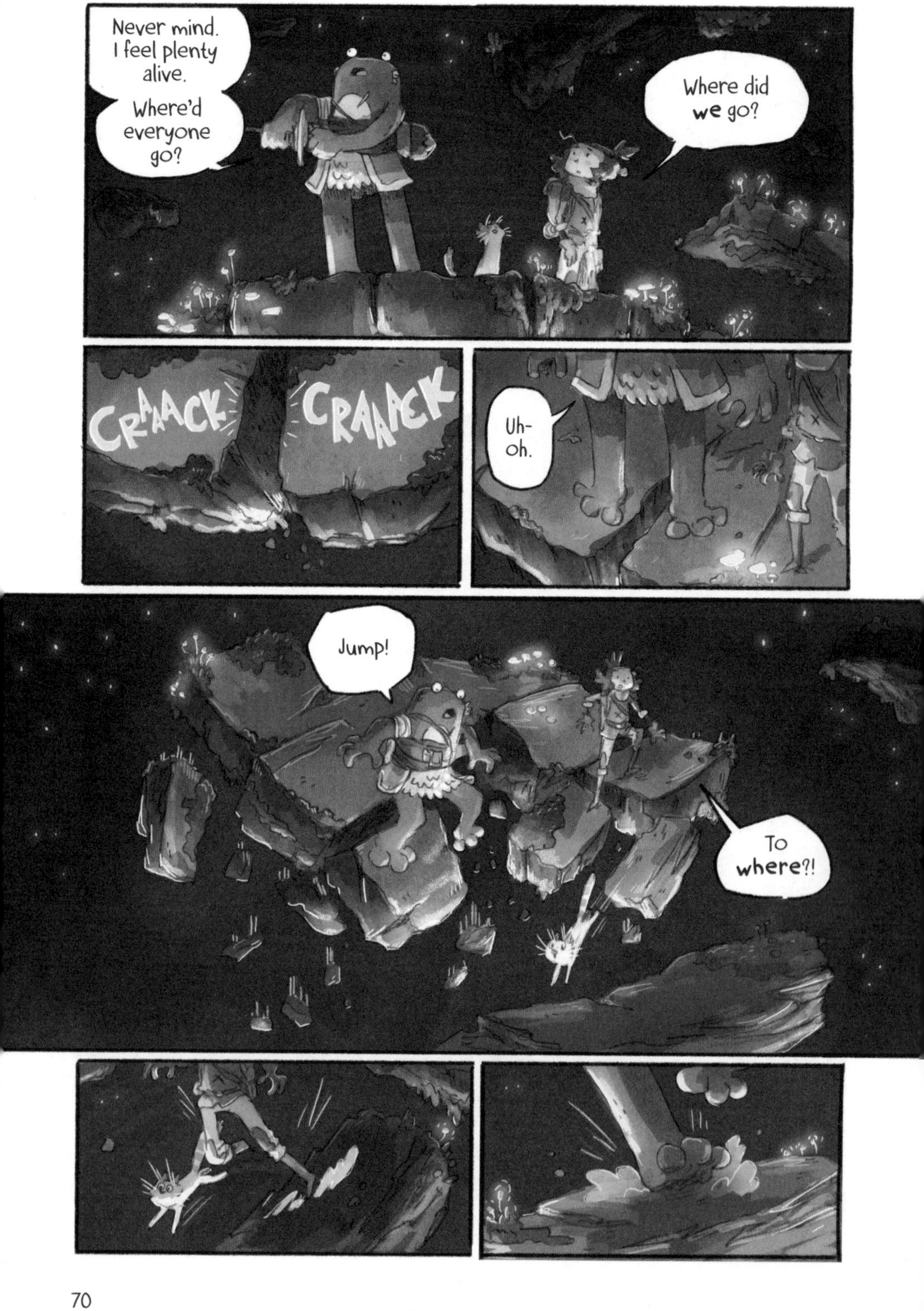
Never mind. I feel plenty alive.
Where'd everyone go?
Where did **we** go?
CRAAACK
CRAAACK
Uh-oh.
Jump!
To **where**?!

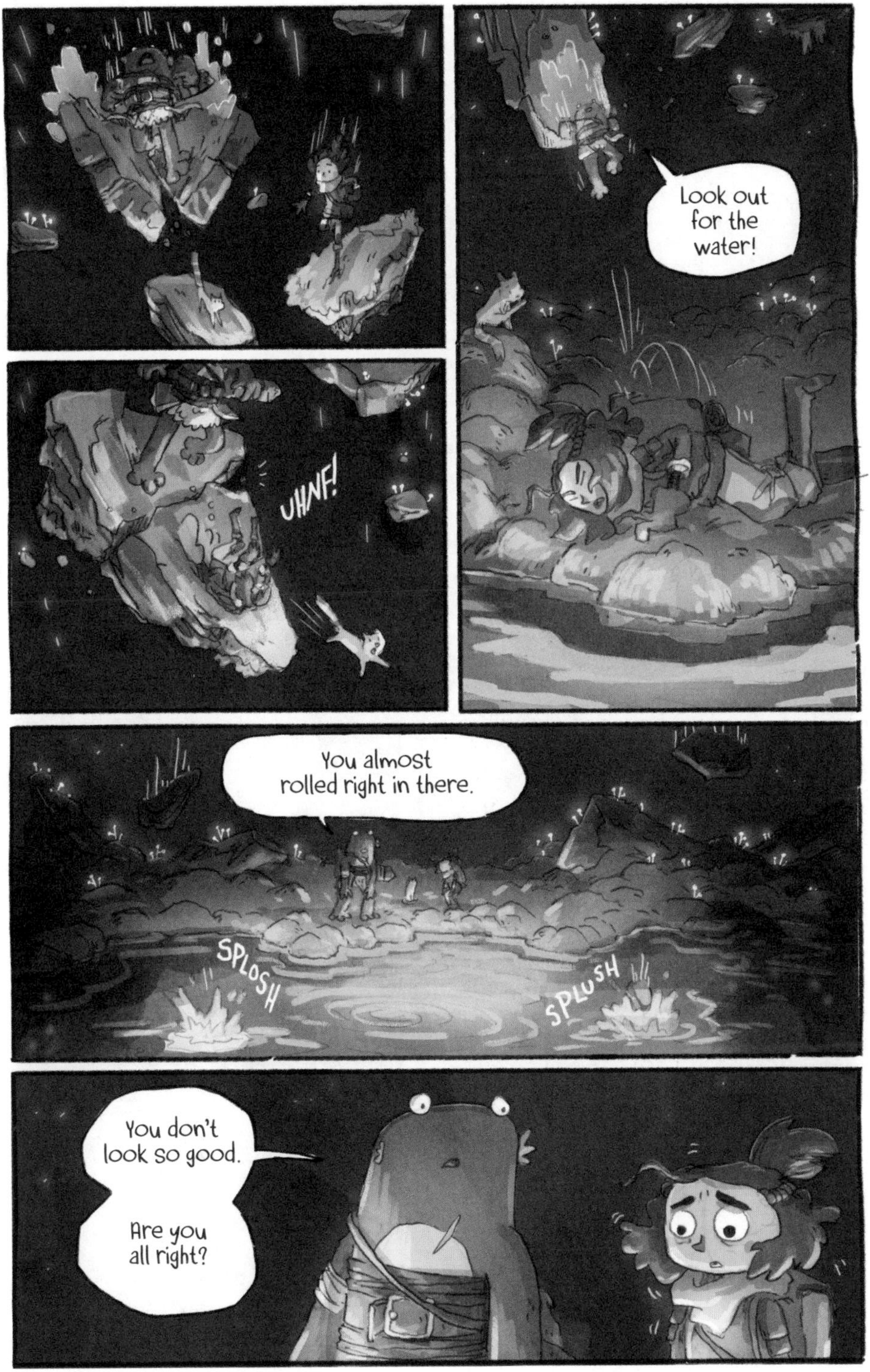
UHNF!
Look out for the water!
You almost rolled right in there.
SPLOSH
SPLUSH
You don't look so good.
Are you all right?

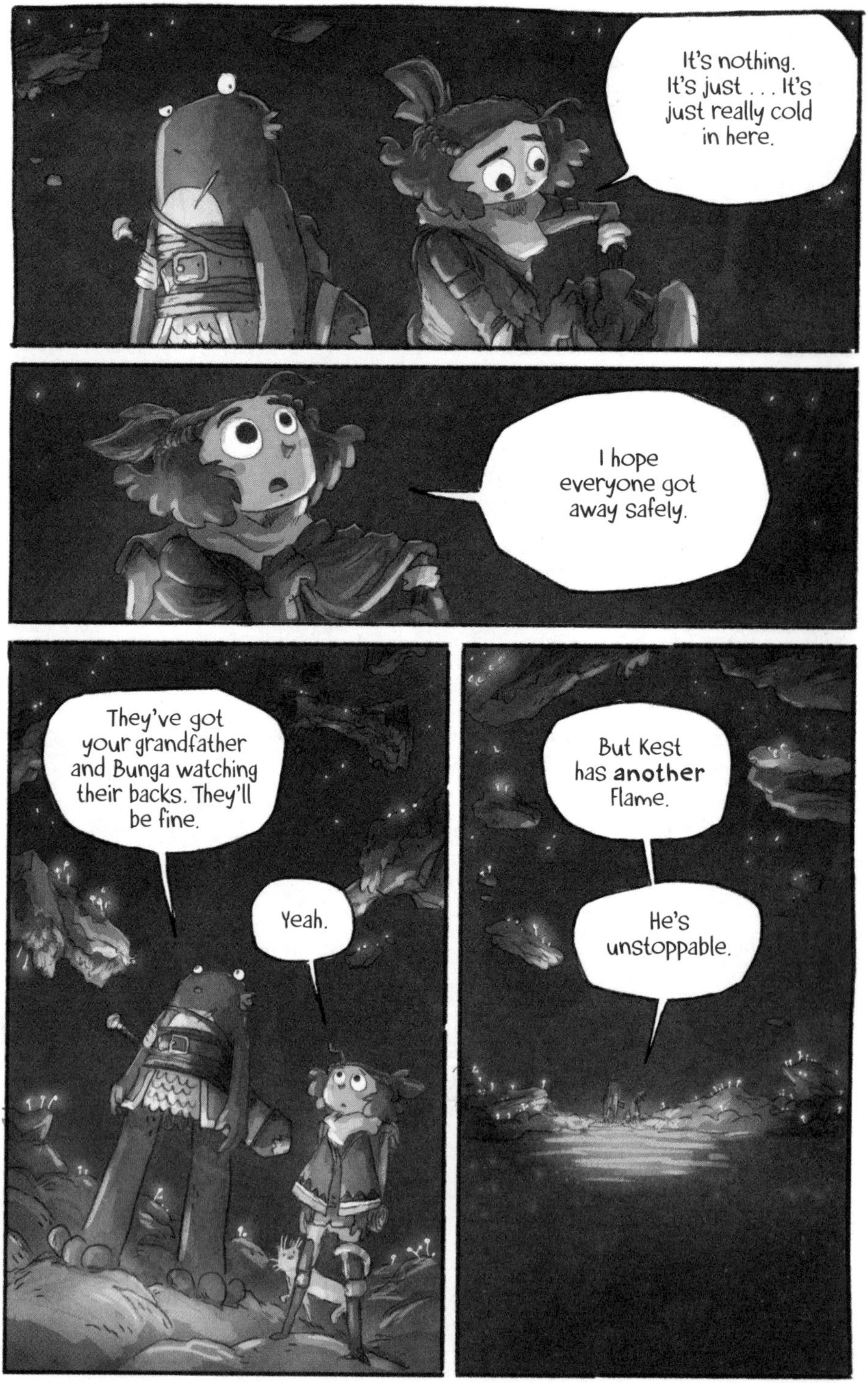
It's nothing. It's just . . . It's just really cold in here.
I hope everyone got away safely.
They've got your grandfather and Bunga watching their backs. They'll be fine.
Yeah.
But Kest has **another** Flame.
He's unstoppable.

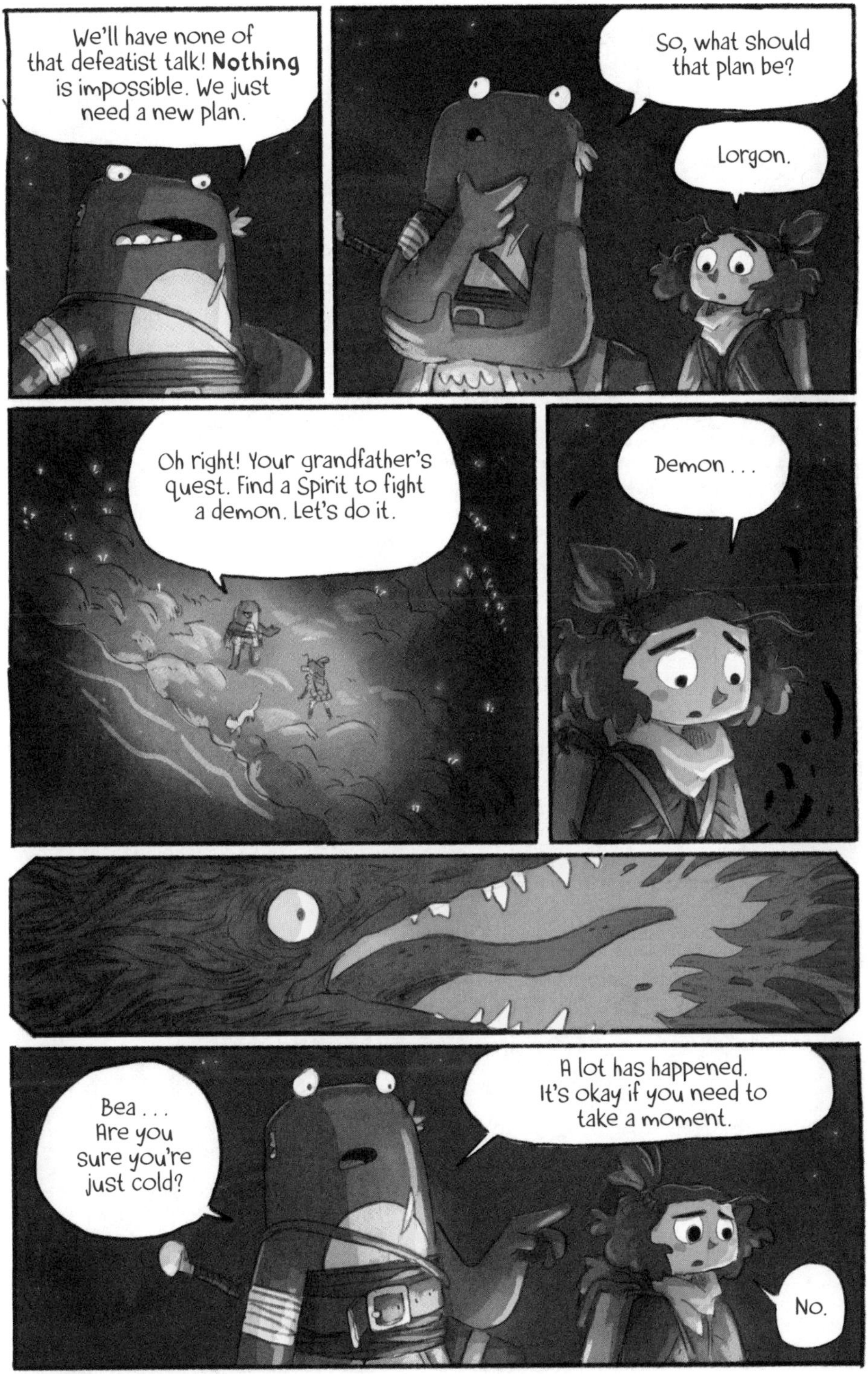
We'll have none of that defeatist talk! **Nothing** is impossible. We just need a new plan.
So, what should that plan be?
Lorgon.
Oh right! Your grandfather's quest. Find a Spirit to fight a demon. Let's do it.
Demon . . .
Bea . . . Are you sure you're just cold?
A lot has happened. It's okay if you need to take a moment.
No.

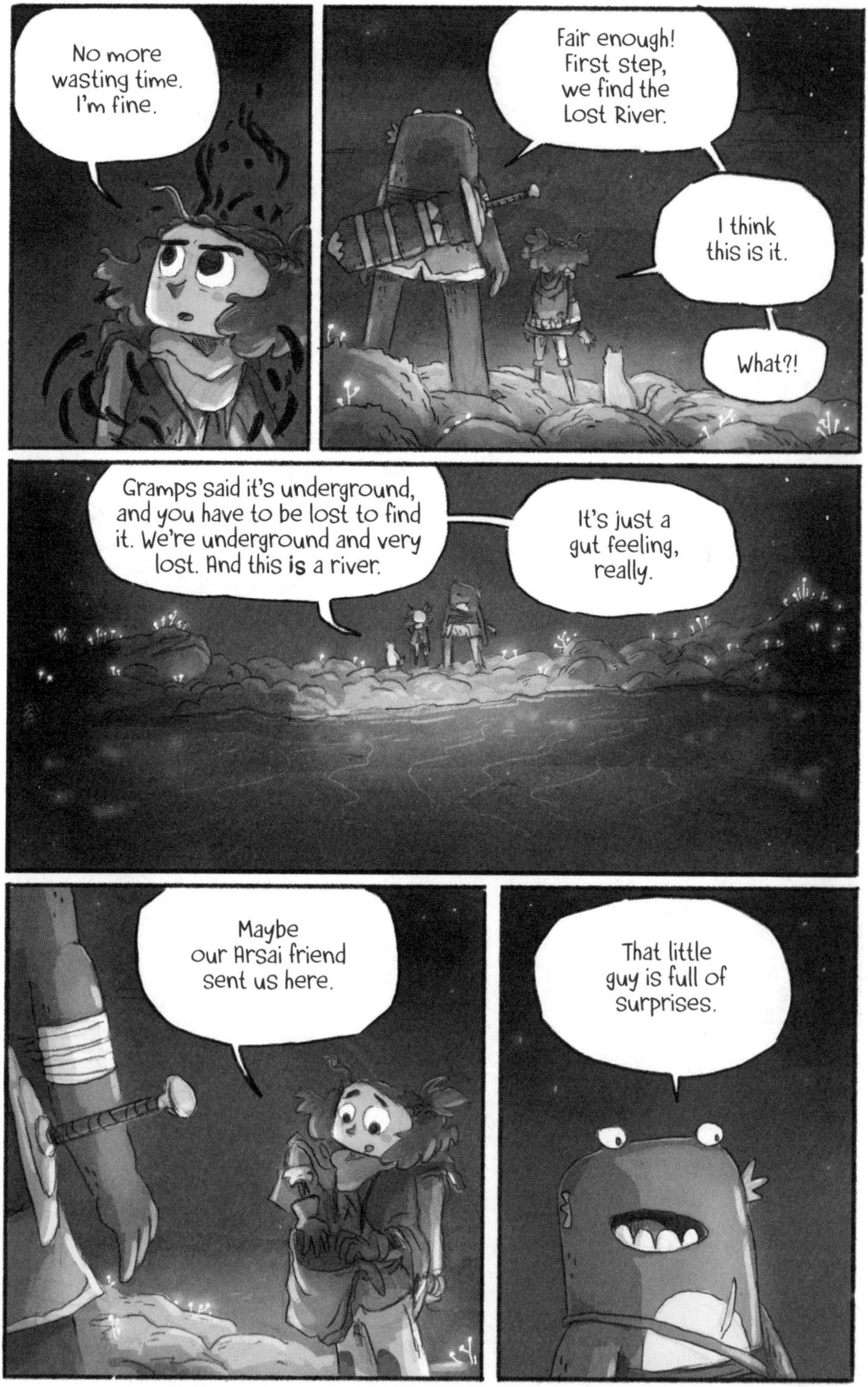
No more wasting time. I'm fine.
Fair enough! First step, we find the Lost River.
I think this is it.
What?!
Gramps said it's underground, and you have to be lost to find it. We're underground and very lost. And this **is** a river.
It's just a gut feeling, really.
Maybe our Arsai friend sent us here.
That little guy is full of surprises.

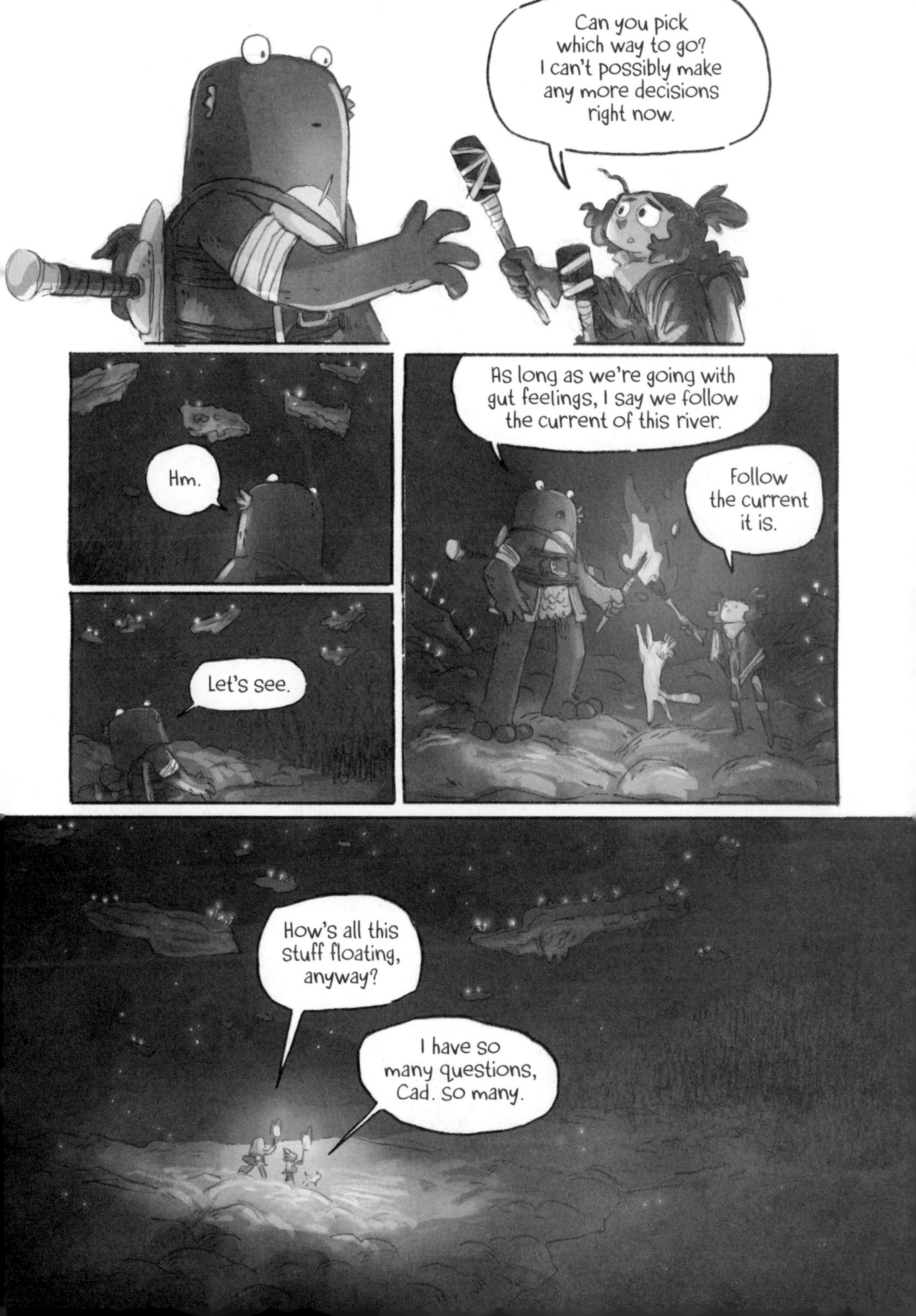
Can you pick which way to go? I can't possibly make any more decisions right now.
Hm.
Let's see.
As long as we're going with gut feelings, I say we follow the current of this river.
Follow the current it is.
How's all this stuff floating, anyway?
I have so many questions, Cad. So many.

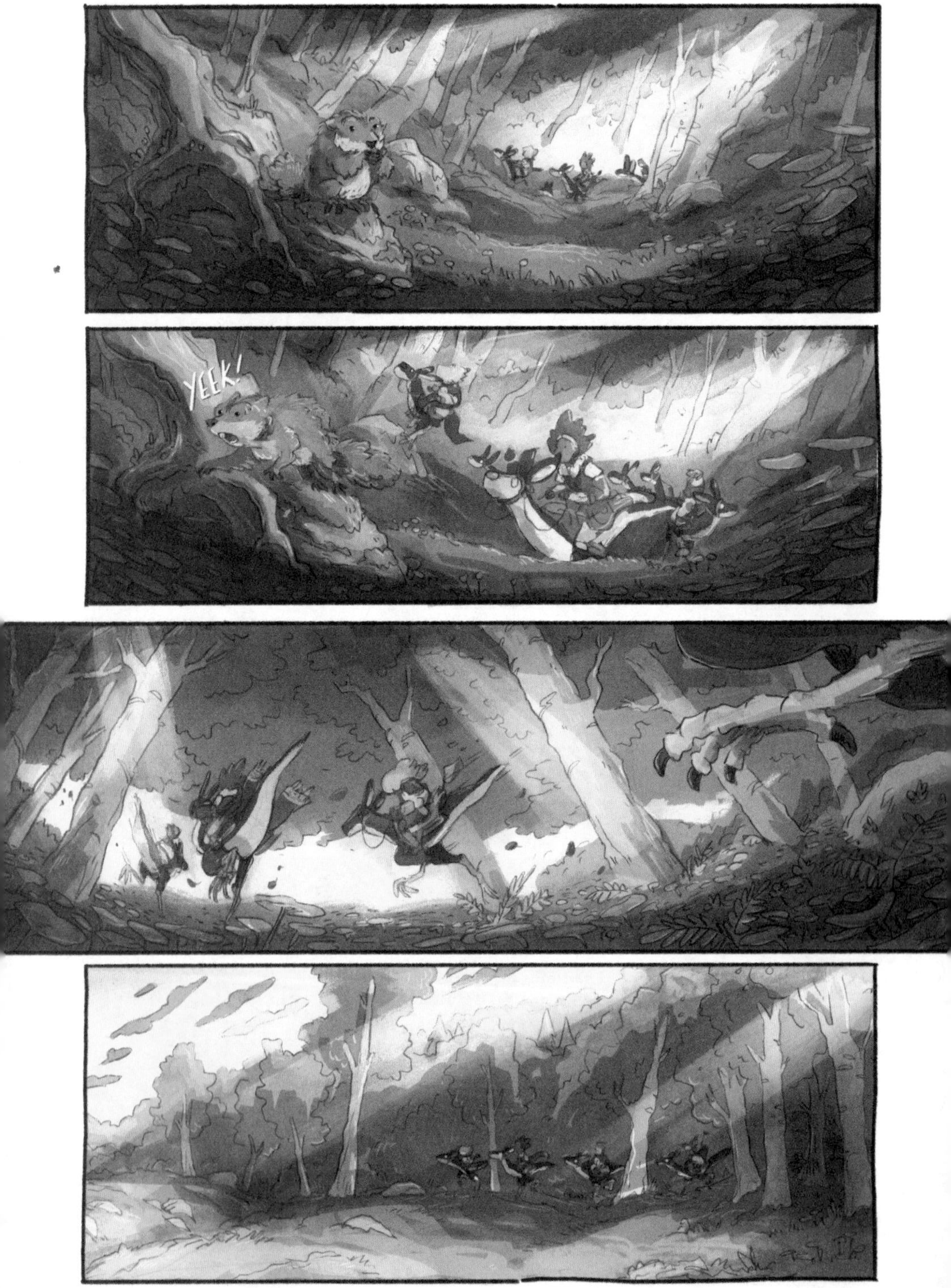
YEEK!

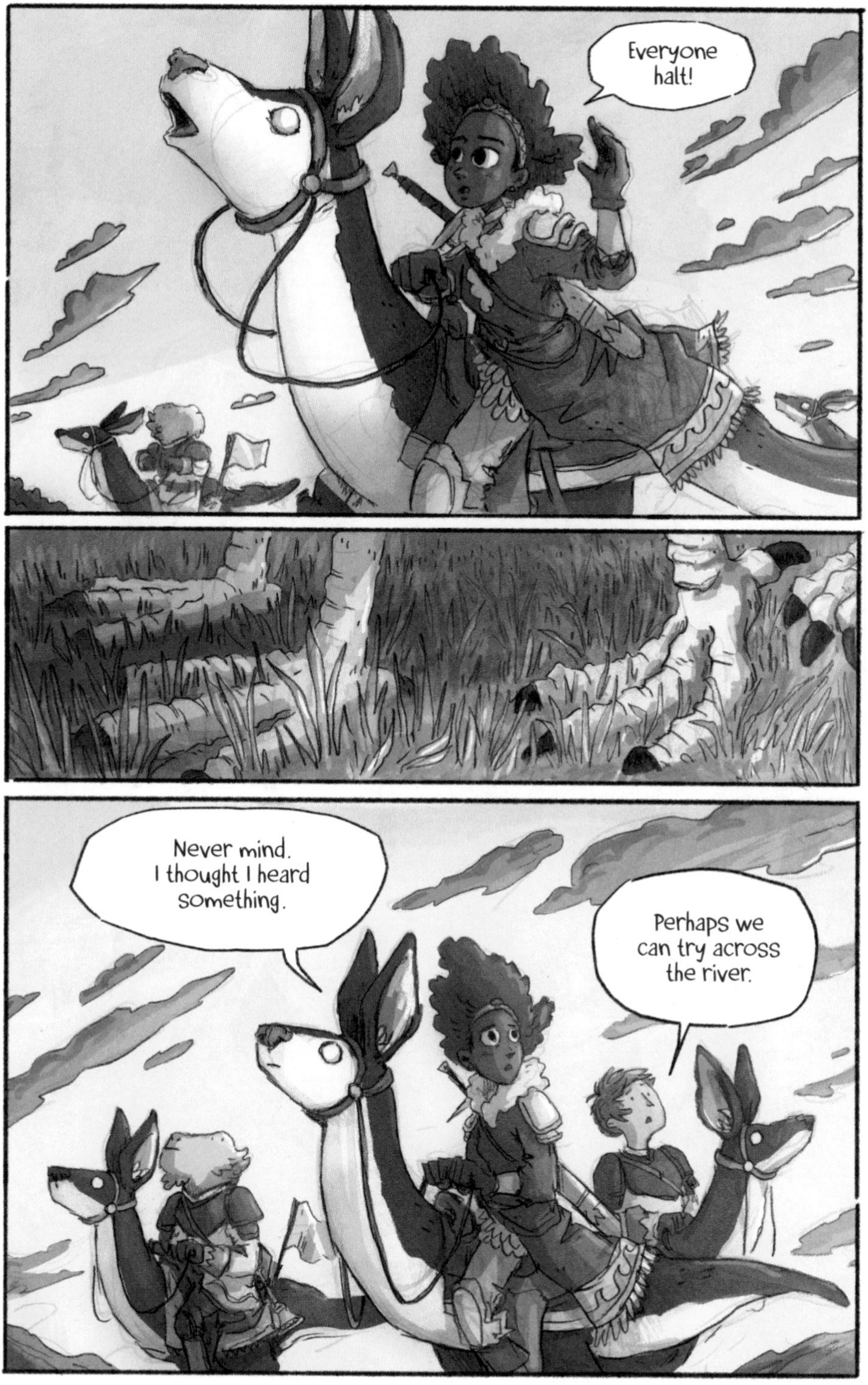
Everyone halt!
Never mind. I thought I heard something.
Perhaps we can try across the river.

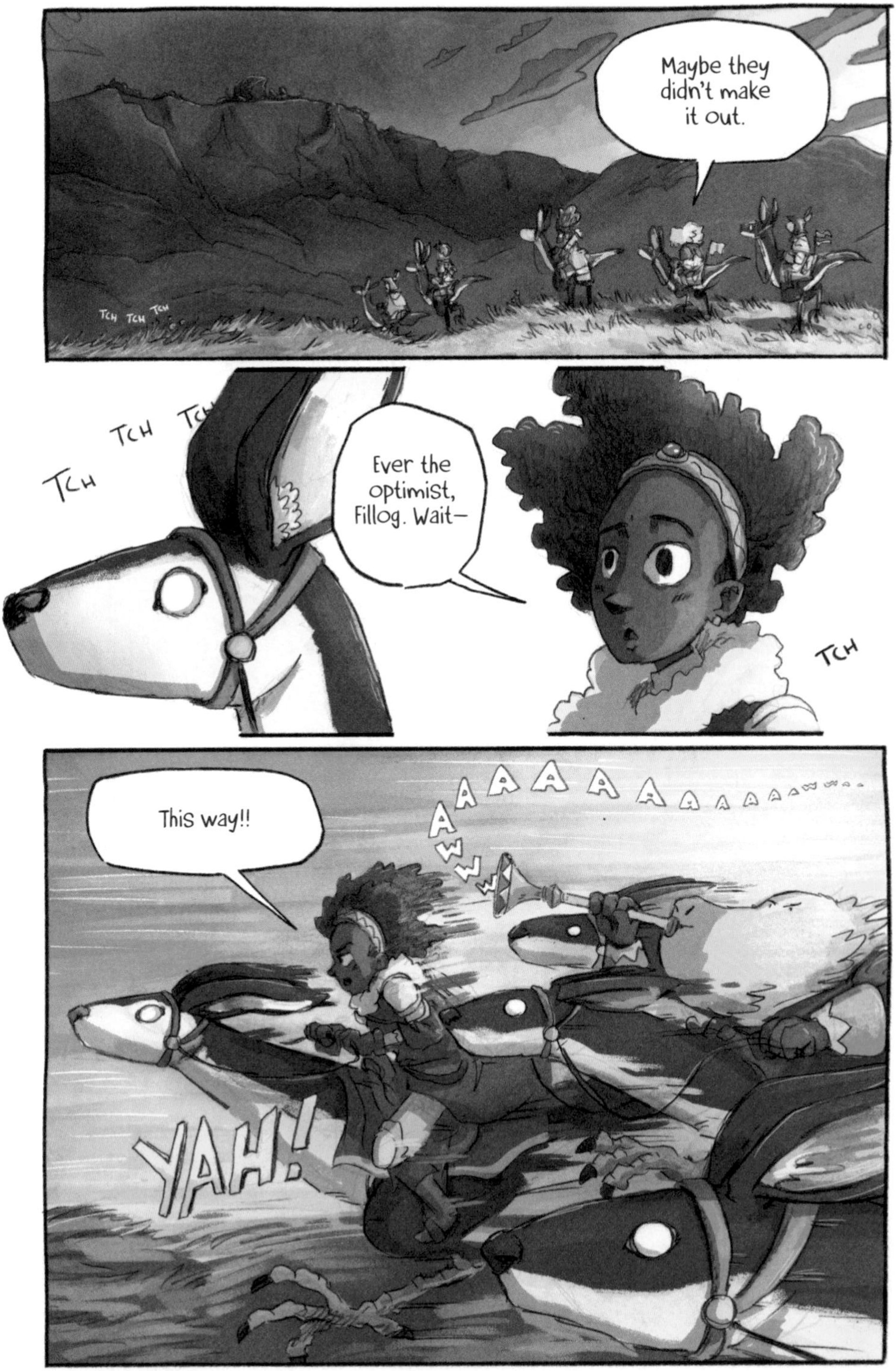
Maybe they didn't make it out.
TCH TCH TCH
TCH TCH TCH
Ever the optimist, Fillog. Wait—
TCH
This way!!
AAAAAAAAAAAAAAWWW
AWWW
YAH!

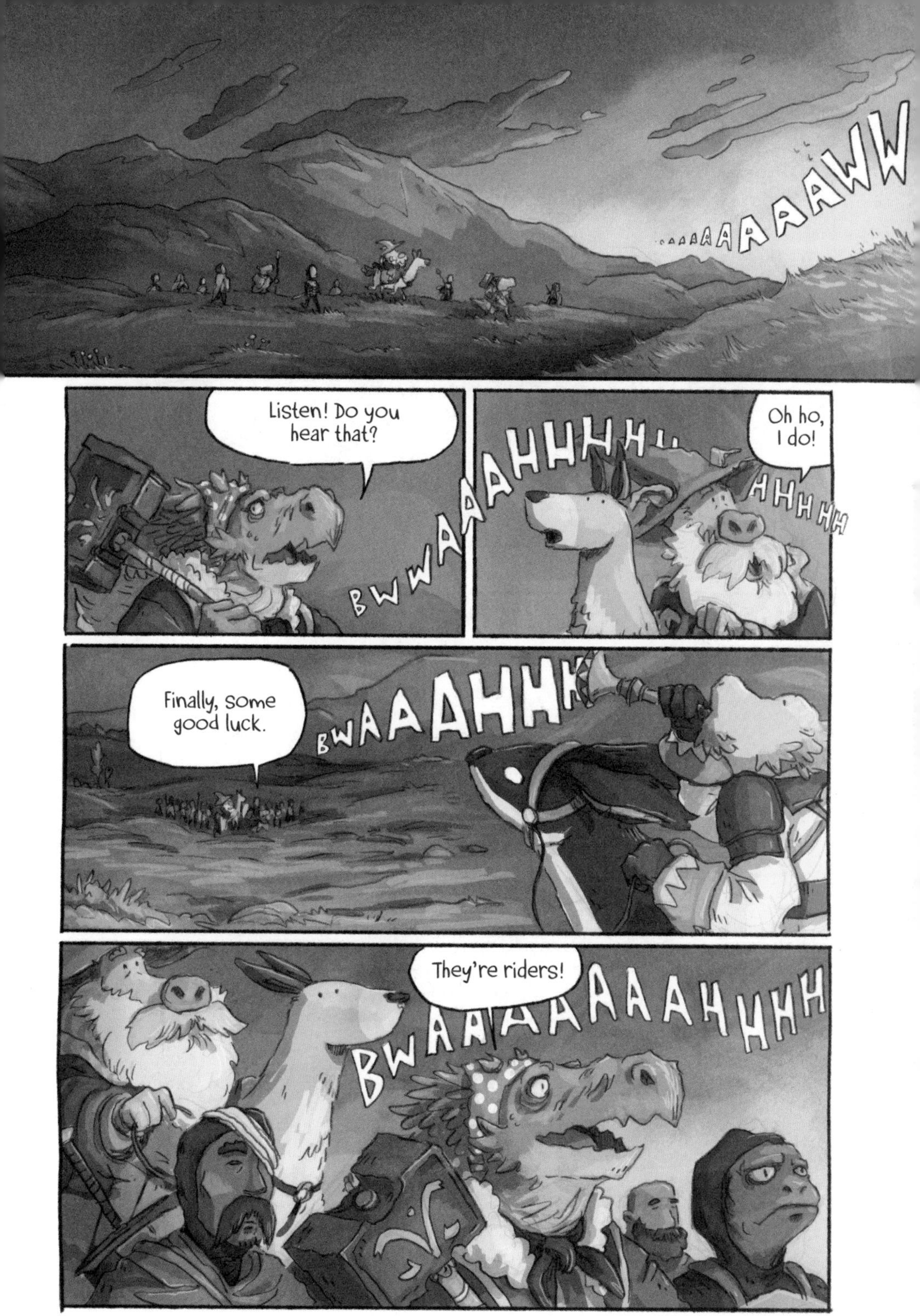

...AAAAAAAAAWW
Listen! Do you hear that?
BWWAAAHHHHHH
Oh ho, I do!
Finally, some good luck.
BWAAAHHHH
They're riders!
BWAAAAAAAAHHHHH

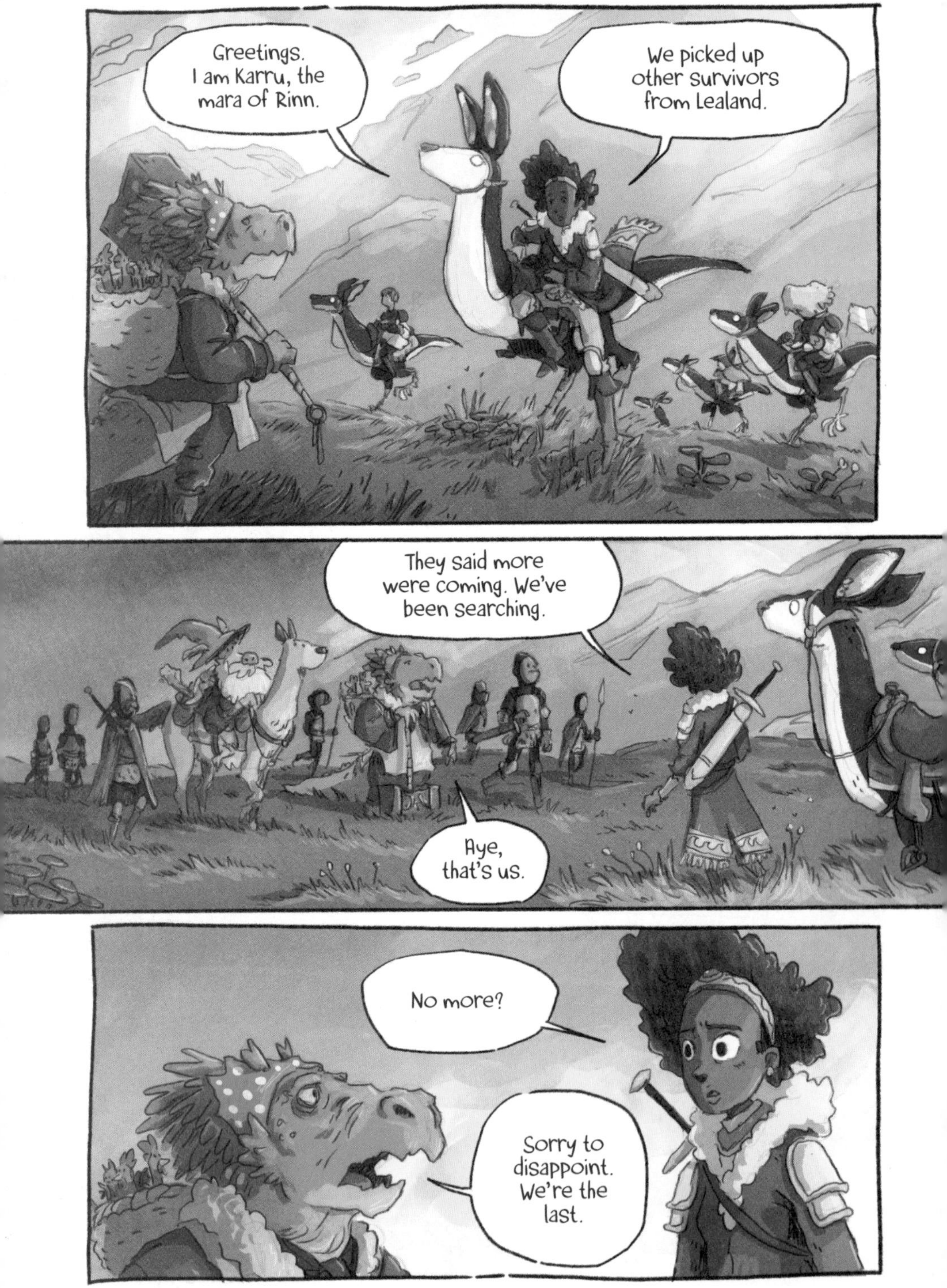
Greetings.
I am Karru, the mara of Rinn.
We picked up other survivors from Lealand.
They said more were coming. We've been searching.
Aye, that's us.
No more?
Sorry to disappoint. We're the last.

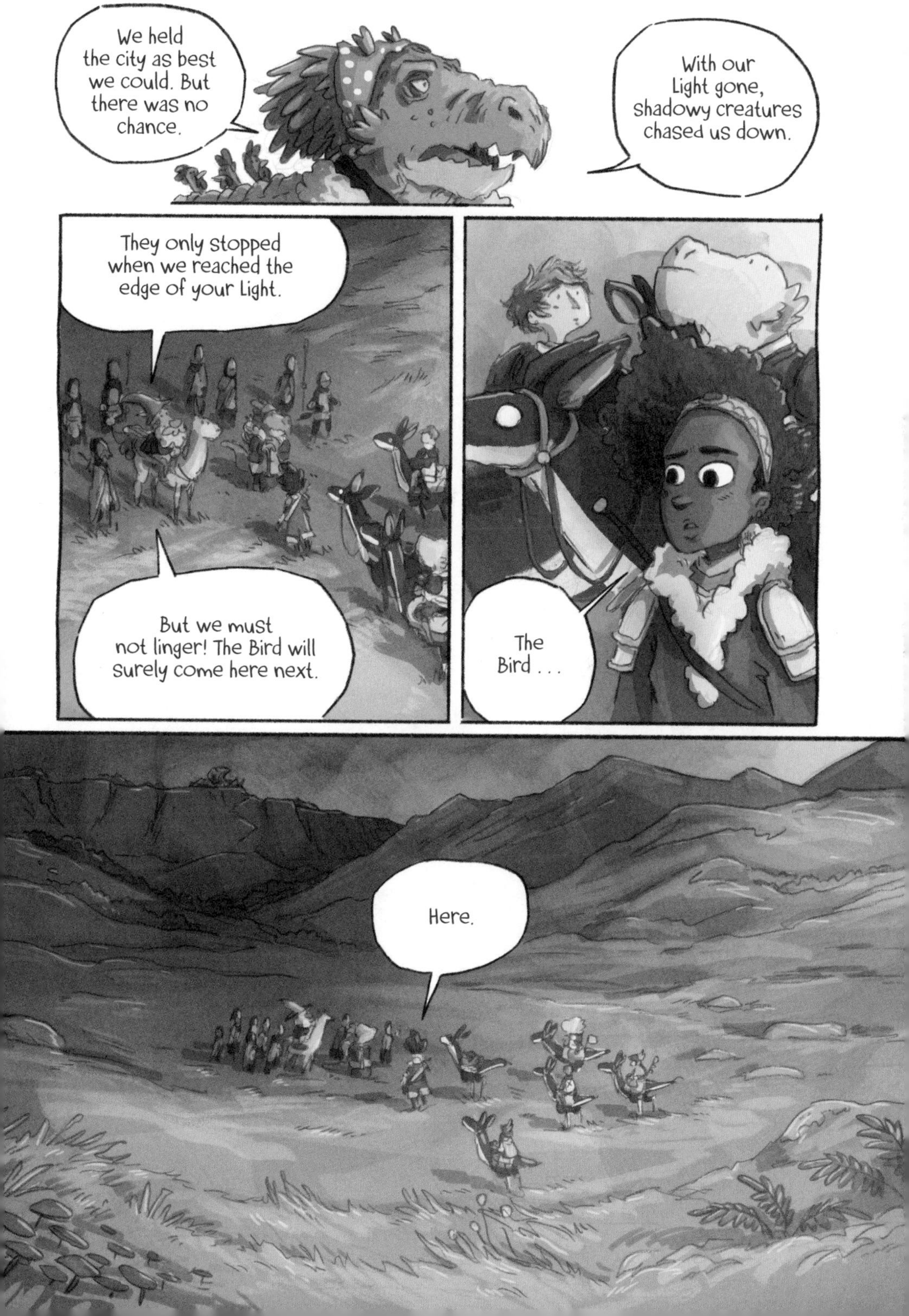
We held the city as best we could. But there was no chance.
With our Light gone, shadowy creatures chased us down.
They only stopped when we reached the edge of your Light.
But we must not linger! The Bird will surely come here next.
The Bird . . .
Here.

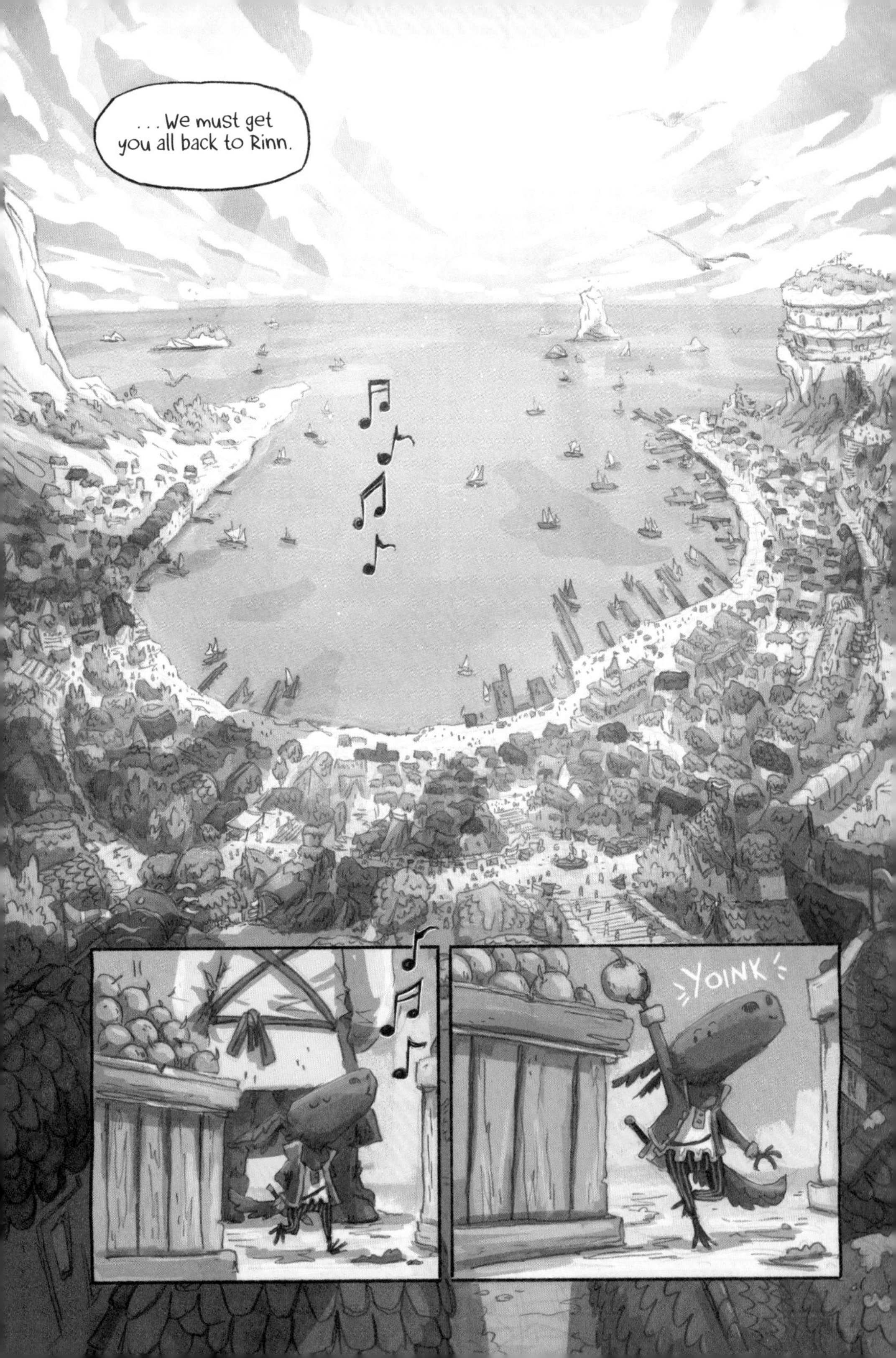
. . . We must get you all back to Rinn.
YOINK

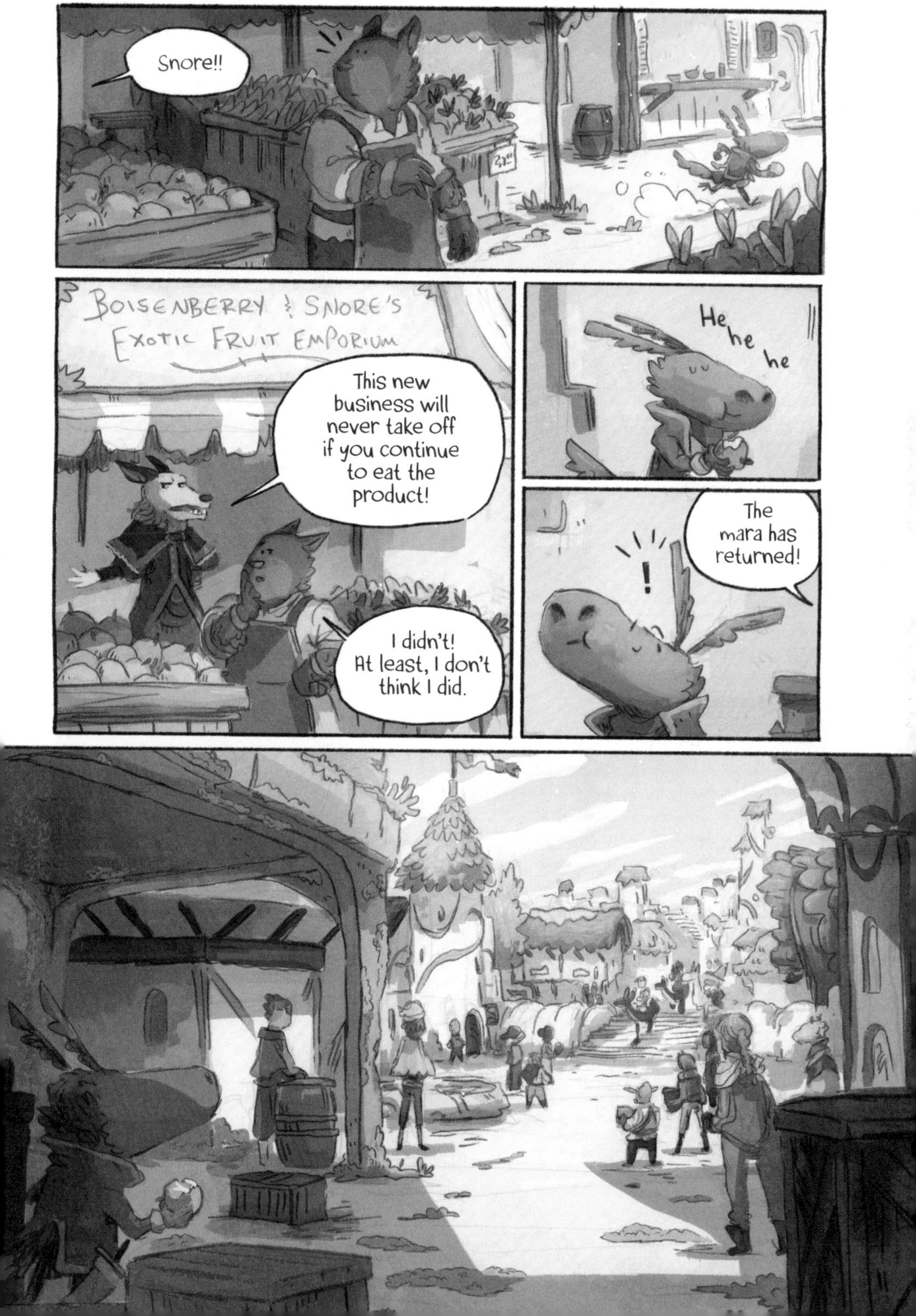
Snore!!
BOISENBERRY & SNORE'S EXOTIC FRUIT EMPORIUM
This new business will never take off if you continue to eat the product!
I didn't! At least, I don't think I did.
He he he
!
The mara has returned!

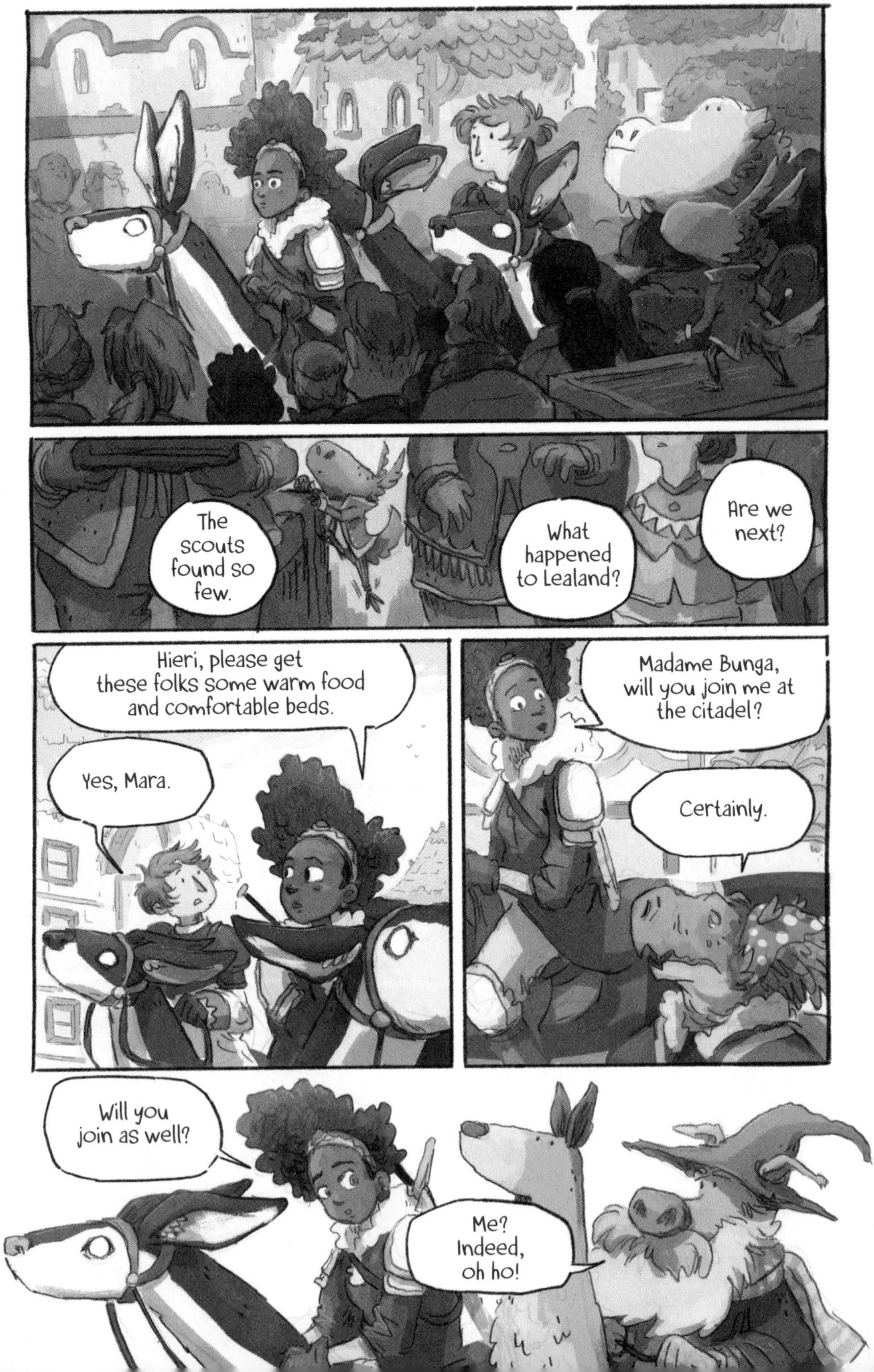
The scouts found so few.
What happened to Lealand?
Are we next?
Hieri, please get these folks some warm food and comfortable beds.
Yes, Mara.
Madame Bunga, will you join me at the citadel?
Certainly.
Will you join as well?
Me? Indeed, oh ho!

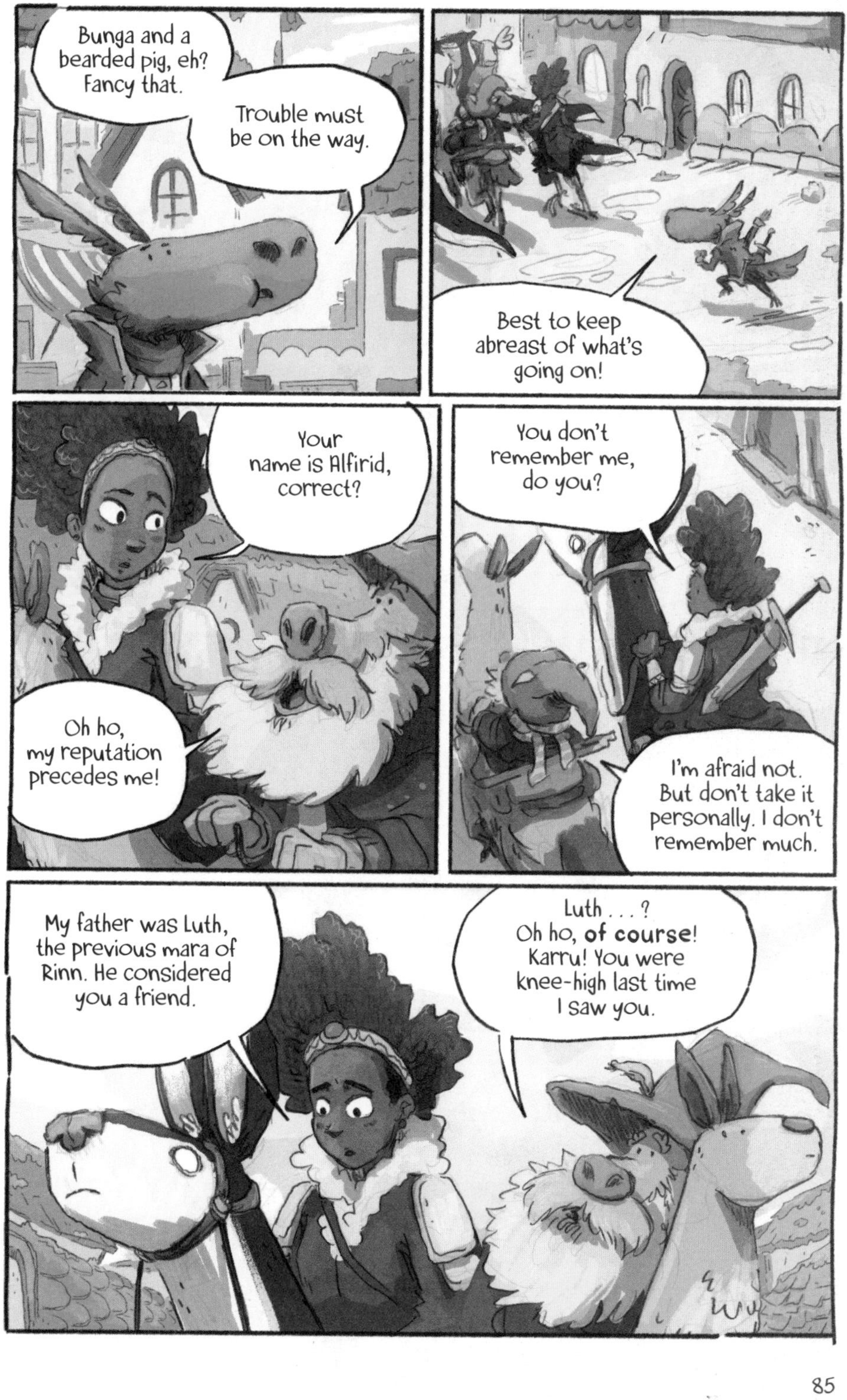
Bunga and a bearded pig, eh? Fancy that.
Trouble must be on the way.
Best to keep abreast of what's going on!
Your name is Alfirid, correct?
Oh ho, my reputation precedes me!
You don't remember me, do you?
I'm afraid not. But don't take it personally. I don't remember much.
My father was Luth, the previous mara of Rinn. He considered you a friend.
Luth . . . ? Oh ho, **of course**! Karru! You were knee-high last time I saw you.

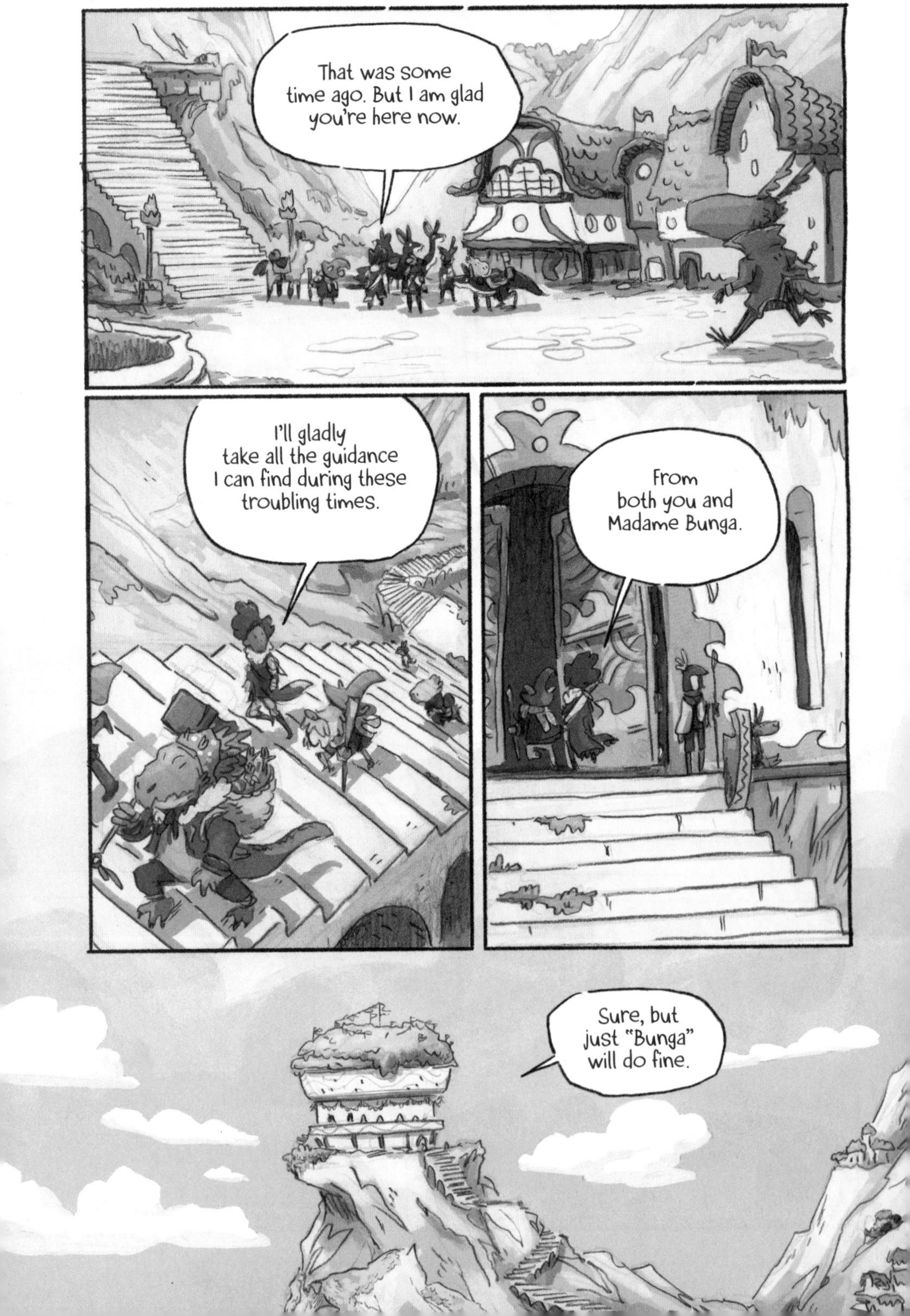
That was some time ago. But I am glad you're here now.
I'll gladly take all the guidance I can find during these troubling times.
From both you and Madame Bunga.
Sure, but just "Bunga" will do fine.

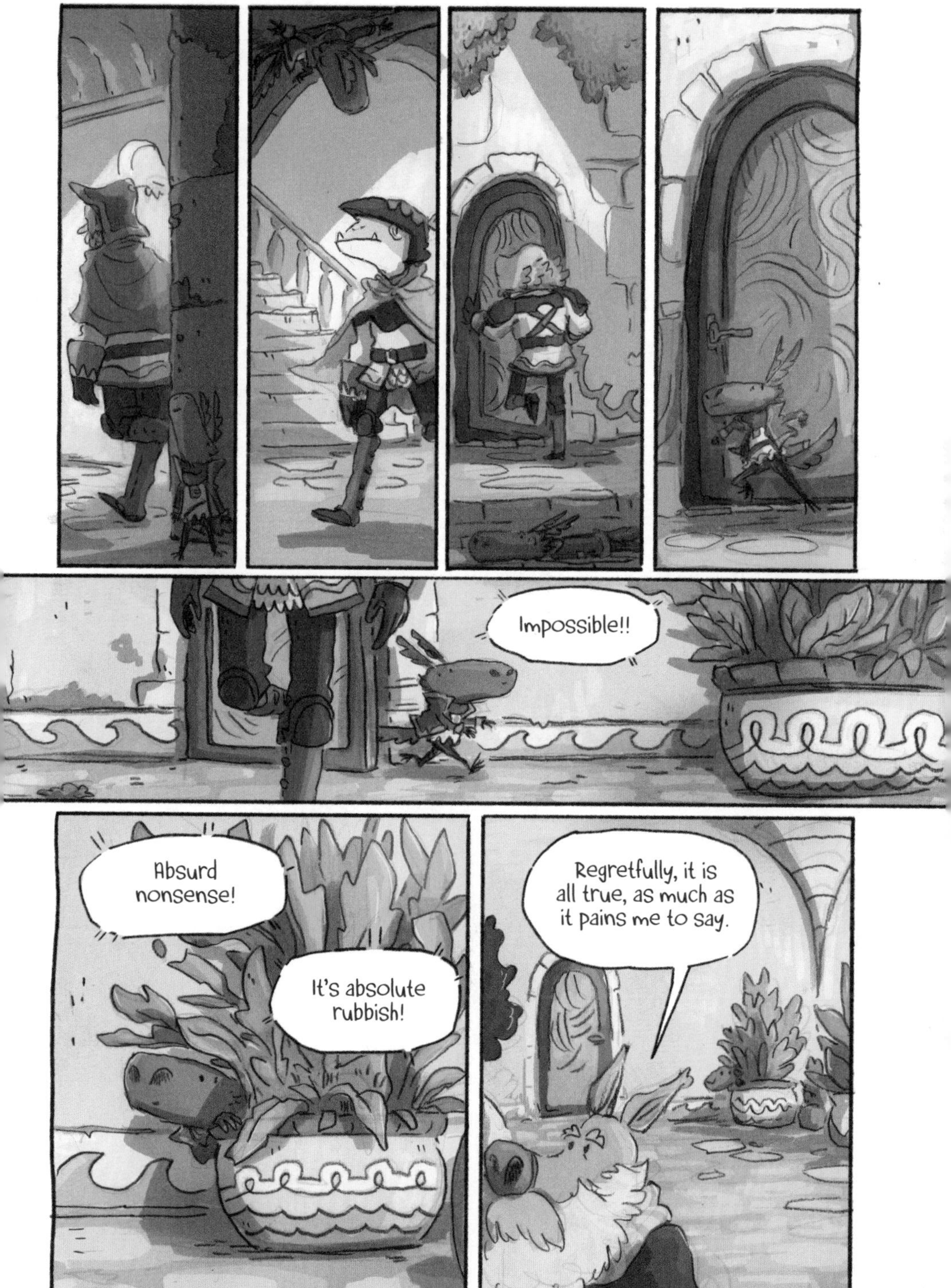
Impossible!!
Absurd nonsense!
It's absolute rubbish!
Regretfully, it is all true, as much as it pains me to say.

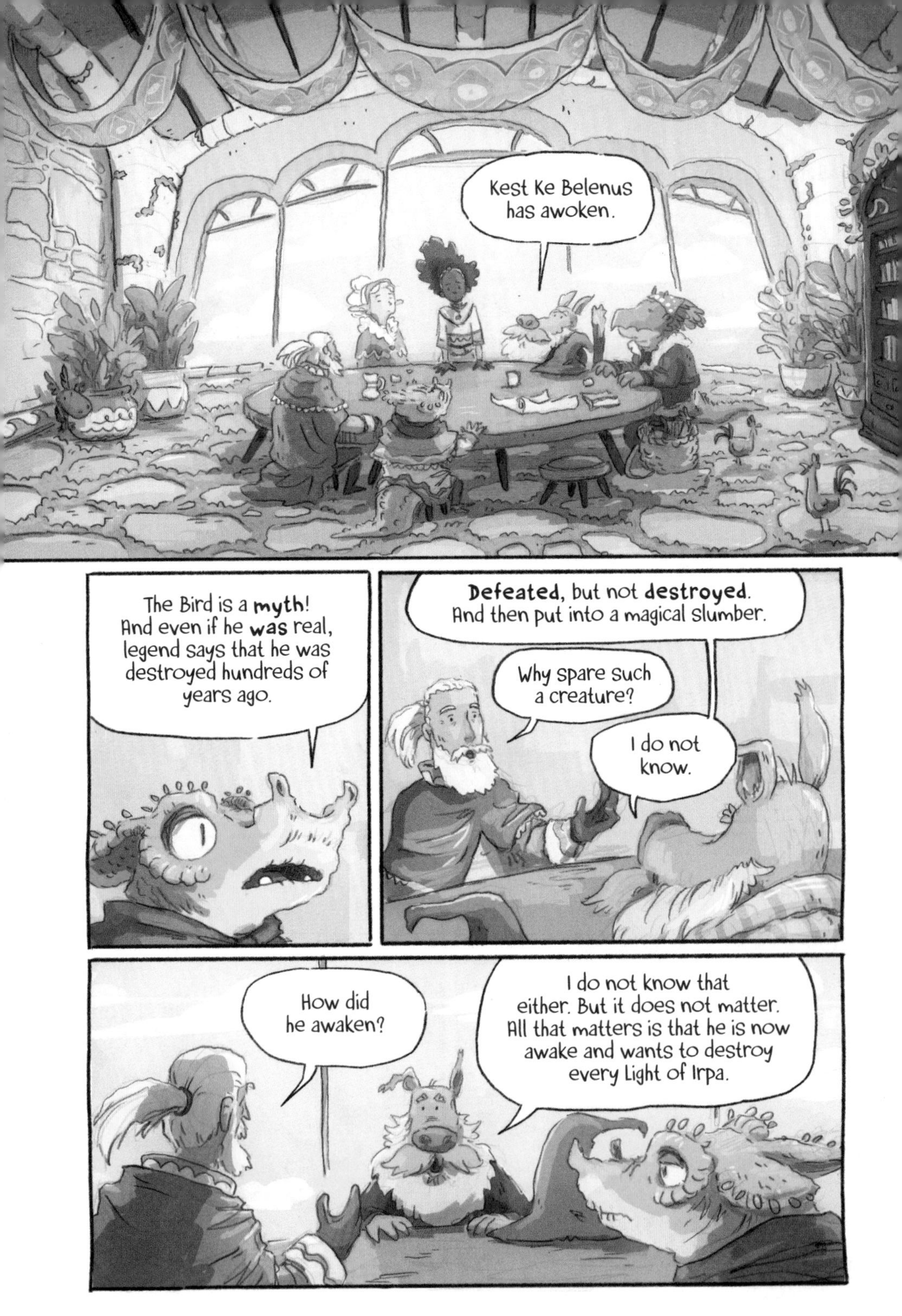

Kest Ke Belenus has awoken.
The Bird is a **myth**! And even if he **was** real, legend says that he was destroyed hundreds of years ago.
Defeated, but not **destroyed**. And then put into a magical slumber.
Why spare such a creature?
I do not know.
How did he awaken?
I do not know that either. But it does not matter. All that matters is that he is now awake and wants to destroy every Light of Irpa.

Heh Heh
Heh

Tell us, Pig Wizard . . . How is it that you know so much about this bird?

Because I'm the one who found him.

In my youth, I set out on a quest to find a way to revive the sun.

My first discovery was the Lost Flame from the Light of Tarian. A critical step in the right direction . . .

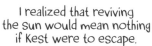

But my next discovery changed everything.

I found Kest, asleep in a crystal cage.

I realized that reviving the sun would mean nothing if Kest were to escape.

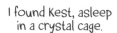

So I appointed myself as guardian of both the Flame and the slumbering bird.

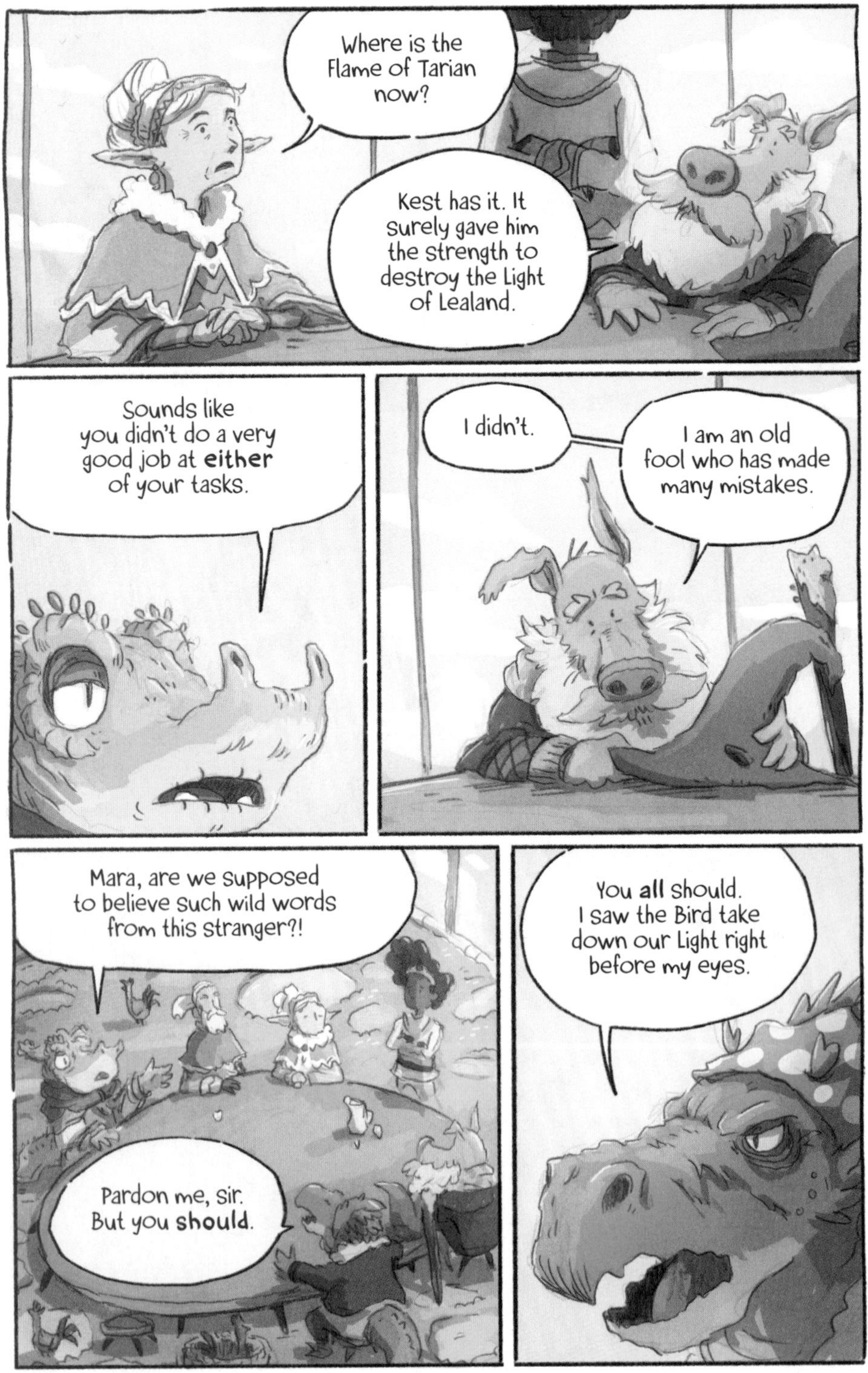
Where is the Flame of Tarian now?
Kest has it. It surely gave him the strength to destroy the Light of Lealand.
Sounds like you didn't do a very good job at **either** of your tasks.
I didn't.
I am an old fool who has made many mistakes.
Mara, are we supposed to believe such wild words from this stranger?!
Pardon me, sir. But you **should**.
You **all** should. I saw the Bird take down our Light right before my eyes.

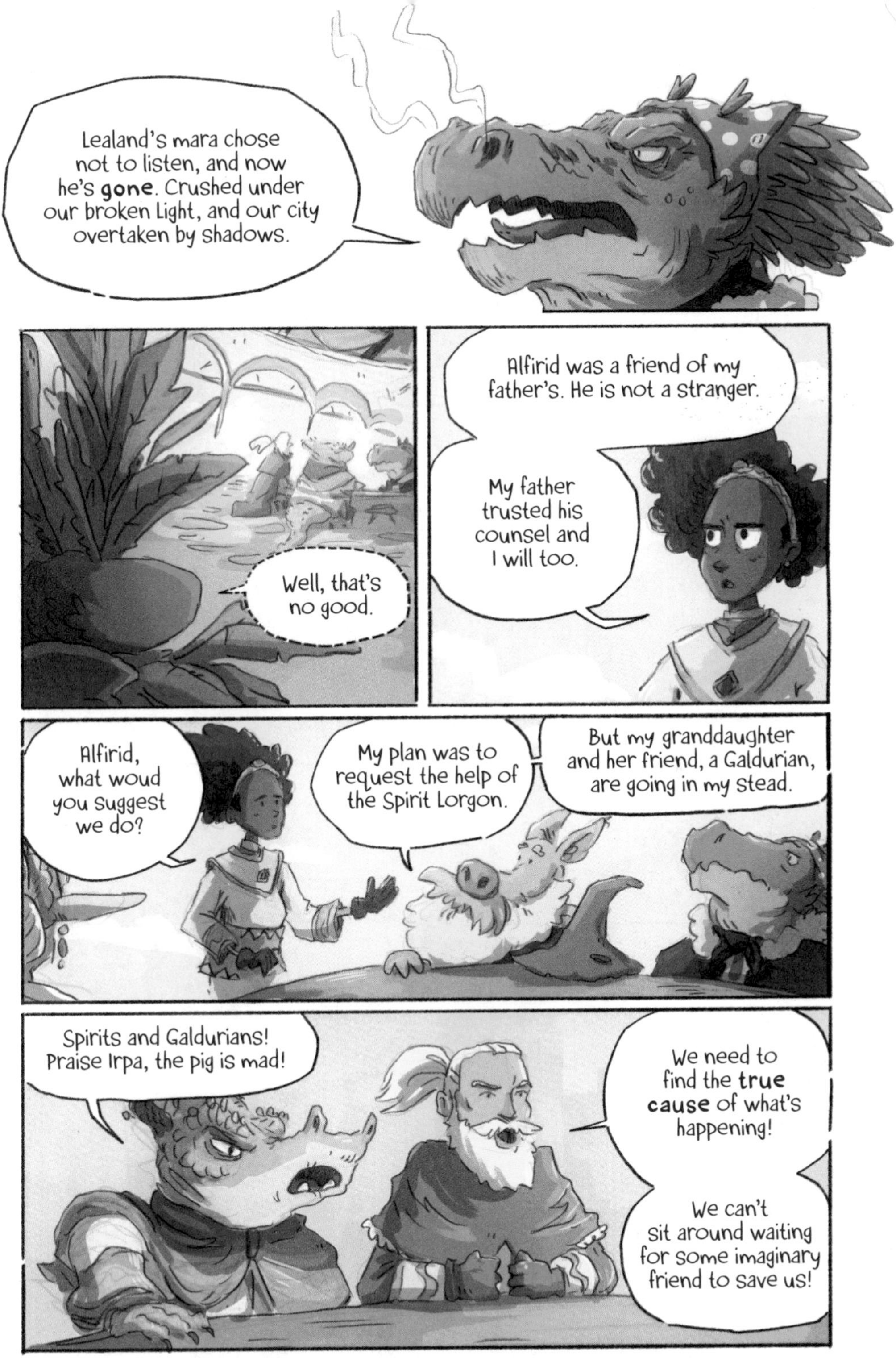

Lealand's mara chose not to listen, and now he's **gone**. Crushed under our broken Light, and our city overtaken by shadows.
Well, that's no good.
Alfirid was a friend of my father's. He is not a stranger.
My father trusted his counsel and I will too.
Alfirid, what woud you suggest we do?
My plan was to request the help of the Spirit Lorgon.
But my granddaughter and her friend, a Galdurian, are going in my stead.
Spirits and Galdurians! Praise Irpa, the pig is mad!
We need to find the **true cause** of what's happening!
We can't sit around waiting for some imaginary friend to save us!

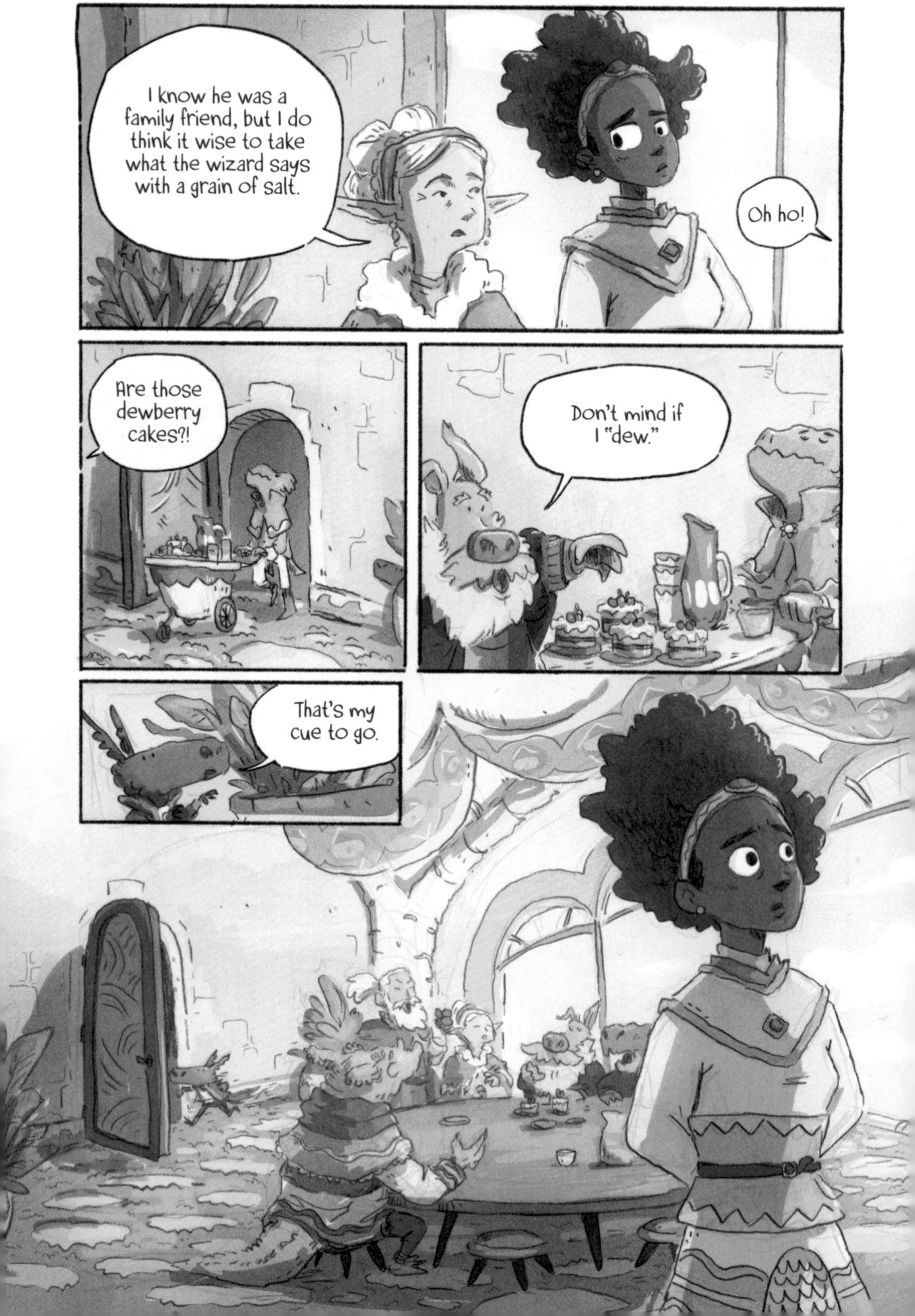
I know he was a family friend, but I do think it wise to take what the wizard says with a grain of salt.
Oh ho!
Are those dewberry cakes?!
Don't mind if I "dew."
That's my cue to go.

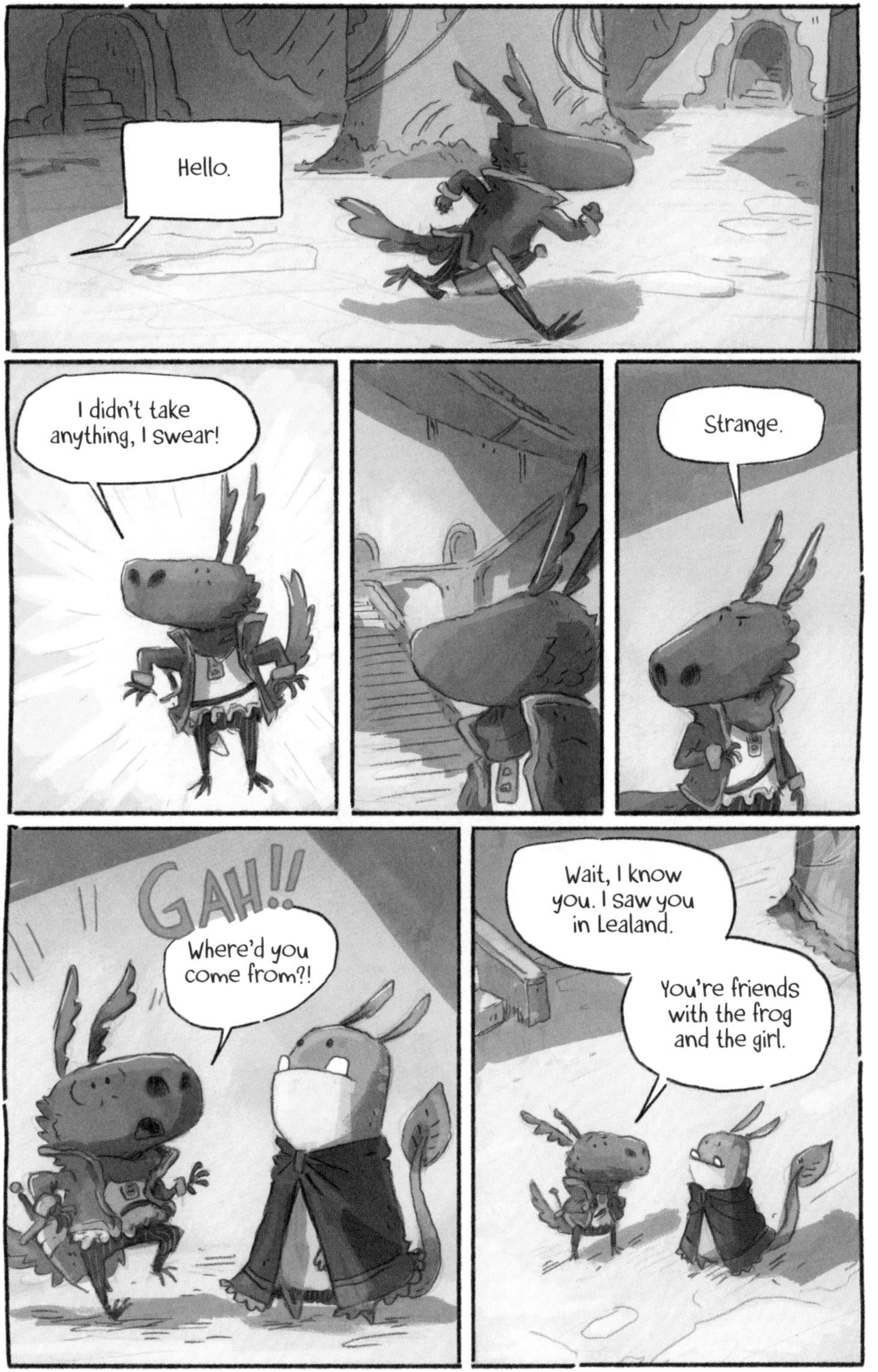
Hello.
I didn't take anything, I swear!
Strange.
GAH!!
Where'd you come from?!
Wait, I know you. I saw you in Lealand.
You're friends with the frog and the girl.

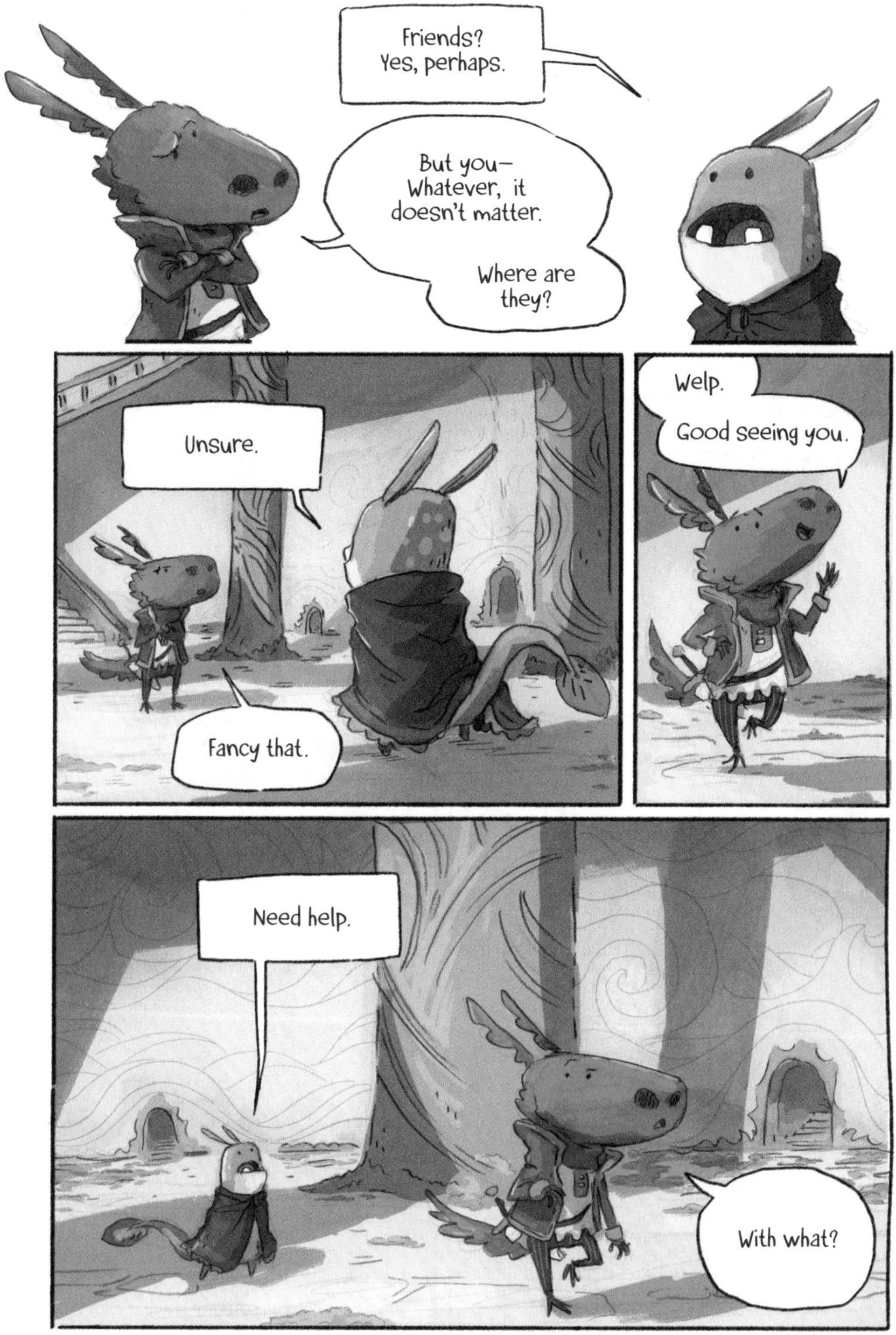
Friends?
Yes, perhaps.
But you— Whatever, it doesn't matter.
Where are they?
Unsure.
Fancy that.
Welp.
Good seeing you.
Need help.
With what?

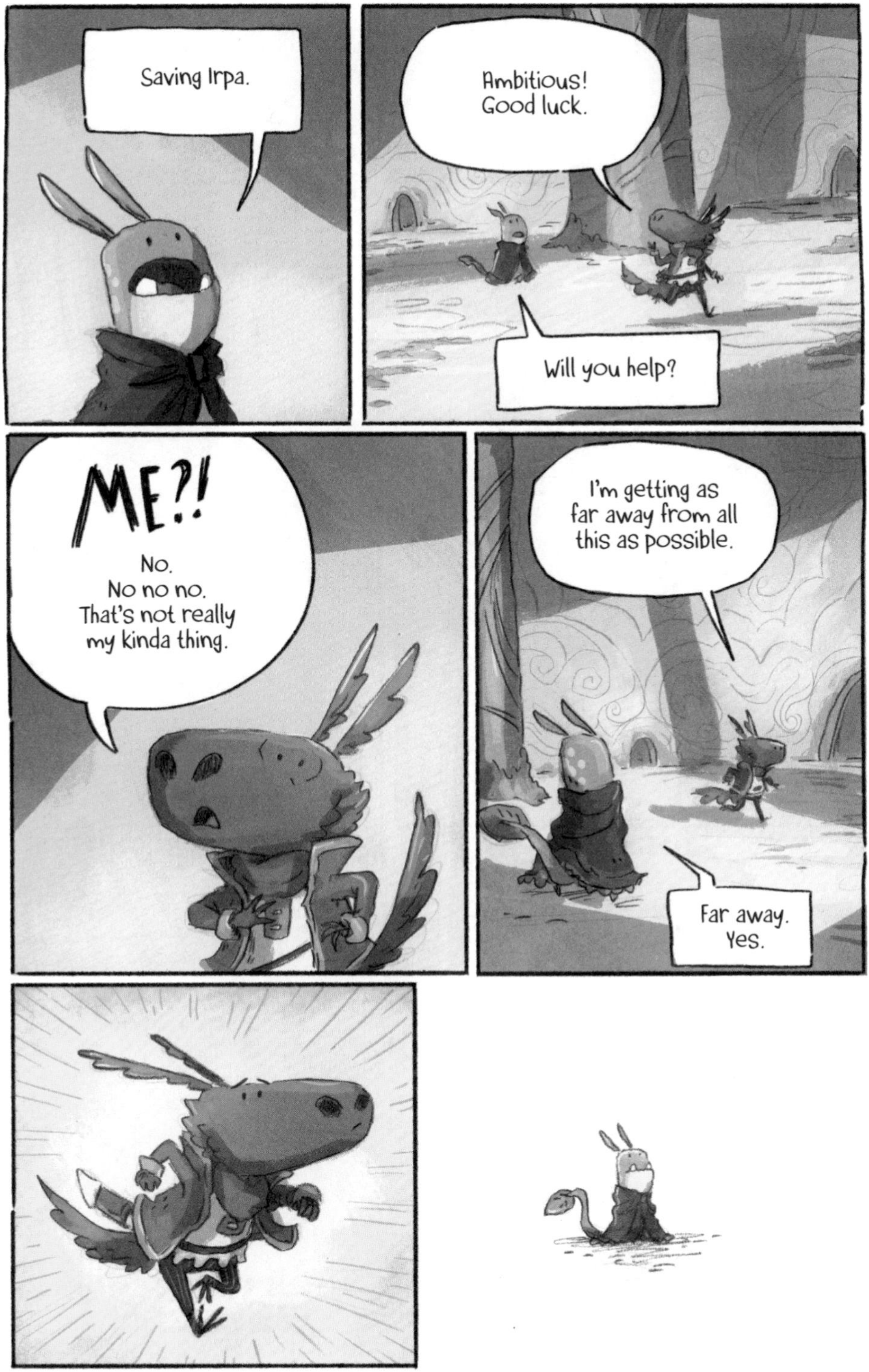

Saving Irpa.
Ambitious! Good luck.
Will you help?
ME?!
No. No no no. That's not really my kinda thing.
I'm getting as far away from all this as possible.
Far away. Yes.

Look.

This place is about to go under.

Murderous demons and shadow monsters and all sorts of unsavory things I'd really like to avoid will be here in a matter of time.

But your lightning trick in Lealand bought me time to escape, so I owe you one.

Rogue's honor and all . . .

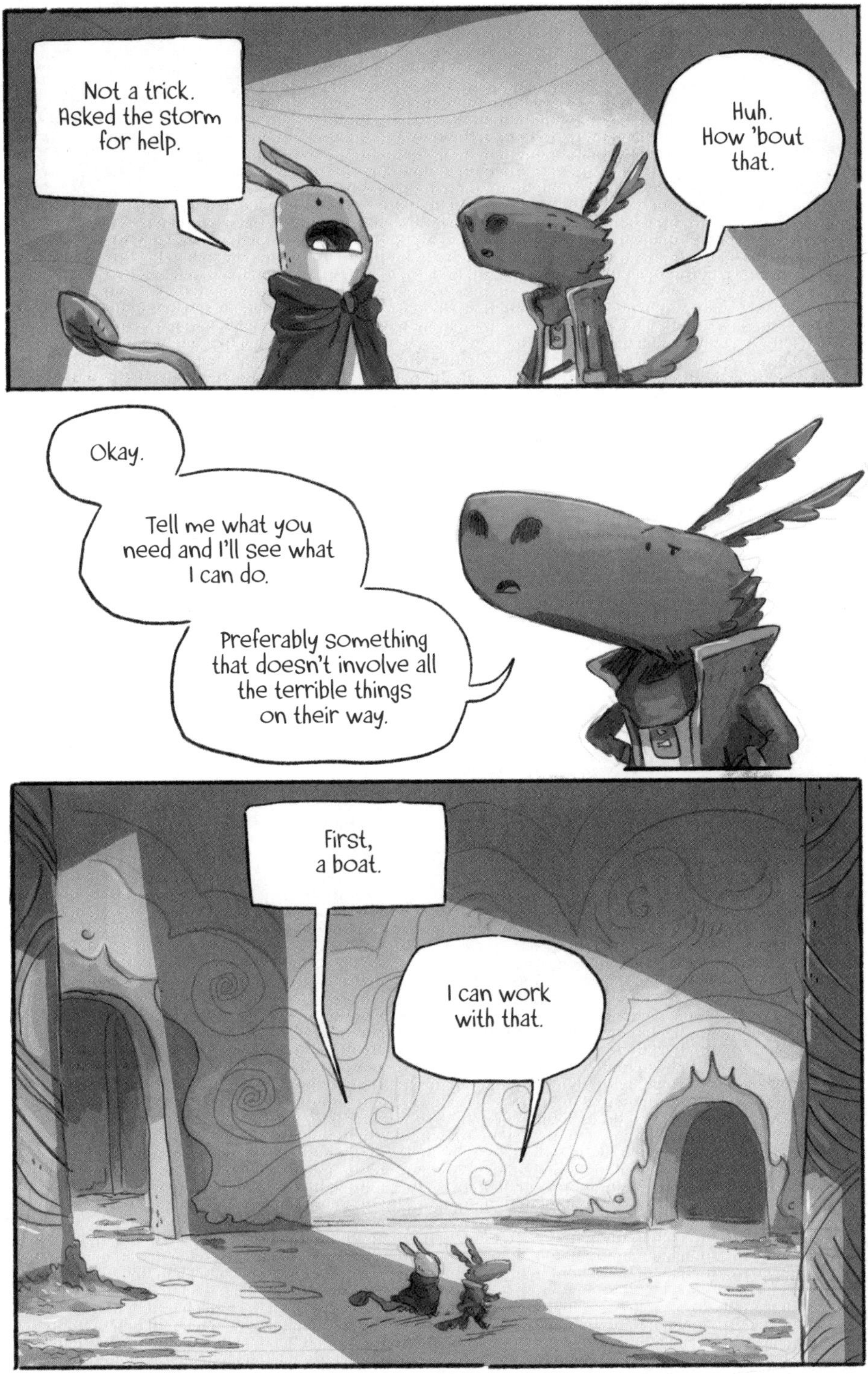
Not a trick. Asked the storm for help.
Huh. How 'bout that.
Okay.
Tell me what you need and I'll see what I can do.
Preferably something that doesn't involve all the terrible things on their way.
First, a boat.
I can work with that.

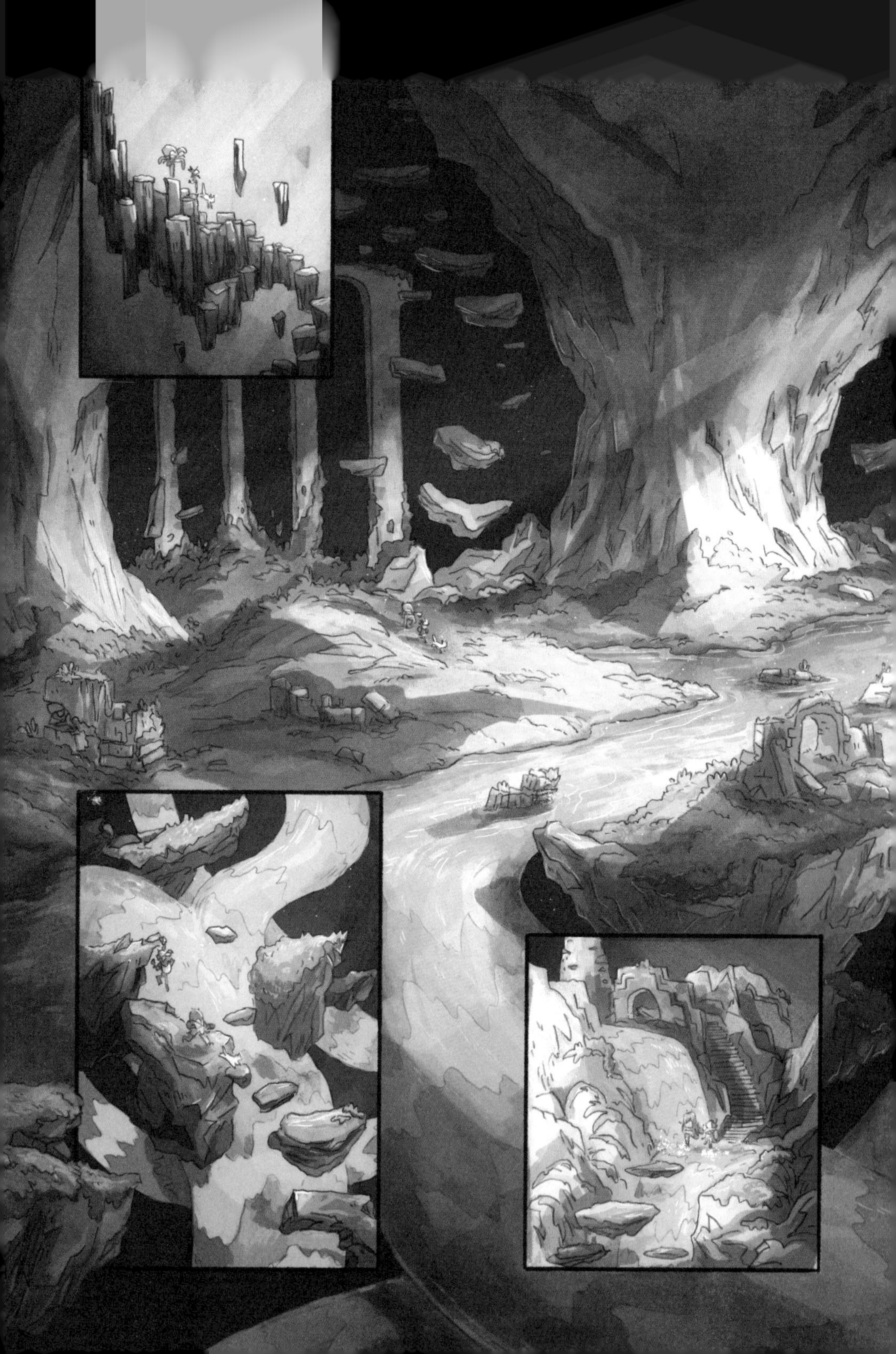

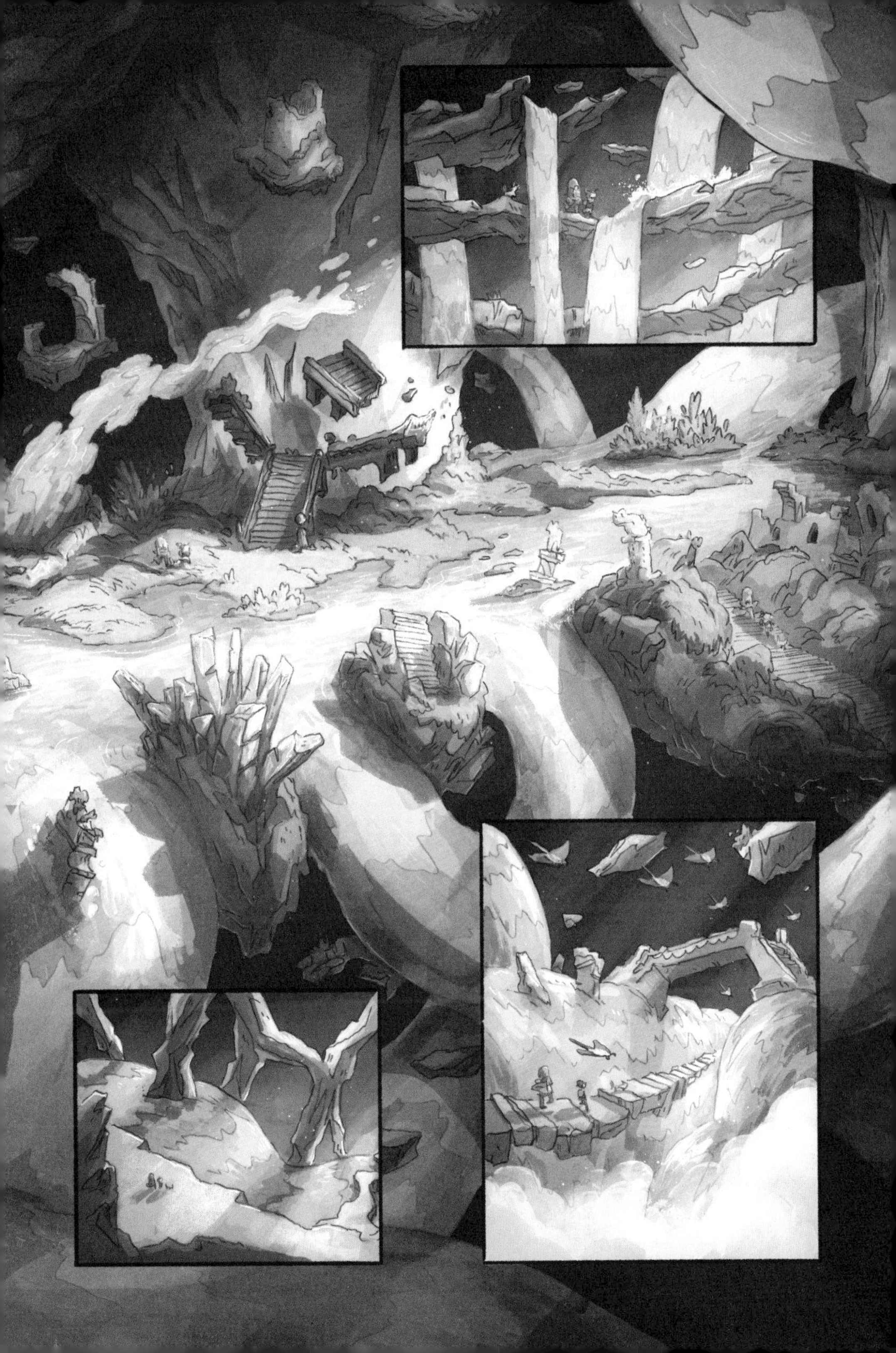

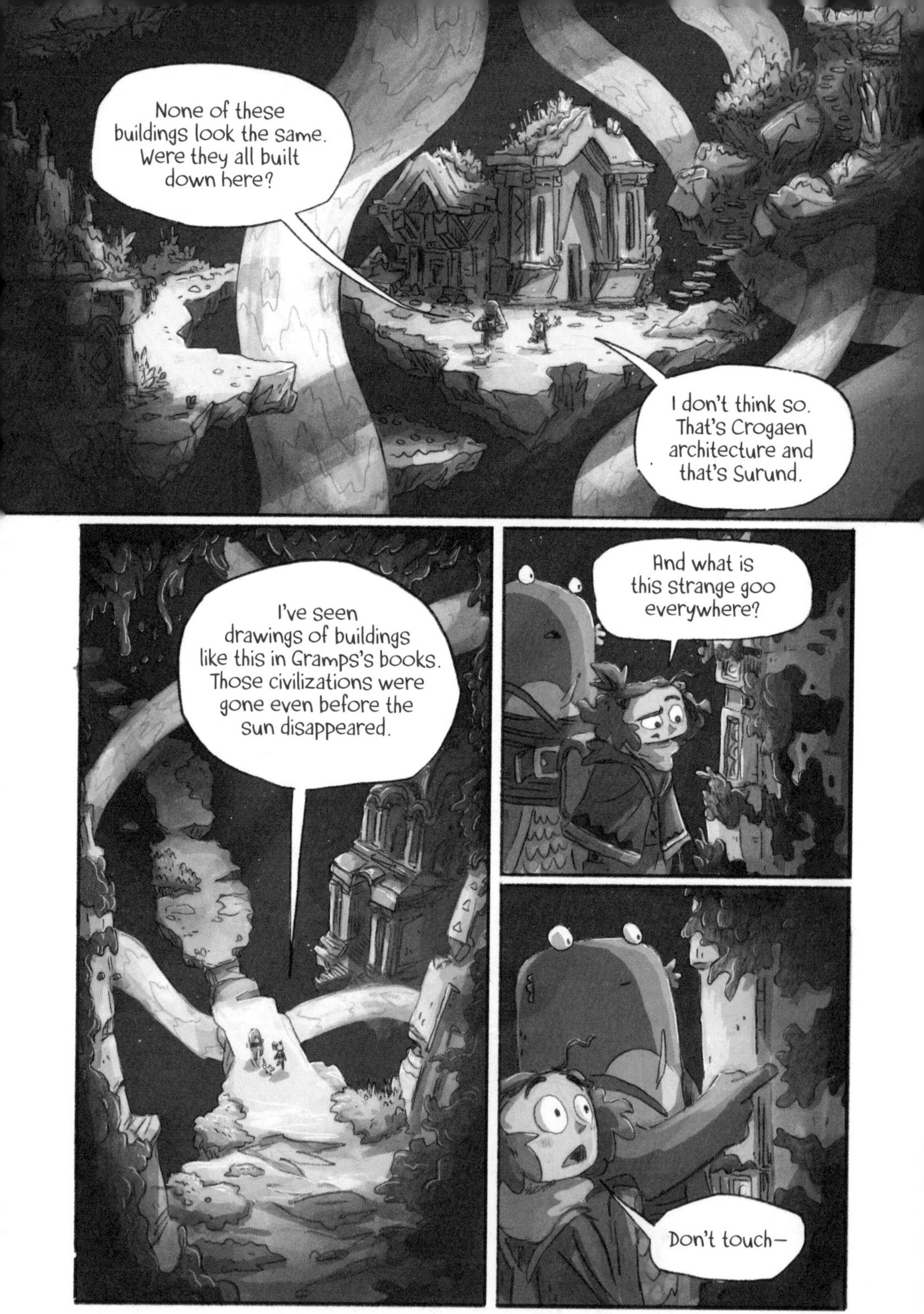
None of these buildings look the same. Were they all built down here?
I don't think so. That's Crogaen architecture and that's Surund.
I've seen drawings of buildings like this in Gramps's books. Those civilizations were gone even before the sun disappeared.
And what is this strange goo everywhere?
Don't touch—

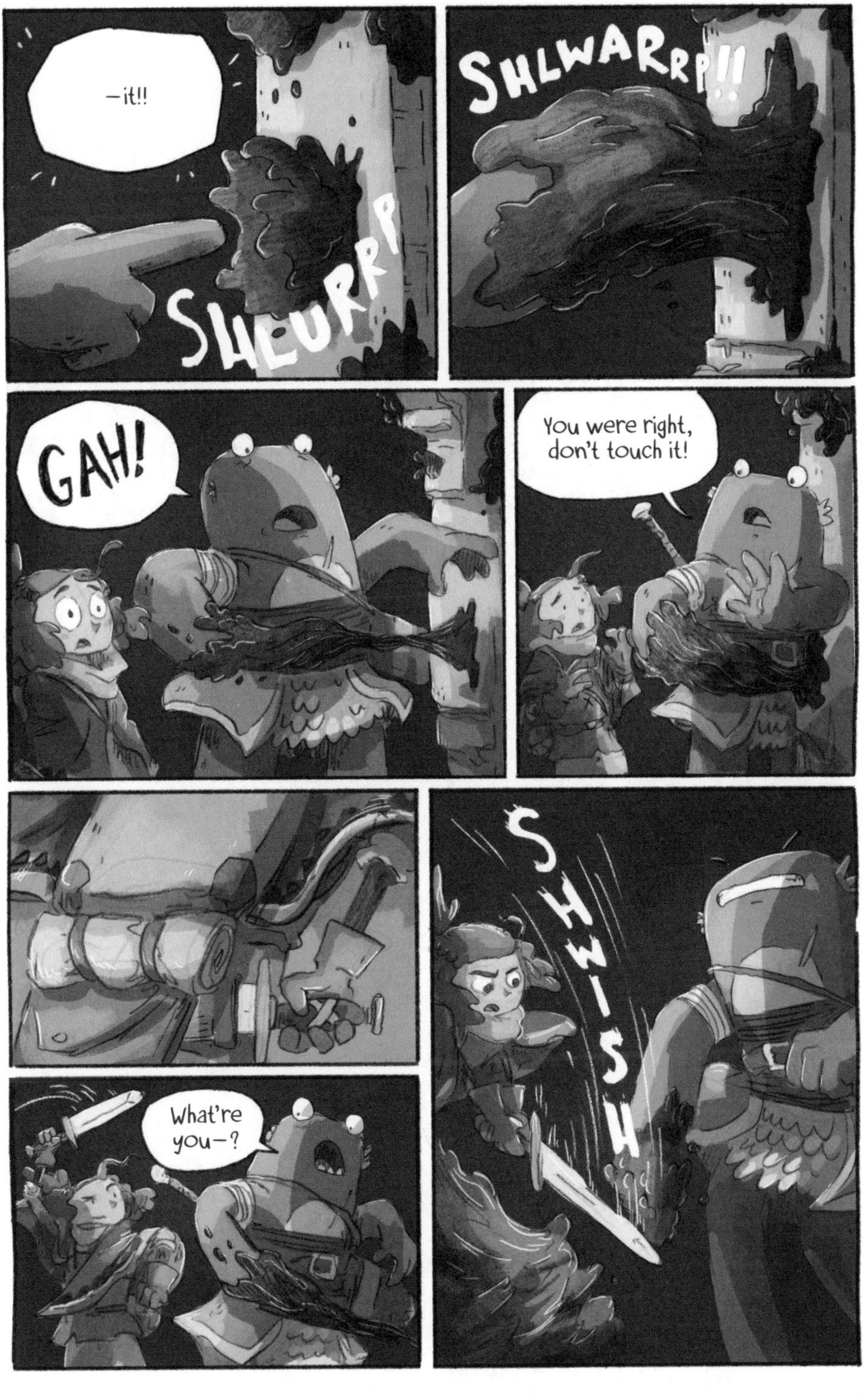
—it!!
SHLURRP
SHLWARRP!!
GAH!
You were right, don't touch it!
SHWISH
What're you—?

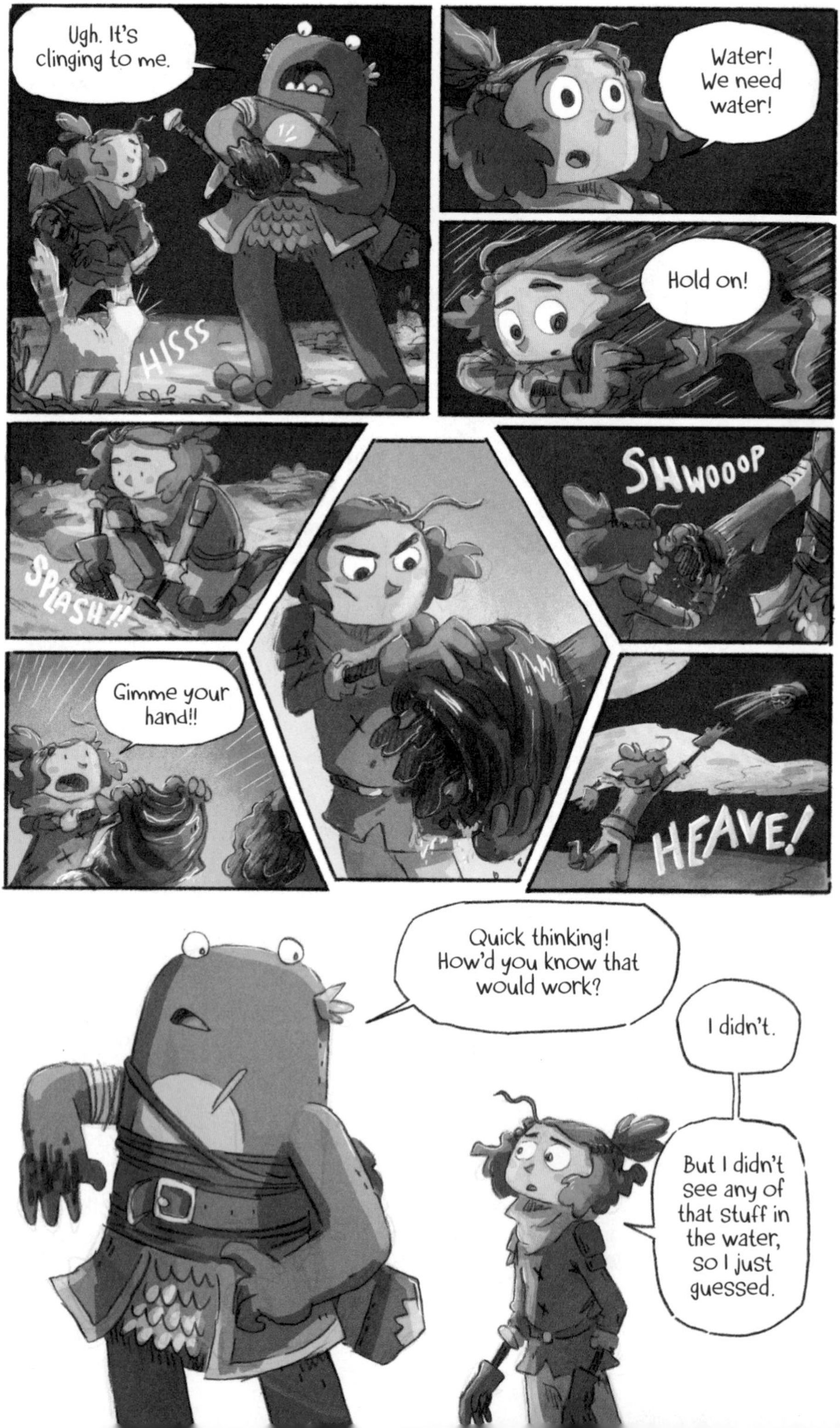
Ugh. It's clinging to me.
HISSS
Water! We need water!
Hold on!
SPLASH!!
SHWOOOP
Gimme your hand!!
HEAVE!
Quick thinking! How'd you know that would work?
I didn't.
But I didn't see any of that stuff in the water, so I just guessed.

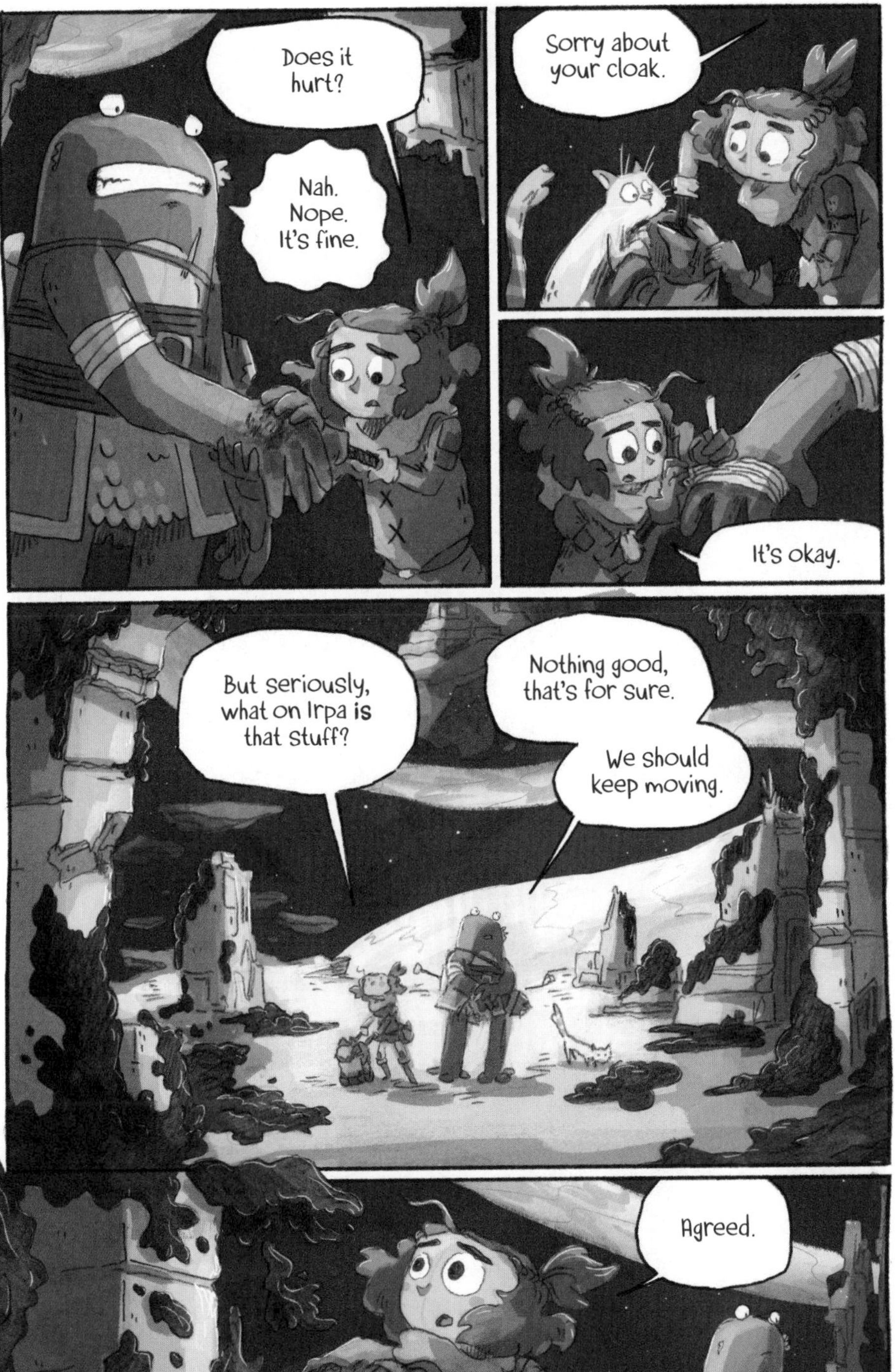
Does it hurt?
Nah. Nope. It's fine.
Sorry about your cloak.
It's okay.
But seriously, what on Irpa **is** that stuff?
Nothing good, that's for sure.
We should keep moving.
Agreed.

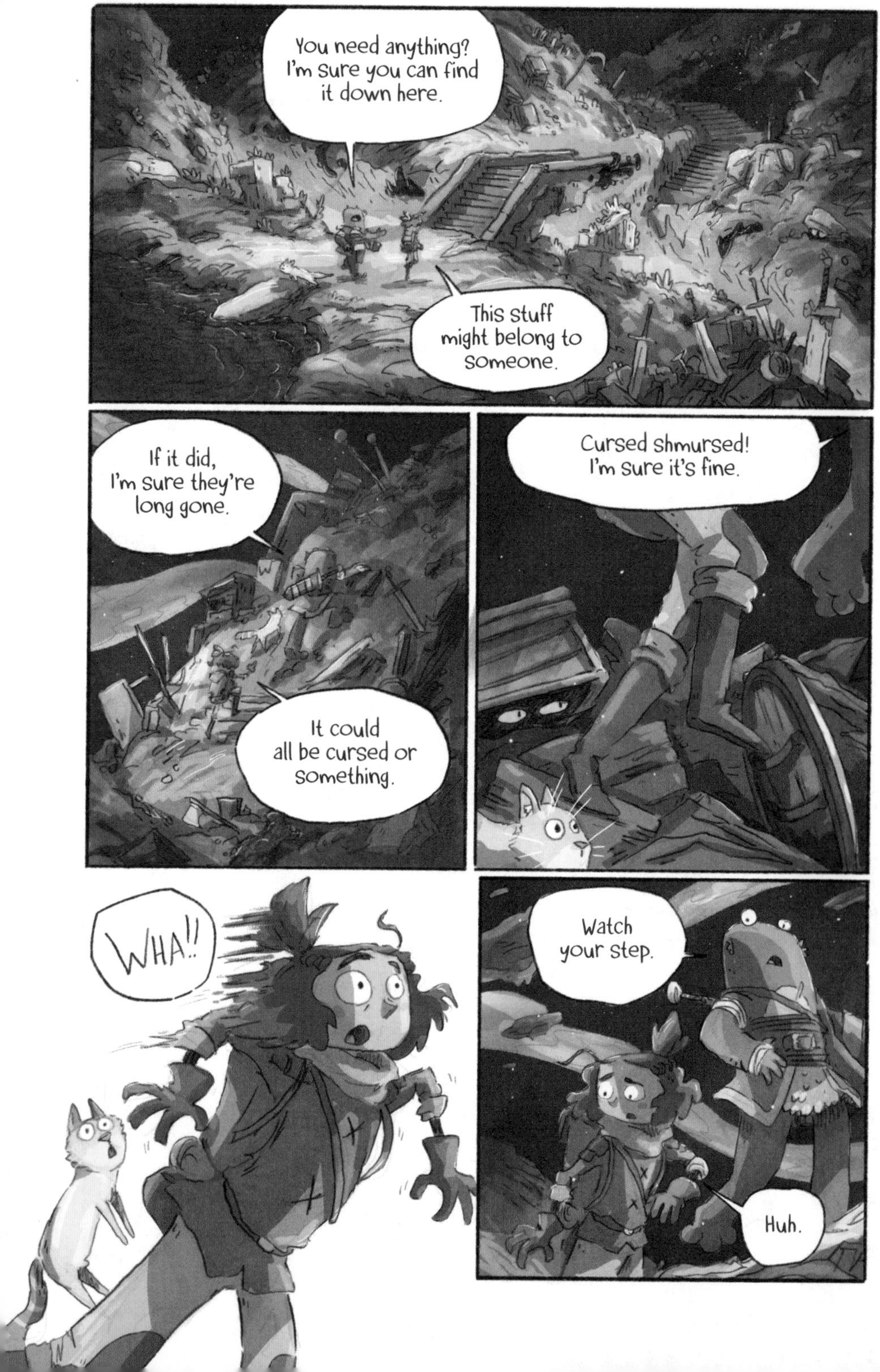
You need anything? I'm sure you can find it down here.
This stuff might belong to someone.
If it did, I'm sure they're long gone.
It could all be cursed or something.
Cursed shmursed! I'm sure it's fine.
WHA!!
Watch your step.
Huh.

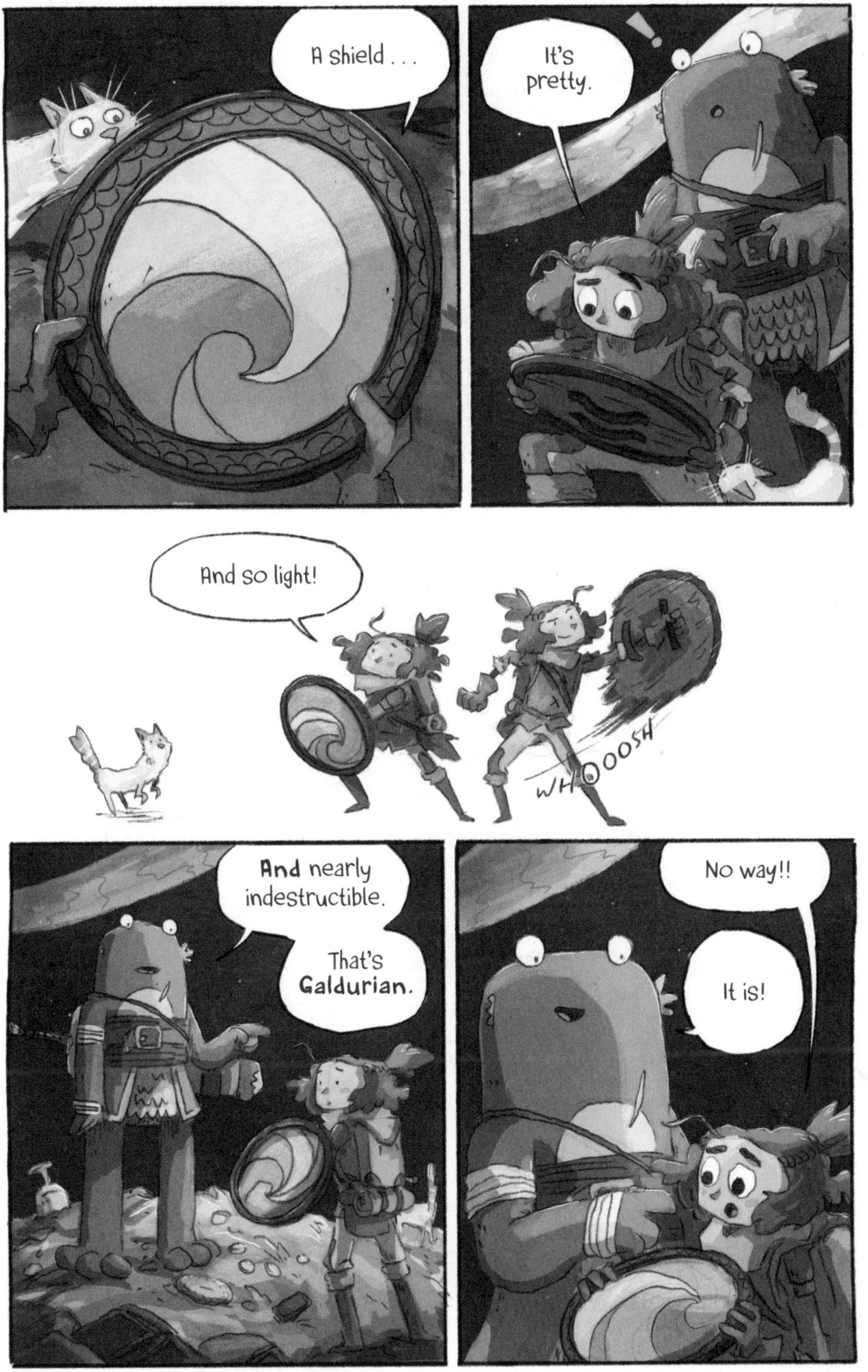
A shield . . .
It's pretty.
And so light!
WHOOOOSH
And nearly indestructible.
That's **Galdurian**.
No way!!
It is!

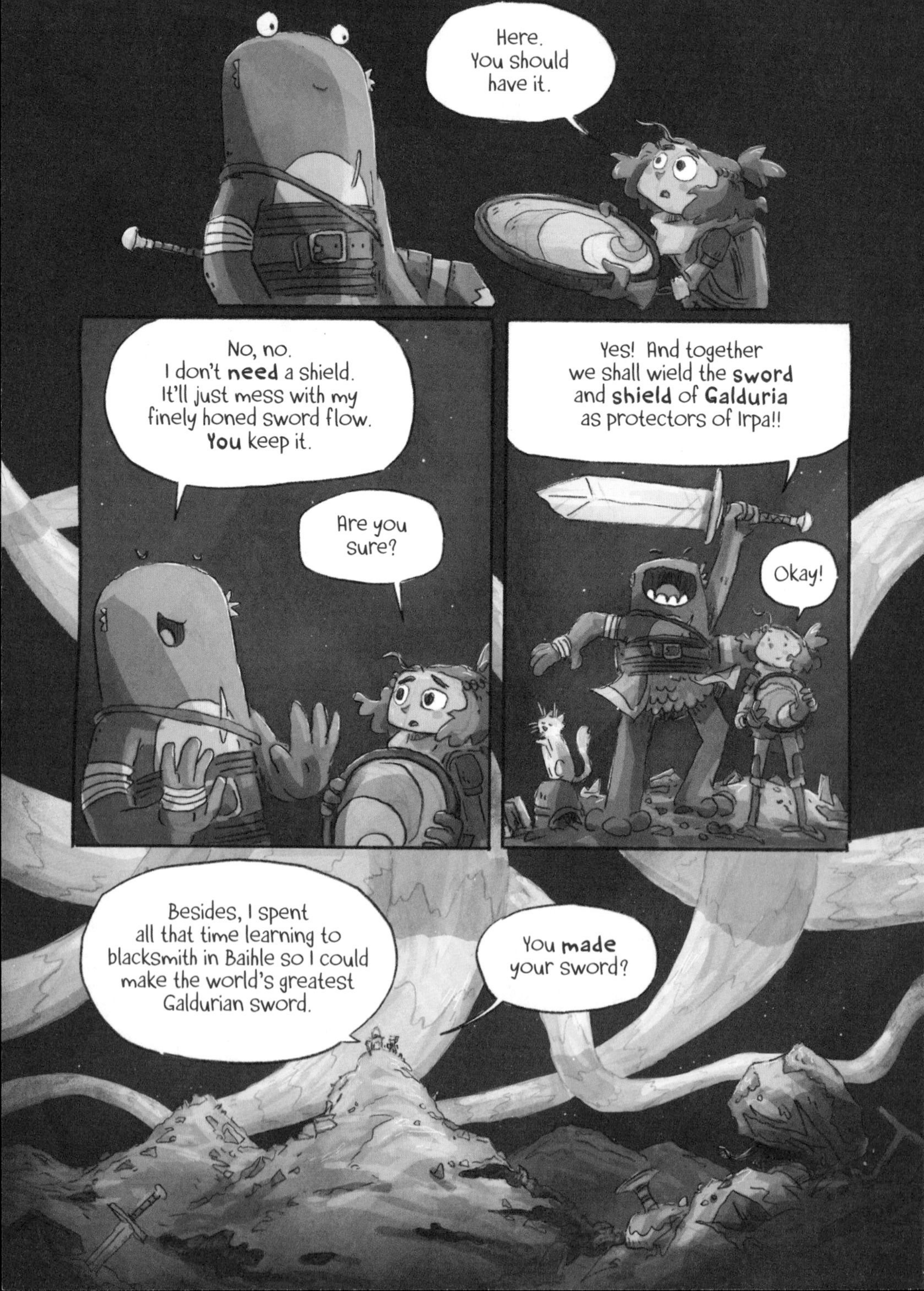
Here. You should have it.
No, no. I don't **need** a shield. It'll just mess with my finely honed sword flow. **You** keep it.
Are you sure?
Yes! And together we shall wield the **sword** and **shield** of **Galduria** as protectors of Irpa!!
Okay!
Besides, I spent all that time learning to blacksmith in Baihle so I could make the world's greatest Galdurian sword.
You **made** your sword?

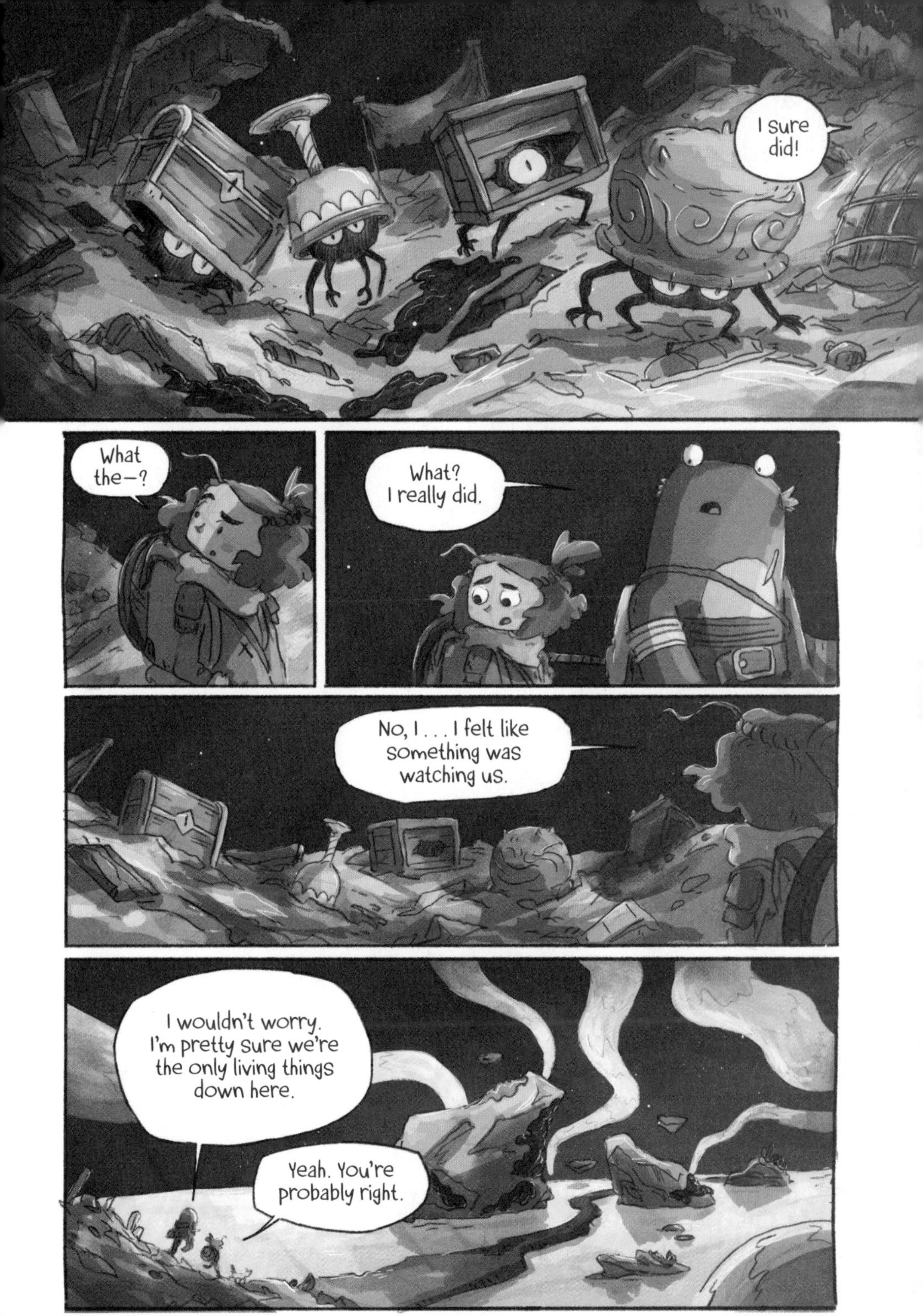

I sure did!
What the—?
What? I really did.
No, I . . . I felt like something was watching us.
I wouldn't worry. I'm pretty sure we're the only living things down here.
Yeah. You're probably right.

So . . . back to your sword . . .

How long did it take to make?

Not long. My teacher said I was the best student she ever had.

Wow.

Actually, that might not be entirely true. Maybe I drove her into early retirement. Who's to say?

But I did make this sword, and it'll never leave my side. It has seen me through many perilous situations.

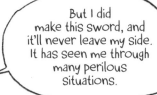

Scrit Scrat

Did you hear that?

Eh?

No. I didn't hear anything.

Are you just tired of my stories?

No.

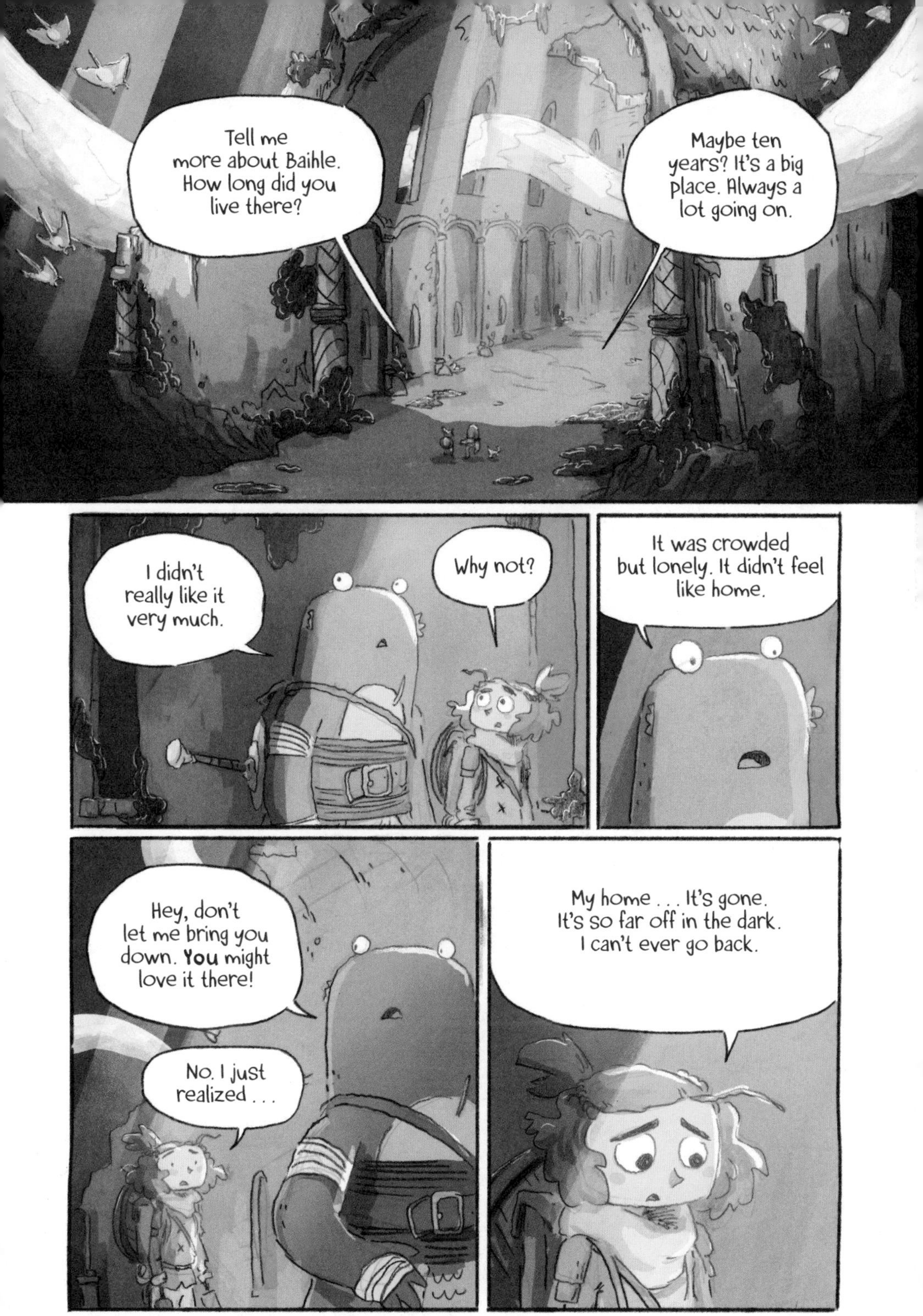

Tell me more about Baihle. How long did you live there?
Maybe ten years? It's a big place. Always a lot going on.
I didn't really like it very much.
Why not?
It was crowded but lonely. It didn't feel like home.
Hey, don't let me bring you down. **You** might love it there!
No. I just realized . . .
My home . . . It's gone. It's so far off in the dark. I can't ever go back.

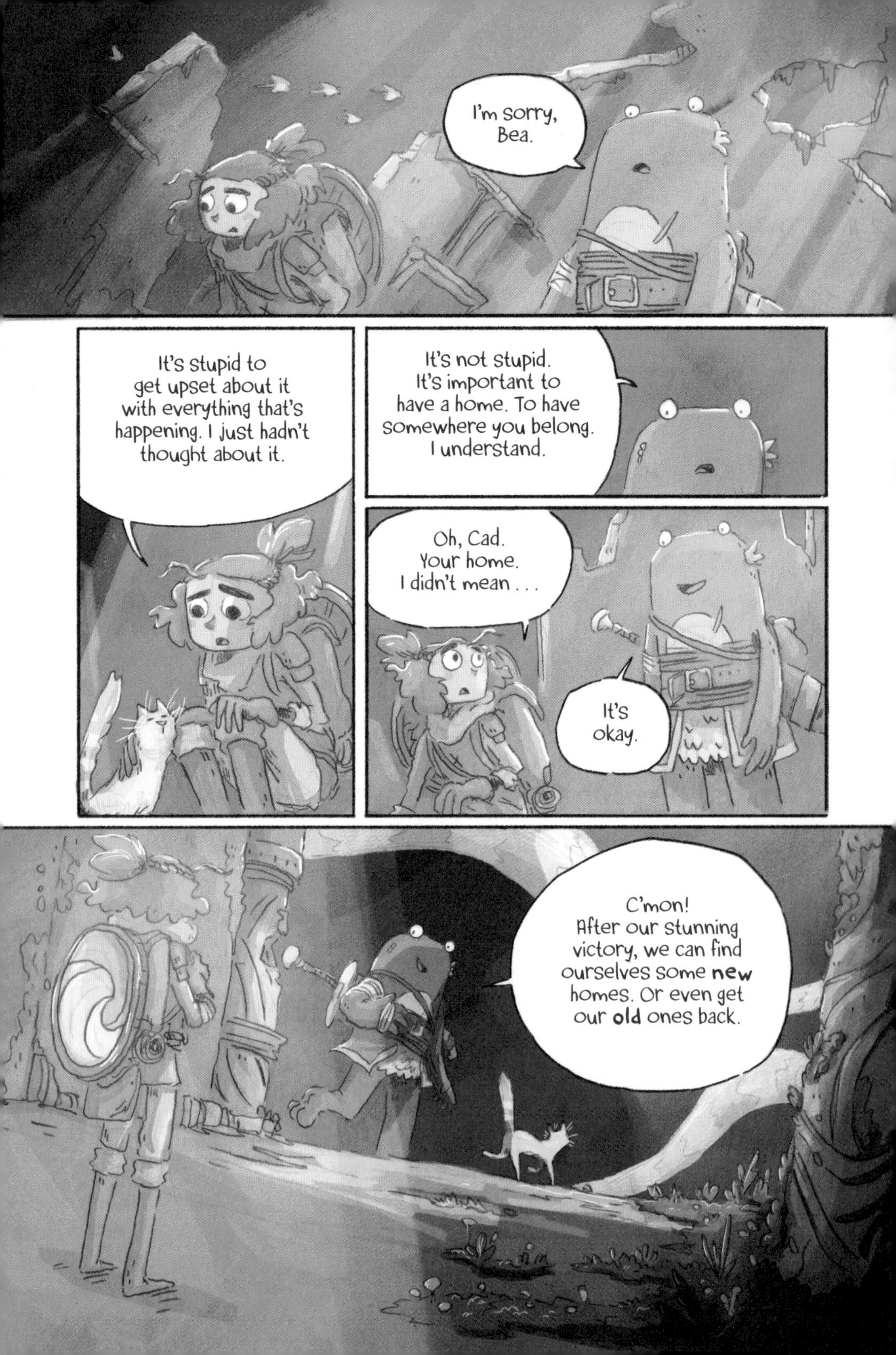
I'm sorry, Bea.
It's stupid to get upset about it with everything that's happening. I just hadn't thought about it.
It's not stupid. It's important to have a home. To have somewhere you belong. I understand.
Oh, Cad. Your home. I didn't mean . . .
It's okay.
C'mon! After our stunning victory, we can find ourselves some **new** homes. Or even get our **old** ones back.

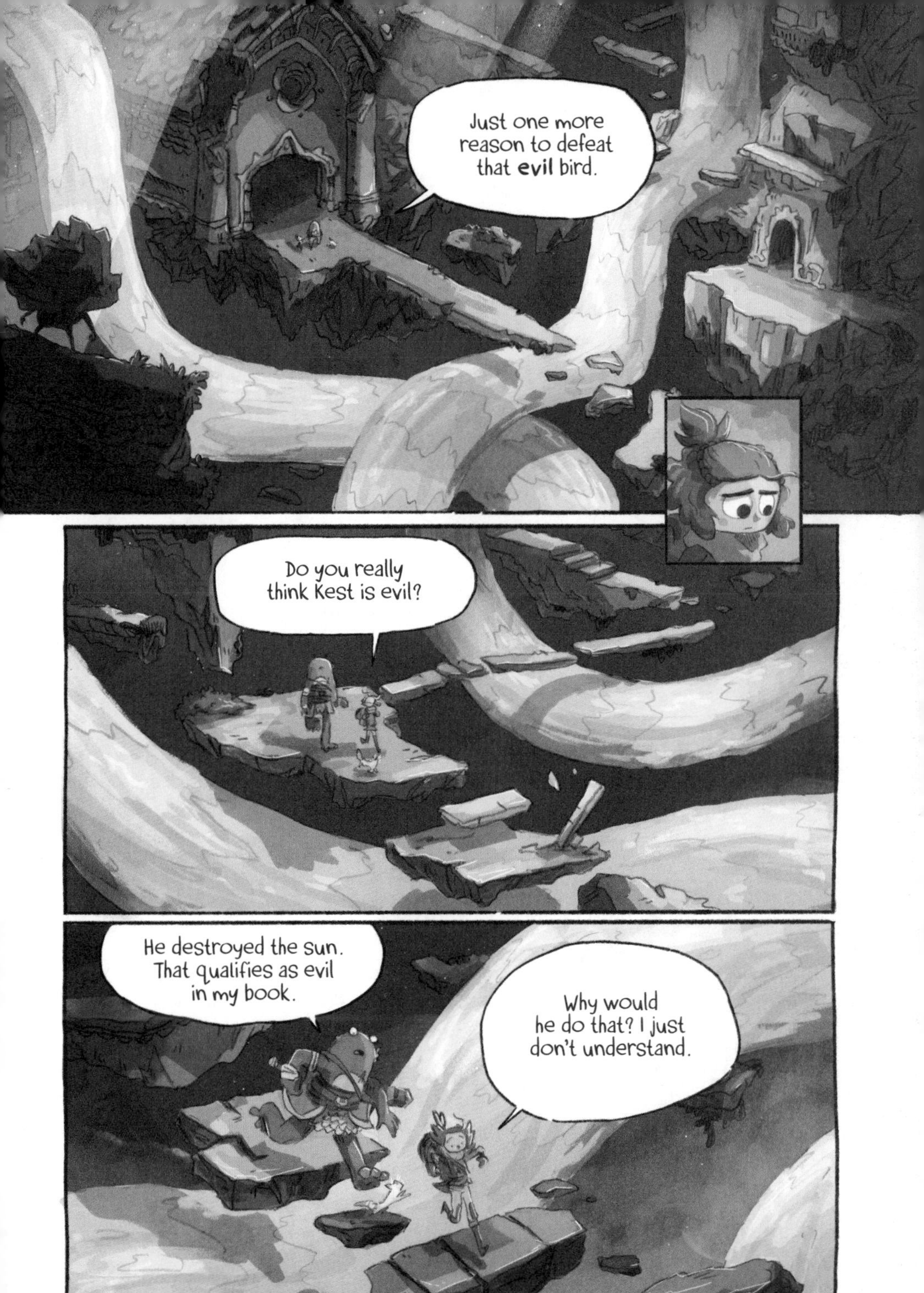

Just one more reason to defeat that evil bird.
Do you really think Kest is evil?
He destroyed the sun. That qualifies as evil in my book.
Why would he do that? I just don't understand.

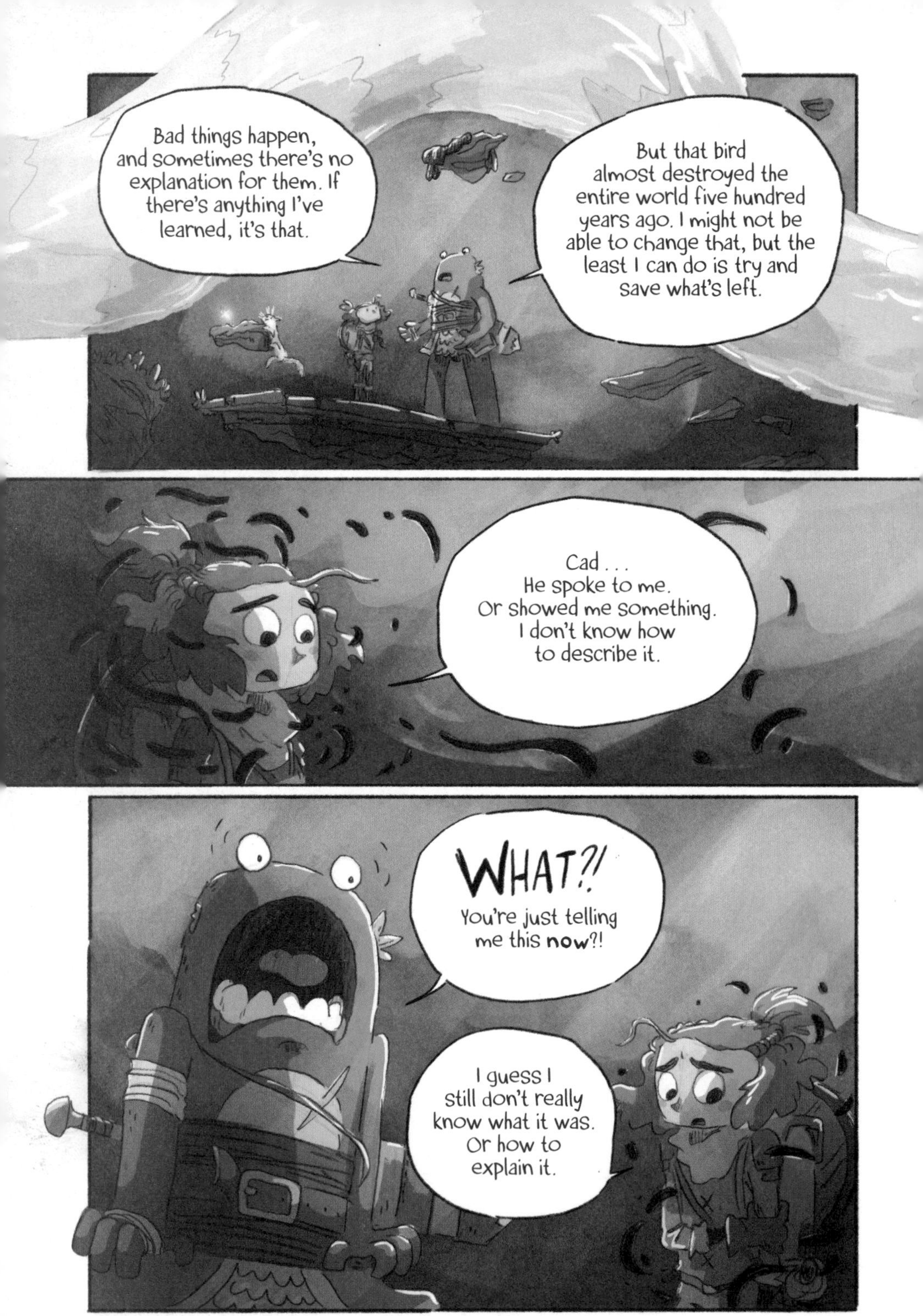
Bad things happen, and sometimes there's no explanation for them. If there's anything I've learned, it's that.
But that bird almost destroyed the entire world five hundred years ago. I might not be able to change that, but the least I can do is try and save what's left.
Cad . . . He spoke to me. Or showed me something. I don't know how to describe it.
WHAT?! You're just telling me this **now**?!
I guess I still don't really know what it was. Or how to explain it.

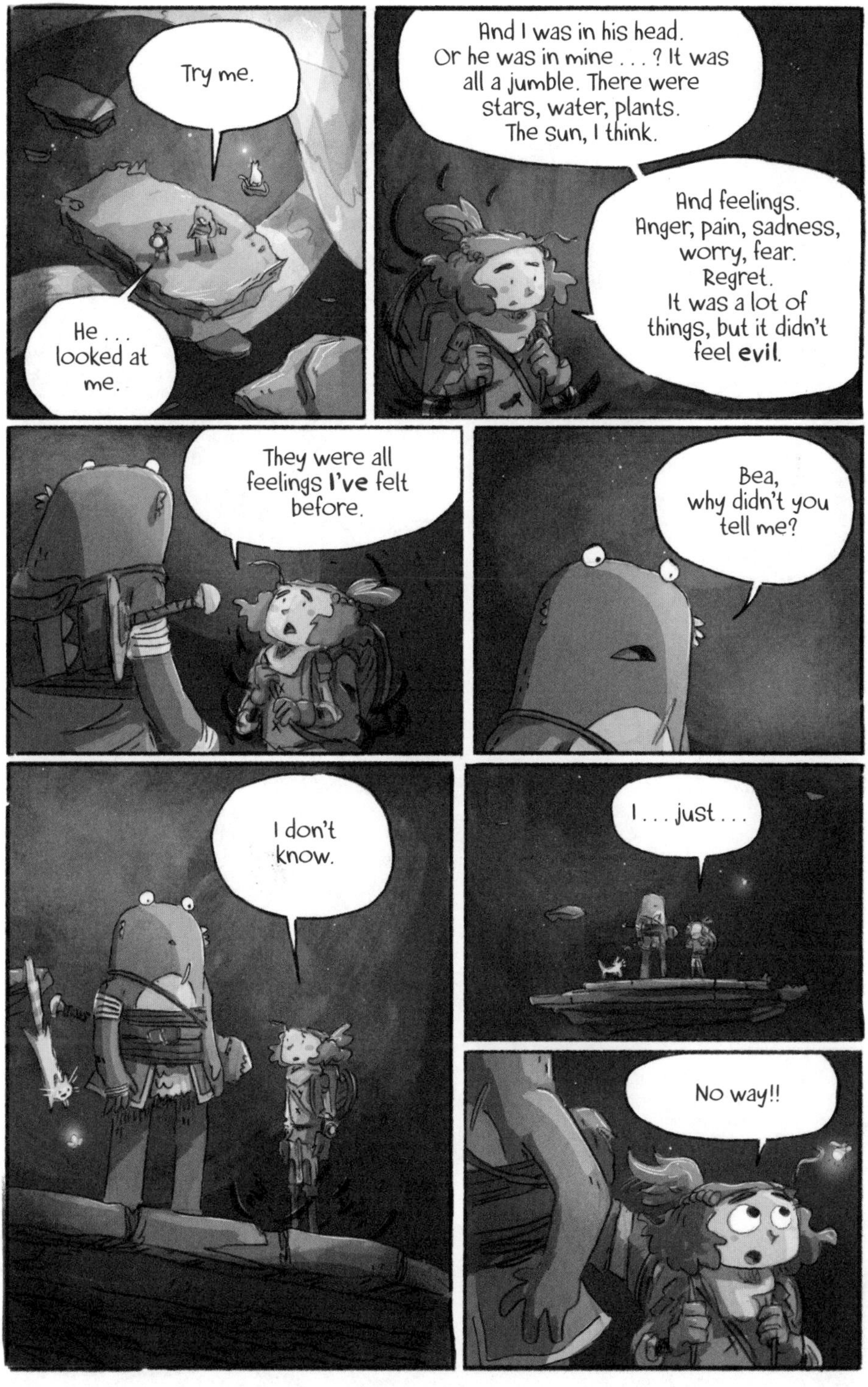
Try me.
He . . . looked at me.
And I was in his head. Or he was in mine . . . ? It was all a jumble. There were stars, water, plants. The sun, I think.
And feelings. Anger, pain, sadness, worry, fear. Regret. It was a lot of things, but it didn't feel **evil**.
They were all feelings **I've** felt before.
Bea, why didn't you tell me?
I don't know.
I . . . just . . .
No way!!

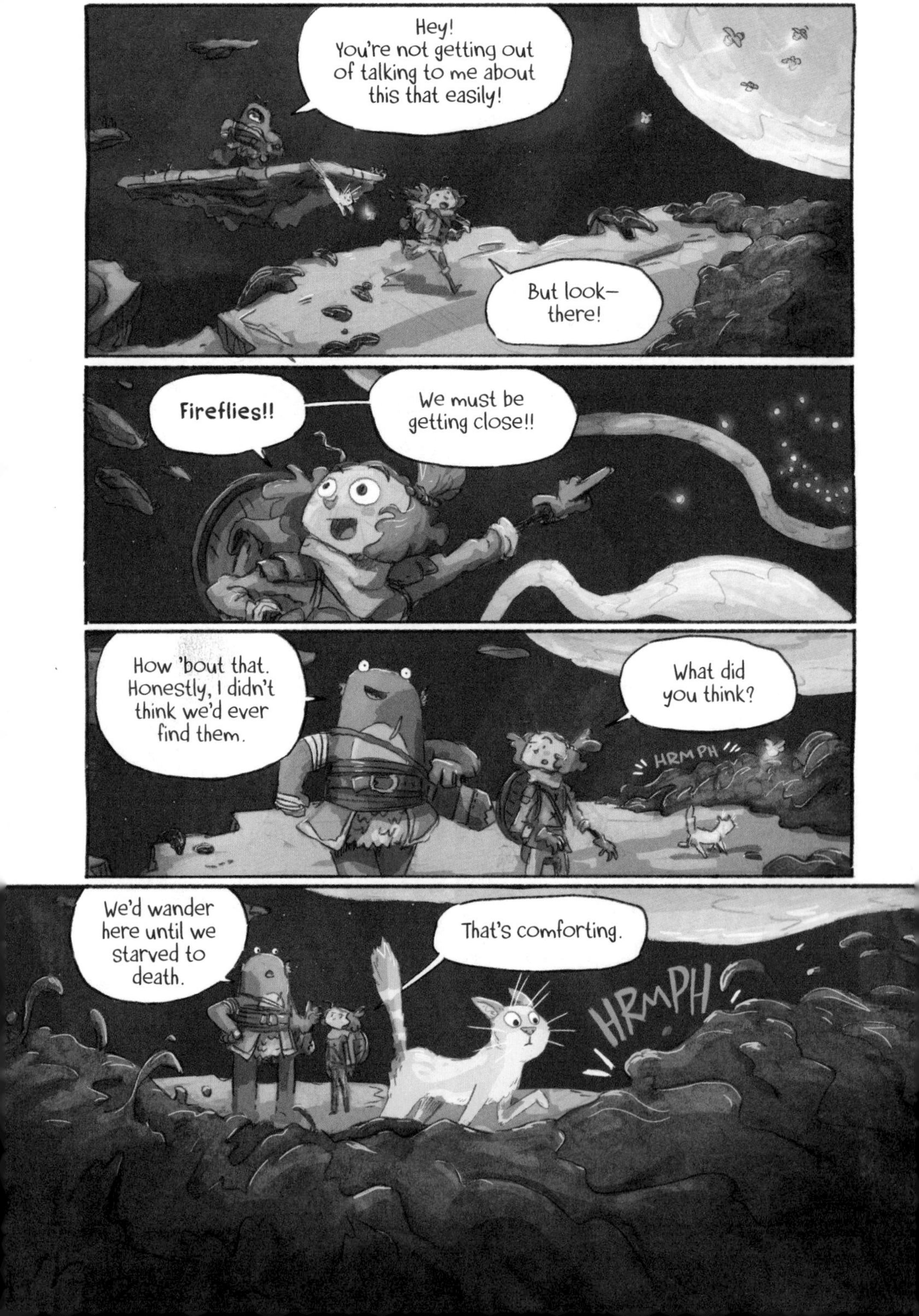
Hey!
You're not getting out of talking to me about this that easily!
But look—there!
Fireflies!!
We must be getting close!!
How 'bout that. Honestly, I didn't think we'd ever find them.
What did you think?
HRMPH
We'd wander here until we starved to death.
That's comforting.
HRMPH

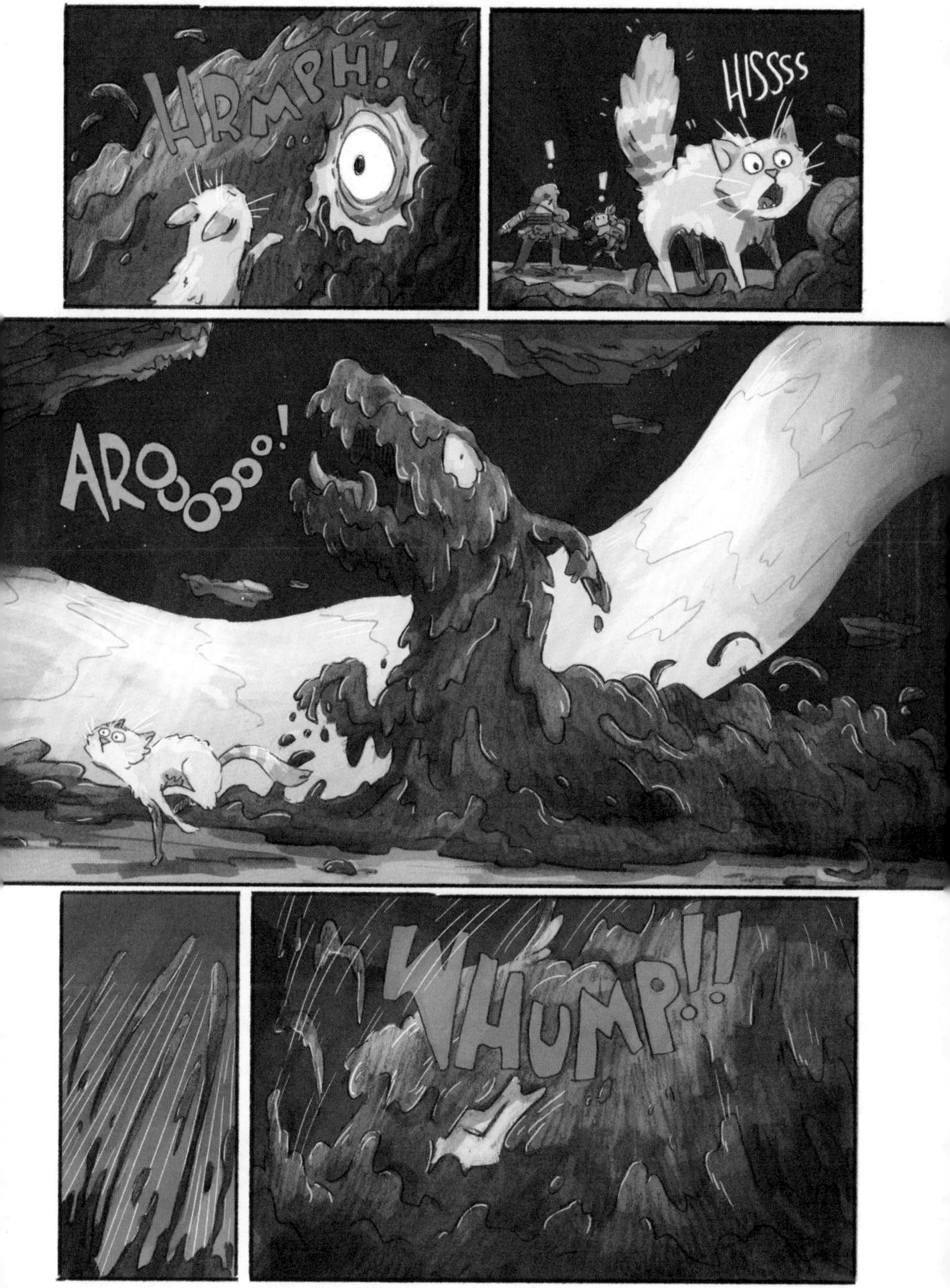
HRMPH!
HISSSS
!
!
AROOOOOO!
WHUMP!!

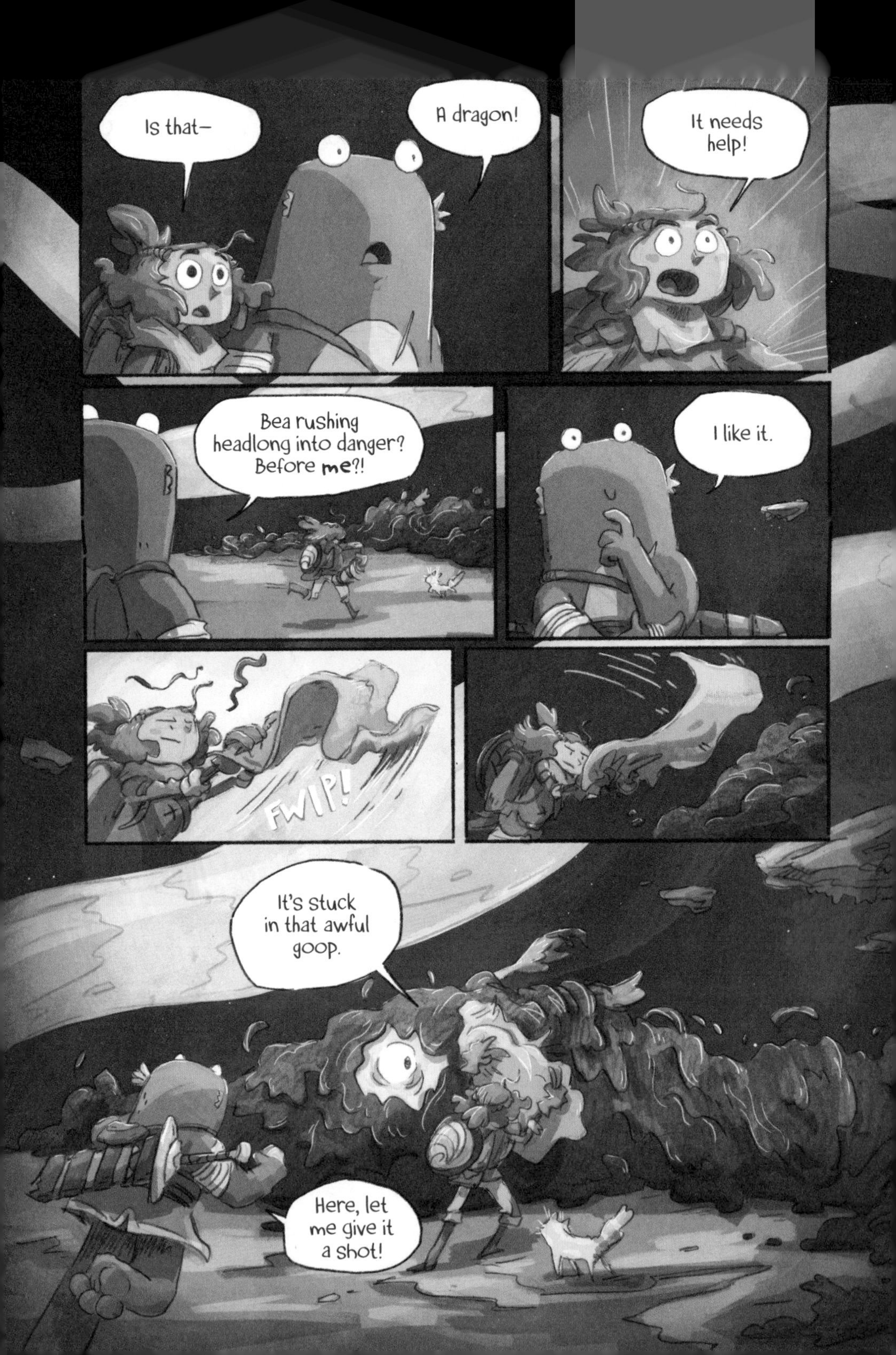
Is that–
A dragon!
It needs help!
Bea rushing headlong into danger? Before **me**?!
I like it.
FWIP!
It's stuck in that awful goop.
Here, let me give it a shot!

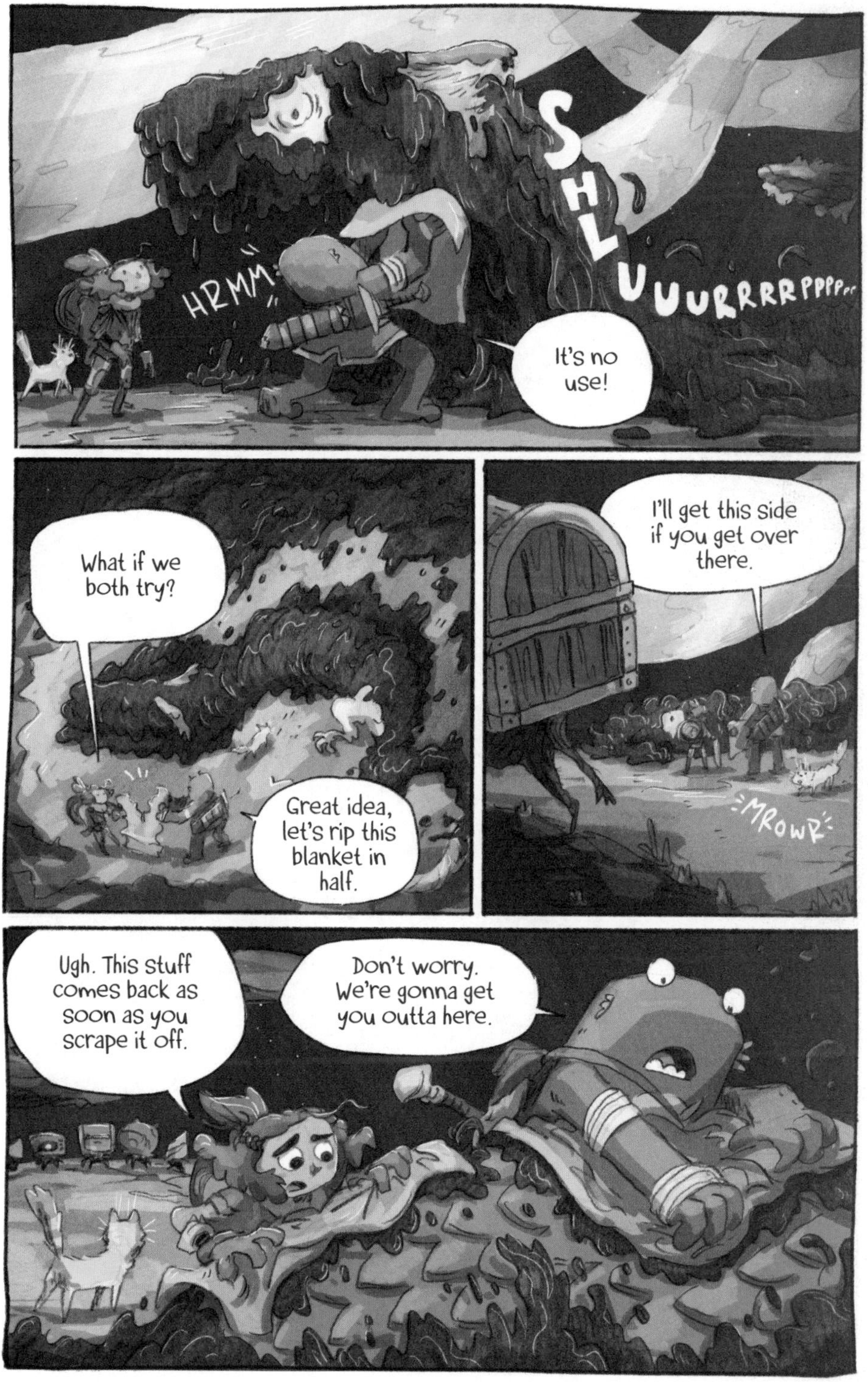
SHLUUURRRRPPPPrr
HRMM
It's no use!
What if we both try?
Great idea, let's rip this blanket in half.
I'll get this side if you get over there.
MROWR
Ugh. This stuff comes back as soon as you scrape it off.
Don't worry. We're gonna get you outta here.

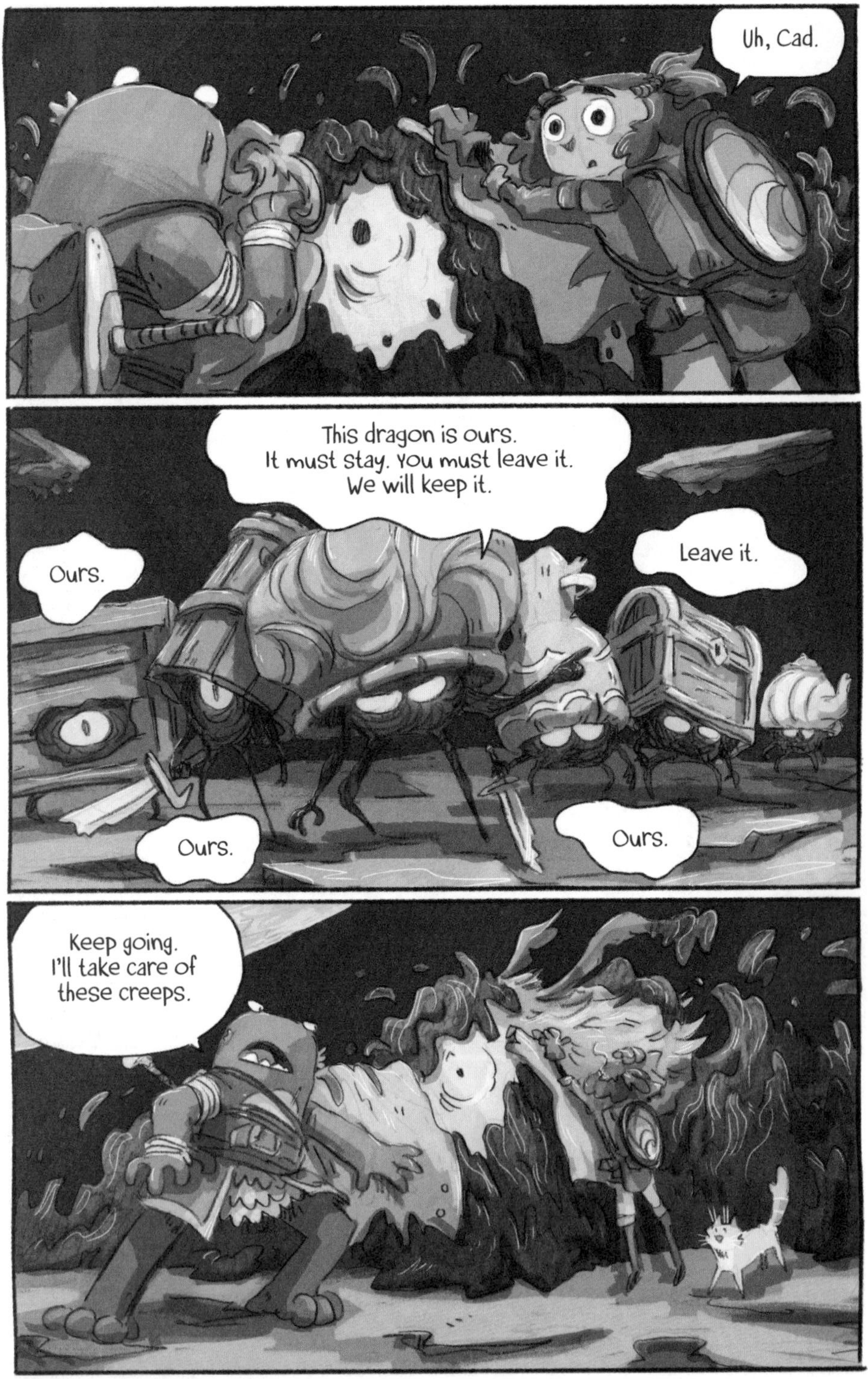
Uh, Cad.
This dragon is ours.
It must stay. You must leave it.
We will keep it.
Ours.
Leave it.
Ours.
Ours.
Keep going.
I'll take care of
these creeps.

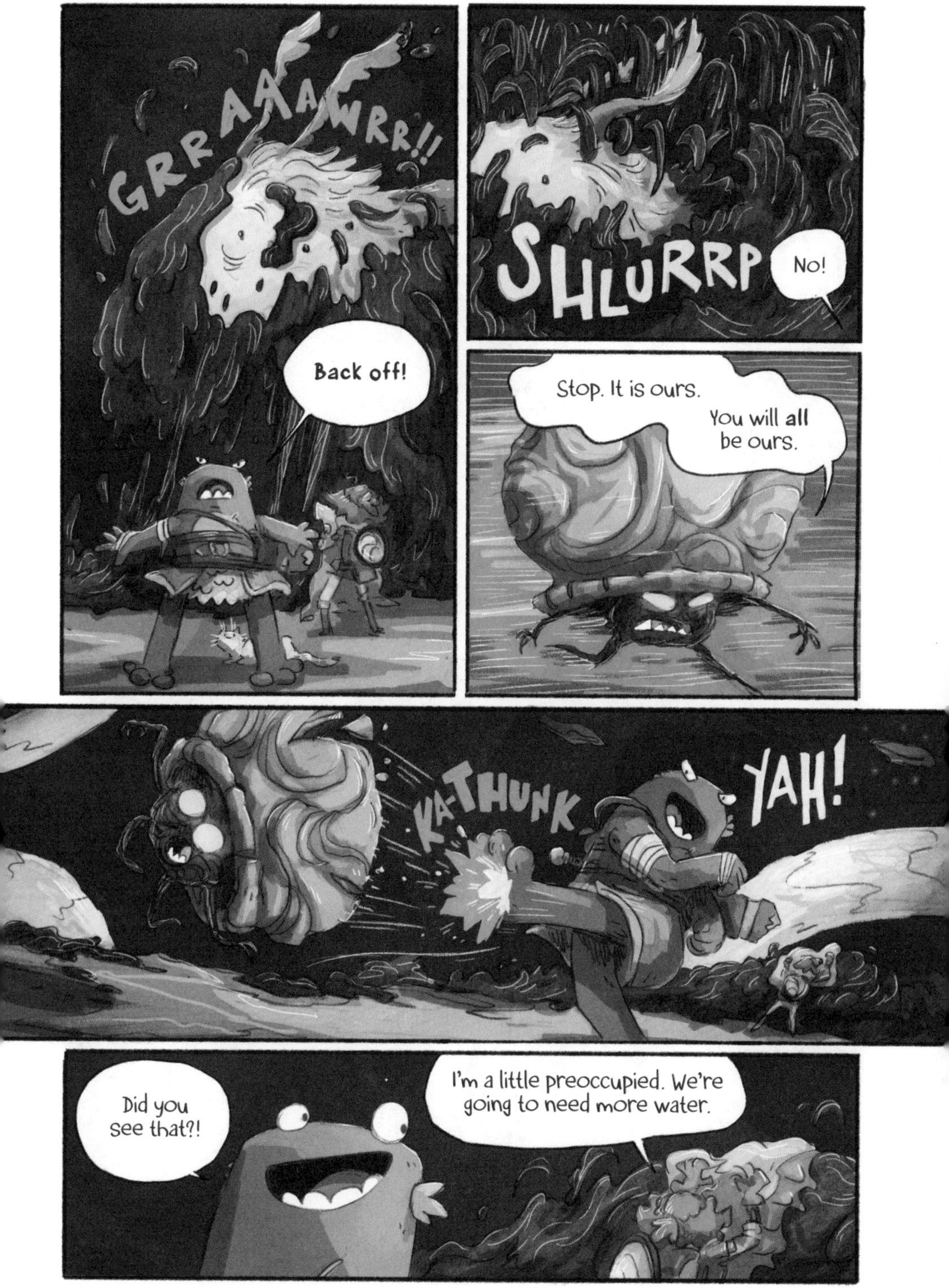
GRRAAAAWRR!!
Back off!
SHLURRP
No!
Stop. It is ours.
You will all be ours.
KA-THUNK
YAH!
Did you see that?!
I'm a little preoccupied. We're going to need more water.

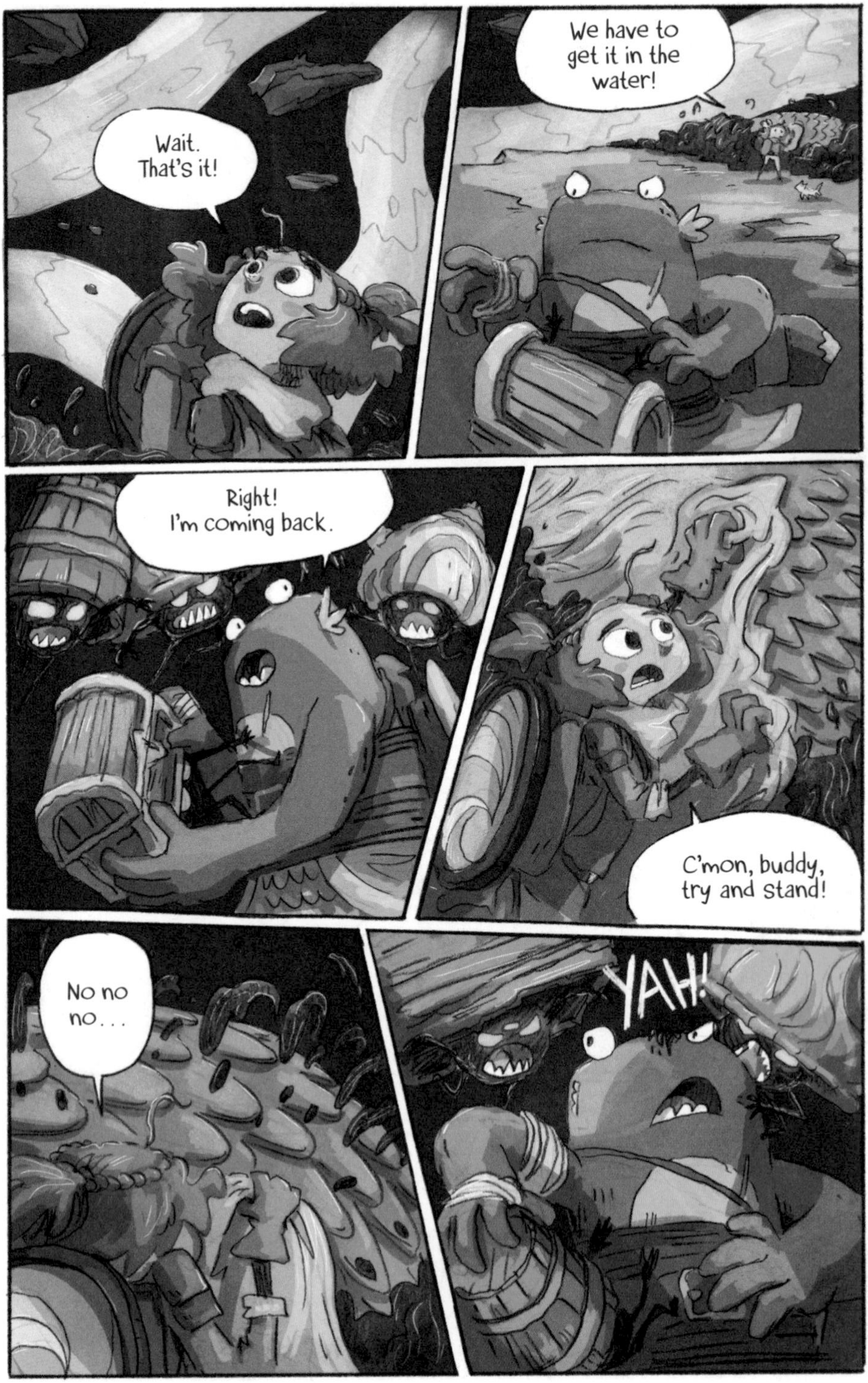
Wait.
That's it!
We have to get it in the water!
Right!
I'm coming back.
C'mon, buddy, try and stand!
No no no...
YAH!

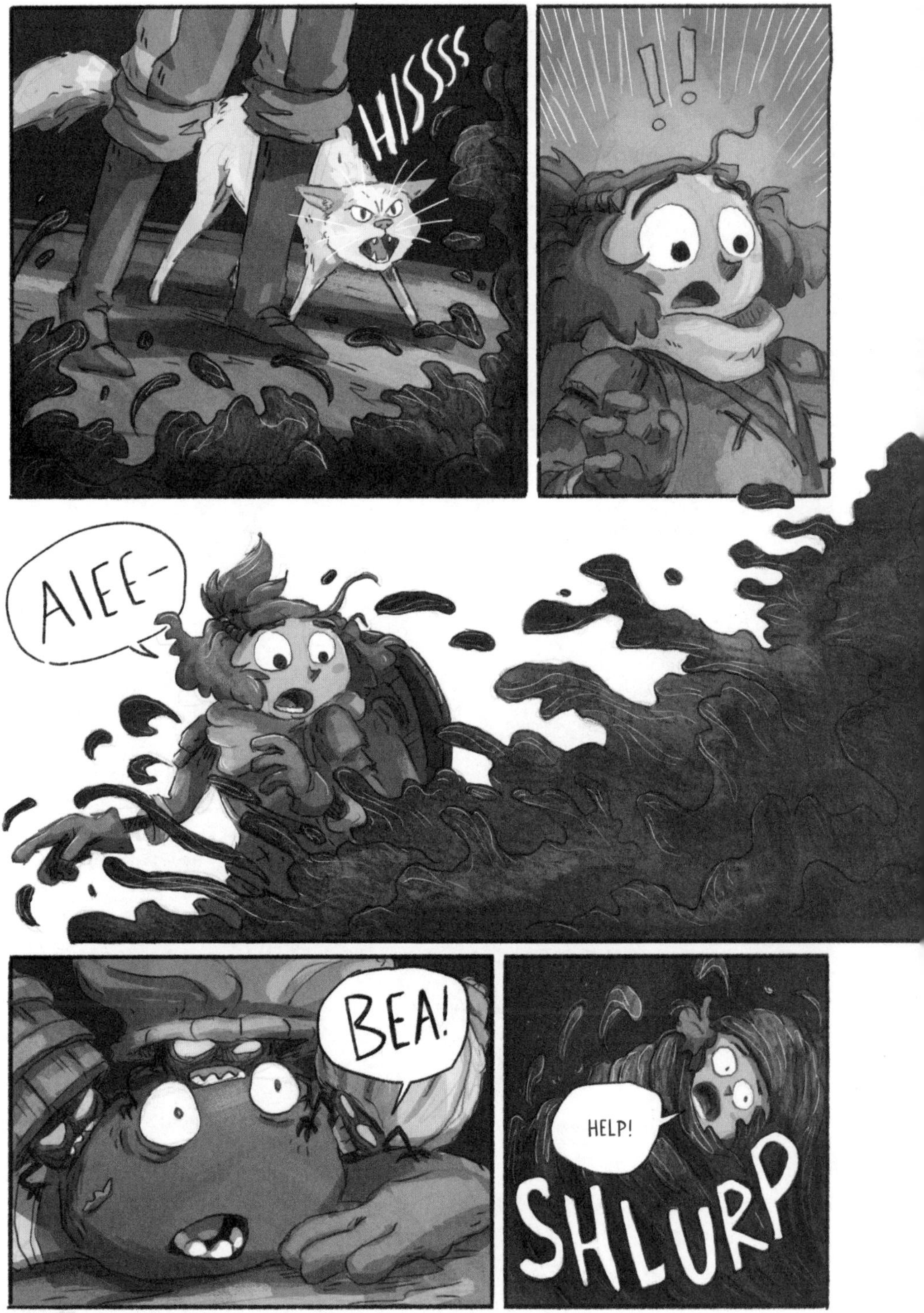
HISSSS
!!
AIEE-
BEA!
HELP!
SHLURP

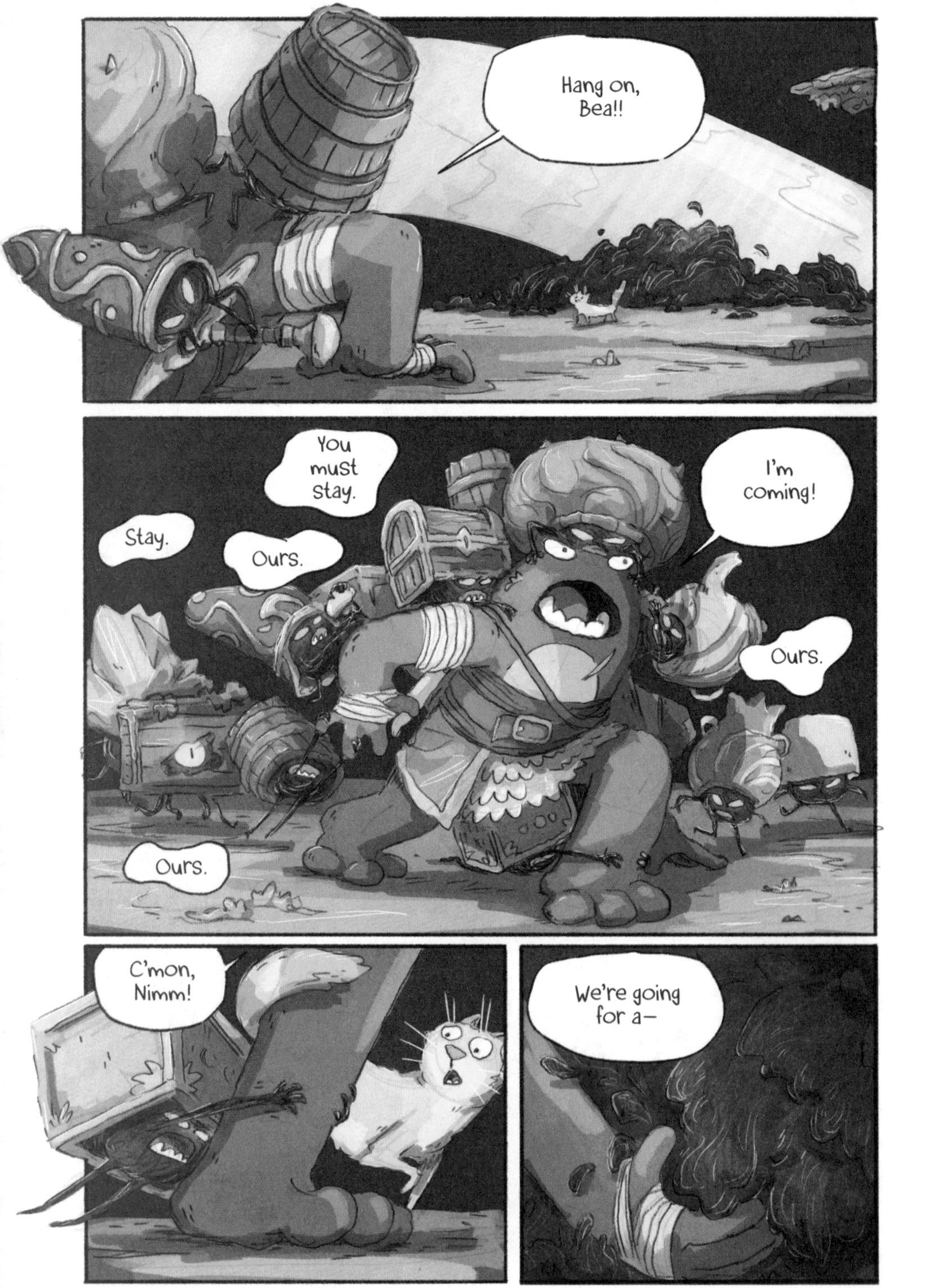
Hang on, Bea!!
You must stay.
Stay.
Ours.
I'm coming!
Ours.
Ours.
C'mon, Nimm!
We're going for a—

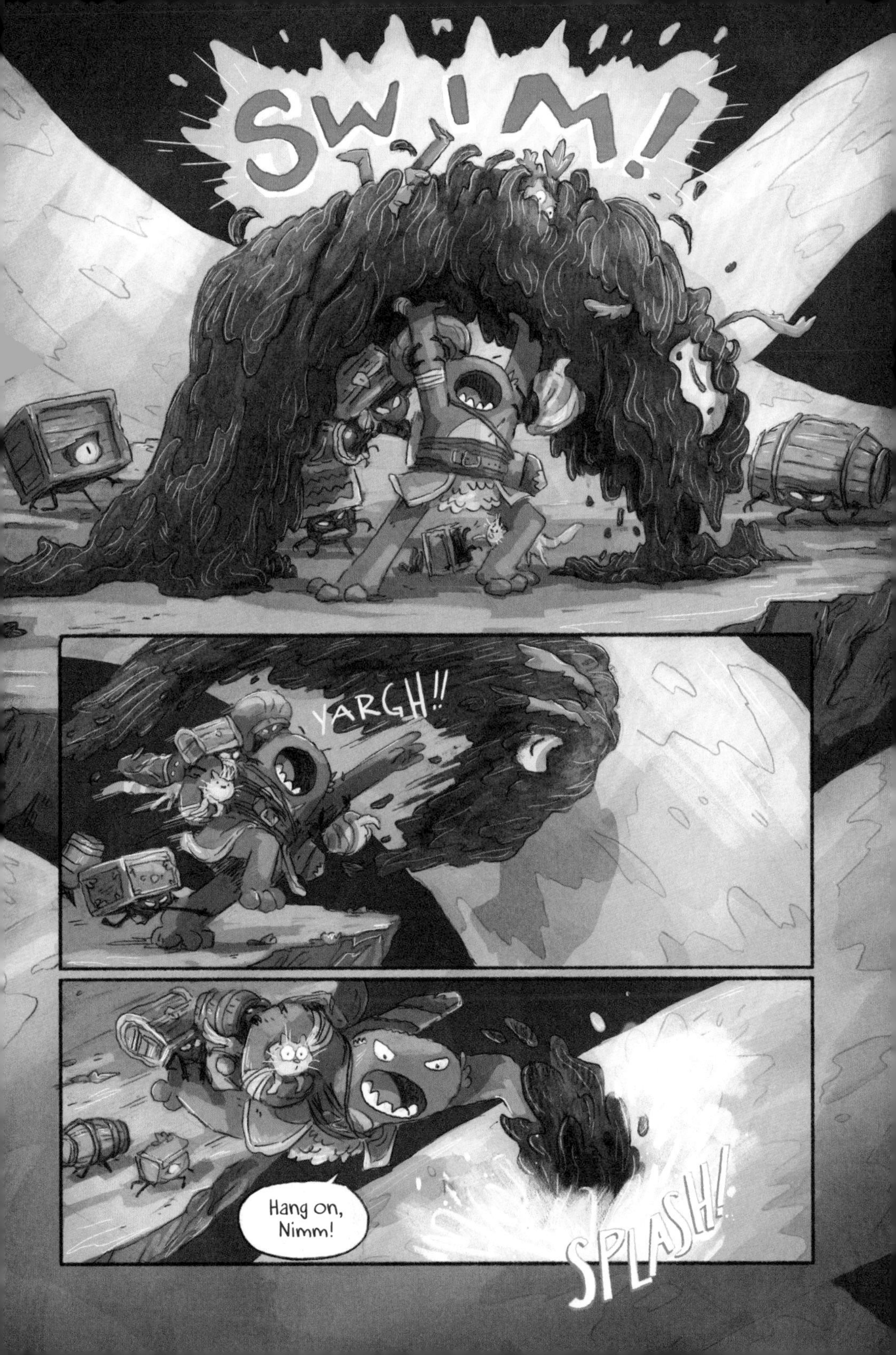
SWIM!
YARGH!!
Hang on, Nimm!
SPLASH!

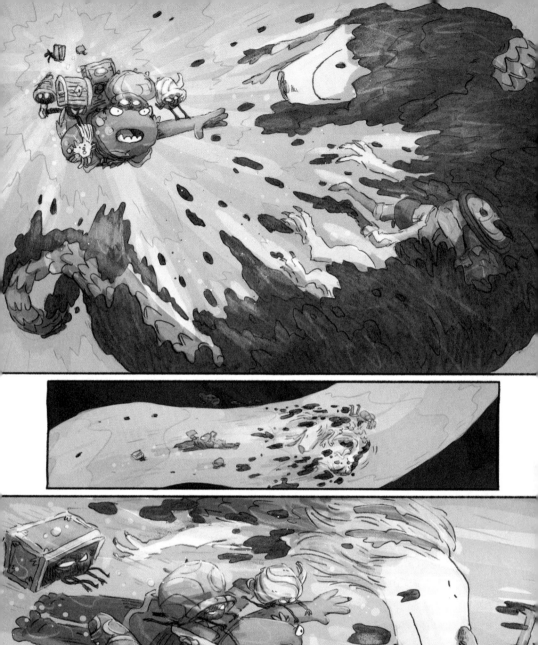

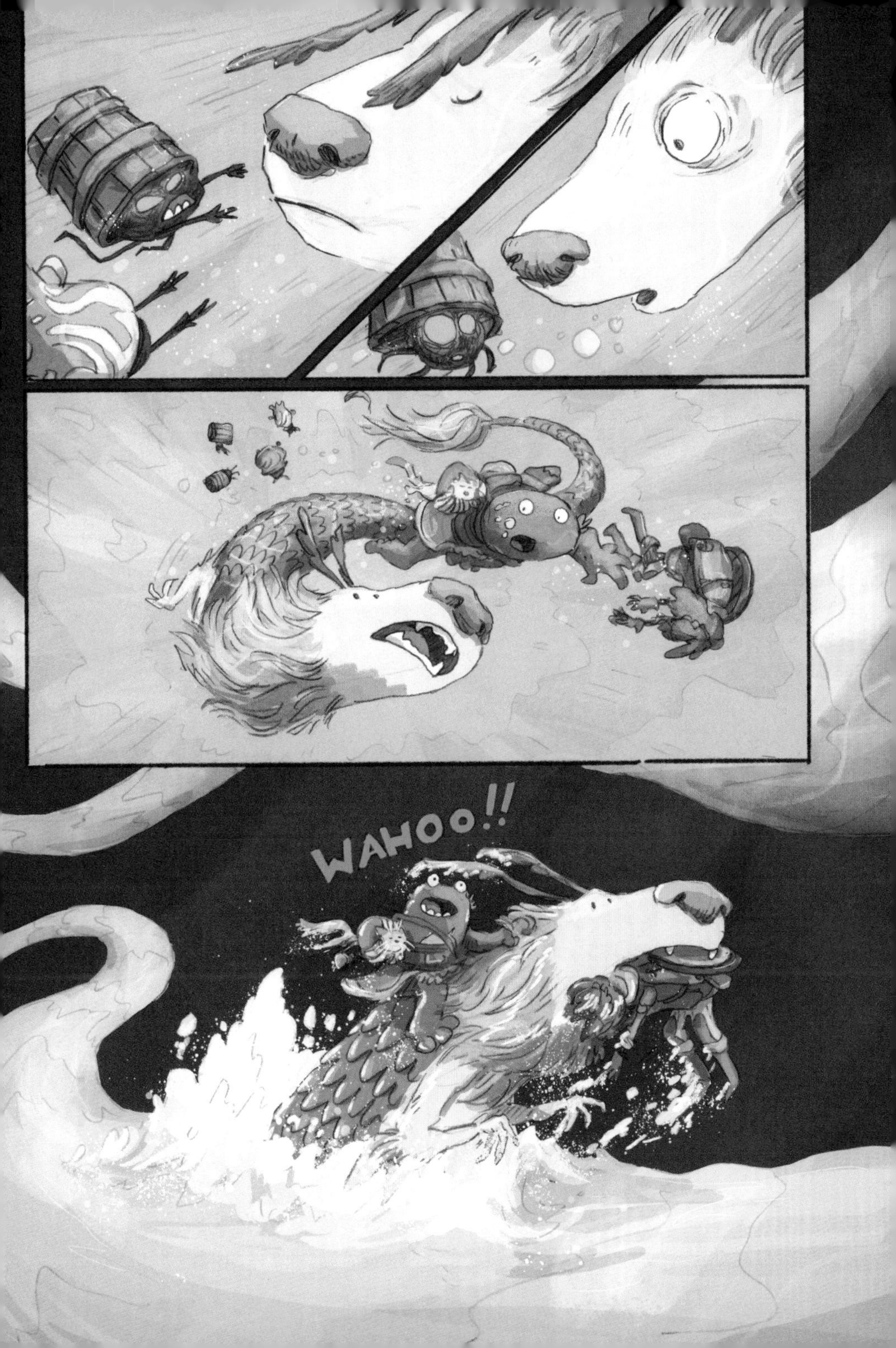
WAHOO!!

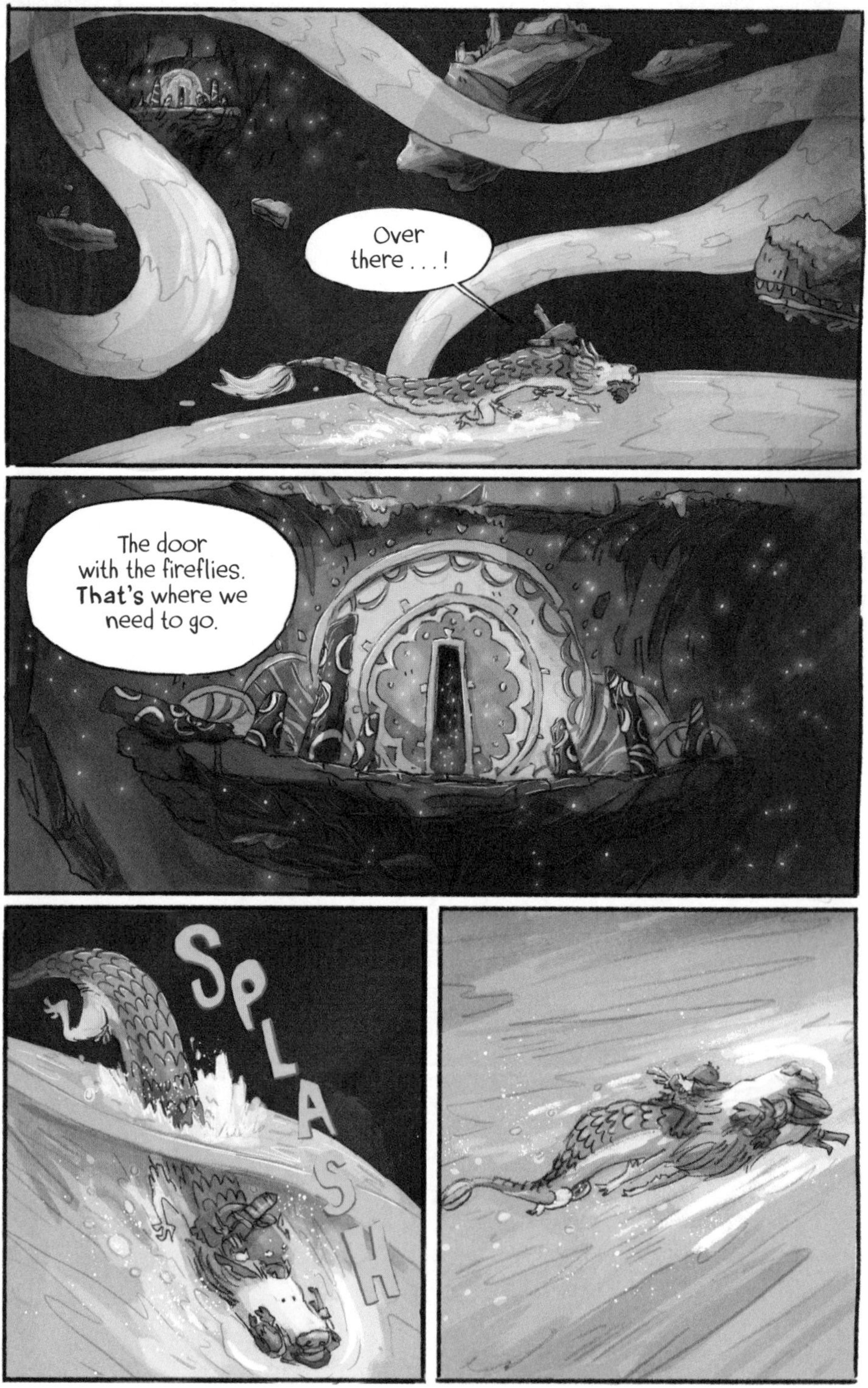
Over there . . . !
The door with the fireflies. **That's** where we need to go.
SPLASH

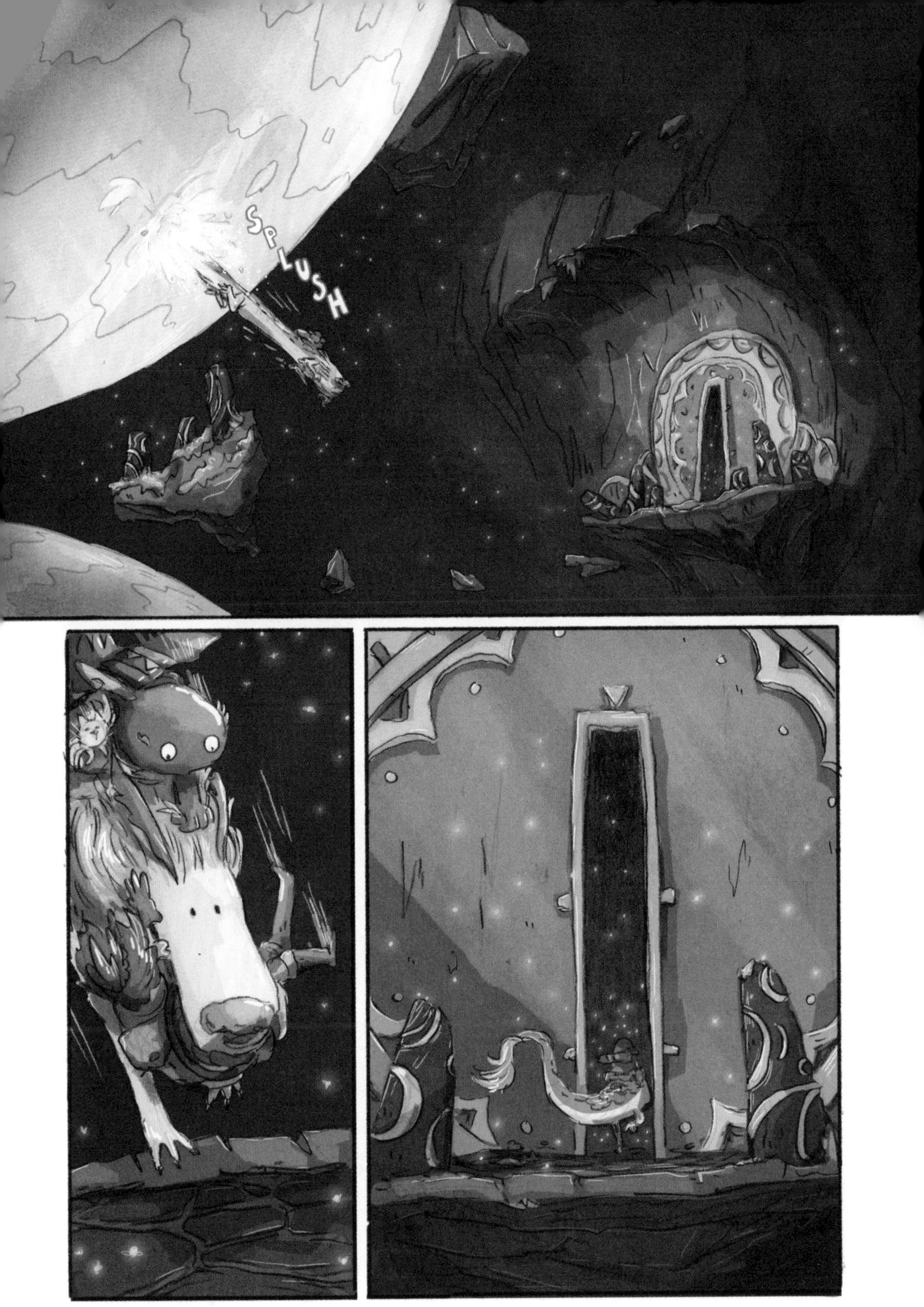
SPLUSH

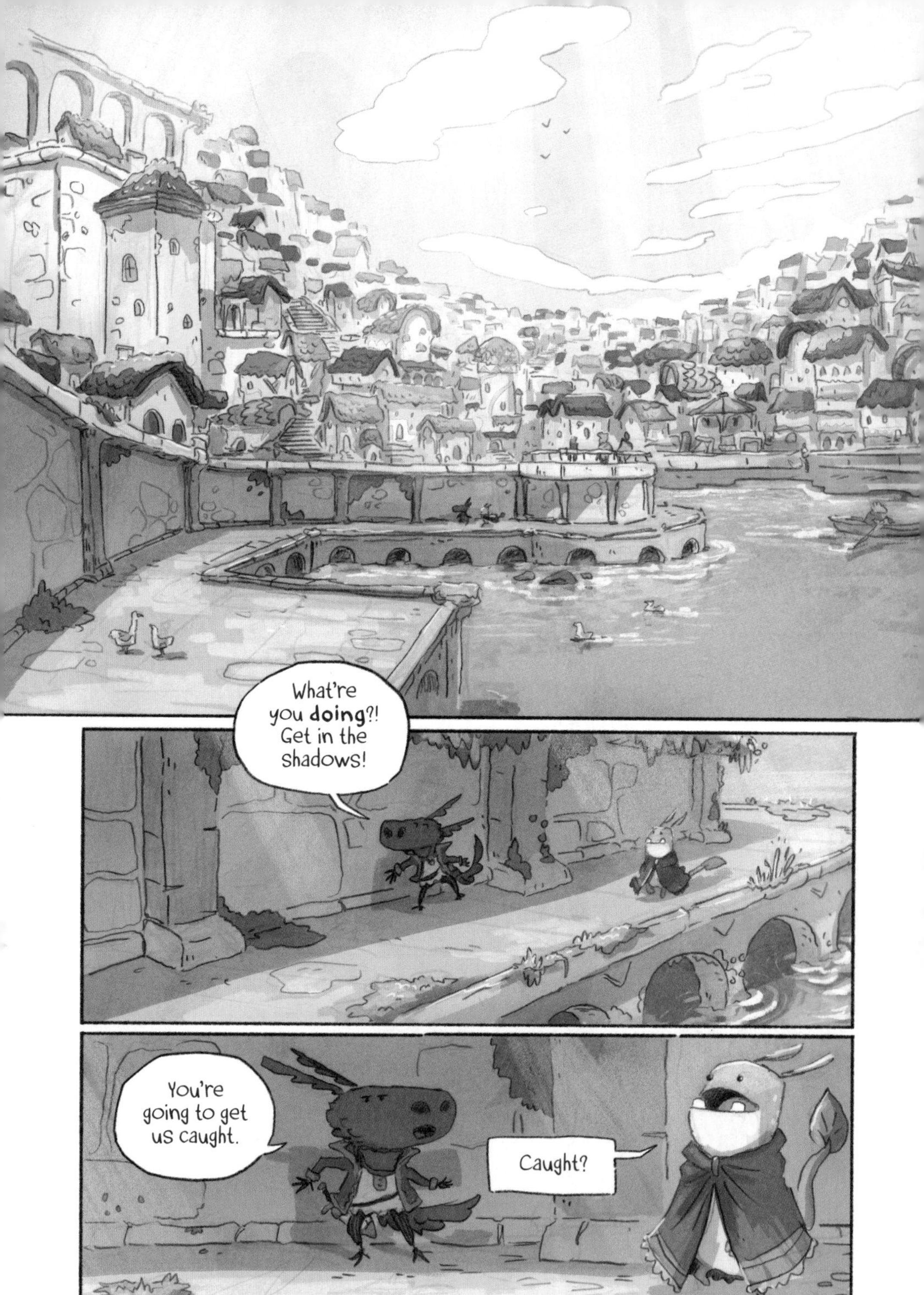
What're you **doing**?! Get in the shadows!
You're going to get us caught.
Caught?

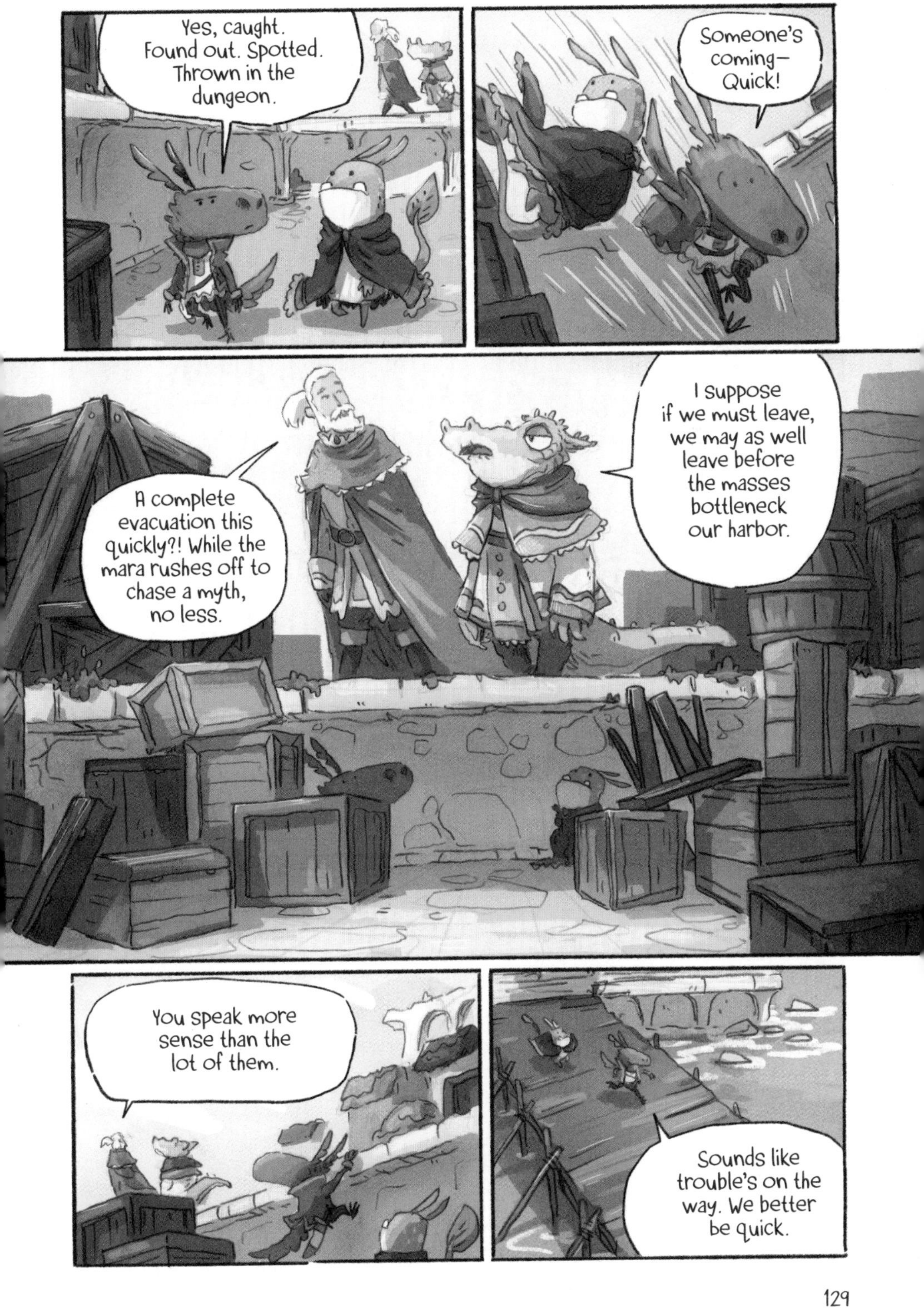
Yes, caught. Found out. Spotted. Thrown in the dungeon.
Someone's coming— Quick!
A complete evacuation this quickly?! While the mara rushes off to chase a myth, no less.
I suppose if we must leave, we may as well leave before the masses bottleneck our harbor.
You speak more sense than the lot of them.
Sounds like trouble's on the way. We better be quick.

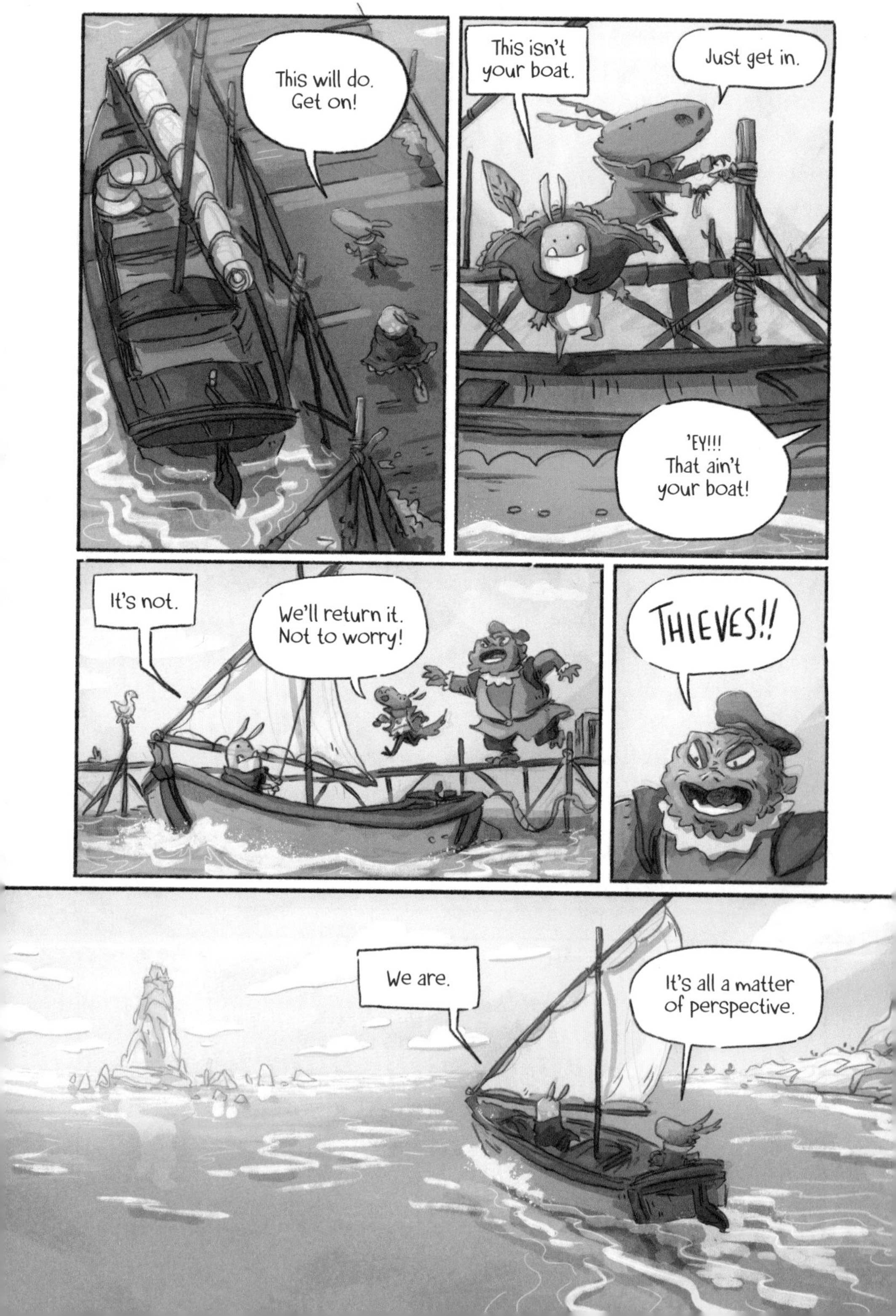

This will do. Get on!
This isn't your boat.
Just get in.
'EY!!! That ain't your boat!
It's not.
We'll return it. Not to worry!
THIEVES!!
We are.
It's all a matter of perspective.

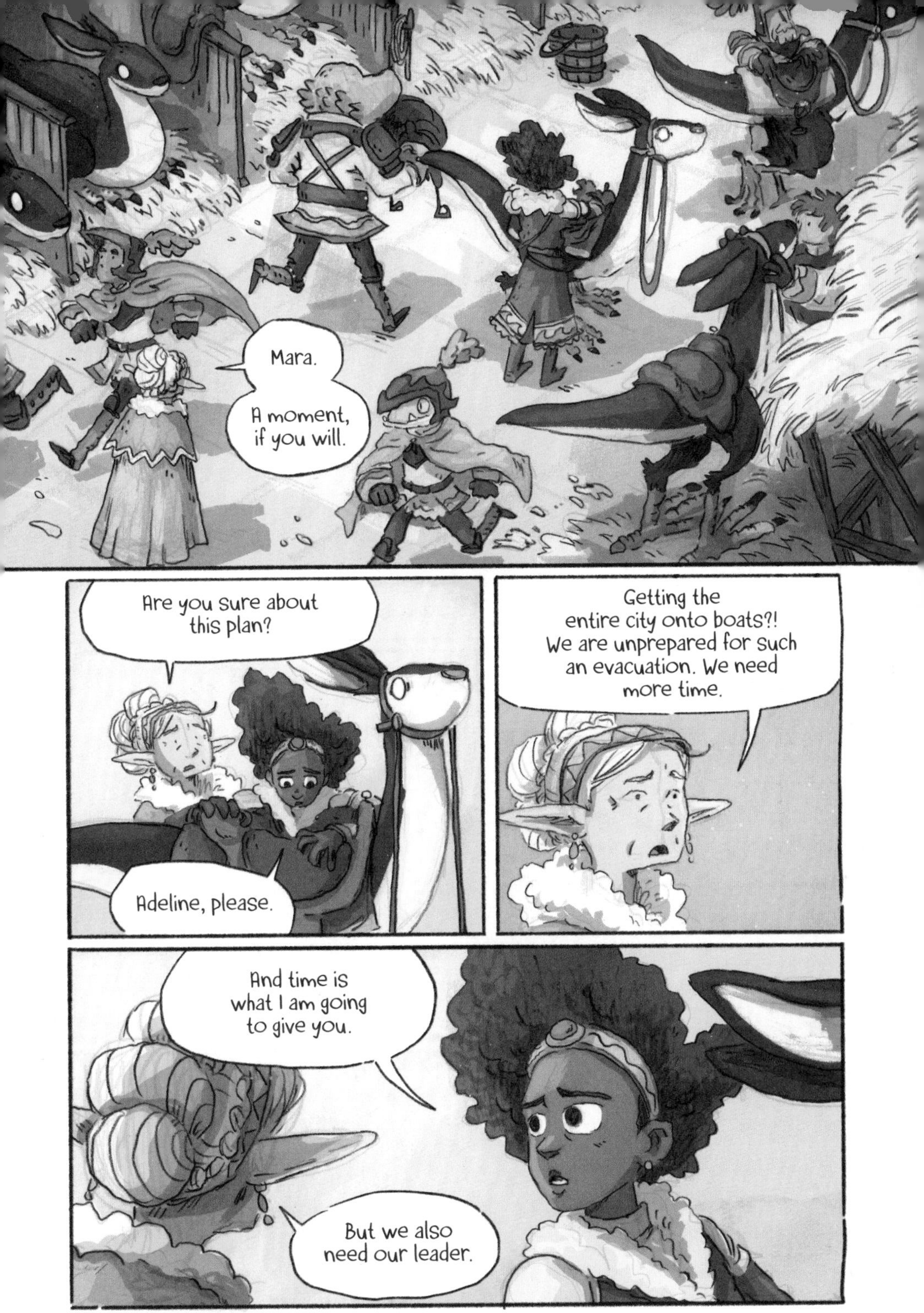

Mara.
A moment, if you will.
Are you sure about this plan?
Adeline, please.
Getting the entire city onto boats?! We are unprepared for such an evacuation. We need more time.
And time is what I am going to give you.
But we also need our leader.

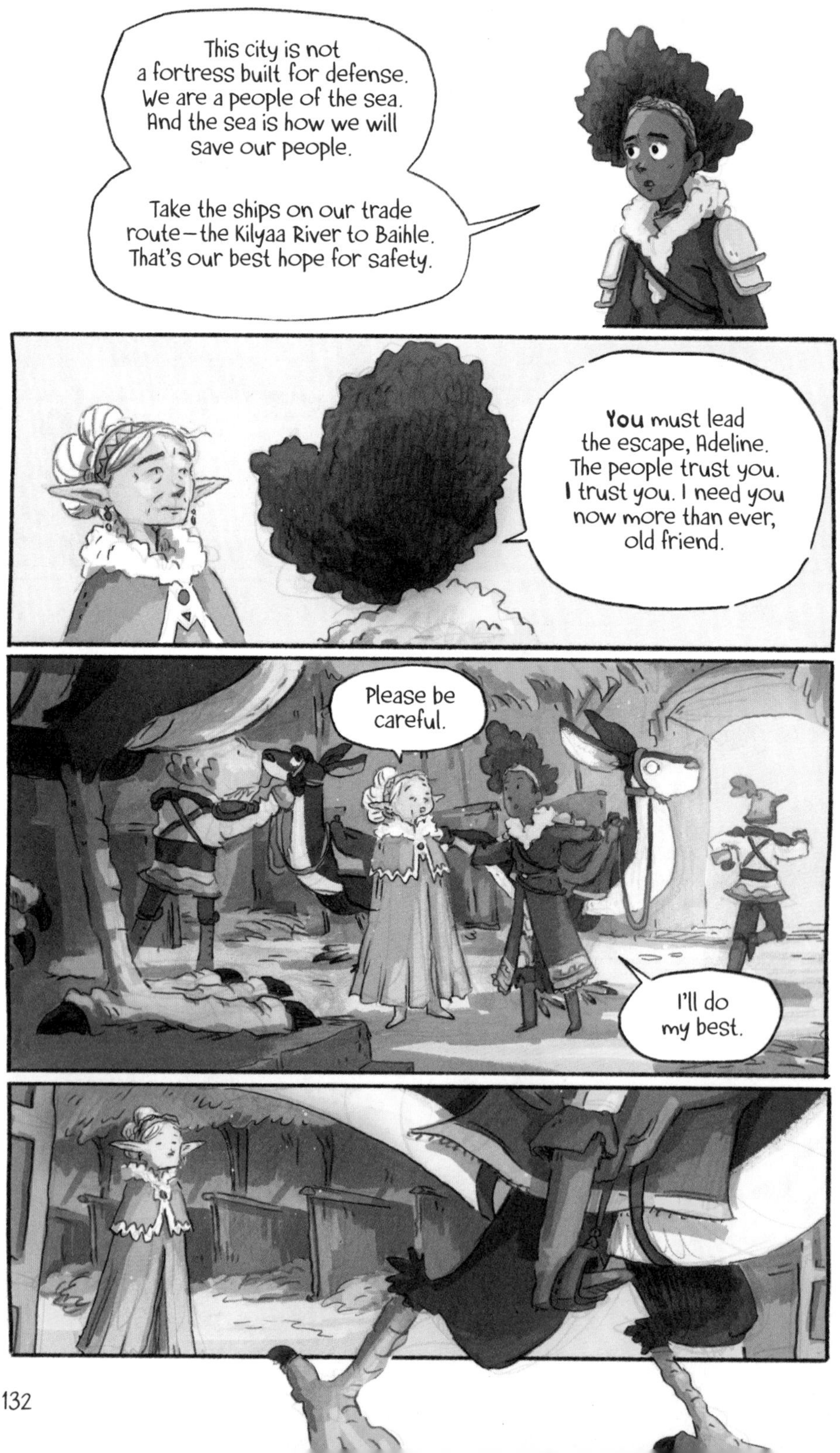
This city is not a fortress built for defense. We are a people of the sea. And the sea is how we will save our people.
Take the ships on our trade route—the Kilyaa River to Baihle. That's our best hope for safety.
You must lead the escape, Adeline. The people trust you. I trust you. I need you now more than ever, old friend.
Please be careful.
I'll do my best.

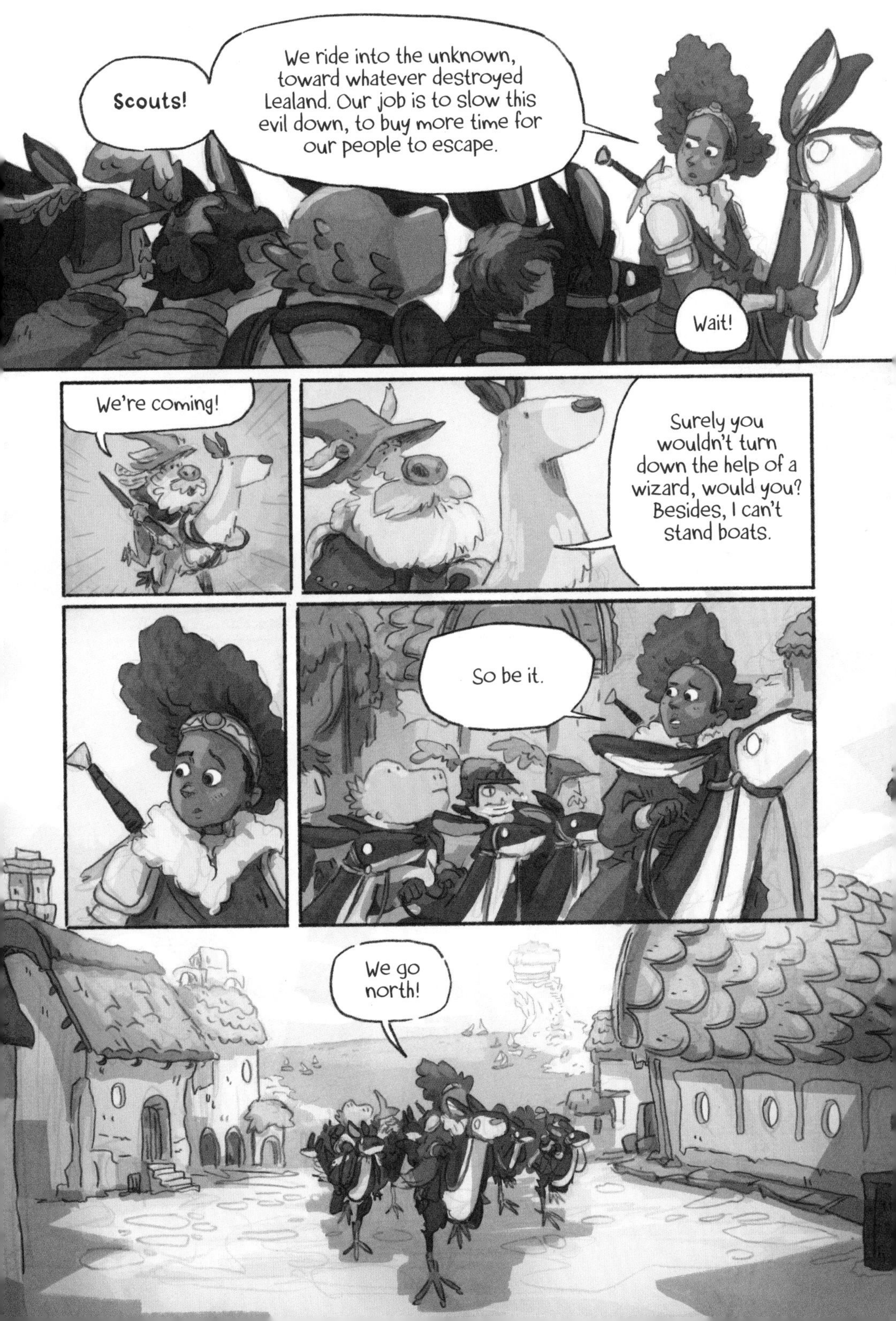
Scouts!
We ride into the unknown, toward whatever destroyed Lealand. Our job is to slow this evil down, to buy more time for our people to escape.
Wait!
We're coming!
Surely you wouldn't turn down the help of a wizard, would you? Besides, I can't stand boats.
So be it.
We go north!

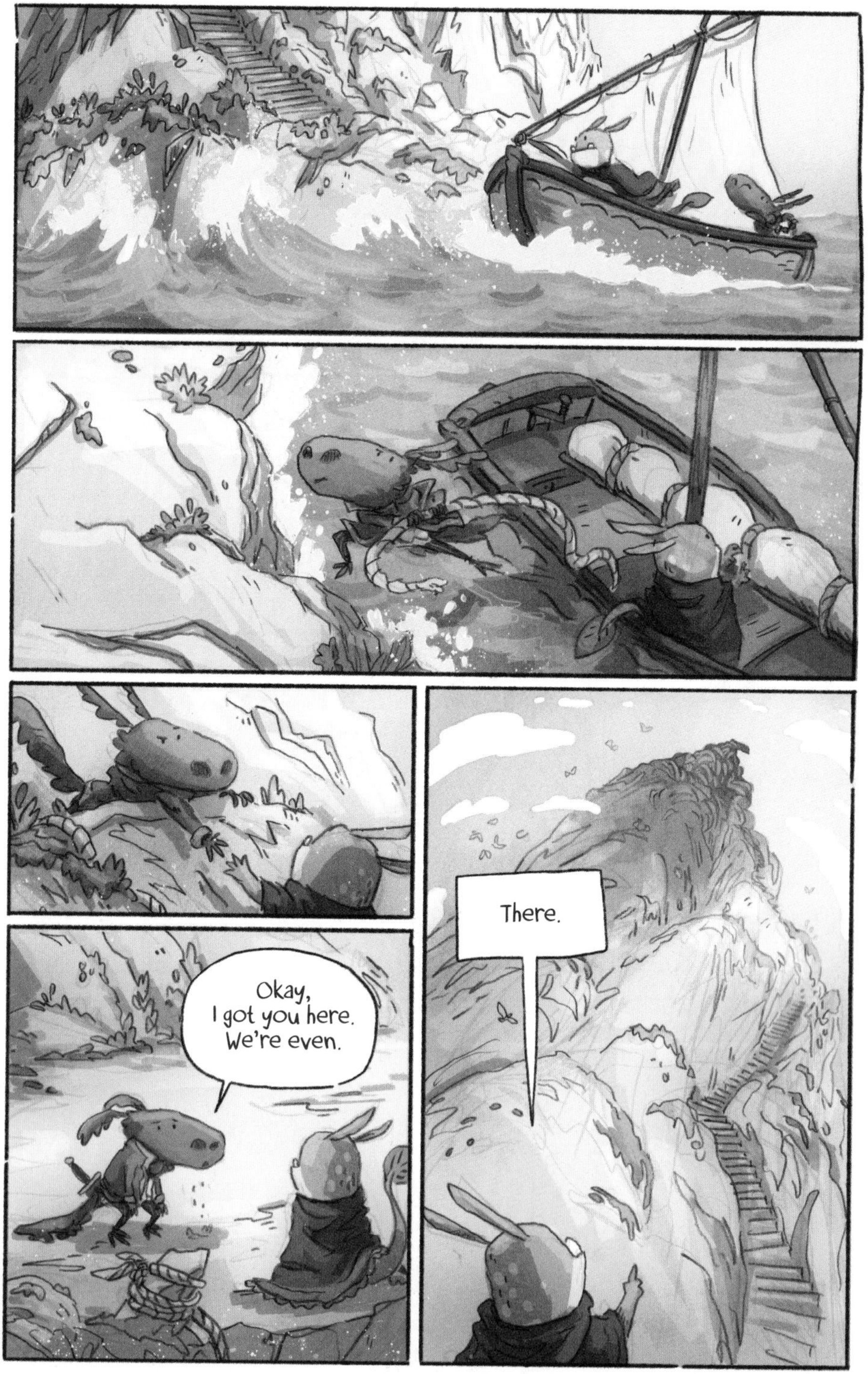
Okay, I got you here. We're even.
There.

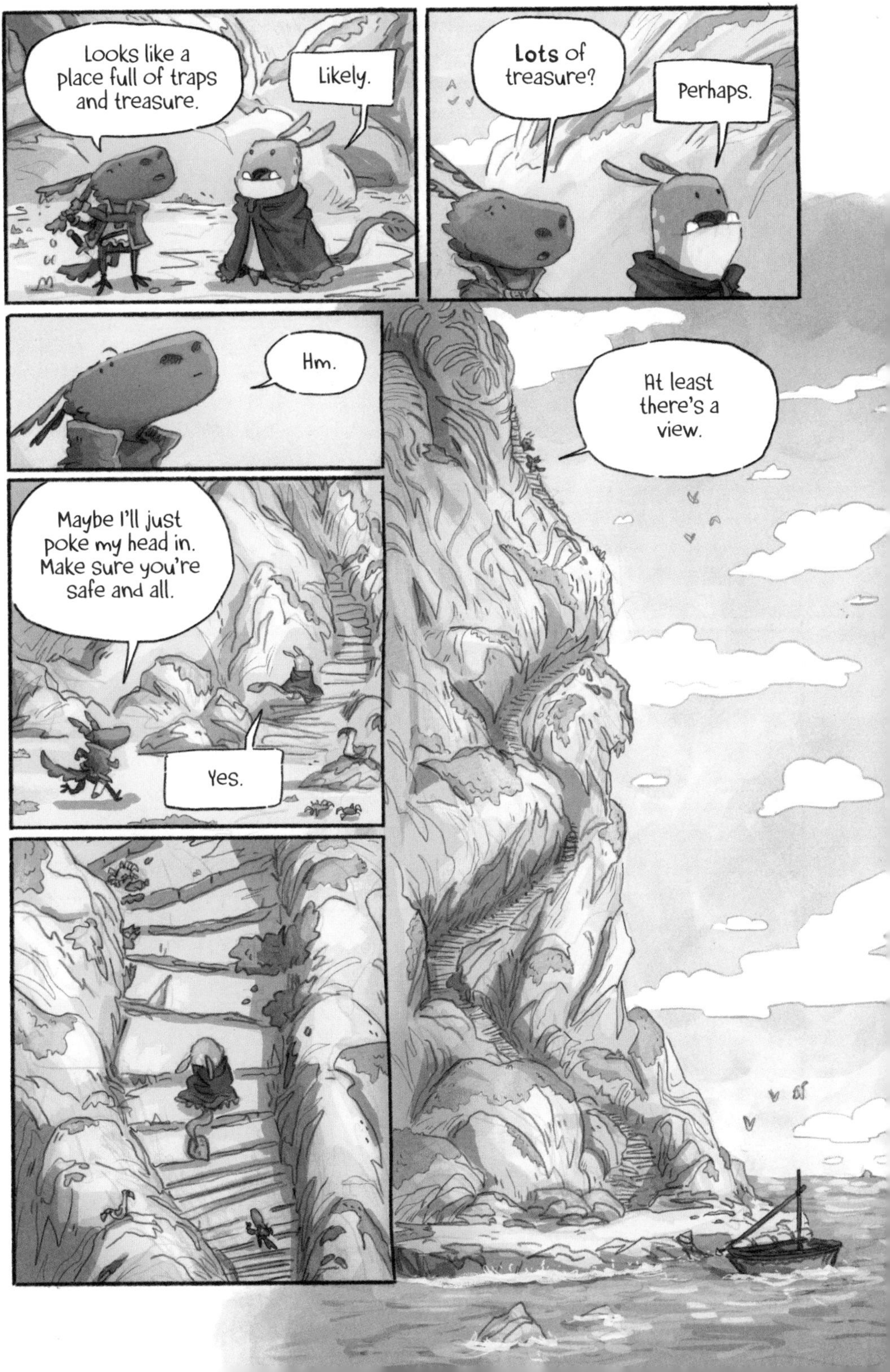
Looks like a place full of traps and treasure.
Likely.
Lots of treasure?
Perhaps.
Hm.
At least there's a view.
Maybe I'll just poke my head in. Make sure you're safe and all.
Yes.

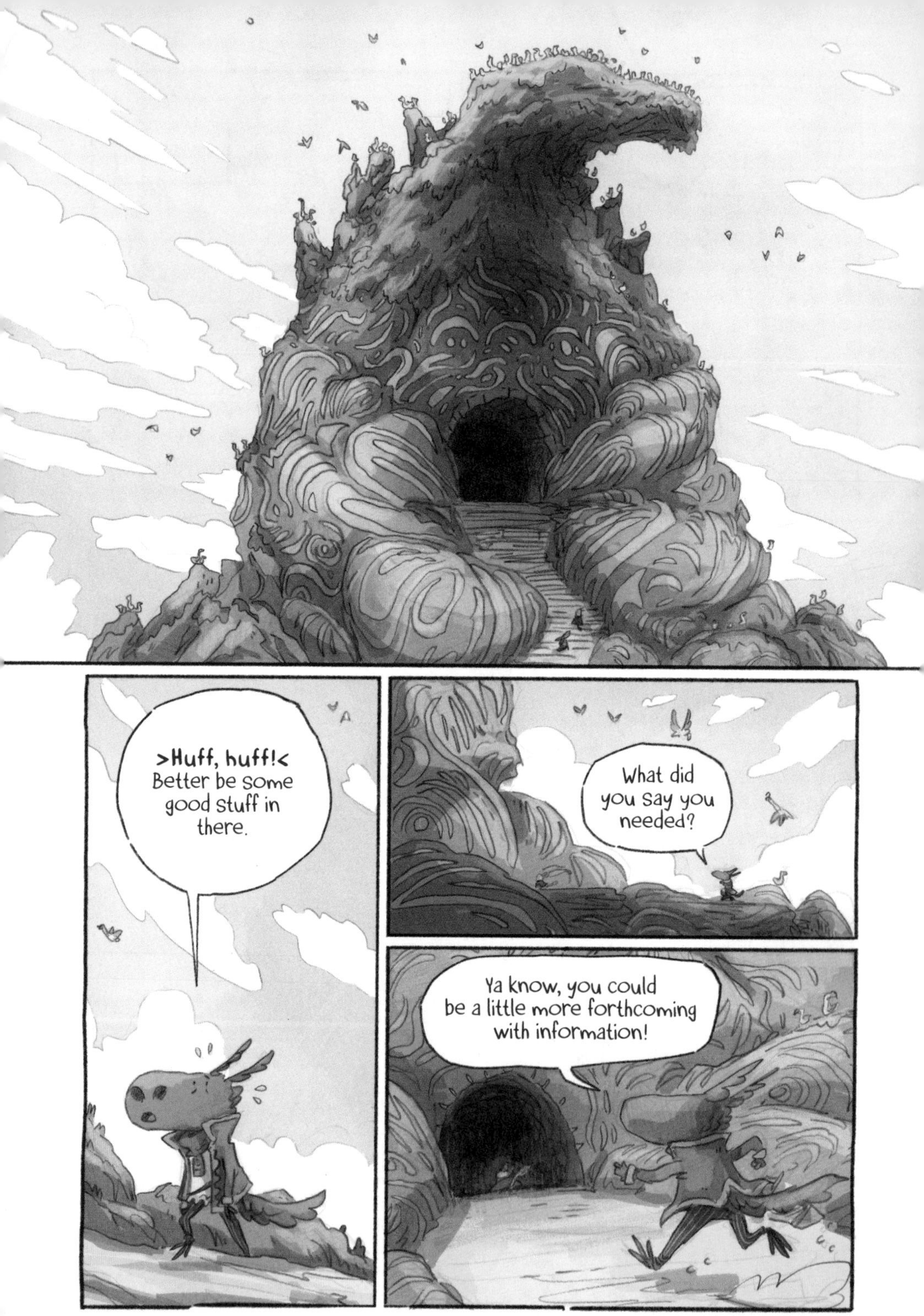
>Huff, huff!< Better be some good stuff in there.
What did you say you needed?
Ya know, you could be a little more forthcoming with information!

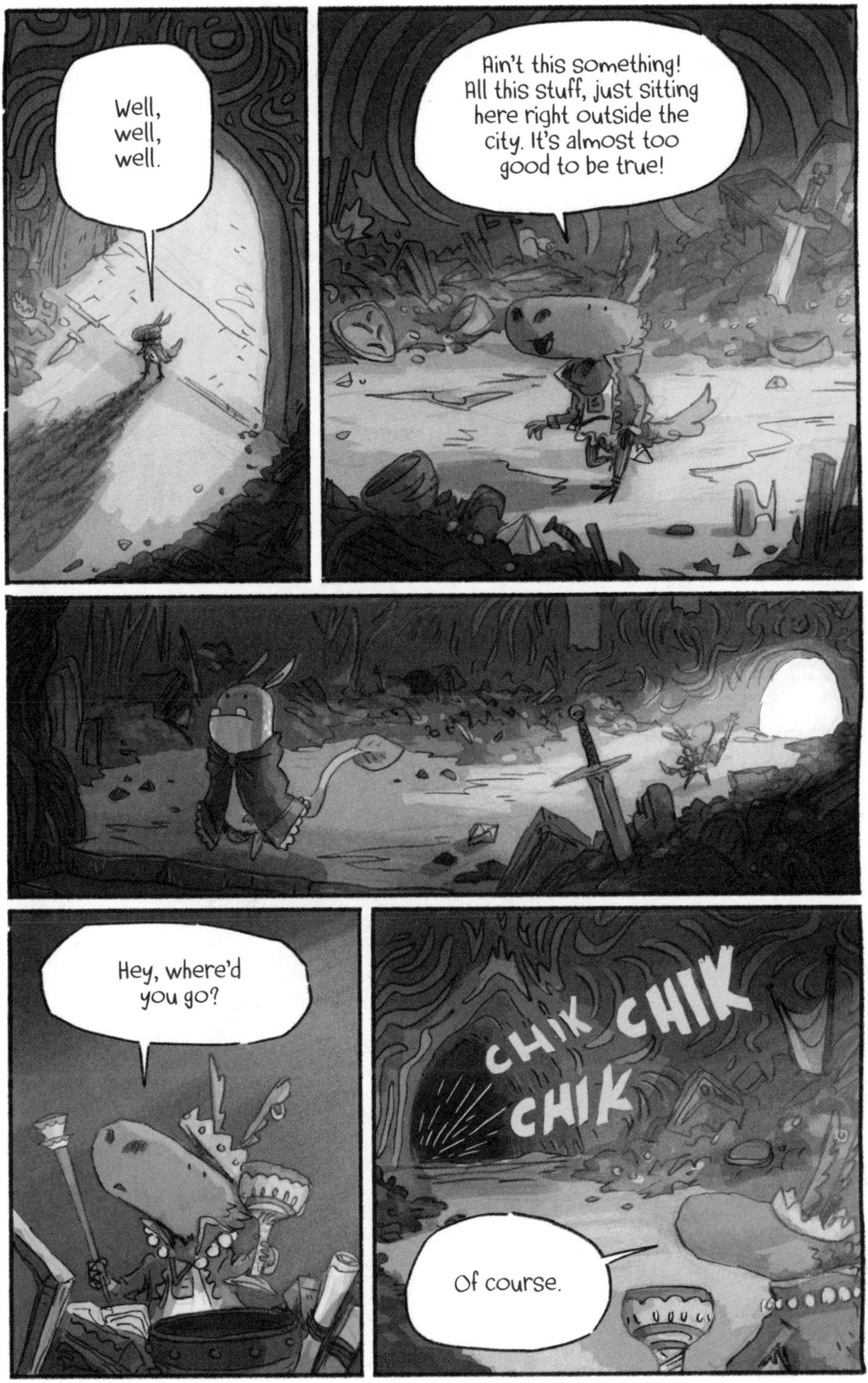
Well, well, well.
Ain't this something! All this stuff, just sitting here right outside the city. It's almost too good to be true!
Hey, where'd you go?
CHIK CHIK
CHIK
Of course.

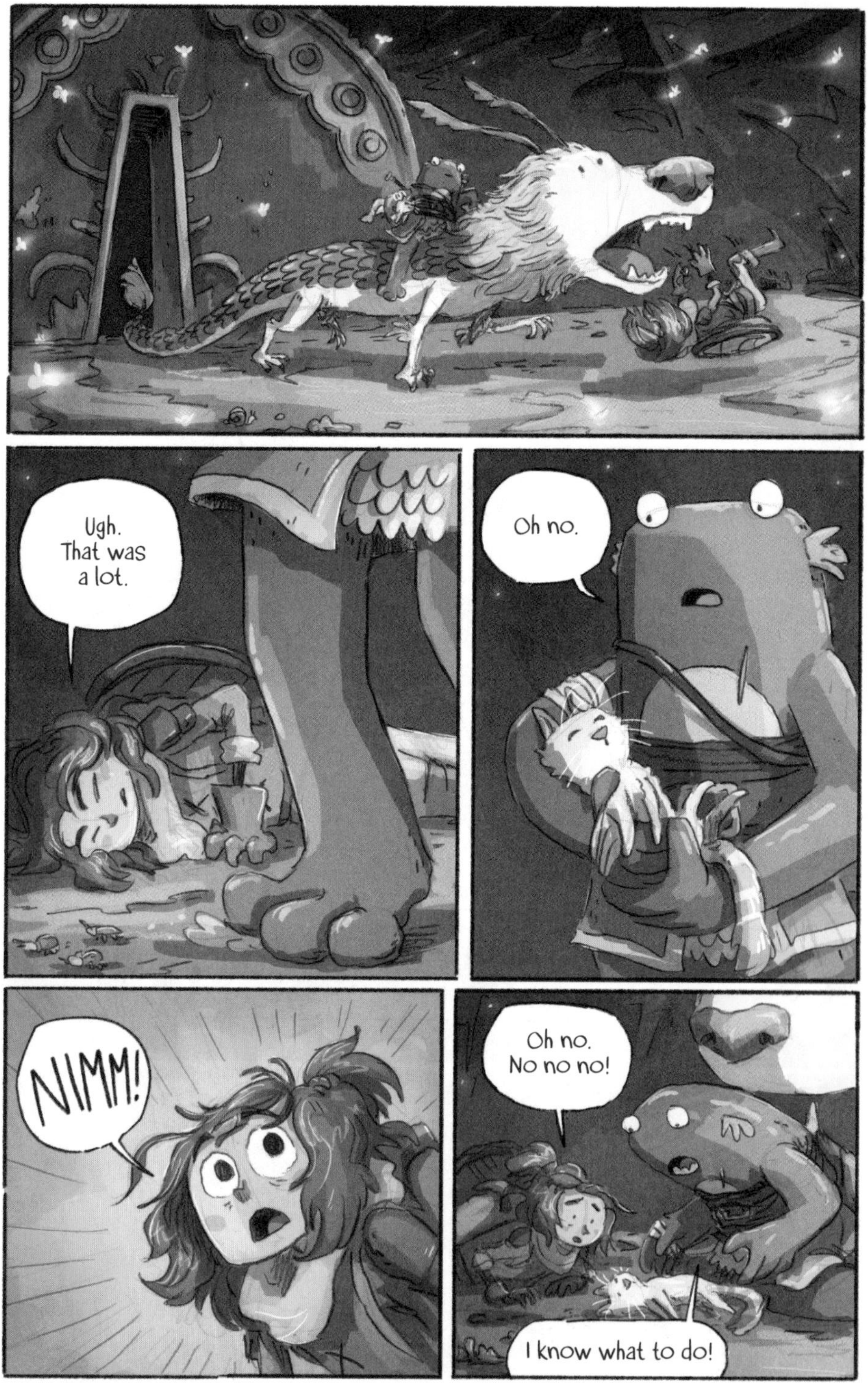
Ugh. That was a lot.
Oh no.
NIMM!
Oh no. No no no!
I know what to do!

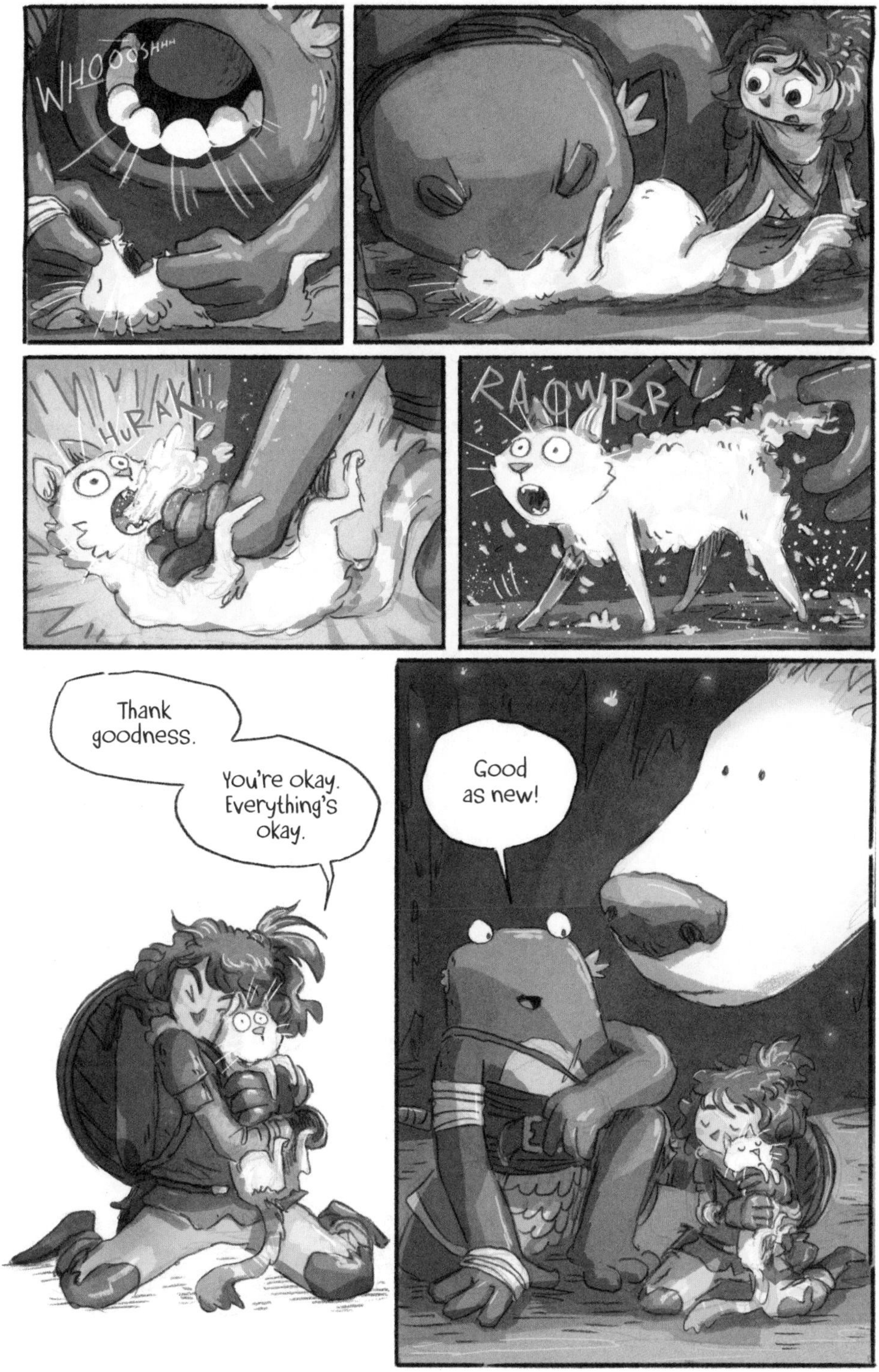
WHOOOSHHH
HURAK!!
RAOWRR
Thank goodness.
You're okay. Everything's okay.
Good as new!

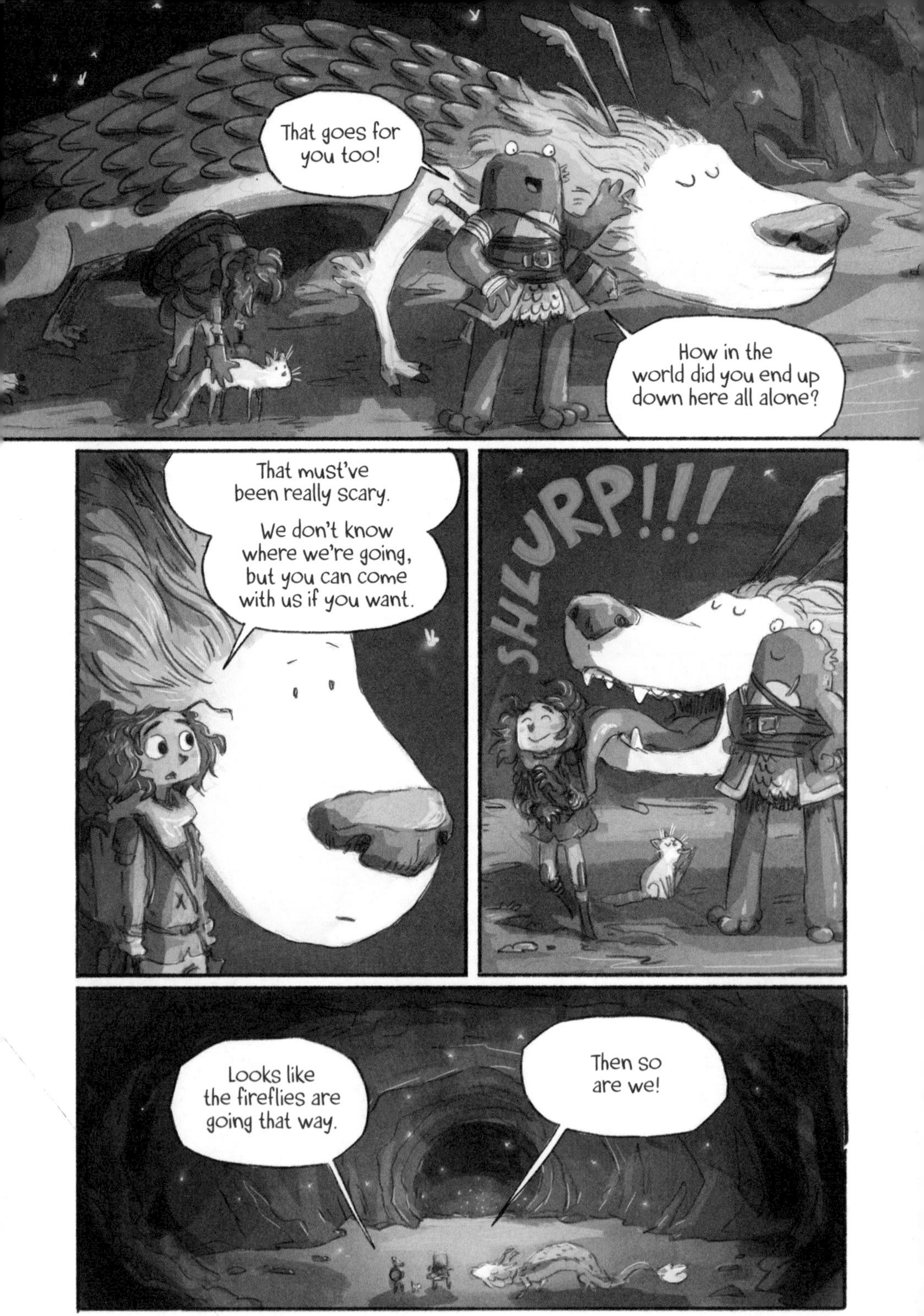
That goes for you too!
How in the world did you end up down here all alone?
That must've been really scary.
We don't know where we're going, but you can come with us if you want.
SHLURP!!!
Looks like the fireflies are going that way.
Then so are we!

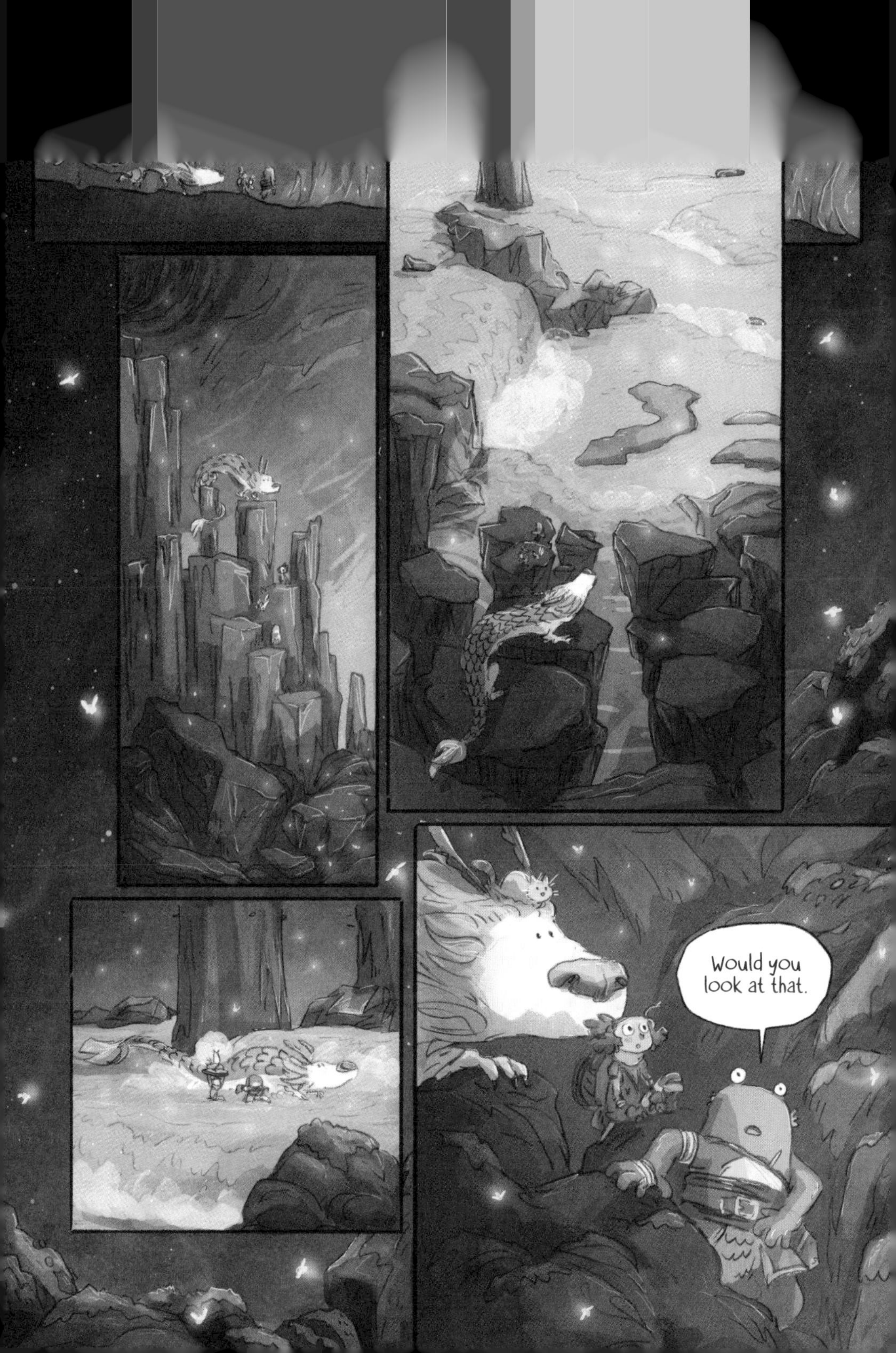
Would you look at that.

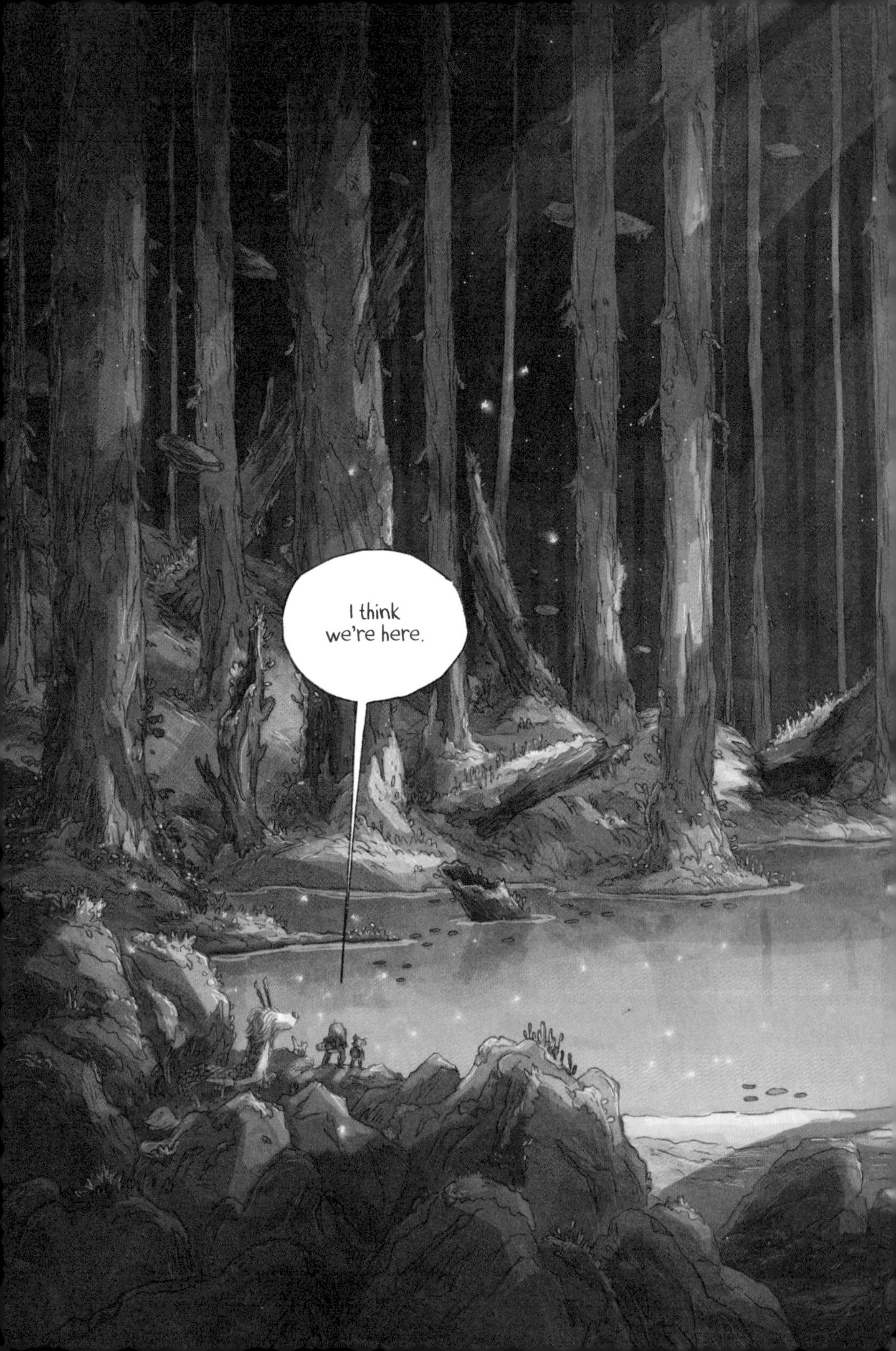
I think we're here.

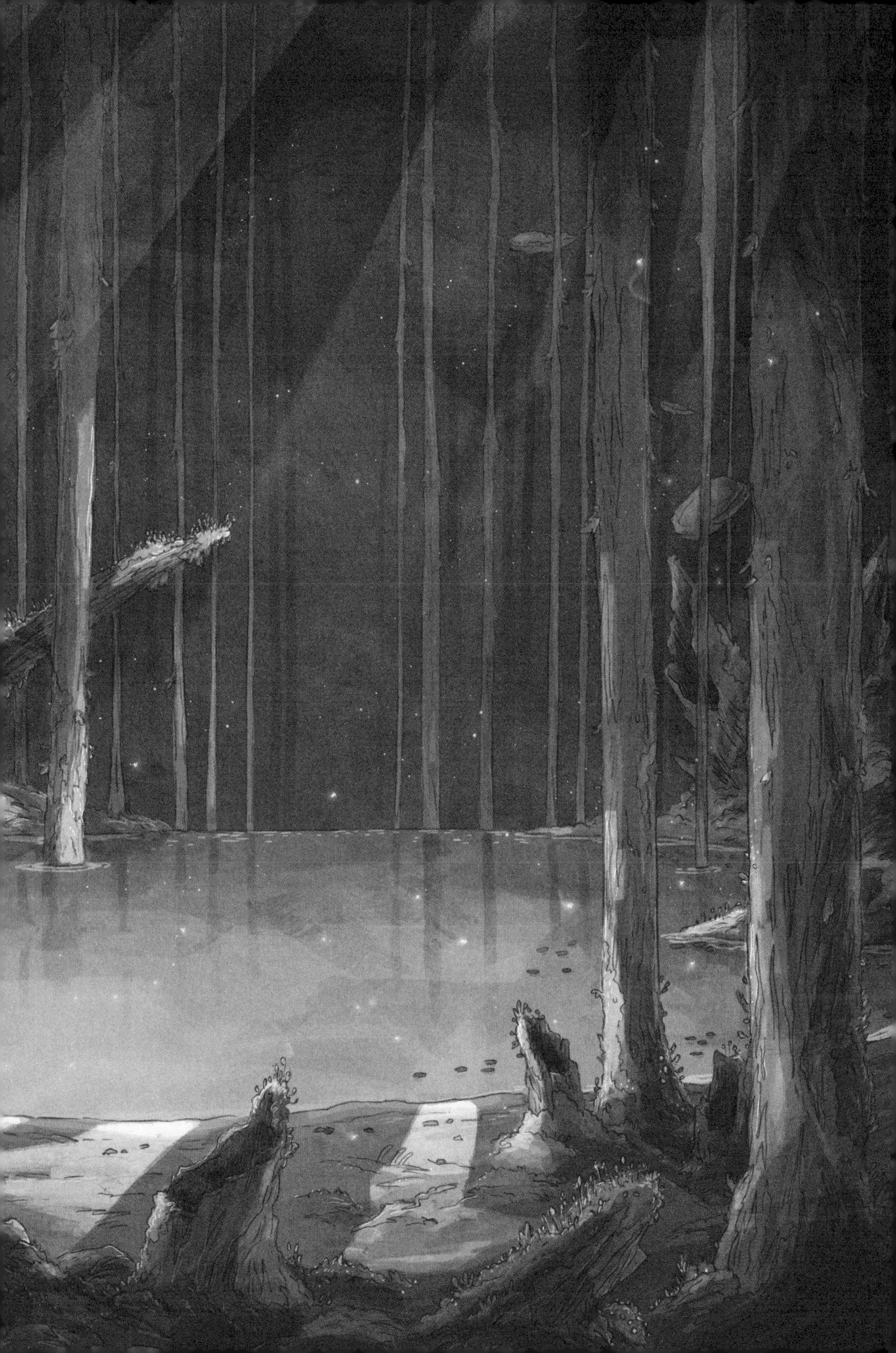

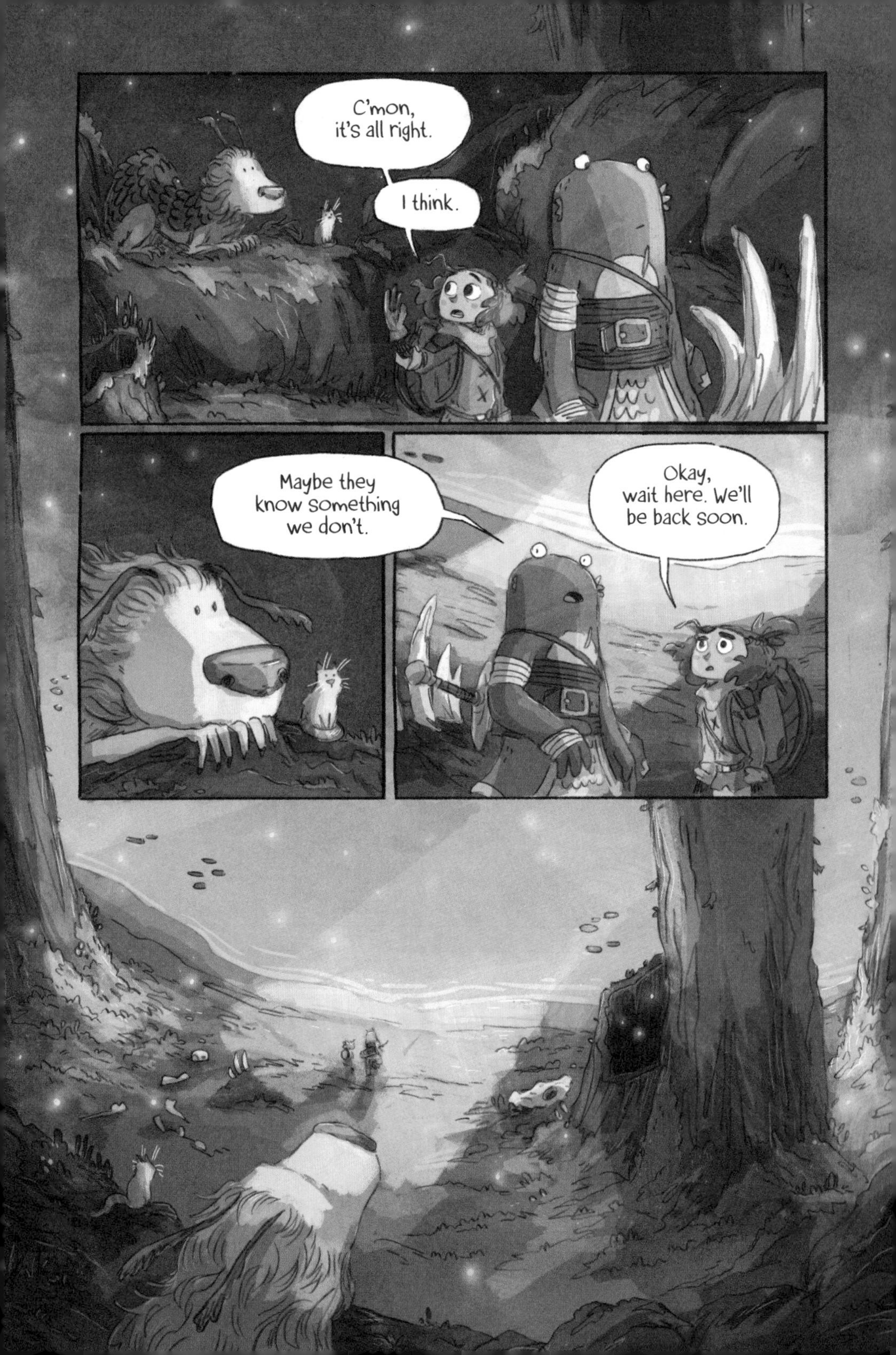
C'mon, it's all right.
I think.
Maybe they know something we don't.
Okay, wait here. We'll be back soon.

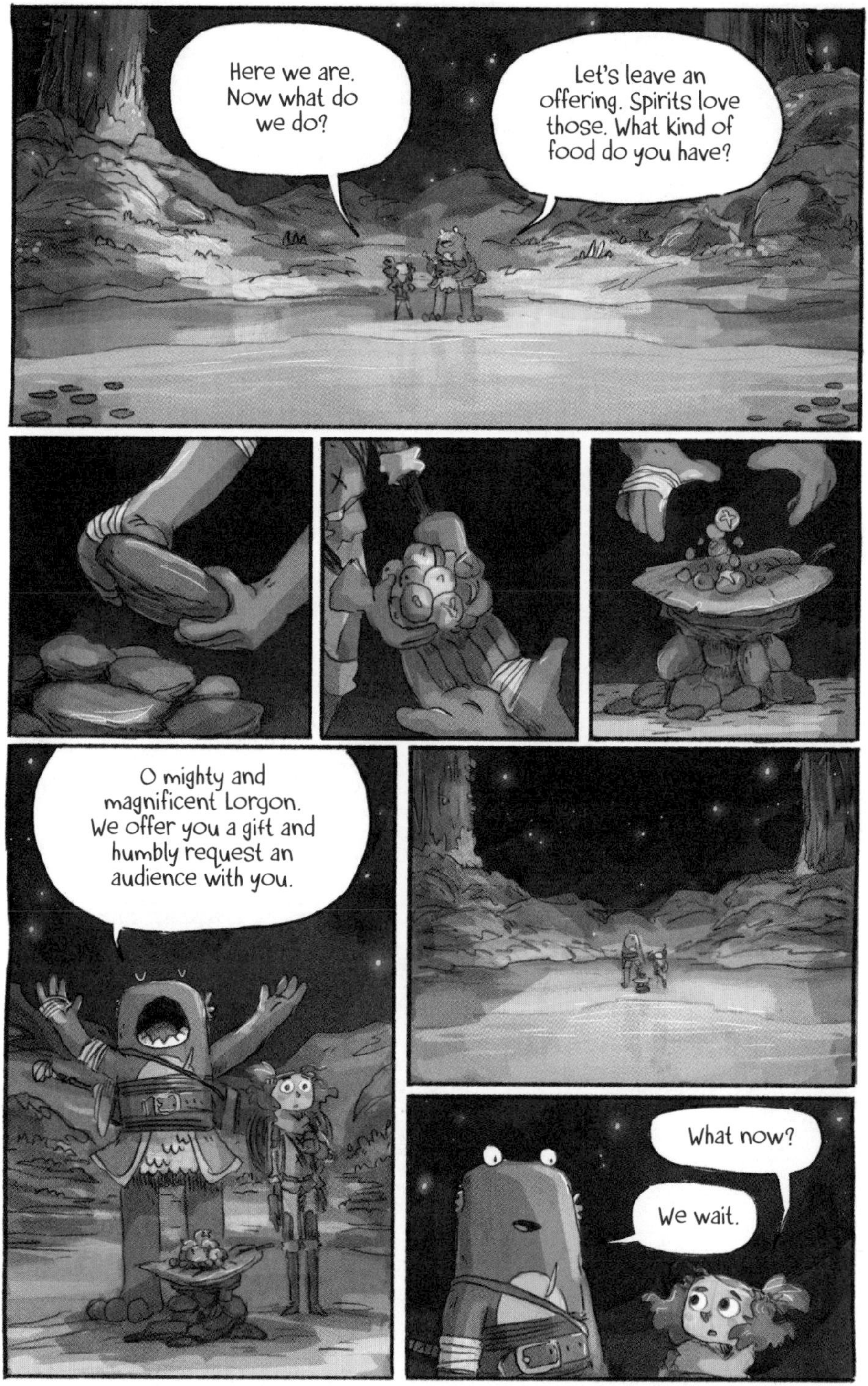

Here we are. Now what do we do?
Let's leave an offering. Spirits love those. What kind of food do you have?
O mighty and magnificent Lorgon. We offer you a gift and humbly request an audience with you.
What now?
We wait.

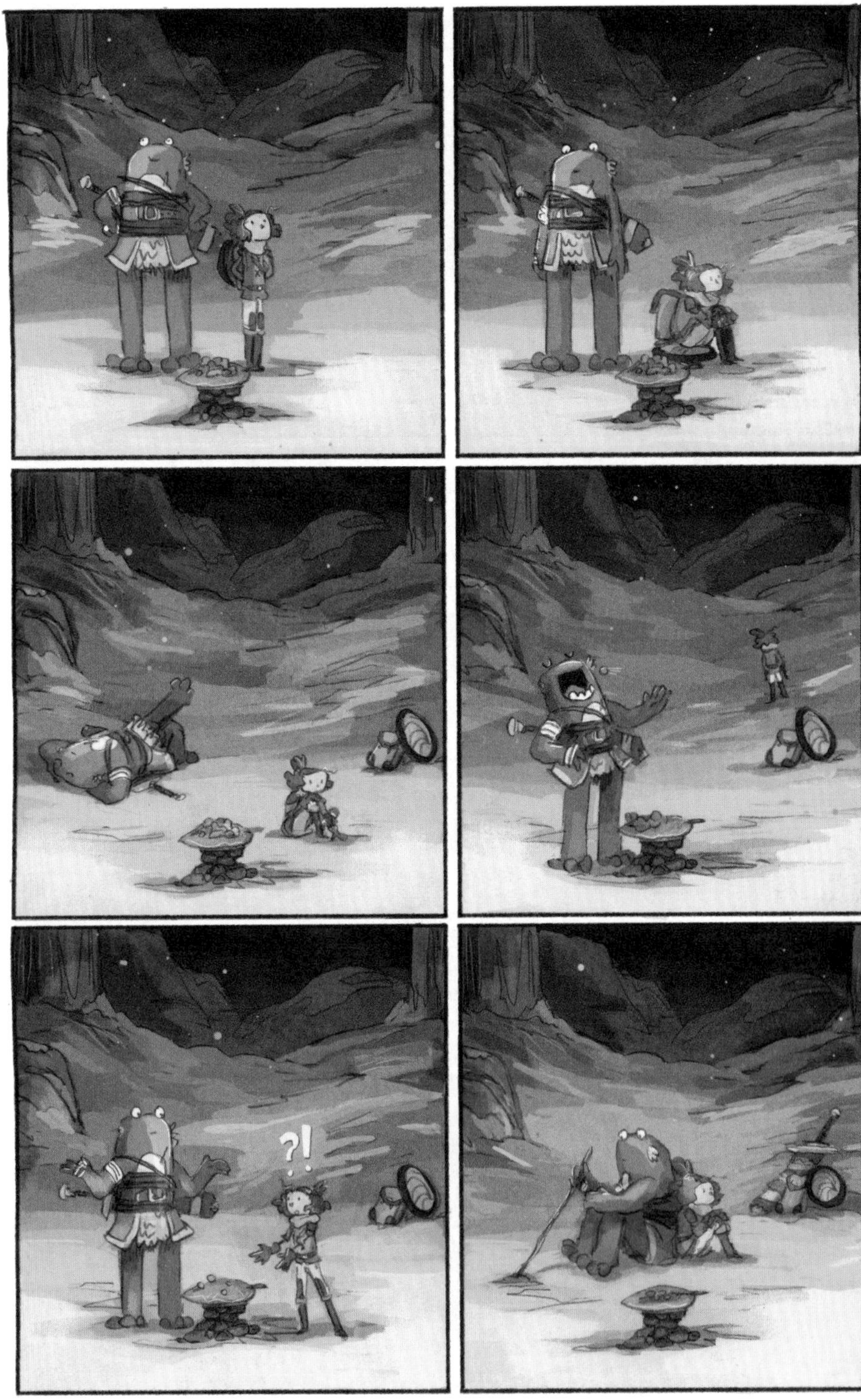
?!

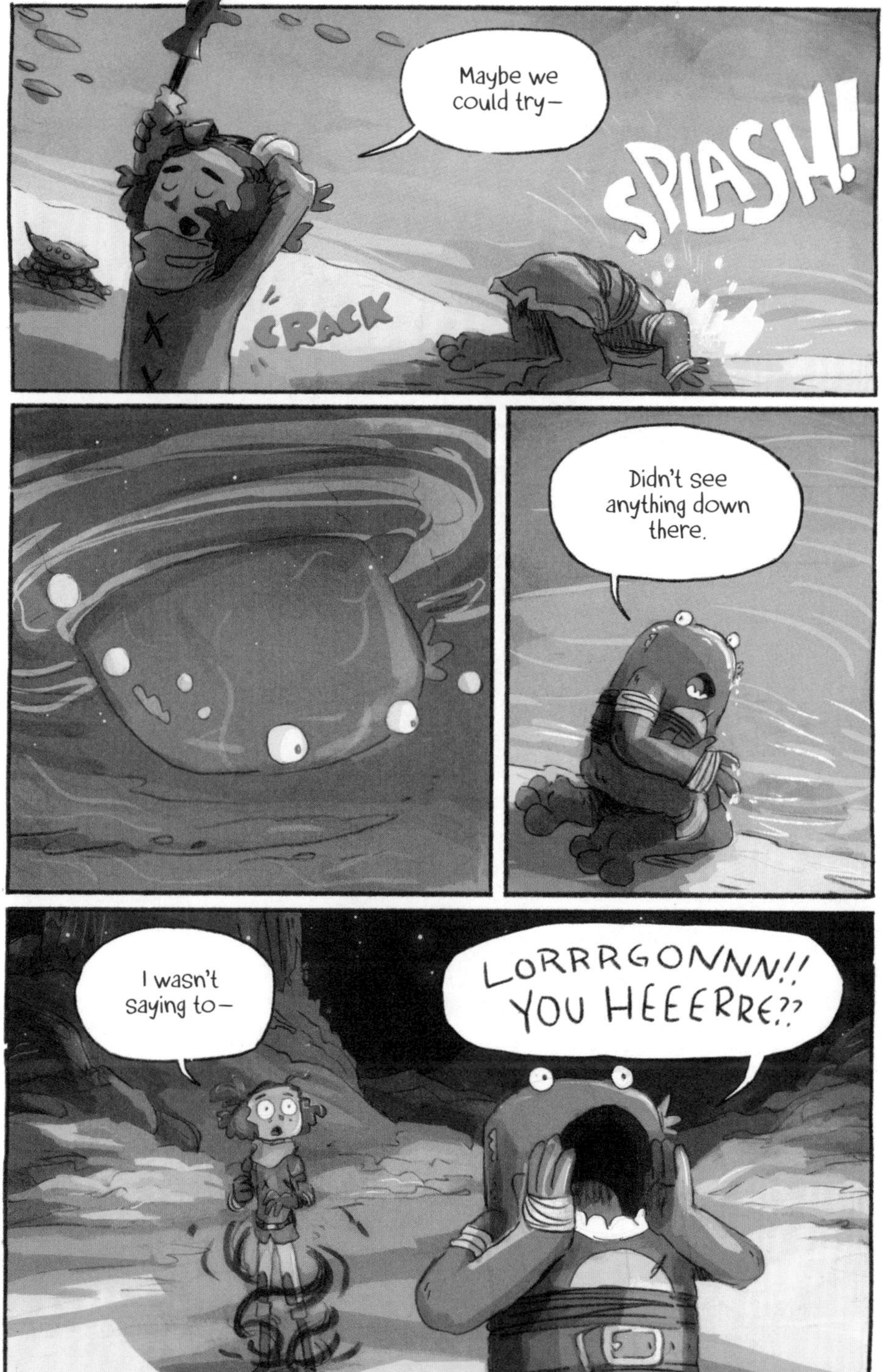
Maybe we could try—
SPLASH!
CRACK
Didn't see anything down there.
I wasn't saying to—
LORRRGONNN!! YOU HEEERRE??

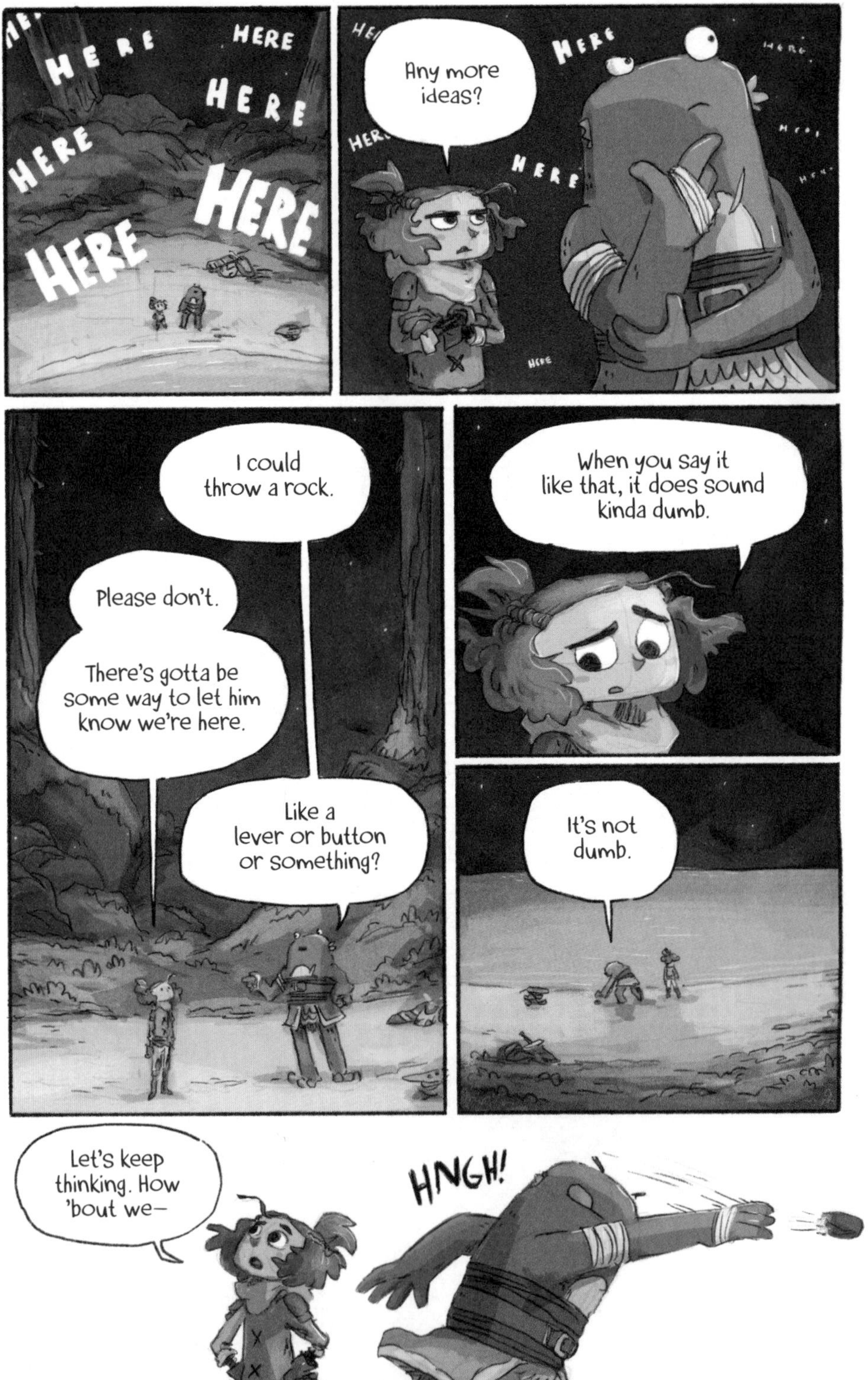
HERE
HERE
HERE
HERE
HERE
HERE
Any more ideas?
HERE
HERE
I could throw a rock.
Please don't.
There's gotta be some way to let him know we're here.
Like a lever or button or something?
When you say it like that, it does sound kinda dumb.
It's not dumb.
Let's keep thinking. How 'bout we–
HNGH!

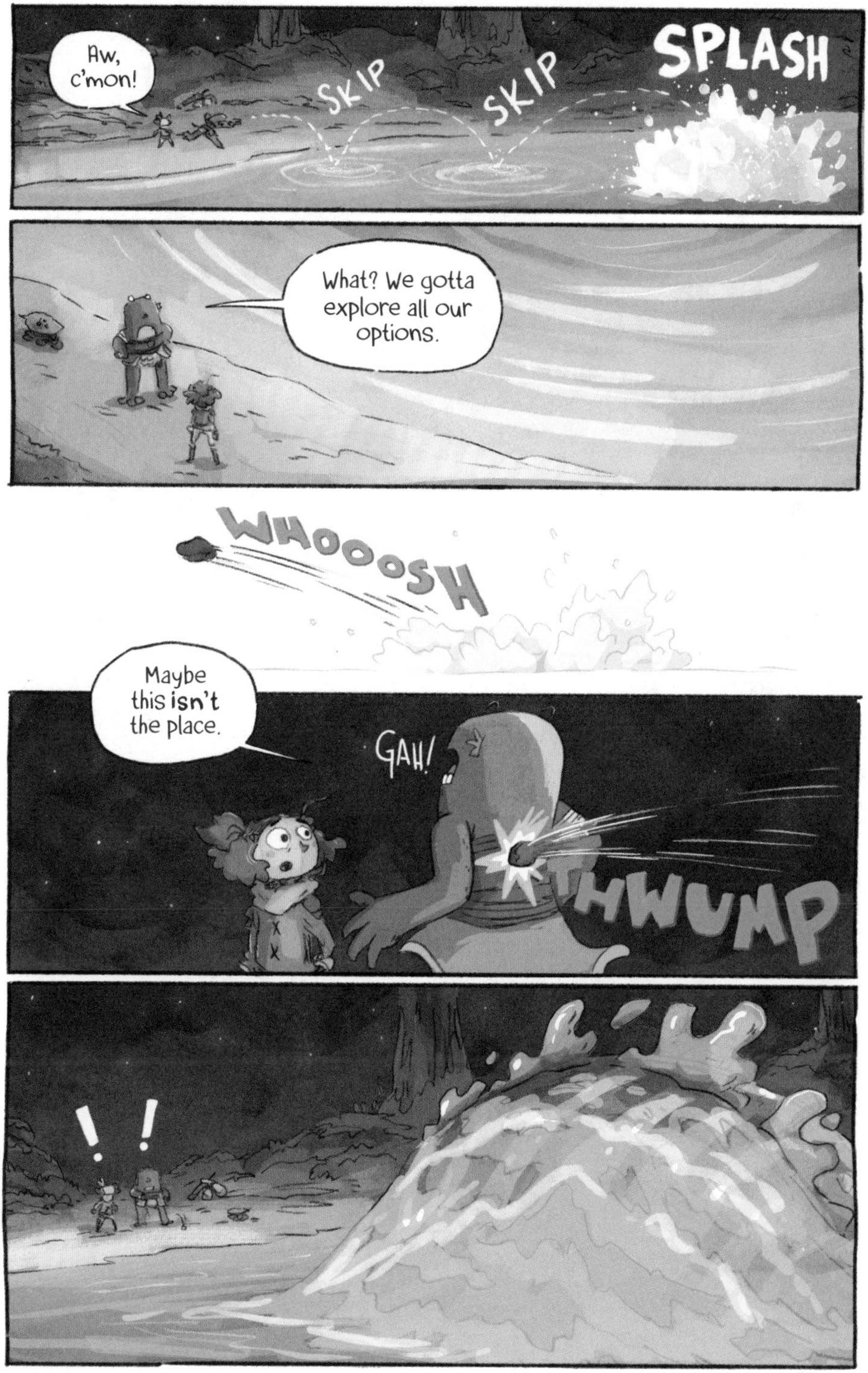
Aw, c'mon!
SKIP
SKIP
SPLASH
What? We gotta explore all our options.
WHOOOSH
Maybe this **isn't** the place.
GAH!
THWUMP
! !

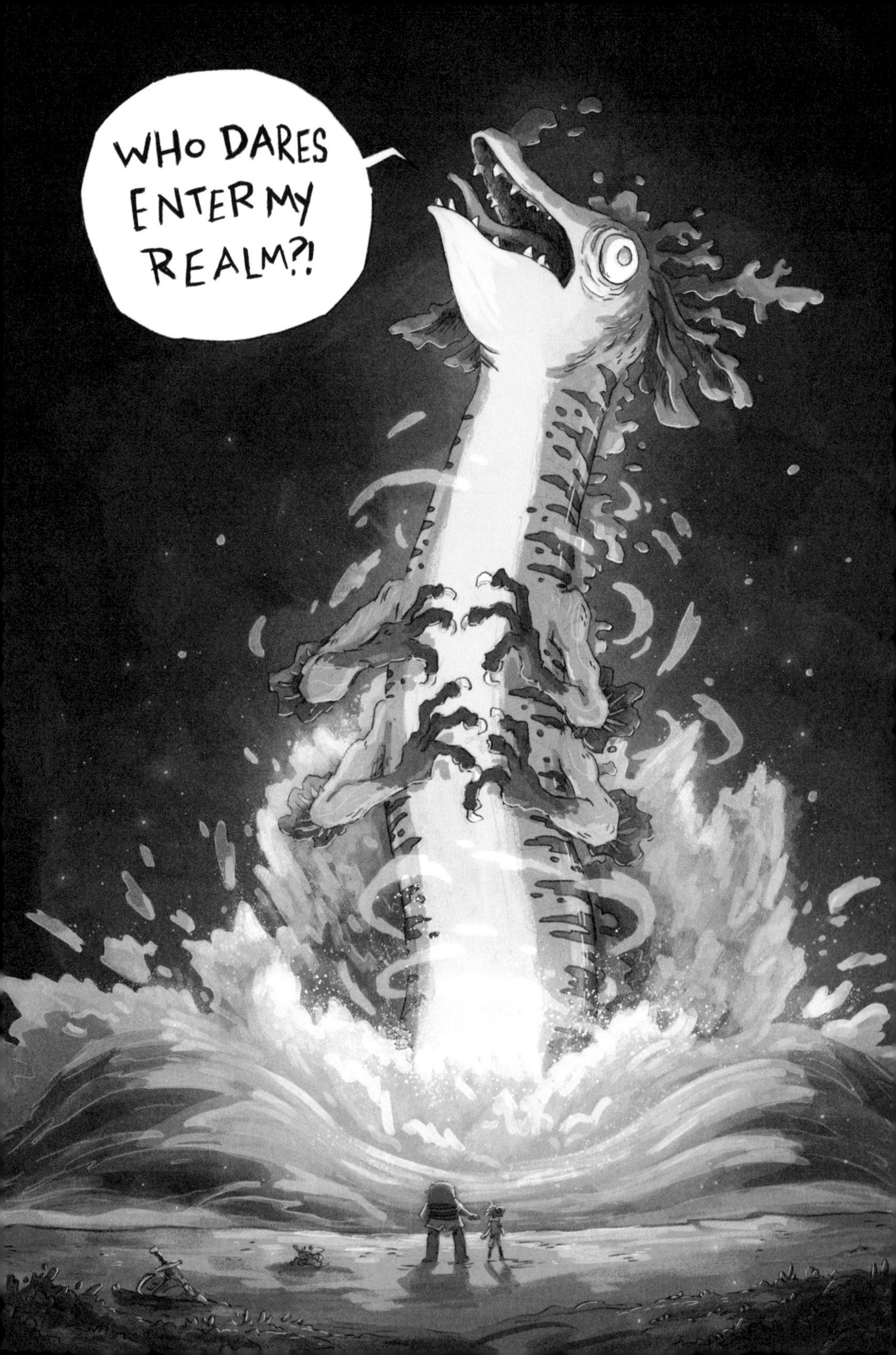
WHO DARES ENTER MY REALM?!

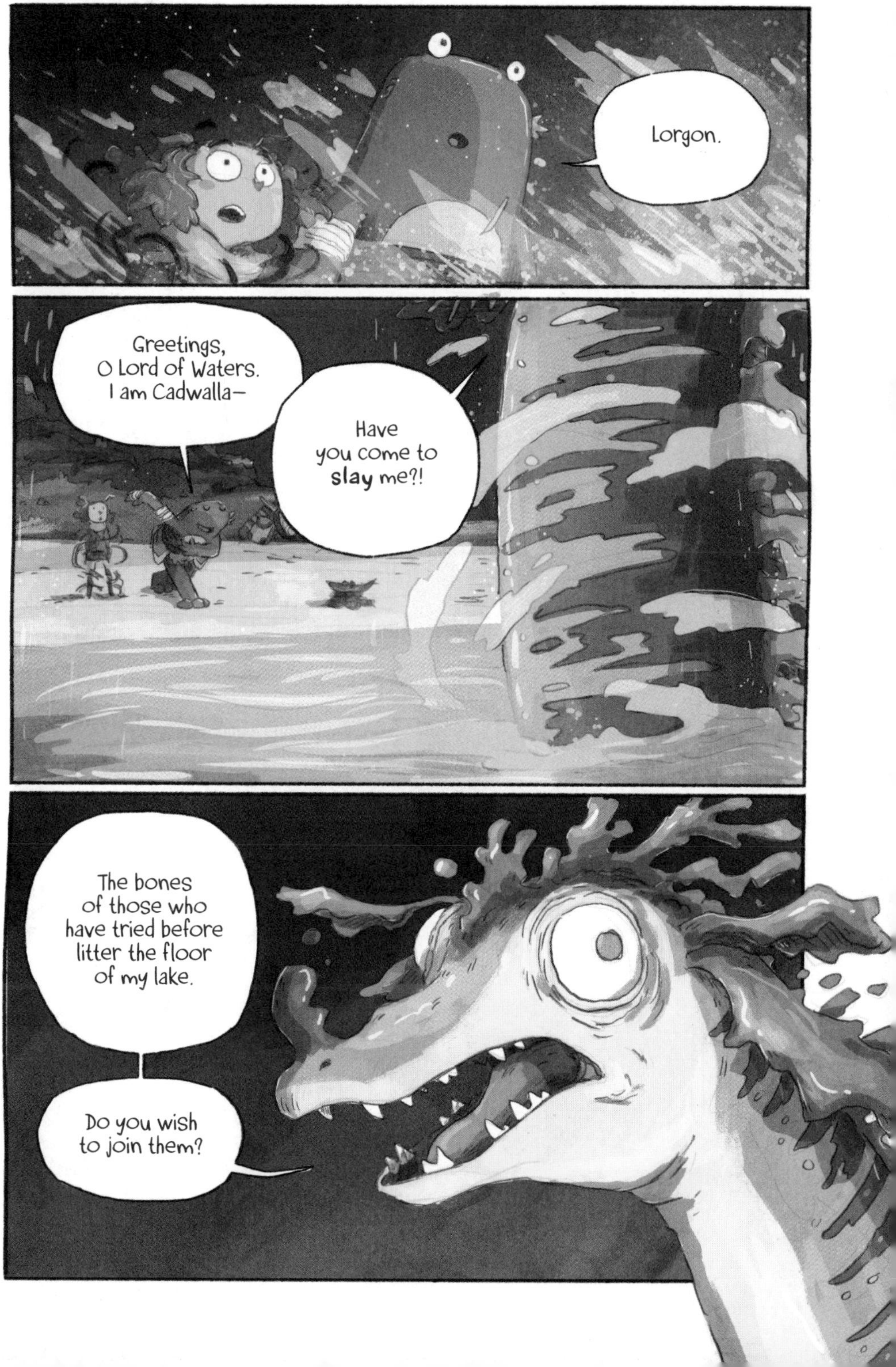
Lorgon.
Greetings, O Lord of Waters. I am Cadwalla–
Have you come to **slay** me?!
The bones of those who have tried before litter the floor of my lake.
Do you wish to join them?

No.
We aren't
here to—

You doubt
the veracity
of my claim?!
Insolent
knave!

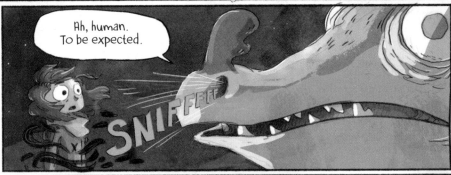

WHOOOSH

Ah, human.
To be expected.

SNIFFFF

But this . . .
Impossible.

SNUFF

Your nose doesn't fail you.
I'm a **Galdurian**. There's a dragon
and a cat with us too.

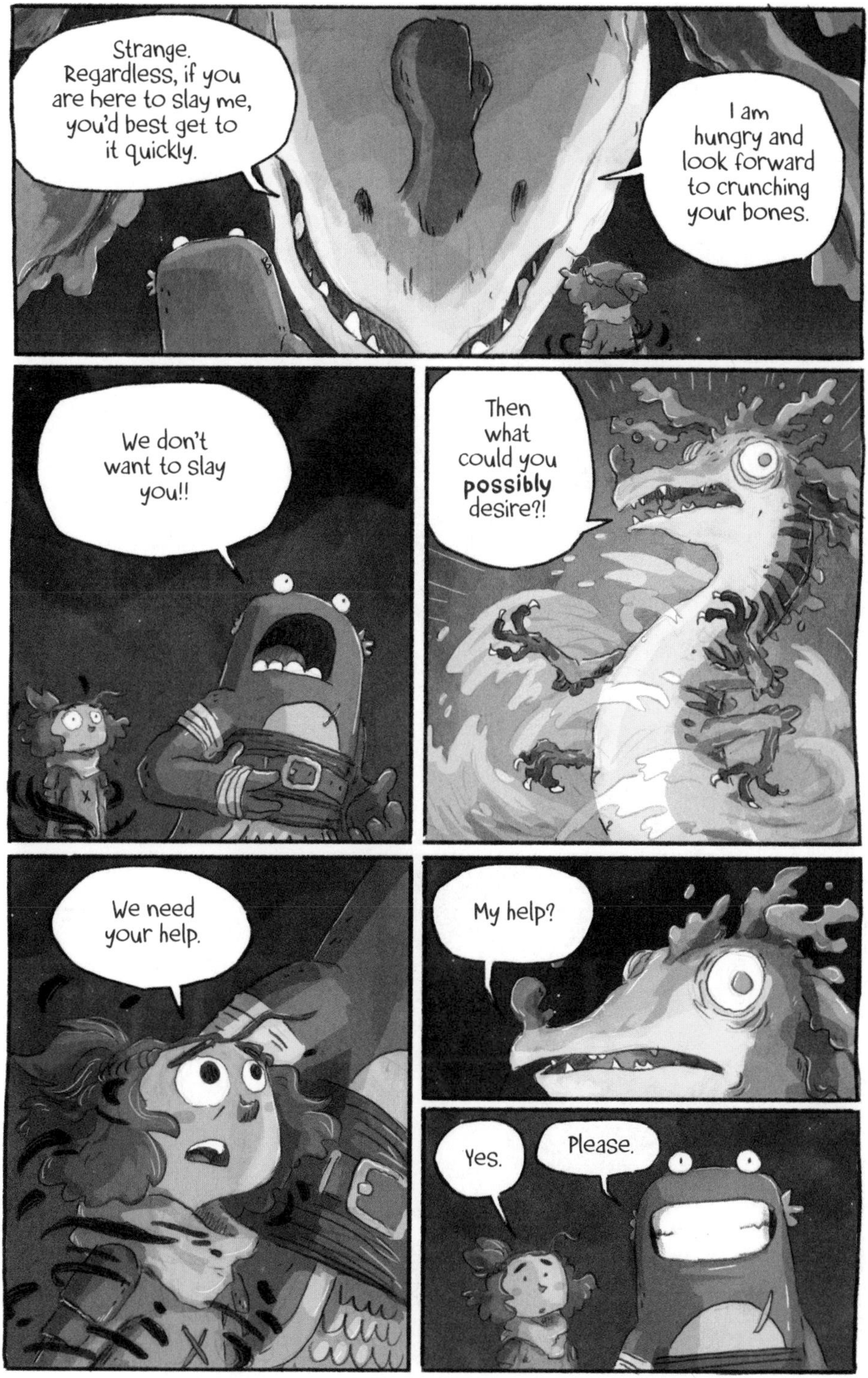
Strange. Regardless, if you are here to slay me, you'd best get to it quickly.
I am hungry and look forward to crunching your bones.
We don't want to slay you!!
Then what could you **possibly** desire?!
We need your help.
My help?
Yes.
Please.

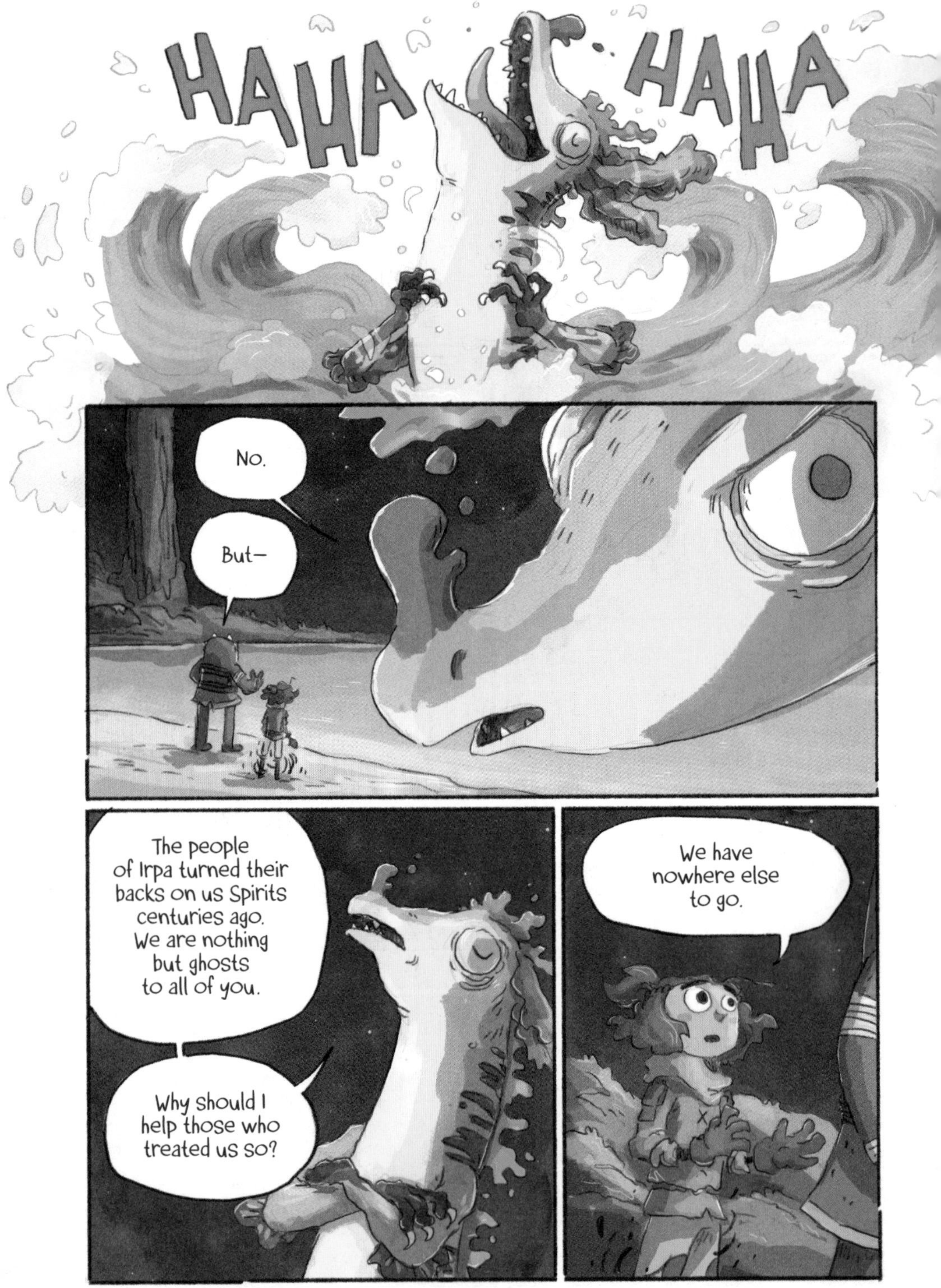
HAHA HAHA
No.
But—
The people of Irpa turned their backs on us Spirits centuries ago. We are nothing but ghosts to all of you.
Why should I help those who treated us so?
We have nowhere else to go.

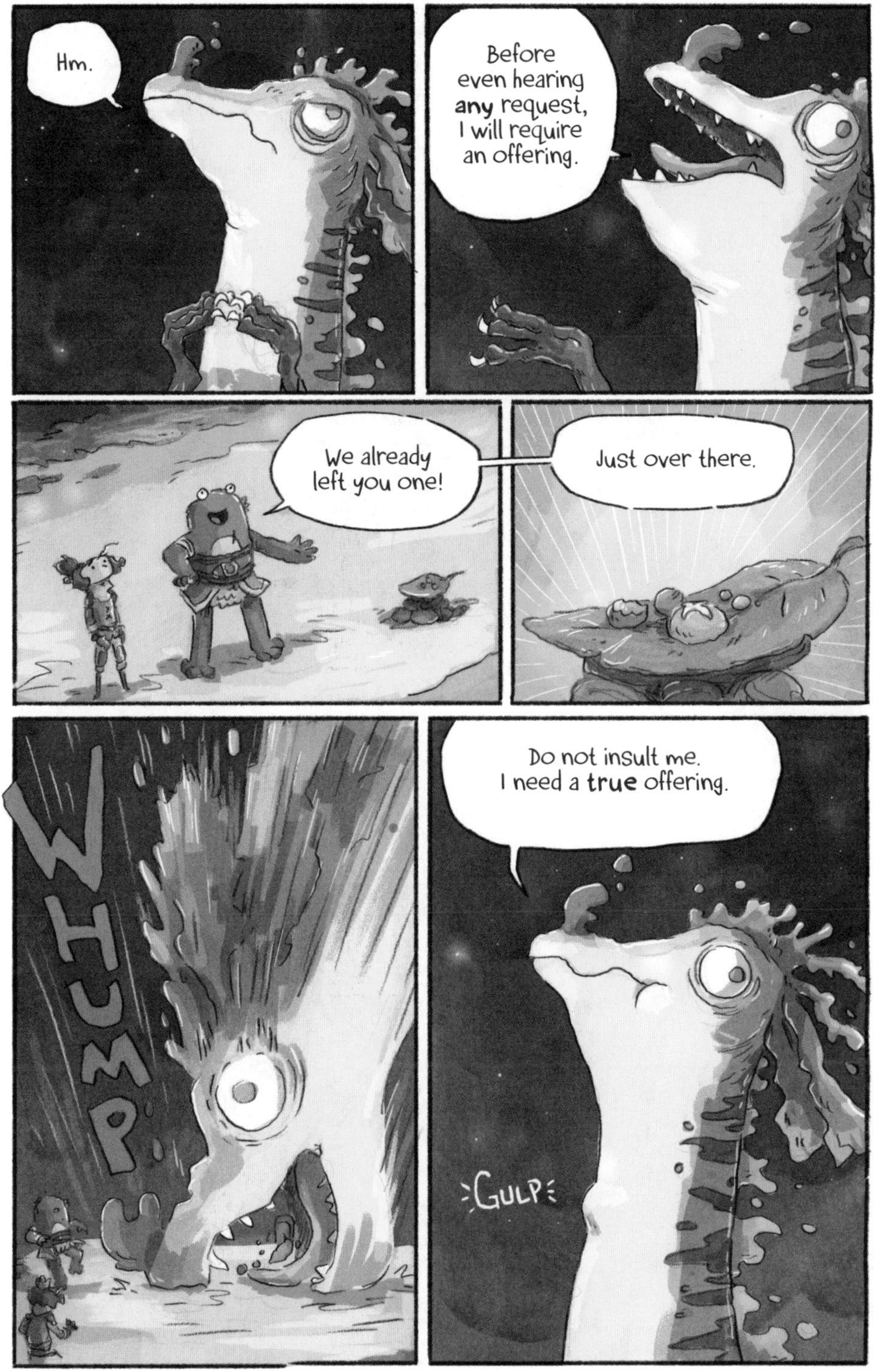
Hm.
Before even hearing **any** request, I will require an offering.
We already left you one!
Just over there.
WHUMP
Do not insult me. I need a **true** offering.
GULP

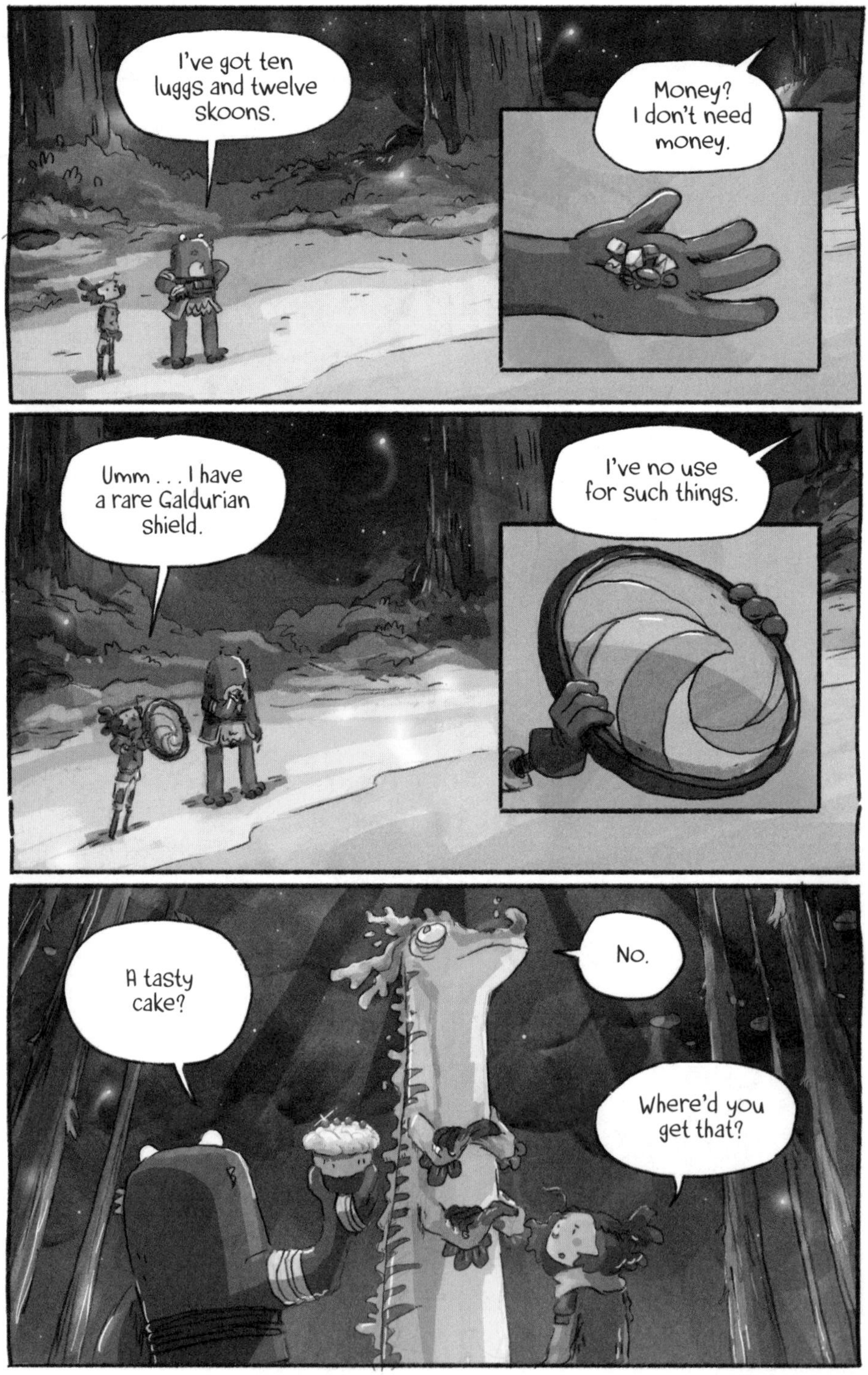
I've got ten luggs and twelve skoons.
Money? I don't need money.
Umm . . . I have a rare Galdurian shield.
I've no use for such things.
A tasty cake?
No.
Where'd you get that?

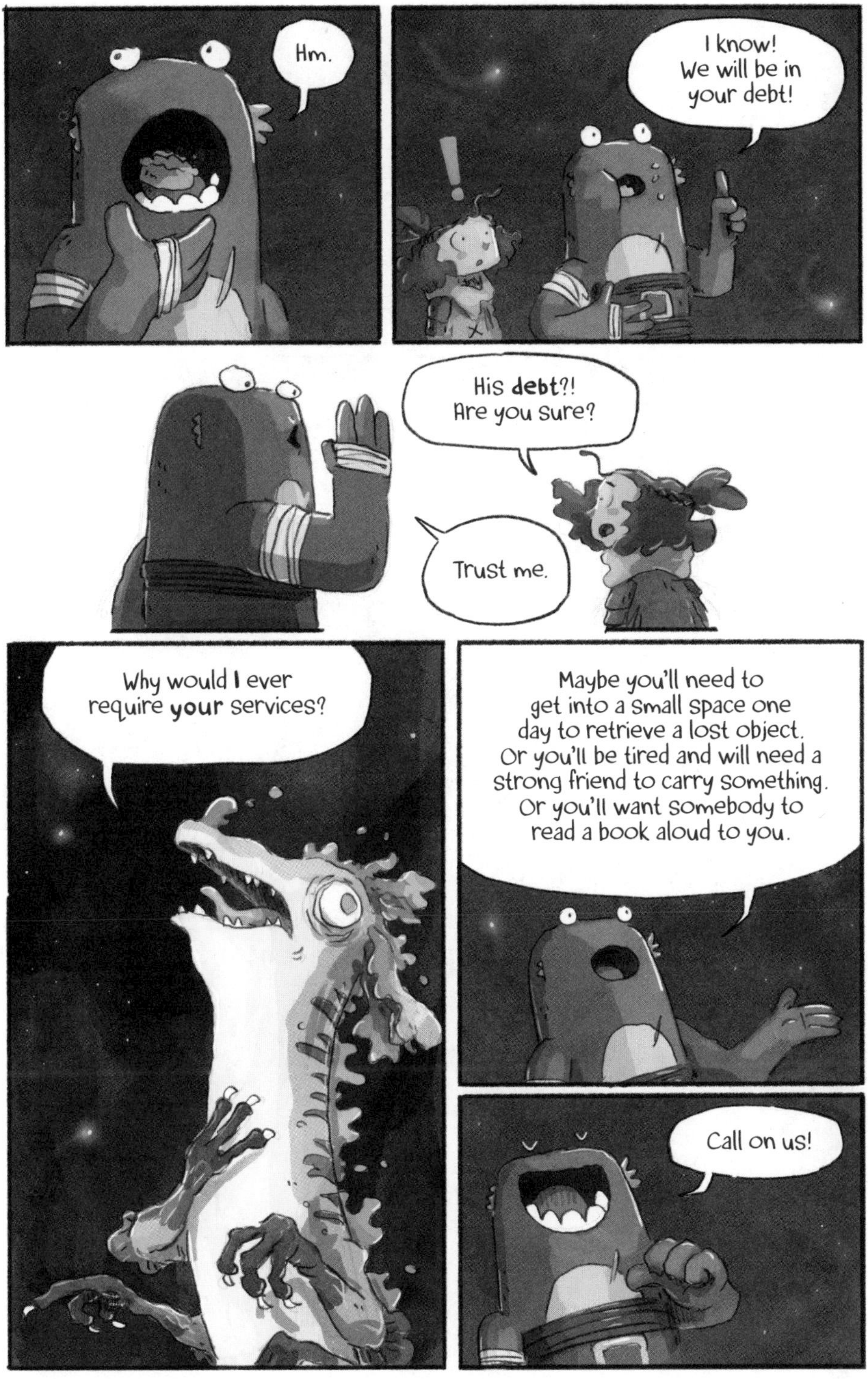
Hm.
I know! We will be in your debt!
!
His **debt**?! Are you sure?
Trust me.
Why would **I** ever require **your** services?
Maybe you'll need to get into a small space one day to retrieve a lost object. Or you'll be tired and will need a strong friend to carry something. Or you'll want somebody to read a book aloud to you.
Call on us!

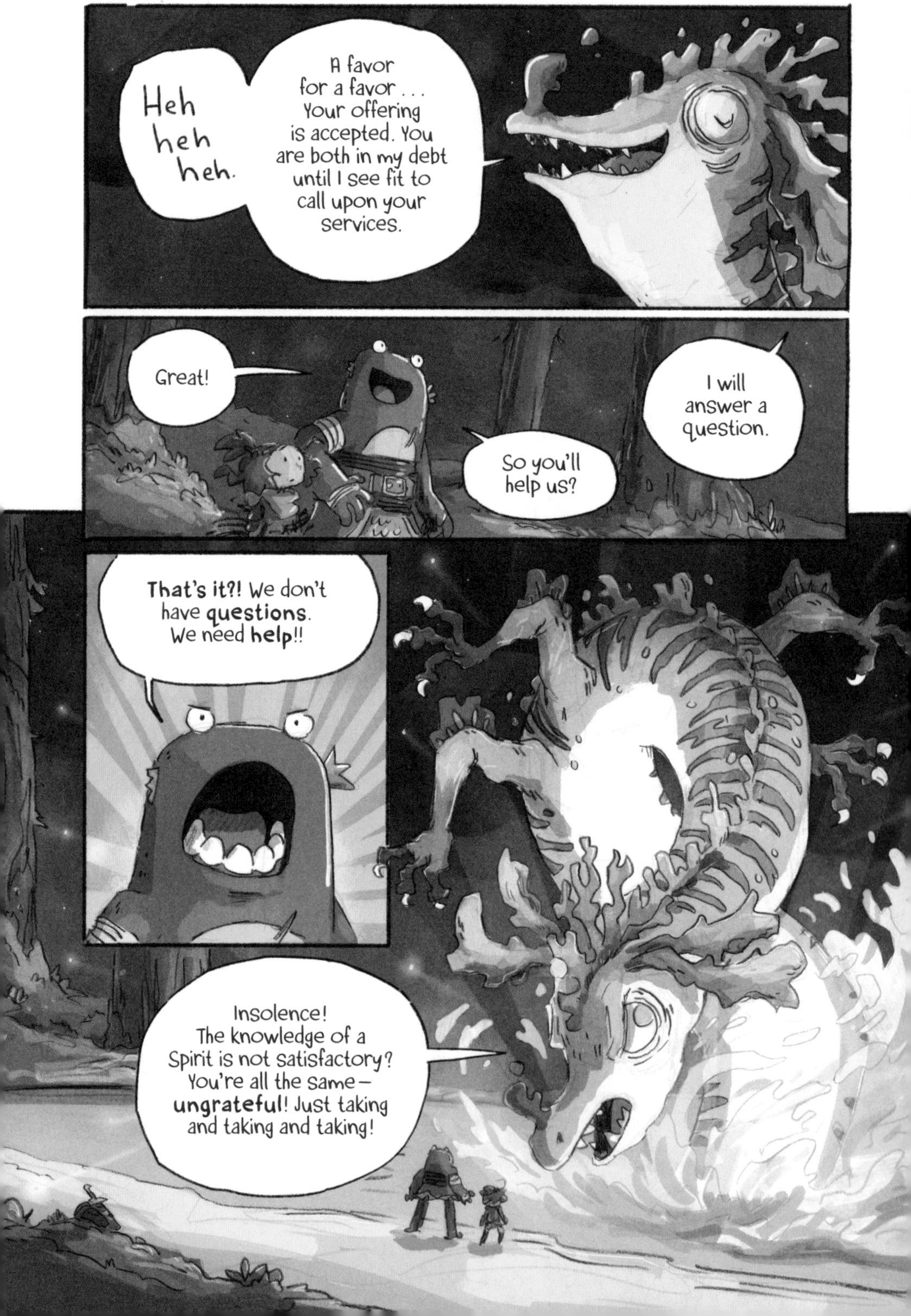
Heh heh heh.
A favor for a favor . . . Your offering is accepted. You are both in my debt until I see fit to call upon your services.
Great!
So you'll help us?
I will answer a question.
That's it?! We don't have **questions**. We need **help**!!
Insolence! The knowledge of a Spirit is not satisfactory? You're all the same— **ungrateful**! Just taking and taking and taking!

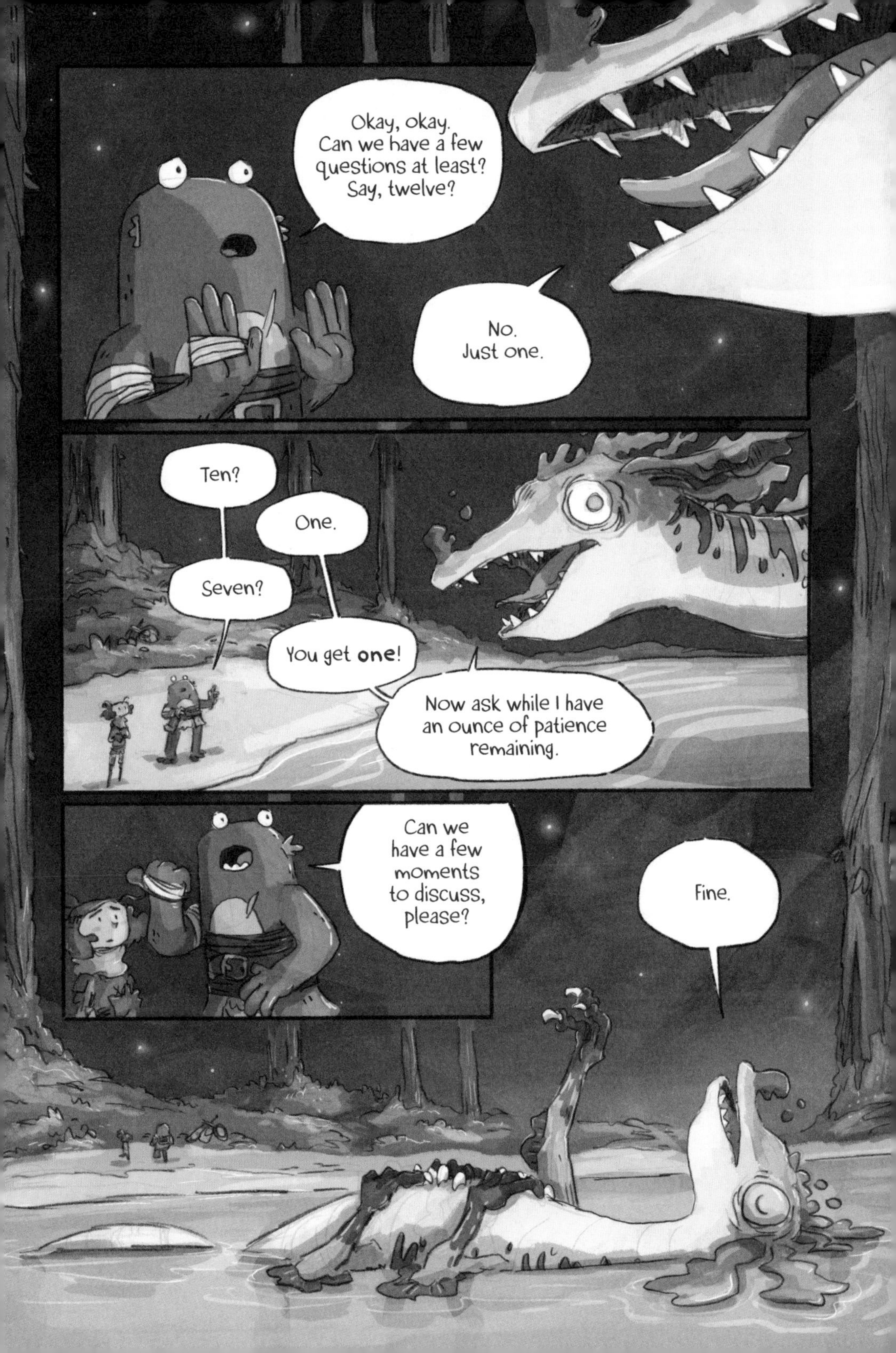
Okay, okay. Can we have a few questions at least? Say, twelve?
No. Just one.
Ten?
One.
Seven?
You get **one**!
Now ask while I have an ounce of patience remaining.
Can we have a few moments to discuss, please?
Fine.

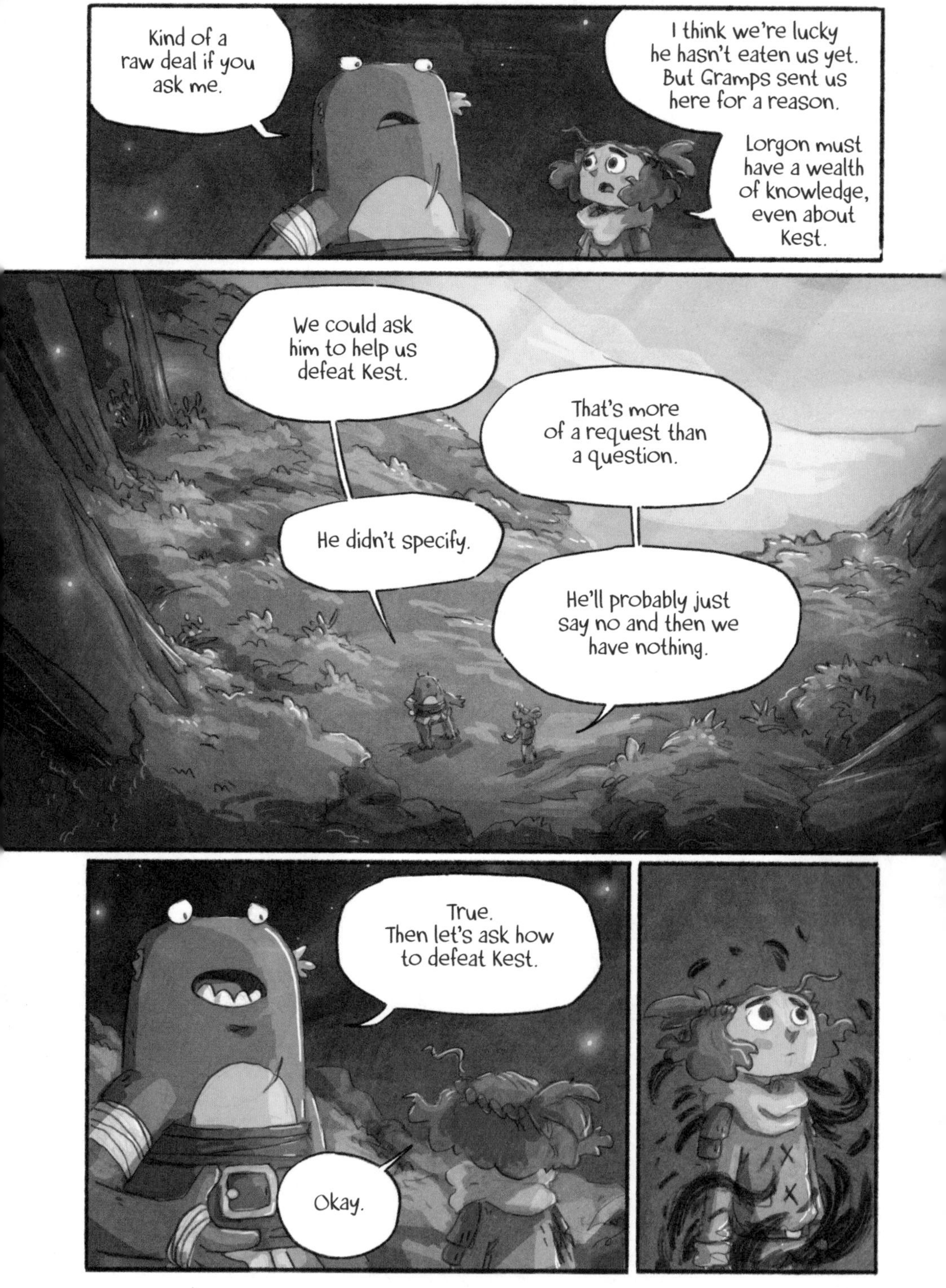
Kind of a raw deal if you ask me.
I think we're lucky he hasn't eaten us yet. But Gramps sent us here for a reason.
Lorgon must have a wealth of knowledge, even about Kest.
We could ask him to help us defeat Kest.
That's more of a request than a question.
He didn't specify.
He'll probably just say no and then we have nothing.
True. Then let's ask how to defeat Kest.
Okay.

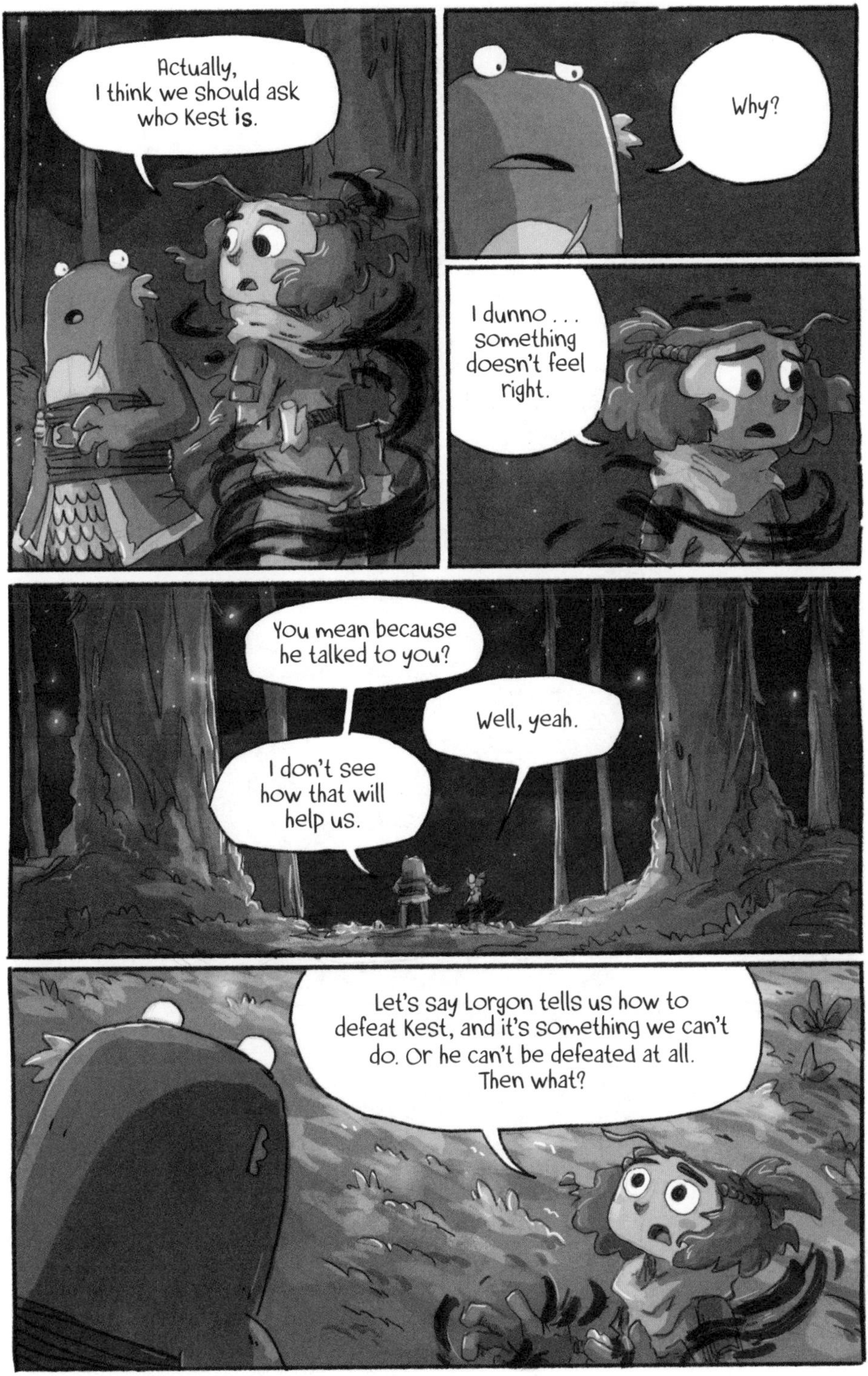
Actually, I think we should ask who Kest **is**.
Why?
I dunno . . . something doesn't feel right.
You mean because he talked to you?
Well, yeah.
I don't see how that will help us.
Let's say Lorgon tells us how to defeat Kest, and it's something we can't do. Or he can't be defeated at all. Then what?

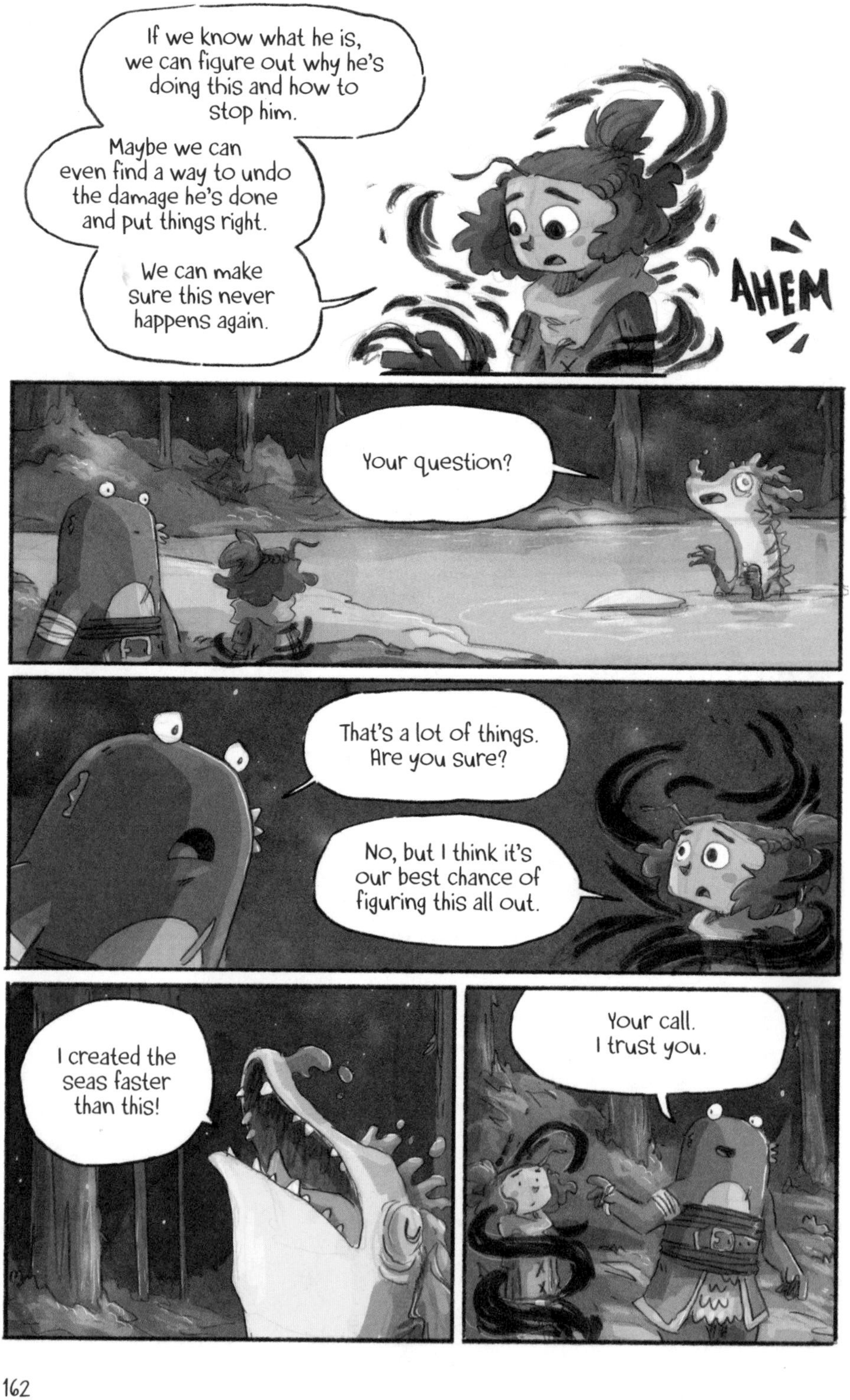

If we know what he is, we can figure out why he's doing this and how to stop him.
Maybe we can even find a way to undo the damage he's done and put things right.
We can make sure this never happens again.
AHEM
Your question?
That's a lot of things. Are you sure?
No, but I think it's our best chance of figuring this all out.
I created the seas faster than this!
Your call. I trust you.

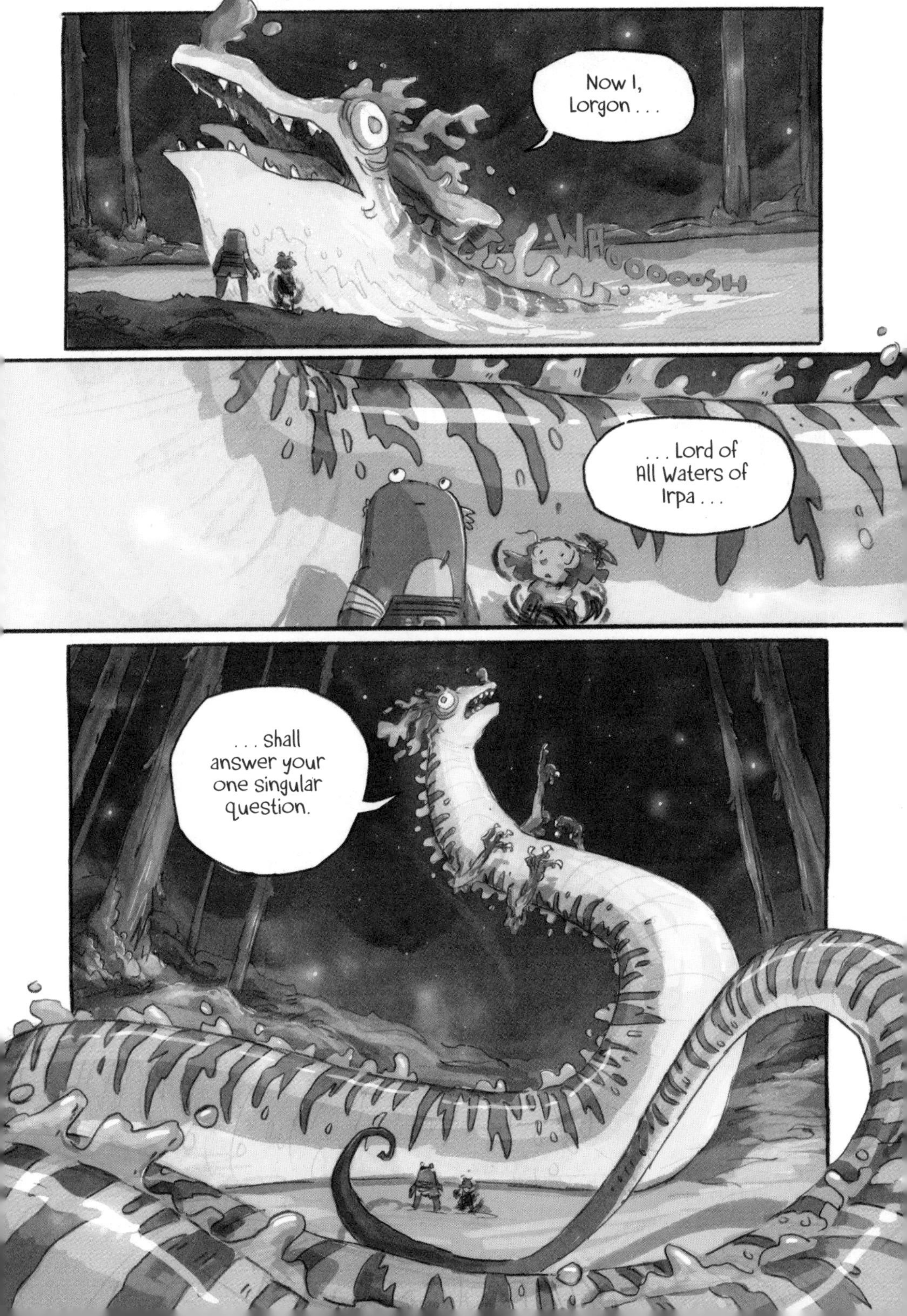
Now I,
Lorgon . . .
WHOOOOOOSH
. . . Lord of
All Waters of
Irpa . . .
. . . shall
answer your
one singular
question.

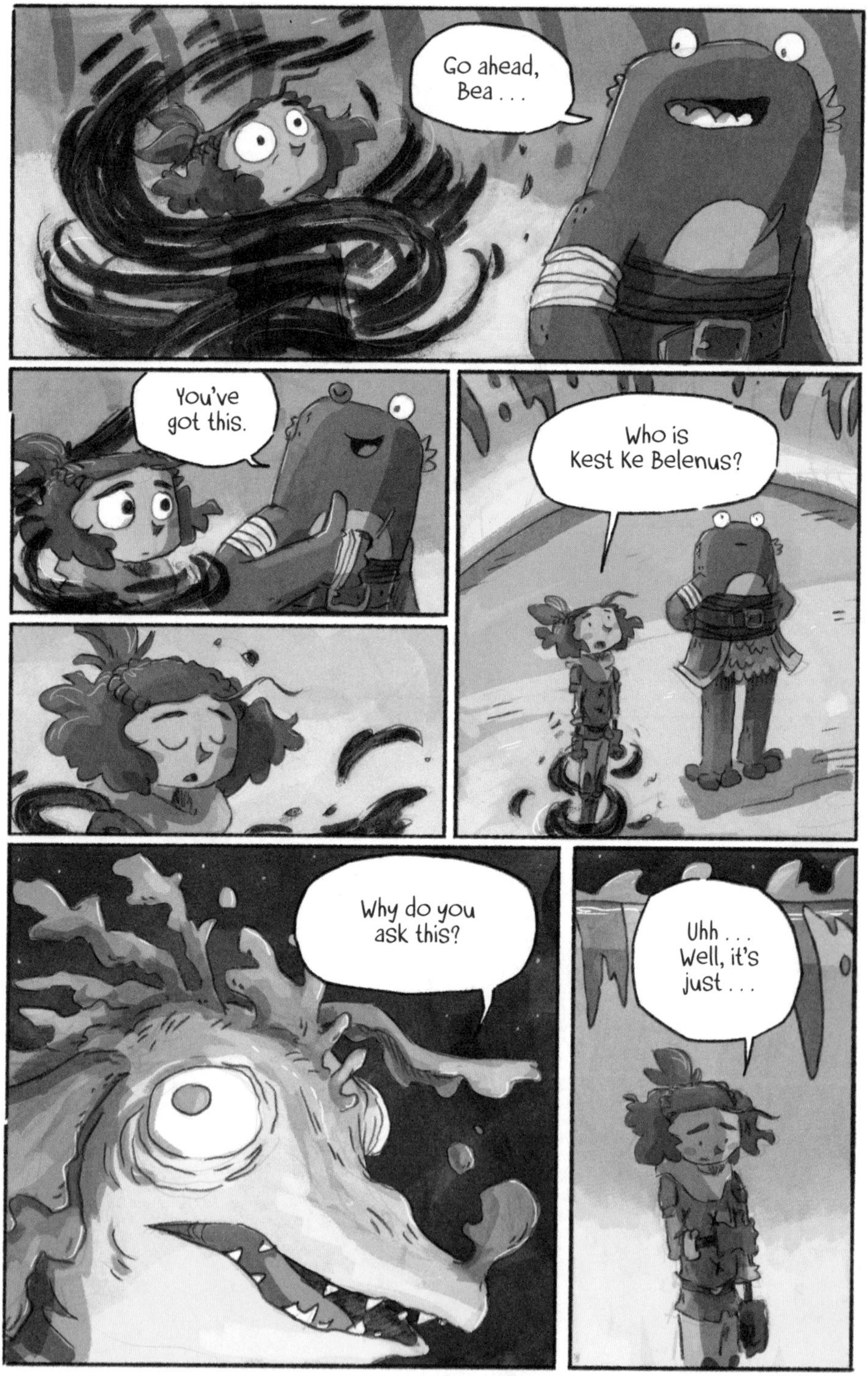
Go ahead, Bea . . .
You've got this.
Who is Kest Ke Belenus?
Why do you ask this?
Uhh . . . Well, it's just . . .

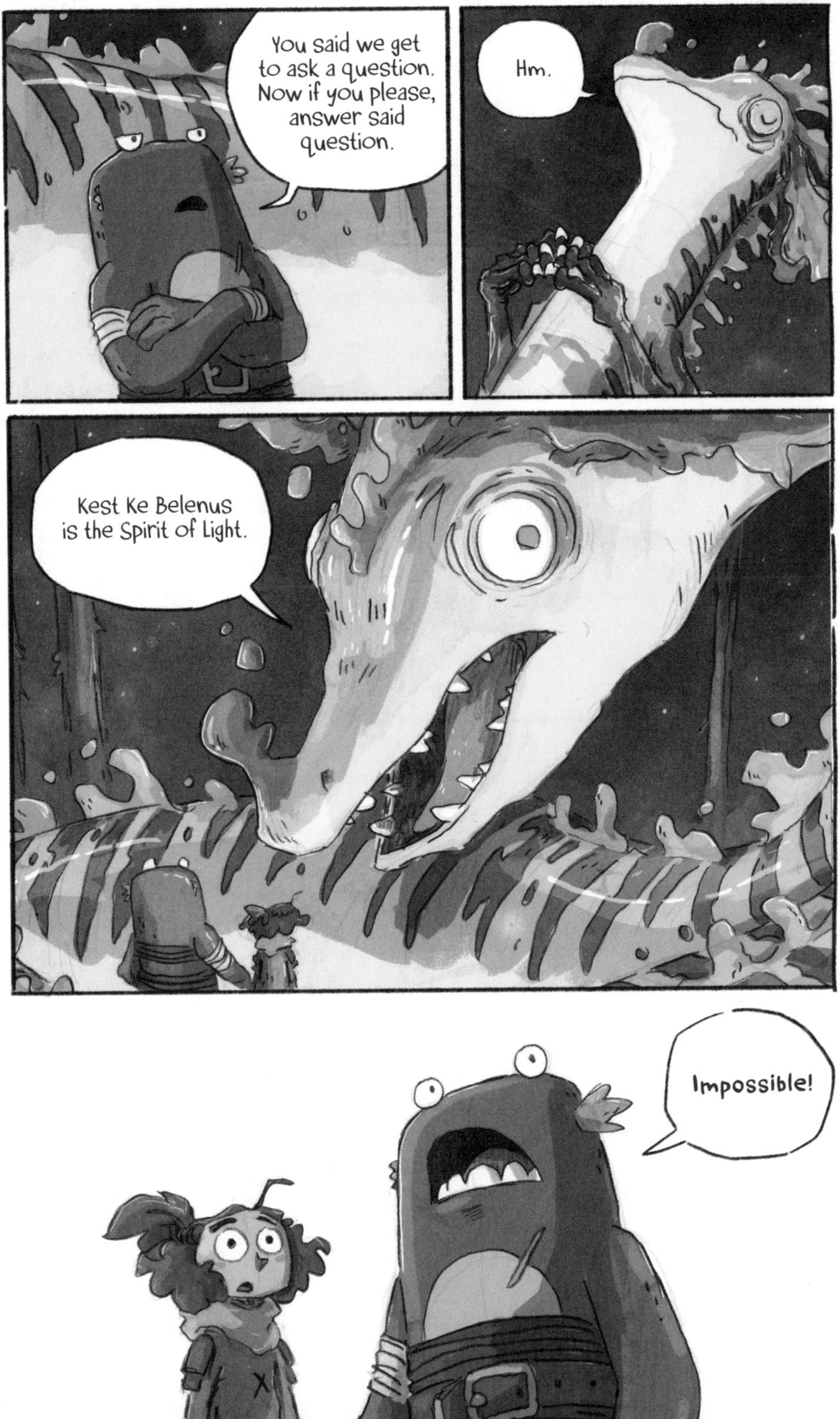
You said we get to ask a question. Now if you please, answer said question.
Hm.
Kest Ke Belenus is the Spirit of Light.
Impossible!

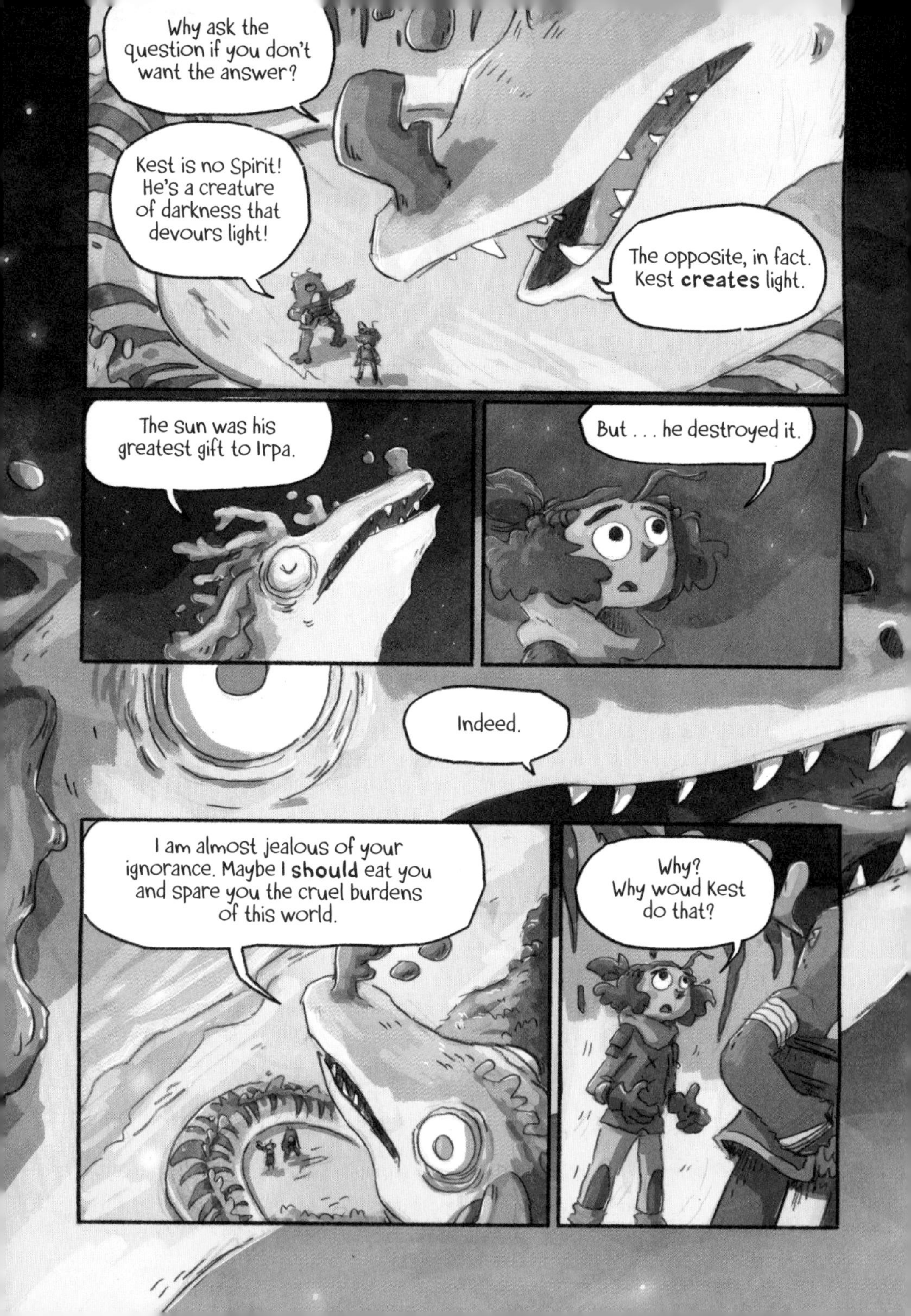
Why ask the question if you don't want the answer?
Kest is no Spirit! He's a creature of darkness that devours light!
The opposite, in fact. Kest **creates** light.
The sun was his greatest gift to Irpa.
But . . . he destroyed it.
Indeed.
I am almost jealous of your ignorance. Maybe I **should** eat you and spare you the cruel burdens of this world.
Why? Why woud Kest do that?

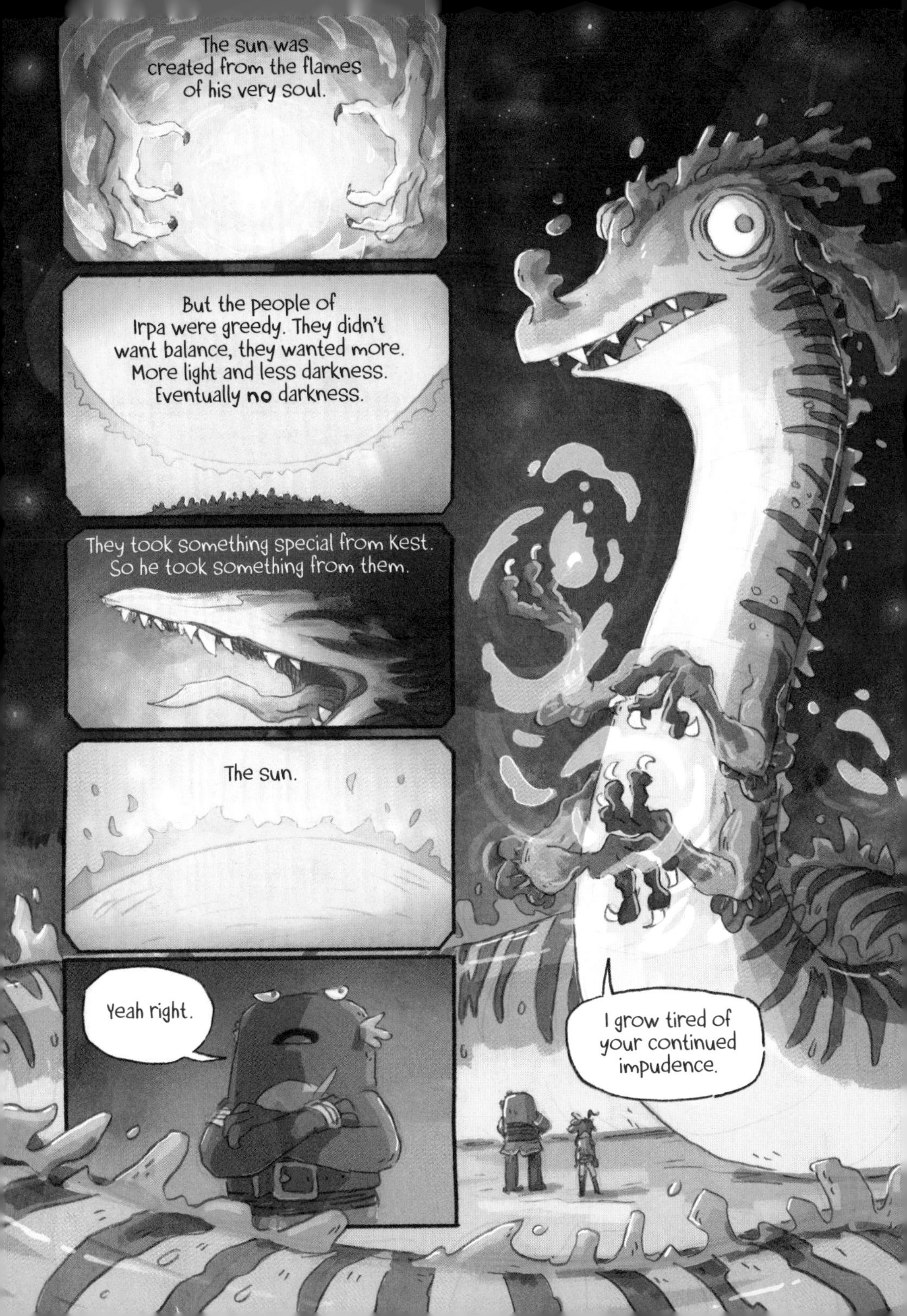
The sun was created from the flames of his very soul.
But the people of Irpa were greedy. They didn't want balance, they wanted more. More light and less darkness. Eventually **no** darkness.
They took something special from Kest. So he took something from them.
The sun.
Yeah right.
I grow tired of your continued impudence.

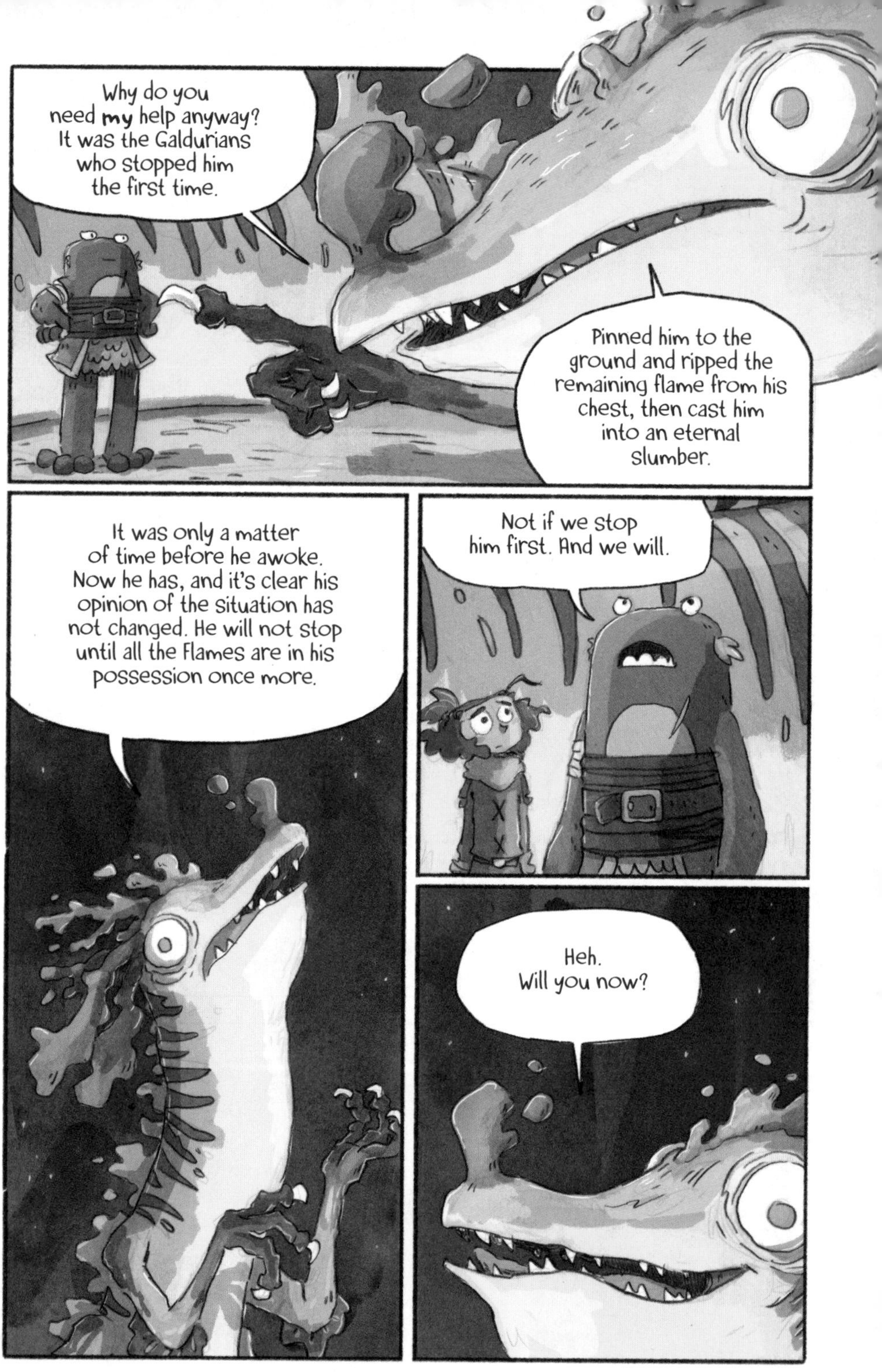
Why do you need **my** help anyway? It was the Galdurians who stopped him the first time.
Pinned him to the ground and ripped the remaining flame from his chest, then cast him into an eternal slumber.
It was only a matter of time before he awoke. Now he has, and it's clear his opinion of the situation has not changed. He will not stop until all the Flames are in his possession once more.
Not if we stop him first. And we will.
Heh. Will you now?

Yes! I will finish what my people started and rescue the light of this world from evil!

And pray tell, how do you plan on doing that?

I will destroy Kest if it's the last thing I do.

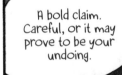

A bold claim. Careful, or it may prove to be your undoing.

But can it be done? How do we stop him?

Kill him, you mean? Oh yes, stab him in the heart, drop a boulder on him, chop off his head . . .

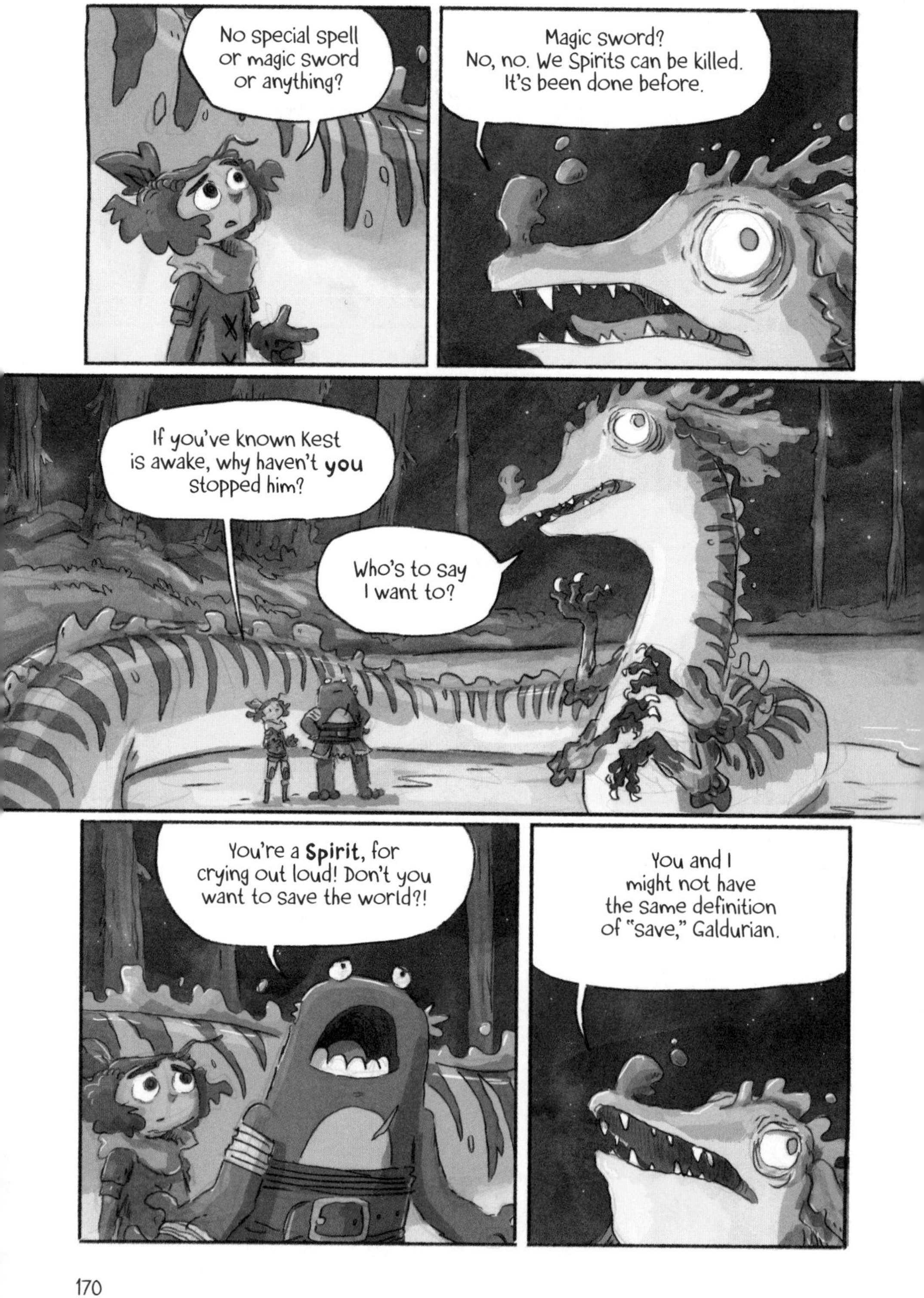
No special spell or magic sword or anything?
Magic sword? No, no. We Spirits can be killed. It's been done before.
If you've known Kest is awake, why haven't **you** stopped him?
Who's to say I want to?
You're a **Spirit**, for crying out loud! Don't you want to save the world?!
You and I might not have the same definition of "save," Galdurian.

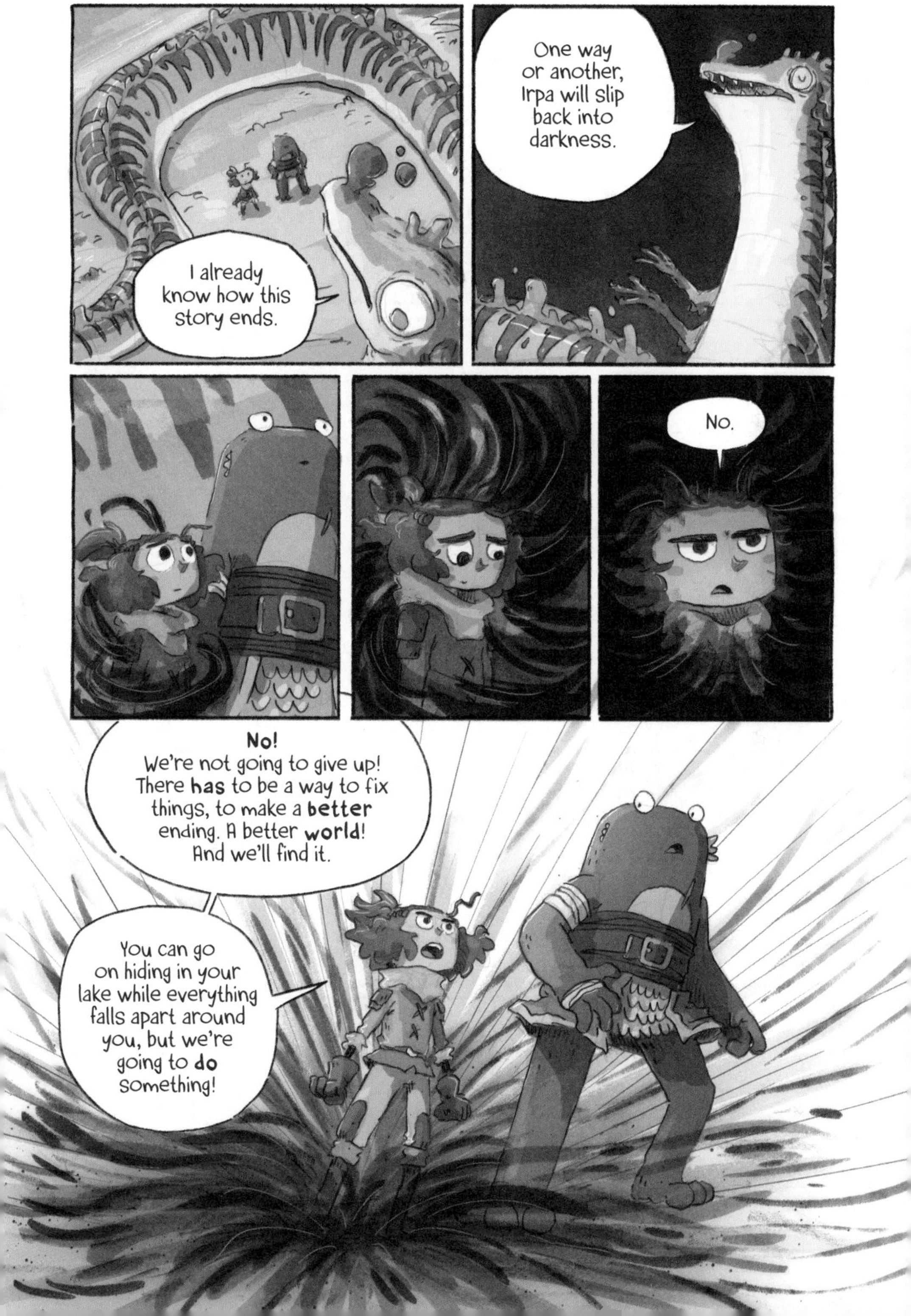
I already know how this story ends.
One way or another, Irpa will slip back into darkness.
No.
No! We're not going to give up! There has to be a way to fix things, to make a better ending. A better world! And we'll find it.
You can go on hiding in your lake while everything falls apart around you, but we're going to do something!

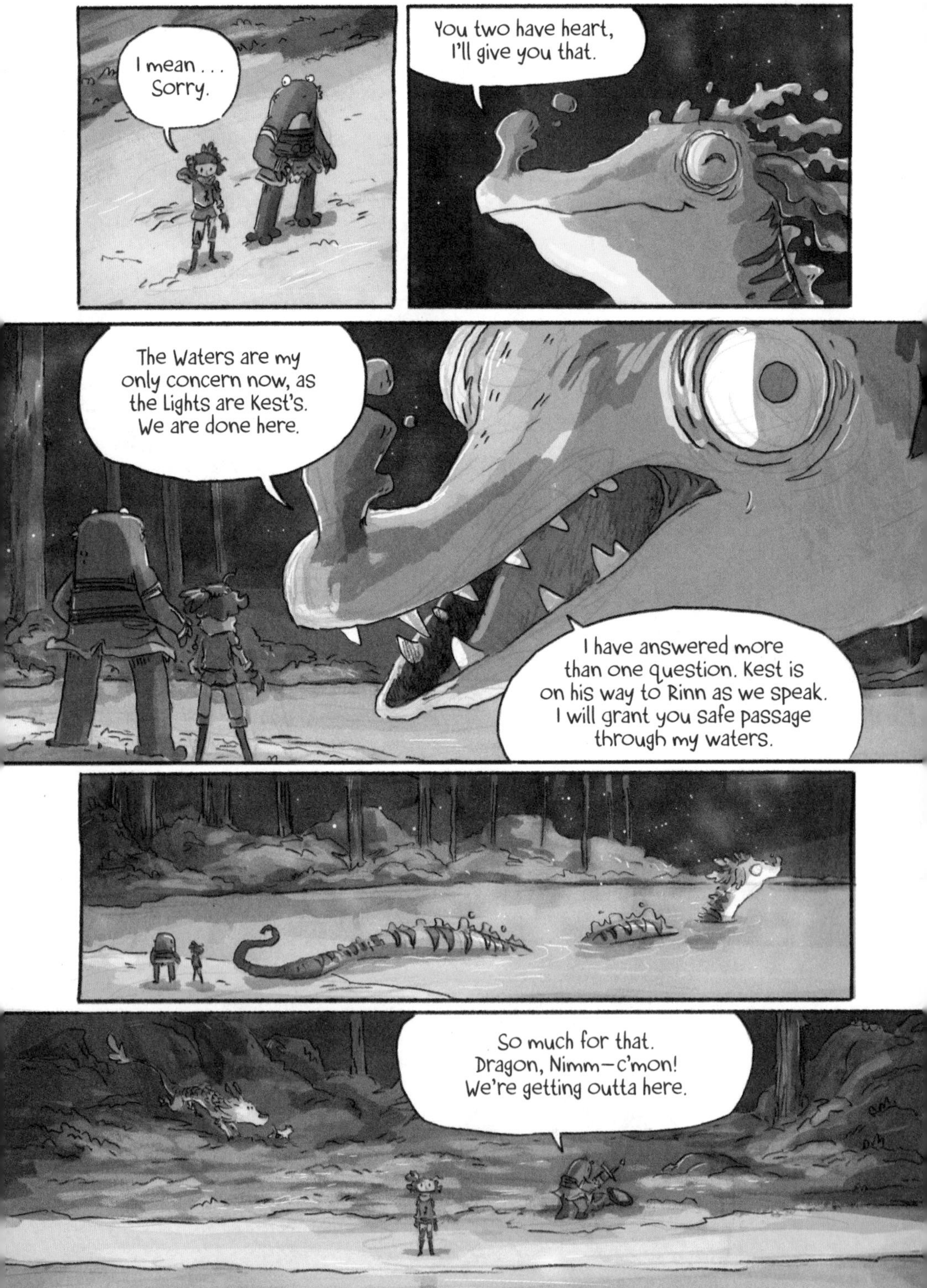
I mean . . . Sorry.
You two have heart, I'll give you that.
The Waters are my only concern now, as the Lights are Kest's. We are done here.
I have answered more than one question. Kest is on his way to Rinn as we speak. I will grant you safe passage through my waters.
So much for that. Dragon, Nimm—c'mon! We're getting outta here.

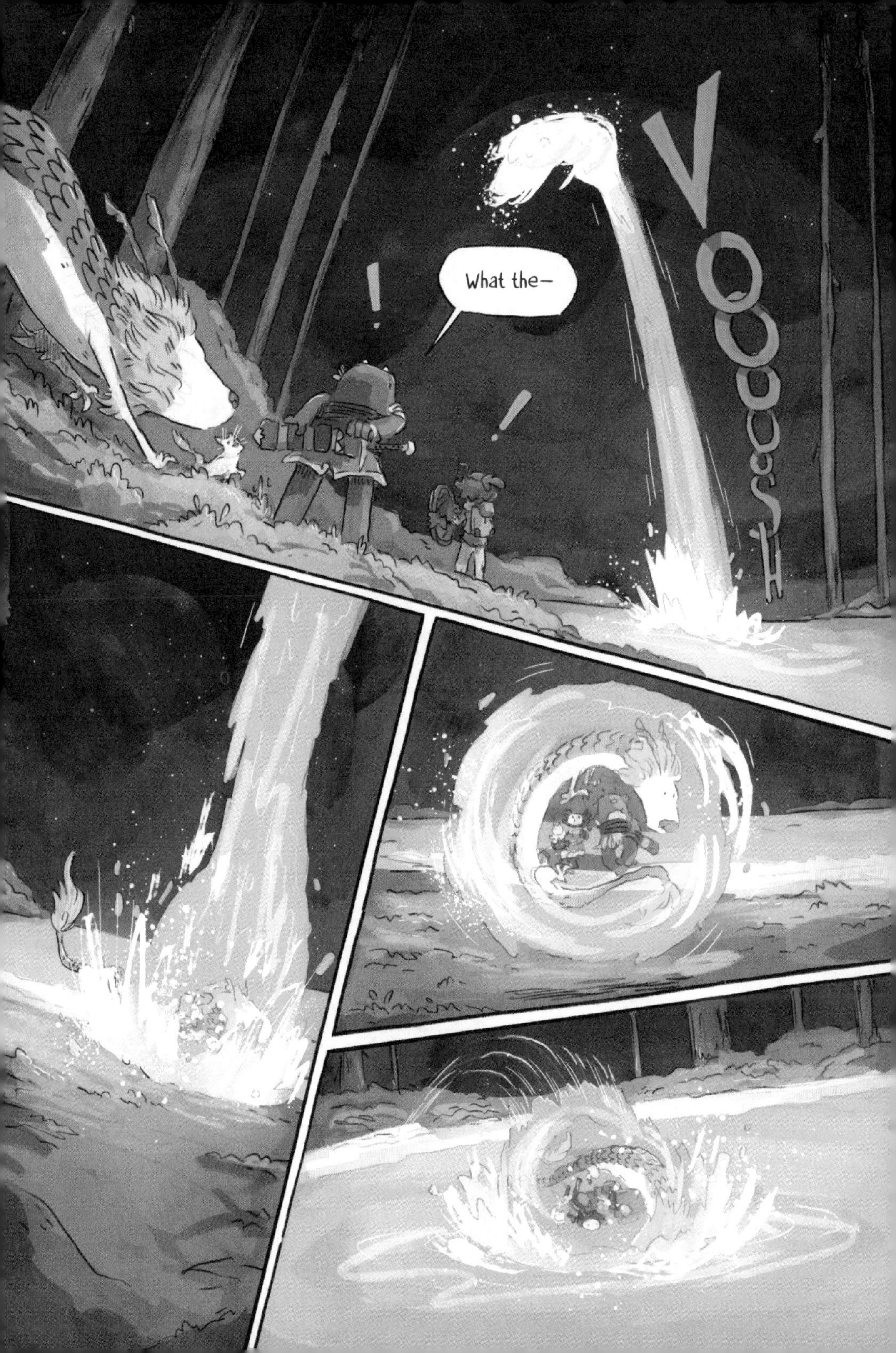
!
What the–
!
VOOOOOSH

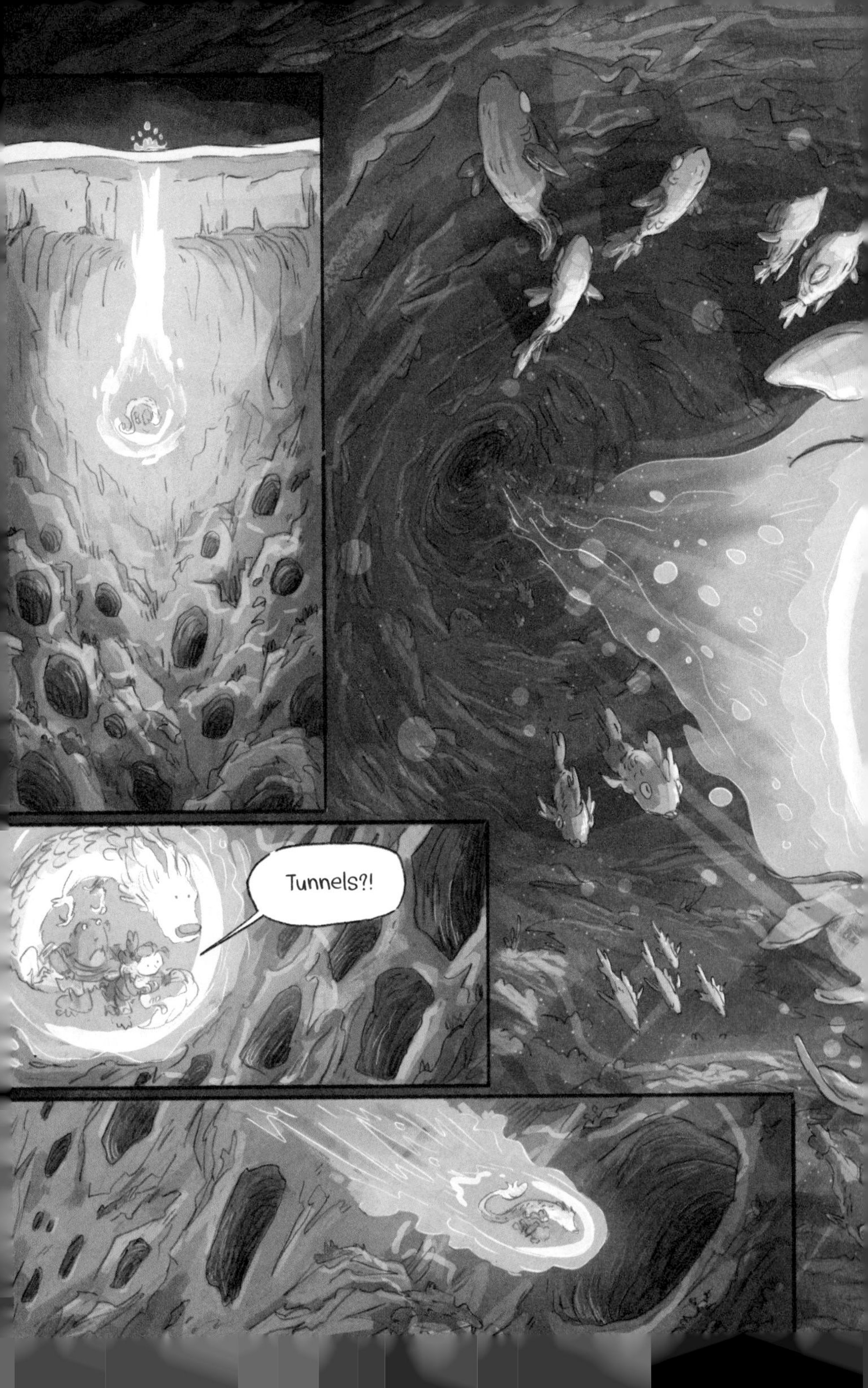
Tunnels?!

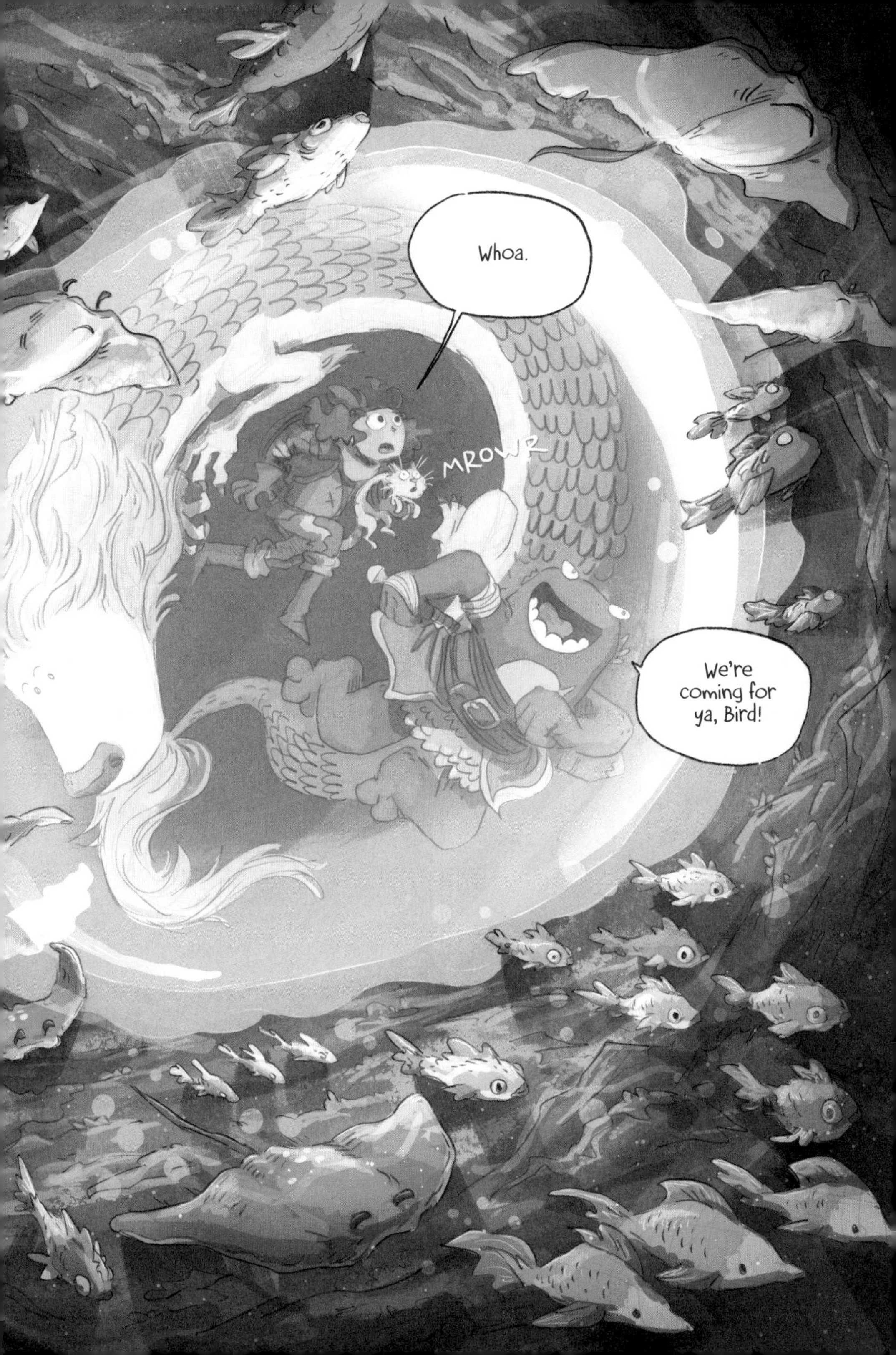
Whoa.
MROWR
We're coming for ya, Bird!

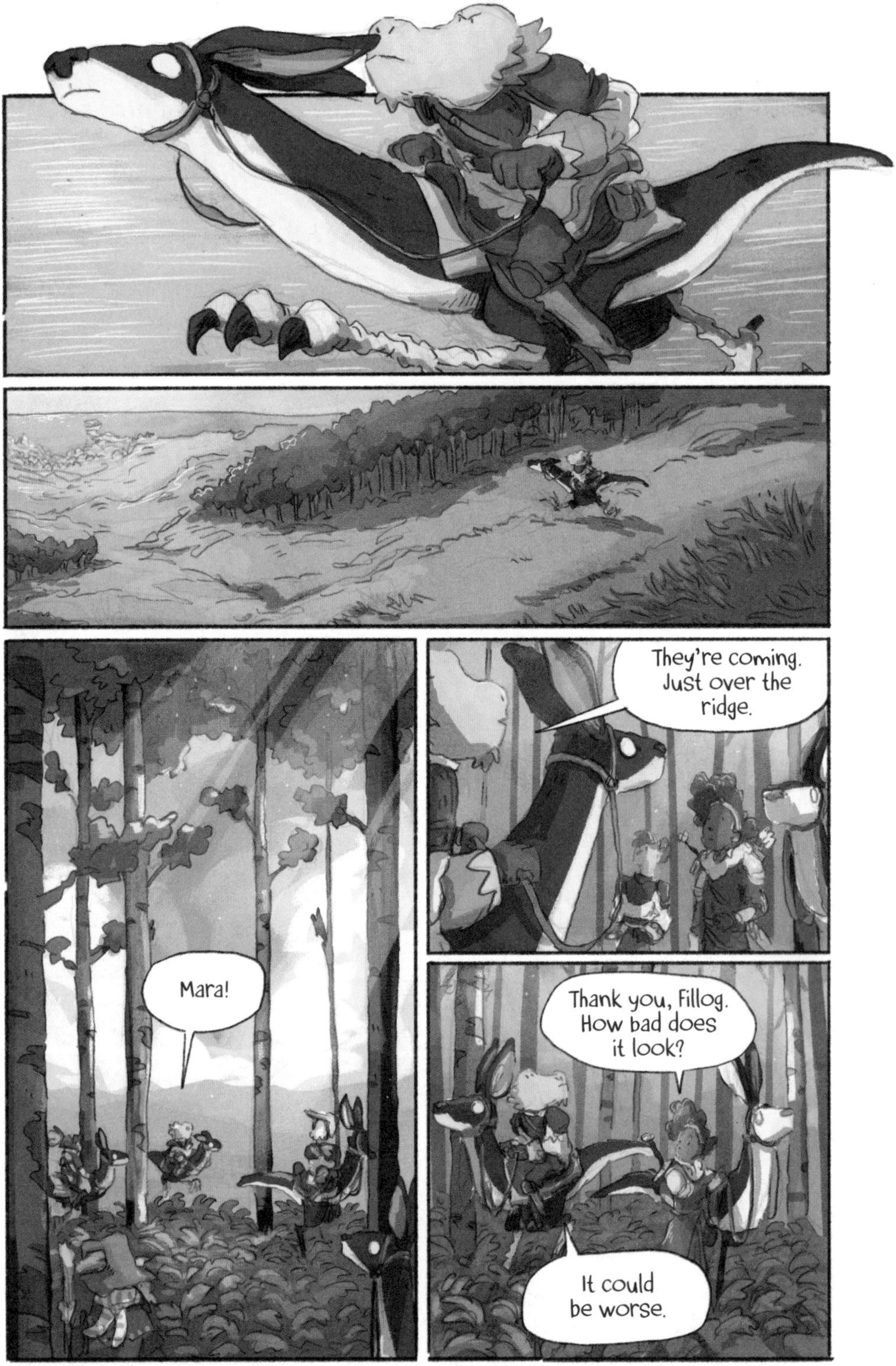

Mara!
They're coming. Just over the ridge.
Thank you, Fillog. How bad does it look?
It could be worse.

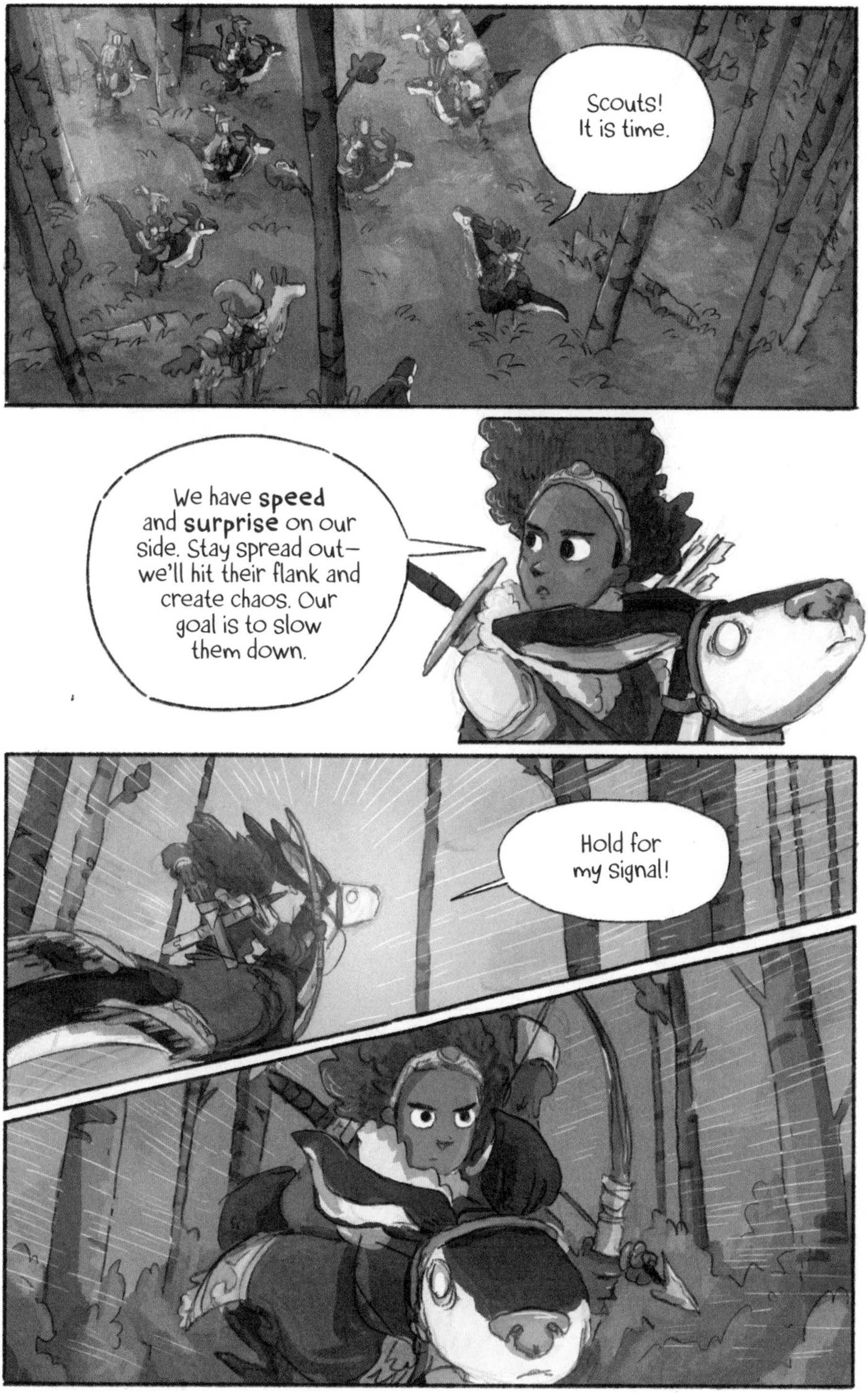
Scouts! It is time.
We have **speed** and **surprise** on our side. Stay spread out—we'll hit their flank and create chaos. Our goal is to slow them down.
Hold for my signal!

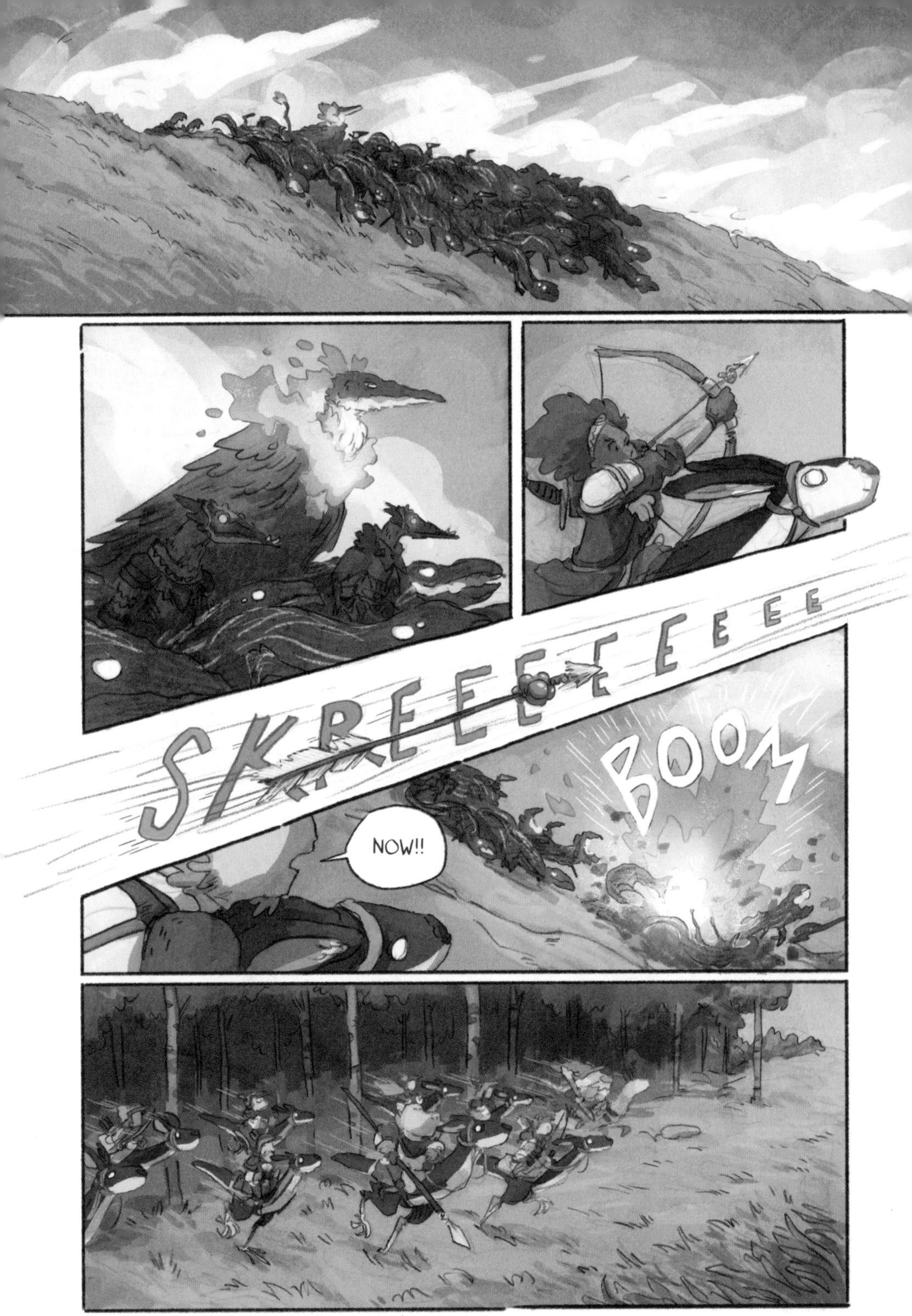
SKREEEEEEEEE
NOW!!
BOOM

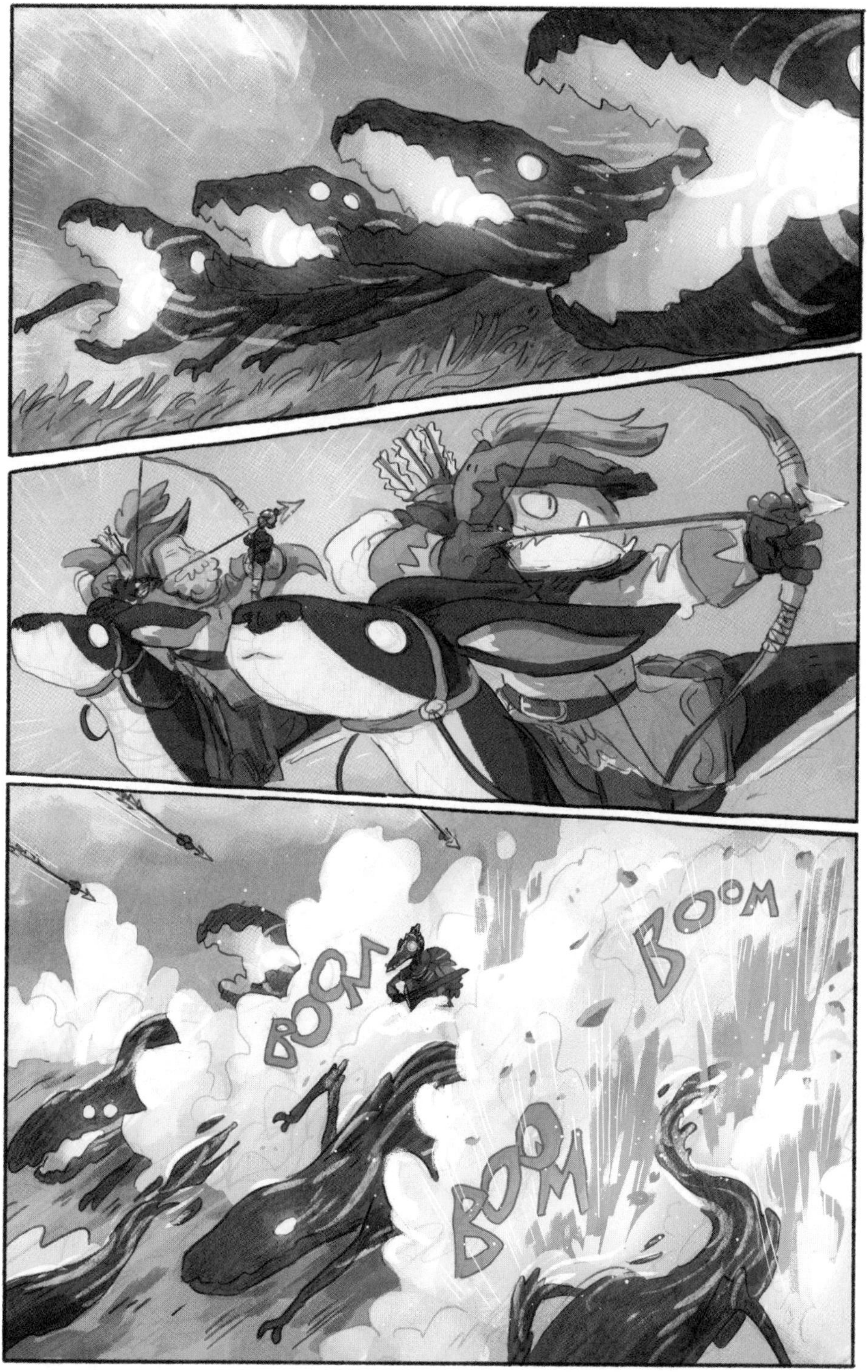
BOOM
BOOM
BOOM

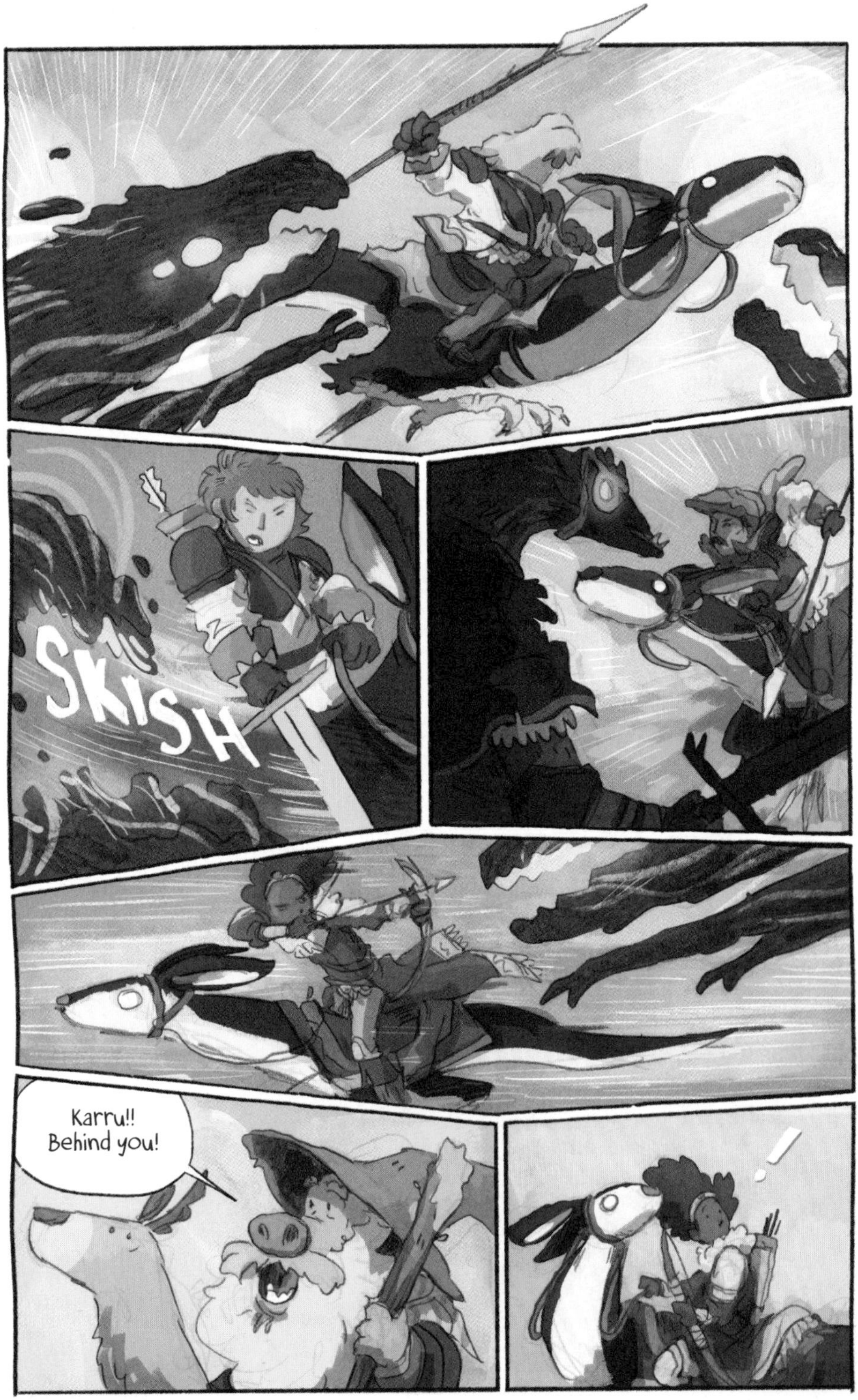
SKISH
Karru!! Behind you!
!

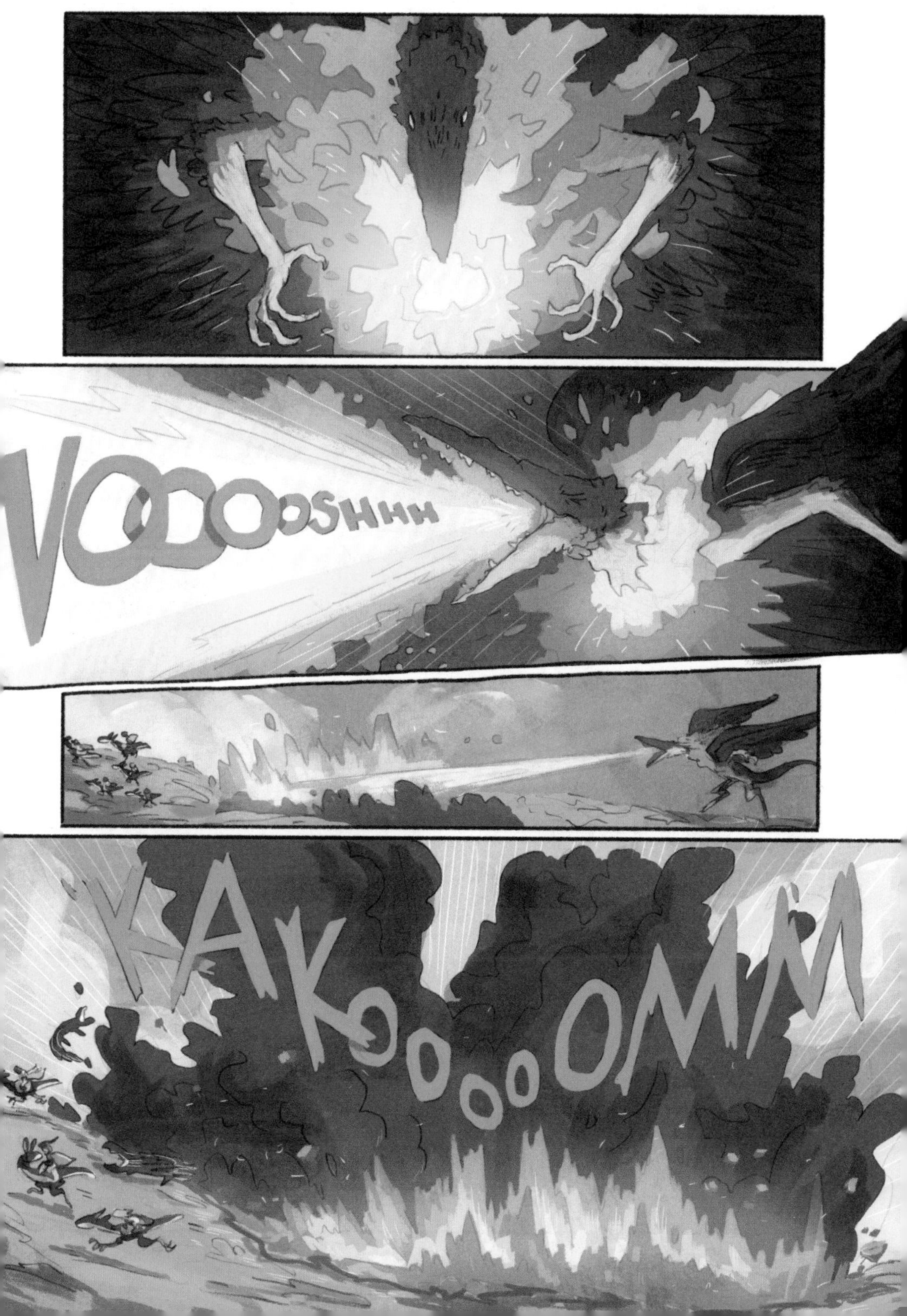
VOOOOOSHHH
KAKOOOOOMM

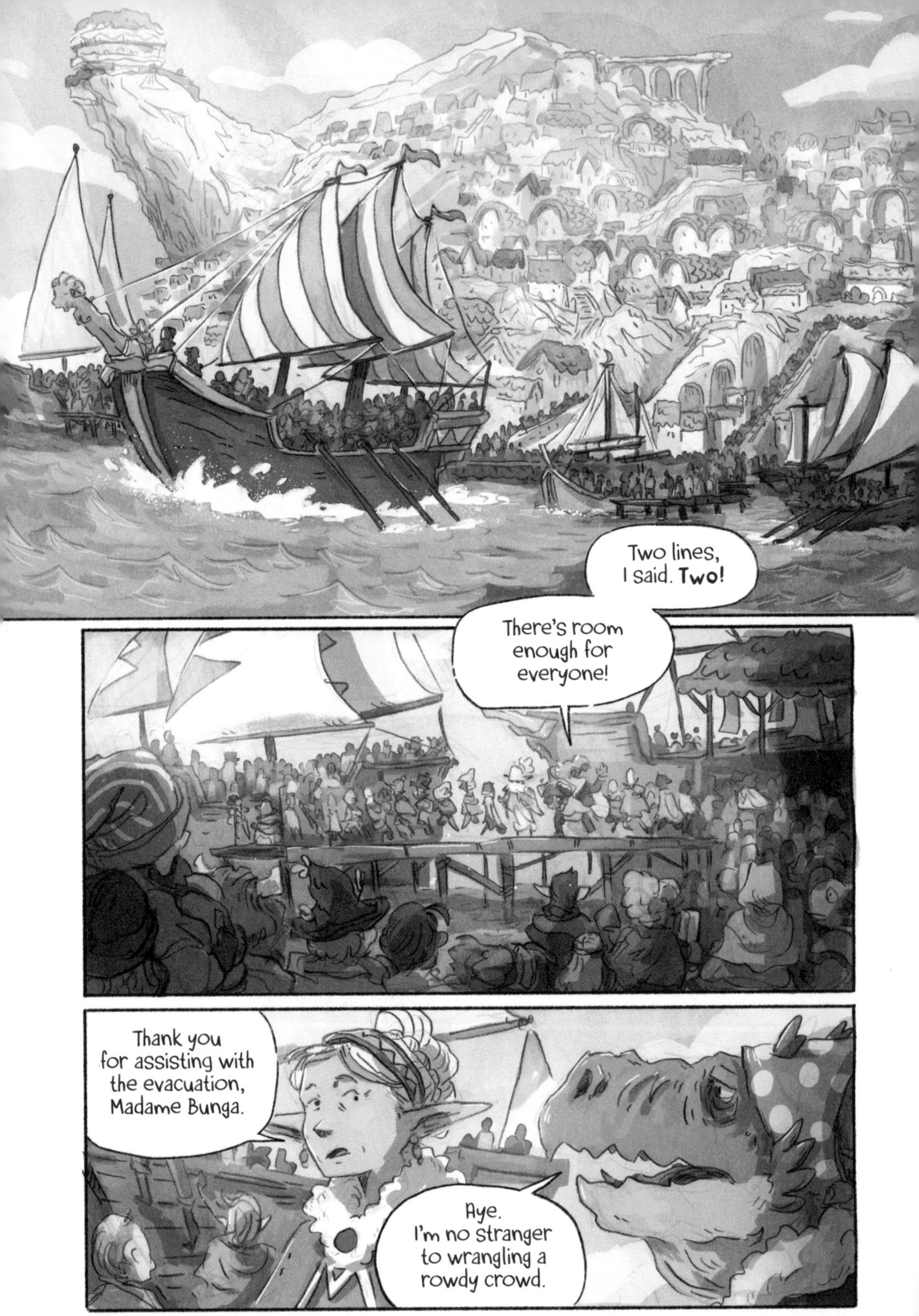
Two lines, I said. Two!
There's room enough for everyone!
Thank you for assisting with the evacuation, Madame Bunga.
Aye. I'm no stranger to wrangling a rowdy crowd.

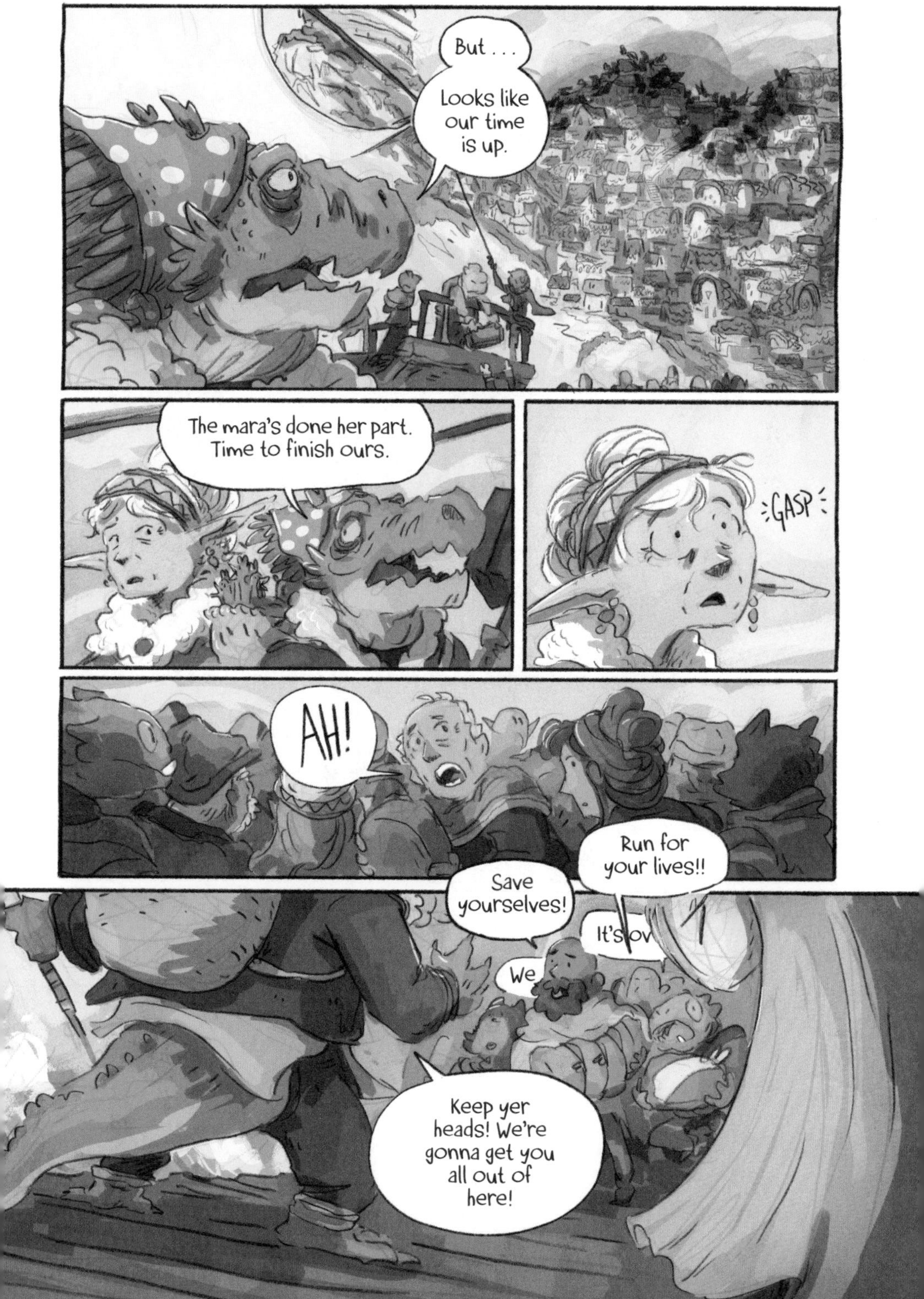

But . . .
Looks like our time is up.
The mara's done her part. Time to finish ours.
GASP
AH!
Run for your lives!!
Save yourselves!
It's ov
We
Keep yer heads! We're gonna get you all out of here!

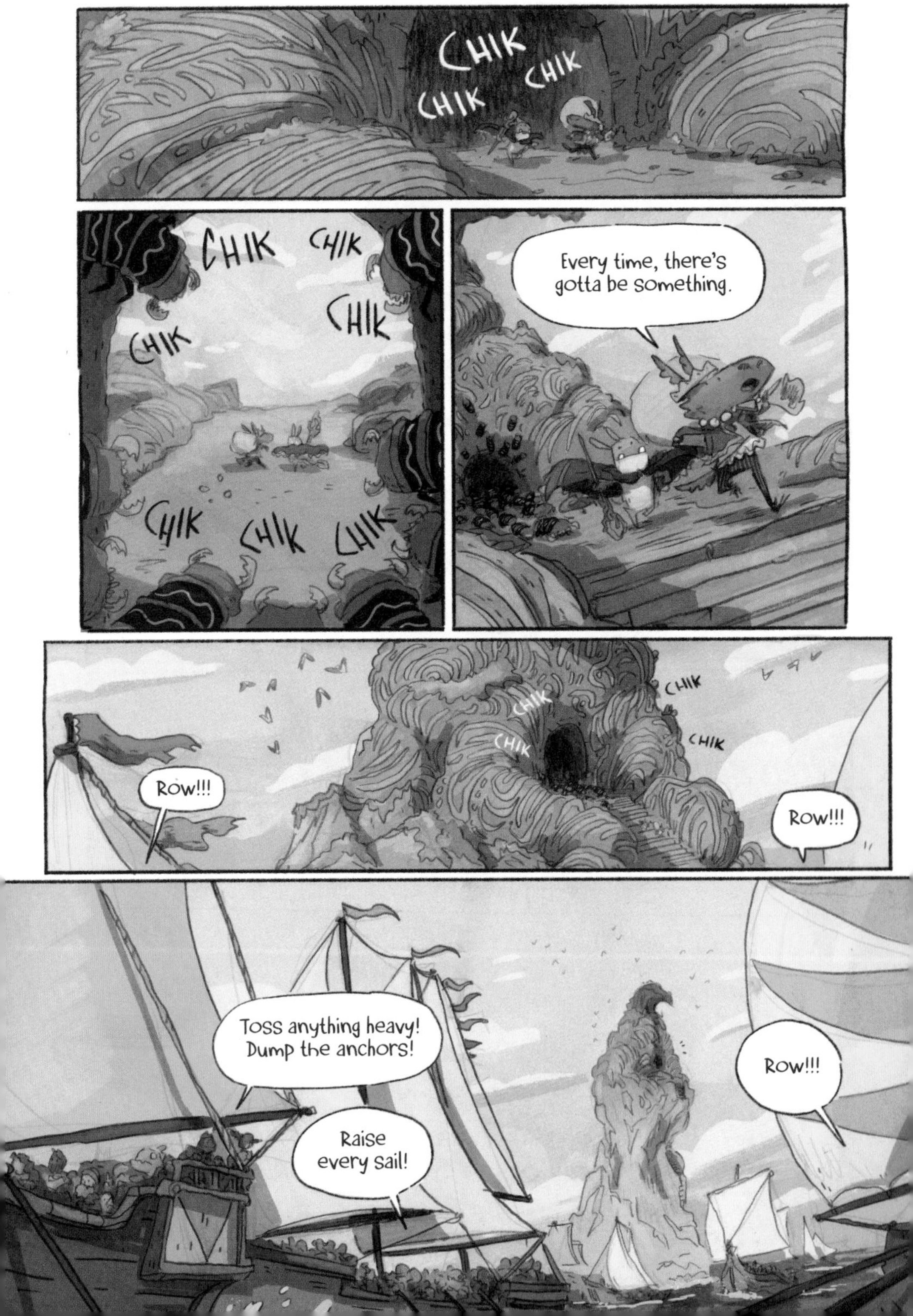
CHIK
CHIK
CHIK
CHIK
CHIK
CHIK
CHIK
CHIK
CHIK
CHIK
Every time, there's gotta be something.
CHIK
CHIK
CHIK
CHIK
Row!!!
Row!!!
Toss anything heavy! Dump the anchors!
Raise every sail!
Row!!!

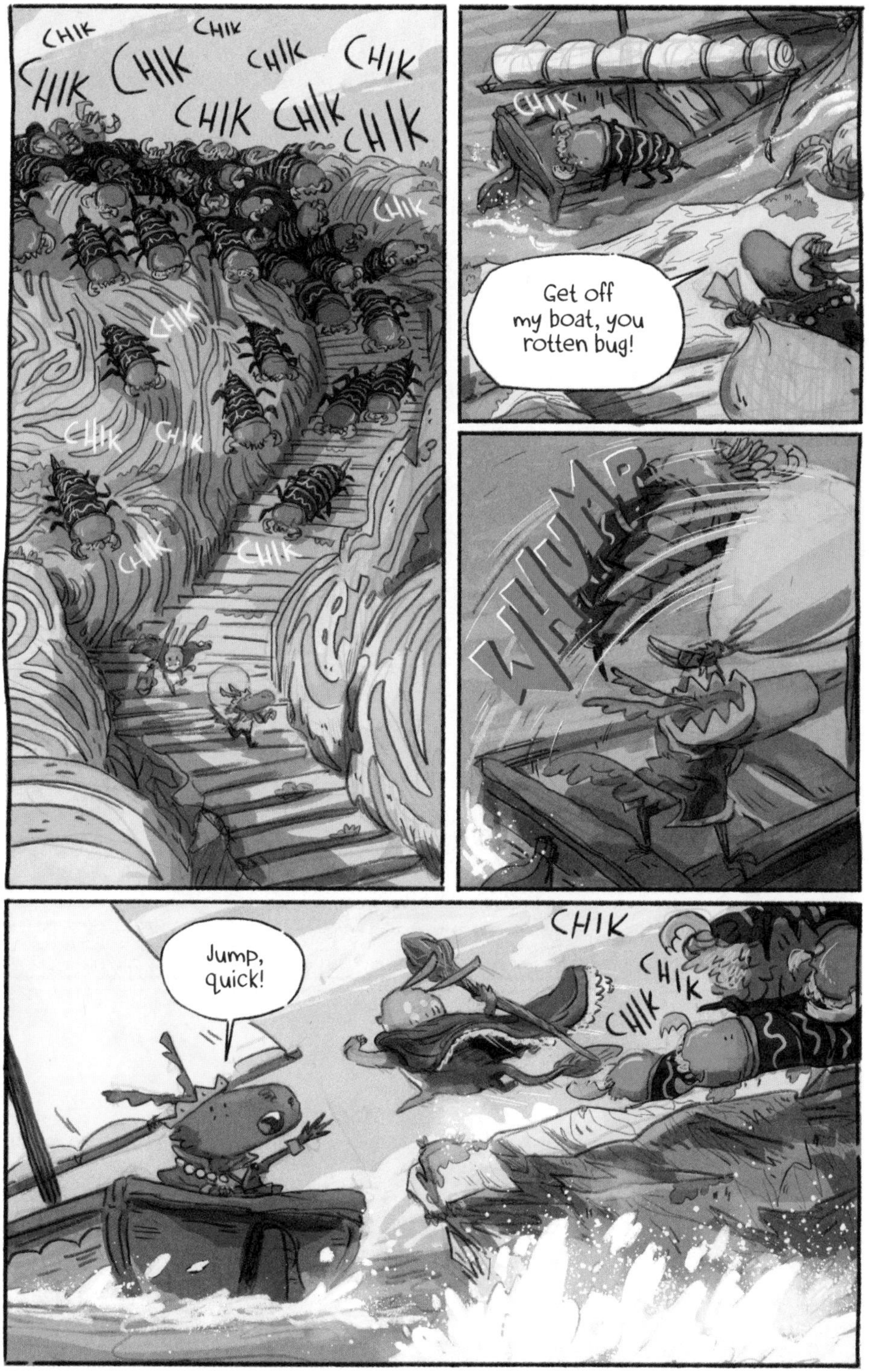
CHIK CHIK CHIK CHIK CHIK CHIK CHIK CHIK CHIK
CHIK
CHIK
CHIK CHIK
CHIK
CHIK
CHIK
CHIK
Get off my boat, you rotten bug!
WHUMP
CHIK
Jump, quick!
CHIK
CHIK

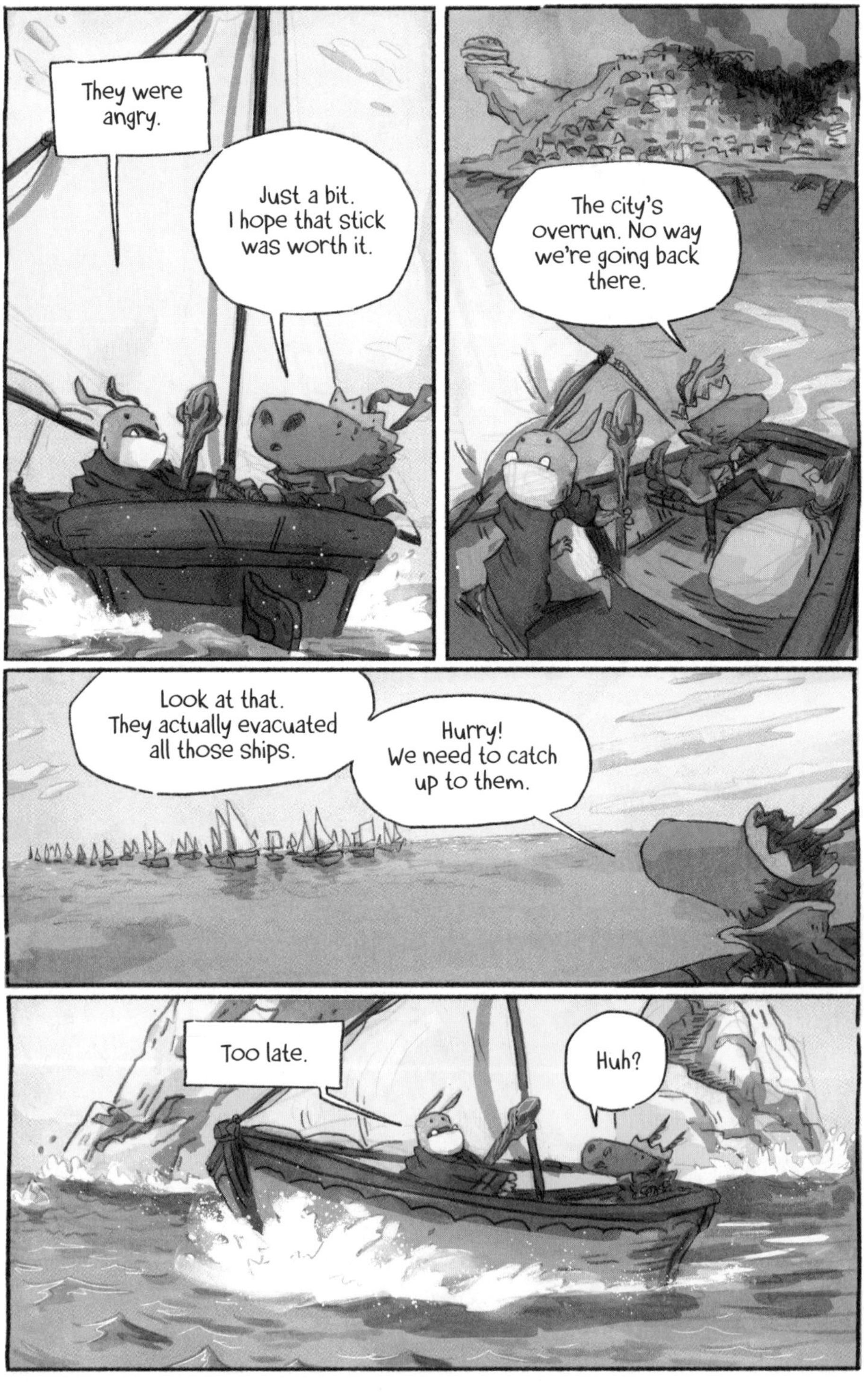
They were angry.
Just a bit. I hope that stick was worth it.
The city's overrun. No way we're going back there.
Look at that. They actually evacuated all those ships.
Hurry! We need to catch up to them.
Too late.
Huh?

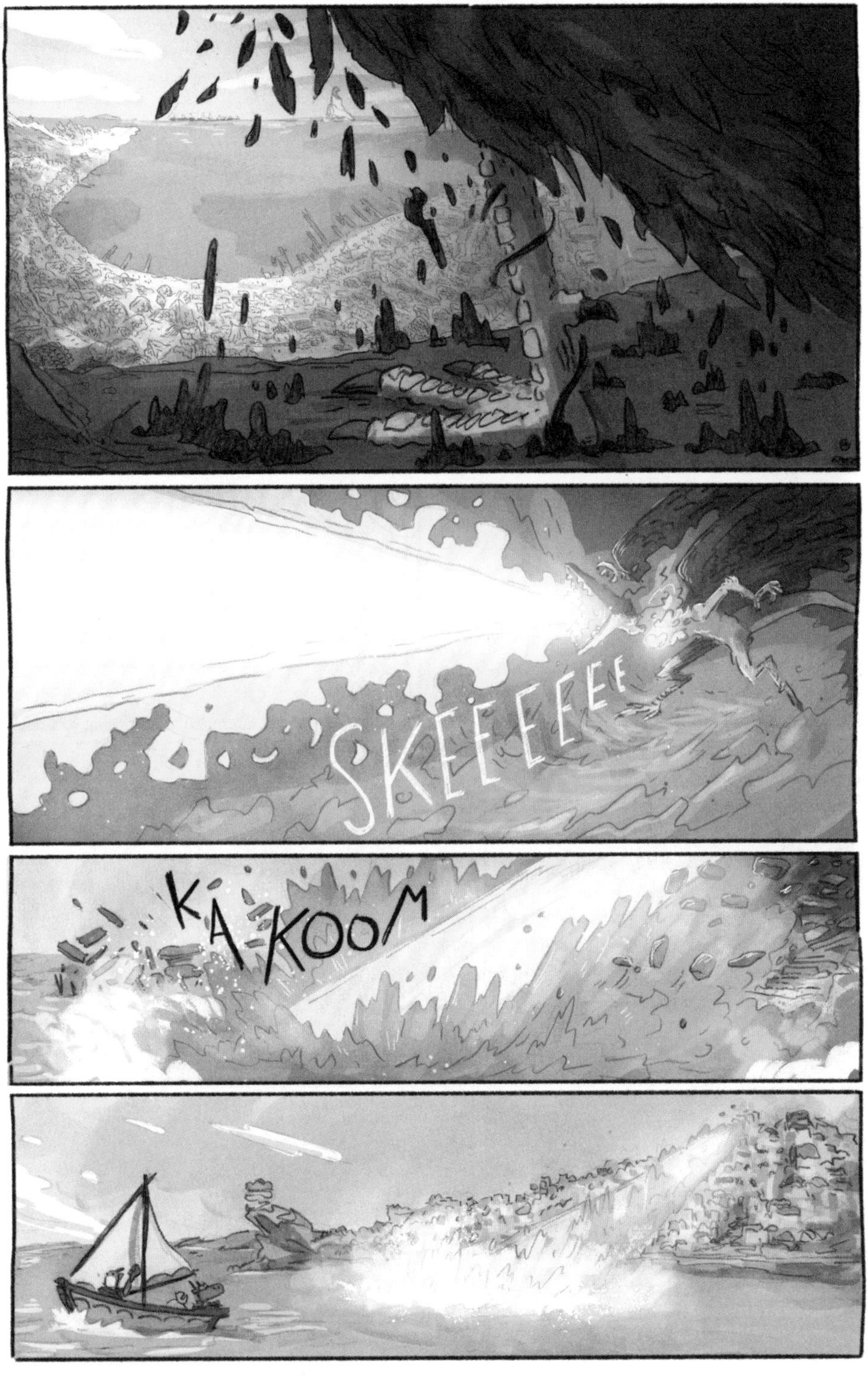
SKEEEEEE
KA-KOOM

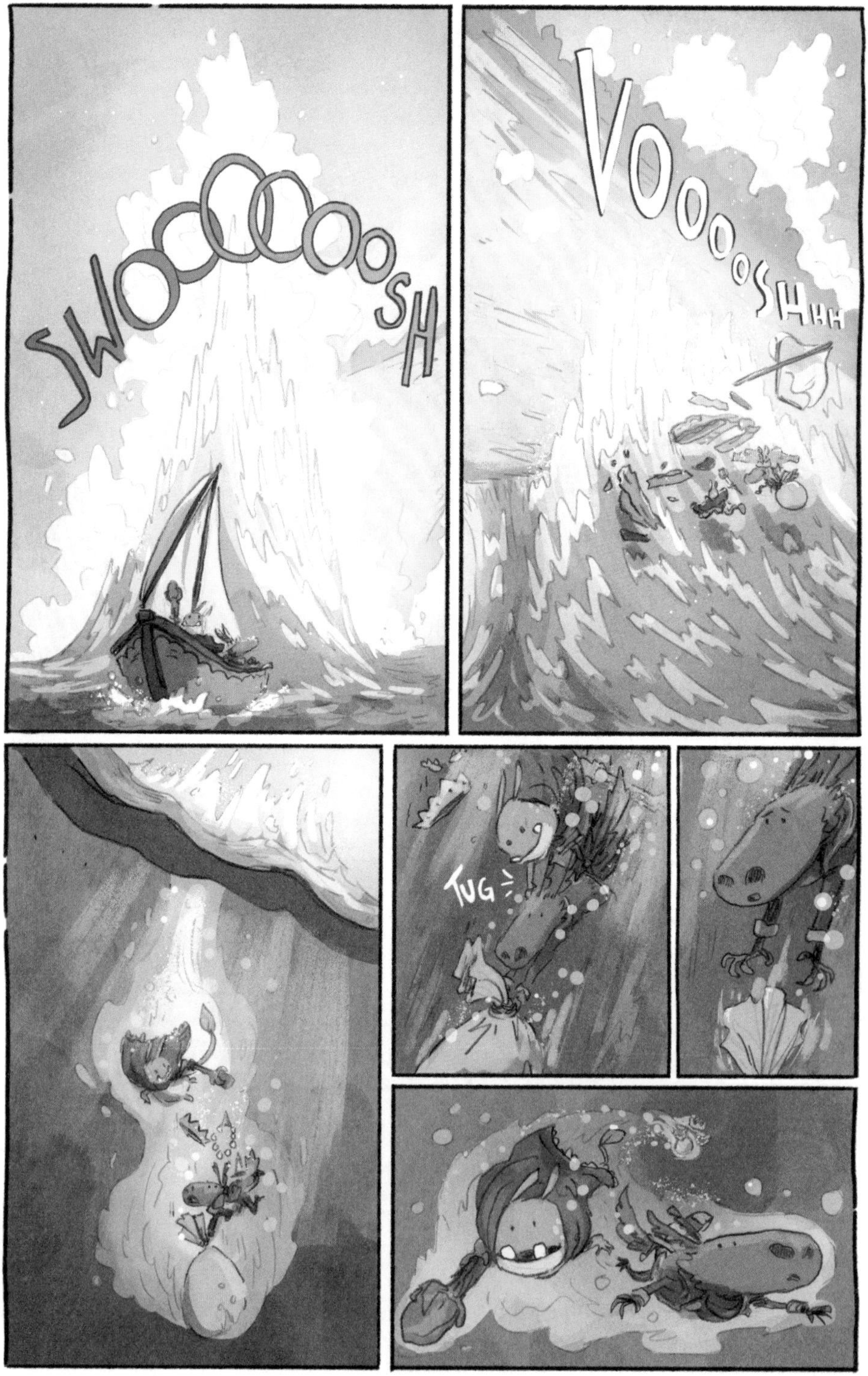
SWOOOOOOSH
VOOOOSHHH
TUG

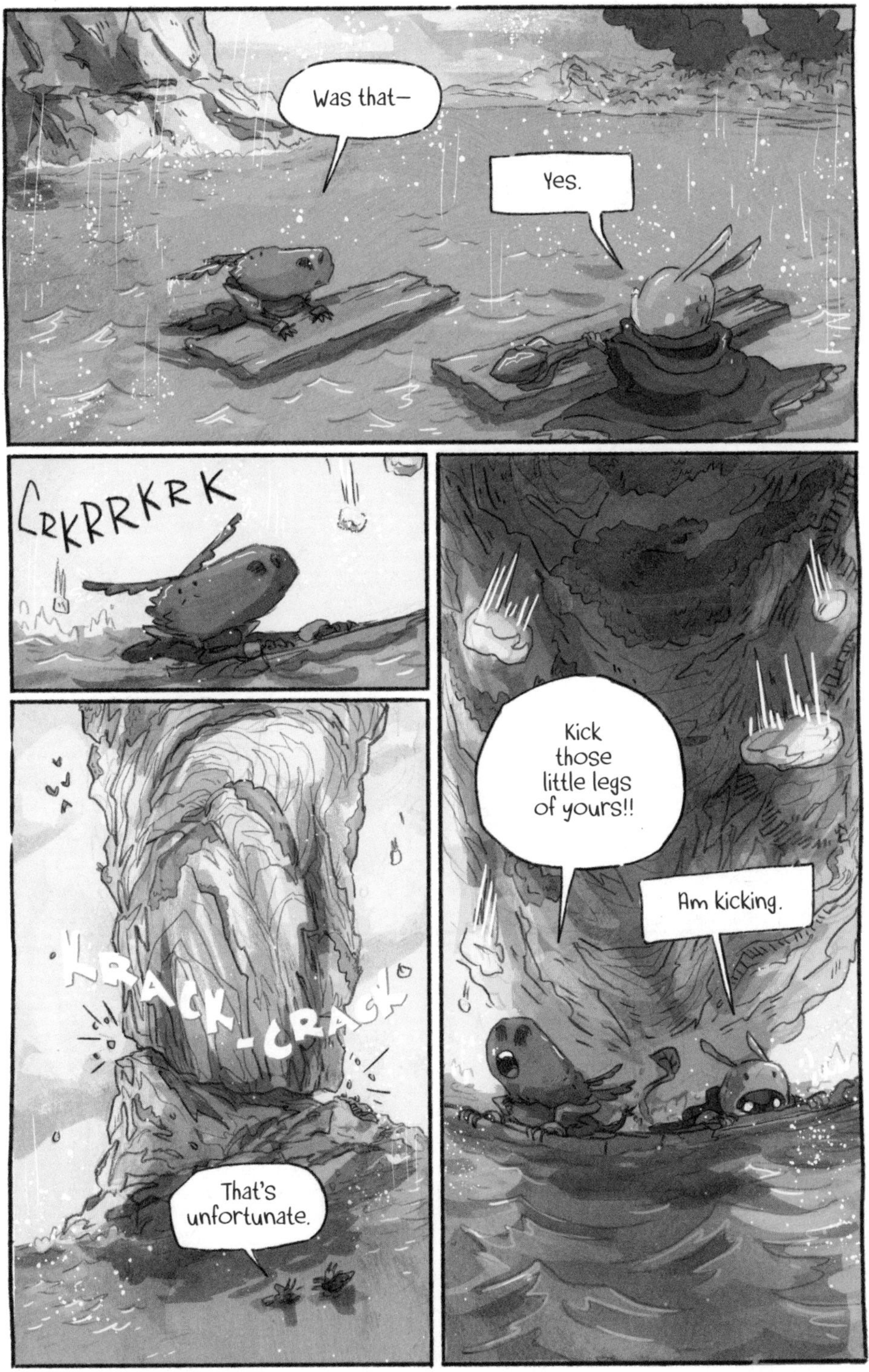

Was that—
Yes.
CRKRRKRK
KRACK-CRACK
That's unfortunate.
Kick those little legs of yours!!
Am kicking.

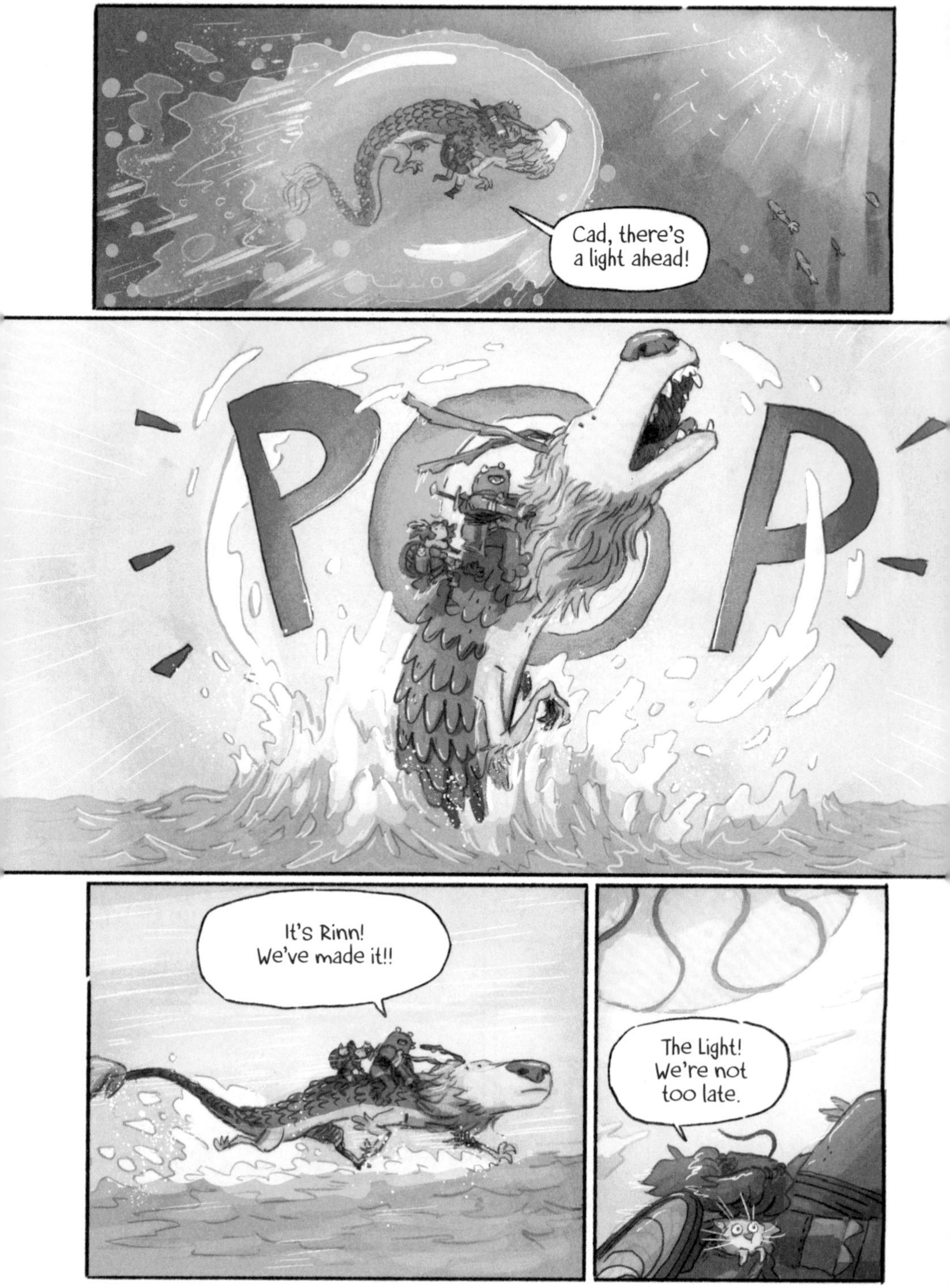
Cad, there's a light ahead!
POP
It's Rinn! We've made it!!
The Light! We're not too late.

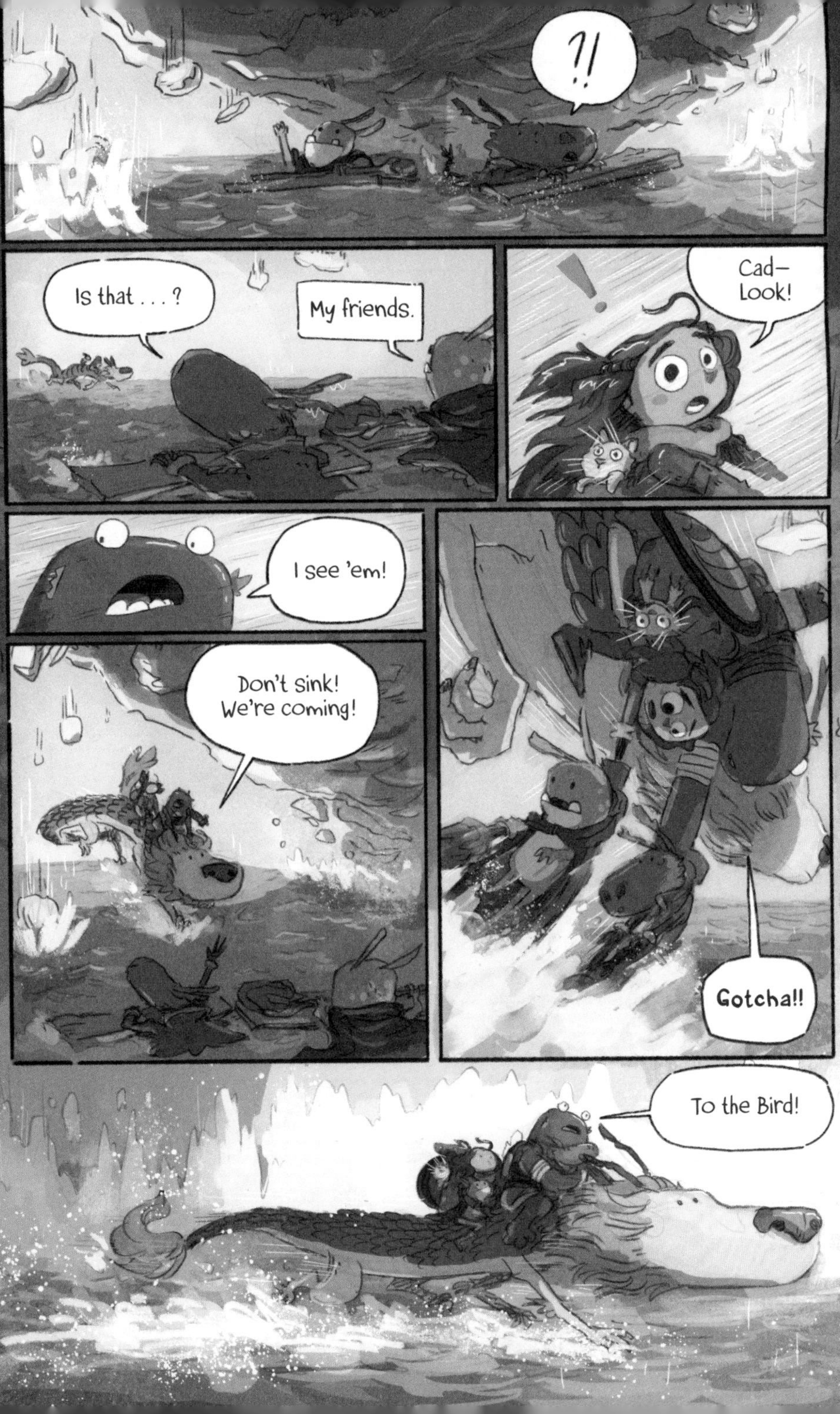
?!
Is that . . . ?
My friends.
Cad—
Look!
I see 'em!
Don't sink!
We're coming!
Gotcha!!
To the Bird!

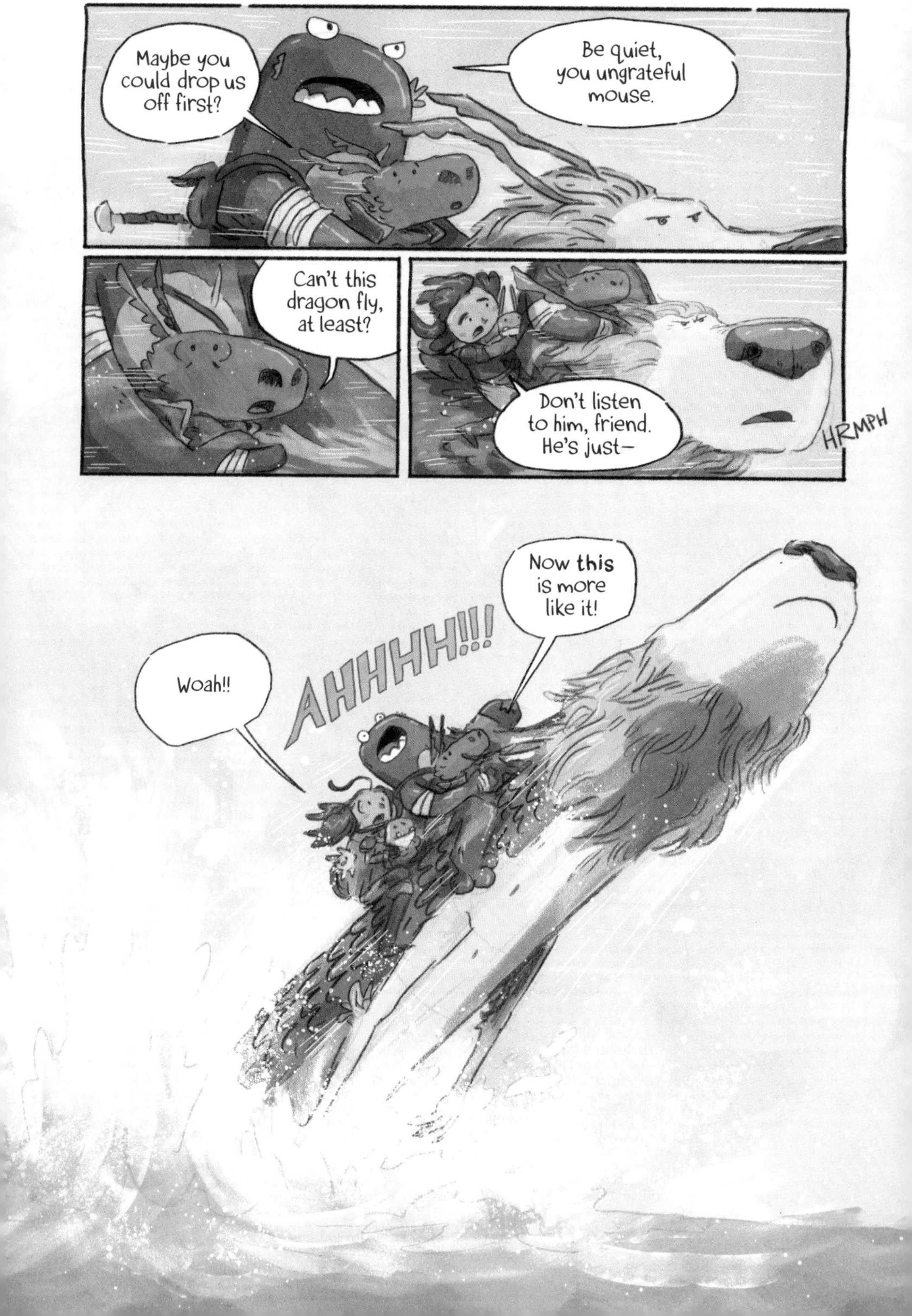
Maybe you could drop us off first?
Be quiet, you ungrateful mouse.
Can't this dragon fly, at least?
Don't listen to him, friend. He's just—
HRMPH
Now **this** is more like it!
Woah!!
AHHHH!!!

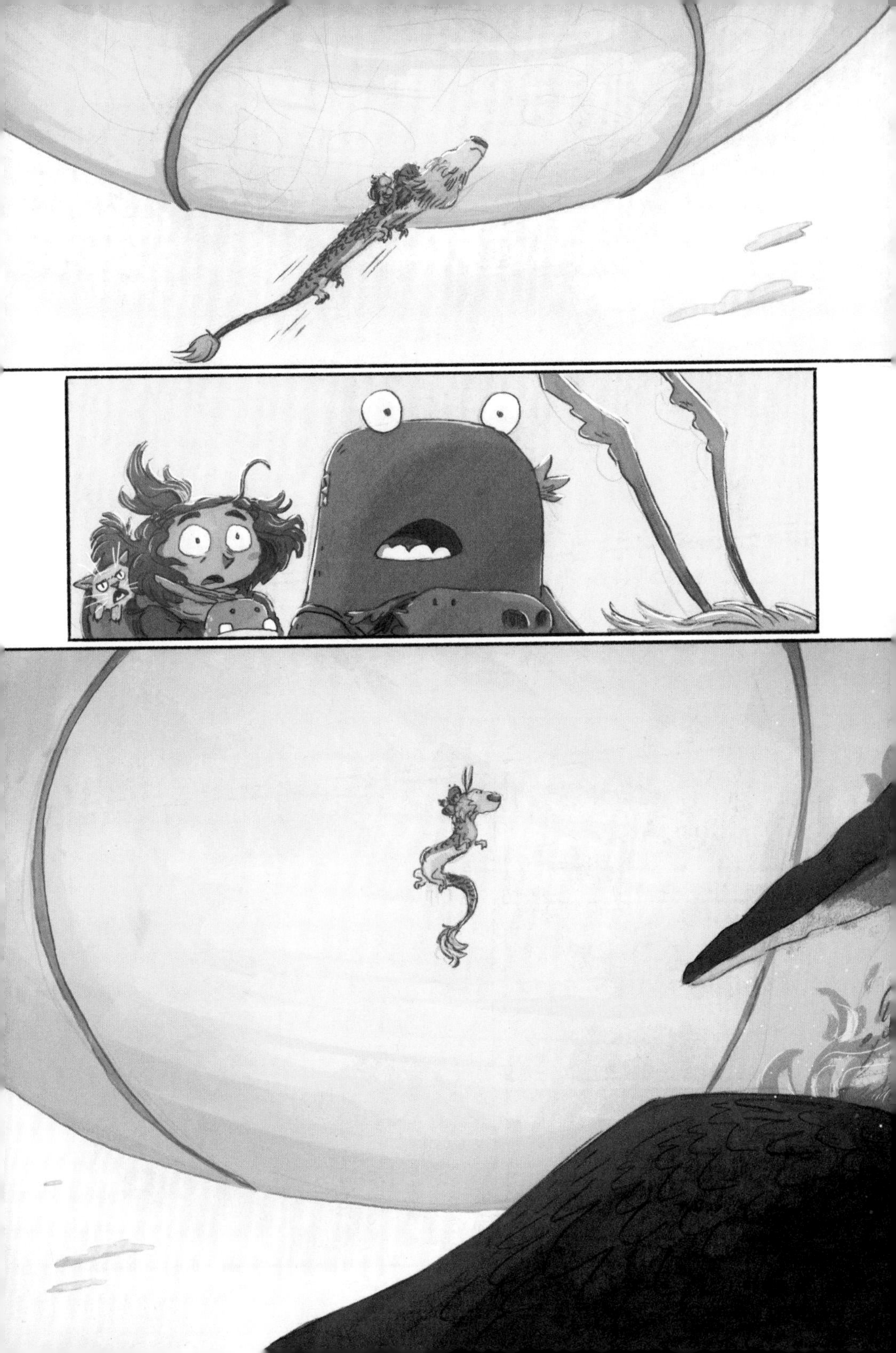

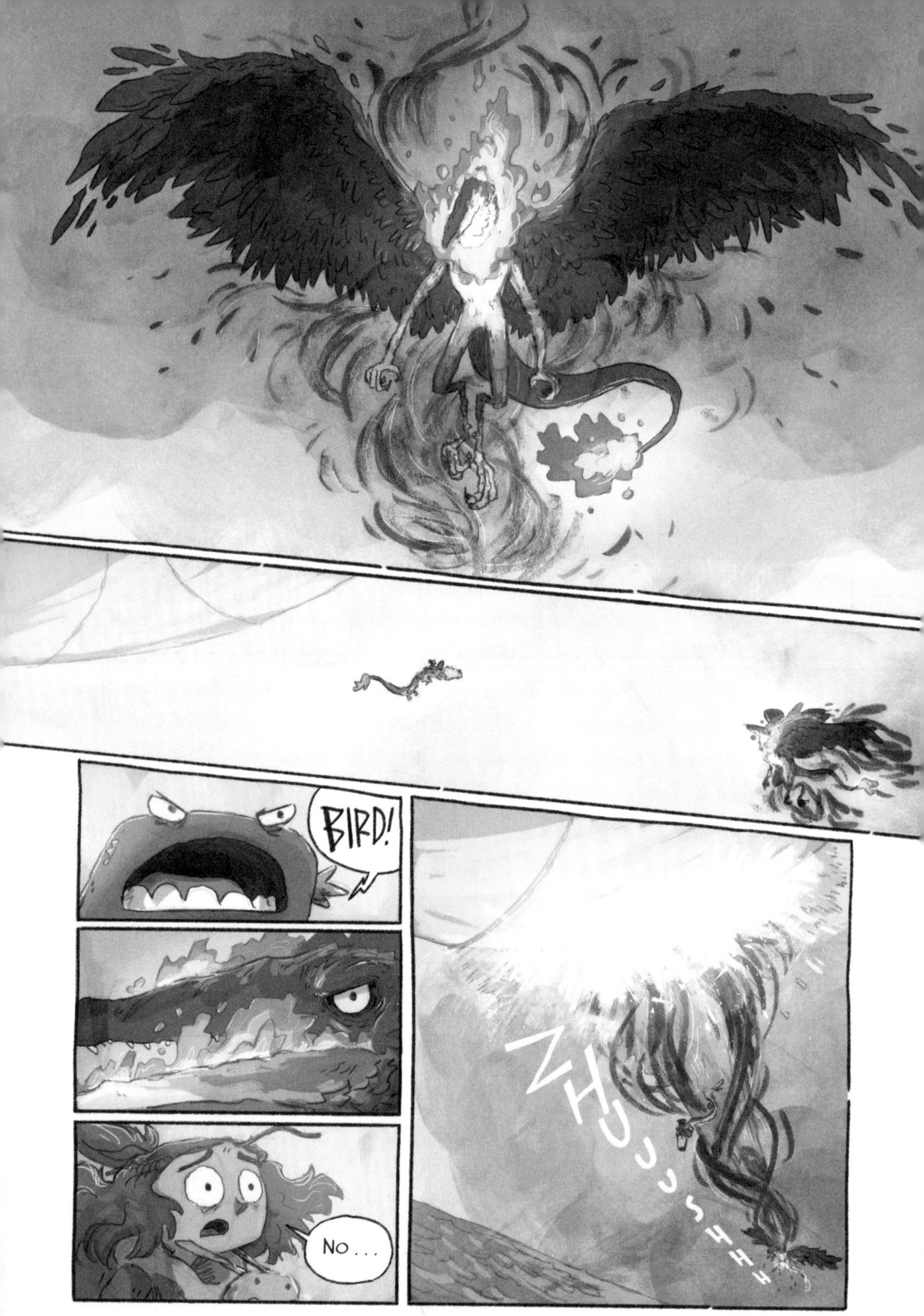
BIRD!
No . . .
ZHUUUUSHHH

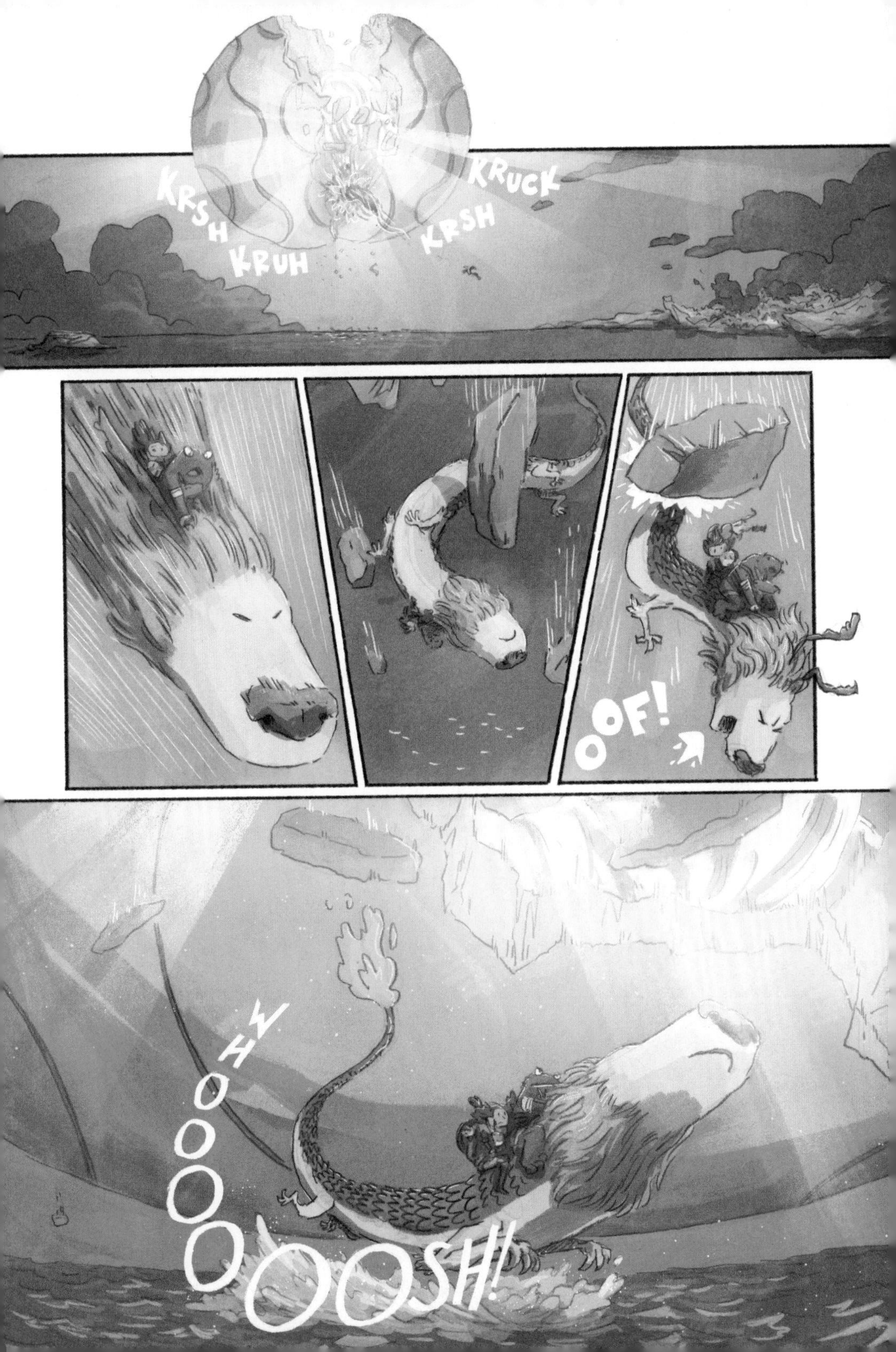
KRSH
KRUH
KRSH
KRUCK
OOF!
WHOOOOOOOSH!

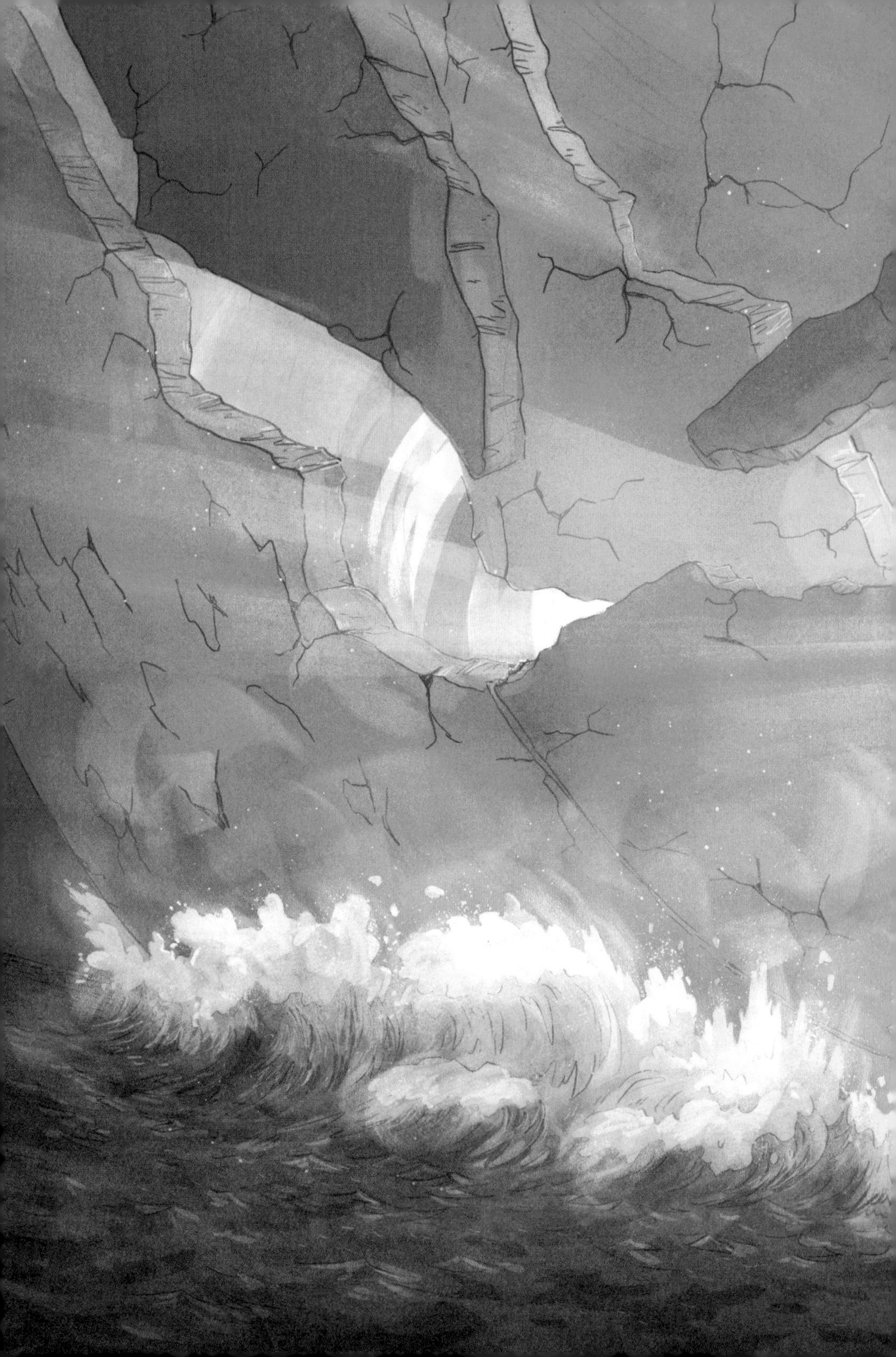

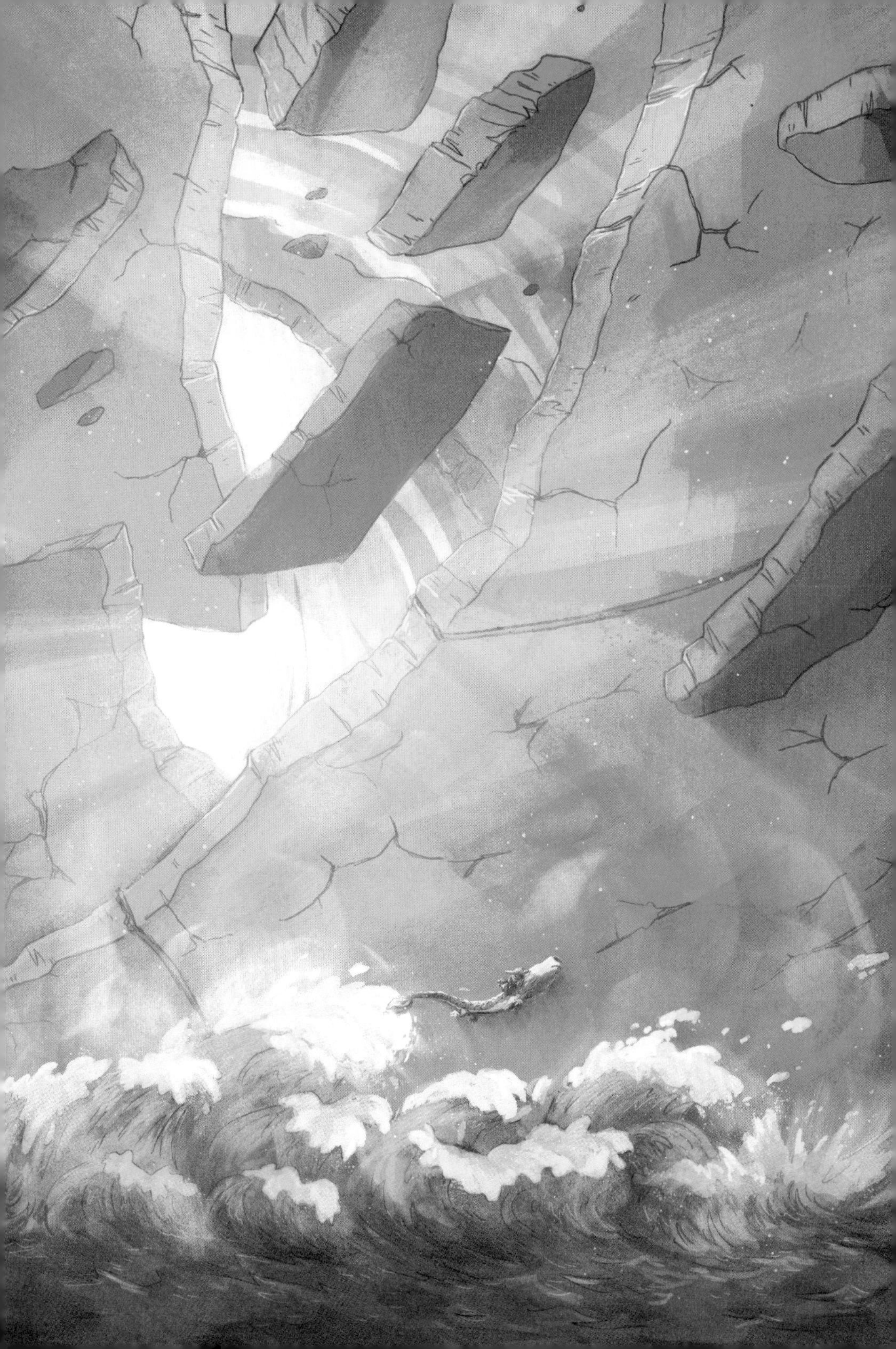

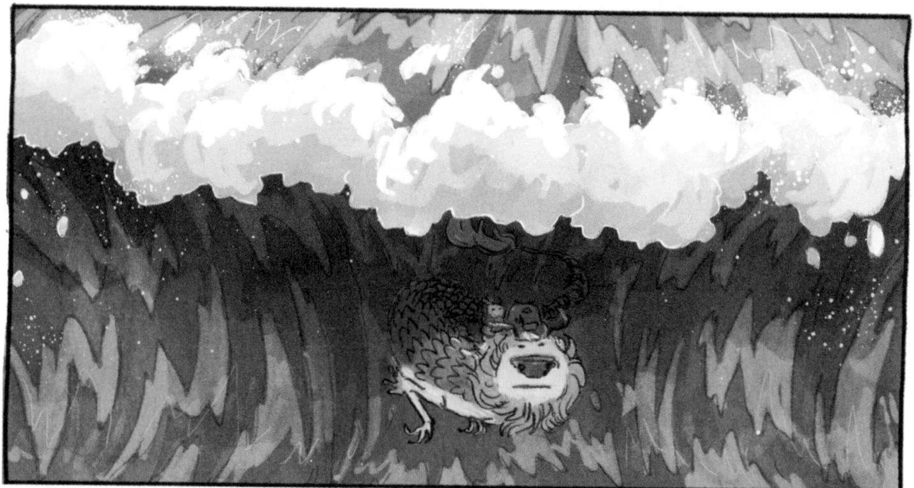

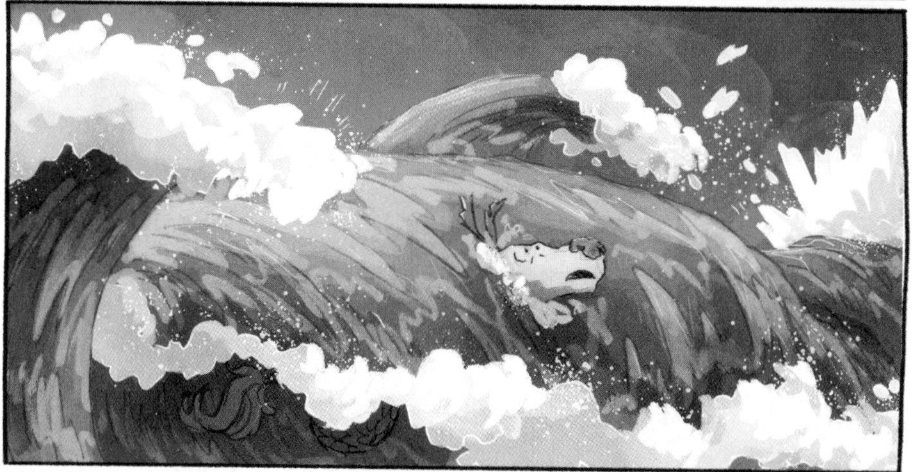

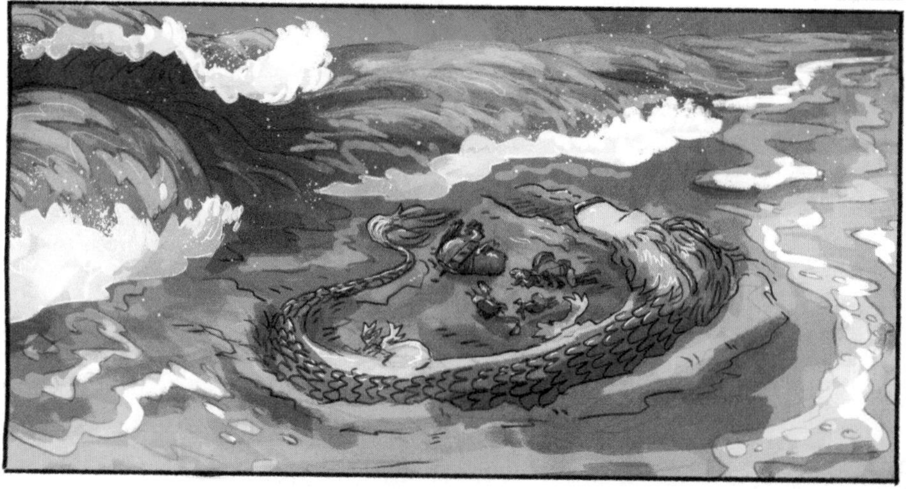

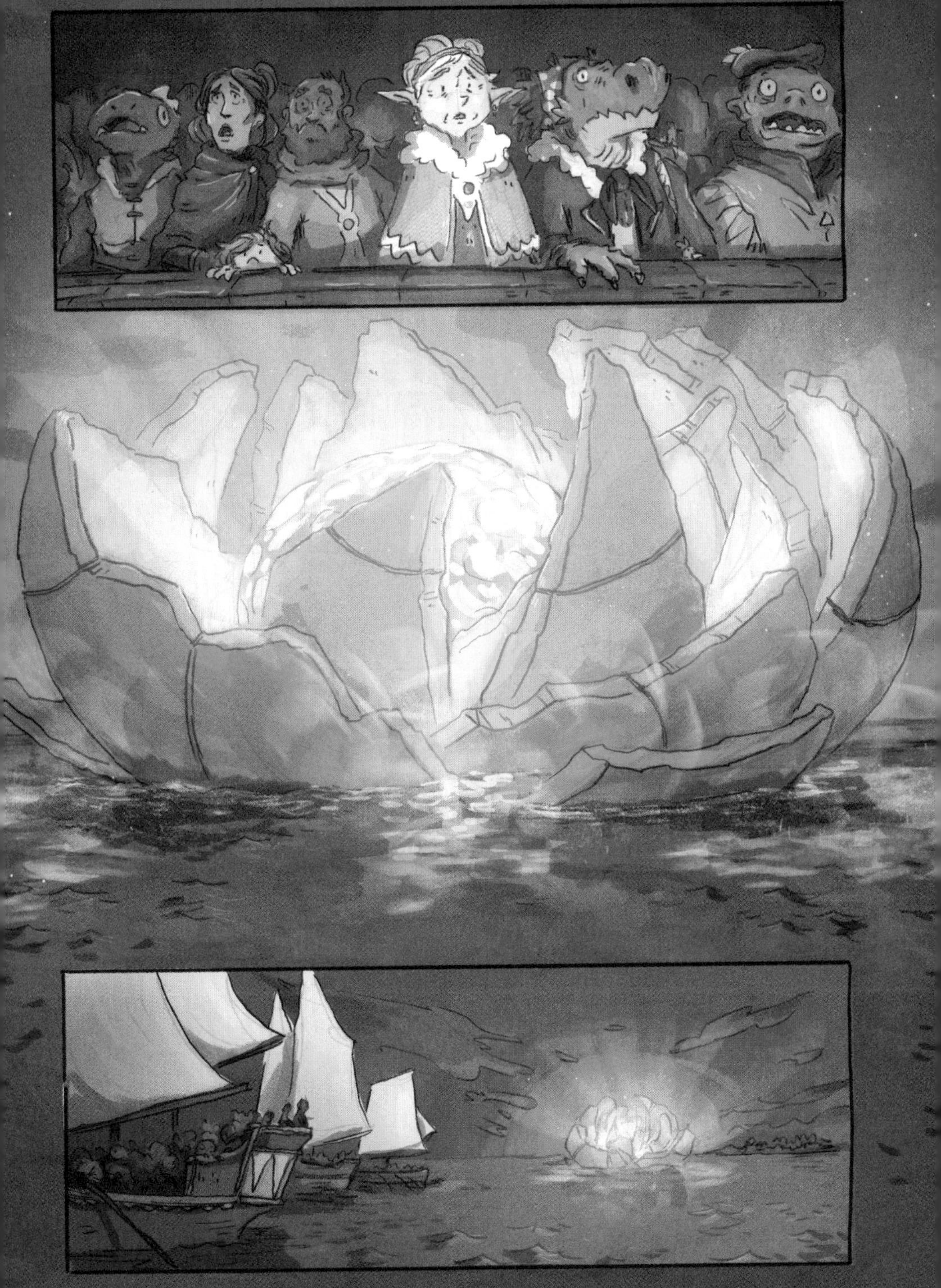

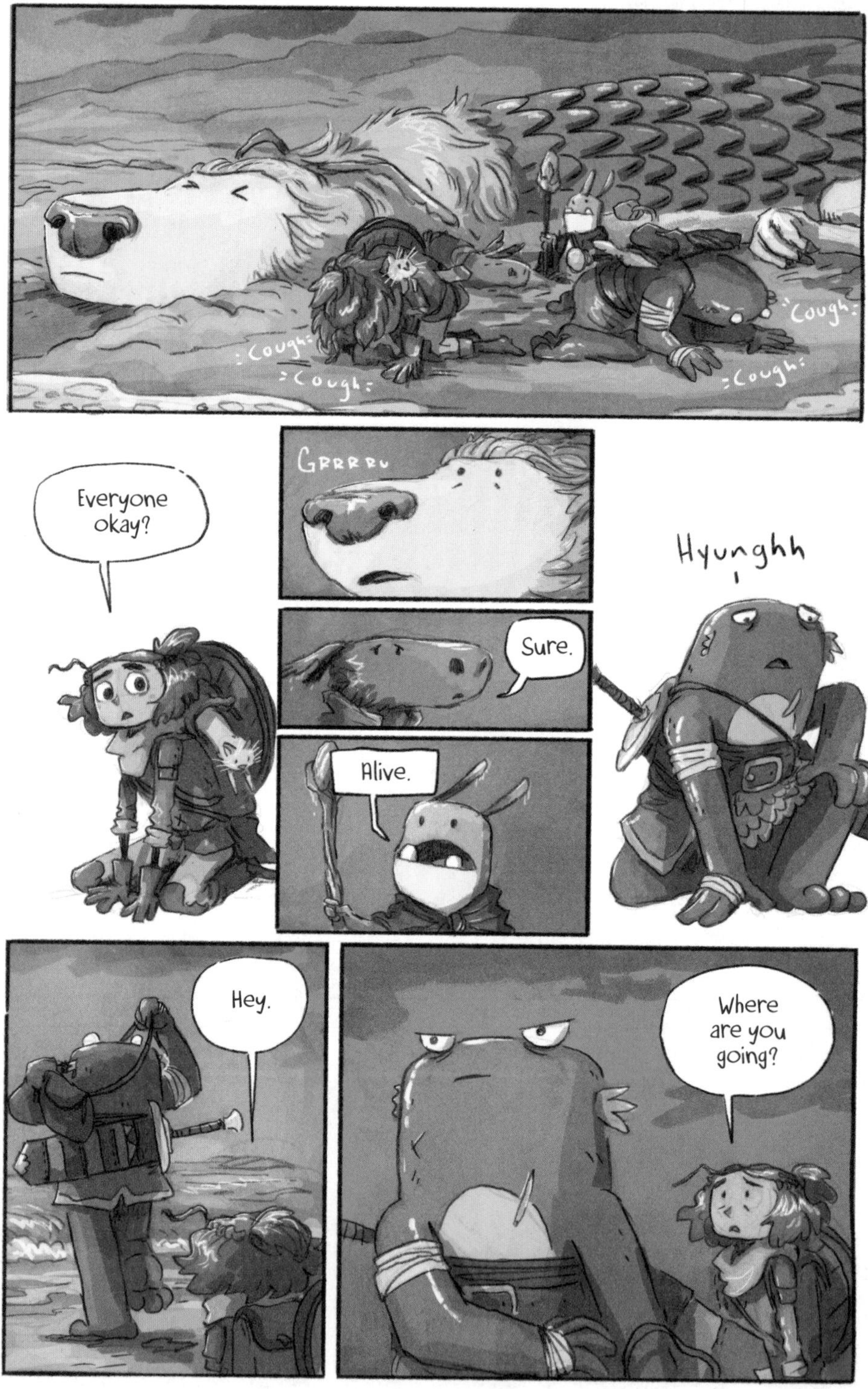
:Cough:
:Cough:
:Cough:
:Cough:
Everyone okay?
GRRRRU
Sure.
Alive.
Hyunghh
Hey.
Where are you going?

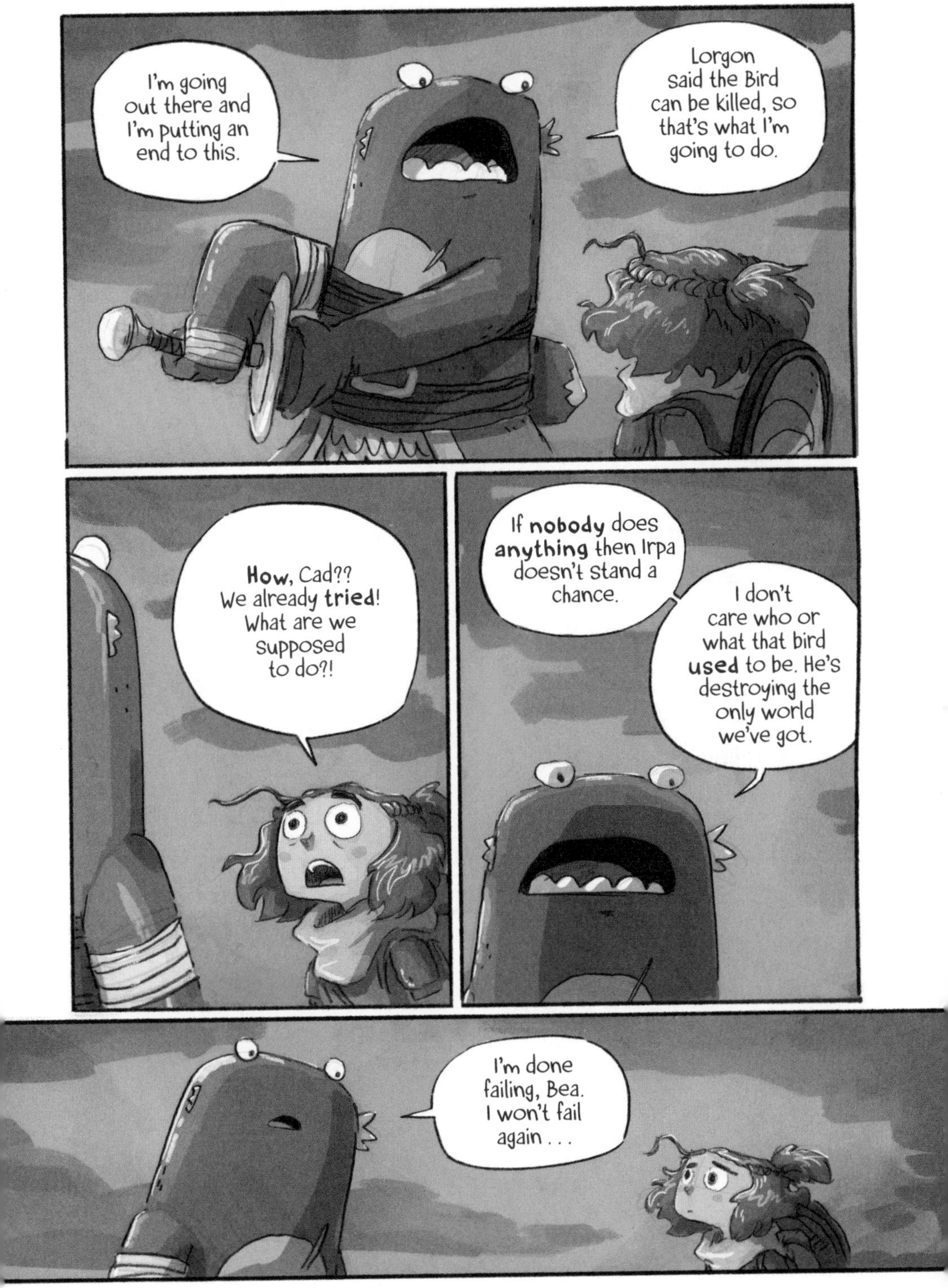
I'm going out there and I'm putting an end to this.
Lorgon said the Bird can be killed, so that's what I'm going to do.
How, Cad?? We already **tried**! What are we supposed to do?!
If **nobody** does **anything** then Irpa doesn't stand a chance.
I don't care who or what that bird **used** to be. He's destroying the only world we've got.
I'm done failing, Bea. I won't fail again . . .

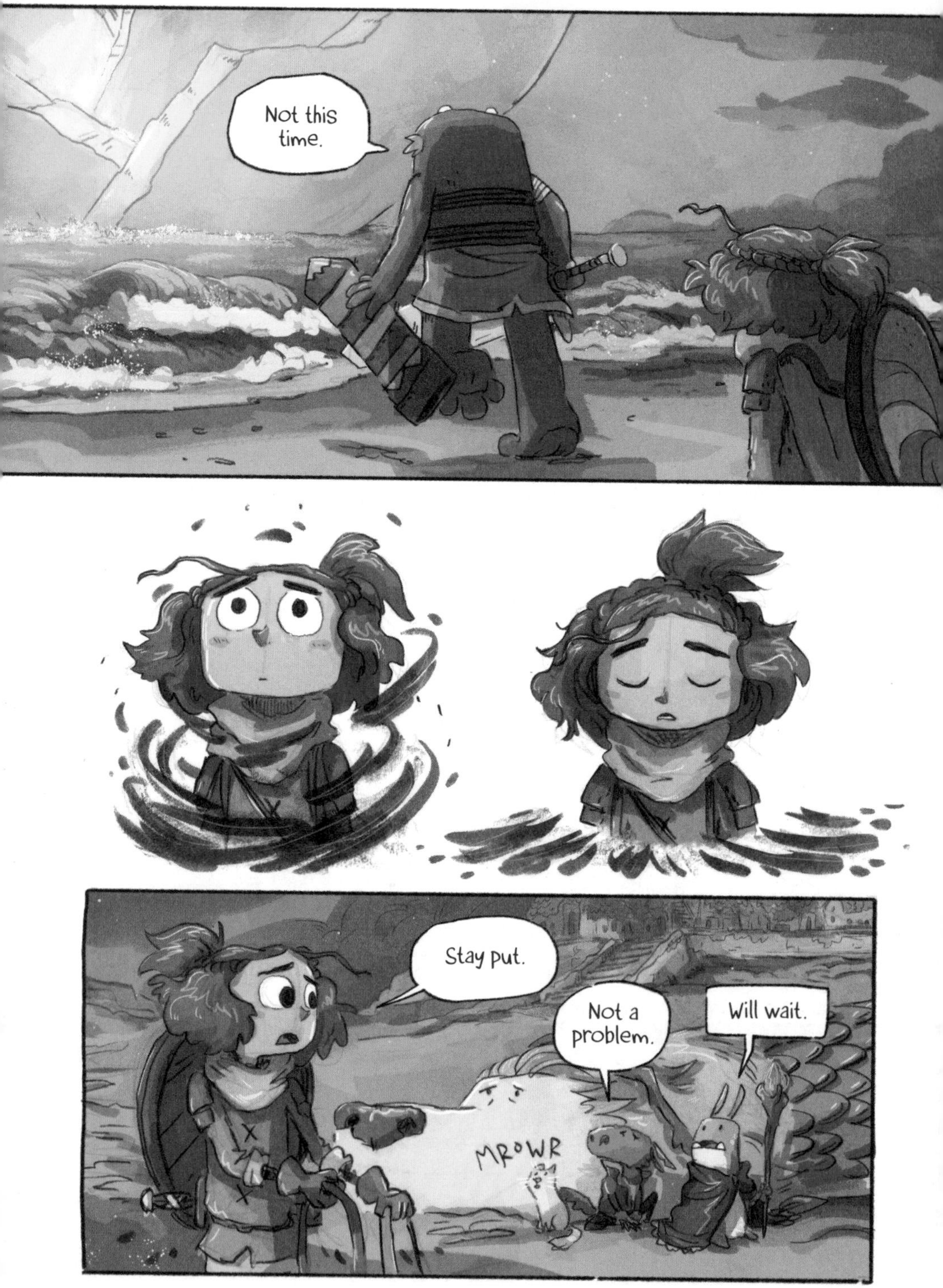
Not this time.
Stay put.
Not a problem.
Will wait.
MROWR

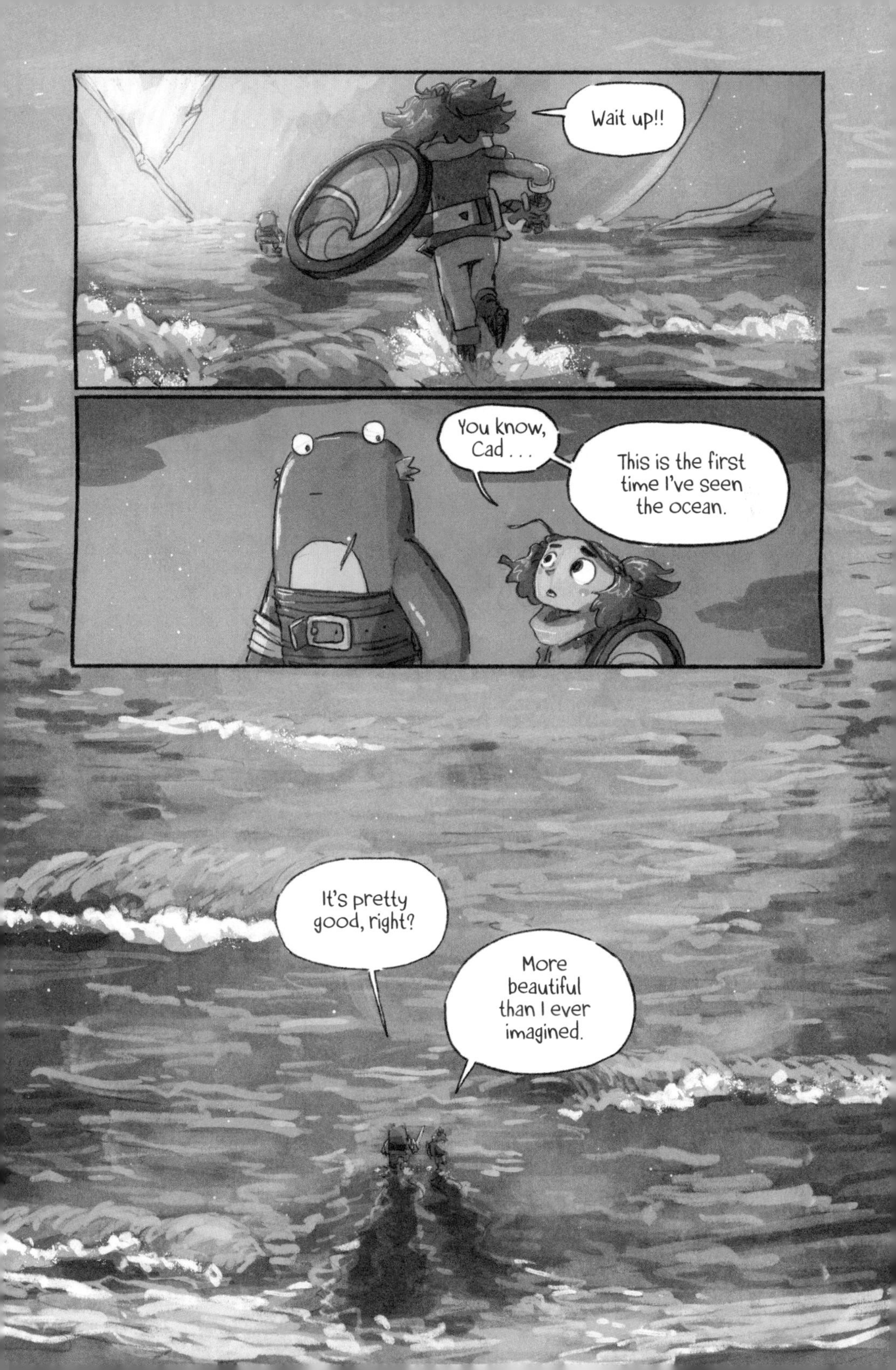
Wait up!!
You know, Cad . . .
This is the first time I've seen the ocean.
It's pretty good, right?
More beautiful than I ever imagined.

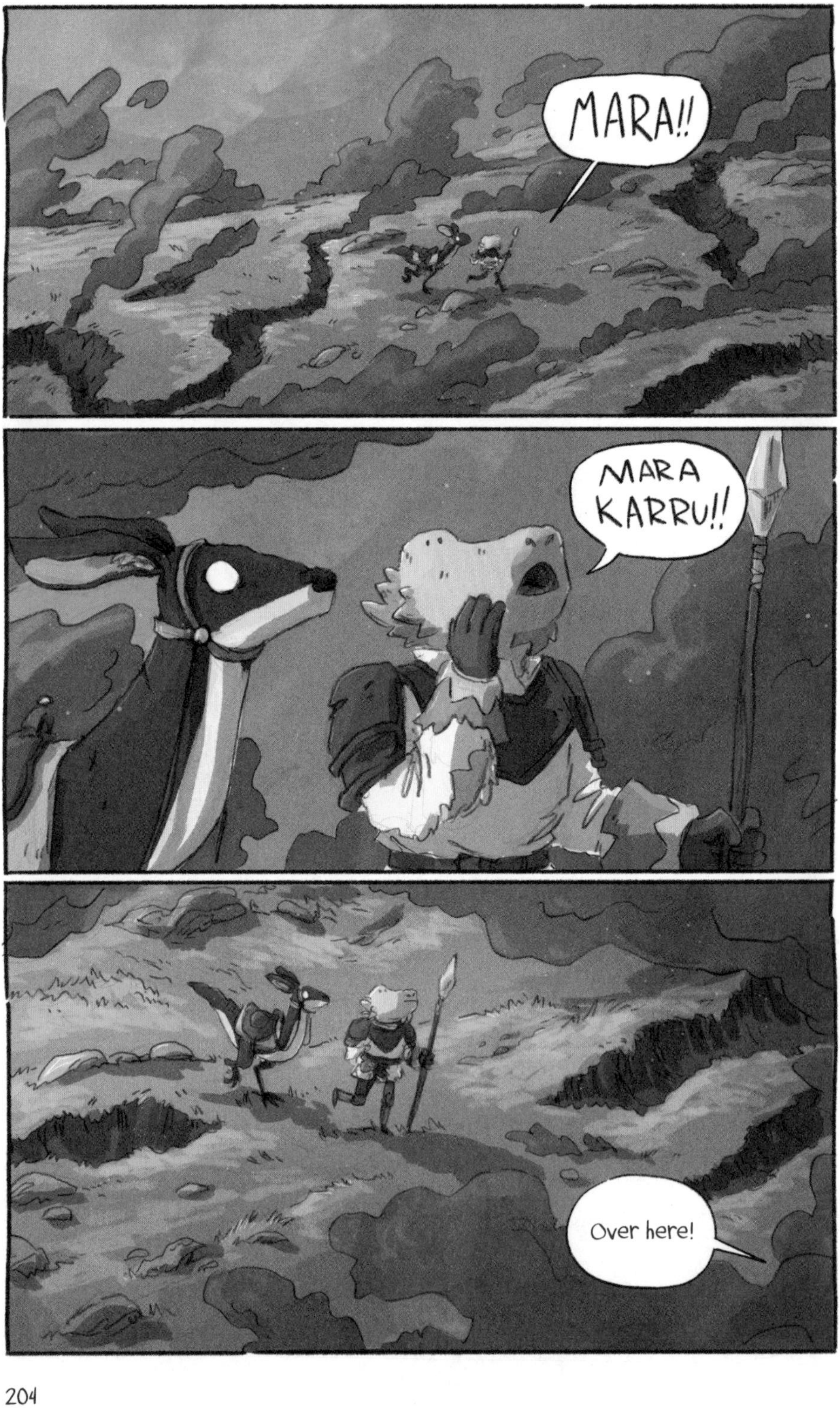
MARA!!
MARA KARRU!!
Over here!

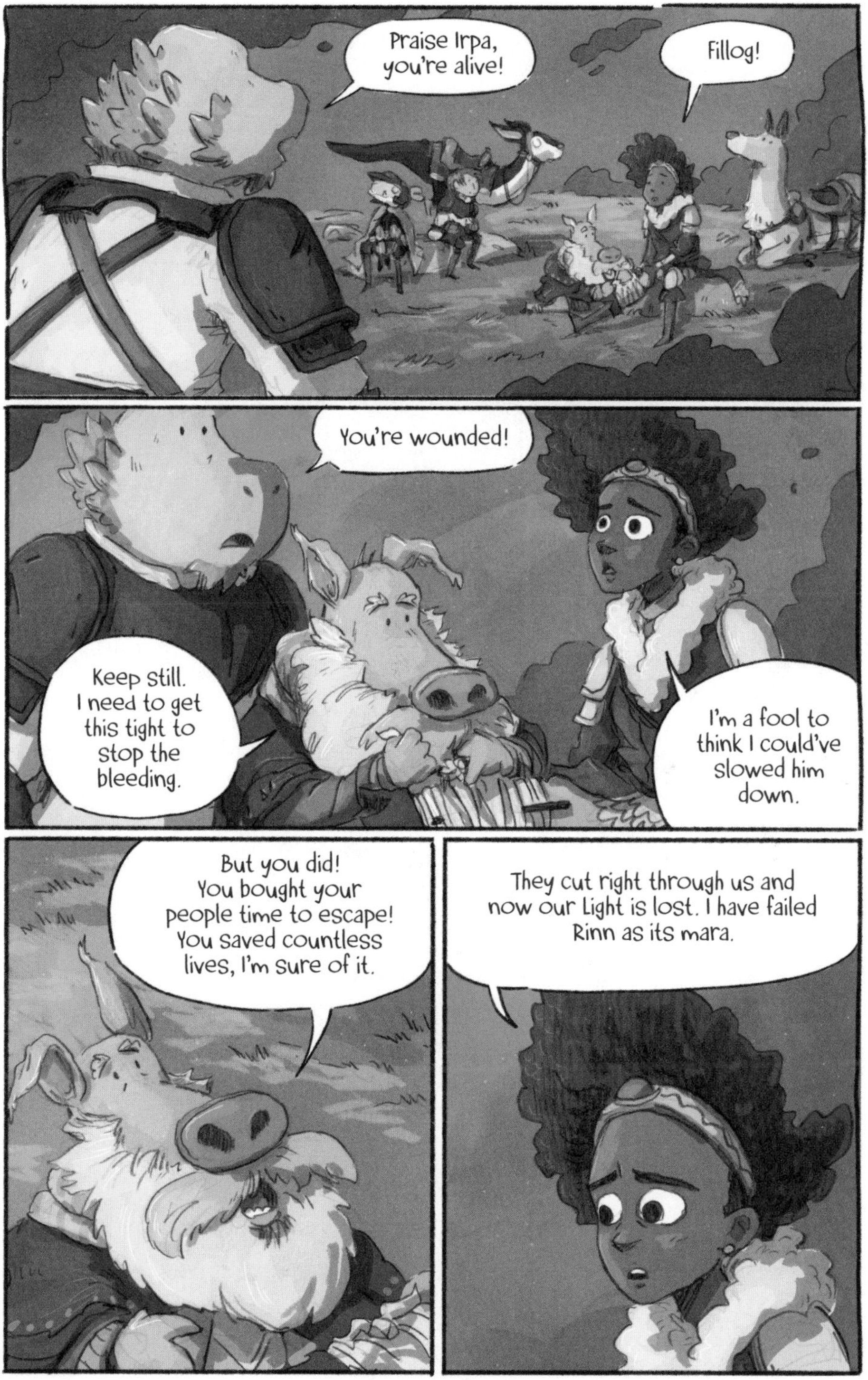
Praise Irpa, you're alive!
Fillog!
You're wounded!
Keep still. I need to get this tight to stop the bleeding.
I'm a fool to think I could've slowed him down.
But you did! You bought your people time to escape! You saved countless lives, I'm sure of it.
They cut right through us and now our Light is lost. I have failed Rinn as its mara.

Nonsense! The people of Lealand paid for their mara's lack of leadership. You were faced with an impossible choice. The bravery of you and your scouts saved your people.

The Light is gone, but there's still a glow in the distance.

How?

Kest must not have retrieved the Flame from within the Light yet.

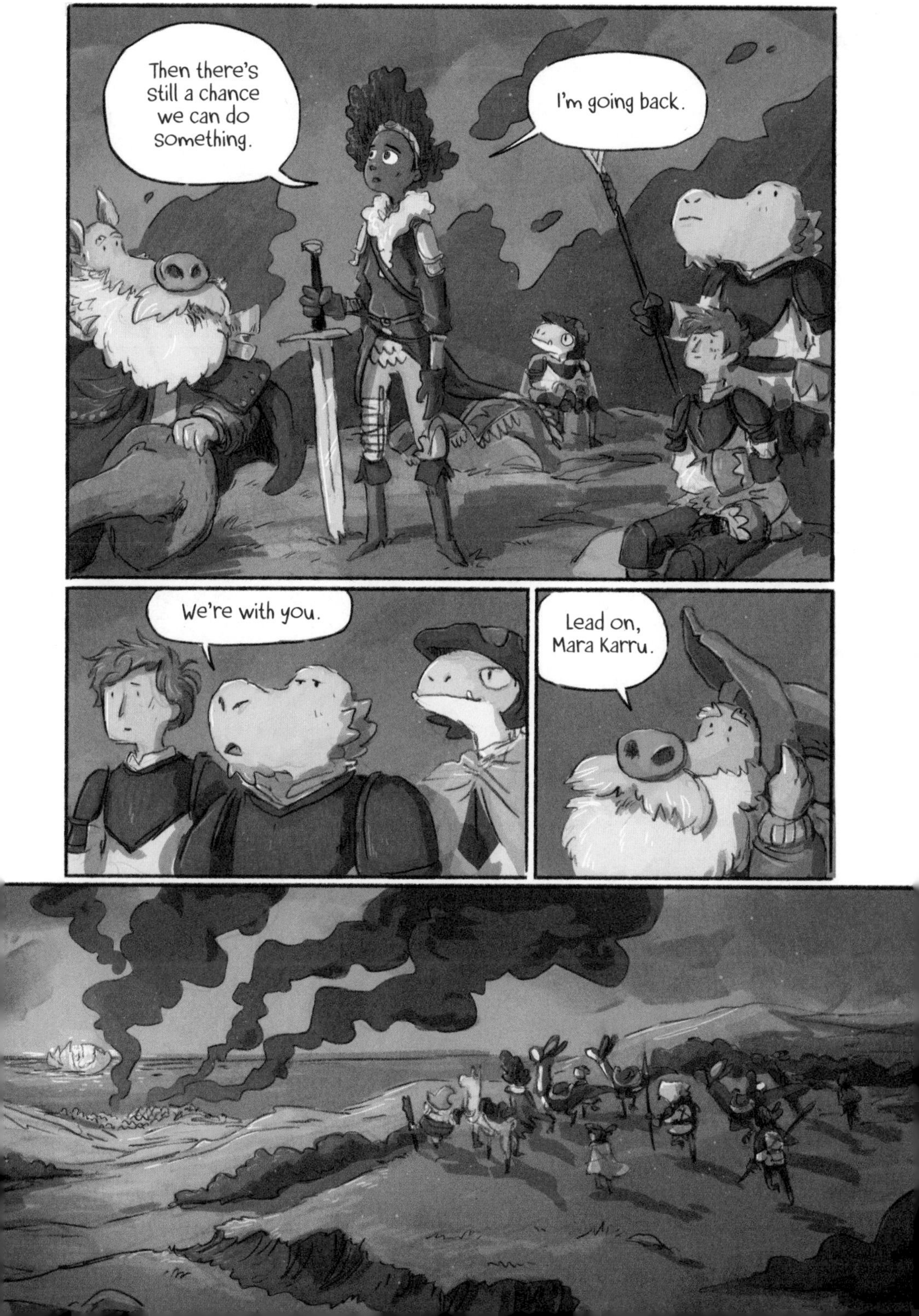
Then there's still a chance we can do something.
I'm going back.
We're with you.
Lead on, Mara Karru.

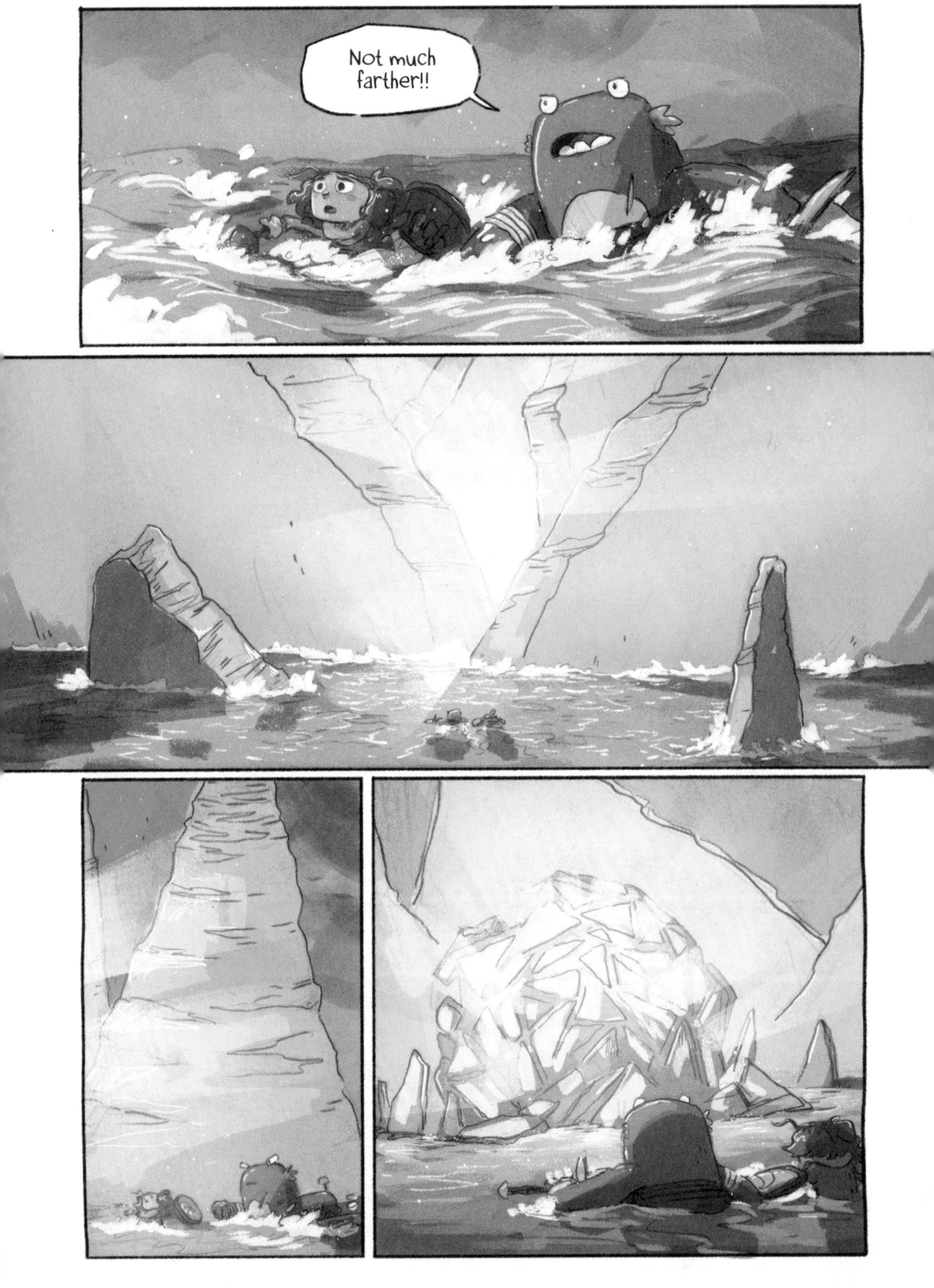
Not much farther!!

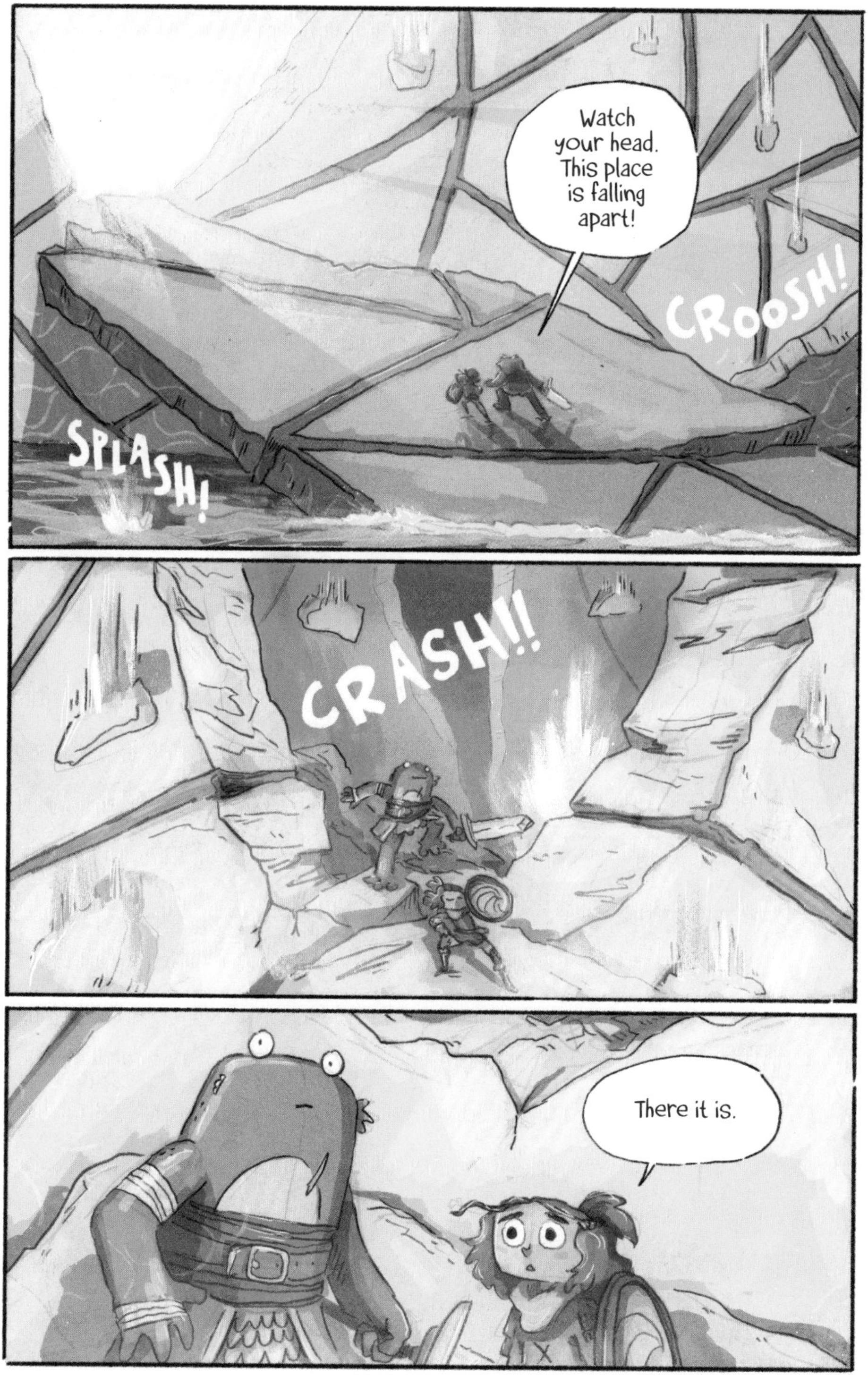
Watch your head. This place is falling apart!
CROOSH!
SPLASH!
CRASH!!
There it is.

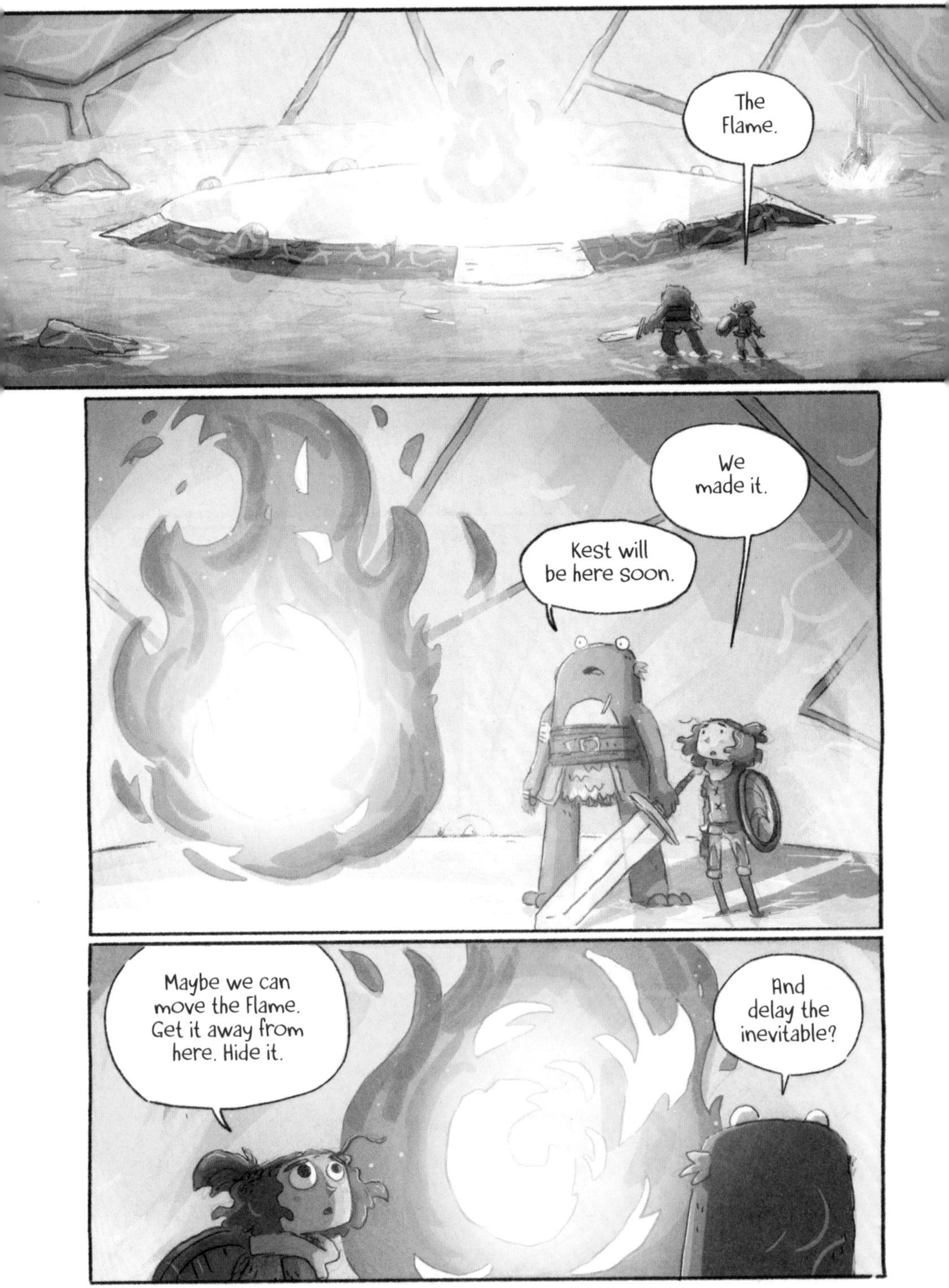
The Flame.
We made it.
Kest will be here soon.
Maybe we can move the Flame. Get it away from here. Hide it.
And delay the inevitable?

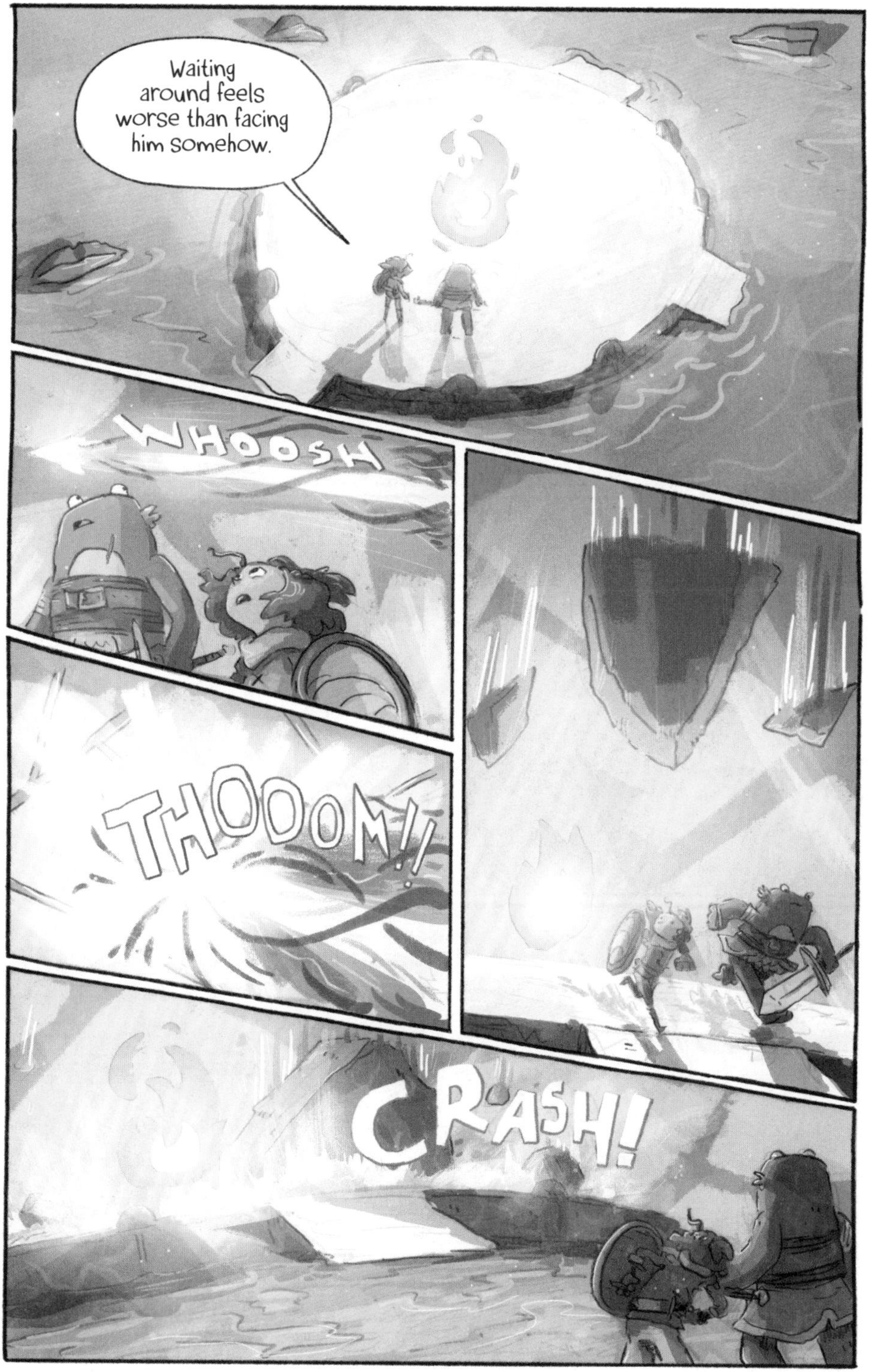
Waiting around feels worse than facing him somehow.
WHOOSH
THOOOM!!
CRASH!

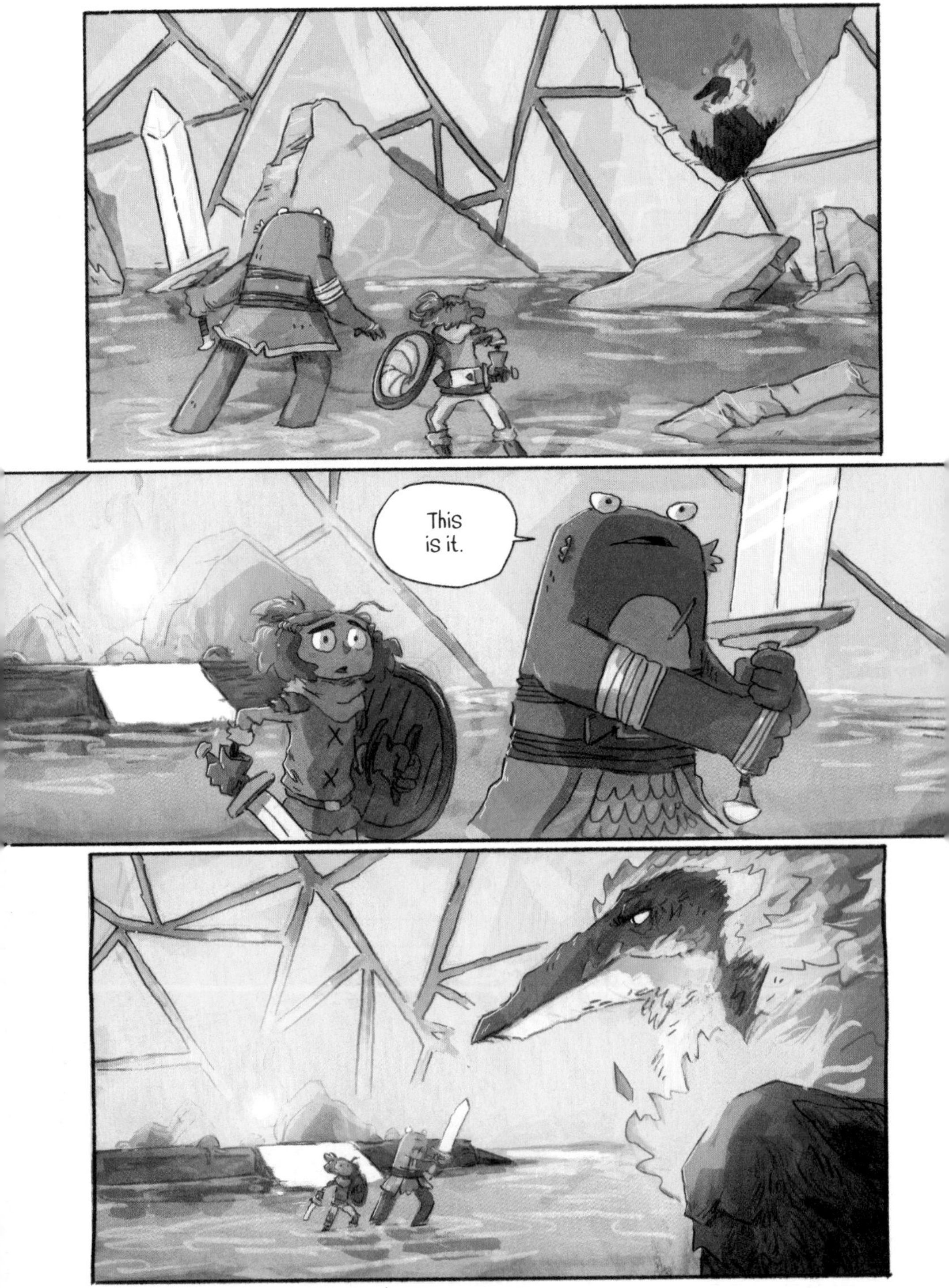
This is it.

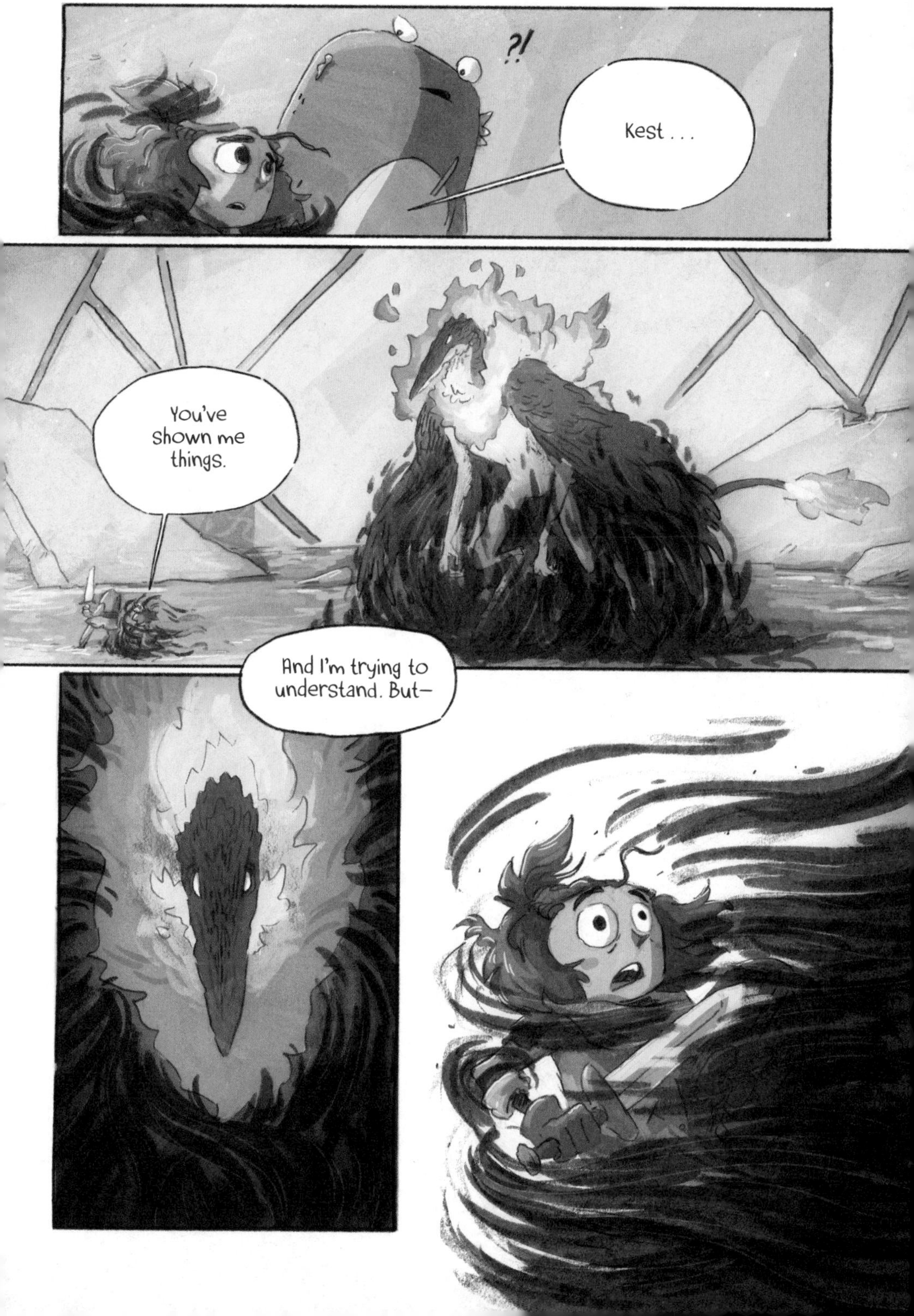
?!
Kest . . .
You've shown me things.
And I'm trying to understand. But—

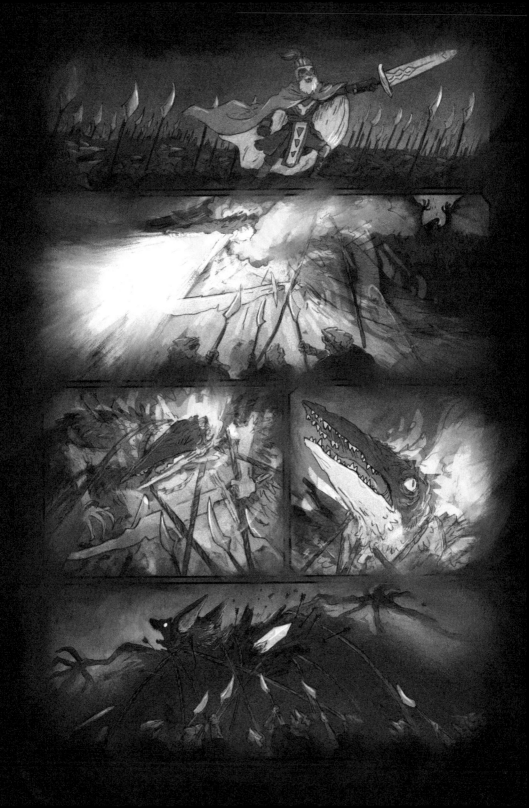

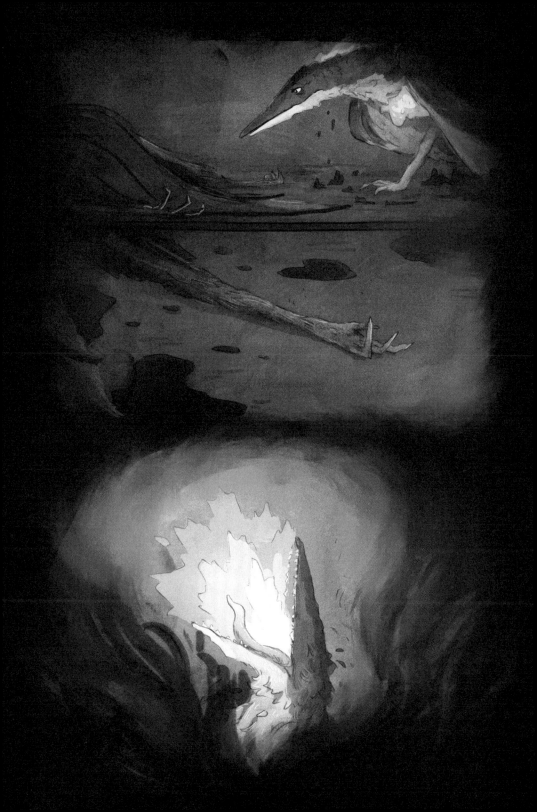

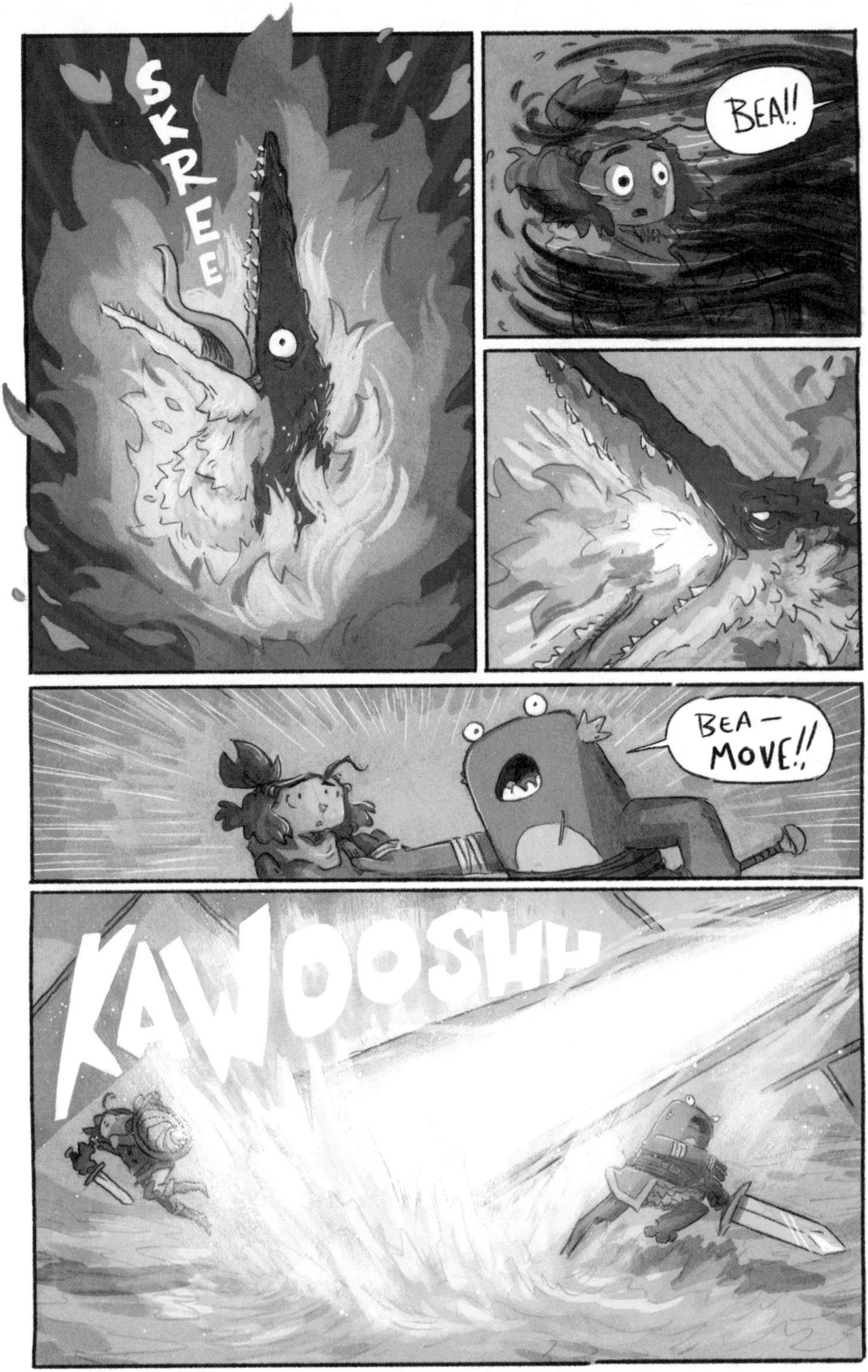
SKREE
BEA!!
BEA—MOVE!!
KAWOOSHH

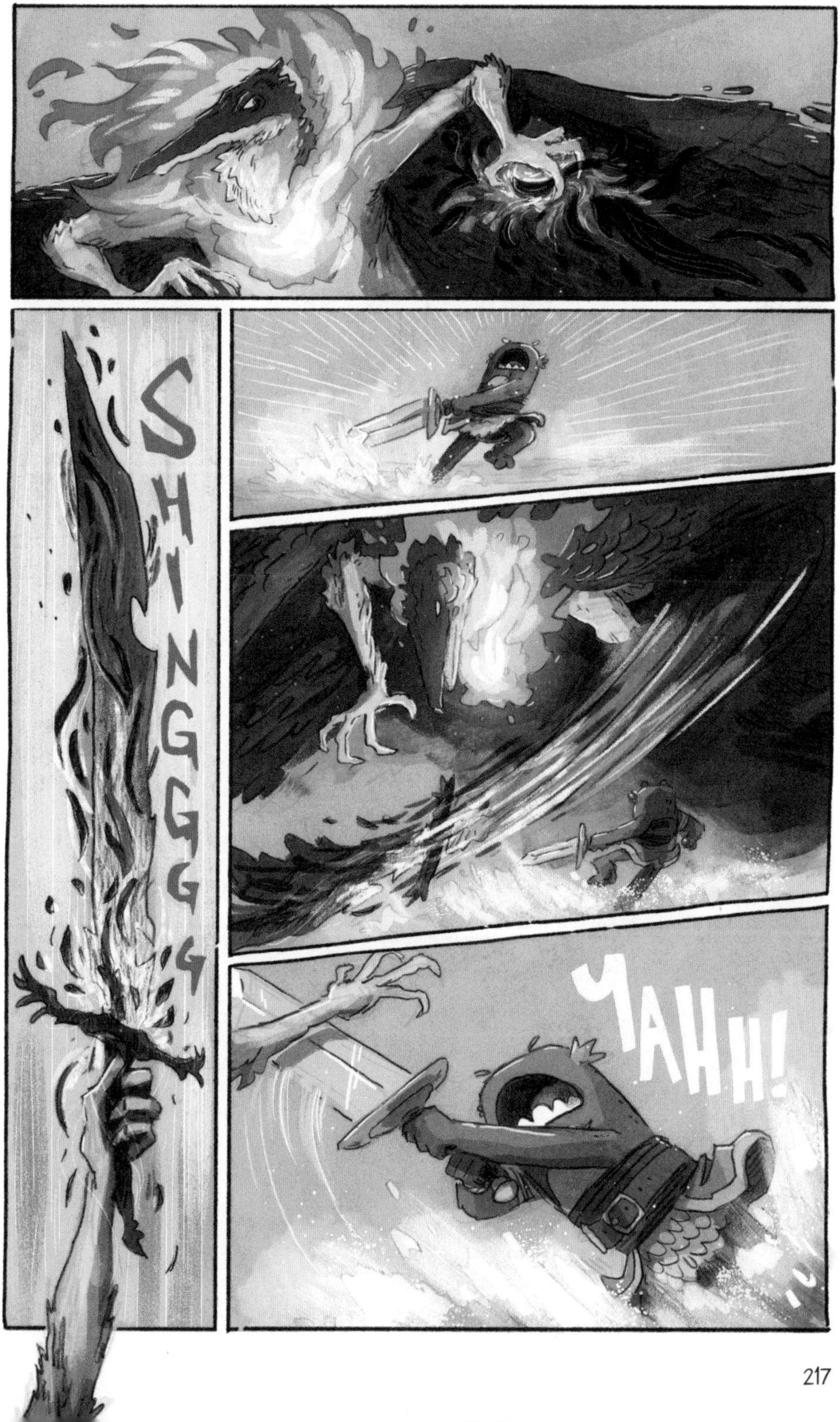
SHINGGGG
YAHH!

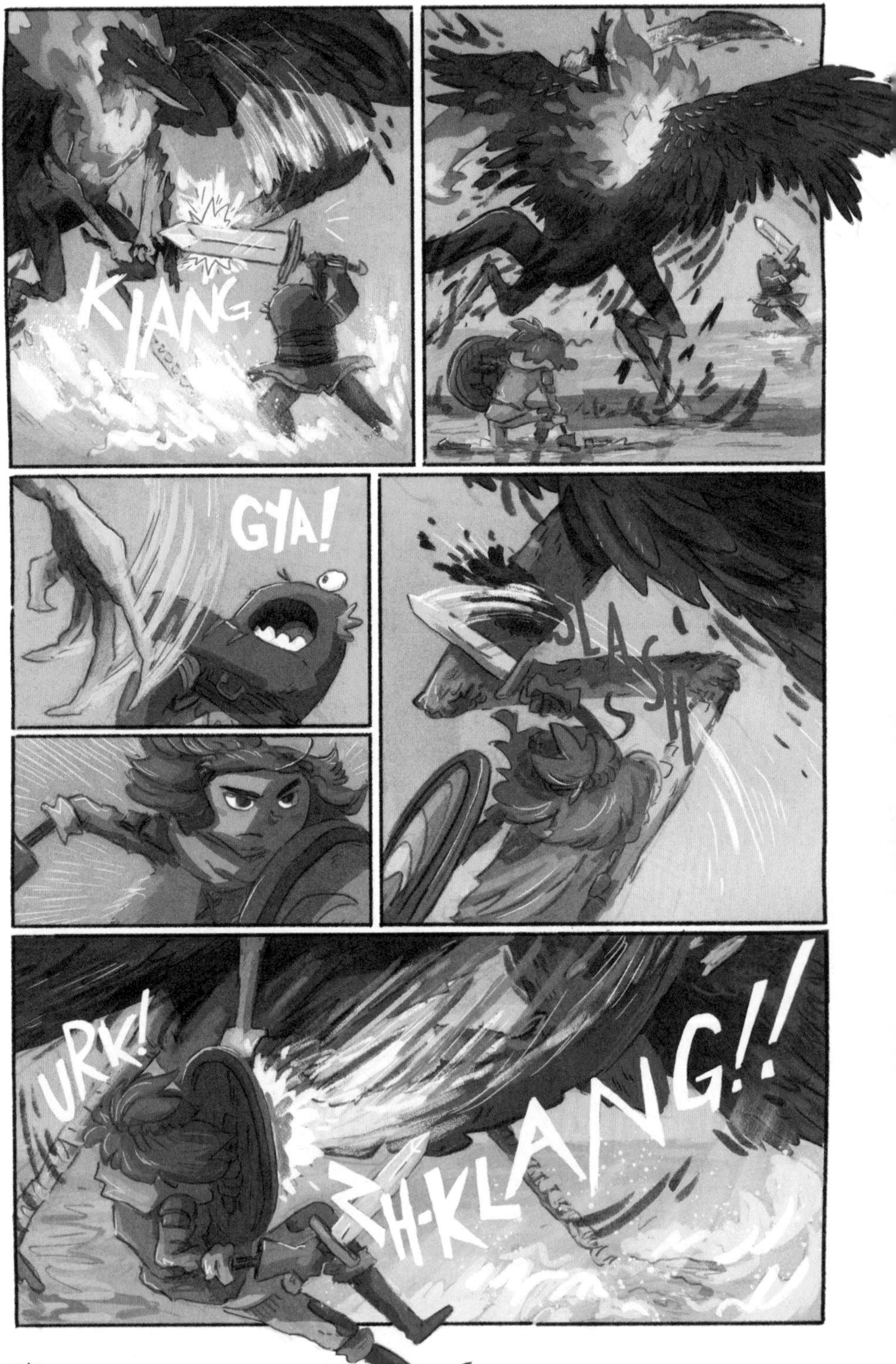
KLANG
GYA!
SLASH
URK!
ZH-KLANG!!

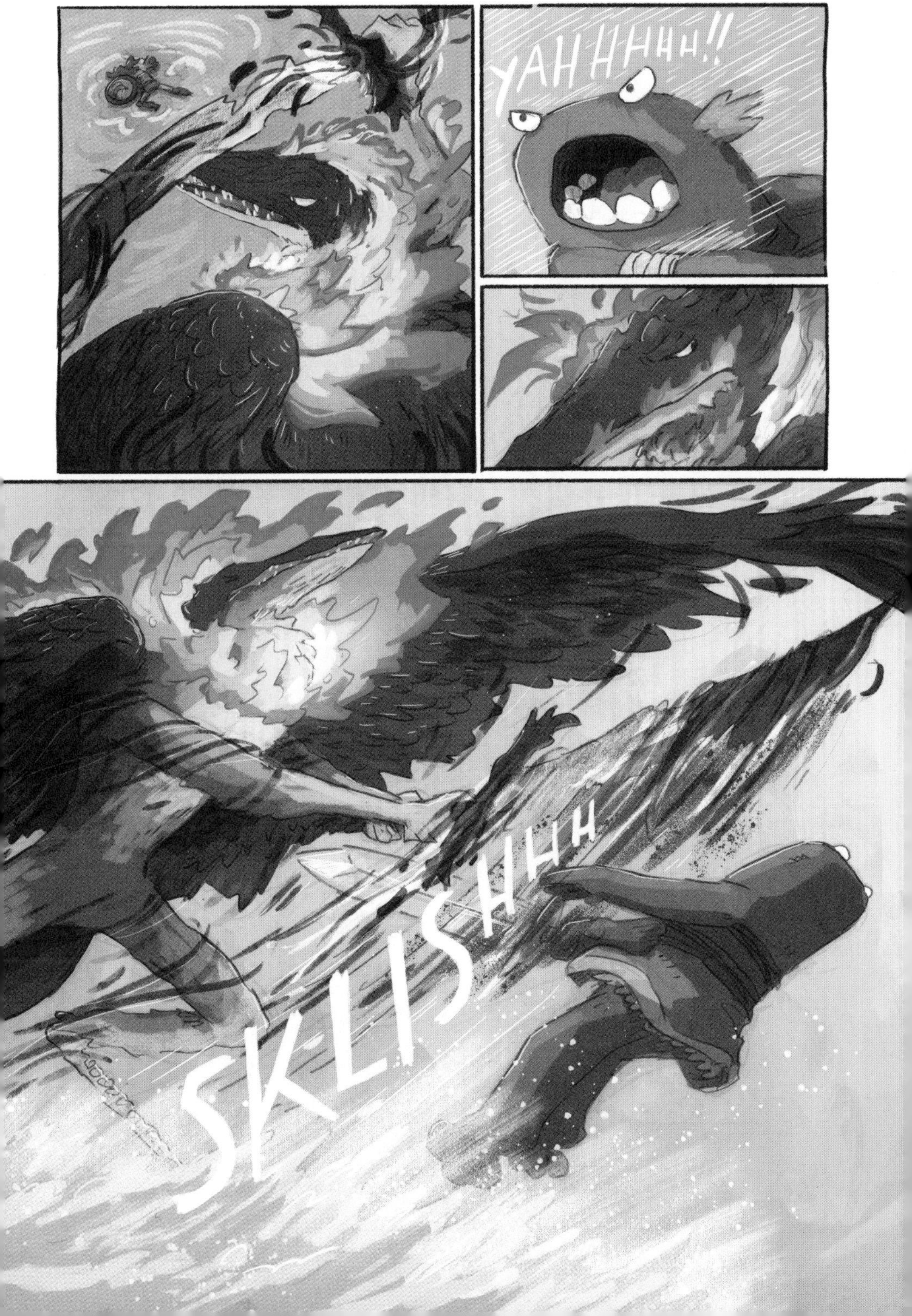
YAHHHHH!!
SKLISHHH

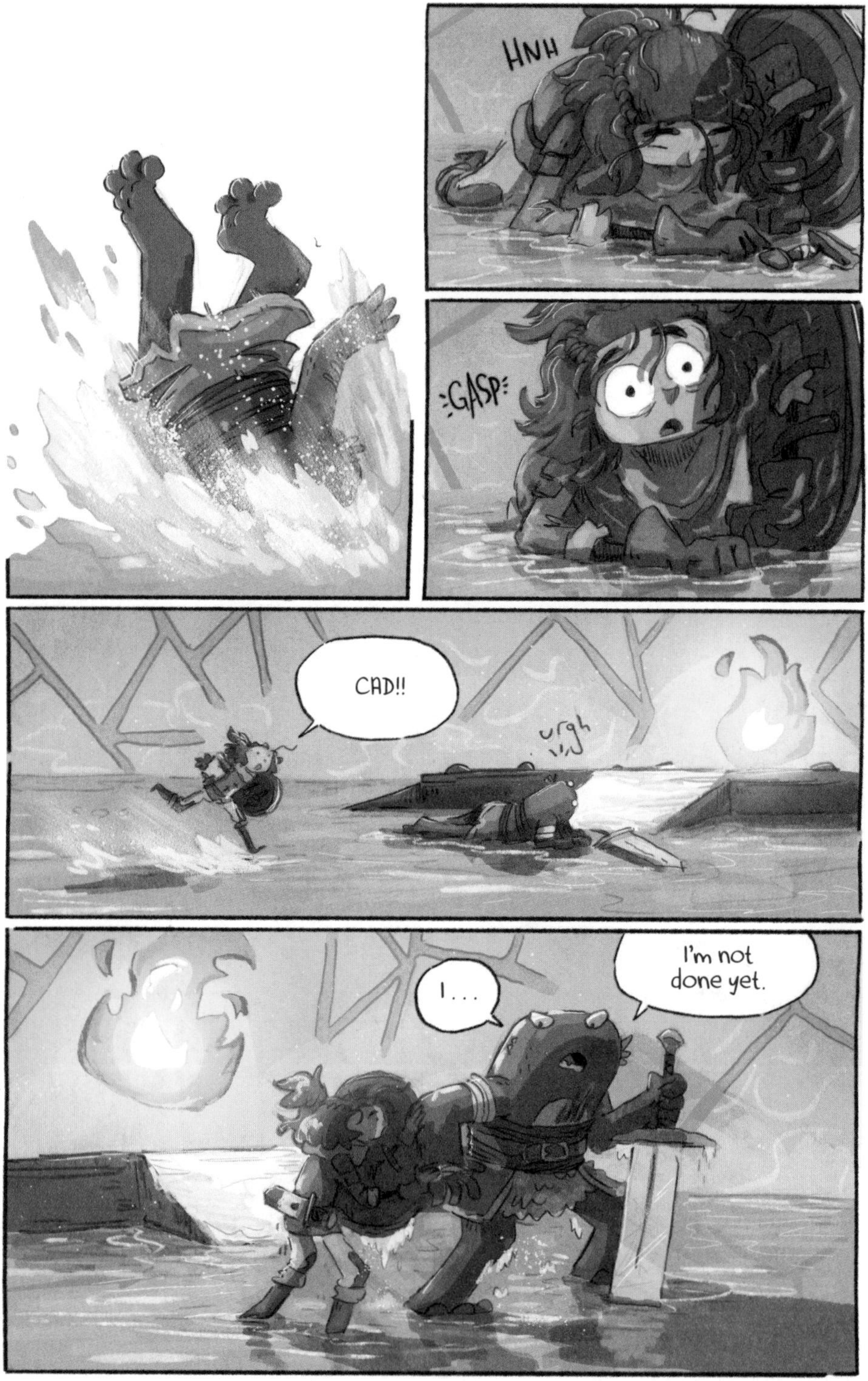
HNH
GASP
CAD!!
urgh
I...
I'm not done yet.

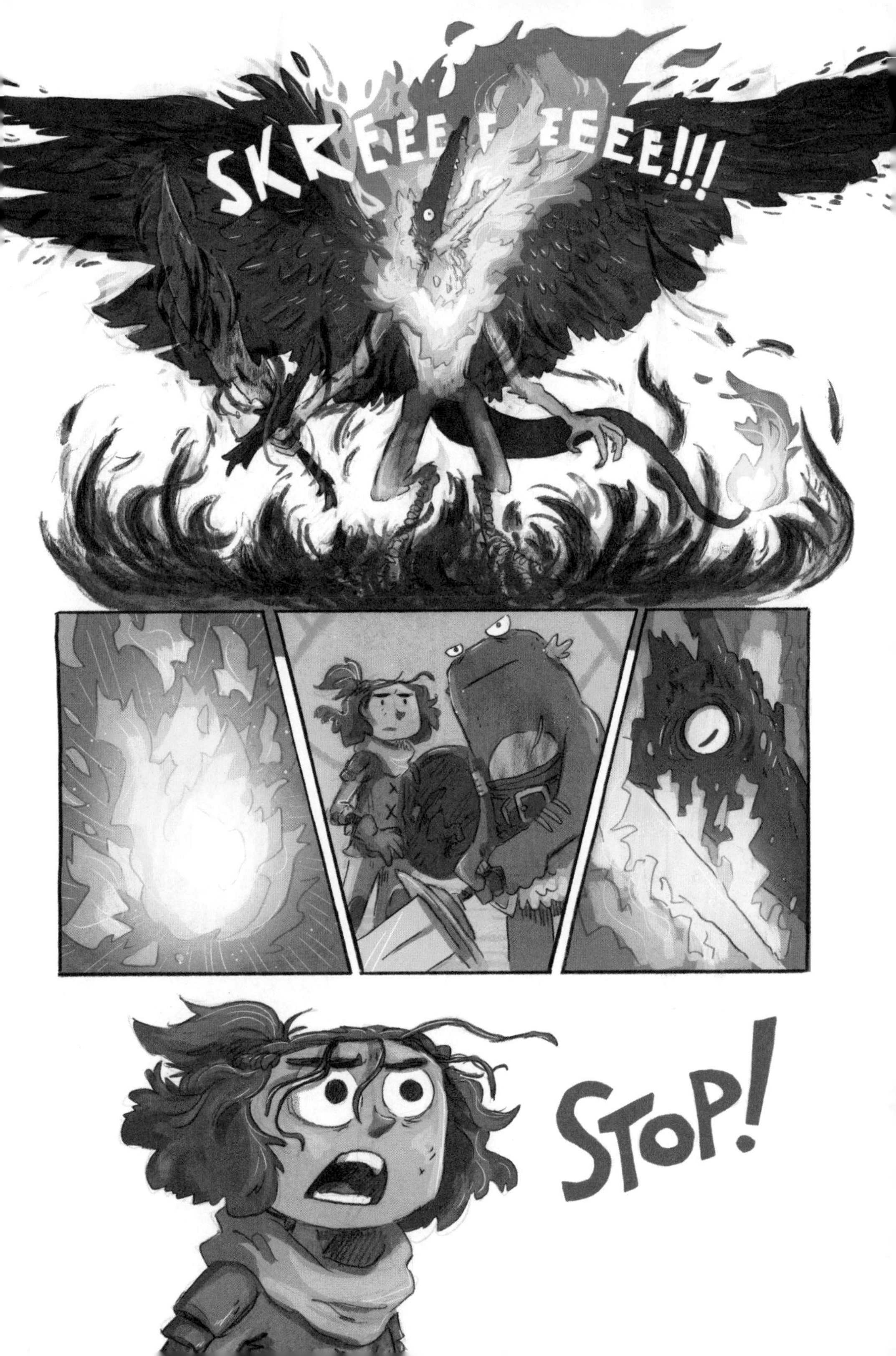
SKREEEEEEEE!!!
STOP!

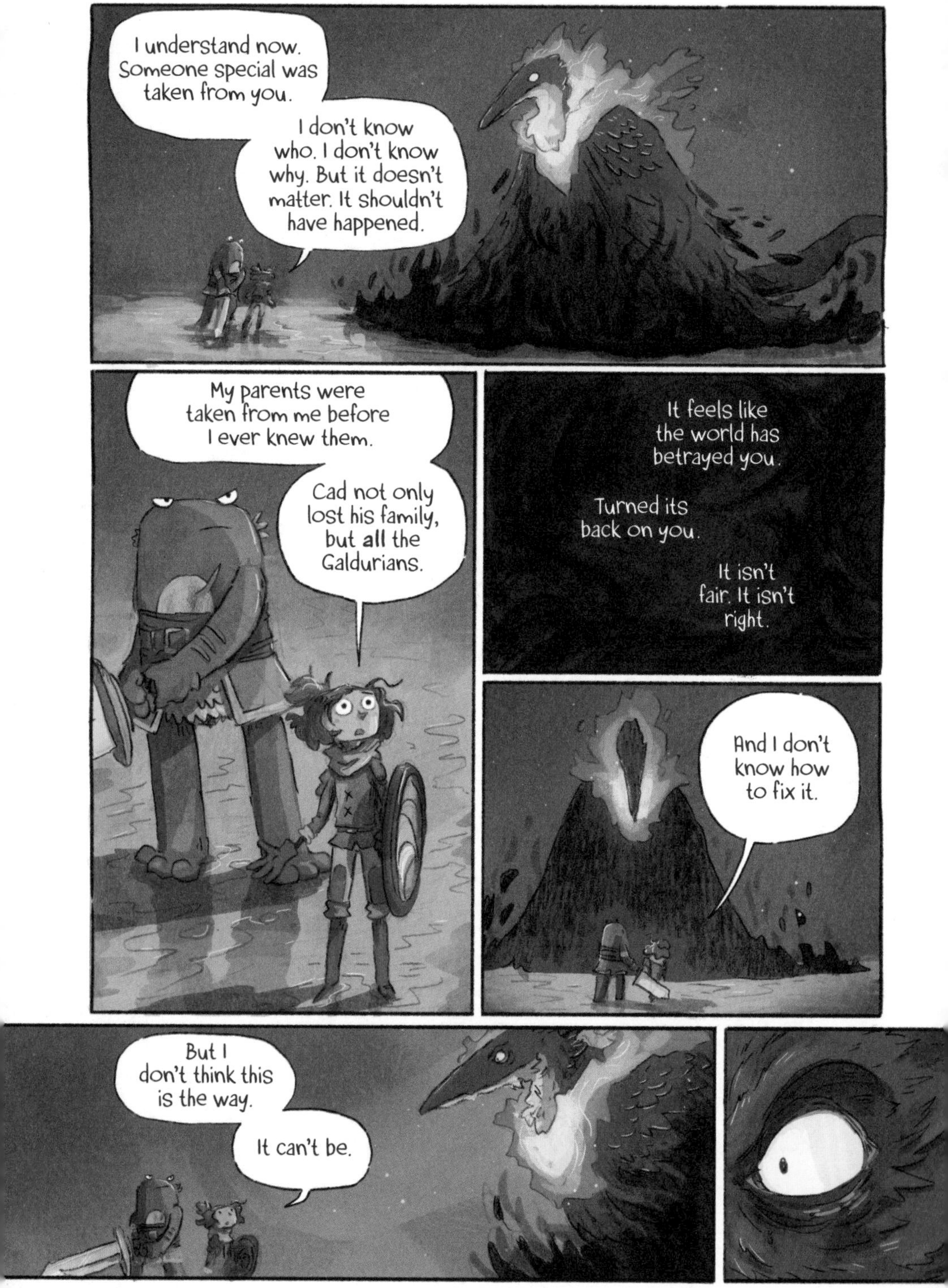
I understand now. Someone special was taken from you.
I don't know who. I don't know why. But it doesn't matter. It shouldn't have happened.
My parents were taken from me before I ever knew them.
Cad not only lost his family, but **all** the Galdurians.
It feels like the world has betrayed you.
Turned its back on you.
It isn't fair. It isn't right.
And I don't know how to fix it.
But I don't think this is the way.
It can't be.

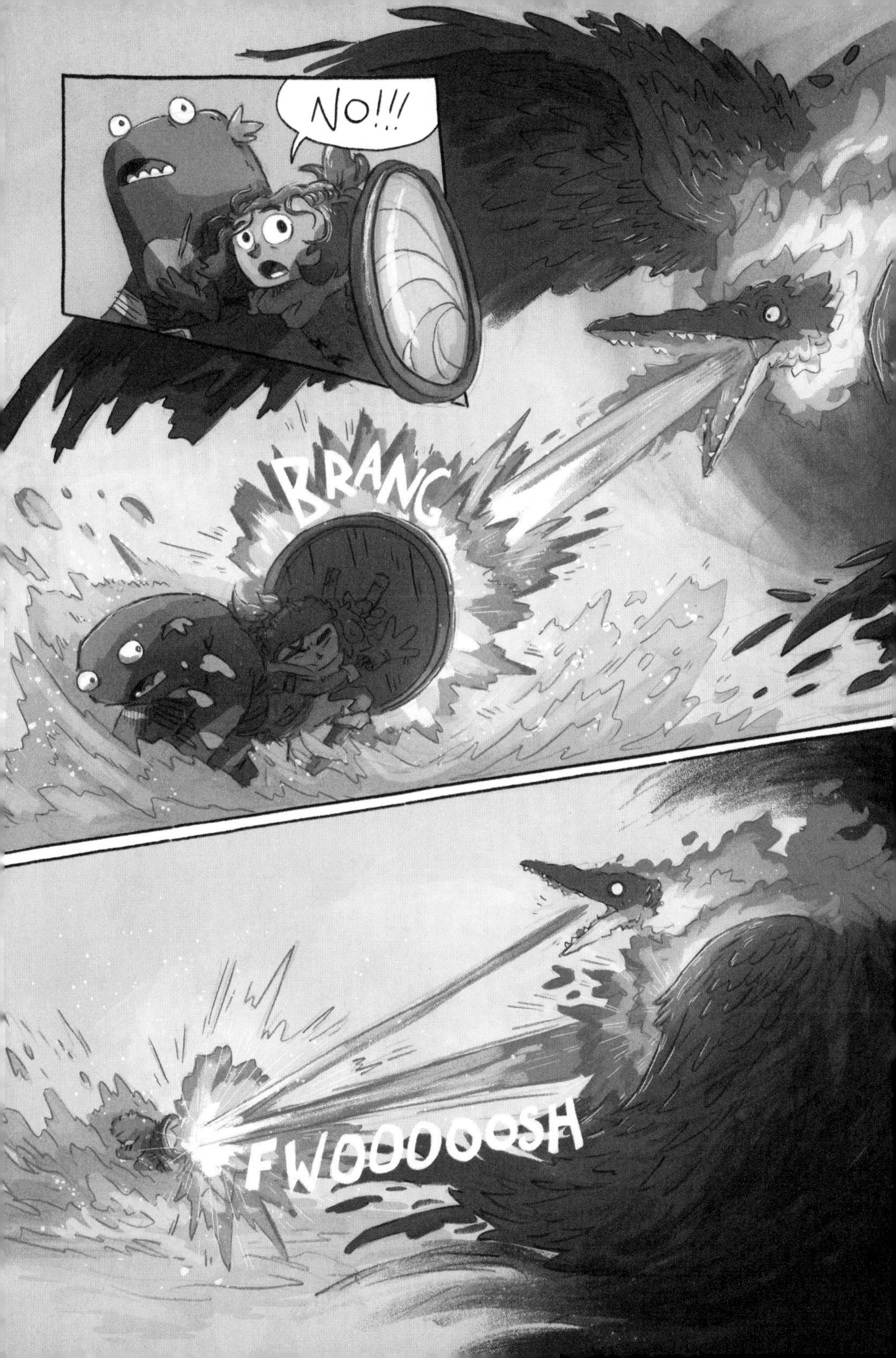
NO!!!
BRANG
FWOOOOOSH

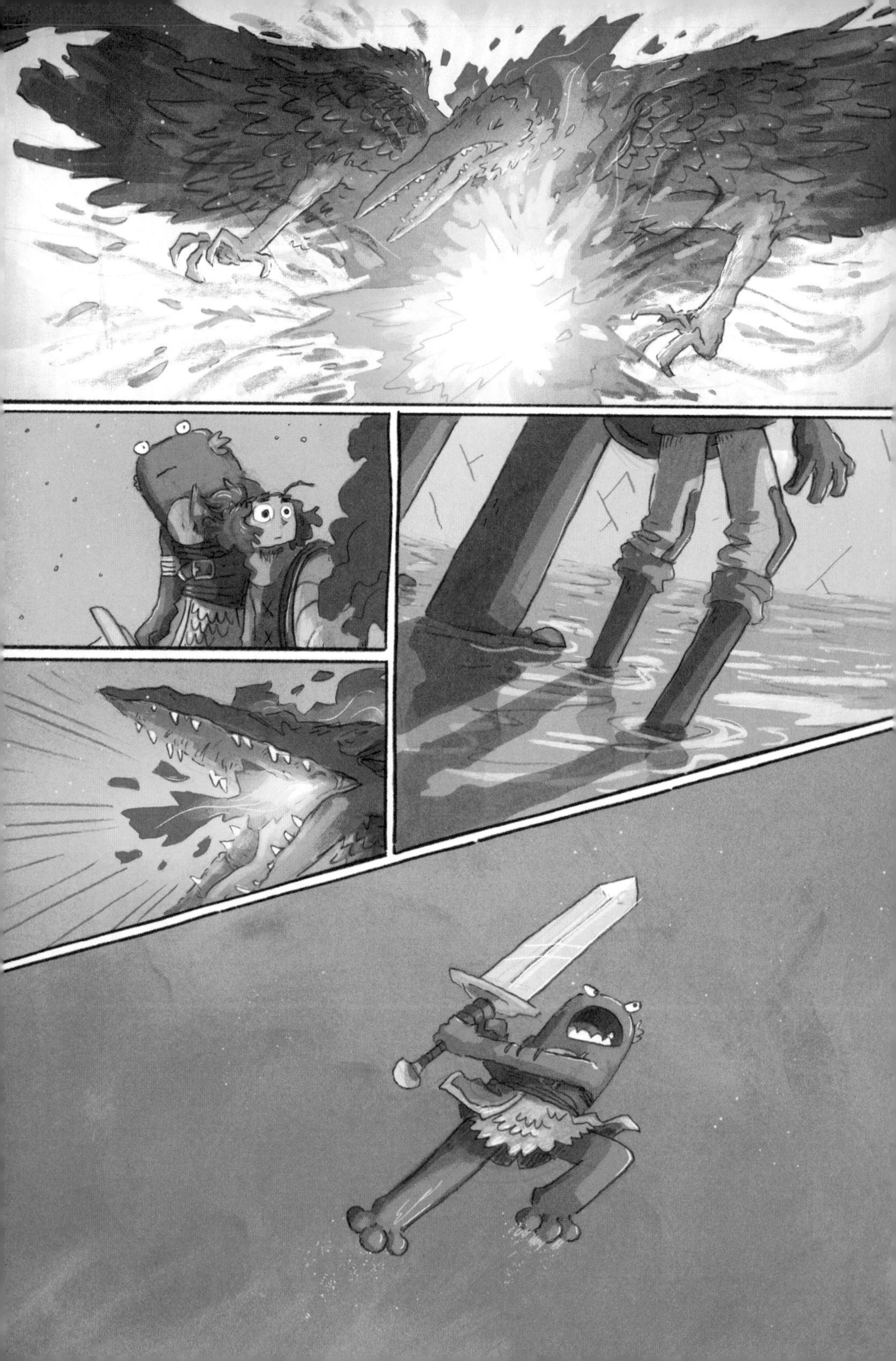

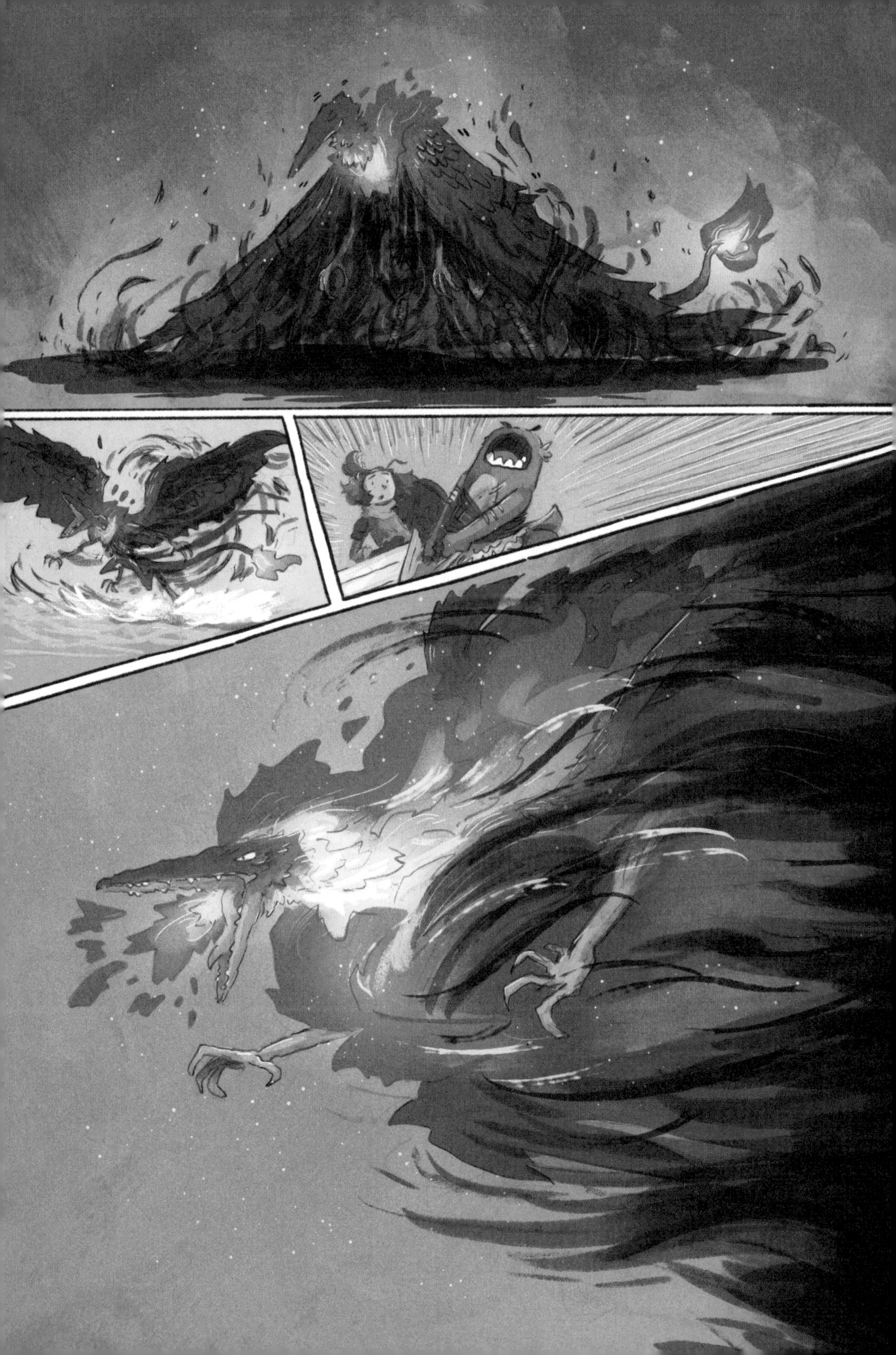

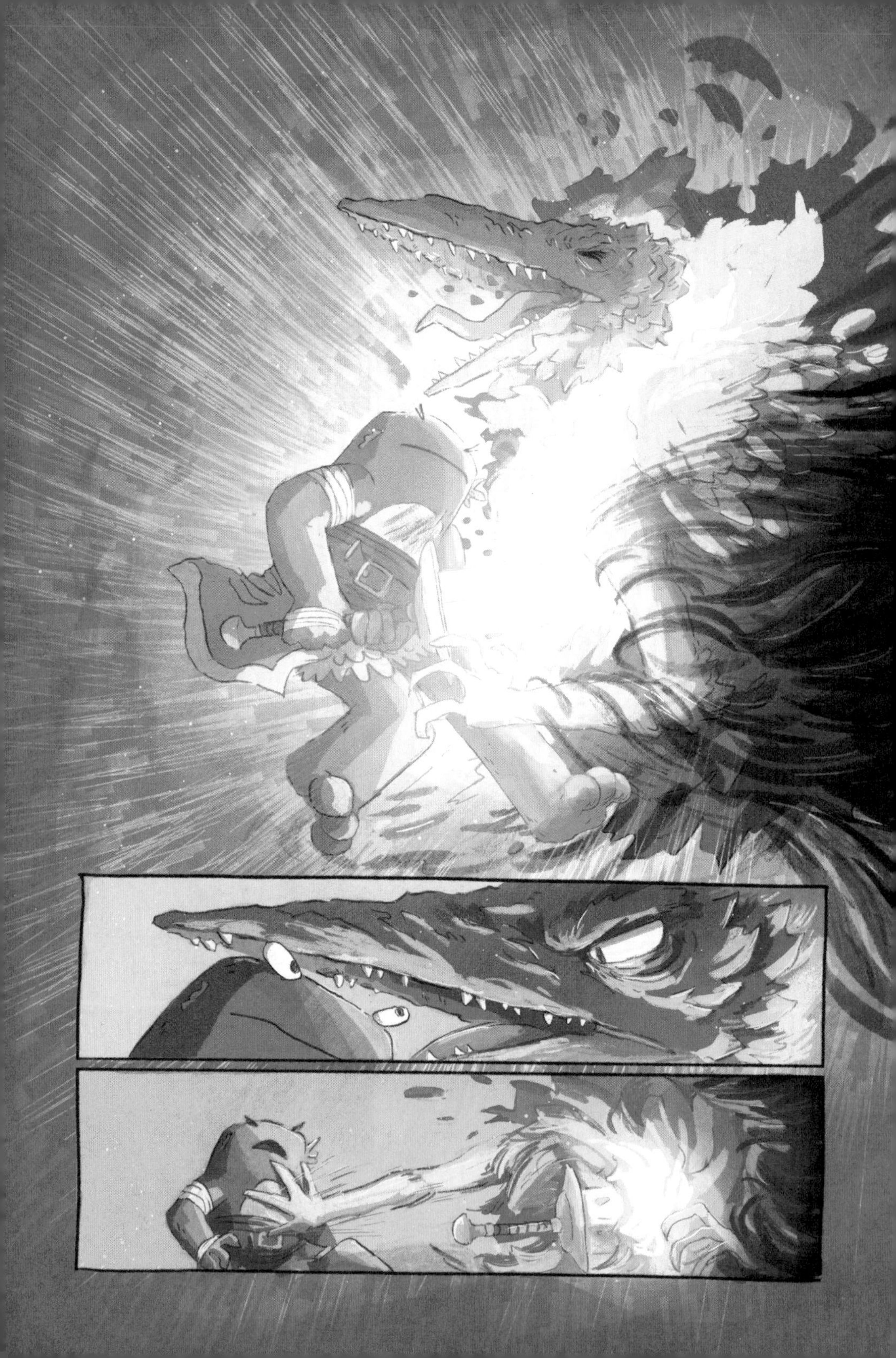

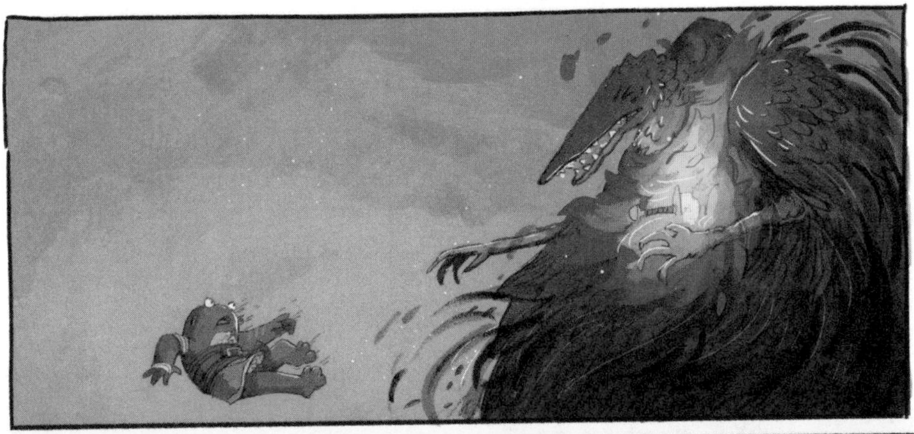

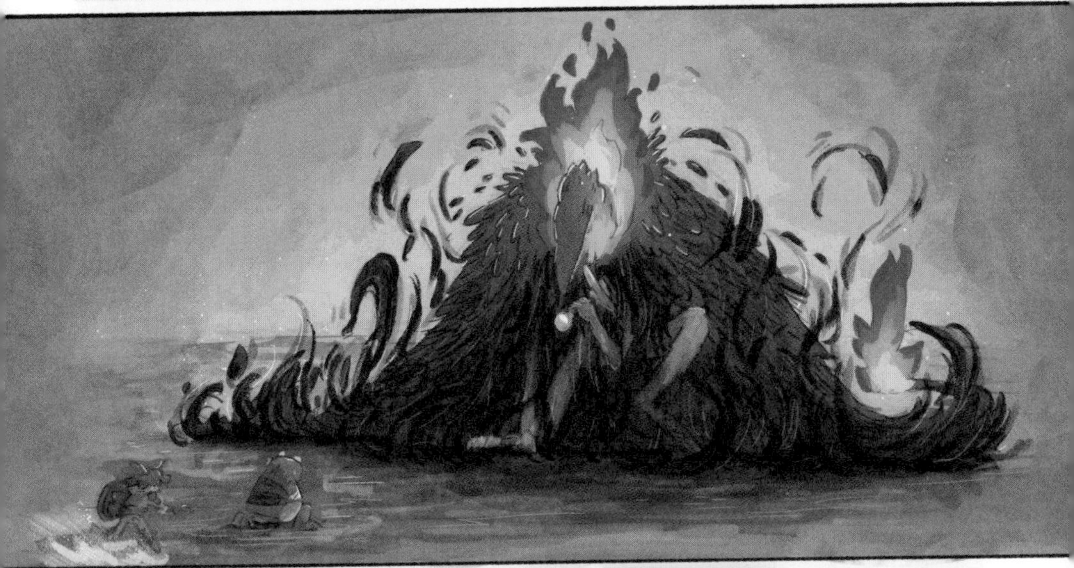

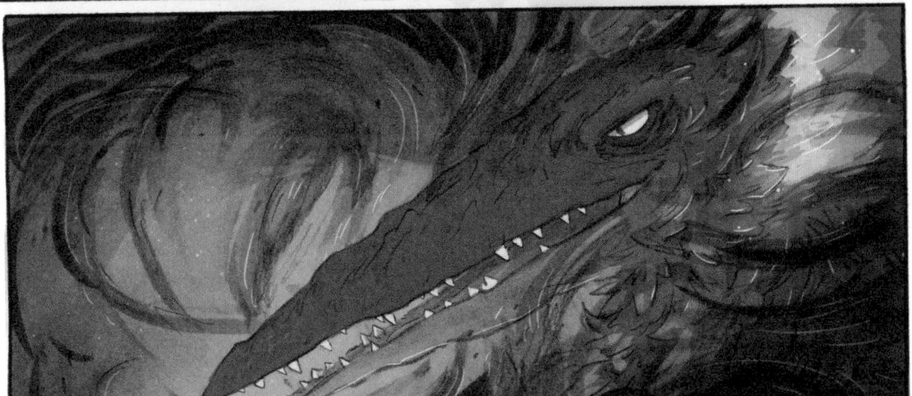

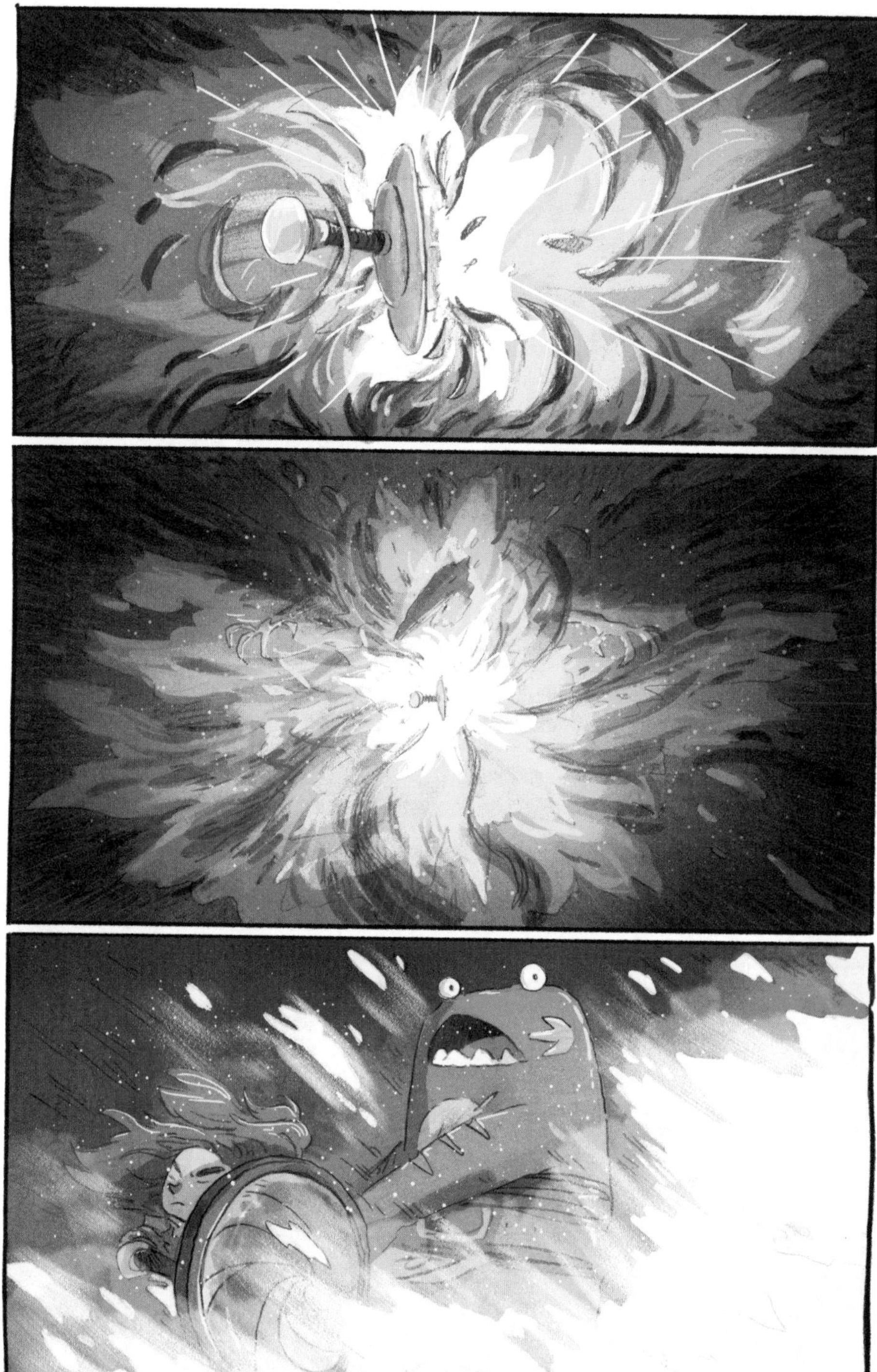

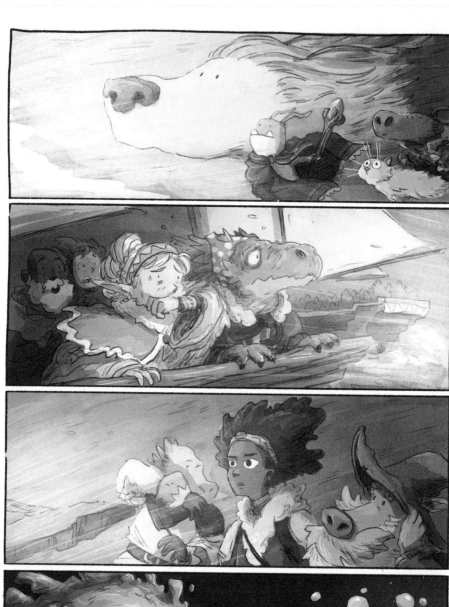
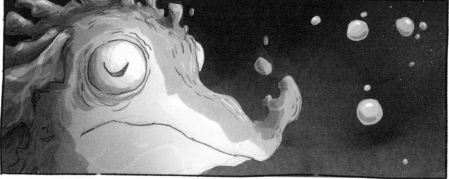

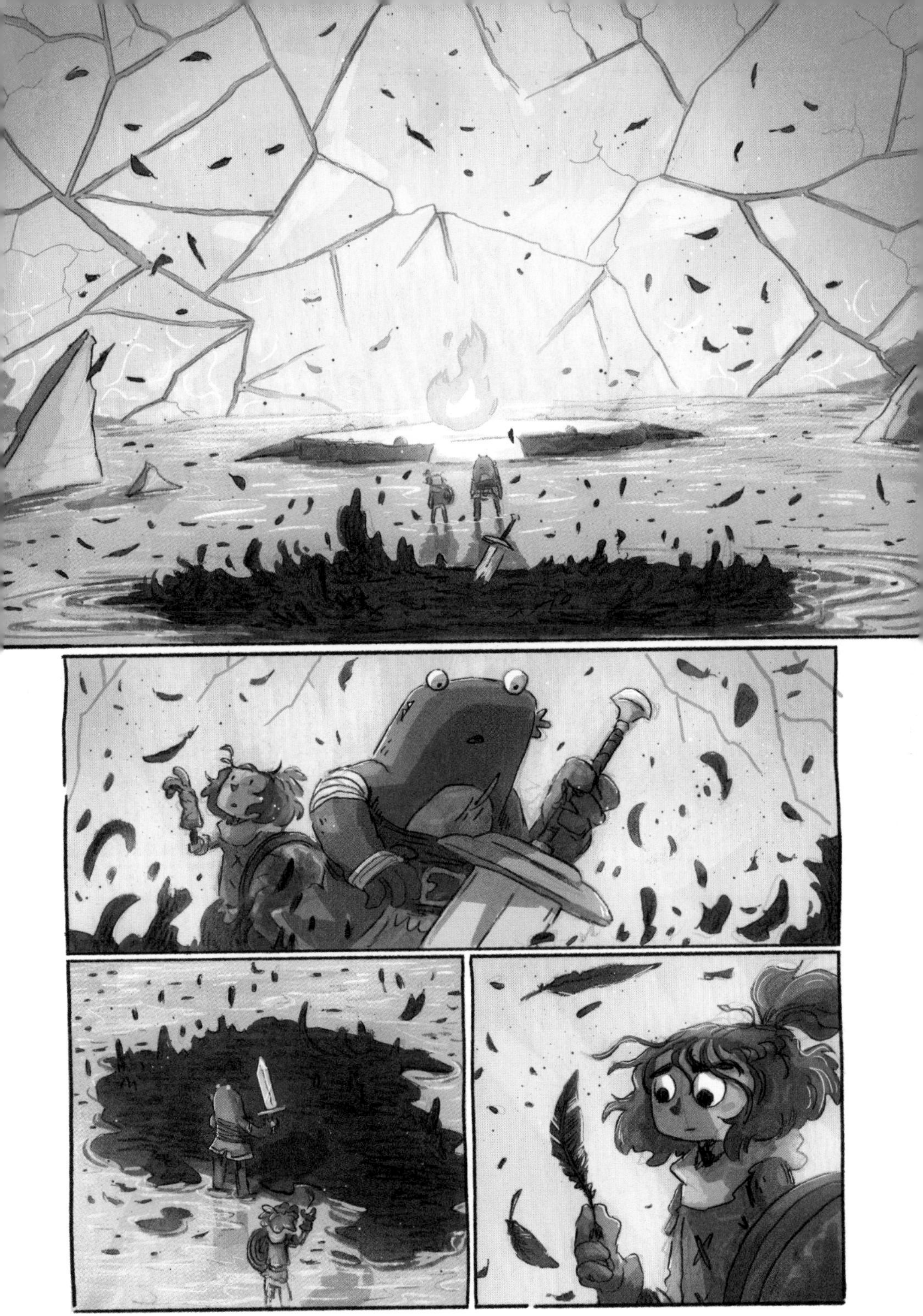

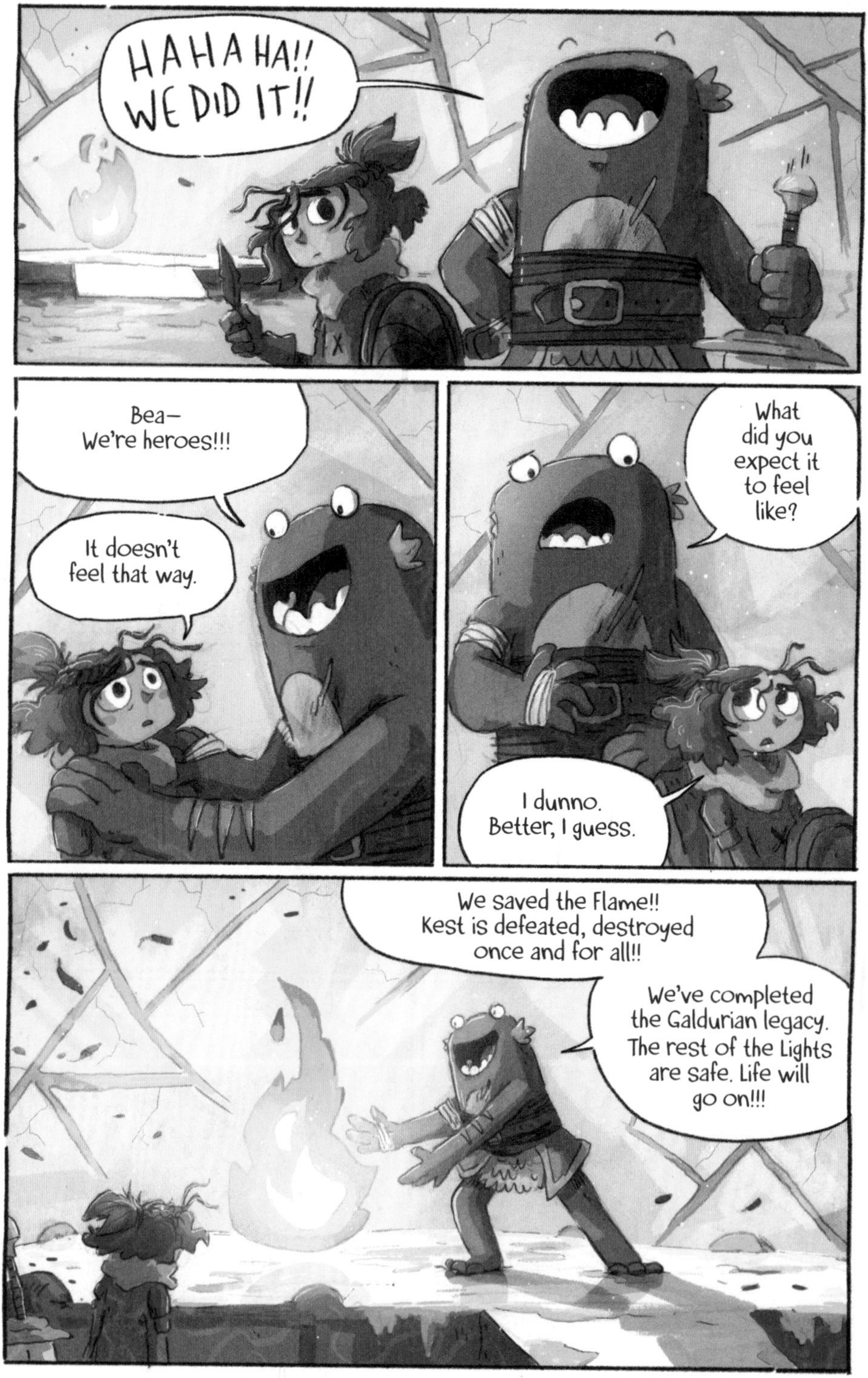
HAHAHA!!
WE DID IT!!
Bea—
We're heroes!!!
It doesn't feel that way.
What did you expect it to feel like?
I dunno. Better, I guess.
We saved the Flame!! Kest is defeated, destroyed once and for all!!
We've completed the Galdurian legacy. The rest of the Lights are safe. Life will go on!!!

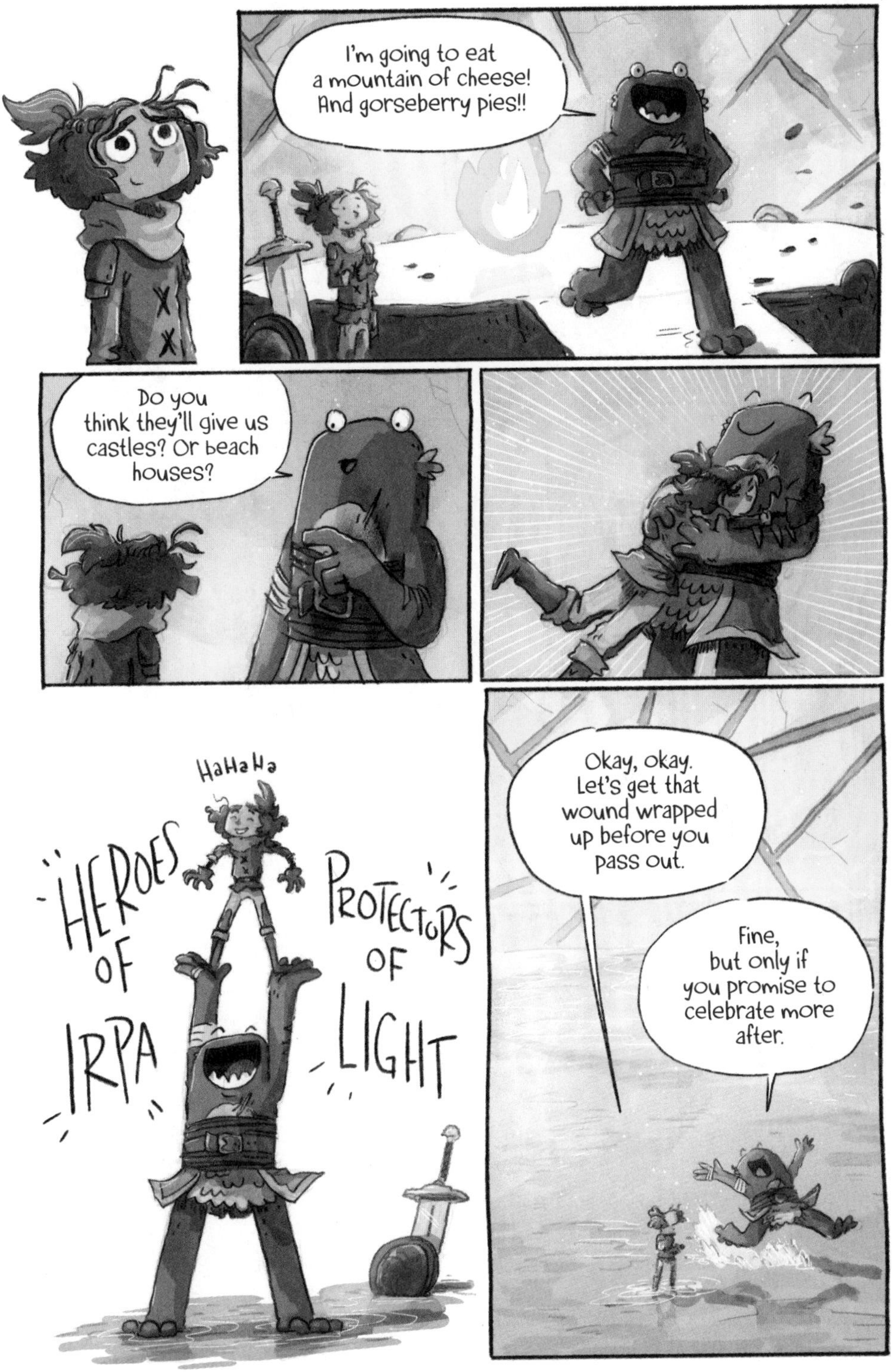
I'm going to eat a mountain of cheese! And gorseberry pies!!
Do you think they'll give us castles? Or beach houses?
HaHaHa
HEROES OF IRPA
PROTECTORS OF LIGHT
Okay, okay. Let's get that wound wrapped up before you pass out.
Fine, but only if you promise to celebrate more after.

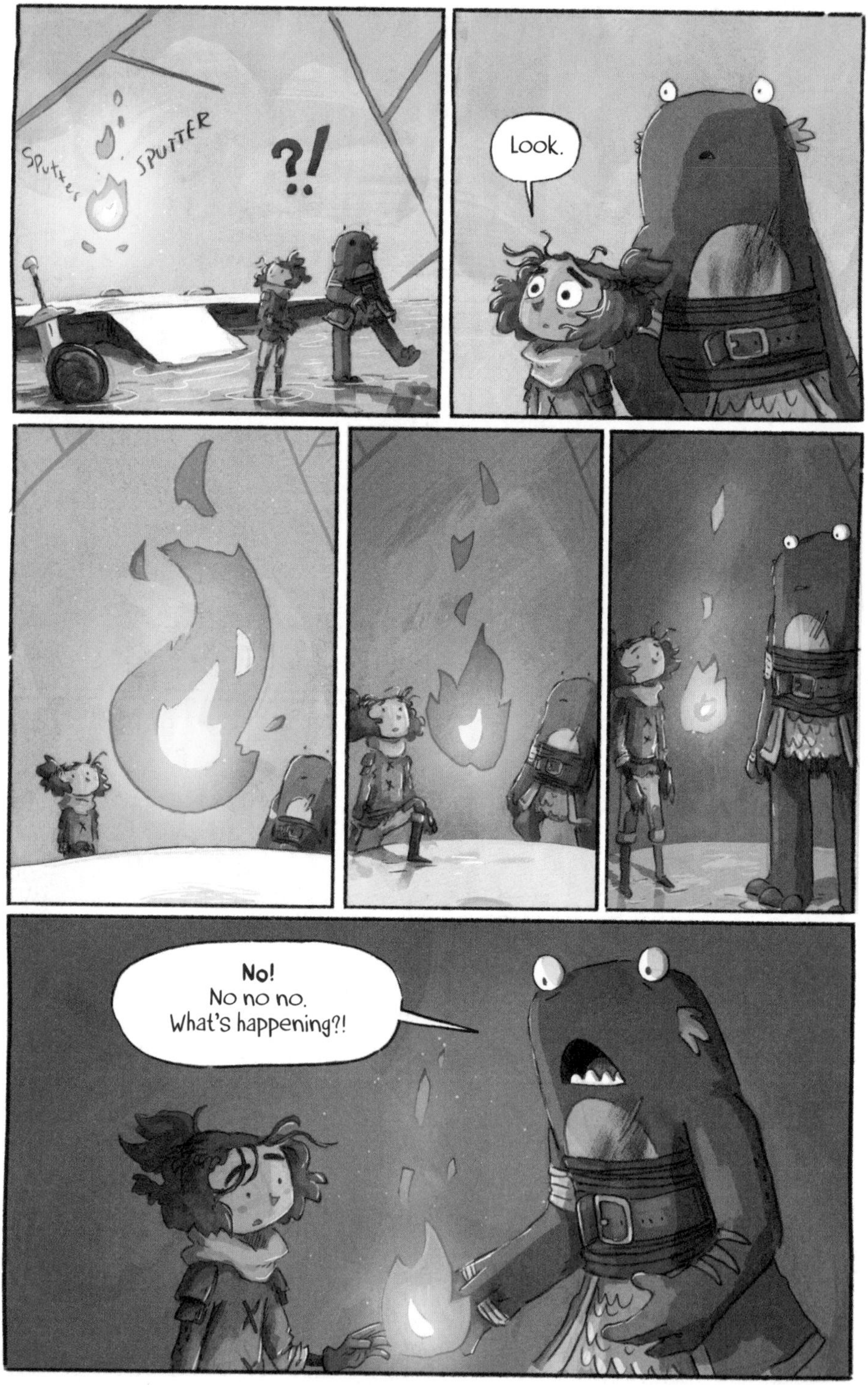
Sputter
SPUTTER
?!
Look.
No!
No no no.
What's happening?!

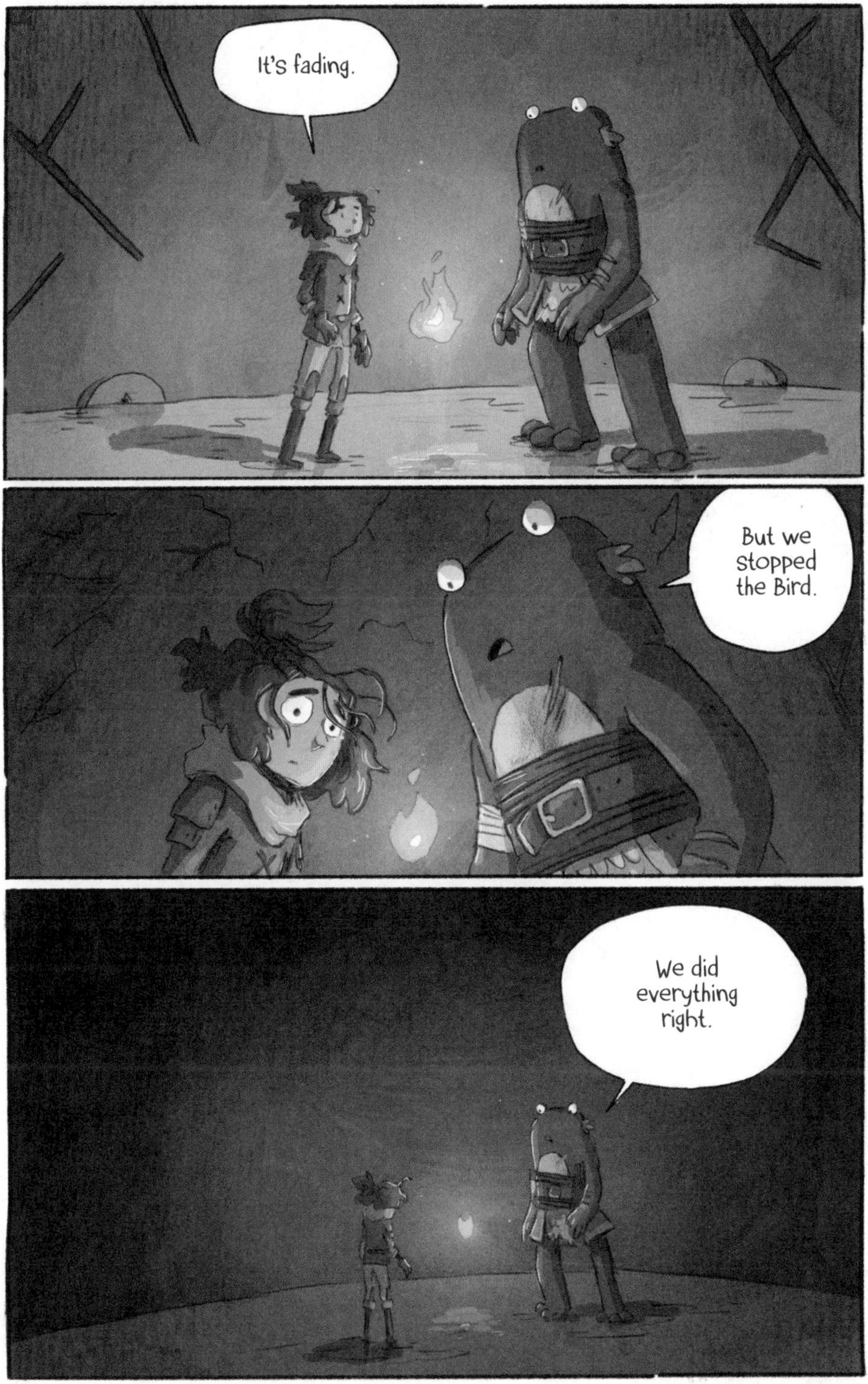
It's fading.
But we stopped the Bird.
We did everything right.

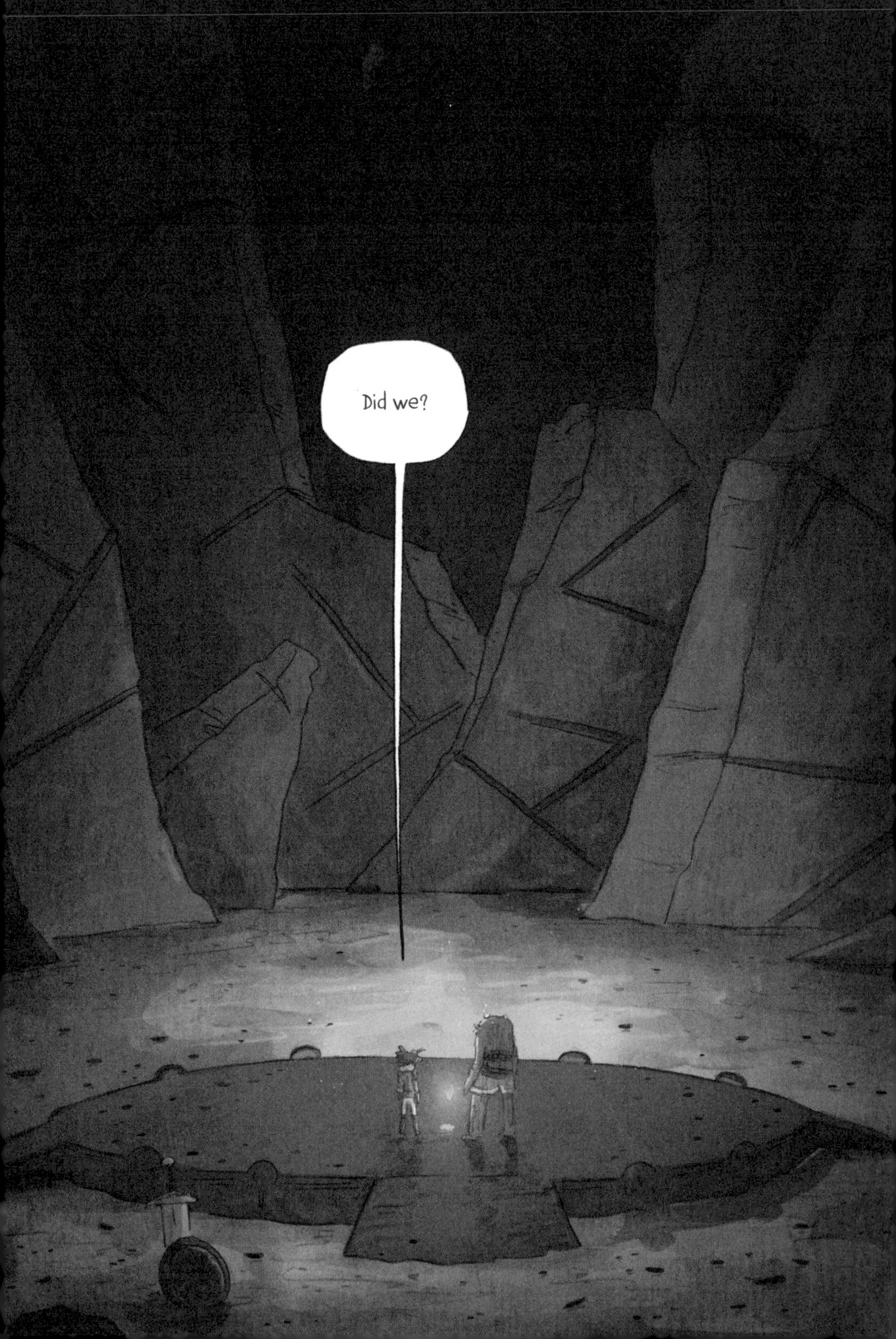
Did we?

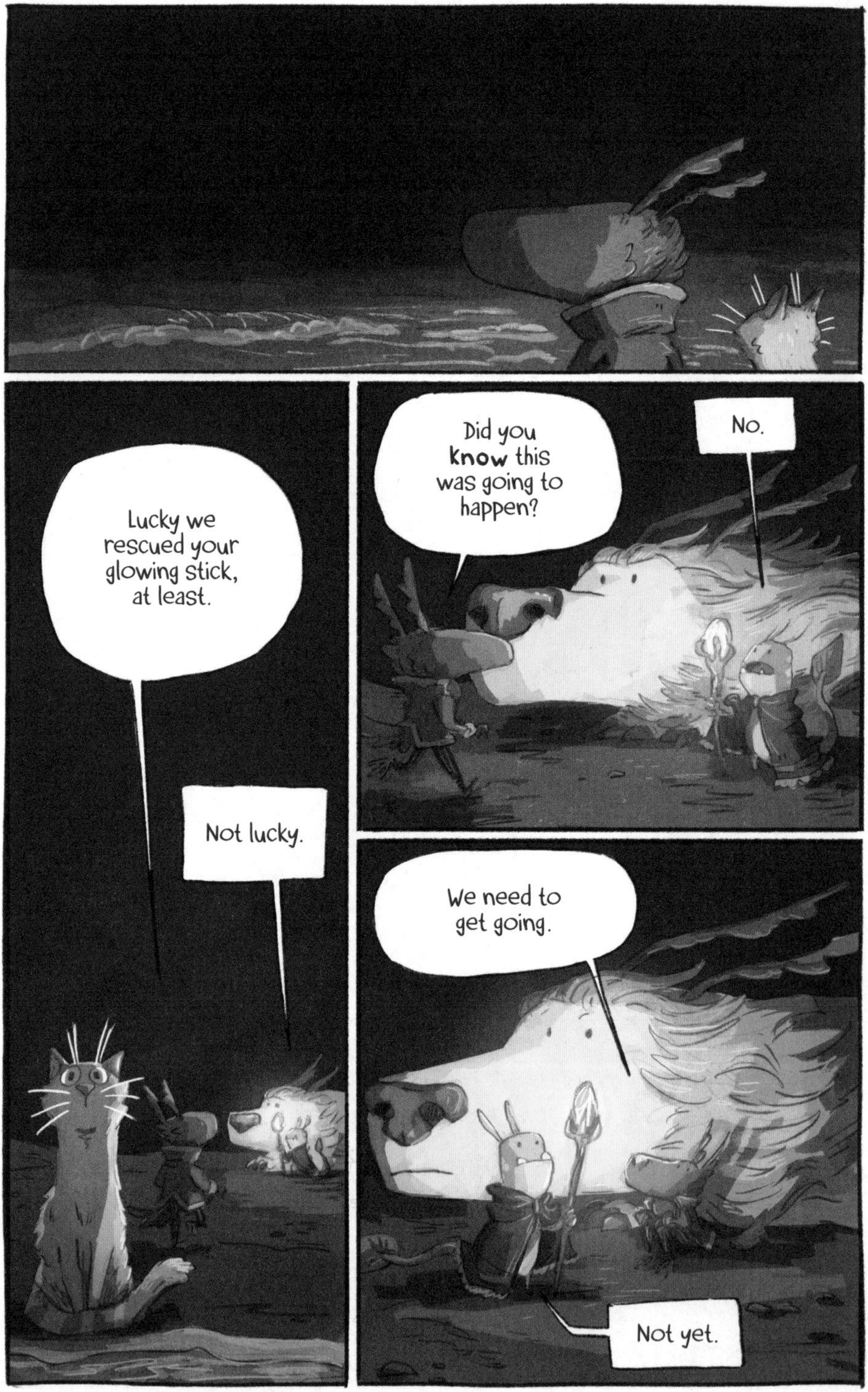

Lucky we rescued your glowing stick, at least.
Not lucky.
Did you **know** this was going to happen?
No.
We need to get going.
Not yet.

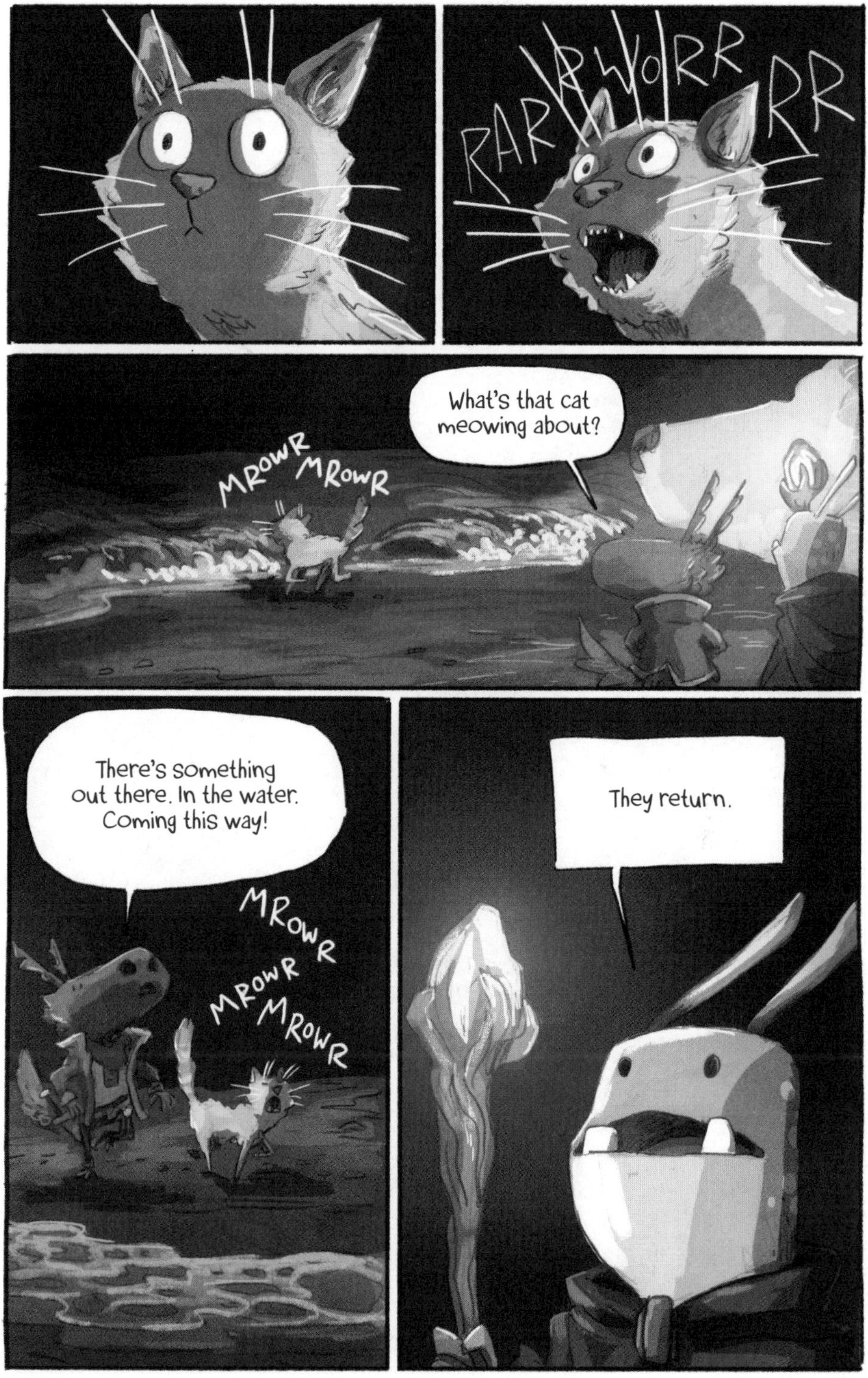
RARRWORRRRR
What's that cat meowing about?
MROWR MROWR
There's something out there. In the water. Coming this way!
MROWR
MROWR MROWR
They return.

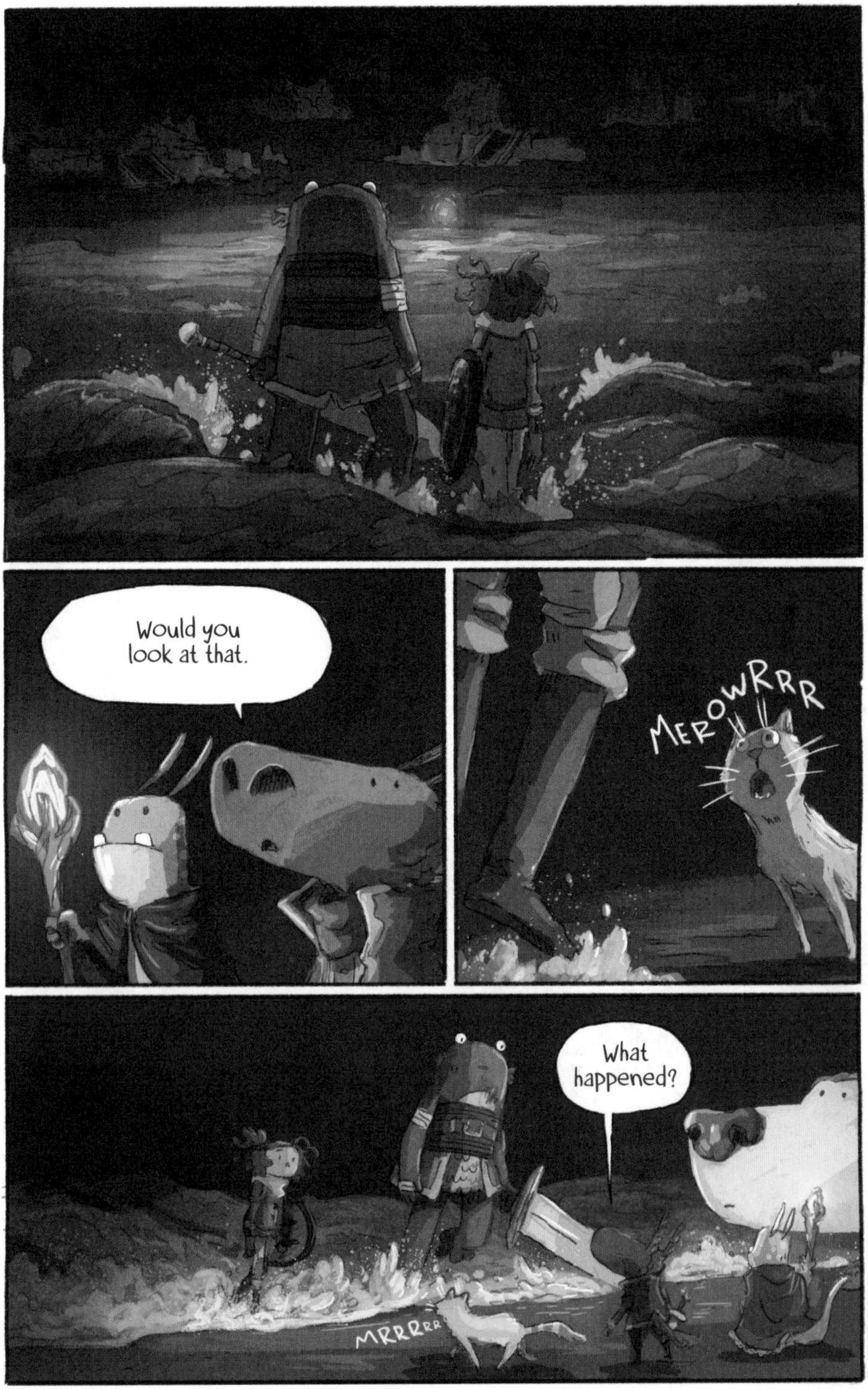
Would you look at that.
MEROWRRR
What happened?
MRRRRR

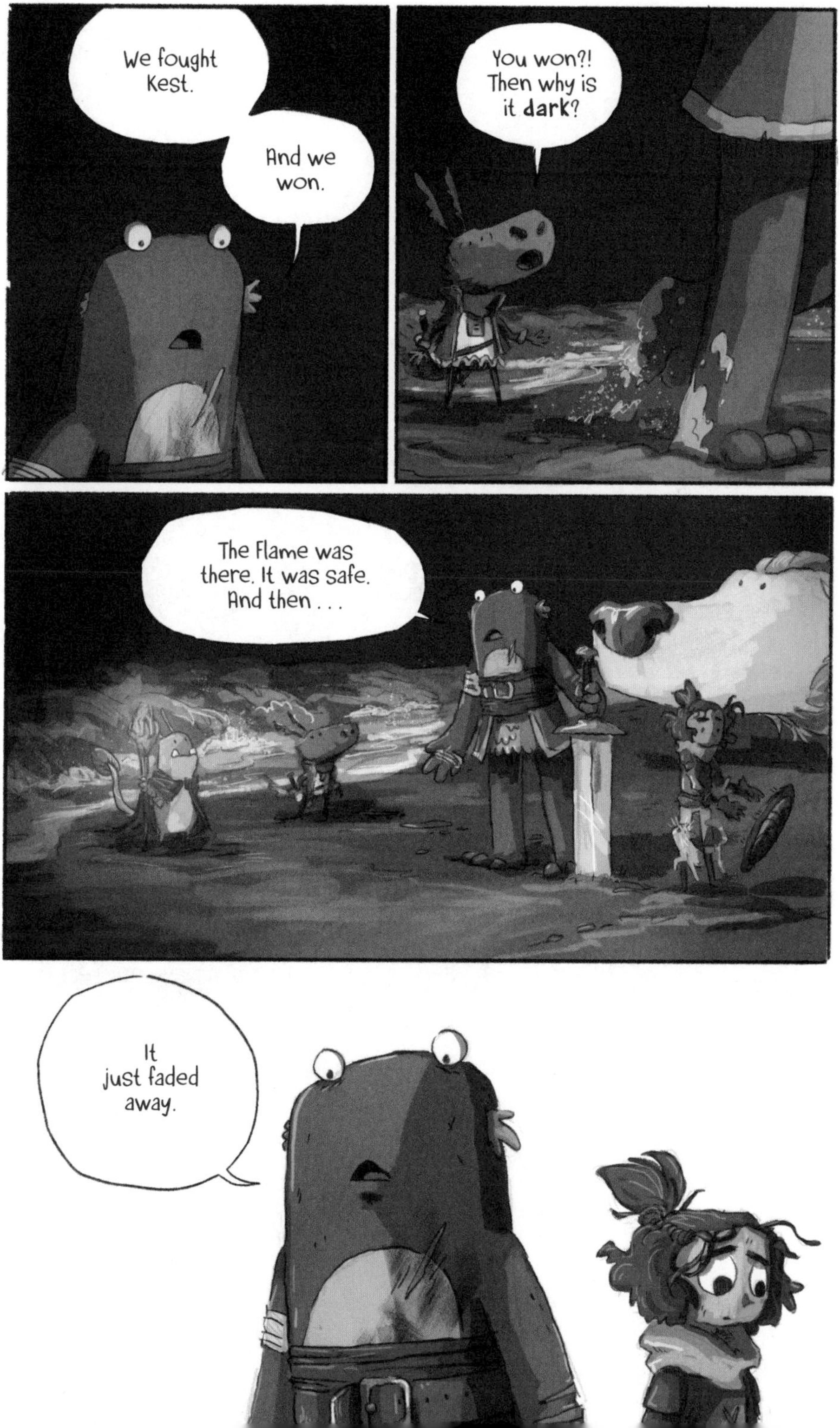
We fought Kest.
And we won.
You won?! Then why is it **dark**?
The Flame was there. It was safe. And then . . .
It just faded away.

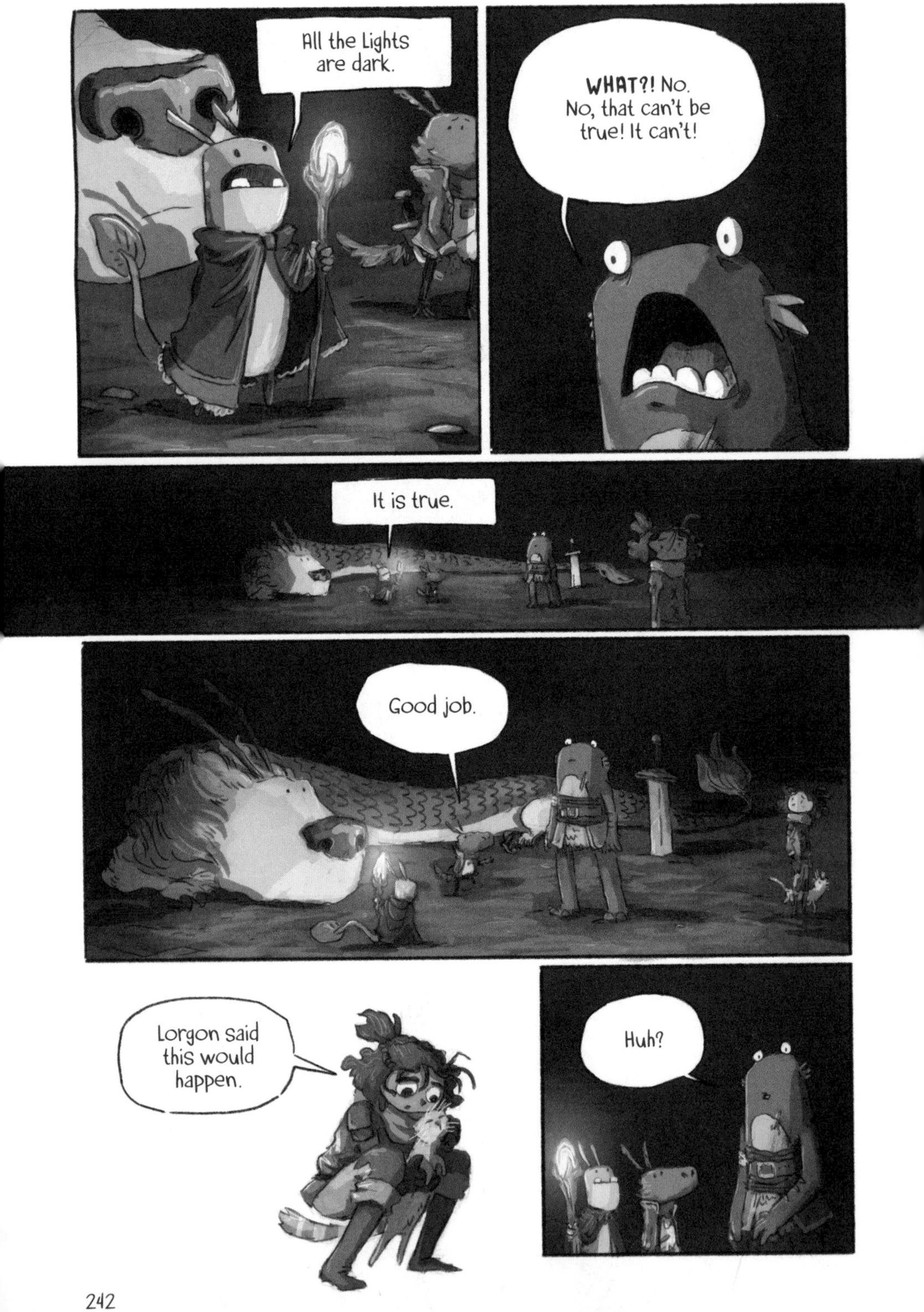
All the Lights are dark.
WHAT?! No. No, that can't be true! It can't!
It is true.
Good job.
Lorgon said this would happen.
Huh?

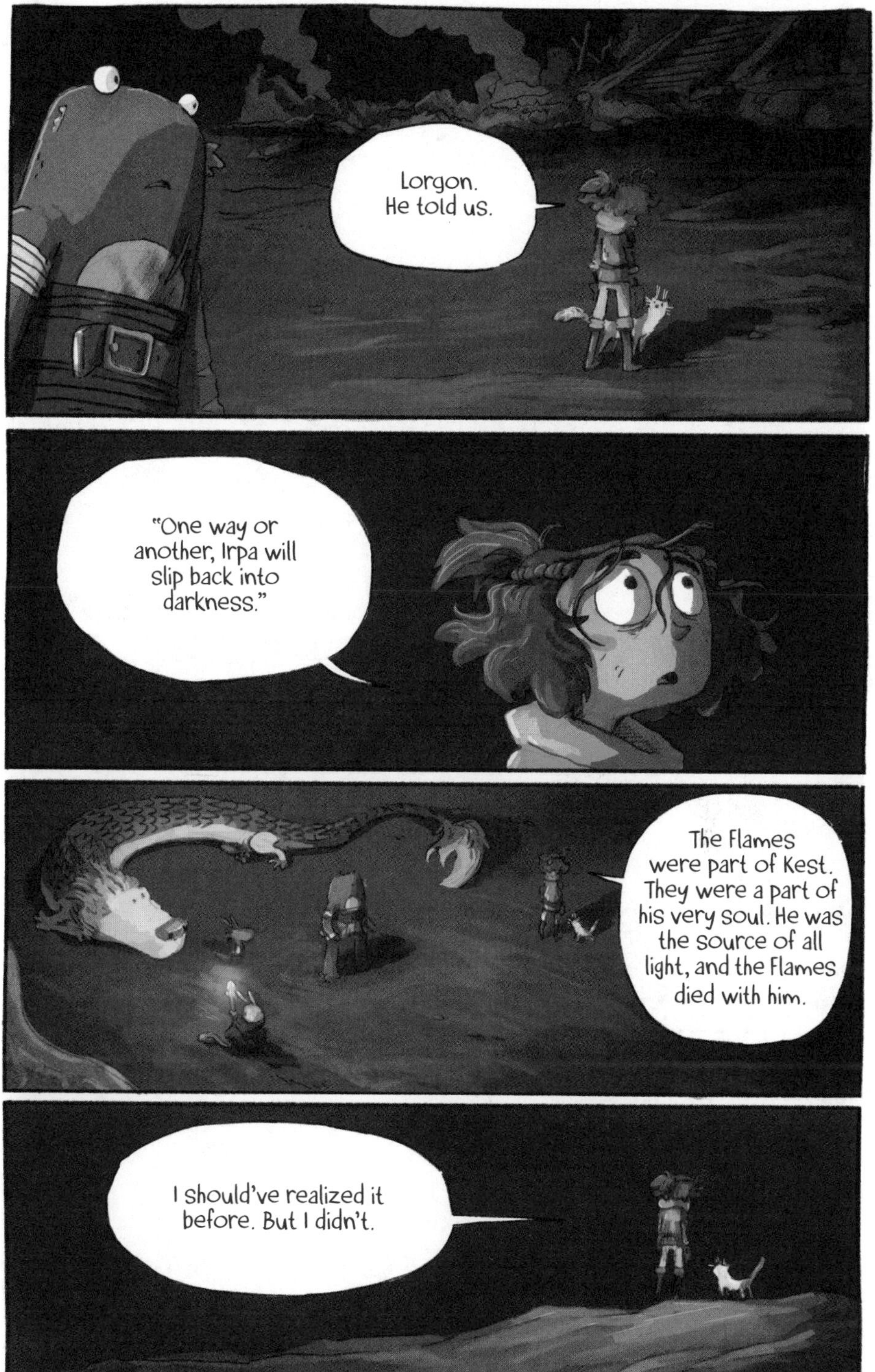
Lorgon. He told us.
"One way or another, Irpa will slip back into darkness."
The Flames were part of Kest. They were a part of his very soul. He was the source of all light, and the Flames died with him.
I should've realized it before. But I didn't.

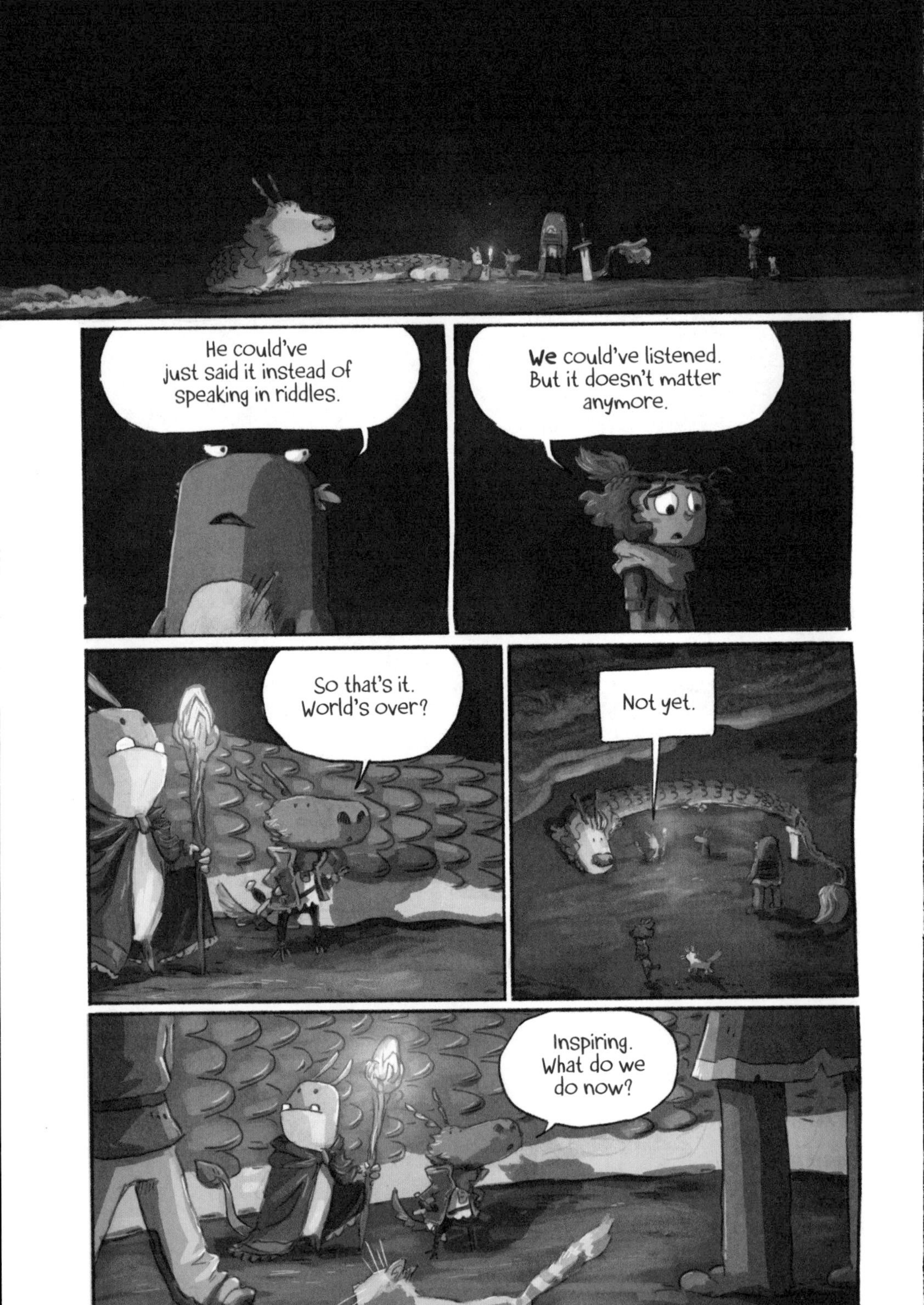
He could've just said it instead of speaking in riddles.
We could've listened. But it doesn't matter anymore.
So that's it. World's over?
Not yet.
Inspiring. What do we do now?

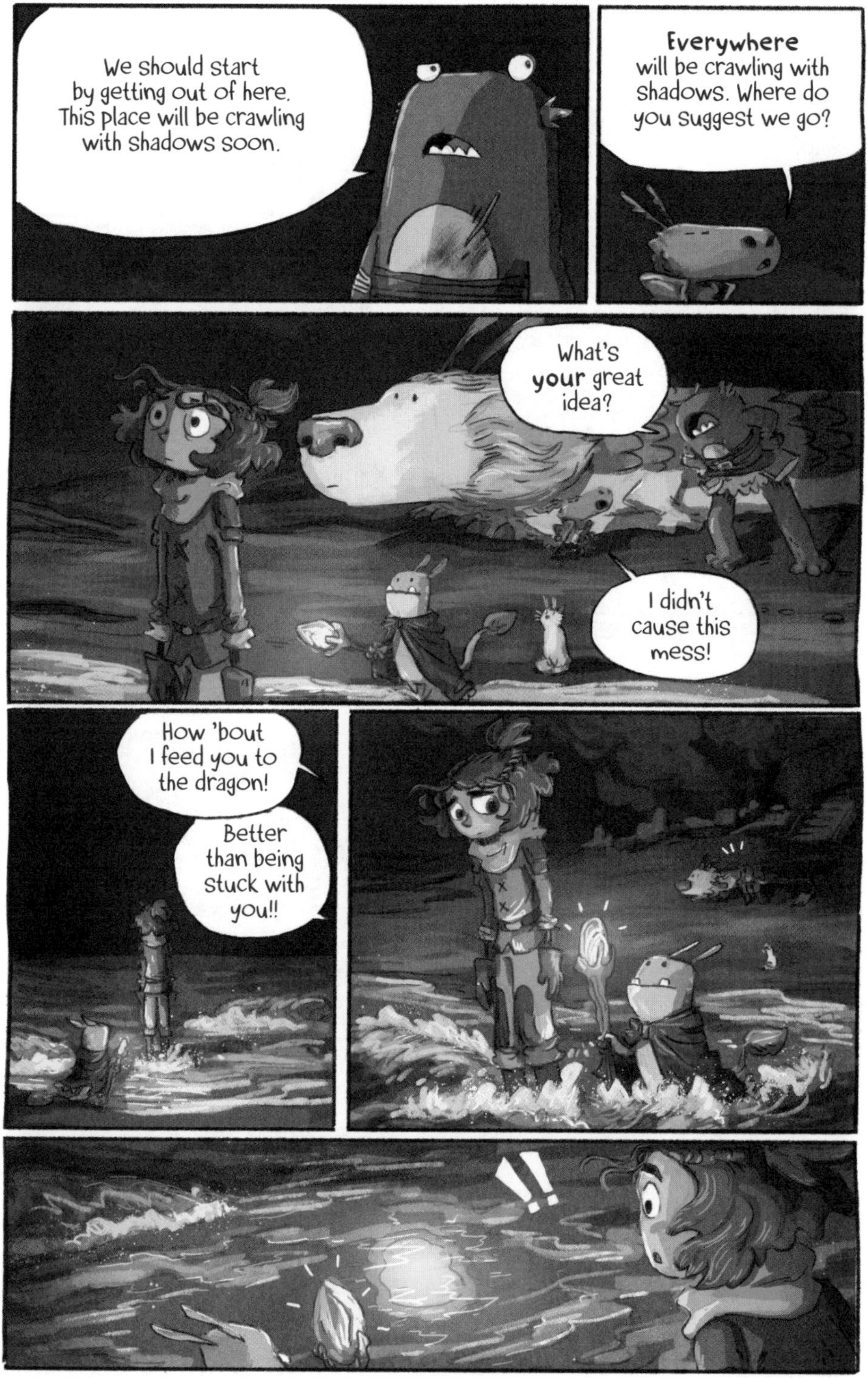

We should start by getting out of here. This place will be crawling with shadows soon.
Everywhere will be crawling with shadows. Where do you suggest we go?
What's **your** great idea?
I didn't cause this mess!
How 'bout I feed you to the dragon!
Better than being stuck with you!!
!!

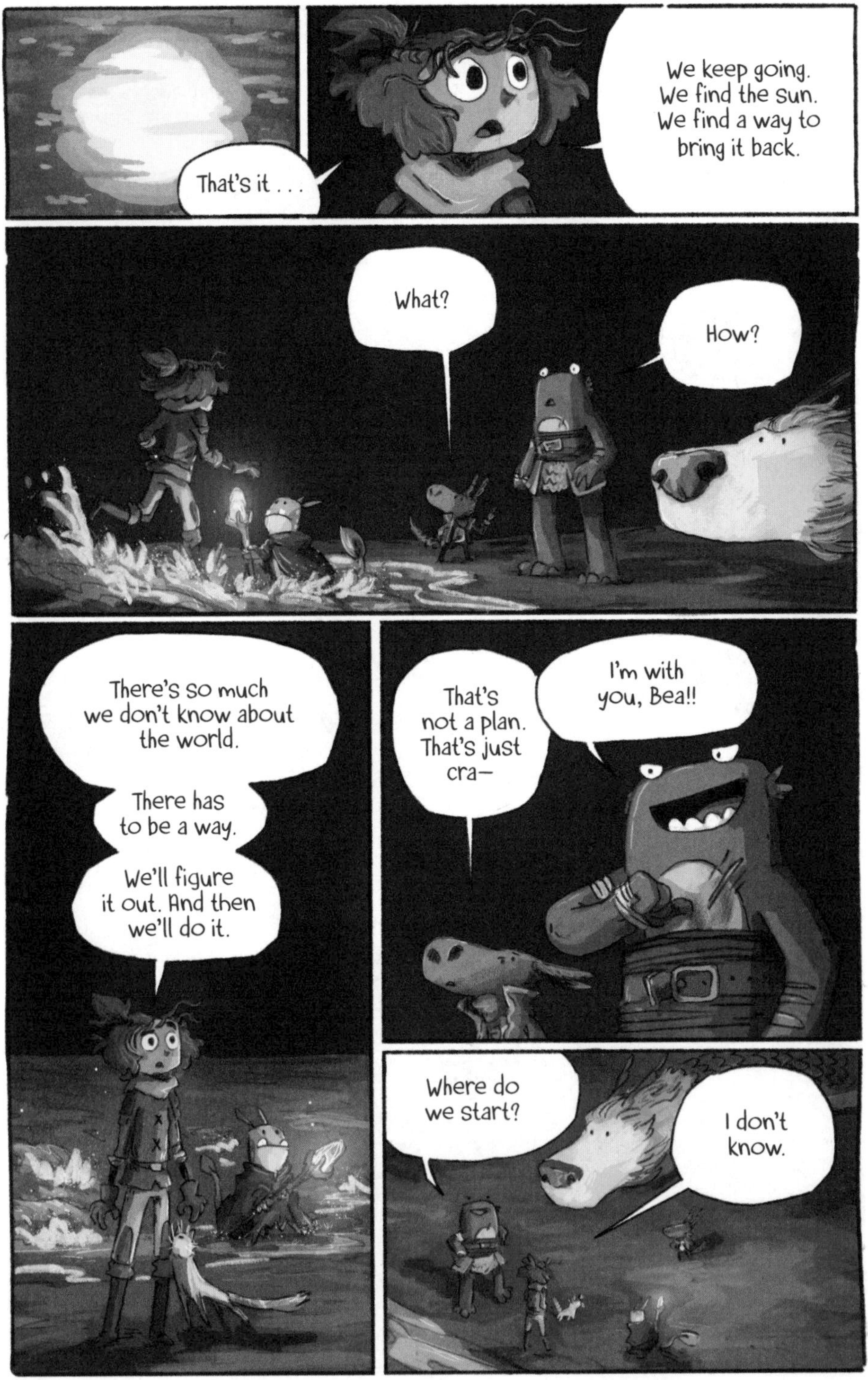
That's it . . .
We keep going. We find the sun. We find a way to bring it back.
What?
How?
There's so much we don't know about the world.
There has to be a way.
We'll figure it out. And then we'll do it.
That's not a plan. That's just cra—
I'm with you, Bea!!
Where do we start?
I don't know.

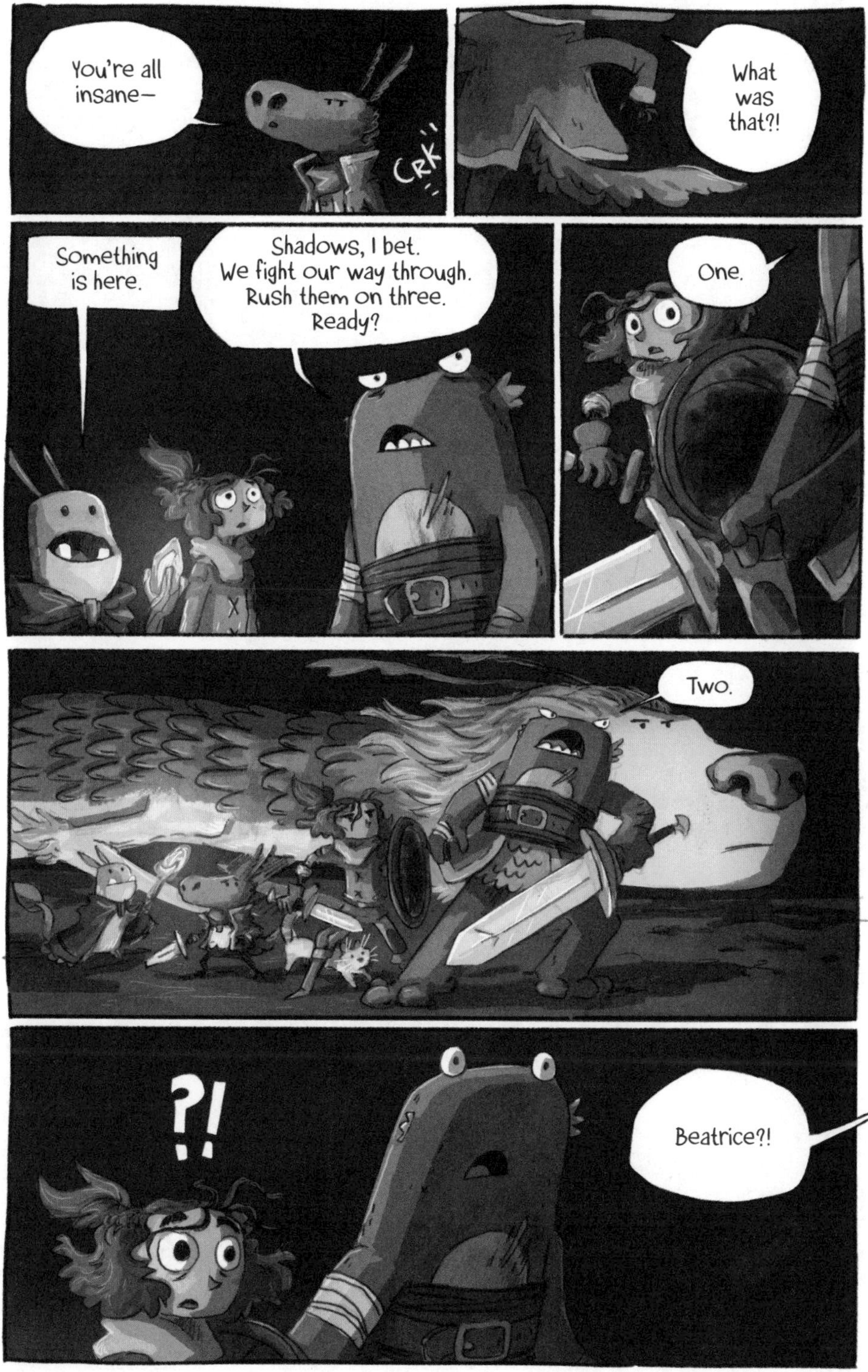
You're all insane—
CRK
What was that?!
Something is here.
Shadows, I bet. We fight our way through. Rush them on three. Ready?
One.
Two.
?!
Beatrice?!

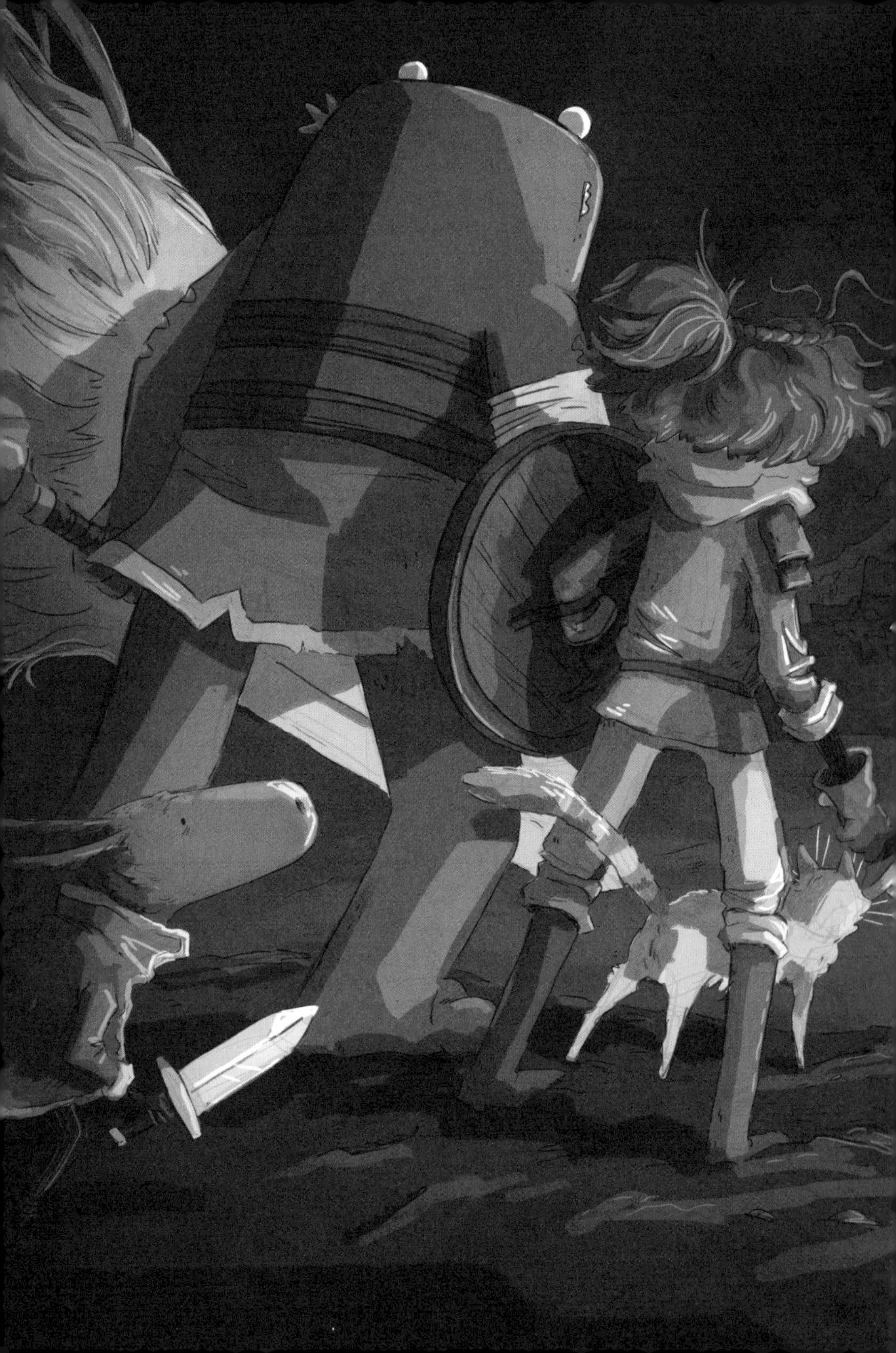

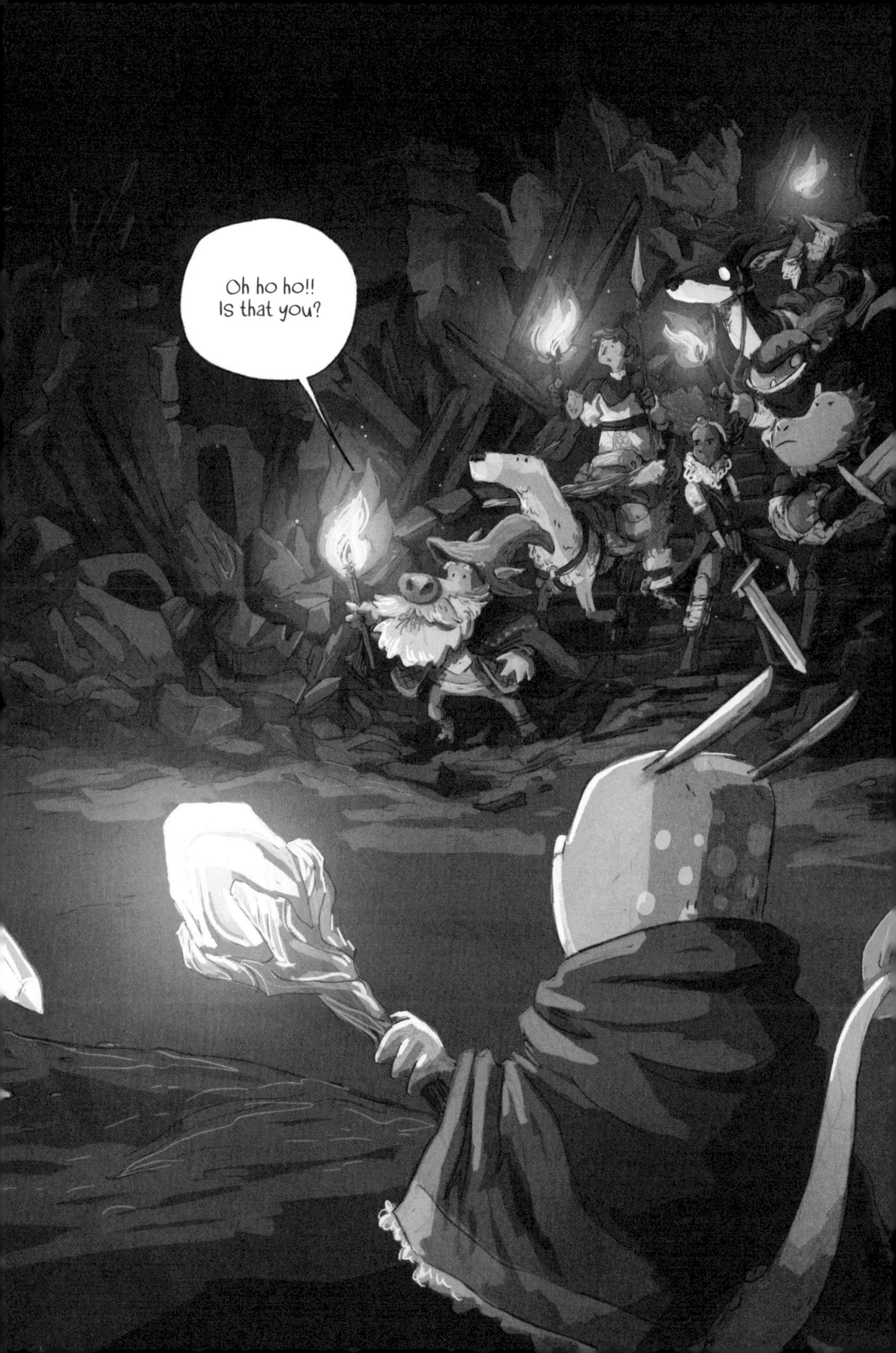
Oh ho ho!! Is that you?

For Jodi

Thanks to
Mom and Dad; Bryan Probert, flatting extraordinaire;
Andrew Arnold, Rose Pleuler, Erica De Chavez,
Caitlin Lonning, Rick Farley, Anna Bernard, and everyone
at HarperAlley; Joe Burrascano, Tom Beatty, Kevin Frodell;
Kazu Kibuishi and Faith Erin Hicks.

HarperAlley is an imprint of HarperCollins Publishers.

Lightfall: Shadow of the Bird
Copyright © 2022 by Tim Probert

Library of Congress Control Number: 2021948113
ISBN 978-0-06-299050-1 — ISBN 978-0-06-299048-8 (pbk.)

The artist used Prismacolor pencil, mechanical pencil, and
Photoshop to create the digital illustrations for this book.
Typography by Tim Probert and Erica De Chavez
21 22 23 24 25 RTLO 10 9 8 7 6 5 4 3 2 1
❖
First Edition